THE WORLD'S CLASSICS

AN ACCIDENTAL FAMILY

FYODOR MIKHAILOVICH DOSTOEVSKY was born in Moscow in 1821, the second in a family of seven children. His mother died of consumption in 1837 and his father, a generally disliked army physician, was murdered on his estate two years later. In 1844 he left the College of Military Engineering in St Petersburg and devoted himself to writing. *Poor Folk* (1846) met with great success from the literary critics of the day. In 1849 he was imprisoned and sentenced to death on account of his involvement with a group of utopian socialists, the Petrashevsky circle. The sentence was commuted at the last moment to penal servitude and exile, but the experience radically altered his political and personal ideology and led directly to *Memoirs from the House of the Dead* (1861–2). In 1857, whilst still in exile, he married his first wife, Maria Dmitrievna Isaeva, returning to St Petersburg in 1859. In the early 1860s he founded two new literary journals, *Vremia* and *Epokha*, and proved himself to be a brilliant journalist. He travelled in Europe, which served to strengthen his anti-European sentiment. During this period abroad he had an affair with Polina Suslova, the model for many of his literary heroines, including Polina in *The Gambler*. Central to their relationship was their mutual passion for gambling—an obsession which brought financial chaos to his affairs. Both his wife and his much loved brother, Mikhail, died in 1864, the same year in which *Notes from the Underground* was published; *Crime and Punishment* and *The Gambler* followed in 1866 and in 1867 he married his stenographer, Anna Snitkina, who managed to bring an element of stability into his frenetic life. His other major novels, *The Idiot* (1868), *Devils* (1871), *An Accidental Family* (1875), and *The Brothers Karamazov* (1880) met with varying degrees of success. In 1880 he was hailed as a saint, prophet, and genius by the audience to whom he delivered an address at the unveiling of the Pushkin memorial. He died six months later in 1881; at the funeral thirty thousand people accompanied his coffin and his death was mourned throughout Russia.

RICHARD FREEBORN, Emeritus Professor of Russian Literature at the University of London, is well known for his translations of Turgenev, which in World's Classics include *First Love and Other Stories*, *A Month in the Country*, and *Fathers and Sons*. He is also the author of several novels.

THE WORLD'S CLASSICS

═══

FYODOR DOSTOEVSKY
An Accidental Family

═══

Translated with an Introduction and Notes by
RICHARD FREEBORN

Oxford   New York
OXFORD UNIVERSITY PRESS
1994

Oxford University Press, Walton Street, Oxford OX2 6DP

Oxford New York Toronto
Delhi Bombay Calcutta Madras Karachi
Kuala Lumpur Singapore Hong Kong Tokyo
Nairobi Dar es Salaam Cape Town
Melbourne Auckland Madrid
and associated companies in
Berlin Ibadan

Oxford is a trade mark of Oxford University Press

British Library Cataloguing in Publication Data
Data available

Library of Congress Cataloging in Publication Data
Dostoyevsky, Fyodor, 1821–1881.
[Podrostok. English]
An accidental family / Fyodor Dostoevsky ; translated with an
introduction and notes by Richard Freeborn.
p. cm.—(World's classics)
I. Freeborn, Richard. II. Title. III. Series.
PG3326.P5 1994 891.73'3—dc20 93–4129
ISBN 0–19–282836–3

1 3 5 7 9 10 8 6 4 2

Typeset by Cambridge Composing (UK) Ltd
Printed in Great Britain by
BPCC Paperbacks Ltd
Aylesbury, Bucks

CONTENTS

INTRODUCTION

An Accidental Family is a translation of Dostoevsky's last completed novel, *Podrostok* (1875), first translated by Constance Garnett as *A Raw Youth* and as *The Adolescent* by Andrew R. MacAndrew. It is a first-person novel ostensibly written as 'Notes' by a 20-year-old narrator about his 19-year-old self. Dostoevsky's use of the term *podrostok* or 'under-ager', 'juvenile', 'teenager' as a title for his novel poses certain problems for a contemporary English translation. Nowadays a 20-year-old writing about his 19-year-old self could legally regard himself as a young adult writing about his young adulthood, not as a raw youth or adolescent writing about his juvenile or teenage experience.

What identifies this particular young narrator is his illegitimacy. He is described at the end of the novel as '*a member of an accidental family*', a phenomenon characteristic, in Dostoevsky's view, of society at the time he was writing. The young narrator's 'Notes' as '*a member of an accidental family*' can be said to provide a means of guessing 'at the innermost spiritual world of someone on the eve of manhood at that tumultuous time—an insight of no mean value, since it is from those on the eve of manhood that the generations are made . . .'. The making of generations, which is what this novel is about, is simultaneously about the making of families, of fatherhood and motherhood, and the ensuing relationships between parents and children. So that the young narrator seeks desperately for membership of a family in order to achieve an identity, a sense of commitment and security. It is through his eventual membership of *an accidental family* that he manages to transcend the hurt of his illegitimacy and come to terms with the bruising indignities of his upbringing. By the very accident of his birth, like his membership of an accidental family, he appears symptomatic of the immaturity of a society afflicted, as Dostoevsky would have it, by chaos and disorder.

Few great writers' lives seem to have been characterized by such disorder as was Dostoevsky's. There was the misfortune which overtook him in his twenties when he was arrested in 1849 as a member of the Petrashevsky group and sentenced to death, only for the sentence to be commuted at the last moment to penal servitude and exile in Siberia. On his release in 1859 still more tribulations beset him. The literary journals begun by him in collaboration with his brother either suffered official closure or went bankrupt. His brother died and Dostoevsky assumed responsibility for his debts. In an effort to recoup his fortunes, he went abroad, gambled, lost more money, and by 1865 he was stranded penniless in Wiesbaden. A letter to Katkov, editor of the liberal-conservative journal *The Russian Messenger*, offering a new novel about a student who murders a money-lender, helped him with his immediate money troubles. The result was *Crime and Punishment*. Written for serial publication, it appeared during 1866 and completely relaunched his literary career. It was the first of Dostoevsky's great novels and marked the start of his reputation as a novelist of world stature.

Despite this success, he continued to have money worries. A draconian agreement entered into with the publisher Stellovsky to complete a novel by 1 November 1866, forced him to interrupt his work on *Crime and Punishment*. In order to meet the deadline, he took the unusual step of hiring a young stenographer and dictating a novel entitled *The Gambler*. The terms of the agreement were met, if narrowly, and he was saved from having to forfeit all rights to his own work.

At this point the tone of black farce which had coloured his life so far yielded to more fairy-tale hues. He and his young stenographer, Anna Snitkina, fell in love. His junior by twenty-five years, she proved not only invaluable to him for his day-to-day work as a writer but in due course she also succeeded in bringing order to his financial affairs. Even so, practically as soon as they were married early in 1867 they were forced to flee abroad to escape Dostoevsky's creditors. This proved to be a second exile lasting more than four years. It naturally had the effect of cutting him off from Russia at a time when rapid changes were occurring in Russian society.

The most important of such changes concerned the new generation of the intelligentsia which had arisen largely as a result of Russia's defeat in the Crimean War of 1854–5. Chiefly under the influence of the journal *The Contemporary* and its leading writer, N. G. Chernyshevsky (1828–89), a younger generation had emerged which challenged the liberalism of the older generation by asserting far more radical policies. Materialist, atheist, dismissive of such institutions as the church and the family, and generally contemptuous of anything that could not be understood through the laws of the natural sciences, this younger generation had the overthrow of tsarism and the liberation of the peasantry as the chief items on its agenda. They were first portrayed in literature in the figure of Bazarov, hero of Turgenev's masterpiece, *Fathers and Sons* (1862), and it was also in this novel that they were first branded as 'nihilists'.

Dostoevsky was mesmerized by nihilists and nihilism. He saw them as arrogant examples of a humanity consumed by a conviction of its own superiority. They were creatures of self-will who repudiated God and sought to become total arbiters of right and wrong in the moral sphere. His attitude to Chernyshevsky and the latter's chief protégé on *The Contemporary*, N. S. Dobrolyubov (1836–61), was one of extreme hostility, chiefly because he felt that their materialism, their anthropological diagnosis of human nature, was simplistic in the extreme. He attacked Chernyshevsky's views for the first time in a cogent, literary sense in his famous *Notes from the Underground* (1864), but his diagnosis of the problem was treated much more fully in *Crime and Punishment*.

Essentially Dostoevsky's novels are dialogical. They pose issues as choices which counterbalance each other and confront the central protagonist—and the reader—with an existential dilemma. At its simplest this may be presented as a choice between God and the devil, but it is never as clear-cut as this. The complexity of human motivation, of human psychology and emotional commitment in its most aberrant forms, always blurs and complicates the issues. In *Crime and Punishment*, for example, Dostoevsky did not really succeed in making the vision of an all-merciful and forgiving God offered by Sonya counterbalance the demonic, self-willed nihilism of the hero, Raskolnikov. From his exile in Europe during the late 1860s he sought to rectify this. In his second great novel, *The Idiot* (1868), he created for the first time an image of a Russian Christ who would redeem the world by beauty. If Prince Myshkin, the simple-minded 'idiot' of the title, is a memorable creation as an innocent abroad in a society dominated by nihilism and avarice, he is scarcely portrayed as strong enough in his redemptive role to withstand the dark and murderous forces that are pitted against him.

The longer Dostoevsky spent abroad, the stronger grew his conviction that Europe was becoming corrupted by capitalism and a jingoistic nationalism. The Franco-Prussian War of 1870–1 appeared to provide ample justification for such a view. His eyes forever directed towards his own country, which he learned about through newspapers, journals, and correspondence with friends, he could not fail to be appalled at what he discerned as signs of a similar corruption spreading there. He saw it as a pestilence of Western free-thinking and godlessness which had infected sections of his own generation, the first generation of the Russian intelligentsia. They in turn had influenced the next generation and split them, on the one hand, into devout nihilists, men possessed by the idea that they had a right to usurp the place of divinity in the moral universe, and, on the other, into bewildered, uncertain seekers after a divine truth that perhaps revealed itself in the idea of a nation or people as 'god-bearing'. Given a political meaning, this divide between generations and attitudes became, in Dostoevsky's picture of it in *Devils* (or *The Possessed*, 1872), a darkly parodic study of a fanatically politicized intelligentsia into whom devils had entered as they entered into the herd of swine in the parable from St Luke's gospel. No redemptive force, let alone a Russian Christ, was strictly speaking offered as a counterbalance in this analysis. His publisher, Katkov, even prevented Dostoevsky from including a chapter in which some ideological redress was to be made because it also contained the notorious 'Confession' by the novel's hero, Stavrogin. In it he described his rape of a defenceless young girl who hangs herself out of shame.

On his return to Russia in July 1871, Dostoevsky was able, with his wife's help, to keep the creditors at bay. Even though still prone to epileptic fits and bouts of ill health, and with the infant death of his firstborn, Sonya, still a painful memory, he was overjoyed by the birth of a son, Fedya, in the very month of his return to his homeland. It was an omen of a more secure future awaiting him during the remaining years of the decade. The return, though, meant that he was able to achieve as a writer what he most wanted: a close acquaintanceship with the topical. He could now confront the reality of Russia, the superficially higgledy-piggledy confusion of its rapid transition from semi-feudal to capitalist forms of social relationship, and discern beneath it the deeper, less obvious, signs of social and intellectual change which were possibly heralding the emergence of a new generation of the intelligentsia.

The completion of *Devils* in 1872 turned his young wife into his publisher. She took charge of the publishing of the separate edition of the novel (as distinct from the version first serialized in Katkov's journal) and within a year had begun to achieve a real increase in the family's income. Another new feature in their lives was the renting of a holiday home in Staraya Russa (not far from Novgorod). This small provincial town, noted for its healthy surroundings, became both the place where Dostoevsky could replenish his energies and a source of material for his novels. A family of the nobility called Versilov, prominent local landowners, provided the name of the hero's father in *An Accidental Family* and Staraya Russa became the setting for his last great—unfinished—novel, *The Brothers Karamazov*. Regular work and regular income to support his family were essential, however, and he was fortunate to find both through his appointment late in 1872 as editor of a right-wing journal, *The Citizen*, owned by Prince Meshchersky.

On the face of it this was precisely what Dostoevsky wanted. It brought him directly in touch with the most topical issues of the day. He could respond to them through publication in *The Citizen* of his own opinions in a section he entitled 'The Diary of a Writer'. Yet the daily grind of editorial work took its toll. Heavy smoking caused emphysema and the reactionary views of the journal's proprietor tended to worsen Dostoevsky's mood, a circumstance not mitigated in any way by the hostility of the censorship to any dissident note in editorial policy. He was scrupulous and touchy and as a consequence overworked. By the spring of 1874 he was only too happy to free himself of the burden of editorship and return to what he was best at: the writing of fiction.

The spring and summer of 1874 saw him making plans for a new novel. His poor health necessitated a prolonged visit to the German spa town of Ems, which he profoundly disliked because it kept him away from his family in Staraya Russa, and—what is more—seemed to inhibit the gestation of his ideas, as his copious notebooks bear witness. The problem was partly due to a new, less reactionary and less political orientation in his own views. Day-to-day acquaintance with Russian life had given him a better appreciation of the idealism of the younger generation and made him more sympathetic to left-wing opinion. When his old friend and editor, N. A. Nekrasov, the man who had first published his work thirty years before, offered to publish his new novel in the leading left-wing journal, *Notes of the Fatherland*, Dostoevsky seized the opportunity gladly.

An Accidental Family (Podrostok) ends by posing a challenge to the family chronicle type of novel which Tolstoy had brought to such a pitch of perfection in his historical epic, *War and Peace* (1869). Long jealous of Tolstoy's reputation, just as he felt rivalled by Turgenev's, Dostoevsky sought in his new novel both to write his own 'Fathers and Sons' and to show the way in which the 'ideal' concept of the family of the Russian nobility, as offered by Tolstoy, had been eroded by social change and become 'accidental'. In the process the very idea and role of the nobility in Russian society had been discredited. Two counterbalancing concepts seem to have been paramount in Dostoevsky's thinking when confronting this issue. They are summed up in two terms—*bezobrazie* and *blagoobrazie*—which recur in his novel but are not easily translatable. They may be understood as an opposition of 'ugliness' and 'beauty', of the spiritually malformed and the spiritually perfect, of the 'ignoble' and the 'noble'; and it is the erosion of the spirit of true nobility (or *blagoobrazie*) in the life of the Russian upper class, in the life of the Russian nobility, and therefore, to a great extent, in Russian society generally, that Dostoevsky deplored most bitterly and sought to expose in his novel.

Published references in *The Diary of a Writer* and jottings in his notebooks for the novel show that he perceived signs of a universal dissolution occurring in Russian society. One such jotting reads: 'The main thing is that the idea of dissolution is everywhere, because everyone is cut off and no connections remain not only in the Russian family but even simply between people. Even children are cut off.' Or 'Look, here we are, a

Russian family. Yet we speak different languages and do not understand each other at all. Society is in a state of chemical dissolution.' Such utterances, with their suggestions of threat to the Russian family as a nucleus of society, were by no means exclusive to Dostoevsky—indeed they were shared by many others during the 1870s, particularly by publicists and not least by Tolstoy (as his *Anna Karenina* was to show) and Saltykov-Shchedrin (as we can see from his *The Golovlovs*)—but Dostoevsky saw the problem as related very specially to 'fathers' and 'sons' and the choices which had to be made by the younger generation of the intelligentsia, by the 'sons', in their search for a guiding idea in life. When, in his notebooks for his novel, he finally hit upon the main theme, he wrote triumphantly: 'THE MAIN IDEA. The young man arrives with a ready-made idea, but the entire point of the novel is that he is *seeking* a guiding thread for his behaviour, *between good and evil*, which is not to be found in our society; this is what he thirsts for, what he feels his way towards, and that is what the novel is about.'

In retrospect, writing in 1876 immediately after the novel had just been published, Dostoevsky was prepared to concede that it was merely 'the first try-out' of his idea of writing about contemporary fathers and sons. The exploration of the idea was to be carried much further in *The Brothers Karamazov* (1880). But in the case of *An Accidental Family*, Dostoevsky added, the 'son', or narrator,

appeared only as an unprepared man, boldly and shyly wishing to take his first step in life as soon as possible. I chose a blameless soul, but one already tainted by the awful likelihood of corruption, both by an early loathing for his own insignificance and 'accidental' birth and by that very breadth which allows even the purest person to become conscious of vice in his thoughts, nourish it in his heart and feel its allure in shameful, but stormy and audacious day-dreams—all that having been left solely to his own efforts and his own power to work out and, true, to God as well. All such are society's rejects, 'accidental' members of 'accidental' families (*The Diary of a Writer*, January 1876).

In concept, then, the novel was to have some of the features of a *Bildungsroman* describing a young man left largely to his own devices in groping towards a guiding idea and achieving some measure of emotional and intellectual maturity. If the young man was blameless, the society in which he found himself was clearly

xiii

at the mercy of a great many evils. Most conspicuous among these was the frequency of suicide and murder. *The Citizen* under Dostoevsky's editorship reported such cases in number after number, lamenting all the while the 'disorder' in Russian life which such incidents revealed. The principal lament centred on the way in which the élite of Russian society, the nobility and the intelligentsia, had become divorced from 'living life' (*zhivaya zhizné*), a somewhat vague, emotive concept (spoken of slightingly by Versilov in the course of the novel) which presupposed that only the peasantry, the 'people', were truly and traditionally in touch with life in any spiritual sense. By contrast, the majority of those present in the largely urban society described in the novel, set as it is mostly in the 'fantastic' city of St Petersburg, are portrayed as human rejects like the novel's narrator. Some may be earnest young intellectuals like the members of the Dergachev group, based on A. V. Dolgushin and his associates who were brought to trial in July 1874 accused of publishing criminal broadsheets with the aim of inciting popular discontent. Some may be engaged in more heinous, if unpolitical, criminal activity such as blackmail and extortion, like Lambert; or there are those involved in the forgery of railroad shares (in which Prince Seryozha is implicated); others (depicted in the novel by Stebelkov and his associates) are seen to be engaged in various nefarious and murky activities—all of which, incidentally, were based on court cases and reports in the press. Even the supposedly most respected of establishment figures in the novel, the 'old prince' Sokolsky, though close to caricature in his portrayal, is represented as having a shady and rather unhealthy, if not actually criminal, interest in the upbringing of young ladies and their preparation for marriage.

Into this maelstrom, much as Prince Myshkin was plunged as a kind of fool in God's name into the maelstrom of St Petersburg life in *The Idiot*, Arkady, the young narrator, finds himself plunged after travelling from Moscow. The choice he has to make between '*good and evil*' can be seen in Dostoevsky's notebooks to develop—through many a trial and error—into a choice between the two ideas embodied in his two fathers, his natural father, Versilov, and the father whose name he bears, Makar Dolgoruky.

The inspiration for Versilov's portrait clearly owed something to P. Ya. Chaadaev (1794–1856). His first 'Philosophical Letter' (1836) concentrated the minds of a whole generation of thinking Russians by laying such stress on the cultural backwardness of the country and the inadequacy of the Eastern Orthodox Church by comparison with the Roman Catholic. A. I. Herzen (1812–70), the leading liberal spokesman among the 'men of the forties', as the intellectuals of the 1840s came to be known, was also a prototype of Versilov. In short, Dostoevsky deliberately based this most influential of characters in his novel on prominent figures in the history of the Russian intelligentsia. Of course, he created in Versilov a composite figure to which were added a number of typically Dostoevskian features, in terms of both ideas and psychology, but the main intent of the characterization was its topicality and its relevance as the portrait of a contemporary 'father' to the much larger novelistic function of portraying a contemporary 'son'.

In the case of Makar Dolgoruky, we have a literary composite. There can be little doubt that the topicality in this instance relates to Dostoevsky's rivalry with Tolstoy's *War and Peace*. Among the sources for the character is Platon Karataev, the simple peasant philosopher who so influenced Pierre Bezukhov. Makar's utterances evidently owe something to the Tolstoyan original. That he is in a line of other literary 'holy men', from the priest Tikhon in the banned chapter of *Devils* to Zosima in *The Brothers Karamazov*, must also be obvious. There can equally be no doubt that he mirrors, if in a particularly Dostoevskian sense, a resurgent interest in religion and the spiritual life common to Russian society in the 1870s and best exemplified by Vladimir Solovyov, whom Dostoevsky knew and whose influence, especially with his 'Lectures on Godmanhood', was to prove crucially important later.

The young narrator, then, was cast in the mould of his time, but he can be seen to transcend those confining influences through being, in a uniquely sustained sense, their first-person witness, their hot line to the reader if not, strictly speaking, their 'onlie begetter'.

Arkady Makarovich Dolgoruky is a young bastard. His chip-on-shoulder, angry, sometimes aggressive, always self-conscious, disconcertingly honest, self-protective character expresses itself in what is usually an uncomplicated but slightly out-of-focus, shorthand manner of narration. It exudes breathlessness. He cannot contain himself. He must tell all, without literary embellishment, always promising only facts and frequently missing out or failing to realize the most important ones; and, being ignorant, he often misunderstands and misinterprets and chatters on about this and that to the sometimes forgivable impatience of the reader; but, then, he will confess engagingly that he never intended his 'Notes' to be read and no one will probably ever read them, etc., etc.; and of course the reader is again ensnared, because nothing is more readable than the supposedly unreadable, the honest, unembellished account that no one is supposed to know about.

As a young bastard, the narrator creates himself. He employs language of deliberate crudeness to express his indignation and his passion (straining in the process an English translator's normal thesaurus of invective). Despite this, there is little that might be called self-righteous in his manner or attitude for all its intense prickliness and gaucheness. Emotionally he often seems naked. But at the centre of his hurt, the breeding-ground of his whole attitude of mind, is his intense vulnerability as an illegitimate son saddled incongrously with the princely name of Dolgoruky.

Why that name? Dostoevsky undoubtedly knew that his readers would see the irony at once. The name belonged to the founder of Moscow, was instantly recognized as princely— 'Prince Dolgoruky?' Arkady is asked as a boy. 'No, *simply* Dolgoruky,' he is obliged to reply—and would be known by many as covertly referring to the most important 'accidental family' in the Russian empire. The family in question belonged to the Emperor Alexander II and his young mistress, Catherine Dolgoruky (or Dolgorukaya), whom he was to marry morganatically after the death of Empress Marie in 1880. The name, in other words, had scandal attaching to it at the very summit of the state. Its use in Dostoevsky's novel could seem both ironic and ambiguous. The surreptitiously seditious aspect of its meaning, in its covert implications that accident of birth and illegitimacy percolated down through Russian society from the very top, might seem to be counterbalanced by the fact that the most truly saintly and positive figure in the novel has the name and has bequeathed it as an emblem of true nobility to the novel's narrator.

By the time the novel opens and Arkady begins his 'Notes', he had left Moscow, the city of which his namesake was founder, and had already been in the imperial capital some weeks. Sexually innocent, if conscious how silly such sexual inexperience can seem in a 20-year-old, he had set about discovering his own 'accidental family' and the reasons for his illegitimacy. The story naturally broached the whole issue of serfdom and the seigneurial rights enjoyed by a member of the serf-owning nobility. The significant difference in this case was that Versilov did not abandon Arkady's mother, Sonya Dolgoruky, after seducing her, even if, on the face of it, he abandoned his illegitimate son. It certainly led to a brooding resentment in Arkady, but outweighed by an intense, almost sexual infatuation with the long-lost father figure which was in spirit as much hero-worshipping as filial. It ended with him becoming his father's rival—or double—in his love for Katerina Nikolaevna, the beautiful widowed daughter of the 'old prince' Sokolsky.

What Arkady sought, as he says, was not just legitimacy, he wanted 'the whole of Versilov, what I wanted was a father . . . that's what I demanded!' He arrived in St Petersburg armed with two means for achieving this. One, essentially an item of blackmail, could not fail to involve him in the nefarious activities of blackmailers. He had brought with him a 'secret' sewn into his jacket pocket. It was a letter from Katerina Nikolaevna to a lawyer seeking advice on how to have her elderly and attractively dotty father, the 'old prince', committed to a lunatic asylum. Should this letter become known, it could mean that Prince Sokolsky would disown his daughter and cut her off without a penny. In a scarcely legitimate sense, therefore, Arkady arrived in St Petersburg with a powerful 'secret' which could eventually suborn the father and virtually criminalize him.

Arkady's other 'secret' was his Idea. Basically it was an 'idea-emotion' and to that extent a means of compensating for his sense of inferiority. It sprang from a need to find a niche or corner in life, a dilemma shared by many other 'dreamers' in Dostoevsky's works (like the narrator of his early novella *White Nights*). Obliquely it acquired a national frame of reference when the 'idea-emotion' propounded by Kraft about the Russians being a second-class race of people so excited him at the meeting of the Dergachev group. The compensatory socialist ideal raised in the subsequent discussion at once posed a challenge to Arkady's image of himself and he responded in terms typical of an 'underground man': 'For that little bit of average good which your rational society promises me,' he declared, 'for a bit of bread and warmth, you take in exchange all my individuality!' His individuality and his Idea, like his personal character and his illegitimacy, were to prove inseparable.

His Idea was to become as rich as Rothschild. In Moscow, before arriving in St Petersburg, he had devoted himself whole-heartedly to rigorous self-denial with the aim of accumulating capital penny by penny. He had persuaded himself that by this means he was mathematically bound to succeed. The naïve literalness of such thinking was proof enough that his Idea was not really rational. It was chiefly an assertion of his individuality and a recognition above all that, in the society of his time, money was the only means of taking even a nonentity '*right to the very top*'. It alone would ensure him freedom from humiliation and an independent awareness of his own strength.

Life naturally challenged his Idea. It only took his compassion for an abandoned baby girl to undermine the intellectual rigour of his idea, if not exactly to bring it tumbling down in ruins. But a more fundamental paradox associated with his Idea was that in order to pursue it he had to isolate himself from his 'accidental family', whereas what he most sought were precisely the emotional security and 'legitimacy' that a family environment had to offer. Chapters V and VI of Part I describe successively Arkady's Idea and the humiliations he suffered at the Touchard school when his illegitimacy was discovered. The Idea, when he finally hit upon it, had a liberating effect. It liberated him from the humiliation of illegitimacy, from self-negation and, above all, from suicide. Kraft's suicide, by contrast, was largely due to his self-image being shattered through his pathological belief that the Russians were a second-rate people; and Olya also commit-ted suicide because her precariously balanced self-esteem was finally destroyed by the threat of prostitution and Versilov's inept benevolence. Arkady was saved by his Idea and by his contradic-tory need for his 'accidental family'.

By the beginning of Part II the situation had changed dramatically. Ignorant of the real cause of Prince Seryozha's befriending of him, Arkady had nevertheless acquired the trappings of wealth largely at the prince's expense. In this upperclass ambience, with Arkady temporarily separated from his family environment, what became spotlighted was the significance of the nobility as a class. Versilov, for instance, saw it as a potential upper-class meritocracy, but the air of caricature attaching to establishment figures in Dostoevsky's picture of Russian life could not fail to colour the betrayal of Prince Seryozha by emphasizing the absence of true nobility of spirit (*blagoobrazie*) in his character. Corrupted by money, he seemed to be a brittle personification of what was most wrong with Russian society; and through his association with Liza, Arkady's sister, he was to prove more damaging to her and to Arkady himself than any of the more obvious reprobates in the novel. In short, had he stood up for Arkady when the latter was accused of theft at the gambling table, Arkady might not have spent a night out in the frost and might then not have confessed so much, particularly about his 'secret', to Lambert. And had the prince not unwisely shopped the Dergachev group to the authorities, Liza might have had a better chance of real happiness with Vasin.

Arkady's 'Idea' proved no real guide to him in life, in the sense that money, when he had it in some abundance, did not strictly speaking liberate him from anything. He simply remained himself. It is testimony to Dostoevsky's genius that he created in Arkady Dolgoruky as narrator a real and extraordinarily likeable personality despite his own admitted faults, backslidings, and bloody-mindedness. His relations with women exemplify this best.

With his mother he played the affectionate 'young bastard' role very successfully, just as he seemed cast always in the role of ungrateful young puppy whenever he was in the company of his 'auntie' Tatyana Pavlovna (whose verbal abuse of him he finally castigates as the possible cause of his own recalcitrance). Towards his own true sister, Liza, he felt nothing but love and affection, mixed with pity (and some misunderstanding). With his half-sister Anna Andreevna he had a more ambivalent relationship. It hardly seemed that he could be fond of her, particularly towards the end when he became pivotal to her plan to marry the 'old prince' Sokolsky, but he clearly took pleasure from knowing her. There was a general recogniton among the women who knew him that, for all his talkative exhibitionism, he had something most precious, doubtless inherited from his mother—purity of spirit, a natural nobility. It informed his passion for Katerina Nikolaevna with an appealing directness and honesty. Their relationship, for all its 'forbidden' character and likely inequality, had a complexity and depth that seemed to have the makings of a true love. Mixed into it, of course, were such potentially volatile ingredients as his own awareness of his libidinous instincts, the shame and lust implicit in the plan to blackmail her, and his own spider-like soul that led him to marvel 'at a man's capacity . . . to nurse in his heart the highest of ideals alongside the greatest lasciviousness and to do so quite innocently'.

At its darkest this ambivalence was mirrored in his father's—Versilov's—relationship with the same woman. It coloured and obviously complicated their own relationship. Consumed by so passionate a desire to know and understand his father, Arkady was almost turned into a voyeur; he did not fully understand, it seems, precisely that obsessive and lustful infatuation which impelled Versilov in his jealous pursuit of Katerina Nikolaevna. In seeking 'the whole of Versilov' Arkady sought to penetrate the often impenetrable character of the man—the evident intellectual arrogance, the apparent suavity, the secretiveness and apartness as well as the grand, seigneurial assumption that he, Andrey Petrovich Versilov, was inherently superior despite the way he had run through fortunes, disregarded his common-law wife, abandoned his illegitimate son, and become involved in socially harmful scandals. However annoying or 'ridiculous' (as Katerina Nikolaevna herself felt bound to describe him) this Versilov was, he exerted an enigmatic fascination on his narrator-son which perhaps inhibited an unbiased portrayal. But what Arkady perceived in him eventually was, on the one hand, a deep, tender, and ultimately redemptive love for the peasant girl he had seduced, Sonya, Arkady's mother; and, on the other hand, he achieved a complex insight into that 'true nobility' (*blagoobrazie*) which was at the core of Versilov's being. Ironically the threat to both noble qualities came from the same source: Versilov's natural male proneness to be sexually blinded by female beauty, Katerina Nikolaevna's in this case, though initially it had been Sonya Dolgoruky's.

'A Russian woman', said Versilov, 'gives her all when she falls in love—her immediate life, her destiny, her present and future because she can't economize, can't think of putting anything by and her beauty quickly goes into whoever she loves. Those [i.e. Sonya's] sunken cheeks are the beauty that has gone into me, into giving me a bit of pleasure . . .' And the initial sacrifice made to bring this about affected most deeply of all the wronged husband, Makar Dolgoruky.

His was indeed a message of humility and acceptance, the obverse of Versilov's though of the same coin. 'For you must know,' Makar declared, 'it is impossible to be a man and not bow down and worship. A man cannot tolerate himself, no man can. And if he rejects God, then he will bow down before an idol—a wooden one or a gold one or one made of ideas.' The manner of Old Testament prophecy which informed his utterances can seem too pious and high-flown, but what he stood for in terms of a counterbalancing idea to Versilov and a countervailing model for Arkady was disavowal of riches and money and pursuit of the pilgrim's way to grace. Once divested of material riches, he declared, 'you will become countless times richer than you ever were, because it's not by what you eat, by fine clothes, by pride and envy that you will be made happy, but by love multiplied over and over in countless ways . . . Nowadays it is no rare thing for the richest and most important to be indifferent to the number of their days and not even to know how to invent a new way of passing the time. But in the time to come hours and days will multiply a thousand times and you will not want to miss a single minute and you will experience each one with joy in your heart. Then you will obtain true wisdom not merely from books, but from being face to face with God. And the earth will shine brighter than the sun, and there will be neither sadness, nor lamentation, but only a paradise beyond all price . . .'

The simplistic—not to say communistic—essence of his message had less effect than his awful story of Slaughterer, the merchant, but if his vision of paradise had something in common with Versilov's vision of a lost Golden Age at the beginning of European civilization—ideologically the high point of the novel—his role was basically that of a reconciler. With his death

Versilov could be reconciled with Arkady's mother, as Arkady hoped. But Versilov was not reconciled, no more than he was successful in deluding himself into imagining that, as a Russian wandering through Europe in the aftermath of the Franco-Prussian War, he was the only European in Europe at that time. His dream of humanity's paradise on earth—a black dream for all its Attic idyll, which Dostoevsky explored both in Stavrogin's 'Confession' and in his frightening study of suicide, 'The Dream of a Foolish Young Man'—was, as Versilov acknowledged, 'the most implausible dream of all, but one for which people would give up their lives and all their strength, for which prophets would die and be killed, without which nations had no desire to live and yet couldn't die!'

What, then, was Versilov's ideal? Principally the ideal of a higher cultural type unique to Russia who, as he believed, had 'acquired the capacity to become first and foremost Russian the more European he becomes'. For Versilov, as a member of the Russian intelligentsia orientated towards the West, the European heritage was immensely precious, unappreciated though it may have been by the jingoistic Europeans themselves, and he lamented the passing of the old assurances of belief. He could discern what he called a 'jackboot mentality' at work in Europe—'reality', he suggested, 'always resounds with jackboots, even when men are most striving towards an ideal'—and the process could lead not merely to rejection of God but also to a universal recognition that humanity had become orphaned. At this point Versilov's real *credo* emerged:

'You know, my dear boy, I could never imagine that people could be stupid and ungrateful. These orphaned people would immediately cleave to each other more closely and lovingly. They would seize each other by the hand on the understanding that they were now all they had. The great idea of immortality would have gone for good and would have to be replaced, and all the great abundance of earlier love for what had been immortality would have become directed by men towards nature, towards the world, towards people and every blade of grass. They would come to love the earth and life with an irrepressible love and to that very extent they would gradually become aware of their transience and finiteness and feel a particular love for it quite unlike their former love ... Suppose tomorrow is my last day, everyone would think as he watched the setting sun, then it doesn't matter, I'll die, but all the others will remain, and their children after them—and the idea that others would remain, loving each other just the same and trembling for one another, would take the place of the idea of meeting beyond the grave. Oh, they would be in such a hurry to love one another in order to extinguish the great sorrow in their hearts! . . .

Arkady's verdict on his father and his ideal showed a dutiful respect for the idealism and a healthy scepticism of the blather:

I wasn't at all worried about his praise of the nobility and his words '*Je mourrai gentilhomme*—I will die a gentleman'. I considered what kind of a *gentilhomme* he was. He was a type of gentleman who gave up everything and became a prophet of universal citizenship and the main Russian concept of 'the coming together of ideas'. And although it was all so much nonsense—this 'coming together of ideas', I mean (which, of course, made no sense at all)—the good thing was that he had spent all his life subservient to an idea and not to some stupid golden calf. My God, hadn't I, in conceiving my 'Idea', bowed down before a golden calf, had I really just needed money? No, I swear, all I'd needed was the idea! I swear that, if I'd had a hundred million roubles, I wouldn't have upholstered a single chair or a single divan in velvet and I'd have eaten just the same kind of beef soup I eat now!

The idea, however, in a Dostoevskian novel is never bloodless. In this novel especially it is always an 'idea-emotion', a compulsion both emotional and mental. Both Arkady's 'fathers', like Arkady himself, were driven by compulsions. They led disordered, footloose lives, governed by the compulsion in Makar's case to seek grace and purity of soul as a pilgrim and, in Versilov's, to discover the Europe whose history and culture were so essential for his own identity as a Russian. To that extent Versilov was 'split in half', as he himself admitted. The crisis came when he recognized that he would have to choose between them, the compulsion, that is to say, of his passionate infatuation for Katerina Nikolaevna and his love for the 'angel', Arkady's mother, whom he could marry once Makar was dead. The issue, of course, was complicated by Arkady's possession of his 'secret'. To Arkady, Katerina Nikolaevna represented both an object of love, yearned for however disgracefully, and a very likely impediment to his fond hope of a reconciliation between his parents and the creation of a true, not an accidental, family. To this end his 'secret' had a role to play in ensuring Katerina

xxiii

Nikolaevna's compliance, whether for his own or for his father's purpose.

Versilov's act of iconoclasm in smashing the miracle-working icon in two expressed the compulsive ambivalence within him and in his relationships. Arkady tried to explain the act, even excuse it, but the idea of a 'double' acting on his behalf, common after all to other Dostoevskian portrayals, hardly seemed satisfactory in this case. In the passionate farewell scene between Versilov and Katerina Nikolaevna the depth of his enslavement emerged not just as infatuation but as the torment of love, the deepest of commitments that cannot help seeming almost a mockery of itself. As he put it: 'I always imagine you're with me when I'm alone. I spend all the time talking to you. I wander through slums and visit dives and you're always right there in front of me like a kind of exact opposite. But you're always laughing at me, just as you are now ...' The rawness of his honesty in this confession was unsparing. He was capable, he admitted, of hating her a great deal more than he loved her, but 'I think I'd spend thirty years standing on one leg if it would please you ...' Jealously possessive as much as pathologically compulsive, his love could kill if necessary. Yet it was redeemed by its sheer craziness.

Craziness surrounded all that happened subsequently—Arkady's conniving with Lambert, the discovery that his 'secret' was no longer his, the helter-skelter dashing about, and the ensuing melodrama of the confrontation. A sleaze factor inherent in the ambience of the novel, in a high proportion of its characters and their relationships, finally dictated the squalid—and essentially humourless—denouement. It was left to the 'authorial' voice quoted by Arkady in the Epilogue to point up the larger moral of his 'Notes' which otherwise seemed to end in such chaos.

The 'authorial' voice, though attributed to Arkady's Moscow mentor to whom he had sent his manuscript, must be assumed to be Dostoevsky's. He it is who goes to some lengths to make clear that the 'Notes' have a quasi-historical significance. They reflect the experience of 'a great many boys like you' who, under the chaotic influences of their upbringing and the society of the time, would either cravenly conform or develop a covert desire to overthrow the status quo.

'But this desire to overthrow the status quo springs more often than not from a likely covert yearning for order and "nobility" [*blagoobrazie*] (I use your term). Youth is pure because it is youth. Perhaps it is precisely in such early, youthful outbursts of madness that the yearning for order and the seeking after truth really originate, and who is to be blamed if certain young people today see this order and this truth in such silly, such comic things that you haven't the faintest idea how they could ever have any faith in them at all!'

There was only one solitary bulwark, as it were, against the disorder and haphazardness of Russian life, as Dostoevsky saw it, and that was, in Pushkin's words, 'the traditions of a Russian family', the only milieu where beauty and finished forms of honesty and duty prevailed. Moreover, such qualities had evolved in that milieu of themselves, out of the life of the Russian nobility itself—and

'My God, the most important thing we can have is some orderly pattern of life we can call our own! It is what we have hoped for, so to speak, our chance to have a rest—something really finished, really constructed and not the everlasting piles of rubbish, not the woodchips flying everywhere, not the trash and garbage from which absolutely nothing has come in the last two hundred years!

Arkady Makarovich Dolgoruky, like so many of his generation, did not have the advantage of a nobility background, just as Dostoevsky did not want to be merely a historical novelist (as was Tolstoy in *War and Peace*) in writing about 'the traditions of a Russian family'. Conditions had changed. Undoubtedly legitimate Russian families had begun transforming themselves into *accidental* families.

'Yes, Arkady Makarovich, you are *a member of an accidental family* in complete contrast to all our recent types of legitimate hero who had boyhoods and youths quite unlike yours.

'I confess I would not want to be a novelist trying to describe a hero from an accidental family!

'. . . But what choice does a writer have who has no wish to write historical novels but longs to write about matters of current importance? He has to guess . . . and get it wrong!'

Whether or not Dostoevsky got it wrong in this novel, for critical opinion in the West has generally neglected the novel or dismissed it as scarcely worthy of a place beside his last four great novels, there can be no doubt that he dared much in writing it. He dared to challenge the whole tradition of the 'family chronicle' novel with its setting within the nobility. More importantly, he dared 'to guess at the innermost spiritual world of someone on the eve of manhood' in a period of rapid socio-economic and political change in Russian life and to offer 'an insight of no mean value, since it is from those on the eve of manhood that the generations are made . . .'. He was not to know, though his prophetic sense may have told him, that the generation to which Arkady Makarovich Dolgoruky belonged was to become renowned for its 'great endeavours', its 'going into the people' in an endeavour to politicize the Russian peasantry, its idealistic populism, its hope of creating a just society in a country only recently liberated from centuries of serfdom, its search for a Russian rather than a European way forward, for a way to 'overstep' capitalism and achieve socialism before the West, and, finally, for its desperate resort to the weapon of terrorism in the struggle against the tsarist autocracy, culminating in the terrible assassination of Emperor Alexander II on 1 March 1881 (after Dostoevsky's own death in January of that year). It is against this background of chaos in Russian life, of a generation faced by grave and tormenting choices and forced eventually to abandon its great endeavours in favour of the 'small endeavours' celebrated in the work of Chekhov, that Dostoevsky's novel is to be read.

He also dared to write a sustained first-person novel. The chatterbox narrator, conjuring with such a variety of themes, has to strain credulity with his fortuitous eavesdropping and remarkable capacity for total recall. The conjuring does not always work. More than once, especially towards the end, consequences have to be anticipated, sequences violated. The multiplicity of characters referred to chattily by their first name and patronymic in typical Russian fashion (Andrey Petrovich, Tatyana Pavlovna, etc.) can leave a reader bewildered—a descriptive list of characters in alphabetical order of first names has therefore been provided—but sometimes those most familiar to the narrator, such as Nikolay Semyonovich, Arkady's Moscow mentor, remain almost unknown quantities for the reader. A notorious example of narratorial forgetfulness is Darya Onisimovna, Olya's mother, who inexplicably acquires the name Nastasya Yegorovna.

If these are blemishes, they do not negate the narrator's strengths. His gusto, the sheer brio of his manner, lacking felicity and often careless as it is, races his reader along, usually from one scene of dialogue to the next in which the emphasis falls always on the characters as voices. Never strictly speaking formal occasions, rarely giving a sense of being 'staged', such scenes of dialogue have the presence and participation of the narrator as their justification and his commentary, his appraisal more often than not dictates their purpose. The polyphony is here controlled and filtered. As for the chronology of events, the narrator's sense of time is grounded in immediacy, in an intense concentration of events within a maximum time frame of a few days at most. His autobiographical material supplies the prehistory and framework for this essentially dramatic manner. Prodigious in its virtually unselective recall of the 'present' time, the narrator's memory is, however, quite selective in its treatment of the 'past'. This is where his real strength as narrator/autobiographer emerges. His recall of his mother, the unhappiness of his boyhood and schooling, his dream of his father—these, as well as the brilliant codas devoted to St Petersburg as a fantasy city or to the meaning of laughter, provide the enriching and poignant detail for what is the narrator's main purpose, a portrait of himself as a young bastard seeking legitimacy and a family of his own.

RICHARD FREEBORN

TRANSLATOR'S NOTE

DOSTOEVSKY is 'so obscure and so careless a writer that one can scarcely help clarifying him—sometimes it needs some penetration to see what he is trying to say'. Any translator of Dostoevsky is bound to sympathize with these words by Constance Garnett. I have tried not to intensify the obscurity or exaggerate the carelessness, but there have been times when clarification in a sense of 'improvement' has been necessary and, I think, forgivable. The greatest challenge has been presented by the vigour of the dialogue. Here I have tried to make the speech transfer into an idiomatic, contemporary English. Throughout I have tended to replace the semi-colon with the full stop and give the punctuation a slightly more contemporary appearance without, I hope, altering or disrupting the copious and often elaborate construction of Dostoevsky's sentences.

Finally, I would like to thank Catherine Clarke, editor of World's Classics, for having the courage and foresight to commission a new translation of this neglected Dostoevsky novel. That it is unjustly neglected is hopefully what this translation will demonstrate. That it is remarkably vital as the picture of an age and a *tour de force* as a sustained, realistic, first-person narrative there can be no doubt.

SELECT BIBLIOGRAPHY

Catteau, Jacques, *Dostoyevsky and the Process of Literary Creation*, trans. Audrey Littlewood (Cambridge, 1989).

Dostoevsky, F. M., *The Notebooks for A Raw Youth*, ed. and with an introduction by Edward Wasiolek, trans. Victor Terras (Chicago, 1969).

Frank, Joseph, *Dostoevsky: The Seeds of Revolt 1821–1849* (Princeton, NJ, 1976).

—— *Dostoevsky: The Years of Ordeal 1850–1859* (Princetown, NJ, 1983).

—— *Dostoevsky: The Stir of Liberation 1860–1865* (Princeton, NJ, 1986).

Hingley, Ronald, *Dostoevsky: His Life and Work* (London, 1978).

Kjetsaa, Geir, *Fyodor Dostoevsky: A Writer's Life*, trans. Siri Hustvedt and David McDuff (London, 1988).

Leatherbarrow, W. J., *Fedor Dostoevsky* (Boston, Mass., 1981).

Mochulsky, K., *Dostoevsky: His Life and Work*, trans. Michael Minihan (Princeton, NJ, 1967).

Peace, Richard, *Dostoyevsky: An Examination of the Major Novels* (Cambridge, 1971).

CHRONOLOGY OF
FYODOR DOSTOEVSKY

Italicized items are works by Dostoevsky listed by year of first publication. Dates are Old Style, which means that they lag behind those used in nineteenth-century Western Europe by twelve days.

1821   Fyodor Mikhailovich Dostoevsky is born in Moscow, the son of an army doctor (30 October).

1837   His mother dies.

1838   Enters the Chief Engineering Academy in St Petersburg as an army cadet.

1839   His father dies, possibly murdered by his serfs.

1842   Is promoted Second Lieutenant.

1843   Translates Balzac's *Eugénie Grandet*.

1844   Resigns his army commission.

1846   *Poor Folk*
         The Double

1849   *Netochka Nezvanova*
         Is led out for execution in the Semenovsky Square in St Petersburg (22 December); his sentence is commuted at the last moment to penal servitude, to be followed by army service and exile, in Siberia.

1850–4 Serves four years at the prison at Omsk in western Siberia.

1854   Is released from prison (March), but is immediately posted as a private soldier to an infantry battalion stationed at Semipalatinsk, in western Siberia.

1855   Is promoted Corporal.
         Death of Nicholas I; accession of Alexander II.

1856   Is promoted Ensign.

1857   Marries Maria Dmitrievna Isaeva (6 February).

1859   Resigns his army commission with the rank of Second Lieutenant (March), and receives permission to return to European Russia.
         Resides in Tver (August–December).
         Moves to St Petersburg (December).
         Uncle's Dream
         Stepanchikovo Village

1861   Begins publication of a new literary monthly, *Vremia*, founded by himself and his brother Mikhail (January).
         The Emancipation of the Serfs.

The Insulted and the Injured
A Series of Essays on Literature

1861–2   *Memoirs from the House of the Dead*

1862   His first visit to Western Europe, including England and France.

1863   *Winter Notes on Summer Impressions*
Vremia is closed by the authorities for political reasons.

1864   Launches a second journal, *Epokha* (March).
His first wife dies (15 April).
His brother Mikhail dies (10 July).
Notes from the Underground

1865   *Epokha* collapses for financial reasons (June).

1866   Attempted assassination of Alexander II by Dmitry Karakozov (April).
Crime and Punishment
The Gambler

1867   Marries Anna Grigorevna Snitkina, his stenographer, as his second wife (15 February).
Dostoevsky and his bride leave for Western Europe (April).

1867–71 The Dostoevskys reside abroad, chiefly in Dresden, but also in Geneva, Vevey, Florence, and elsewhere.

1868   *The Idiot*

1870   *The Eternal Husband*

1871   The Dostoevskys return to St Petersburg. Birth of their first son, Fyodor (16 July).

1871–2 *Devils* (also called *The Possessed*)

1873–4 Edits the weekly journal *Grazhdanin* (*The Citizen*).

1873–81 *Diary of a Writer*

1875   *An Accidental Family* (also called *A Raw Youth*)

1878   Death of Dostoevsky's beloved three-year-old son Alesha (16 May).

1879–80 *The Brothers Karamazov*

1880   His speech at lavish celebrations held in Moscow in honour of Pushkin is received with frenetic enthusiasm on 8 June, and marks the peak point attained by his reputation during his lifetime.

1881   Dostoevsky dies in St Petersburg (28 January).
Alexander II is assassinated (1 March).

LIST OF CHARACTERS

In alphabetical order of first names

Grisha Vasin, *intellectually very gifted friend of Arkady, member of Dergachev circle and keen on Arkady's sister, Liza*

Ippolit Aleksandrovich Nashchokin, *young gambling acquaintance of Prince Seryozha*

Katerina Nikolaevna (or Nikolavna) Akhmakov, *beautiful daughter of old Prince Sokolsky and widow of General Akhmakov*

Kraft, *member of Dergachev circle and associate of Andronnikov*

Lambert, *friend of Arkady from his schooldays. Of French origin*

Lavrovsky, *Arkady's schoolboy acquaintance*

Lizaveta (Liza) Makarovna Versilov, *Arkady's sister*

Lukerya, *maidservant in the Versilov apartment*

Lydia Akhmakov, *daughter of General Akhmakov, a girl with whom Versilov was associated in Ems*

Makar Ivanovich (Ivanych) Dolgoruky, *Arkady's 'spiritual' father and husband of Sofya (Sonya) Andreevna Dolgoruky, Arkady's mother*

Marie (Marya), *Tatyana Pavlovna's Finnish cook-housekeeper*

Marya Ivanovna, *wife of Nikolay Semyonovich, blood relative and ward of the Moscow lawyer, Andronnikov. Arkady's Moscow landlady*

Matvey, *dare-devil driver employed by Arkady*

Maxim Ivanovich Slaughterer (Skotoboynikov), *merchant in Makar Dolgoruky's story*

Nastasya Stepanovna Salomeev, *woman given to spiritualism, mentioned by the old Prince Sokolsky*

Nastasya Yegorovna, *mother of Olya, the suicide (also known as* Darya Onisimovna)

Nikolay Ivanovich Sokolsky, *the 'old prince', father of Katerina Nikolaevna*

Nikolay Semyonovich, *Arkady's Moscow landlord and respected mentor*

Osetrov, *retired midshipman in Tatyana Pavlovna's building*

Olya, *daughter of Darya Onisimovna (also known as* Nastasya Yegorovna)

Pelishchevs (*see* Boris Mikhailovich)

Pete (Petya) (*see* Trishatov)

'Pock-marked chap' (*see* Semyon Sidorych)

Pyotr Ippolitovich, *Arkady's St Petersburg landlord*

Pyotr Stepanovich, *alcoholic teacher employed by Maxim Ivanovich in Makar Dolgoruky's story*

Pyotr Valeryanych, *retired lieutenant-colonel mentioned by Makar Dolgoruky*

Savin Markanov, *headman of Aleksandr Malgasov*

Semyon Sidorych, *'pock-marked chap', acquaintance of Lambert*

Sergey Petrovich Sokolsky, 'Prince Seryozha'

Sofya (Sonya) Andreevna Dolgoruky, *Arkady's mother*

Stebelkov, *stepfather of Grisha Vasin, self-professed medical practitioner, money-lender, and confidence trickster*

An Accidental Family

PART I

CHAPTER I

I

I CANNOT contain myself. I have sat down to write this story of my first steps in life when I could very well not have done so. I know one thing for sure: I'll never again sit down to write my autobiography, even if I live to be a hundred. One's got to be too grossly in love with oneself in order to write about oneself without shame. I only excuse myself with the thought that I'm not writing for the reason others write, which is to receive the reader's praise. If I've suddenly thought of writing down word for word what's happened to me in the past year, then I've done it out of inner necessity, because I've been so shocked by it all. I am only going to describe events, doing everything I can to avoid digressions and—most of all—literary embellishments. A writer writes for thirty years and in the end hasn't the faintest idea why he's been writing so long. I'm not a writer, don't want to be a writer, and would consider it vulgarly indecent to exhibit in the market-place of writing the innermost parts of my soul and beautiful descriptions of my feelings for all to see. However, I foresee with annoyance that it'll be impossible to get away completely without describing feelings and without a few thoughts of my own (perhaps even trashy ones), so depraved does any kind of writing make one, though undertaken solely for oneself. And one's thoughts can be very trashy too, since it's more than likely that what one values oneself has no value at all to someone else. But all that's by the way. The preliminaries are now done with. There'll be nothing more of this. Down to business . . . Though there's nothing more peculiar than getting down to business—to any business, for that matter.

II

I'm beginning my story—that's to say, I'd like to begin my story—on 19 September last year, the very day when I first met . . .

But to explain who I met right away, just like that, when no one knows anything, would be trashy. I even think this way of

5

saying things is trash. Having promised to avoid literary embellishments, I'm falling into that trap from the start. Apart from that, I think it's no good just wanting to write clearly. I will also remark that I don't think there's a single European language in which it's so difficult to write as Russian. I've just read through what I've written and I see that I'm a lot cleverer than what I've written. How is it that what is expressed by a clever man is a lot sillier than what is still inside him? I've often noticed this about myself and my verbal relations with people throughout the whole of this last fateful year and I've been through real hell.

Although I'll begin from 19 September, I'll still insert a couple of words about who I am, where I came from, and, of course, what might have been going on in my head, if only partially, on that morning of 19 September, in order to make things clear to the reader and perhaps to myself as well.

III

I've finished school, I'm pre-university, and I'm 20. My name's Dolgoruky and legally my father is Makar Ivanovich Dolgoruky, a former serf of the Versilovs. So I'm legitimate, though in the highest degree I'm an illegitimate son and there's not the least doubt about where I come from. It happened this way: twenty-two years ago Versilov the landowner (who is my real father), then 25, visited his estate in Tula province. I assume at that time he was very much a nonentity. It's interesting that this man, who had amazed me from earliest boyhood and had had such a fundamental influence on my spiritual self and even perhaps infected my whole future, this man remains even now, in an extraordinary number of ways, a complete enigma to me. But more about that later. You can't talk about it just like that. In any case, my whole notebook will be full of him.

He'd just at that time been widowed, aged 25. He had been married to a high-society lady, but not all that rich, a Fanariotov, and had had a son and daughter by her. Information about this wife of his who died at such an early age is scanty and is lost among my papers. In fact, many of the personal circumstances of Versilov's life have eluded me, so offhand has he always been with me, so distant, withdrawn, and casual, despite times when he has been astonishingly considerate. I mention now, however,

6

for clarification later, that in the course of his life he has gone through three fortunes—and large ones at that, four hundred thousand roubles or so and maybe even more. Now of course he hasn't got a penny . . .

At that time he went to his estate 'God knows why', at least that's how he expressed it to me later. His little children weren't living with him but with relatives, as was usual. That's how he always treated his children, legitimate or illegitimate. There were a good many serfs on the estate and among them was a gardener Makar Ivanovich Dolgoruky.

I'll say here right away, so as to be rid of it once and for all: few people can have so loathed their name as I have throughout my life. It's been silly, of course, but that's how it's been. Every time I went to a new school or came up against someone who, owing to my age, I had to explain myself to—in short, every little teacher person, tutor, inspector, priest—whoever it might be, having asked my name and heard it was Dolgoruky, always found it necessary to ask:

'Prince Dolgoruky?'

And each time I was obliged to explain to all these futile people:

'No, *simply* Dolgoruky.'

That word *simply* began eventually to drive me out of my mind. I'll remark in this connection, in view of such a phenomenon, that I don't remember a single exception—they all asked it. Some people would have found it completely unnecessary—and who the devil would want to know it anyhow? But they all asked it without exception. Having heard that I was *simply* Dolgoruky, the questioner would usually measure me with a dull and stupidly indifferent look, evidence of the fact that he didn't himself know why he'd asked, and then be done with me. My fellow classmates asked most insultingly of all. You know how they question a new boy. The new boy, confused and lost on his first day at school (it doesn't matter what kind it is), is fair game for everyone. He gets ordered about, teased, and treated like dirt. A healthy, plump bully suddenly stops in front of him and studies him for several seconds intently with a long, stern, and supercilious gaze. The new boy stands in front of him in silence, glances at him askance if he's not a coward, and waits to see what'll happen.

'What's your name?'

'Dolgoruky.'

'Prince Dolgoruky?'

'No, simply Dolgoruky.'

'Oh, *simply*! You're a fool!'

And he'd be right—there's nothing sillier than being called Dolgoruky when you're not a prince. I bear this mark of silliness on me without any sense of guilt. Later, when I'd got really annoyed, I always answered the question 'Are you a prince?' with:

'No, I'm the son of an estate worker, formerly a serf.'

Later still, when I'd been driven really frantic, I'd answer the question 'You're a prince, are you?' by saying firmly:

'No, I'm simply Dolgoruky, the illegitimate son of my former master, Mr Versilov.'

I thought this one up when I was already in the sixth form of high school and though I was soon convinced it was silly I didn't give it up immediately. I remember that one of my teachers—however, he was the only one—found that I was 'full of a vengeful idea of his civil role'. In general my assertion was accepted with what for me was a quite insulting complacency. Finally, one of my fellow classmates, a chap with a very sharp tongue whom I'd only had occasion to talk to once in the whole year, said to me with a serious expression, but glancing a bit to one side:

'Such feelings, of course, do you honour and there's no doubt you've got something to be proud of. You behave as if you've won a prize—but if I were in your position I wouldn't boast about being illegitimate!'

Since then I've stopped *boasting* about being illegitimate.

I repeat that it's very difficult to write in Russian. Here I am having written three whole pages about how I've spent all my life loathing my name—yet the reader's quite certain I really loathe the fact that I'm not a prince but simply Dolgoruky. To offer more explanations and justifications would be beneath me.

IV

Anyhow, among the staff on the estate, of whom there were a great many apart from Makar Ivanov, there was a girl, and she

8

was 18 years old when the 50-year-old Makar Dolgoruky suddenly revealed his intention of marrying her. Marriages among estate workers, as is well known, used only to happen under serfdom with the masters' permission and sometimes directly under their supervision. The estate was then in the charge of an Auntie—no auntie of mine, that is, just the lady landowner herself. I don't know why all her life she'd been known as Auntie, not only to me but to everyone, and equally as much in the Versilov family, to whom she was hardly related at all. She was Tatyana Pavlovna Prutkov. At that time she had thirty-five serfs of her own in that very province and in that very county. She did not exactly manage so much as oversee the neighbouring estate of Versilov's (of 500 souls) and that overseeing, so I heard, was worth every bit as much as would have been management by an expert. Still, her expert knowledge is no concern of mine. I simply want to add, without thought of flattering or ingratiating, that this Tatyana Prutkov was a person of true nobility and even of some originality.

It was she who not only did not discourage the marital inclinations of the solemn Makar Dolgoruky (and at that time he was said to be solemn), but, on the contrary, encouraged them in the highest degree. Sophya Andreevna (the 18-year-old, my mother, that's to say) had been an orphan for several years. Her late father, who had always held Makar Dolgoruky in the most extraordinary respect and was indebted to him in some way, also an estate worker, six years before, as he was dying, within, so it was said, a quarter of an hour of drawing his last breath, so that it could all have been put down to necessity and to delirium if it hadn't been that he had no rights in law in any case, being a serf, summoning Makar Dolgoruky to him before all the servants and in the presence of the participating priest, stated aloud and insistently his last will and testament while pointing at his daughter: 'Bring her up and take her unto you.' Everyone heard him say this. So far as Makar Ivanov was concerned, I don't know in what sense he later got married, with great pleasure, that is, or in fulfilment of an obligation. More than likely he had a look of complete indifference. He was the sort of man who even then had the ability 'to create an impression'. He was not numerate, so to speak, or literate (although he knew all the church services and particularly the lives of some of the saints,

9

mostly through having heard them so often), nor could he be considered a village pump politician, as it were; he was simply a man of stubborn character, at times even brash. He was opinionated, unbending in his judgements, and, in conclusion, 'lived respectfully', as he put it in his amazing way—that's how he was then. Of course, he received universal respect in return, but it was said no one could stand him. It was a quite different matter when he ceased to be a serf. Then he was only remembered as a kind of saint and one who had suffered much. I know that for a fact.

As for the character of my mother, until she was 18 Tatyana Pavlovna had kept her by her, despite the pleas of the estate bailiff that she be sent off to Moscow to learn a trade, and gave her a certain amount of education, that is to say taught her to sew, make clothes, behave like a young lady, and even to read a bit. My mother never learned to write properly. In her eyes marriage to Makar Ivanov was for long a foregone conclusion and all the things that happened to her she found admirable and of the very best. She was as calm for her wedding as she could possibly have been in the circumstances, so that Tatyana Pavlovna herself called her calm as a fish. I learned all this about the character of my mother at that time from Tatyana Pavlovna. Versilov arrived in the estate exactly six months after the wedding.

v

I want simply to say that I have never been able to discover and work out satisfactorily how it all began between him and my mother. I am fully prepared to believe, as he himself assured me last year, with a red face despite the fact that he spoke about it all with the most unconstrained and 'amused' look, that it had not been romantic at all and was just *one of those things*. I can believe it was just like that, and delightfully put, too, but I'd still like to know how it could have happened. Personally I have hated and despised all sexual 'dirt' all my life. Of course, it's not just a matter of shameless curiosity on my part. I will remark that, until last year, I hardly knew my mother at all. As a child I was entrusted to servants, for Versilov's peace of mind (about which much later). After that I simply couldn't imagine what she had looked like at that time. If she hadn't been pretty, what could a man like Versilov as he was then have found so seductive about her? The question is important for me because it reveals an extraordinarily curious side to him. That's why I ask it, not from any salacious motive. He himself, this sombre and reserved man, with his attractive charm which he got from God knows where (literally out of his pocket) whenever he thought it necessary—he himself told me that he had then been a very 'silly young pup' and not so much sentimental as *a pup* (no more) and had just read *Anton the Unlucky* and *Polinka Saks*,* two literary works which had had a vast civilizing effect on our younger generation in those days. He added that it was probably because of *Anton the Unlucky* that he had gone to his estate—and he added this in all seriousness.

How could this 'silly pup' have started up a relationship with my mother? I can just imagine (assuming anyone reads this) that a reader might surely roar with laughter at me as someone idiotically immature who, his innocence still stupidly intact, is trying to make head or tail of things he knew nothing about. Yes, I really know nothing about these things, although I'm not proud to admit this because I know how silly such inexperience is in a 20-year-old. I'll simply tell this reader of mine that he hasn't any idea either and I'll prove it. True, I know nothing about women and don't want to because I've sworn not to—I spit on the whole lot! But I know—I really do—that some women can bowl you over with their beauty and they know they can, in a split second! Other women you've got to spend six months chewing over before you know what they've got! To study that kind and fall in love with them it's not enough to look and be ready for whatever happens, you've got to be gifted in some way. I'm certain about that, even though I know nothing about it, and if it were different you'd have to turn all women into simple domestic animals and keep them around the place in that form. Perhaps a lot of men would like that.

I know positively, from several sources, that my mother was no beauty, although I've never seen the portrait of her in those days which is still about somewhere. It seems you wouldn't have fallen in love with her on sight. For simple 'relaxation' Versilov could have chosen another, and there was such a one, and

11

unmarried, the housemaid Anfisa Konstantinovna Sapozhkov. But a man who arrived on his estate with *Anton the Unlucky* under his arm in order to destroy, on the strength of his proprietorial rights, the sanctity of marriage, even if only of one of his serfs, would be bound to be thoroughly ashamed of himself because, I repeat, it was only a few months ago—i.e. twenty years later—that he'd talked extremely seriously about this *Anton the Unlucky*. In Anton's case only a horse was taken away, but in this case it was a wife! It meant that something special occurred, which meant that Mademoiselle Sapozhkov missed out (in my opinion, it was she who won). I tackled him once or twice about this last year, when there was a chance of talking to him (because there wasn't always) about all these questions and I noticed that, despite all his sophistication and the twenty years that had elapsed, he was somehow extraordinarily evasive. But I insisted. At least, wearing that look of sophisticated negligence which he frequently permitted himself in my presence, I remember that he once mumbled rather strangely something about my mother being one of those *defenceless* people whom you don't so much fall in love with—on the contrary, you don't at all—but whom you suddenly *take pity on* for their meekness—what else?—and you never know why, but you go on feeling pity for them, until pity grows into attraction . . . 'In short, my dear fellow, it sometimes happens you can't stop being attracted.' That's what he told me. And if it really was like that, then I'm bound to think of him not at all as the 'silly pup' he made himself out to be in those days. I wanted it to be like that.

However, he then started assuring me that my mother fell in love with him 'out of sheer submissiveness'—a pure invention of his, as if it had all been due to serfdom! He lied blatantly just to be chic, lied against his conscience, against his honour, and his innate nobility!

I've brought all this up, of course, in order to sing my mother's praises, but I've already admitted I knew nothing about her at that time. Yet I know only too well all the hopelessness of the conditions in which she lived and the miserable idea of humanity which had degraded her since childhood and to which she had to submit for the rest of her life. Nevertheless, the 'bad luck' occurred. And I must make one thing clear. Being carried away

12

as I was, I forgot to mention something I should have made clear to start with—that their relationship began literally with *bad luck*. (I hope the reader won't pretend he doesn't know what I'm talking about.) Briefly, it all began with proprietorial rights being asserted, despite the fact that Mademoiselle Sapozhkov was passed over.

But at this point I must chip in with a word of my own and declare at once that I am not contradicting myself. Because, for heaven's sake, what on earth could a man like Versilov (as he was then) have to talk about to someone like my mother even if it were a case of the most irresistible love? I've heard from depraved people that very often a man, when having it off with a woman, starts off in complete silence—which is, you know, the height of bloody awful behaviour and, to me, quite sickening. Nevertheless, I think Versilov, even if he'd wanted to, couldn't have started having it off with my mother in any other way. I mean, he wouldn't have begun by explaining *Polinka Saks* to her, would he? Above all, I mean, Russian literature didn't come into it. On the contrary, according to him (he once came clean about it), they used to hide away in corners, meet on staircases, springing away from each other red-faced like rubber balls when someone passed by, and the 'tyrant master' would be in fear and trembling of the meanest floor-cleaner despite all his proprietorial rights. But even if it began with the exercise of proprietorial rights, it worked out that way and yet not that way and in all essentials there isn't anything to be explained. To do so would make it even more obscure. The extent of their love would be guesswork because the first principle of people like Versilov is to abandon everything the moment they've got what they want. But it didn't work out like that. To fuck a pretty, flirtatious serf girl (though my mother wasn't a flirt) would be for a depraved 'young pup' (and they were all depraved, the very last one of them, both progressives and reactionaries) not just allowed but almost the 'done thing', especially in view of my father's romantic position as a young widower with time on his hands. But to love her for the rest of his life—that'd be too much. I can't swear he loved her, but he dragged her around with him for the rest of his life—that's true enough.

I asked a host of questions, but there was one very important one which I didn't dare ask my mother directly, despite the fact that I got to know her very well last year and, above all, like a rude and ungrateful pup who thinks *the world owes him*, didn't spare her feelings. The question was: how could she, she herself, already married six months and under the weight of all the ideas of the legality of marriage, literally crushed beneath their weight like a helpless fly, how could she, who revered her Makar Ivanovich hardly less than a sort of God, how could she in just a couple of weeks be seduced into sin? Surely my mother wasn't a depraved woman? On the contrary, I'll say now right away it'd be hard to imagine a purer soul—and so she has been all her life. It might be possible to explain it by saying she didn't know what she was doing—not in the sense that defence lawyers nowadays plead for murderers and thieves, but in the sense of a strong influence which, in view of the notorious naïvety of people subject to it, takes possession of them tragically and fatally. Who knows, maybe she fell in love until her dying breath with ... with the cut of his coat, the Parisian parting in his hair, his French accent (precisely his French one, of which she never understood a word), the romance he sang at the piano. Maybe she fell in love with something she'd never seen or heard of before (after all, he was very handsome) and because of it fell hopelessly in love with everything about him, his fashionable clothes and his romances included. I've heard this happened sometimes to serf girls under the serf system—and to nice girls, too. I can understand it, and whoever puts it all down to serfdom and 'sheer submissiveness' is a bloody fool! So could this young man have had in him such straightforward seductive power as to attract such a hitherto pure creature to such obvious danger, someone so completely different from him, from such a completely different world and environment? That it was to an obvious danger my mother was aware, I hope, all her life. Except that when she went with him, she didn't think about the danger at all—that's the way it always is with the *defence-less* ones: they know there's danger but they still take the plunge.

Once the sin was committed, they repented. Wittily he told me how he broke down in tears on Makar Ivanovich's shoulder, having summoned him to his study for the occasion, while she—

14

she lay dead to the world in some tiny little room in the servants' quarters.

But enough of questions and scandalous details. Versilov, having purchased my mother from Makar Ivanovich, went off helter-skelter and has ever since, as I mentioned above, dragged her about with him almost everywhere, except on those occasions when he was absent for long periods. Then he mostly left her in the care of Auntie, Tatyana Pavlovna Prutkov, that is, who could always be called on when necessary. They lived in Moscow, in various towns and estates, even abroad, and finally in St Petersburg. About all of that later—or no matter. I'll simply say that a year after my mother left Makar Ivanovich I appeared in the world, and after another year my sister, and then another ten or eleven years later a sickly boy was born, my younger brother, who died only a few months old. My mother's beauty ended with the painful labour of his confinement—so at least I was told. After that she quickly aged and grew frail.

But the relations with Makar Ivanovich were never severed completely. No matter where the Versilovs were, whether they were living in one place or on the move, Makar Ivanovich always kept what he called his 'family' informed of his doings. An odd sort of relationship developed, in part a bit solemn and almost quite formal. Among the landowning classes such relationships invariably had something comic about them, I know this, but there was none of it in this case. Letters were sent about twice a year, no more and no less, and were all extraordinarily alike. I've seen them. There was little personal in them—on the contrary, as far as possible they were limited to solemn accounts of the most ordinary events and most general feelings (if it's possible to talk about feelings being 'general'), that is to say: information first of all about the health of the correspondent, then queries about health, followed by good wishes, humble obeisances, and blessings—and that was all. I think it was precisely on such generalities and such impersonality that the whole orderliness of tone and the whole higher knowledge of behaviour in that society was based. 'To my most esteemed and respected wife, to our dear Sophya Andreevna, I send my humblest greetings . . .' 'To our dear children I send my eternally inviolable blessings.' All the children were always mentioned by name, as their numbers increased, myself among them. I will mention here that Makar Ivanovich was always clever enough not to address 'his excellency, the most esteemed Mr Andrey Petrovich' as his 'benefactor', although he invariably included in each letter his profoundest obeisances, requesting his correspondent's favour in return and divine blessing on himself. Replies were always sent to Makar Ivanovich by my mother as soon as possible and were always couched in precisely the same terms. Versilov, it has to be said, took no part in the correspondence. Makar Ivanovich sent his letters from various parts of Russia, from towns and monasteries in which he sometimes stayed for long periods. He never begged for anything; yet every three years he made a point of turning up and staying with my mother who, as was always the case, occupied separate quarters from Versilov. I'll have more to say about this later, but here I'll simply mention that Makar Ivanovich never flung himself down on a divan in the sitting-room but modestly chose a place for himself behind a screen. He never stayed long—five days or so or a week.

I forgot to mention that he was frightfully fond of his surname 'Dolgoruky' and held it in great esteem. Of course, it was quite silly! It was all the sillier because he liked his name just because there were princes named Dolgoruky. A completely upside-down way of thinking!

If I said that the family was always together, then that was true except for myself. I was like an outcast and from the day of my birth I was lodged with strangers. This had never been deliberate, but it was simply how it worked out. When I was born, my mother was still young and pretty and my father wanted to have her with him. A screaming baby was obviously a hindrance to one and all, especially while travelling. That's how it happened that until I was 19 I hardly saw my mother at all apart from one or two fleeting occasions. It happened not because of my mother's feelings but because of Versilov's arrogant disregard for people.

Now about something quite different.

A month ago—that's to say, about a month before 19 September—I decided in Moscow to have done with the whole lot of them and concentrate on my idea once and for all. That's literally the word—*concentrate* on my idea—because that way of putting it says almost all there is to say about my main idea, the reason why I live on this earth. In the isolation of my many years of daydreaming during my life in Moscow it has grown in me since the sixth form of high school and has never left me for a moment. It has swallowed up my whole life. Before conceiving it I lived my life in day-dreams, lived from childhood on in a kingdom of daydreams of the sort everyone knows. But with the appearance of this main and all-consuming idea my day-dreams came together and flowed instantly in the way they should—from the silly to the sensible. My schooling had no affect on them, nor on my idea. I will add, though, that I completed my schooling badly last year, while up till then I'd been among the top of my year, and it was all a consequence of my idea and the conclusion (maybe a false one) which I drew from it. So it wasn't my schooling that affected my idea, it was my idea that affected my schooling and my going to university. When I left school, I set my heart immediately not only on breaking with everything radically, but also, if necessary, with the whole world, even though I was then only 19. I wrote to everyone concerned, via everyone concerned in St Petersburg, saying I wanted to be left completely alone, didn't want any money sent to me, and, if possible, wanted to be completely forgotten (assuming someone, in any case, still remembered me) and, lastly, didn't want to go to university *at all*. The dilemma facing me was incontrovertible: either I went to university and received a higher education or I postponed for four years the immediate implementation of my idea—and I unhesitatingly opted for my idea, because I was mathematically sure of it.

Versilov, my father, whom I'd seen only once in my life, for an instant, when I was just 10 (and who succeeded in that instant in leaving a lasting impression), Versilov, in answer to my letter (which had not actually been sent to him), wrote to me in his own hand summoning me to St Petersburg and promising me a job there. A summons from this man who was so dry and proud, so casual and condescending towards me and who, ever since fathering me and then abandoning me, not only didn't know me at all but didn't even have a bad conscience about it (who knows, maybe he only had a vague and uncertain awareness of my existence, because it turned out later it wasn't he but others who'd paid for my upkeep in Moscow), the summons from this man, I say, who had suddenly remembered me and done me the honour of writing to me in his own hand—this summons, having flattered me, sealed my fate. Strange to say, what I liked among other things about his short letter (one small sheet of paper only) was that he didn't mention anything about going to university, didn't ask me to change my mind, didn't reproach me for not wanting an education—in short, didn't go in for any of the usual parental blah-blah-blah about such things, but this was just what was bad on his part in the sense that it showed up more clearly than ever his casual attitude towards me. I decided to go because it didn't interfere with my main day-dream. 'I'll see how it works out,' I told myself. 'In any case, I'll get involved with them only for a short time, maybe no time at all. But the moment I see that this step, however temporary and small, is taking me away from *what really matters*, then I'll break with them at once, give it all up and go back into my shell.' Yes, back into my shell! 'I'll hide inside it like a tortoise'—I liked that comparison very much. 'I won't be alone,' I kept on spouting to myself as I walked about like a mad thing during those last days in Moscow, 'I'll never be alone again, as I have been for so many terrible years so far, because I'll always have my idea, which I'll never give up, even if I like them all there and am happy there and spend ten years with them all!' It was just this impression (I'm jumping ahead a bit now), just this ambivalence in my plans and aims which first became apparent in Moscow and never left me for a moment in St Petersburg (because I don't know whether there was a single day in St Petersburg when I didn't set myself a final date for breaking with them and leaving)—this ambivalence, I say, was one of the chief reasons for the many indiscretions I committed during the year, the many beastly things I did, even the underhand things and, naturally, all the silly things.

Of course I'd suddenly have a father, something I'd never had before. This thought went to my head both while getting ready

18

in Moscow and while on the train. A father meant nothing to me as such, and I wasn't fond of displays of affection in any case, but this man hadn't wanted to know me and had humiliated me, while I'd gasped after him in my dreams (if it's possible to dream like that). Every day-dream of mine from childhood on had been full of him, woven its way round him, and ultimately centred on him. I didn't know whether I loved or hated him, but he filled up all my future and all my calculations about life—and it happened of its own accord, it grew as I grew.

I was also influenced in my departure from Moscow by yet another very powerful consideration, by a temptation which, three months already before departure (when there was no thought of St Petersburg at all) had seized hold of my heart and made it beat faster. What drew me into that unknown ocean was the thought that I could enter into it as my own master and captain of the fates of others—and what others! But they were magnanimous, not despotic feelings seething inside me—I want to make that clear now, so my words won't be misunderstood. At the same time Versilov might have thought (if he deigned so much as to think about me) that it was a small boy travelling to him, a former high-school boy, someone so immature he'd be astonished at the whole wide world. But I meanwhile knew all there was to know about him and had with me a most important document for which (I know this now for sure) he'd have given up several years of his life if I'd revealed its secret to him then. However, I see I'm talking in riddles. Without facts you can't describe feelings. Besides, there'll be quite enough about all that when the time comes, which is why I've started writing it all down. But just writing it down makes it cloudy and nightmarish.

VIII

In the end, so as to get to 19 September at last, I'll say briefly and, so to speak, in passing that I discovered them all—Versilov, that is, my mother, and my sister (whom I was meeting for the first time in my life)—in different circumstances, almost in poverty, or on the brink of it. I knew about this already in Moscow, but wasn't prepared for what I saw. From earliest childhood I was accustomed to imagine this man, this 'future father' of mine, as almost bathed in brilliance and simply couldn't imagine him except as someone occupying a top place. Versilov never lived with my mother in the same apartment but always rented a separate one for her. Of course, he did this out of his absolutely loathsome sense of 'decency'! But now they were living all together in a wooden shack down a side street near the Semenovksy Barracks. All their things were in pawn, so that I even gave my mother without Versilov knowing a secret sixty roubles of my own. They were *secret* because they were saved up out of my pocket-money which had been doled out to me at five roubles a month over two years. The accumulation had begun on the very first day of my 'idea'. So Versilov wasn't to know anything at all about this money. I was terrified he might.

This help turned out to be only a drop in the ocean. My mother worked and my sister took in sewing while Versilov lived an idle, self-indulgent life and kept up many of his former, fairly expensive habits. He grumbled appallingly, particularly at dinner, and his entire behaviour was completely despotic. But my mother, sister, Tatyana Pavlovna, and the innumerable women-folk of the family of the late Andronnikov (head of a civil service department and the man who had been looking after Versilov's affairs, deceased only three months before my arrival) simply worshipped him like some kind of idol. I couldn't have imagined such a thing. I will note that nine years before he was incomparably more elegant. I've already admitted that in my day-dreams he was bathed in brilliance, and so I couldn't imagine how he could have aged so much and become so worn out in a mere nine years—and this at once made me feel sad, wretched, and ashamed. The sight of his face was one of the most oppressive of my initial impressions after arriving. However, he was certainly not an old man, being no more than 45. But on closer study I found in his good looks something even more astonishing than I had remembered from seeing him before. There was less of the former gloss, less of outward show and even elegance about him, but life had as it were etched in his features something much more interesting than before.

Anyhow, poverty was only a tenth or twentieth part of his misfortunes, and I knew all too much about that. Apart from poverty, there was something far more serious—not to mention that there were still hopes of winning the court case over the inheritance between Versilov and the Princes Sokolsky (it had

20

already been going on a year), which meant that Versilov might obtain in the near future an estate valued at seventy—or possibly more—thousand roubles. I mentioned above that Versilov had already run through three fortunes—and here was another about to come to his aid! The case would be decided very shortly. That's what I'd arrived to find. True, no one had high hopes that he'd get any money, none was obtainable anywhere and so everyone was waiting to see what happened.

But Versilov never went out to see people, even though he was sometimes away the whole day. It was already about a year since he had become a social *outcast*. The story surrounding this, despite all my efforts, remained for me in the main unexplained even after being in St Petersburg a whole month. Whether or not Versilov was to blame—that's what I wanted to know, that's why I'd made the trip to Moscow! Everyone had turned their backs on him, among them all the influential titled people whom he'd always known how to cultivate all his life, as a consequence of rumours about an extremely horrid and—what was far worse in the eyes of high society—an extremely scandalous thing he had allegedly done just over a year ago in Germany and even about an all-too-public slap in the face which he had then received from one of the very same Princes Sokolsky and which he had not reacted to by calling on the perpetrator to fight a duel. Even his children (the legitimate ones), a son and a daughter, had turned their back on him and lived apart. True, his son and daughter moved in the highest circles, through the help of the Fanariotovs and old Prince Sokolsky (formerly a friend of Versilov). However, studying him closely throughout the whole of this month, I saw a haughty man who had not been excluded by society so much as one who had driven society away from him, so independent did he seem. But did he have a right to be so independent?—that's what bothered me! I had to discover the whole truth as soon as possible because I'd come here to pass judgement on this man. I still kept my secret powers from him, but I had either to recognize him or reject him completely. But the latter choice was too much for me and I agonized over it. Anyhow, I'll come absolutely clean: this man was very dear to me!

But meanwhile I lived with them all in the same apartment, went out to work, and could hardly stop myself saying rude

21

things about them. And sometimes even did say them. After living there a month, I became convinced as each day went by that I couldn't turn to him for any final explanations. The arrogant man had become to me a riddle which insulted me to the depths of my being. He was even charming to me and joked, but I'd rather have quarrelled with him than had those jokes. All my conversations with him always had a certain ambiguous character—that's to say, on his side he simply seemed to be laughing at me. From the very start of my coming from Moscow he treated me frivolously. I couldn't understand why he did this. True, he got what he wanted—he seemed an enigma to me. But I wasn't going to stoop to asking him to take me seriously. What's more, he had certain amazing and unassailable tricks of behaviour which I didn't know how to deal with. In short, he treated me just like the most immature kid, which I could barely stand, though I knew that's how it would be. As a consequence, I myself ceased to talk seriously and waited. I even almost gave up talking altogether. I waited for one person, whose arrival in St Petersburg could finally reveal to me the truth. That was my last hope. In any case, I'd made plans to break with them once and for all and had already taken practical steps. I was sorry for my mother, but it was to be 'either him or me'—or that's how I wanted to put it to her and my sister. I'd even fixed the day. But meanwhile I went to work as usual.

CHAPTER II

I

ON the 19th I was also due to receive my first salary for my first month in my St Petersburg job. No one had asked me about this job, it had just been given to me, it seemed, the day I arrived. This had been very rude and I was almost in duty bound to protest. It was a job in the house of the old Prince Sokolsky. But if I'd protested then, it would have meant that I'd have cut myself off from them at the start, which didn't bother me in the least but would have harmed my basic aims, so I accepted the job without saying anything and by my silence kept my dignity.

I will explain right away that this Prince Sokolsky, a wealthy man and a privy councillor, was not related to the Moscow Princes Sokolsky (who had been impoverished nonentities for several generations), with whom Versilov was engaged in litigation. They simply had the same name. Nevertheless, the old prince took a great deal of interest in them and was particularly fond of one of them, the first in the line, so to speak, a young officer. Quite recently Versilov had had enormous influence on the old man's affairs and was a friend of his—a strange friend, because the poor prince, as I've already mentioned, was absolutely terrified of him not only when I first took the job but apparently always had been, throughout their friendship. However, they hadn't seen each other for some time. The dishonourable affair, for which Versilov had been blamed, concerned precisely this Sokolsky family, but Auntie Tatyana Pavlovna had come to the rescue and through her I had been given the job with the old man, who wanted 'a young fellow' to work with him in his study. Along with this it turned out that he was also dreadfully keen to help Versilov, as a kind of first step in his direction, and Versilov had *allowed* it. The old prince had done this in the absence of his daughter, the widow of a general, who very probably wouldn't have allowed him to take this first step. More about this later, but I'll mention that the strange state of his relations with Versilov struck me so much that it endeared me to him. I toyed with the idea that if the head of the offended family still continued to nurture such respect for Versilov, then all the widespread rumours about the foul things Versilov had done must be either silly or at least ambivalent. This was partly what made me refrain from protesting when I took the job and, having taken it, I hoped to test the truth of it all.

Tatyana Pavlovna was playing an odd role when I first encountered her in St Petersburg. I had almost forgotten about her completely and never expected that she would have such significance. I had already encountered her three or four times during my Moscow life when she had appeared from God knows where on someone's bidding, each time when I had had to settle in somewhere new—on entering the Touchard school or later, after two and a half years, when I was going on to high school and was finding a place in the apartment of the unforgettable

Nikolay Semyonovich. Having appeared, she would spend the whole day long with me, checking on my underwear and my clothing, travelling to Kuznetsky* and buying everything I needed—in short, arranging all my earthly goods down to the last carrying-case and penknife, all the time hissing at me, scolding me, blaming me for this and that, testing me, and quoting to me the example of other fantastic boys she knew or were related to her, who were all better than me, and, what's more, she'd pinch me and slap me about and sometimes quite painfully. Having fixed me up and settled me in, she'd vanish for several years at a time. On my arrival in St Petersburg, she immediately put in an appearance again to help me settle in. She was a dryish, tiny little person, with a birdlike beaky little nose and sharp birdlike little eyes. She was a slave to Versilov and bowed down to him as if he were the Pope, but through conviction. But I soon noticed that everywhere she was held in most definite respect and, above all, everyone knew her. The old Prince Sokolsky treated her with unusual respect, as did her family, the proud Versilov children as well and the Fanariotovs, yet all the while she took in sewing, did lace-washing and shop work for a living. She and I quarrelled from the very first word because she instantly took it into her head, as she had done six years ago, to start hissing at me. Ever since we quarrelled each day, but it didn't stop us sometimes having a talk and I confess that by the end of a month I had begun to like her—for her independence of character, I think. However, I never let her know this.

I understood at once that I'd been given my job with the sick old man simply in order to be a 'comfort' to him and that this was what my work amounted to. Naturally, this hurt me and I would have done something about it, but the eccentric old fellow quickly produced an unexpected impression on me, something a bit like pity, and by the end of the month I had become oddly attached to him and at least I had given up my intention of being rude. He was, by the way, no more than 60. The whole thing had come out into the open at that point. A year and a half previously he had suddenly had a fit of some kind. He had been travelling somewhere and had gone mad, so that a scandal of sorts occurred which had been the subject of gossip in St Petersburg. As happens in such cases, he was instantly whisked off abroad, but about five months later he suddenly reappeared and was completely recovered, although he had given up his job in the civil service. Versilov made the serious claim (and with evident heat) that there had been no madness of any kind and that it had only been an attack of nerves. I immediately noted the heat with which Versilov made his claim. Still, I'll also note that I almost shared his opinion. The old man seemed sometimes no more than remarkably frivolous for his years, something which hadn't been the case earlier, it was said. It was said that earlier he had been used to giving advice in certain quarters and had on one occasion proved almost too outstanding in the fulfilment of a particular task.

Having known him for a month, I couldn't have supposed that he had any particular strengths as an adviser. It was commonly remarked of him (though I didn't notice it myself) that, after his fit, he had developed a special proclivity for getting married as quickly as possible and had already done something about this more than once in the past eighteen months. People apparently knew about this in the best society and showed an interest, as was right and proper. But as this half-baked urge was contrary to the interests of certain people surrounding the prince, the old man was kept under surveillance from all sides. He had little family of his own. He had been a widower for about twenty years and had only one daughter, the general's widow who was now expected from Moscow any day, a young woman whose character he was undoubtedly frightened of. But he had a mass of various distant relatives, chiefly from his late wife, who were almost all on the poverty line. Apart from that, there was a multitude of male and female children who had been fostered by him and who all expected a cut from his will and consequently all did their bit to help the general's widow keep tabs on him. Above all, he had had one odd eccentricity ever since his youth, though I'm not sure whether it was comic or not—the giving in marriage of impoverished young ladies. He had been doing this for twenty-five years at a stretch—either distant female relatives or the stepdaughters of his wife's cousins or goddaughters, even, once, the daughter of his doorkeeper. He used to take them into his own home as little girls, bring them up with the help of governesses and French teachers, then have them educated at the best schools, and finally marry them off with a dowry. All of

25

them constantly crowded round him. Naturally, those he had fostered produced more girls in their marriages, all of whom sought to be fostered by him, and he had to be constantly attending christenings, was constantly showered with congratulations on his birthday, and enjoyed it all immensely.

Having started working for him, I noted at once that the old man had become fixed in the oppressive conviction—and one couldn't fail to notice it—that everyone in the best society had begun giving him strange looks and that they had stopped treating him as they had done previously when he was well. At even the most entertaining social gatherings this impression never left him. The old man became hypersensitive and started seeing something in people's eyes. The thought that they all still suspected him of being out of his mind evidently tormented him and he would even sometimes peer at me mistrustfully. And if he happened to learn that so-and-so had been spreading such a rumour about him or asserting it to someone, then this most inoffensive of men would become his enemy for life. I ask the reader to take note of this. I will add that this decided me from the very first day not to be rude to him. I was even glad if an occasion arose sometimes to cheer him up and take his mind off it. I don't think that admission casts a shadow on my self-esteem.

A large part of his money was in investments. Since his illness he had become a partner in a large joint-stock company, but a very secure one. And although others looked after the business, he was also extremely interested in it, attended shareholders' meetings, was elected a founding member, sat on committees, made lengthy speeches, overturned decisions, and evidently had great fun making a lot of noise. He loved speechifying, because at least everyone could see what a mind he had. And in general he was terribly fond of dropping into his conversation, even on the most intimate of occasions, particularly profound remarks or *bon mots*, which is something I can understand only too well.

In his house, on the ground floor, he had set up a kind of office with an official to look after the accounts, keep the books, and also run the house itself. This official, though working part-time in the civil service, would have been quite sufficient for such work, but on the express wish of the prince I was added as well, supposedly to help the official; but I was immediately transferred to his study upstairs and often, even for outward show, had no occupation whatever, neither papers, nor books.

I am writing now like someone who has long since sobered up and is in many respects scarcely more than an outsider. But how can I describe the anguish of that time (which I can still vividly recall), deep-rooted as it was in my heart, and above all the excitement I felt then, rising to such turbulent and feverish heights I couldn't sleep at night—the excitement of my impatience, of all the mysteries I'd made for myself?

II

To ask for money is bloody awful, even if it's a salary, if you have the feeling somewhere in the recesses of your conscience that you haven't earned it. In the mean time, the day before, my mother, after whisperings with my sister so that Versilov shouldn't hear ('in order not to upset Andrey Petrovich'), had intended to pawn an icon which was especially dear to her for some reason. I was due to get fifty roubles a month, but I had no idea how I was to receive it—nobody'd told me when I started my job. Three or so days previously, coming across the official downstairs, I asked him who I got my salary from. He looked at me with a smile of astonishment (he didn't like me) and said:

'So you're being paid a salary, are you?'

I thought that after my answer he would add:

'What on earth for, sir?'

But he simply answered drily that he 'didn't know a thing' and stuck his nose back into a lined ledger into which he was entering accounts from some receipts.

However, it wasn't news to him that I had a job to do. A couple of weeks earlier I'd spent just on four days working at something he'd passed on to me—a copying job, but it had turned out to be almost a case of rewriting it. It was a whole mass of the prince's 'ideas' which he was preparing to submit to a shareholders' committee meeting. It had all to be properly arranged and given some semblance of style. I spent a whole day with the prince afterwards over this thing and he argued vigorously with me. Still, he was pleased in the end. I simply don't know whether he submitted it or not. As for two or three letters, also on business matters, that I wrote on his orders, I won't even mention them.

So it was disagreeable for me to have to ask for my salary, particularly as I'd already made up my mind to give up the job in anticipation of being forced to leave there due to unavoidable circumstances. Waking up that morning and dressing in my attic room, I felt my heart was beating wildly and, though I didn't give a damn, on going to the prince's house I once more felt the same old excitement because that morning the arrival was awaited of the very person, the woman, from whom I was expecting an explanation of everything that bothered me. I am referring to the prince's daughter, Mrs Akhmakov, the young general's widow whom I've already mentioned and who was in bitter contention with Versilov. At last I've actually written her name! Of course, I'd never seen her and couldn't even imagine what she looked like or what I'd say to her. But I had imagined (perhaps with good grounds, too) that when she arrived the obscurity surrounding Versilov in my eyes would be dispersed. I couldn't be sure of this because I was frightfully annoyed that, from the very start, I'd been so faint-hearted and awkward; I was frightfully inquisitive and, above all, quite repelled—all three feelings coexisted in me. I can remember the whole of that day by heart!

My prince still knew nothing about his daughter's likely arrival and supposed she'd be returning from Moscow in a week or so. I had already learned about it quite by accident the day before, because Tatyana Pavlovna, who had received a letter from Mrs Akhmakov, had mentioned it to my mother in my presence. Although they whispered together about it and used vague terms, I guessed what it was. Of course, I wasn't listening in, I just simply couldn't fail to hear something when I saw that my mother, on learning of this woman's arrival, grew suddenly so excited. Versilov was not at home.

I didn't want to convey any of this to the old man because I couldn't fail to notice how anxious he had been about her arrival during this whole period. He had even, about three days ago, mentioned, in a shy, vague way, that he was fearful of her arrival on my account, because she might give him a dressing-down for employing me. However, I must add that in his relations with his family he still retained his independence and authority, especially over money matters. To start with, I had reached the conclusion that he was a complete old woman, but then I'd had to change my ideas in the sense that, if he was an old woman, there still remained the occasional streak of stubbornness if not of actual manliness in him. There were moments when, in view of his character—outwardly cowardly and submissive—there was nothing to be done with him. Versilov later explained all this to me in greater detail. I'll mention now only out of curiosity that we almost never talked about his daughter, as if deliberately avoiding the subject. I particularly avoided the subject and he avoided talking to me about Versilov, and I was quite sure he wouldn't answer me if I asked him one of those ticklish questions which so intrigued me.

If you want to know what he and I talked about throughout the whole of that month, then I'll say it was essentially about every topic imaginable but most of all about certain strange things. I much enjoyed the extraordinary good nature with which he treated me. Sometimes I would look at this man with extraordinary bewilderment and ask myself: 'How on earth could he have earlier sat on committees? He should really be at high school, in the fourth form, say—and then he'd have been a delightful friend to have.' More than once I'd been astonished by the appearance of his face. To look at, it would seem extraordinarily serious (and almost handsome) in a dry way; thick grey curly hair and wide-open eyes; and his whole, well-built figure had a dry look about it; but his face had an unpleasant, almost indecent way of suddenly changing its expression from an unduly serious one to one that was excessively frivolous, so that someone seeing him for the first time would be caught out. I mentioned this to Versilov who listened to me with interest. I think he hadn't expected me to be capable of noticing such things, but he remarked by the way that this had only occurred in the prince's case since his illness and therefore very recently.

We talked chiefly about two abstract matters—about God and His existence, whether or not He exists, and about women. The prince was very religious and emotional. He had a large icon stand in his study with a lamp burning in front of it. But suddenly he would have moods and he'd suddenly begin doubting the existence of God and start making astonishing remarks, obviously in order to stir me up. To the idea itself I was pretty indifferent, generally speaking, but we would still get carried away, both of us, and always quite sincerely. I recall all these conversations even now with pleasure. But what he enjoyed most was chatting about women and because I, through my dislike of talking about this topic, couldn't join in properly, he sometimes even got annoyed.

He started talking on this very topic the moment I arrived that morning. I found him in a playful mood, although the day before I'd left him in an extraordinarily depressed state of mind. Anyhow, I had at all costs to have it out with him about my salary—before certain others arrived. I calculated that we'd be bound to be *interrupted* that day (my heart wasn't beating wildly for nothing) and if that happened I'd very likely not dare raise the question of money. But because nothing was being said about money, I naturally grew furious at my own silliness and, as I recall it now, in annoyance at some unduly jolly question of his, let fly at him with my views on women and with extraordinary fervour. As a result, he unburdened himself even more fulsomely.

III

'. . . I hate women because they're rude, because they're awkward, because they haven't got minds of their own and because they dress indecently!' I concluded my long tirade disjointedly.

'Have a heart, my dear chap!' he cried out, terribly delighted, which made me angrier than ever.

I am submissive and petty only in petty matters, but in important matters I never submit at all. In such petty matters as decorous social behaviour I can be made to do God knows what and I always deplore this characteristic of mine. Out of a kind of shitty goodwill I've sometimes been ready to kowtow to some social dandy, only because I've been seduced by his politeness, or I've found myself being drawn into an argument with some complete idiot, which is all the more unforgivable. All this is because I haven't got sufficient staying power and had a hole-and-corner upbringing. I go away angry and swear I won't do the same thing tomorrow, but tomorrow it's just the same. That's why I've sometimes been mistaken for a 16-year-old. But instead of cultivating staying power I now prefer to lock myself away all the more securely into a corner, although that may seem very misanthropical: 'All right, so I'm socially awkward—to hell with all that!' I say this in all seriousness and once and for all. However, I'm not writing this on account of the prince and not even because of the conversation we had then.

'I'm not saying this just to delight you,' I almost screamed at him. 'I'm simply saying what I believe.'

'But what's this about women being rude and dressing indecently? This is new.'

'Yes, they're rude. Go to the theatre, go to a party. Every man knows his right-hand side when coming and going, he steps to the right and I step to the right. A woman, by which I mean a lady—I'm talking only about ladies—literally goes straight for you, not even noticing you, just as if you're constantly obliged to jump aside and let her pass. I'm ready to give way as a member of the weaker sex, but what's right got to do with it, why's she so sure I've got to give way? That's what's so insulting! That's why I could never give a damn when I come across them. And after that they go around shouting that they're oppressed and demanding equality. What sort of equality is it when I always get trampled on and have grit flung in my mouth!'

'Grit!'

'Yes. Because they're dressed indecently—only a pervert wouldn't see it. In courts of law they lock the doors when cases of indecency are being heard. Then why do they allow it on the streets where there are far more people? They stick all kinds of frills on their behinds to show what *belles femmes* they are! And quite openly! After all, I can't help noticing and youngsters'll notice too and lads and boys who are just beginning to . . . It's filthy! Let old perverts admire them and run about after them with their tongues hanging out, but the purity of the young must be safeguarded. It just makes me spit! She walks along the boulevard and behind her she's got a train a metre and more long and it sends up a cloud of grit. What do you do if you're behind her? Either you try running ahead to pass her, or just jump away from her, otherwise she'll give you a nose-full or a mouthful of grit! What's more, it's silk she's traipsing round in

31

for mile after mile, simply because it's the fashion, while her husband only gets five hundred roubles annually for his Senate job! That's where all the bribe-taking starts! That's why I always spit on them and do so out loud and swear at them!'

Although I record this conversation a bit humorously and in a way characteristic of that time, this is still what I think.

'And you've always got away with it?' the prince enquired.

'I spit and I walk away. It goes without saying she's aware, but she doesn't show it and goes on her way grandly without turning her head. But I've only used swear words completely seriously once—with a couple of ladies on the boulevard, both wearing trains—not, I mean, really foul language, but I've simply remarked out loud that trains were insulting.'

'That's literally what you said?'

'Of course. In the first place, they flout social conventions and, in the second place, they cause dust. But the boulevard's for everyone's use, mine, someone else's, a third, Fyodor's, Ivan's—everyone's. That's what I said. And in general I dislike the way women walk, especially when seen from behind. I also said that, or hinted as much.'

'My friend, you could've landed in serious trouble. Couldn't they have whisked you off to the police?'

'No, they couldn't. There was nothing to complain about. Someone was walking along beside them and talking to himself. Everyone's got the right to say what he believes out loud. I spoke in the abstract, without addressing them in particular. It was they who turned on me and started swearing a great deal worse than I did, calling me a wimp, that I ought to have my food taken away from me, that I was a nihilist and they'd report me to the police, that I'd picked on them because they were poor weak women and if there'd been a man with them I'd have soon run away with my tail between my legs. I announced to them coolly and calmly that they should stop pestering me and that I would cross to the other side. And in order to show them that I wasn't frightened of their menfolk and was ready to face a challenge to a duel, I said I would accompany them to within twenty paces of their home and then stand outside and wait for their men to appear. And that's what I did.'

'You didn't!'

'Of course, it was silly, but I was furious. They traipsed off

32

with me following for a couple of miles, in the heat, until they got to the Institutes and they went into a single-storey wooden house—very nicely kept, I've got to admit—with a great many flowers visible in the windows and a couple of canaries, three small dogs, and framed engravings. I stood in front of the house for about half an hour. They glanced out two or three times covertly and then lowered all the blinds. At last some official or other came out of the gate, a middle-aged chap. Judging by his appearance he'd been sleeping and had been deliberately woken up. He wasn't exactly in a dressing-gown, but in something a bit like it, very homely. He stood by the gate, put his arms behind his back, and stared at me—and I at him. Then he'd look away, then look back at me again and suddenly he started smiling at me. I turned round and walked off.'

'My friend, that's positively Schilleresque! I've always wondered why you, so red-cheeked, your face literally bursting with health, should be so repelled, as it were, by women! How can it be that a woman hasn't had the usual effect on you at your age? *Mon cher*, when I was only 11, my tutor noticed that I was showing far too much interest in the statues in the Winter Garden.'

'You'd absolutely love it if I went with some local whore and then came and told you all about it! No way! I myself was 13 when I saw a woman completely naked—completely! Ever since I've been repelled.'

'Really? But, *cher enfant*, a beautiful fresh woman smells as sweet as an apple—what's repulsive about that?'

'In my boarding school, at Touchard's, before I went to high school, I had a friend, Lambert. He hit me the whole time because he was three years older than me and I did things for him, even took his shoes off and so on. When he was being confirmed, a priest called Rigaud came to congratulate him on his first communion, and both of them fell on each other's shoulders in tears and the priest Rigaud began pressing him terribly hard to his chest, making all sorts of gestures. I also cried then and felt very envious. When his father died, he left and I didn't see him for two years, but then I met him one time on the street. He said he'd come and see me. I was at high school then and living at Nikolay Semyonovich's. He came one morning, showed me five hundred roubles, and ordered me to come away with him. Although he'd been hitting me two years before, he'd always needed me, and not just to take off his shoes. He'd always been used to telling me everything.

'He said he'd taken the money that day out of a box his mother had, after he'd made a key for it, because the money left by his father was all his in law and she wouldn't dare not give it to him, and he said the priest Rigaud had come yesterday to give him a ticking off—he'd come into the room, stood over him and started whining, showing how horrified he was and raising his arms to heaven and saying: "And, lo, I did take out a knife and said I will cut your thwoat." (He couldn't pronounce his 'r's properly.)

'We went off to Kuznetsky. On the way he told me that his mother was having an affair with the priest Rigaud and he knew about it and didn't care a damn and that all the stuff they said about communion was rubbish. He said a lot of other things and I grew frightened. In Kuznetsky he bought a twin-barrelled gun, a game pouch, cartridges, a riding whip, and a pound of sweets. We went out of town to do some shooting and on the way we met a birdcatcher with some cages and Lambert bought a canary from him. In a wood he released the canary, because it couldn't fly far after being caged, and started shooting at it but missed. It was the first time he'd shot in his life, but he'd long wanted to buy a gun, even when he'd been at Touchard's, and it had long been a dream of ours. He was literally choking with excitement. He had terrifically black hair, a white face with pink cheeks like a mask, a long hooked nose like a Frenchman, white teeth, and jet-black eyes. He tied the canary to a branch and gave it two blasts from both barrels at close range and it flew into a hundred feathery pieces.

'Then we returned to town, went to a hotel, took a room, and started having some food and champagne. Along came a woman ... I remember I was amazed how sumptuous she looked in a green silk dress. It was then I saw everything I've just told you about ... When we started drinking again, he started taunting her and swearing at her. She was sitting there without her dress on—he'd taken it away—and when she kicked up a fuss and asked for it back so she could get dressed he began whipping her as hard as he could on her bare shoulders. I jumped up and seized him by his hair so hard he was flung down to the ground at one go. He grabbed a fork and stuck it in my thigh. At my

34

shout people rushed in and I was able to run away. Ever since I've been revolted by the thought of nakedness and, believe me, she was a beauty.'

As I was speaking the prince's expression gradually changed from the playful to the sad.

'*Mon pauvre enfant*! I've always been certain that your boyhood had many unhappy days in it.'

'Please don't worry about that.'

'But you were all alone, you told me that yourself, despite this Lambert. The way you described it all—the canary, the confirmation with all the tears, and then, in a year or so, how he found out about his mother and the priest ... Oh, *mon cher*, the question of children in our time is an awful one—all these charming little golden-headed children, with their curls and their innocence, dancing in front of you in their early childhood and looking at you with their bright laughter and their bright little eyes, looking just like angels or delightful little birds ... And then ... and then it would've been better if they'd never grown up at all!'

'What an old sentimentalist you are, prince! You sound as if you have children of your own. But you haven't got any small children and never will have.'

'*Tiens!*' His whole face changed instantly. 'Just the day before yesterday Aleksandra Petrovna—just the day before yesterday!— Aleksandra Petrovna Sinitsky—I think you must have met her here three weeks ago—just imagine, the day before yesterday, when I made the jolly remark that if I get married I can at least be sure there won't be any children, she suddenly turned on me and even said with a certain malice: "On the contrary, you will have them, it's with people like you they *invariably* come along from the start, you wait and see!" Ha-ha-ha! For some reason everyone imagines I'll suddenly get married. But even if that was a nasty thing to say, you've got to agree it was clever!'

'Clever and offensive.'

'Well, *cher enfant*, you can't take offence at every little busybody. I think what counts in people most of all is cleverness, which is visibly disappearing among us, and whatever Aleksandra Petrovna says can hardly be counted, can it?'

'What was that you said?' I pestered him. 'You can't take offence at every little busybody ... That's just it! Not every little busybody's worth paying attention to—an excellent rule of life! It's just what I need. I'll write it down. Sometimes, prince, you say the most delightful things!'

He literally glowed.

'*N'est-ce pas? Cher enfant*, true cleverness is vanishing and the less there is, the worse it'll be. *Eh, mais . . . C'est moi qui connait les femmes*. Believe me, the life of any woman, no matter what she may profess, is an eternal search for someone to bow down to, a thirst, so to speak, to kowtow. And take note—there are no exceptions to this rule!'

'Absolutely true! Marvellous!' I shouted with delight. At any other time we would have launched into a philosophical discussion of this topic lasting a whole hour, but suddenly I was bitten by my conscience and went red. It struck me that with all my praise for his *bons mots* it might seem I was sucking up to him for his money and that he would think this as soon as I started asking for it. I'd like to make this clear at this point.

'Prince, I most humbly ask you now to let me have the fifty roubles owing to me for this month!' I fired off all at one go and with an irritability amounting to rudeness.

I remember (because I remember everything that happened that morning down to the last detail) there then occurred, truth to tell, a very nasty scene between us. He didn't understand me at first and then spent a long time looking at me without understanding what money I meant. Naturally he hadn't imagined that I was receiving a salary—and for what? True, he later started assuring me he'd forgotten and, when he guessed what I was on about, instantly started bringing out twenty-five roubles, but in a great hurry and with a red face. Confronted by this, I stood up and declared sharply that I couldn't take the money because I had evidently either been misinformed about receiving a salary or deceived about it in order to make me take the job, and that I was now only too aware that I had nothing to be paid for because I had done nothing. The prince took fright at this and started assuring me that I'd been of frightfully great service to him and would continue to be in the future and that fifty roubles was so little he'd have to add to it because he was obliged to and he'd arranged it all with Tatyana Pavlovna but had 'unforgivably forgotten all about it'. I flared up and finally announced that it was beneath me to receive a salary for telling

36

scandalous anecdotes about traipsing after two ladies down to the Institutes and that I hadn't been hired just to pass the time of day with him but to do something serious and if there was nothing serious to be done, then I'd have to give in my notice, and so on and so forth. I hadn't imagined that he'd have become as frightened as he was on hearing these words of mine. It goes without saying that it ended with my abandoning my protests and his handing me fifty roubles—and I still go red in the face when I remember that I took them! Everything on earth always ends in baseness and, what's worst of all, he then managed almost to prove to me that I deserved it all unreservedly and I was silly enough to believe him and, what's more, to decide it was impossible not to take it.

'*Cher, cher enfant!*' he exclaimed, kissing me and embracing me (I confess I was just on the point of tears for some reason and restrained myself just in time and even now, as I write, I feel the colour rising in my cheeks), 'dear friend, you're now a relation of mine, in the past month you've become as dear to me as a piece of my own heart! In high society everything's for show and nothing else. My daughter Katerina Nikolaevna is a brilliant woman and I'm proud of her, but she often, very, very often, my dear chap, insults me ... Still, these little girls (*elles sont charmantes*) and their mothers who come on birthdays—all they do is bring their embroidery and don't know how to say a thing. I've accumulated enough embroidery to cover sixty cushions, all dogs and deer. I'm very fond of them, but I feel I'm almost related to you—not like a son so much as a brother and I particularly enjoy it when you object to things, because you're literary, you've read a lot and you know how to express your enthusiasm ...'

'I've read nothing and I'm certainly not literary. I've just read whatever came my way, and in the last two years I've read nothing at all and I won't be reading anything in the future.'

'Why won't you?'

'I have other aims.'

'*Cher* ... It'd be a pity if you said to yourself at the end of your life as I do: "*Je sais tout, mais je ne sais rien de bon.*" I really don't know why I've lived on this earth! But ... I'm so obliged to you that I ... I even wanted ...'

He suddenly broke off, gave up, and fell into a reverie. After being shaken by emotion (and such shakings could occur from moment to moment, God knows why) he usually lost the balance of his mind for a time and stopped being in control of himself. However, he would quickly regain an even keel and no harm would come of it. We sat silent for a moment or so. His very full, lower lip drooped conspicuously ... What had astonished me most of all was that he had suddenly mentioned his daughter—and with such candour as well. Naturally I attributed this to his unsettled state.

'*Cher enfant*, you're not angry with me that I'm so familiar with you, are you?' he suddenly burst out.

'Not at all. I admit that, to start with, I was a bit insulted and wanted to get my own back on you, but I saw that was silly because you weren't being familiar with me to insult me, were you?'

He had stopped listening and had forgotten his question.

'Well, what about your *father*?' He suddenly gave me a thoughtful look.

I literally jumped. In the first place, he was referring to Versilov as my *father*, which he had so far never permitted himself to do in my presence, and secondly he had actually mentioned Versilov, which had never happened before.

'He's at home, penniless and depressed,' I answered briefly, but I was burning with curiosity.

'Yes, about the money ... His court case is being heard today and I'm waiting for Prince Seryozha, he'll be coming with something. He promised to come straight here from the court. Their whole fortune's involved, sixty or eighty thousand roubles. Of course, I've always wished Versilov the best and I think he'll be the winner and the princes won't get a thing. That's the law for you!'

'It'll be in court today?' I cried in amazement.

The thought that Versilov had even neglected to tell me about this struck me as extraordinary. 'Very likely he hasn't told mother or anyone,' I thought immediately. 'What a man!'

'Is Prince Sokolsky in St Petersburg then?' I asked, struck by another thought.

'He's been here since yesterday. He came straight here from Berlin to be here today.'

This was also an extraordinarily important piece of news for me. 'So he'll be coming here today,' I thought, 'this man who had given *him* the slap in the face.!'

'Yes, well . . .' The look on the prince's face changed suddenly '. . . he'll be professing his belief in God as usual and . . . and, very likely, he'll be going after little girls, fledgling little girls, eh? Ha-ha-ha! There might be a very amusing story in that! Ha-ha-ha!'

'Who's professing God? Who's going after little girls?'

'Versilov! Believe it or not, in the past he used to pester all of us with questions about what we ate, what we thought. He was almost as bad as that. He'd scare you and scold you with questions like: "If you're religious, why haven't you become a monk!" He'd almost demand it of you. *Mais quelle idée!* Even if he were right, that was a bit too much, wasn't it? He particularly liked frightening me with the Last Judgement, me of all people!'

'I've never noticed any of this, and I've been living with him for a month,' was my reaction after listening impatiently. I was terribly annoyed that he wasn't right yet and was mumbling away so incoherently.

'It's simply that he doesn't talk like that now, but, believe me, he did. He's a clever man without doubt and very erudite, but is he in his right mind? It's all because of the three years he spent abroad. And I admit I was shocked, very shocked . . . and everyone was . . . *Cher enfant, j'aime le bon Dieu* . . . I'm a believer, as much as I can be, but I . . . I really did lose control of myself then. Granted that I might have seemed frivolous, but I did it deliberately, in annoyance—and the essence of my objection was anyhow just as serious as when the world began: "If there is a higher being," I told him, "and he exists *in person* and not in the form of some spirit flowing throughout creation, like some liquid or other (because that's even more difficult to understand), then where does he live?" My friend, *c'était bête*, without doubt, but all objections boil down to this, don't they? *Un domicile*—it's an important matter. He was terribly angry. He'd become a Catholic while abroad.'

'I've also heard about this. It's probably nonsense.'

'I assure you by all that's holy. Just take a look at him . . . Still, you say he's changed. But how he used to torture us in those days! Believe it or not, he used to behave as if he were some kind of saint and his holy relics would be appearing any moment!

He used to demand we keep an account of our behaviour, I swear to you! Talk of relics! *En voilà une autre!* Well, some monk or hermit might . . . but here was a chap walking about in white tie and tails and all that—and, all of a sudden, he had *relics*! An odd thing for a man of the world to want and, I admit, in rather strange taste. I'm not saying anything against it—of course, there is saintliness and anything can happen . . . Besides it's all *de l'inconnu*, but for a man of the world it's even a bit improper. If it ever happened to me, or I was offered it, then I swear to you I'd refuse it. Well, I mean, what if suddenly I were having dinner in my club and then all at once afterwards *I became a saint*? Oh, I'm just joking! I said all this to him then . . . He used to wear chains, you know.'

I went red with anger.

'You actually saw his chains, did you?'

'I myself didn't see them, but . . .'

'I tell you this is all a lie, a tissue of foul slanders and libels by enemies of his—that's to say, by one enemy, the chief and most inconsiderate one, because he has only one enemy—and it's your daughter!'

It was the prince's turn to flare up.

'*Mon cher*, I beg you and I insist that you never again in my presence mention the name of my daughter in association with this foul story.'

I stood up. He was beside himself, his chin quivering.

'*Cette histoire infame!* . . . I never believed it and I never wanted to, but I've been told again and again: believe it, believe it . . .'

At this point a footman suddenly entered and announced we had visitors. I dropped back into my chair.

IV

Two ladies entered, both young, the one a stepdaughter of a cousin of the prince's late wife, or something of the kind, one of his wards to whom he'd already allotted a dowry and who (I mention this for the future) had money of her own; and the other Anna Andreevna Versilov, Versilov's daughter, three years older than me who lived with her brother at the Fanariotovs and whom I'd seen only once before in my life, fleetingly, out on the

40

street, although I had already had an encounter, also fleeting, with her brother in Moscow (very likely I'll mention this encounter later, if I can find the space for it, because it was really very unimportant). From childhood on, Anna Andreevna had been a particular favourite of the prince's (Versilov's friendship with the prince had begun an awfully long time ago). I was so embarrassed by what had just happened that, on their entering, I did not even get up, although the prince rose to greet them. Then I thought it'd be shameful to get up, so I remained where I was. The main thing was I was stunned by the way the prince had shouted at me just three minutes before and I still couldn't make up my mind whether I ought to go or not. But the old man had already forgotten all that, as usual, and grew pleasantly invigorated at the sight of the young ladies. He had even, with one of his quick changes of facial expression and giving me a mysterious wink, managed to whisper to me just before they came in:

'Take a look at Olimpiada, watch her closely . . . I'll tell you about it later . . .'

I took a pretty close look at her and found nothing remarkable. She was a short girl, plump and red-cheeked. Her face, however, was fairly pretty, of the sort that appeals to materialists. Her expression may have been kindly, but it was furrowed. She couldn't have had any particular intellectual brilliance, but only in a higher sense, because cunning was evident from her eyes. She was no more than 19. In short, nothing outstanding. At high school we'd have called her 'frumpy'. (If I describe her in such detail, it's solely because it'll be needed for the future.) Besides, everything I've described so far in such unnecessary detail leads on to what'll be necessary later. Everything'll be appropriate in its place. I don't know how to avoid describing it this way. If it's boring, then I beg you not to read it.

Versilov's daughter was a completely different person. Tall and even slightly emaciated, she had an elongated and remarkably pale face, but her hair was black and abundant; she had large, dark eyes and a profound look; her lips were small and crimson and her mouth attractively fresh. She was the first woman not to disgust me by the way she walked. However, she was lean and fine-boned. The expression of her face was not entirely kindly, but it was dignified. She was 22. There was no outward mark of similarity to Versilov, but, as if by a kind of miracle, her facial expression was unusually like his. I don't know whether she was beautiful—that's a matter of taste.

Both of them were dressed very modestly, so there's no point in describing their clothes. I expected that I would instantly be humiliated by some look from Miss Versilov or a gesture and was ready for it. Her brother had humiliated me in Moscow at our very first encounter. She couldn't have known me to look at, but of course she knew I was going to the prince's. Everything that the prince proposed or did aroused interest among his mass of relations and 'expectant ones' and constituted an event—his sudden attachment to me, all the more so. I knew for certain that the prince took a great interest in Anna Andreevna's future and was looking for a husband for her. But it was more difficult finding a husband for Miss Versilov than for the expectant embroiderers.

And then, against all my expectations, Miss Versilov, after shaking the prince's hand and exchanging a few words with him, looked at me with unusual curiosity and, seeing that I was also looking at her, suddenly bowed to me with a smile. True, she had only that moment entered and made her bow, but her smile was so kind that it evidently must have been intended. And I remember that I experienced an extraordinarily pleasant sensation.

'And this is ... this is ... my nice young friend Arkady Andreevich Dol ...' the prince babbled, noticing that she had bowed to me but I had remained seated, and then came to a sudden stop. Perhaps he was confused over whether or not to introduce me (to introduce, that is, a brother to a sister). The frump also bowed to me. But suddenly, quite idiotically, I jumped up in a huff—in an access of completely senseless, pretend pride, and total vanity.

'Forgive me, prince, I am not Arkady Andreevich, but Arkady Makarovich,' I declared sharply, entirely forgetting that I should have returned the ladies' bows. The devil take such momentary improprieties!

'*Mais ... tiens!*' cried the prince, striking a finger against his forehead.

'What school were you at?' rapped out the silly, whining voice of the frump, who had walked directly up to me.

'At high school, in Moscow, ma'am.'

'Ah, yes, so I heard! Did they teach you well?'

'Very well.'

I remained standing there like a soldier on parade.

The young lady's questions were certainly not imaginative, but, in asking them, she managed to turn attention from my silly gaffe and make it easier for the prince, who was meanwhile listening with happy smile to something Miss Versilov was whispering in his ear—evidently not about me. But the question still remained why this young lady, who was entirely unknown to me, had tried to distract attention from my gaffe. Still, it was hard to imagine that she should have asked her questions on the spur of the moment. There must have been something deliberate about it. She was looking at me far too curiously, just as if she very much wanted me to take all the more interest in her. I thought about all this later and I wasn't wrong.

'What? Surely not today!' the prince cried out suddenly, jumping up.

'Didn't you know?' Miss Versilov asked in astonishment. 'Olympe! The prince didn't know that Katerina Nikolaevna will be here today! We were on our way to her. We thought she'd come by the morning train and would already be home. Just now we and she both drove up to her house simultaneously and she told us to come and see you and she'd be along immediately . . . And here she is!'

A side door opened and—*in came that woman*!

I recognized her from the astonishing portrait hanging in the prince's study. I had been studying it all month. During the three minutes I spent in the study in her presence I didn't take my eyes off her face once. But if I'd not known the portrait and someone had asked me after those three minutes who she was, I wouldn't have said a thing because everything became blurred.

I only remember from those three minutes a really beautiful woman whom the prince kissed and made the sign of the cross over and who suddenly started giving me rapid glances the moment she came in. I clearly overheard the prince, obviously pointing at me, mutter something with a little laugh about a new secretary and utter my name. She jerked her face up, gave me a nasty look, and smiled so scornfully that I suddenly took a step forward, went up to the prince, and stammered, trembling terribly, unable to finish a single word, my teeth chattering:

'Ever since I . . . I have things to . . . I am going.'

And I turned round and went out. No one said a word to me, not even the prince. The prince told me later that I'd gone so white he felt 'quite frightened'.

Not to worry!

CHAPTER III

I

THERE was indeed nothing to worry about. Higher considerations had swallowed up all the incidentals and one powerful feeling contented me for everything. I left in a kind of excitement. Going out on to the street I was ready to burst into song. Quite deliberately it was a delightful morning with sunshine, passersby, noise, traffic, joyfulness, and crowds of people. Surely, though, that woman had insulted me, hadn't she? From whom would I have endured such looks and such a scornful smile without immediately protesting, even though in the silliest way? Yet I didn't mind, did I? After all, she'd come just to insult me as quickly as possible, never having set eyes on me before, because to her I'd been sent by Versilov and she was sure both then and long afterwards that Versilov held her entire fate in his hands and had the means of ruining her if he wanted to by means of one particular document—at least that's what she suspected. For her it was a duel to the death. And yet I wasn't insulted! There had been an insult, but I hadn't felt it! Not at all—I even felt glad that, having gone there to hate her, I was even feeling I was beginning to love her!

'I don't know,' I wondered, 'whether the spider hates the fly which it has aimed at and caught? Poor, dear little fly! I think people love their victims; at least I think it's possible to love them. You see, I am in love with my enemy—for instance, I'm terribly pleased she's so beautiful. I'm terribly pleased, my dear lady, you're so haughty and grand, because if you'd been less grand it wouldn't have been anything like the pleasure. You've

44

spat on me but I've triumphed. Even if you'd literally spat in my face, I probably wouldn't have been angry, because you're my victim—*mine*, not *his*. What an enchanting idea! Yes, secret consciousness of power is far, far more pleasant than open domination! If I were a rich man worth a hundred million roubles, I think I'd still get pleasure from walking about in my oldest clothes and letting people take me for the most miserable creature almost on the brink of poverty, shoving me about and despising me—just knowing who I really was would be enough!'

That's how I expressed my thoughts and my joy at that time and much of what I felt. I'll only add that here, in what I've written, it's all come out much more frivolously than it was, because really I felt it all much more deeply and shamefully. Perhaps at this moment I'm much more ashamed of myself than I am in what I write and do. God grant I am!

Perhaps I've done a bad thing in sitting down and writing. Far, far more remains insde than comes out in the words. Your thoughts, though bad ones, are always much deeper so long as they're with you, but written down they're much more silly and dishonest. Versilov told me that the exact opposite occurs with really nasty people. It's easy for them, they're used to telling lies, but I'm trying to write the whole truth and nothing but the truth and that's terribly hard!

II

On the 19th I also took another 'step'.

For the first time since my arrival I had money in my pocket because the sixty roubles I'd saved over the last two years I'd given to my mother, as I mentioned earlier. But a few days before I'd decided that on the day I received my salary I'd make the 'experiment' which I'd long dreamed of. The day before I'd cut out of the newspaper an address—it was in an announcement by 'the Clerk of the St Petersburg Municipal Court' and so on and so forth that 'on the nineteenth day of September, at twelve o'clock midday, in the Kazan District' and so on and so forth 'at No. so-and-so a sale will be held of the personal effects of Mrs Lebrecht' and 'the goods and chattels may be inspected on the day of the sale' and so on and so forth.

It was just after one o'clock. I hurried to the address on foot.

For a couple of years I had vowed not to take cabs (otherwise I wouldn't have saved up sixty roubles). I never went to auctions because I hadn't *allowed* myself to. Although my present 'step' was only *experimental*, I had decided that I could only take it when I was finished with the high school, after breaking with all the others, when I could literally break through my shell and become completely free. True, I was far from being in a 'shell' of any kind and far from being free. But then the step I had decided on was only a kind of probe—simply to see how it might be, to fantasize about it a bit and perhaps go no further until the time came to embark on it seriously. For everyone else it was simply a silly, insignificant auction, but for me it was like laying the keel of the ship in which Columbus set out to discover America. That's how I felt about it then.

Reaching the place, I went into the depths of the courtyard of the house named in the address and entered Mrs Lebrecht's apartment. It consisted of an entrance-hall and four small, low-ceilinged rooms. In the first room by the entrance there was a crowd of as many as thirty people. Half of them were in the trade and the other half, judging by their appearance, were there out of curiosity or because they enjoyed auctions or had been sent by the Lebrechts. There were merchants, Jews giving gold objects the once-over, and a few well-dressed types. Even the physiognomies of some of these gentlemen became etched in my memory. In the room to the right a table had been placed between the open doors to prevent access because there all the listed and saleable items had been set out. There was another room on the left, but the doors were closed, although from time to time they were opened slightly for someone to peer out—evidently one of Mrs Lebrecht's numerous family, for whom this was a very shameful episode. Behind the table set between the doors, facing the public, sat a court bailiff, judging by his insignia, engaged in selling the goods. I arrived at a half-way stage. As soon as I entered I pushed my way towards the table. Bronze candlesticks were being sold. I started watching.

I watched and immediately started wondering what I could buy. What the hell could I do with bronze candlesticks? Would they achieve what I wanted and would my calculations work out? And were my calculations just childish? I had all these thoughts and waited. My feelings were much like those at a gaming table just before laying a bet but in readiness for it: 'If I want to I will, or if I want to I'll go away—it's all up to me.' My heart still hadn't begun beating fast, but was slightly faltering and quivering—quite a pleasant feeling. But indecisiveness can quickly begin to weigh you down and you can start going blind—stretching out your hand, picking a card, but mechanically, almost against your will, as if someone else were guiding you. Finally, having decided and put down your stake, your feeling is quite different—it's great! I'm not writing generally about auctions but simply about myself—who else could feel like that at an auction?

There were some who grew excited, some who waited in silence, some who made purchases and then regretted them. I felt no pity for one man who, through mishearing, had bought by mistake a cupro-nickel milk jug instead of a silver one and paid five roubles instead of two. I even felt gleeful about it. The bailiff varied the items: after the candlesticks he produced earrings, after the ear-rings a cushion in tooled morocco leather, after the cushion a box—evidently to ring the changes and to suit the needs of the traders. I'd hardly been there ten minutes and thought of doing something about the cushion and the box, but each time I'd failed at the last moment because these items had seemed to me quite impossible. Finally an album turned up in the bailiff's hands.

'A family album, in red morocco binding, a bit worn, with water-colour and pastel drawings, in a carved ivory case with silver clasps—two roubles!'

I stepped up to inspect it. The item had an elegant appearance, but a part of the carved ivory was missing. I was the only one who went to inspect it and everyone else was silent. I had no rivals. I could have undone the clasps and taken the album out of its case to look at it, but didn't and simply waved my hand vaguely, as much as to say: 'So what!'

'Two roubles, five copecks,' I said, my teeth, I think, once again chattering.

It was mine. I instantly took out my money, paid for it, seized hold of the album and retired to a corner of the room. There I took it out of its case and started feverishly inspecting it. Without its case it was the most worthless thing in the world—the size of a small sheet of writing paper, the little album was thin, with

47

worn gilt edging to the pages, the sort of thing that used to be common among young ladies who had just left their institutes. There were water-colours and pastels of temples on hills, cupids, and ponds with swans swimming on them; there was also a poem:

> I have on a journey long to go,
> Far will I be from dear Moscow,
> Long away from all I know,
> To the Crimea by coach I go.

(To think it's stuck in my memory!) I decided I'd made a complete fool of myself: if there was one thing I didn't need, it was that album.

'No matter,' I decided. 'You invariably lose with the first card, it might even be a good sign.'

I was in really good spirits.

'Oh, I'm too late! You've got it, have you? Did you buy it?' resounded the voice of someone beside me in a blue topcoat, a handsome, well-dressed man, a late arrival.

'I missed it. Oh, what a pity! How much?'

'Two roubles, five copecks.'

'Oh, what a pity! Would you consider letting me have it?'

'Let's go outside,' I whispered to him, overwhelmed.

We went out on to the stairs.

'I'll let you have it for ten roubles,' I said, feeling a chill running up my spine.

'Ten roubles! For heaven's sake!'

'It's as you wish.'

He looked me full in the eyes. I was well dressed, looking quite unlike a Jew or a dealer.

'For heaven's sake, it's just a worthless old album. Who'd want something like that? The case really isn't worth anything and you wouldn't be able to sell it to anyone, would you?'

'You're the one who wants to buy it.'

'Yes, but this is special, I only learned about it yesterday. After all, I'm the only one after it! For heaven's sake!'

'I would have asked twenty-five roubles for it, but because there was a risk you might give up at once I only asked for ten. I won't take a copeck less.'

I turned round and began walking away.

'Look, take four,' he said, catching me up in the courtyard. 'Well, five.'

I said nothing and went on walking.

'All right, then, take it!' He took out ten roubles and I gave him the album. 'But you'd agree it's not right, wouldn't you? Paying two roubles and getting ten . . .'

'What's wrong with it? Supply and demand!'

'What sort of supply and demand?' (He was growing angry.)

'There's only a market for goods when they're in demand. If you hadn't wanted it, I probably wouldn't have got forty copecks for it.'

Although I didn't burst out laughing and was outwardly quite serious, I laughed inwardly—laughed not exactly out of excitement, I don't know out of what, and caught my breath slightly.

'Listen,' I muttered at him completely beside myself, but in a friendly spirit and feeling a rush of fondness for him, 'listen, when the late James Rothschild of Paris, who left a fortune of one thousand, seven hundred million francs'—he gave a nod of the head—'when he learned by chance as a young man, a few hours before anyone else, about the murder of the Duc de Berry,* he immediately let the right people know about it and in an instant had made several millions—that's the way it's done!'

'So you think you're a Rothschild, do you?' he shrieked at me in annoyance, as if I were a fool.

I walked quickly out into the street. At one stroke I had made seven roubles ninety-five copecks' profit! It had been a senseless step to take, just child's play, I admit, but it fitted in exactly with my idea and couldn't fail to excite me extremely deeply . . . Still, there's no point in trying to describe my feelings. The ten-rouble note was in my coat pocket and I stuck two fingers in to feel it and literally walked along without removing my hand. After going a hundred or so steps along the street, I took the note out to look at it, looked at it, and was just about to give it a kiss. Suddenly a carriage rolled up to the entrance of a house. The hall porter was opening the doors and a woman came out of the house to get into the carriage—a young woman, sumptuously dressed, beautiful and rich, in silk and velvet and with a train more than a metre long. Suddenly a pretty little handbag jumped

49

out of her hand and fell on the ground. She took her seat. A footman bent down to pick up the handbag, but I dashed forward, retrieved it, handed it to her, and raised my hat. (I had on a top hat and wasn't badly dressed for a young man.) In a restrained way but with the most charming of smiles the lady said '*Merci, monsieur*'. The carriage rumbled off. I gave the ten-rouble note a kiss.

III

That day I had to see Efim Zverev, one of my former schoolmates who had dropped out and entered a special higher education establishment in St Petersburg. He isn't worth describing and I'd never been friendly with him, but I'd been looking for him in St Petersburg. He would be able (due to various circumstances which also aren't worth talking about) to give me the address of Kraft, someone extraordinarily vital to me, as soon as the latter returned from Vilno. Zverev was expecting him either today or tomorrow, as he'd informed me the day before yesterday. I had to cross over to the Petersburg side,* but I didn't feel at all tired.

I found Zverev (he was also 19) in the courtyard of his aunt's house where he was temporarily residing. He had only just had dinner and was walking about the yard on stilts. He told me right away that Kraft had arrived back the day before and was at the place where he'd been living before, right there on the Peters-burg side, and wanted to see me as soon as possible in order to give me some vital news.

'He's planning to be off somewhere again,' Efim added.

Because it was of capital importance for me in present circumstances to see Kraft, I asked Efim to take me at once to his apartment, which turned out to be only a couple of steps away down a side street. But Zverev announced that he'd met him only an hour ago and that he'd gone to Dergachev's.

'So let's go to Dergachev's. What's bugging you—scared?'

It's true, Kraft could be at Dergachev's a long time, so where could I wait for him? I wasn't scared of going to Dergachev's, but I just didn't want to go there despite the fact that Efim had dragged me round there a couple of times already. Anyhow, he always said 'scared' to me with a very nasty smile. It wasn't a case of my being scared, I'll say that straight out, and if I was frightened it was to do with something quite different. But this time I was determined to go. It was also only a couple of steps away. As we went I asked Efim if he still intended to run away to America.

'Maybe I'll wait a bit,' he said with a light laugh.

I'd never liked him much, even rather disliked him. He had very fair hair, with a full, chalky white face, almost indecently white, like a small child's, but he was even taller than me and could hardly be taken for anything other than a 17-year-old. There was nothing much to talk to him about.

'So what's going on there? Will there be a crowd?' I asked for starters.

'Why're you always so scared?' he giggled again.

'Go to hell!' I lost my temper.

'There won't be a crowd. It'll only be friends, people we know. Relax.'

'It doesn't matter a damn whether we know them or not! Am I one of them? Why should they be sure of me?'

'I've brought you, that's enough. They've even heard a bit about you. Kraft can also vouch for you.'

'Listen, will Vasin be there?'

'I don't know.'

'If he is, as soon as we go in, give me a nudge and point him out—as soon as we go in, d'you hear?'

I'd heard a fair bit about Vasin and had long been interested in meeting him.

Dergachev lived in the small courtyard wing of a wooden house belonging to a merchant's wife, but he occupied the whole of the wing. It consisted of just three rooms. The blinds were down in all four windows. He was a technician and had a job in St Petersburg. I'd heard that he'd been offered a lucrative private post in the provinces and was going to be off there.

As soon as we entered the tiny hallway we heard voices. They seemed to be engaged in heated argument and someone was shouting:

'Quae medicamenta non sanant—ferrum sanat, quae ferrum non sanat—ignis sanat!'*

I was really in some confusion. Of course I was unused to society, no matter what kind it was. In high school I'd been on familiar terms with fellow classmates, but I'd not really been

51

friends with any of them because I'd made a corner for myself and lived in it. But that wasn't what embarrassed me. No matter what happened I'd made myself promise not to get involved in arguments and to say only essential things, so that no one could come to any conclusion about me; but the main thing was to avoid arguments.

The room, altogether too small for them, contained seven men and, counting the ladies, ten people in all. Dergachev was 25 and married. His wife had a sister, and there was another female relation who also lived with him. The room was furnished so-so, but adequately and it was even clean. There was a lithograph portrait hanging on the wall, though a very cheap one, and in the corner an icon without a frame, but with a little lamp burning in front of it. Dergachev came up to me, shook my hand, and asked me to sit down.

'Have a seat, we're all friends here.'

'Please,' added immediately a reasonably pretty young woman, dressed very modestly, who, after slightly bowing to me, at once left the room. This was his wife, who had apparently also been taking part in the argument but had now gone out to feed her baby. This still left two other women in the room—one very small, about 20, in a black dress and far from bad-looking, and the other a woman of about 30, dried-up and sharp-eyed. They sat, intently listening but taking no part in the argument.

So far as the men were concerned, they were all on their feet, and the only ones sitting apart from myself were Kraft and Vasin. Efim pointed them out to me then and there, because I was even seeing Kraft now for the first time in my life. I stood up and approached him to introduce myself.

I will never forget Kraft's face. It had no special beauty, but it had something almost too mild and delicate about it, although a feeling of personal dignity shone in every feature. Twenty-six, fairly lean, above average in height, fair-haired, with a serious, but soft face, there was something so calm and quiet about every part of him. But if you'd asked me, I wouldn't have swopped my own—perhaps very commonplace—face for his, which seemed to me so attractive. There was something in his face I wouldn't have wanted in my own, something altogether too complacent in a moral sense, a kind of secret haughtiness of which it was unaware. However, I couldn't judge things so literally at that time. It seems to me now that I judged it like that then—with hindsight, that's to say.

'I'm very glad you've come,' said Kraft. 'I've got a letter which concerns you. We'll be a little longer here and then you come to my place.'

Dergachev was of medium height and a broad-shouldered, muscular, dark-haired man with a large beard. The look in his eyes showed he was quick in the uptake and displayed restraint and a certain persistent caution in everything. Although he was quiet for the most part, he was obviously in charge of the discussion. Vasin's appearance didn't greatly impress me, though I had heard he was exceptionally clever—fair-haired, with large light-grey eyes, a very open face, but at the same time there was something unduly hard about it, as if one could anticipate he'd be uncommunicative—but his expression was intelligent, more intelligent than Dergachev's and deeper and cleverer than all others in the room. Still, I may be exaggerating everything. Of the rest I recall only two faces belonging to the young men there—one tall, swarthy man with black side-whiskers, about 27, a teacher of some kind who talked a lot and the other a young chap my age dressed in a Russian-style shirt who had a furrowed face, was taciturn, and belonged to the group of listeners. He turned out later to be of peasant origin.

'No, that's not the way it ought to be put,' began the teacher with black side-whiskers, evidently renewing an old argument and growing more heated than anyone else. 'I'm not talking about mathematical proofs, but it's the idea I'm prepared to believe in without mathematical proofs . . .'

'Hold on, Tikhomirov!' Dergachev loudly interrupted. 'The new arrivals won't understand. It's like this, you see . . .' He suddenly turned to me alone (and I confess that if he'd been intending to examine me like a new boy or make me answer, he did just the right thing, because I was aware of this at once and at the ready) '. . . you see, here's Mr Kraft, someone reasonably well known to us for his character and the solidity of his convictions. As a consequence of a very ordinary fact he has come to a very extraordinary conclusion, with which he has surprised us all. He has concluded that the Russian people are a second-rate people . . .'

'Third-rate!' someone shouted.

'. . . a second-rate people who are destined to serve simply as material for a much nobler race and not to have their own role in the destinies of mankind. In view of this—probably a justified outcome of his thinking—Mr Kraft has come to the conclusion that any further activity by any Russian person must be paralysed by this idea and so everyone, so to speak, has to give up what he's doing and . . .'

'Allow me, Dergachev—that's not how it should be put!' Tikhomirov again chimed in impatiently (Dergachev at once yielded to him). 'In view of the fact that Kraft has made serious researches and come to conclusions on the basis of physiology which he recognizes as mathematically correct and expended about two years, perhaps, on his idea (which I would have accepted quite calmly a priori), in view of this, in view—that is—of Kraft's concerns and seriousness, this matter is to be considered a real phenomenon. There arises from all this a question, which Kraft cannot comprehend, and that's what we must concern ourselves with—Kraft's lack of comprehension, that is, because this is a real phenomenon. We have to decide whether this phenomenon is clinically unique or is an attribute which can normally be repeated in others. This is of interest in view of our common cause. I will believe Kraft so far as Russia is concerned and I will even say that I'm probably glad of it. If this idea were accepted by everyone, it would free people's hands and liberate many people from the prejudice of patriotism . . .'

'Patriotism was not my concern,' said Kraft with a certain tenseness. I think all these debates were unpleasant for him.

'Patriotism or not, that can be put on one side,' said Vasin who had been very silent.

'But in what way, tell me, can Kraft's conclusion weaken the striving for a common human cause?' shouted the teacher (he was the only one who shouted, all the others talked quietly). 'So Russia is condemned to be second-rate, but one doesn't have to work only for Russia! And, apart from that, how can Kraft be a patriot if he's already ceased to believe in Russia?'

'Anyhow he's German,' a voice was again heard to say.

'I'm Russian,' said Kraft.

'It's a question which isn't directly relevant,' Dergachev remarked to the interrupter.

'Get away from the narrowness of your idea . . .' Tikhomirov did not listen to what was said. 'If Russia is simply material for nobler races, why shouldn't it be? That's still a worthy role to have. Why not be content with this idea in view of the widening of the task? Humanity is on the eve of its regeneration, which has already begun. Only a blind man would deny the task awaiting us. Leave aside Russia if you've ceased to believe in it and work for the future—for a future unknown people, but one which will consist of the whole of humanity without any differentiation between races. Russia would in any case die some time. Peoples, even the most gifted of them, only last for one and a half to two thousand years. What's it matter whether it's two thousand or two hundred years? The Romans didn't last more than one and a half thousand years in a vital sense and were then also turned into raw material. They haven't existed for a long time, but they left behind an idea and it has become an element in the ongoing destiny of mankind. How can one tell someone there was nothing to be done? I can't imagine a situation when there was nothing to be done! Do what you can for humanity and don't worry about the rest! When you look around you, there's so much to be done that a lifetime's not long enough.'

'One must live by the law of nature and truth,' said Mrs Dergachev from behind the door. The door was slightly ajar and it could be seen that she was standing there breast-feeding her baby, her bosom covered, as she listened avidly.

Kraft had listened to it all with a faint smile and at last said, with a rather agonized look, although with powerful sincerity:

'I cannot understand how, if one is under the influence of some dominant idea, to which both your mind and heart are completely in thrall, you can live by something outside that idea?'

'But if it is proved to you logically and mathematically that your conclusion is erroneous, that you have not the slightest right to exclude yourself from universally useful activity simply because Russia is doomed to be second-rate, if it is demonstrated to you that instead of a narrow horizon you are in full view of infinity, instead of the narrow idea of patriotism . . .'

'Oh, I told you . . .' Kraft gave a gentle wave of the hand '. . . patriotism's got nothing to do with it.'

'There's obviously a misapprehension here,' Vasin suddenly broke in. 'The error lies in the fact that Kraft hasn't reached just a logical conclusion but a conclusion, so to speak, that has turned into an emotion. Human nature is not always the same. With many people a logical conclusion is sometimes transformed into a very strong emotion which seizes hold of their entire being and which is very hard to drive out or alter. In order to cure someone of this you have to change the emotion itself, which can only be done by substituting another one of equal strength. This is always difficult and in many cases impossible.'

'No, that's wrong!' yelled his adversary. 'A logical conclusion of itself liquidates prejudice! Intellectual conviction is what gives birth to feeling. An idea comes from a feeling and in its turn, on being introduced into someone, formulates a new feeling!'

'People are very different. Some can change their emotions easily, others with difficulty,' responded Vasin, as if unwilling to continue the argument. But I was ecstatic about his idea.

'That's it, it's just as you said!' I turned suddenly to him, breaking the ice as I started talking. 'You've got to put one emotion in place of another to change it. In Moscow four years ago a general . . . you see, gentleman, I didn't actually know him, but . . . maybe it was simply that he couldn't arouse enough respect for himself . . . and in any case facts can seem irrational, but . . . Still, you see, his child died—that's to say, in fact it was two little girls, one after the other, from scarlet fever . . . Well, he was suddenly so heart-broken by this that he grieved and grieved and you didn't dare look at him as he walked about the place in such a state—and he ended by dying almost six months later. The fact is he died from this! What could have brought him back to life? The answer is—an emotion of equivalent strength! You'd have had to have dug up those two little girls and given them to him—that's all you could have done, or something of the kind. So he died. But you could have offered him some marvellous conclusions—that all life is short, that we're all mortal, that statistics can show how many children die of scarlet fever . . . He was a retired man . . .'

I stopped, catching my breath and looking round.

'That's got nothing to do with it,' somebody said.

'The fact you've quoted, although it's not absolutely identical with the matter under discussion, is still relevant and helps to clarify it,' said Vasin, turning to me.

At this point I must confess why I was delighted by Vasin's argument for an 'idea-emotion' and at the same time I must confess I was as ashamed as hell. Yes, I'd been scared of going to Dergachev's, though not for the reason Efim supposed. I was scared because I'd been frightened of them even when I was still in Moscow. I knew that they (they, that's to say, or others of the same kind—it doesn't really matter) were dialecticians and would demolish my own 'idea'. I was firmly convinced in myself that I would not give away my 'idea' and tell them. But they (or—again—others like them) could probably tell me something which would make me disillusioned with my own 'idea' without my giving them any hint of what it was. My 'idea' contained queries which I had not resolved, but I didn't want anyone beside myself to resolve them. In the last couple of years I had even given up reading books, fearing that I might hit upon some passage out of tune with my 'idea' which might shake me to the core. And here suddenly was Vasin solving my problem at a stroke and dispelling my worries in the highest sense. In fact, what was I frightened of and what could they do to me with whatever dialectics they might employ? I was perhaps the only one there who understood what he meant by an 'idea-emotion'! It's no big deal to overturn a fine idea, what you must do is put an equally fine one in its place—so no more would I, having no desire to give up my emotional attachment to it, overturn forcibly in my heart their rejection of my idea no matter what they might say. And what could they put in place of it? So I could be bolder, I had to be more courageous. Going into an ecstasy at what Vasin said, I still felt ashamed and thought I was nothing but a worthless kid!

This is just what made me so ashamed. It wasn't any bloody desire to show off intellectually that made me break the ice and start joining in, but a wish to be friends with them. I consider this desire of mine to be recognized as a good chap and have people hug me and so on (in short, all such nastiness) was the very worst of all the things I could be ashamed of and yet I suspected this had been lurking in me a long time and precisely ever since I'd chosen to live in a corner for so many years, though I didn't regret that. I knew I had to be much more dead serious in the presence of people. What consoled me every time such a shameful episode occurred was simply the fact that I still had my 'idea', secret as ever, and I hadn't given it away. I would sometimes imagine with a sinking feeling that when I did give my 'idea' away to someone I would suddenly have nothing left to me, I would be like the rest and perhaps I'd then even give up my 'idea' altogether. So I kept it to myself and cherished it and was terrified of giving it away in a lot of chatter. And here, at Dergachev's, at almost the very first encounter, I hadn't restrained myself—I'd given nothing away, of course, but I'd chattered unforgivably and covered myself with shame. What a bloody awful thing! No, I just can't live among people—that's what I think now and I'll say the same thing in forty years. My idea is the corner I live in.

V

Vasin had no sooner praised me than I suddenly had an irresistible desire to talk.

'To my mind everyone has a right to his own feelings . . . if out of conviction . . . so that no one can blame him for them,' I said to Vasin. Although I spoke out boldly, it was exactly as if it wasn't me, but a stranger in my mouth who had set my tongue wagging.

'So what?' interrupted with an ironic drawl the very same voice which had interrupted Dergachev and shouted that Kraft was a German.

Since I considered him a complete nonentity, I turned to the teacher as if he had been the speaker.

'It is my conviction that I shouldn't dare to judge anyone,' I said in a trembling voice, already aware that I was letting myself in for it.'

'What's so secret about that?' the nonentity's voice rapped out again.

'Everyone has his own idea,' I said, looking fixedly at the teacher who, for his part, said nothing and studied me with a smile.

'Have you got one?' cried the nonentity.

'It would take too long to explain . . . But my idea is partly to do with being left alone. So long as I've got a couple of roubles I can call my own, I want to live on my own, not depending on anyone—don't worry, I know the sort of things you can say against this—and not doing anything, even for the benefit of that great future humanity which you've called on Mr Kraft to work for. Personal freedom—my own freedom, that's to say— is my first priority and I don't want to know about anything else.'

I had made the mistake of losing my temper.

'So you're proclaiming the quiet life of a contented cow, are you?'

'What if I am? Cows are inoffensive. I don't owe anyone anything, I pay my taxes so that I can be protected from being robbed and beaten and killed and no one should dare ask anything more of me. I may personally have other ideas, and I may want to be of service to humanity, and perhaps I will be of ten times greater service than all the people who talk so much about it. But all I want is that *no one should dare ask anything more* of me or force me to do anything, as you've been demanding of Mr Kraft. It is my completely free right to raise my finger or not. But to rush and fall upon everyone's shoulder out of love for humanity and to shed burning tears for it is all a matter of fashion. And why should I have to love my neighbour or your future humanity, which I will never see, which will never know a thing about me and which will rot away without being remembered by anyone (time means nothing here), when the earth will turn into an icy lump of stone and will fly about space with an infinite number of other icy lumps—can you imagine anything more senseless? That's what your teaching amounts to! Tell me, why must I be a noble human being if everything lasts only a minute?'

'Bah!' a voice shouted.

I had shot all this off with a tetchy irritability, breaking all bounds. I knew I was rushing headlong, but I rushed for fear of objections. I felt only too well that I was sieving it all out disconnectedly and jumping from idea to idea, but I was hurrying to convince them and overwhelm them. It was so important to me! I'd been getting ready for this for three whole years! But it was remarkable how they suddenly fell silent, said absolutely nothing, and just listened. I went on addressing myself to the teacher:

'Precisely, sir. One very intelligent man used to say, among other things, that nothing was more difficult than answering the question: "Why must I be a good and noble man?" You see, there are three classes of evil men in the world: the naïve ones, those who are convinced, that is, that what they do is noble in the highest degree; the ones who are ashamed of themselves, ashamed, that is, of their own evil-doing but are absolutely intent on doing it; and, lastly, evil men pure and simple. Let me give you an example. I had a schoolfriend, Lambert, who told me when he was 16 that, if he was rich, it would be his greatest pleasure to feed his hounds bread and meat when the children of the poor were dying of hunger and, when they had nothing to heat their stoves with, to buy up a whole timber yard, build a bonfire in a field, and set light to it and not give the poor a single log. That's how he felt! Tell me, what should I say to a really evil man when he asks the question: "Why should I be good and noble?" And particularly now, in our time, when you've changed so many things. Because things have never been worse than they are now. In our society nothing's clear-cut, gentlemen. After all, you deny there's a God and any possibility of performing noble deeds, so what deaf, dumb, mindless dead weight is going to make me want to act properly if it's more to my advantage to do otherwise? You say: "A rational attitude to humanity is also to my advantage"—but what if I find all these rational ideas are irrational, all these communal barracks and phalansteries and so on?* Devil take them and all their changes, when I've only got one life to live on earth! Let me find out for myself what's best for me—that's a lot nicer. Why should it concern me what will happen to this humanity of yours in a thousand years' time, if all you allow me under your rules is no love, no life after death, and no possibility of being noble and self-sacrificing? Well, if that's it, then in the crudest possible way I will live only for myself— and the rest of the world can go to hell!'

'Bloody marvellous!'

'Still, I'm always ready to go to hell, too.'

'So much the better!' (It was the same voice.)

The remainder all kept silent, all looking at me and eyeing me. But gradually from different corners of the room there came a sniggering, quiet to start with, and then they started sniggering right into my face. Only Vasin and Kraft refrained. The one with

60

the black side-whiskers just grinned. He stared at me fixedly and listened.

'Gentlemen!' I was shaking all over. 'I will not tell you my idea, but I will ask you, on the contrary, from your own point of view—and don't imagine that I'm speaking just from my own point of view, because I probably love humanity a thousand times more than all of you put together!—and you really must answer me now, you've got to, because you're laughing—tell me: what'll you tempt me with to follow your doctrines? Tell me, how'll you prove to me that with you everything'll be better? What'll you do in your communal barracks about my protest that I'm an individual? Gentlemen, I've wanted to confront you with this for a long, long time! You'll have communal barracks, communal living quarters, everything'll be according to the rules—*stricte necessaire*—with atheism and childless women being common property—yes, I know very well that's the final thing! And for all this, for that little bit of average good which your rational society promises me, for a bit of bread and warmth, you take in exchange all my individuality! Let me ask you this, sir. Say you take my wife away, will you then take away my individual self-esteem so I won't bash my rival's head into a pulp? You will say that I will then be much wiser in myself. But what'll my wife say about such a rational husband if she's got any self-respect left? That is unnatural, gentlemen, and you ought to be ashamed!'

'You're a specialist on women, are you?' the nonentity's voice rapped out sarcastically.

For an instant I thought I'd fling myself at him and let my fists fly. He was small in stature, with reddish hair and freckles—anyhow, to hell with what he looked like!

'You needn't worry, I've never had a woman!' I snapped, turning to him for the first time.

'What priceless information, which could have been divulged more politely in view of the ladies present!'

But everyone all at once began stirring. They all started picking up caps and preparing to leave—not on account of me, of course, but because the time had come. Their silent disregard of me crushed me with shame. I also jumped up.

'May I ask you your name since you were looking at me all the time?' the teacher said suddenly, approaching me with the wickedest of smiles.

'Dolgoruky.'

'Prince Dolgoruky?'

'No, simply Dolgoruky, son of the former serf Makar Dolgoruky and illegitimate son of my former master, Mr Versilov. Don't worry, gentlemen, I've not said this so that you can immediately fling yourselves on my neck and howl like calves at my plight!'

A loud and most unceremonious salvo of laughter greeted this, so that the baby sleeping on the other side of the door woke up and started crying. I was in a quivering rage. They all shook Dergachev's hand and left without paying me any attention.

'Let's be going,' Kraft nudged me.

I went up to Dergachev, squeezed his hand as hard as I could and also pumped it several times as hard as possible.

'I'm sorry that Kudryumov'—he was the chap with the reddish hair—'needled you all the time,' Dergachev said to me.

I went out behind Kraft. I wasn't ashamed of anything.

VI

Of course, between me as I am now and me as I was then there's nothing in common at all.

Continuing in my 'I wasn't ashamed of anything' mode, I caught up with Vasin on the stairs, having hung back from Kraft as a second-rater, and with the most complete naturalness, as if nothing had happened, asked:

'I think you know my father—I mean Versilov—don't you?'

'I don't know him personally that well,' Vasin answered instantly (and without any of that hurtful, affected politeness which sensitive people assume when talking to someone who's just been disgraced). 'But I know him a little. I've met him and heard him speak.'

'If you've heard him speak, then you know him of course, because you are who you are! What do you think of him? Forgive such a quick question but I must know. I must know what *you* think, what *your* opinion is.'

'You're asking a lot of me. I think he's a man capable of making great demands on himself and perhaps of fulfilling them—but without accounting to anybody else.'

'That's true, that's very true—he's a very proud man! But is he pure in heart? Listen, what do you think of his Roman Catholicism? However, I've forgotten that you perhaps don't know . . .'

If I hadn't been so excited, it goes without saying I wouldn't have shot such questions at someone I'd never talked to before but only heard about. I was astonished that Vasin didn't seem to notice my craziness.

'I've heard something about it, but I don't know how true it is,' he answered as ever calmly and in a level voice.

'It's nonsense, it can't be true of him! You surely don't think he can believe in God?'

'He's a very proud man, as you yourself have just said, and many very proud people like to believe in God, particularly if they like to look down on other people. I think many strong people have a sort of natural compulsion to find someone or something to worship. A strong man often finds it very difficult to endure his own strength.'

'Hey, that's terribly true!' I exclaimed again. 'Only I'd love to understand . . .'

'It's quite clear why. They choose to worship God so as not to worship people—of course without realizing that in their case it's not so humiliating to worship God. They make extraordinarily fervent believers—or, to be more accurate, they fervently want to be believers, but they mistake their desire for the faith itself. Very often they end up being thoroughly disillusioned. I think Mr Versilov has extraordinarily sincere traits in his character and in general I find him an interesting man.'

'Vasin,' I cried, 'you've pleased me no end! I'm not surprised at your intellect, I'm astonished that you, a man so pure in heart and so far above me, that you can walk with me and talk with me so simply and politely, as if nothing at all had happened!'

Vasin smiled.

'You're being too generous—and what happened back there happened because you're simply too fond of abstract talk. You've probably spent a long time not saying anything at all.'

'I've not said anything for three whole years. I've been getting myself ready to speak all that time . . . Because you are yourself extraordinarily intelligent, I don't imagine I could seem a fool to you, though no one could have behaved more stupidly, but I might well seem an out-and-out bastard!'

'A bastard?'

'Sure! Tell me, don't you secretly despise me for saying I was the illegitimate son of Versilov—and priding myself on being the son of a serf?'

'You're being too hard on yourself! If you find you've made a mess of what you wanted to say, then don't talk like that next time. You've got fifty years ahead of you!'

'Oh, I know I've got to be very cautious with people! The very worst of all vices is always wanting to be friends with people. Only a moment ago I said that to them and now I'm wanting to be friends with you! But there's a difference, isn't there? If you've understood it and are capable of understanding it, then I say Thank God!'

Vasin smiled again.

'Come to my place any time you like,' he said. 'I've got work to do now and I'm busy, but do let me have the pleasure of seeing you.'

'I thought from the look of you, from your face, that you were exceptionally stern and uncommunicative.'

'That could be very true. I got to know your sister, Lizaveta Makarovna, last year in Luga . . . Look, Kraft has stopped, I think, and is waiting for you. He'll be going round the corner.'

I firmly shook Vasin's hand and raced after Kraft, who had been walking ahead of us all the time I had been talking to Vasin. We walked in silence to his apartment. I had no desire—and was anyhow quite unable—to talk to him. One of the strongest traits in Kraft's character was consideration for others.

CHAPTER IV

I

KRAFT had been in government service somewhere and had at the same time assisted the late Andronnikov (for a consideration) in conducting certain private court cases, in which he had been constantly involved over and above his official work. What was important for me was that Kraft, through his particularly close association with Andronnikov, could know a great deal about what interested me. But I knew from Marya Ivanovna, wife of Nikolay Semenovich, with whom I'd stayed so many years when I'd been going to high school (and who had been a blood relative, ward, and favourite of Andronnikov), that Kraft had even been 'entrusted' with conveying some information to me. I had already been waiting a whole month for him to do so.

He lived in a tiny apartment of two rooms, completely by itself, and at that moment, having only just arrived back, was even without a servant. Although his trunk was open, it was as yet unpacked and things were lying about on chairs and on a table in front of a sofa were deposited a suitcase, a travelling case, a revolver, and other items. As he entered, Kraft was completely lost in thought, as if he had forgotten about me altogether. He had perhaps also not noticed that I hadn't said a word to him on the way there. He immediately started searching about for something, but, having glanced in passing at a mirror, stopped in front of it and for a whole minute studied his face intently. Though I noted this peculiarity (and thought about it a great deal later), I was in a gloomy mood and very confused. I hadn't the strength to concentrate on anything. For a moment I was seized by a sudden wish to take what I could and be gone and to abandon the whole thing for good and all. And what the hell was it all anyway? Hadn't I just pretended the whole thing? I was becoming desperate at the thought that I was probably expending my energies on a lot of unworthy nonsense simply out of sentimentality when I was faced by a real task requiring energetic treatment. In the mean time, my inability to do anything serious was obvious from what had happened at Dergachev's.

'Kraft, will you be going there again?' I suddenly asked him. Kraft slowly turned to me as if he hadn't understood. I sat down on a chair.

'Be forgiving!' Kraft said suddenly.

Of course, I thought this was a joke. But, looking closely at him, I saw such an odd and even astonishing look of magnanimity on his face that I was even amazed myself at the serious way he had asked me to 'forgive' them. He moved a chair and sat down beside me.

'I know I'm probably just full of myself,' I began, 'but I'm not going to apologize to them . . .'

65

'There's absolutely no need to,' he said quietly and seriously. He always spoke quietly and very slowly.

'Say I have a bad conscience . . . I like having a bad conscience. Kraft, forgive me being your guest and talking such rubbish. Tell me, are you also a member of that group? That's what I wanted to ask you.'

'They're no sillier than others and no cleverer. They're mixed up, like all of them.'

'Surely they're not all mixed up?' I turned to him with spontaneous interest.

'All the better people nowadays are mixed up. It's the mediocrities and worthless ones that are kicking up all the fuss . . . Still, it's not worth talking about it.'

As he talked he gazed up in the air, beginning a phrase and breaking it off. What particularly struck me was the despondency in his voice.

'Vasin can't be one of them, can he? Vasin's got brains, he's got moral purpose!' I cried.

'There's no moral purpose nowadays. It's suddenly transpired there is none and the main thing is one's got the impression there never was any.'

'Never was?'

'Let's forget about it,' he said with evident apathy.

I was touched by his air of serious melancholia. Ashamed of my own egotistic feelings, I began to share the way he felt.

'The present time,' he began after a couple of minutes silently staring up in the air, 'the present time is a time of the golden mean and insensitivity, of a passion for ignorance and laziness, of an inability to do anything and a demand for everything to be ready-made. No one stops to think. It's rare for anyone to work out an idea for himself.'

He again broke off and said nothing for a time. I was content to listen.

'Now Russia is being stripped of its forests, its soil is being depleted, it's being turned into a steppe and fit only for Kalmucks. Should someone hopefully turn up and plant a tree, he'd be laughed at. He'd be told: "You're not expecting to live long enough to get anything out of that, are you?" On the other hand, all well-intentioned people are just going on about what it'll be like in a thousand years' time. Any kind of unifying idea has completely gone. It's as if we're all waiting for transport and tomorrow we'll get the hell out of Russia. Everyone's living simply to ensure they'll have enough . . .'

'One moment, Kraft, you said people are worrying about what it'll be like in a thousand years. Well, your own despair, er, about the fate of Russia, er, isn't that the same thing?'

'It's . . . It's the most essential question ever!' he said irritably and stood up. 'Oh, yes, I'd forgotten!' he added instantly in a quite different tone of voice, looking at me in bewilderment. 'I brought you here on business and meanwhile . . . For God's sake forgive me!'

It was as if he had just come to himself after being asleep and was almost in a totally confused state. He extracted a letter from his briefcase, which was lying on the table, and handed it to me.

'This is what I have to give you. It's a document which has a certain importance,' he began carefully and with a certain businesslike air. On recalling it long afterwards I was struck by his capacity—at such a difficult time for him, moreover—to take such heartfelt interest in somebody else's business and to talk about it so calmly and firmly. 'It is a letter from the very Stolbeev whose last will and testament was the cause of the court case between Versilov and the Princes Sokolsky. The case is now being heard and will very probably be decided in Versilov's favour, because the law is on his side. Meanwhile, in this letter—a personal one written a couple of years ago—Stolbeev set out his will or—to be more accurate—his wish and expressed himself rather in the Princes' favour than Versilov's. At least, those points, on which the Princes Sokolsky are depending in contesting the will, receive strong support in this letter. Versilov's opponents would give a great deal for this document, which, however, has no significance in law whatever. Andronnikov, who concerned himself with Versilov's case, kept this letter by him and, shortly before his death, gave it to me with the instruction to "look after it"—probably he was worried about his papers as he felt death approaching. I don't want now to make any judgement about Andronnikov's intentions in the matter and I confess that when he died I found myself in a state of grave indecision as to what to do with this document, particularly in view of the likely outcome of the court case. But Marya Ivanovna, Andronnikov's niece, to whom he entrusted a great deal when he was alive, helped me out of my difficulty. Three weeks ago she wrote to me saying quite definitely that I should give you the document and that this *it seemed*—that's as she put it—would have met Andronnikov's wishes. So here is the document and I'm very glad that I've finally been able to give it to you.'

'Listen,' I said, astonished by such unexpected news, 'what should I do with this letter now? What ought I to?'

'That's up to you.'

'Oh, that can't be so, I'm not free to do what I want! You must agree, surely! Versilov was so waiting for this inheritance . . . and he'll die, you know, without that kind of help . . . And now suddenly here's this document!'

'The only copy in existence is here, in this room.'

'Really?' I looked at him closely.

'If you can't figure out what to do in this case, what can I advise you to do?'

'But I just can't hand this on to Prince Sokolsky. I'd kill all Versilov's hopes and, apart from that, I'd seem like a traitor to them . . . On the other hand, by letting Versilov have it I'm condemning innocent people to poverty and placing Versilov himself in the impossible situation either of renouncing his inheritance or of becoming a thief.'

'You're exaggerating the significance of it all.'

'Tell me one thing: does the document have a final, decisive character?'

'No, it doesn't. I'm no lawyer to speak of, but opposing counsel would know, of course, how to make use of this document and get the most out of it. Andronnikov was positive that once this letter was offered in evidence it wouldn't have any great significance in law, so that Versilov would win the case regardless. The document is more a matter of conscience, so to speak . . .'

'And that's the most important thing of all!' I interrupted. 'That's precisely why Versilov will be in an impossible situation!'

'Still, he can destroy the document and in that way be out of danger.'

'Do you have any particular grounds for supposing he would, Kraft? That's what I want to know! That's why I'm here!'

'I think anyone in his place would do that.'

'And would you?'

'I'm not likely to receive an inheritance and so I don't know about myself.'

'Well, all right,' I said, stuffing the letter into my pocket. 'For the time being that's the end of it. Listen, Kraft. Marya Ivanovna, who, I assure you, has revealed a great many things to me, told me that you—and you alone—could tell me the truth about what had happened in Ems between Versilov and the Akhmakovs eighteen months ago. I've been waiting for you like a sun that would shed light on everything for me. You've no idea what my situation is. I beg you to tell me the whole truth. What I want to know is, what sort of a man is he really? I must know that now, now more than ever!'

'I'm surprised that Marya Ivanovna didn't tell you it all herself. She could have heard it all from Andronnikov before he died and, no doubt, did hear it and probably knows more about it than I do.'

'Andronnikov himself couldn't make head or tail of it, so Marya Ivanovna says. I don't think anyone can unravel it! The devil himself would get in a twist! But I do know you were in Ems at the time . . .'

'I wasn't there the whole time, but I'll gladly tell you what I know. Will that satisfy you, though?'

II

I will not give everything he said word for word, but only its jist.

Eighteen months ago Versilov, having become friendly with the Akhmakovs through the help of the old Prince Sokolsky— they were all abroad in Ems at the time—produced a strong impression, in the first place, on Akhmakov himself, a General and still a young man, but one who had lost the entire rich dowry of his wife, Katerina Nikolaevna, at cards in the course of three years of marriage and had suffered a stroke through leading such a profligate life. He recovered from it and was recuperating abroad, but he was living in Ems on account of his daughter from his first marriage.

She was a sickly girl of 17, suffering from a chest disorder and reputedly having extraordinary beauty as well as a lively imagination. She had no dowry of her own and all hopes were, as usual, pinned on the old prince. Katerina Nikolaevna was reputed to be a good stepmother. But the girl for some reason became particularly attached to Versilov. He was professing at that time 'something passionate', as Kraft expressed it, some kind of new life, and he 'was in a religious mood in a higher sense' (so Andronnikov, as I was informed, put it in an odd and perhaps jocular way). But the remarkable thing was that everyone soon took a dislike to him. The General was even afraid of him. Kraft did nothing to deny the rumour that Versilov had succeeded in instilling in the sick husband's mind the notion that Katerina Nikolaevna was not indifferent to the young Prince Sokolsky (who had at that time left Ems for Paris). He did not do this directly, but 'as was his wont' (Kraft's words), by hints, by implication, and by all manner of insinuations, 'at which he was a past master' (again Kraft's words). I would say generally that Kraft considered him, and wished to consider him, more of a rogue and an inveterate schemer than a man actually consumed by some higher and possibly original ideal. I myself knew, apart from what Kraft said, that Versilov, having initially had an extraordinary influence on Katerina Nikolaevna, gradually brought the relationship to the point of a rift with her. What it was all about I couldn't get Kraft to tell me, but everyone had emphasized the mutual hatred which had arisen between them after they had been friends.

Then something odd occurred: Katerina Nikolaevna's sick stepdaughter apparently fell in love with Versilov, or at least was infatuated by something in him, or was inflamed by his rhetoric, or I don't know what; anyhow it became common knowledge that at one time Versilov would spend almost day after day in the girl's company. It ended by her suddenly announcing to her father that she wanted to marry Versilov. That this was what actually happened was confirmed by everyone—Kraft and Andronnikov and Marya Ivanovna, and on one occasion even Tatyana Pavlovna said the same thing in my presence. They also asserted that Versilov not only wanted, but also insisted on marriage with the girl and that the agreement between these two ill-assorted beings, one young, one old, was mutual. But the idea struck terror in the father. The greater his revulsion at Katerina Nikolaevna, whom he had earlier loved very much, the more he tended to idolize his daughter, especially after his stroke. But the bitterest opponent of the marriage was Katerina Nikolaevna herself. There occurred a very great many secret and extraordinarily unpleasant family quarrels, disputes, bitter recriminations, and, in short, all sorts of nastiness. The father eventually began to yield in view of the stubbornness of his beloved daughter, who had been 'turned into a fanatic' (Kraft's words) by Versilov. But Katerina Nikolaevna continued to object with implacable hatred. It was at this point that the confusion began which no one could make head or tail of. Here, however, is Kraft's guess at what it was all about, based on the known facts, but it is still only a guess.

Versilov had apparently succeeded *in his own way*, delicately and irrefutably, in convincing the young girl that Katerina Nikolavna would agree to the marriage because she was herself in love with him and had for a long while been tormenting him with her jealousy, her pursuit of him, her intrigues, and her professions of love and was now ready to burn him alive for falling in love with someone else—something like that, in short. Worst of all, he had apparently 'hinted' as much to the father, the husband of the 'unfaithful' wife, giving the explanation that the young prince had merely been a passing fancy. It goes without saying that all hell broke loose in the family. According to some versions, Katerina Nikolaevna was frightfully fond of her stepdaughter and now, scandalously defamed in front of her, was in a state of despair, not to mention her relations with her sick husband. But there also existed another version, in which, to my regret, Kraft fully believed and in which I believed also (having already heard all about it). It was asserted (Andronnikov, so it was said, having heard about it from Katerina Nikolaevna herself) that, on the contrary, Versilov—long before, that is, the young girl's feelings were involved—had offered his love to Katerina Nikolaevna and she, being his friend, even exulting in his company for a time, but gradually losing faith in him and turning against him, had met Versilov's declaration of love with extraordinary revulsion and had bitterly mocked him. Her formal grounds for rejecting him were that he had proposed marriage to her directly in anticipation of the general's likely second stroke. Thus, Katerina Nikolaevna would have felt particular hatred for Versilov when she saw later on that he was seeking her stepdaughter's hand so openly. Marya Ivanovna, while telling me all this in Moscow, believed both versions, the whole lot, that

71

is. She would insist that it could all happen at once, that it was a kind of *la haine dans l'amour,* of hurt amorous pride on both sides and so on and so forth—in short, something in the way of a most complicated, romantic entanglement which would be unworthy of any serious and right-thinking man, with something pretty squalid about it as well. But Marya Ivanovna had herself been hooked on novels since her childhood and read them day and night despite her own beautiful nature. As a result, Versilov's baseness, his lying and scheming were exhibited for all to see, as well as something sinister and filthy, all the more obvious since it really ended tragically, so it was said, in the poor, consumptive girl poisoning herself with phosphorous matches. However, I don't even know now whether this last rumour was correct. At least every effort was made to hush it up. The girl was only ill two weeks and then died. The story about the matches remained in some doubt, but Kraft firmly believed it. Then the girl's father died soon afterwards, from grief, it was said, which caused a second stroke, but not until three months later. But after the poor girl's funeral, the young Prince Sokolsky, who had returned to Ems from Paris, gave Versilov a public slap in the face in the public gardens and the latter did not respond with a challenge to a duel. On the contrary, the next day he was out on the promenade as if nothing had happened. It was at this point that everyone turned against him, in St Petersburg as well. Although Versilov continued to be on good terms with some people, it was in a completely different social circle. His acquaintances in high society all held him guilty, although few of them knew the details. They knew only about the romantic death of a young girl and a public slap in the face. Probably only two or three people knew the full facts—and it was the lately deceased Andronnikov who knew more than anyone else, having had long business associations with the Akhmakovs and particularly with Katerina Nikolaevna over a certain matter. But he kept all these secrets even from his own family and revealed only a bit to Kraft and Marya Ivanovna, and that from necessity.

'The chief thing is that there is now in existence a document,' concluded Kraft, 'which Mrs Akhmakov is extremely apprehensive about.'

And this is what he had to inform me on the subject.

Katerina Nikolaevna was incautious enough when the old

prince, her father, was abroad recovering from his 'fit' or 'illness', to send Andronnikov in great secrecy (Katerina Nikolaevna trusted him completely) an extremely compromising letter. At about that time, it was said, the prince in his convalescence had actually shown a tendency to throw his money about in a spending spree. He had begun buying abroad completely unnecessary but valuable things such as pictures and vases, and giving donations and sacrificing large sums on God knows what, even on various local institutions. He almost bought for an enormous sum from some Russian no-good, sight unseen, a ruined and debt-ridden estate. He topped it all by actually beginning to dream of marrying again. And so in view of this, Katerina Nikolaevna, who had not left her father's side through-out his illness, sent a letter to Andronnikov, as a lawyer and 'old friend', asking the question:

'Would it be possible in law to put the prince under custodial care and to declare him incapable? If so, how could this be best achieved without scandal, so that no one is to blame and my father's feelings can be spared? Etc., etc . . .'

Andronnikov apparently made her see sense at the time and advised against. Afterwards, when the prince had fully recovered, there was no going back to that plan; but the letter still remained in Andronnikov's possession. And then, when he died, Katerina Nikolaevna remembered the letter at once, because if it were found among the dead man's papers and fell into the old prince's hands, he woud undoubtedly cast her out forever, deprive her of her inheritance, and not give her a penny for the rest of her life. The idea that his very own daughter did not believe in his own sanity and even wanted him to be declared insane would have turned him from someone meek as a lamb into a ravening beast. Now that she was widowed, she remained without any means thanks to her gambler husband and was solely dependent on her father. She fully hoped to obtain from him a new dowry just as generous as the first one!

Kraft knew very little about the fate of this letter, but remarked that Andronnikov 'never destroyed any essential papers' and, apart from that, was not only broadminded, but also a man 'of broad conscience', so to speak. (I was even a bit surprised at the time by such extraordinary independence of view on the part of Kraft, who had been so fond of Andronnikov and respected him so much.) But Kraft was pretty sure the compromising document had fallen into Versilov's hands through his close association with Andronnikov's widow and daughters. It was common knowledge that they had immediately and obligingly offered Versilov the chance of looking through all the papers left behind by the deceased. He also knew that Katerina Nikolaevna had an idea that Versilov had the letter and was frightened precisely of this, thinking that Versilov would instantly take the letter to the old prince. He knew, too, that on her return from abroad she had been looking for the letter in St Petersburg, had been to see the Andronnikovs, and was still continuing to look for it, because she still entertained the hope that Versilov didn't have it. Finally, she had also gone to Moscow with the sole purpose of begging Marya Ivanovna to look for it among the papers which she still kept. She had only learned about the existence of Marya Ivanovna and her relationship with Andronnikov very recently, after her return to St Petersburg.

'Do you think she found anything at Marya Ivanovna's?' I asked, having my own idea on the subject.

'If Marya Ivanovna didn't reveal anything even to you, then it's likely she's got nothing at all.'

'You mean that Versilov's got the document?'

'Yes, that's the likeliest thing of all. However, I don't know, anything's possible . . .' He said this with evident weariness.

I stopped questioning him. Anyhow, what was the good of it? All the main points had become clear to me, despite the unseemly muddle and fuss. All my fears had been confirmed.

'It's all such a bad dream, such a nightmare,' I said with deep regret and picked up my hat.

'Is the man very precious to you?' asked Kraft with evident and considerable feeling which I read on his face at that moment.

'I literally had a premonition,' I said, 'that I wouldn't learn the whole thing from you. Mrs Akhmakov is my last remaining hope. My hopes had in any case been pinned on her. Perhaps I'll go and see her or perhaps I won't.'

Kraft gave me a look of some bewilderment.

'Goodbye, Kraft! Why suck up to people who don't want you? It'd be better to break with the whole lot, eh?'

'So where to now?' he asked rather severely and stared at the floor.

'Back home, inside oneself! Break with the lot and go home for good!'

'Going to America, you mean?'

'Sure—to America! Back home, to one's own place! That's what my idea is all about, Kraft!' I said enthusiastically.

He gave me a slightly curious look.

'You have a place you can call your own, have you?'

'I have. Be seeing you, Kraft. I'm grateful to you and sorry to have been a bother! If I were you and had such a vision of Russia in my head, I'd tell the whole lot of them to go to hell. I'd tell them all to go to hell and scheme and squabble among themselves—I couldn't care less!'

'Stay a moment,' he said suddenly, having already accompanied me to the door.

I was rather astonished, turned round and again sat down. Kraft sat down opposite me. We exchanged smiles—I can see it all quite clearly now. I recall very clearly that I couldn't help wondering at him.

'What I like about you, Kraft, is that you're such a polite person,' I said suddenly.

'You really think so?'

'I do, because I so rarely know myself how to be polite, though I'd very much like to ... Still, maybe it's better just to insult people. At least it eliminates the misfortune of loving them.'

'What time of day do you like most?' he asked, evidently not having heard me.

'What time? I don't know. I don't like sunset.'

'Is that so?' he said with particular interest, but then at once grew thoughtful again.

'Are you going away somewhere again?'

'Yes ...'

'Soon?'

'Yes.'

'Surely you don't need a revolver, do you, to go to Vilno?' I asked without the slightest ulterior motive—indeed without even thinking! I asked simply because I had caught sight of the revolver and was thinking of something to say. He turned round and looked intently at the revolver.

'No, I just left it there by habit.'

'If I had a revolver, I'd hide it away under lock and key. My

75

God, just think how enticing it could be! Perhaps I don't have much faith in the idea that there's been an epidemic of suicides, but if something like this were staring you in the face there'd be times when you'd feel enticed.'

'Don't talk about it,' he said and suddenly stood up.

'I'm not talking about myself,' I added, also getting to my feet. 'I wouldn't use it. Give me three lives and it still wouldn't be enough for me.'

'Go on living longer and longer, then!'

The remark seemed to burst from him spontaneously. He gave a distracted smile and, strangely, walked straight to the entrance-way just as if he were showing me out and not noticing what he was doing.

'I wish you every success, Kraft,' I said, going out on to the stairs.

'That's as may be,' he answered firmly.

'So long!'

'That's as may be, too.'

I remember well the last look he gave me.

III

So that was the man I'd yearned to see for so long! And what had I expected from Kraft, what new pieces of information?

As I left Kraft, I desperately wanted something to eat. It was already evening and I hadn't had dinner. On the Petersburg side, on Grand Prospect, I went into a low-down pub to spend maybe twenty, certainly no more than twenty-five copecks—I'd never have allowed myself to spend more. I had some soup and I remember that I sat down to look out of the window when I'd finished. The place was packed and had a smell of overcooked meat, dirty table napkins, and tobacco. It was horrid. Above my head a sombre and pensive nightingale without a voice kept on tapping its beak against the bottom of its cage. It was noisy in the adjoining billiard-room, but I sat there and thought hard. The setting sun (why had Kraft been surprised by my dislike of sunset?) evoked in me new and unexpected sensations which were quite inappropriate. I kept on imagining my mother's calm expression, her charming eyes, which had been directed at me always so diffidently throughout the past month. Recently at home I had been very rude, principally to her. I had been wanting to be rude to Versilov, but, being habitually vile as I am, instead of being rude to him I had given her hell. I had even quite terrified her, because she had often given me such imploring looks whenever Andrey Petrovich came into the room, fearful that I'd make some rude remark . . . It was very odd that now, in this pub, I'd realized for the first time that Versilov always addressed me in familiar terms, while she had always been formal and respectful. I had been astonished by this earlier, and not, as it were, to her credit, but now I realized it especially—and all sorts of strange thoughts flowed into my head one after another. I sat for a long time where I was, until it was completely dark. And I also thought about my sister . . .

A crucial time had come. No matter what happened, decisions had to be made! Surely I was capable of making a decision, wasn't I? What was hard about making a complete break if they themselves didn't want me? But my mother and sister? No, I couldn't abandon them no matter how things turned out.

It's true that the appearance of this man in my life, for an instant in my early childhood, delivered the fateful jolt from which my entire consciousness began. If he hadn't crossed my path then, my mind, my ideas, and probably my destiny would have been different, regardless even of the preordained nature of my own character which I couldn't escape.

But then it had turned out that this man was only an illusion of mine, a day-dream left over from childhood. I had invented him, but in fact he had turned out to be someone else who had fallen far short of my fantasies about him. I had travelled to find someone pure, not *this* man. And why on earth had I fallen in love with him, forever and ever, in one short minute when I had seen him only once as a child? That 'forever and ever' had to vanish for good. Some time, if I have the space, I'll describe that first meeting of ours. It was the silliest little episode, of which one couldn't make a thing. But I created a whole pyramid out of it. I began building this pyramid under my bedclothes, when, as I went to sleep, I could cry and dream—about what?—I don't know for sure. That I'd been abandoned? That I'd been made to suffer like hell? But it had only been hell for a little time, no more than two years, in the Touchard school, into which he'd shoved me and then gone away forever. Afterwards no one gave me hell. Even just the opposite. I myself started looking down on my classmates. And I simply can't stand the way orphans whine about themselves! There's nothing more ghastly than orphans— all these illegitimate cast-offs and that sort of rubbish, whom I can't feel an ounce of pity for—when they are suddenly brought before the public gaze and start pitifully, but edifyingly whining: 'Oh, just look how we've been treated!' I'd thrash the whole lot! Not one of this foul official trash can understand that it would be ten times nobler for them to keep quiet and not whine and *not even be worthy* of complaining. As soon as they became worthy, that's where You, the Son of Love, would be needed.

Anyhow, that's what I think!

But what's funny is not that I dreamed under my bedclothes but the fact that I came here for his sake, once more on account of someone I'd invented, having almost forgotten about my main aim. I came to help him demolish scandal about himself and crush his enemies. The document Kraft had been talking about, the letter from this woman to Andronnikov which she was so worried about, which could seal her fate and reduce her to penury and which she thought Versilov had—that letter wasn't in Versilov's possession but in mine, sewn into my side pocket! I had sewn it there myself and no one in the whole wide world knew it was there. That the incurably romantic Marya Ivanovna, who had had the document 'in her keeping', should have chosen to let me have it and no one else, was simply up to her, her view of things and her wish, and I am not obliged to explain her motives. One day perhaps I'll tell all. But so unexpectedly forearmed in this way, I could hardly fail to be enticed by a desire to appear in St Petersburg. Of course, I proposed to help this man only by stealth, without showing off and without getting heated, anticipating neither his praise nor his warm embrace. And never, never would I be *worthy* so much as to reproach him for the least thing! And anyhow was he to blame for the fact that I'd fallen in love with him and turned him into a fantastic ideal? It could be I didn't even love him at all! His original intellect, his unusual character, some schemes of his and scrapes he'd got into and the fact that my mother was with him—none of this, it seemed, could stop me. It was enough that the idol of my imaginings had been smashed to smithereens and that I perhaps couldn't go on loving him any more. So what was stopping me from doing what I'd set out to do? That was the real question. It was turning out that I was the one who was behaving stupidly and not anyone else.

But in demanding honesty from others I will also be honest myself. I have to confess that the document sewn into my pocket did not arouse only a passionate desire to fly to Versilov's assistance. This is now only too clear to me, though thinking about it then I used to go red at the thought. I had dreamed of the woman as a haughty high-society lady, whom I would meet face to face; she would despise me and laugh at me as no better than a mouse without even suspecting that I was the master of her fate. I had been intoxicated by this thought even in Moscow and particularly in the train on the way here—I have admitted as much already. Yes, I hated this woman, but was already in love with her as my intended victim, and this is all true, it's all real. But it was all such childishness, which I hadn't expected from someone like myself. I am describing my feelings at that time— the thoughts, that is, that passed through my head as I sat in the pub listening to the nightingale above me and tried to decide, that very evening, to break with them for good. The thought of the recent meeting with the woman suddenly made me go crimson with shame. How bloody embarrassing! What a shame- ful, stupid little effect I made and—worst of all—it showed how completely ineffective I was! It simply went to prove, I thought then, that I had no power at all to withstand even the stupidest sort of female enticement, when I'd only just told Kraft that I had 'a place of my own', that I knew my own business, and that even if I had three lives to live they wouldn't be enough. And I had been proud of saying that.

The fact that I'd given up my idea and been drawn into Versilov's business could still be forgiven; but the fact that I was rushing about like a startled hare from one side to the other and getting mixed up in every little bit of nonsense was just my stupidity. What the devil had made me go to Dergachev's and jump up and spout my stupid nonsense, when I'd known for ages I didn't know how to say anything sensibly and properly and that it'd be much better to keep quiet? And along comes some Vasin or other and tells me I've still got fifty years ahead of me, so there's nothing to worry about! A fine thing to say, I admit, and every credit to his undeniable intelligence—fine because it was the simplest, and it is always the simplest thing that's really understood in the end after all the more sensible or sillier things have been tried. But I knew that myself long before knowing Vasin. I'd felt that idea at least three years before; it was partly what my own 'idea' was all about.

So that's what I was thinking about in the pub.

I was in a foul mood when, worn out by walking and all my thinking, I got back to the Semenovsky Barracks at eight o'clock that night. It was already dark and the weather had changed. It was dry, but a nasty St Petersburg wind had picked up, blowing in sharp and bitter gusts against my back and stirring up dust and grit. How many grim faces of working people hurried round me as they returned to their nooks and crannies after work! Each one had his own grim concern etched in his features and there was probably not a single common, unifying thought in the whole crowd! Kraft was right—people are all different.

I came across a small boy, so small it was strange he should be out on the street by himself at such an hour. He seemed to have lost his way. A woman stopped for a moment to listen to him, but couldn't understand him, spread her arms and went on her way, leaving him alone in the dark. I was just on the point of going up to him, but for some reason he suddenly took fright at the sight of me and ran off.

As I got home I decided I would never go and see Vasin. When I ascended the outside steps, I desperately wanted to find everyone at home without Versilov so that I might have a chance of saying something kind to my mother or my dear sister, to whom I hadn't said anything special for a whole month. As it turned out, he wasn't at home.

IV

By the way, in introducing into these 'Notes' of mine a new character—I am speaking about Versilov—I will briefly give his curriculum vitae, which doesn't, however, amount to much. I do this so that the reader should have a better understanding and because I can't see where else I can insert it into my account.

He had a university education, but then went into a guards' cavalry regiment. He married a Miss Fanariotov and retired. He went abroad and, on his return, lived in Moscow in good social circumstances. On the death of his wife he visited his estate; that was when the episode occurred with my mother. After that he lived for a long time somewhere in the south. During the Crimean War he again joined up, but he never went to the Crimea and was never directly involved in action. When the war was over, after leaving the service, he went abroad, this time even taking my mother, whom, however, he left in Königsberg. The poor thing would sometimes recount with horror and much head-shaking how she had then spent six months there entirely on her own with her little daughter, with no knowledge of the language, as lost as if she were in a forest, and towards the end with no money. It was then that Tatyana Pavlovna came to her rescue and brought her back to somewhere in Nizhny-Novgorod province. Later Versilov, after the emancipation of the serfs in 1861, became an arbitrator and apparently did the job very well, but soon gave it up and took up the business of conducting various private civil suits in St Petersburg. Andronnikov always set great store by his abilities, had a great deal of respect for him, and would only say that he couldn't understand his character. Afterwards Versilov gave up that as well and once again went abroad, this time for several years. It was then that the close relationship with the old Prince Sokolsky began. Throughout this period his financial affairs changed radically two or three times, either reducing him to beggary or again suddenly lifting him up and making him rich.

However, now, having brought my notes to this point, I am determined to give an account of 'my Idea'. I will describe it in the form it took from its very inception. I am determined, so to speak, to unveil it to the reader and also to clarify it for the sake of what I will have to say later. What's more, it's not only the reader but I myself as well who's beginning to get lost in the difficulty of explaining what I did without explaining what prompted me to do it. Through what might be called 'a technique of concealment' and my own ineptitude, I have once again fallen into the trap of using the 'literary embellishments' of novelists which I scorned at the beginning. As I embark on my St Petersburg novel with all the shaming stories I have to tell, I find these prefatory words essential. But it's not 'literary embellishments' which have made me use 'a technique of concealment' so far, it's the essence of the whole business, it's difficulty, that's to say. Even now, when the past is over and done with, I find an insuperable difficulty in giving an account of my 'Idea'. Apart from that, I have undoubtedly got to set it out in the form it had then—that is to say, as I conceived and thought about it at that time, not as I do now—and that is a further difficulty. It's almost impossible to put some things into words. Precisely those ideas which are simpler and clearer than the rest are the most difficult to understand. If Columbus before his discovery of America had tried describing his idea to others, I am sure they would have taken an awfully long time to understand him. And even then they wouldn't have. In saying this, I have no intention of comparing myself with Columbus, and if anyone thinks so he should be ashamed of himself and that'll be that.

CHAPTER V

I

MY Idea is to become a Rothschild. I urge my readers to be calm and serious about this.

I repeat: my Idea is to become a Rothschild, to become as rich as Rothschild; not rich simply, but as rich as Rothschild. Why, for what purpose—that'll come later. To start with I'll simply demonstrate that the achievement of my aim is guaranteed by mathematics.

It's all very simple. The secret is in the two axioms *Persevere* and *Keep at it*.

People will tell me: 'We've heard all that before. Every German father says the same thing to his children, but meanwhile there was only one Rothschild (I am referring to the late James Rothschild of Paris) while there have been millions of German fathers.'

I would answer:

'You say you've heard it all before, but you've really heard nothing. True, you're right on one thing: if I said it's all "very simple", then I forgot to add that it's also the most difficult thing imaginable. All religions and all moralities in the world boil down to one thing: "One must love virtue and avoid vice." What could be simpler than that? Well, then, go ahead and do something good and virtuous and try and avoid just one of your vices . . . Just you try it, eh? See what I mean?

That's why innumerable good German fathers in the course of innumerable centuries have repeated those two remarkable axioms, which comprise the whole secret of it, while Rothschild remains unique. Which means that it's not the same thing and all the good German fathers have been repeating some other idea . . .

Undoubtedly they have also heard about the need to *persevere* and *keep at it*; but what's needed for the attainment of my aims is not what good German fathers mean by those axioms.

And one more thing: he may be a good father—I'm not only talking about Germans—have a family, live like everybody else, have the same expenses and obligations as everybody else, but you won't make a Rothschild out of him, only an average man. I understand only too clearly that, having become a Rothschild or even having simply wished to become one, not in a fatherly fashion but absolutely seriously, I must at once become an outcast from society.

Some years ago I read in the papers that a beggar had died on one of the boats on the Volga. He used to walk about in rags begging for alms and everyone knew him. After his death they found that he had as much as three thousand paper roubles sewn into his shirt. A few days ago I read about a beggar, formerly an aristocrat, who used to go round the pubs holding out his hand. He was arrested and found to have five thousand roubles on him. Two things may be concluded: firstly, *Persevere* in the accumulation of pennies and you can get huge results (time's of no account), and secondly, the most uncomplicated form of accumulating money, so long as you *keep at it*, is mathematically bound to be successful.

Meanwhile, there are probably a very fair number of respectable, intelligent, and abstemious people, who haven't got (no matter how hard they try) either three or five thousand roubles and would desperately like to have them. Why is this? The answer is clear: because not one of them, no matter how much he desires it, *wants* it enough to resort to begging, if he cannot accumulate enough money otherwise. And not one of them is sufficiently persevering to ensure, even if he becomes a beggar,

83

that he doesn't spend the first pennies he's collected on an unnecessary crust of bread for himself or on his family. In any case, with this way of saving money—by begging, I mean—one's got to feed oneself only on bread and salt and nothing else in order to accumulate anything at all; at least that's how I see it. This was no doubt what the two above-mentioned beggars did— they ate only bread, that is, and lived under the open sky. There is no doubt that they had no intention of becoming Rothschilds. They were only Harpagons or Plyushkins* in their purest form, nothing more; but even conscious accumulation of a completely different kind, with the aim of becoming a Rothschild, demands no less desire for it and strength of will than those two beggars had. A good German father does not have such strength of will. The world contains a whole range of different strengths, particularly in strength of desire and strength of will, just as there is one temperature at which water boils and another at which iron becomes red hot.

It's like the monastic life and performing feats of monastic self-discipline. It's a feeling, not an idea. So what's it all for? Why do it? Is it morally right or morally deforming to go about all your life in rags and eat nothing but black bread, all the time carrying such a load of money around with you? These questions can be left till later, but now I'd like to talk about the possibility of achieving my aim.

When I thought of my 'Idea' (and when it was still red-hot), I started asking myself whether I could be a monk and perform such feats of monastic self-discipline. So for the whole of the first month I lived on nothing but bread and water. This meant daily no more than two and a half pounds of black bread. To achieve this I had to fool clever Nikolay Semyonovich and my well-wisher, Marya Ivanovna. I insisted, to her chagrin and in the face of some bewilderment from the extremely sensitive Nikolay Semyonovich, that my dinner should be brought to my room. There I simply got rid of it. I poured the soup out of the window into some nettles or disposed of it down the WC; the meat I either threw to a dog out of the window or, after wrapping it in paper, put it in my pocket and then got rid of it, and so on. Because there was less than two and a half pounds of bread provided with each meal, I bought more on the side. I got through that first month, perhaps doing no more than upsetting my stomach; but the next month I had some soup with the bread and a glass of tea morning and evening—and I assure you that in that way I spent a whole year in perfect health and contentment, and morally in ecstasy and endless secret delight. I not only didn't regret not having proper meals, I was in a state of great excitement over it. At the end of the year, having made certain that I was capable of withstanding any sort of fast, I started eating like the rest of them and started having dinner with them. Not satisfied with this experiment, I made a second one. Apart from the money given to Nikolay Semyonovich for my keep, I was supposed to have five roubles in pocket money each month. I resolved to spend only half of it. This was a very hard test, but after two or so years, on arriving in St Petersburg, apart from other money, I had in my pocket seventy roubles which I had saved. The result of these two experiments meant a great deal to me, because I knew positively that I could do what I wanted, that I could achieve my aim, and that, I repeat, was what my 'Idea' was all about. All the rest was child's play.

II

Still, we'd better take a look at this child's play.

I have described two of my experiments. In St Petersburg I did a third, as the reader already knows—I went to the auction and at one stroke made a profit of seven roubles, ninety-five copecks. Of course, that wasn't a real experiment, but just child's play. I'd wanted to get an inkling of what the future would be like and test how I'd go about it. Generally speaking, the real launching of my attempt had been postponed right from the start, in Moscow, until I was completely free. I was only too well aware that I had at least to finish high school, for instance. (As I've already said, I'd given up any thought of going to university.) There's no doubt that I travelled to St Petersburg very angry in myself because I'd no sooner done with school and found myself free for the first time than I suddenly saw that Versilov's affairs would distract me from starting to become a Rothschild for God knows how long! But though I was angry, I still made the journey entirely content with my aim.

True, I had no knowledge of the practical side of it, but I had been thinking it over for three years at a stretch and could have no doubts about it. I had imagined a thousand times how I would begin. I would suddenly find myself, as if I had dropped from heaven, in one of our two capital cities (I had set my sights on them from the start, and most of all St Petersburg, to which I'd given priority for some reason); so there I was, dropped from heaven, but completely free, not dependent on anyone, in good health, and having a hundred roubles secreted away in my pocket as the basis of my capital. Without that hundred roubles it would have been impossible to start, because the first likelihood of success would have been too long postponed. Apart from the hundred roubles I had, as I've said, courage, perseverance, a desire to keep at it, absolute independence, and secrecy. Independence—that was the chief thing, because right up to the last I had a hearty dislike of any association or relationship with people. Generally speaking, it was a *sine qua non* that I should embark on my 'Idea' entirely on my own. I find people tiresome and I would have been unsettled, and being unsettled would not have served my purpose. Generally until now, throughout my entire life, in all my dreams of how I will behave with people, things have always worked out very cleverly for me, but the instant I've tried putting them into practice everything's worked out stupidly. I admit this sincerely and with annoyance, because I have always given myself away when it comes to words and been in too much of a hurry, and so I decided to stop seeing people. What I won from this was independence, calmness of spirit, and clarity of purpose.

Despite the frightful St Petersburg prices, I determined once and for all that I would not spend more than fifteen copecks on a meal and I knew that I would keep my promise. I had given lengthy and comprehensive consideration to this question. For example, I decided to eat only bread and salt for two days in a row, but simply in order to spend on the third day what I had saved on the other two. I thought this would be better for my health than everlasting fasting on fifteen copecks. Then, as a place to live, I just needed a corner, literally a corner, somewhere to sleep at night or to shelter in on bad days. I proposed to live on the street and out of necessity I was prepared to spend the nights in shelters where, besides a roof, they would give you a piece of bread and some tea. Oh, I knew only too well how to hide my money and ensure nothing was stolen from me either in my corner or at the shelter! I swear to you they wouldn't even suspect! 'Steal from me? No, I'm more frightened I might steal from someone else!' I once heard someone say jovially on the street. Of course, in my own case I would employ only caution and cunning and had no intention of stealing anything. More than that, while still in Moscow, perhaps from the very first day of my 'Idea', I decided that I would never be a pawnbroker or a money-lender. That's for Jews or those Russians who have neither intellect nor character. Pawnbroking and money-lending are for scum.

As for clothes, I proposed to have two outfits, one for best and one for everyday. Once I had them, I was sure I could make them last. For two and a half years I had deliberately taught myself to wear the same thing and had even discovered a secret. For clothes to stay new and not get worn, you had to brush them as much as possible, five or six times a day. Cloth isn't afraid of brushing, I can say for sure, but it is afraid of dust and dirt. Dust is just small stones when you look at it through a microscope, but a brush, no matter how hard, is virtually the same as animal hair. In the same way I taught myself to look after my boots. The secret lies in placing the sole down flat all at one go and avoiding treading on the side. You can learn to do this in a couple of weeks and after that it becomes second nature. By this means boots can be worn, on average, a third longer. I tested it over two years.

Now for the actual nitty-gritty.

I worked it out like this: I had a hundred roubles. In St Petersburg there are so many auctions and sales going on and so many small shops and so many people in need that it's impossible, having bought something for such-and-such, not to sell it for a little bit more. For the album I got seven roubles and five copecks in profit on an expenditure of two roubles and five copecks' capital. This enormous profit was made without any risk. I saw from his eyes that the purchaser wouldn't give up. It goes without saying that I was only too well aware that this was only a lucky chance. But it was precisely lucky chances I was looking for and why I had decided to live on the street. Such chances were only too rare, so what? Still, my first rule would be not to take any risks and, secondly, to ensure that every day I would make more than the minimum I needed for my subsistence, so that no day would pass without the accumulation of capital.

I'll be told—that's all a lot of day-dreaming, you're not streetwise, you'll be conned right away. But I have will-power and character, and being streetwise involves know-how like anything else and can be acquired by perseverance, by keeping one's eyes open and using one's wits. Right up to nearly the top class in high school I was one of the first and I was always very good at mathematics. Well, it's impossible, isn't it, to idolize experience of the streets and streetwise behaviour to the point where all success becomes impossible? This is what people always say who've never tried to do anything on their own, who've never tried to start a new life, and always vegetated in a familiar rut. 'So-and-so's got a bloody nose and the next one'll get the same,' etc. Well, I won't. I've got character and if I keep my eyes open I'll get by. I mean, how can one possibly imagine that, with ceaseless perseverance, keeping one's eyes skinned and being continuously alert and calculating, being boundlessly active in dashing about the place, you can't discover eventually how to make that extra few pence? Most of all I was determined not to go for the maximum profit but always to be calm and collected. Then, a bit later, having made a thousand or so, I would of course give up street-bargaining and so on. Of course, I knew all too little about the stock-market and shares and banking and the rest. But on the other hand it was as plain to me as my own five fingers that when the time came I'd learn all about stocks and shares and banking as well as anyone, and that this know-how would be quite simply acquired because it would have become my business. Anyhow, does one require all that many brains for it? So much for the wisdom of Solomon! All you need is character; know-how, skill, and knowledge will come of their own accord. Just so long as you don't give up *wanting*!

The main thing is not to take risks and that takes character. Recently in St Petersburg I saw there was a flotation of railway shares. Those who managed to get them made a big profit. For a while the shares boomed. Someone who hadn't managed to buy or was greedy, if he knew I had shares, might propose I sell to him for a given percentage above the going rate. Well, I'd sell them at once. Of course, I'd be a laughing-stock because it would be argued that if I'd waited I could have got ten times more. Maybe, but my profit would be a bird in the hand while yours was still in the bush. So you'll say I won't make much profit that way. Well, that's just where you're wrong and where all your Russian railway magnates are wrong.* You've got to learn the truth that perseverance and stickability in making profits and, above all, in accumulating capital are much more effective than short-term profits of maybe one hundred and more per cent!

Not long before the French Revolution a fellow called Low turned up in Paris and launched what was in principle a scheme of genius (which afterwards flopped quite dreadfully).* The whole of Paris was in a turmoil. Shares in Low's scheme sold like hot cakes and there was enormous demand for them. Sackloads of money from all over Paris poured into the house where the subscription list had opened. But there wasn't enough room in the house and crowds gathered on the streets outside—people of all professions, classes, and ages, the bourgeoisie, the nobility, their children, countesses, marquises, prostitutes—all gathered together in one ferocious, half-crazed mass, as though they'd all been bitten by some rabid dog. Rank, breeding, and dignity, even honour and reputation were all trampled underfoot in the crush. People sacrificed their all (even women) to obtain a few shares. The subscription list was finally passed out into the street but there was nothing to write on. A hunchback was asked if he would offer his back as a makeshift table on which the subscriptions could be written. The hunchback agreed—one can just imagine at what a price! Shortly afterwards (a very short time) everyone was bankrupted, the bubble burst, the whole scheme went to the devil, and the shares were worthless. Did anyone make anything out of it? Only the hunchback, precisely because he had accepted not shares but gold coins. Well, I am like the hunchback! I've still had the strength not to eat and copeck by copeck to save up seventy-two roubles. I'd still have enough, even at the height of a fever which seized everyone else, to hold back and prefer good money to the promise of large sums. I am only trivial about trivialities, but not about what's important. I often haven't had the character to be patient in small matters, even after the birth of my 'Idea', but for big matters there'll always be enough. When, before going to work in the morning, my mother gave me lukewarm coffee, I was angry and rude to her, but I was still the same man who had lived a whole month on nothing but bread and water.

In short, not to make money, not to learn how to make money, would be unnatural. It would also be unnatural, relying on uninterrupted and regular money-making, on uninterrupted attention to detail and common sense, abstemiousness, economy, and ever-increasing energy—it would be unnatural, I repeat, not to become a millionaire. How did the beggar accumulate so much money if not by perseverance and a degree of fanaticism? Am I inferior to him? 'And in the end, suppose I don't achieve anything, suppose my calculations are wrong, suppose I flop and go bust—well, I'll still go on. I'll go on, because that's what I want to do.' That's what I used to tell myself in Moscow.

I'll be told that there's no 'idea' in all this and nothing new at all. And I'll say for good and all there's a whole heap of ideas here and a whole heap of new things!

Oh, I've foreseen how trivial the objections will be and how trivial I'll seem myself in outlining my 'Idea'. So what? I haven't divulged a hundredth part of it. I feel it's all come out looking trivial and crude and superficial and even more juvenile than I am.

III

It remains to answer the questions 'why?' and 'what for?' and 'is it moral or not?' and so on and so forth, to which I promised to give answers.

I feel sad that I must disillusion the reader right at the start—sad, yes, and happy too. It should be realized that there's no feeling of 'vengeance' associated with my 'Idea' and nothing Byronic—no solemn curses, no plaintive pleas of an orphan, no tears of one born to illegitimacy, nothing like that, nothing at all. In short, a romantic lady, if she happened to come across my Notes, would turn up her nose in disgust. The whole point of my 'Idea' is isolation.

'But isolation', it may be objected, 'can be obtained without having to become a Rothschild. What's Rothschild got to do with it?'

'It's got this. Apart from isolation I also need power.'

As a sort of preface, let me say that a reader will perhaps be horrified by my frankness and may well wonder why the writer didn't blush at writing such stuff. My answer is that I'm not writing for publication. I'll probably have a reader in about ten years' time when everything will have been so clarified and so much in the past and over and done with that there'll be no need to blush at all. So if I sometimes turn to a reader in my Notes, then it's just a device. My reader is a creature of my imagination.

No, it wasn't my illegitimacy, which I was teased about at Touchard's, not my sad childhood years, not a desire for vengeance, and not the right to protest that started me off on my 'Idea'. Everything can be blamed simply on my character. Ever since I was 12, I think, since, that is, I've had any proper awareness of things, I've come to dislike people. Not exactly dislike, but somehow they've become tiresome to me. I felt all too sad in myself sometimes, in my purest moments, that I couldn't say everything I wanted even to my nearest and dearest—that's to say, I could, but didn't want to and for some reason refrained from doing so, and was mistrustful, gloomy, and uncommunicative. And another thing—I have long noticed in myself a trait, right from childhood on, that makes me all too often judge others and feel too inclined to blame them. But this would very often be followed by another thought, far too onerous for me: 'Maybe I'm the one to blame, not them?' And how frequently have I blamed myself for nothing! In order to avoid questions like that, I have naturally looked for isolation. What's more, I've not found anything in the society of people, no matter how hard I've tried—and I have tried. At least all my peer group and all my friends—the whole lot—seemed to be intellectually inferior. I don't recall a single exception.

Yes, I'm morose, I'm constantly hiding myself away. I often want to get away from people. Perhaps I may do some good for humanity, but I often don't see the slightest reason for doing so. And people aren't all *so* marvellous that they need to be worried about that much. Why on earth don't they come to me, directly and openly, and why should I always have to be the first to go crawling to them? I'm always asking myself that question. I'm a grateful person and I've proved it a hundred times over in silly ways. I would instantly respond to a frank man with frankness and start being his friend then and there. I've always been like that, but people have always started by taking the mickey out of me and then turning their backs on me with some wisecrack or other. Lambert, who always hit me as a boy, was the most open of the lot, but he was just an out-and-out scoundrel and rogue and his openness was only due to stupidity. Such were my thoughts when I came to St Petersburg.

When I came away from Dergachev's (God knows why I'd stuck my nose in there at all), I went up to Vasin and praised him in an access of enthusiam. And so what? By that evening I already felt I liked him a lot less. Why? Precisely because, having heaped such praises on him, I had demeaned myself by comparison. Really it ought to be the other way round. Someone sufficiently just and magnanimous that he praises another man, even to his own detriment, should be considered superior to anyone else so far as his personal dignity is concerned. I understood this well enough, but I still liked Vasin less, even a lot less. I am deliberately, by the way, choosing an example familiar to the reader. I even remembered Kraft with a bitter taste in the mouth because he had himself virtually seen me out, and that feeling had remained with me until the day when everything had been made completely clear about Kraft's state at the time and it was impossible to be angry. From the lowest class in high school, as soon as a classmate got the better of me at work or in making jokes or in physical strength, I instantly stopped talking to him and had nothing more to do with him. It wasn't that I hated him or wanted him to fail. I simply turned away from him because that was my character.

Yes, I have yearned for power all my life, power and isolation. I dreamed about it even at a time in my childhood when I'd have been laughed in the face if anyone had found out what was going on under my skull. That's why I've been so fond of secrecy. Yes, I dreamed about it with all my might and sometimes to the point when I couldn't think of a thing to say. People concluded from this that I was unsociable and drew all sorts of dirty inferences from my vagueness, but my rosy cheeks proved the exact opposite.

I was particularly happy when, on going to bed and drawing the bedclothes over me, I began by myself, in the most perfect isolation, with no people around me and not a sound from them, to reorganize my life on a different footing. The fiercest kind of day-dreaming was always a part of my life right up to the start of my 'Idea', when all my dreams, far from being silly, all at once became rational and were transformed from a dreamy fiction into a rational reality.

Everything then merged into a single aim. However, my dreams had not been all that silly, though there'd been masses of them, literally thousands and thousands. But I still had favourite ones . . . Besides, this is scarcely the place to talk about them.

Power! I'm sure a great many people would find it very funny if they knew that a complete nonentity like me was intent on acquiring power. But I'll astonish them even more by saying that from my very first day-dreams, right from earliest boyood, I could never imagine myself other than right at the top, in first place, at all times, and in every walk of life. And I'll make another strange admission: maybe that continues right up to the present time. I'll remark that I'm not apologizing for this.

My 'Idea' is this—and that's where its strength lies—that money is the only means of taking even a nonentity *right to the very top*. I may not be a nonentity myself, but I know, for instance by glancing in a mirror, that my appearance is no asset, because I've got a common or garden face. But if I were as rich as Rothschild, who wouldn't do with a face like mine and have thousands of women rush at me with all their charms as soon as I whistled? I'm even sure that they would eventually come to regard me quite sincerely as good-looking. I may be intelligent as well. But even if I were seven times cleverer than most, there'd be bound to be someone around who was eight times cleverer, and then I'd be done for. Yet, if I were a Rothschild, would that eight-times-cleverer chap mean anything next to me? He wouldn't even be allowed to talk next to me! No matter how intelligent I may be, put me next to Talleyrand or Piron* and I'm eclipsed, but if I were a Rothschild where would Piron be, or Talleyrand for that matter? Money, of course, is a despotic power, but at the same time it's the highest kind of leveller and that's its chief strength. Money smoothes out all inequalities. That was the conclusion I reached in Moscow.

You will see in this thought, of course, no more than impertinence and violence, the triumph of nonentity over talent. I agree that it's a bold thought (and therefore a sweet one). But do you really imagine I wanted power at that time just in order to crush everybody underfoot and get my own back? The fact is that's exactly how your scum would act. Moreover, I'm certain that thousands of ever-so-exalted, clever, and talented people, if they suddenly had a windfall of Rothschild's millions, wouldn't be able to contain themselves and would behave like the worst scum and would crush people underfoot worse than anyone. My Idea's not like that. I'm not frightened of money: it won't get the better of me and I won't let it crush others.

What I need isn't money or—better—money isn't necessary to me; even power isn't necessary; I need only what is obtained by power and cannot be obtained without it: an independent and calm awareness of one's strength! That is the fullest definition of the freedom over which there is so much struggle in the world! Freedom! I've finally uttered the great word . . . Yes, an independent awareness of one's strength is both enchanting and beautiful. I have strength of my own and I am content. So long as there are thunderbolts in Jupiter's hands, he is content; after all, how often does he hurl them? A fool might imagine he was asleep. But put some writer or other or a chattering fool of a countrywoman in Jupiter's place—and then see how the thunderbolts would fly!

If only I had power, I reasoned, I wouldn't really need it at all. I can assure you that I myself, of my own accord, would always take a back seat. If I were Rothschild, I would go everywhere in my oldest coat and with an umbrella. It wouldn't matter to me that I was shoved this way and that on the street and had to jump my way through muddy quagmires to avoid the traffic. The awareness that I was Rothschild would even delight me at such moments. The knowledge that I was likely to have a dinner such as no one else might have, made by the finest cook in the world, would be quite sufficient. I would eat some bread and ham and my awareness simply of being Rothschild would be enough. I still feel the same now.

I won't suck up to the aristocracy, but they'll come crawling to me. I won't go chasing after women, but they'll be all over me, offering everything a woman has to offer. The mediocrities of this world will be after me for my money and the clever ones will be drawn to me out of curiosity about such a strange, proud, reclusive, and utterly indifferent human being. I would be courteous to both types and might even give them money, but I would take nothing from them in return. Curiosity excites passion, perhaps, and I would arouse passion. They would go away with nothing, I can assure you, except a few presents. And I would become an object of twice the interest for them.

for me it is enough
To be aware of this . . .*

It is a strange fact that I have been enchanted by the picture of Pushkin's Miserly Knight feasting his eyes on his gold (besides, it's a true one) ever since the age of 17.

I do not want—and never will want—to crush and torture anyone. But I know that if I did want to destroy a certain person who was my enemy, no one would stand in my way and I would get help from every quarter; again, that would be all right. I've never even got my own back on someone. I've always been surprised that James Rothschild should have agreed to become a baron! Why should he have done that, when he was already higher up the social ladder than everyone else? 'So what if that oaf of a general insults me at a post-station when we're both waiting for horses! If he knew who I was, he'd rush to harness my horses himself and help me into my modest tarantass! I've heard that a certain foreign count or baron publicly placed slippers on the feet of a local banker at a Vienna railway station and he was such scum that he let him! Oh, what if this frightful beauty (and there are frightful ones, believe me!), this daughter of a fabulously wealthy and high-born aristocratic lady, on encountering me accidentally on a boat or somewhere, looks askance at me and, turning up her nose in disgust, shows surprise that such a modest and scruffy little man as I am should dare to take first place beside her with some book or paper in my hands? But if only she knew who was sitting beside her! And if she did know, she'd come and sit down beside me herself, all meek and mild and gentle, eager for me to glance at her and radiant at my smile . . .' I deliberately insert these early fantasies of mine at this point in order to express my thoughts more vividly, but fantasies as such are pale and, perhaps, trivial. Only real life can justify it all.

People will say it's silly to live like that. Why not have a hotel, keep open house, collect a society round you, enjoy influence, get married? But then what would Rothschild be in that case? He'd be like everyone else. The entire charm of my 'Idea', all its moral force, would vanish. As a child I learned by heart the monologue spoken by Pushkin's Miserly Knight. Pushkin never conceived anything better than that! I am of the same opinion now.

'But your idea is too paltry,' people will tell me derisively. 'It's just about money and wealth. Where is its benefit to society, its humanitarianism, its heroically self-sacrificial character?'

But who knows how I might use my wealth? What is immoral and paltry about the fact that these millions will flow from a mass of Jewish hands, and other malevolent, dirty hands, into the hands of a sober, strong-minded recluse who keeps a keen eye on the world? In general, all my dreams about the future and all my forecasts are now simply so much fiction and it's probably silly to write them down. Let them stay in my skull. I also know that probably no one will ever read this. But if someone did read it, would he believe that I probably couldn't stand having Rothschild's millions? Not because they might have been too much for me but in a quite different and opposite sense. In my dreams I have more than once confronted that future moment when my consciousness will be satisfied but my power will seem too small. Then—not from boredom and not from some aimless yearning after an ideal—I will give away all my millions. Let society deal with all my wealth any way it likes, but I—I will again fall back into obscurity! Probably I'll even turn into a beggar like the one who died on the ship, with the one difference that they won't find anything sewn into my shirt. The simple consciousness that I had had millions in my hands and then thrown them away like so much garbage will keep me going in the wilderness. I am even ready to think in these terms now. Yes, my 'Idea' is my castle in which I can always take refuge from people, even though I might be a beggar dying on a Volga boat. That's my poetic dream! And take note: I need *every bit* of my corrupt free will simply in order to prove *to myself* that I have the strength to renounce it.

Without doubt it will be objected that this is so much fancy talk and I'll never give up my millions if they were to come my way and I wouldn't turn into some Saratov beggar or other. Maybe I wouldn't let them go. All I've done is to express my ideal thought. But I will add in all seriousness: if in accumulating my wealth I reached a fortune as large as Rothschild's, then I might actually end by giving it all away. (Besides, it would be hard to do this before reaching Rothschild's fortune.) And I wouldn't give away half, because that would simply be vulgar. I would then be a half poorer and nothing else. But I'd dispose of absolutely everything, down to the last penny, because, having become a beggar, I would then be twice as rich as Rothschild! If people can't understand that, then that's not my fault—I'm not going to explain it!

'It's a lot of asceticism, a lot of fancy talk of abnegation and impotence,' people will declare, 'and it'll be the triumph of mediocrity and the common mean!' Yes, I admit it will partly be the triumph of mediocrity and the common mean, but hardly a triumph of impotence. I have always been frightfully amused at the thought of someone—precisely a totally mediocre and average man—standing in front of the world and saying with a smile: 'You, all of you—Galileo and Copernicus, all you Charles the Greats and all you Napoleons, you Pushkins and Shakespeares, you field marshals and high-ranking generals, there you all are—and here am I, illegitimate and ungifted, and yet I'm higher than all of you because you yourselves have acknowledged it!' I know I've carried this imagined scene to such extremes that I've even cancelled out education itself. I thought it would be nicer if the man in question were grossly uneducated. This exaggerated day-dream of mine even influenced my success in the top class at school. I stopped studying precisely out of fantatical devotion to the idea that, without education, my ideal would acquire greater beauty. I have now changed my mind on this point. Education won't get in the way.

Gentlemen, surely independence of thought, no matter how slight, is not all that onerous for you? Blessed is the man who has an ideal of beauty, even if it's a mistaken one! But I believe in mine. It's simply that I haven't expounded it sensibly and systematically. In ten years, of course, I'll be able to do it better. I'll bear that in mind.

IV

I've finished telling about my 'Idea'. If I've described it poorly and superficially, then I'm to blame and not my 'Idea'. I've already given a warning that the simplest ideas are the hardest of

97

all to understand. Now I will add that they are much harder to expound, more especially since I was expounding my idea in its previous form. There is a kind of back-to-front law for ideas: commonplace, jumped-up ideas are understood extraordinarily quickly and always by the crowd, always by the man in the street. What is more, they are considered the greatest and the most original—but only on the day of their appearance. The cheapjack is never durable. When something's quickly understood, it's only a sign of its ordinariness. Bismarck's idea* was instantly thought a stroke of genius and Bismarck himself labelled one, but the rapidity of it all was suspicious. I will wait and see what remains of Bismarck's idea in ten years' time and perhaps what remains of the chancellor himself. I insert this highly digressive and inappropriate note at this point not, of course, in order to make comparisons but as an *aide memoire*. (This explanation is intended for the common or garden reader.)

I will now tell two stories in order to be done with my 'Idea' for good and all and so that it need not get in the way any further.

In the summer, in July, two months before I set off for St Petersburg and when I was already completely free of school, Marya Ivanovna asked me to go to the Troitsky Posad to take a message to an old maiden lady (something terribly uninteresting that isn't worth mentioning in detail). On my way back that same day I noticed in the railway carriage a scruffy young chap, dressed in good but dirty clothes, pimply and dark-haired with a sallow, muddy complexion. He was remarkable for getting out at each station or halt and having a tot of vodka. Towards the end of the journey he became surrounded by a jolly crowd that was, however, extremely tatty. A merchant among them, also a bit drunk, was particularly delighted by the young chap's ability to drink incessantly and remain sober. Also very satisfied with it all was another young fellow, an appallingly silly and appallingly talkative man, dressed in German style and exuding the most filthy odour—a footman I learned later. This fellow struck up a friendship with the tippler and each time the train stopped helped him to his feet with 'Time to have some vodka' and both went off arm in arm. The young tippling chap hardly ever said a word, but more and more chatterers joined his group. He simply listened to them all, ceaselessly grinned and drooled saliva as he giggled and from time to time, but always unexpectedly, produced a sound something like 'Tura-lura-loo' while lifting his finger very comically to his nose. This delighted the merchant and the footman and the rest of them and they guffawed extraordinarily loudly and freely. It's hard to understand what sometimes makes people laugh. I also drew near. I don't know why this young chap amused me as well. Perhaps it was because of such blatant violation of the generally accepted norms of polite behaviour. In short, I didn't think he was a fool. Anyhow, we made friends and, on leaving the carriage, I learned from him that at nine o'clock that evening he'd be on the Tver Boulevard.

It turned out he was a former student. I met him on the boulevard and he taught me a trick of his. We would walk together along the boulevard and on seeing a decent sort of woman we would join up with her the instant there was no one about. Without saying a word to her, we would take our places on either side of her and in the calmest way, as if we were unaware of her presence, we would embark on an obscene conversation. We would call things by their real names and, with the most innocent faces, as it it were quite proper, we would go into such details about a variety of filthy and improper acts that not even the dirtiest pervert could have invented in his dirtiest imaginings. (I, of course, had picked up my knowledge about these things at school, even before high school, but only in word, not in deed.) The woman would be very frightened and try to hurry away, but we would keep up with her and go on with our conversation. Our victim would not do a thing, of course; she couldn't cry out because there was no one about and it would have been an odd thing to complain about, in any case. We spent eight days doing this kind of thing. I can't understand why I enjoyed it. I didn't enjoy it really, but I did it. I thought to start with it was an original thing to do, something quite out of the ordinary. Besides, at that time I couldn't stand women.

I informed the student on one occasion that Jean-Jacques Rousseau admitted in his *Confessions* that as a youth he used to enjoy flashing by uncovering the part of his body which was usually concealed and waiting in a corner for women passing by. The student answered me with his 'Tura-lura-loo'. I had noticed that he was dreadfully ignorant and showed surprisingly little interest in anything. There was no hidden idea, such as I expected to find in him. Instead of any originality, I found only an oppressive sameness. I grew to dislike him more and more. Finally it all came to an end quite unexpectedly. One time, when it was already dark, we fastened on to a girl who was walking briskly and shyly along the boulevard, quite young, perhaps only 16 or even less, very cleanly and modestly dressed, perhaps making her own living and returning home to her old mother, a poor widow with many children—still, there's no need to get sentimental—the girl listened for a while and went hurrying on, her head bent and hidden beneath a veil, fearful and trembling, but suddenly she stopped, threw the veil back from a very good-looking—so far as I can remember—but rather thin face and shouted at us with glittering eyes:

'Oh, what bastards you are!'

By rights she should then have burst into tears, but something else happened. She raised her arm and with her frail little hand delivered the student a slap in the face that was of unparalleled accuracy. It had the force of an explosion! He swore and was just about to fling himself at her, but I restrained him and the girl managed to run away. Left alone we immediately quarrelled. I told him everything that had been boiling up in me in the last few days, that he was just scum and a pitiful no-good and there'd never been any sign of an original idea in him. He called me a bastard . . . (I had once mentioned my illegitimacy to him), we swore at each other and after that I never saw him again.

That evening I was very annoyed with myself, the next day less so, and the day after that I'd forgotten all about it. Sometimes, of course, I used to think about that girl, but only occasionally and briefly. It was only on arriving in St Petersburg two weeks later that I suddenly remembered this scene in all its detail—I remembered it and was suddenly so ashamed that tears literally poured down my cheeks. I was tortured by it a whole evening long and a whole night long, and in part I still am. I couldn't understand to start with how I could have stooped so shamefully low at the time and—most of all—I couldn't understand how I could have forgotten it and not been ashamed of it and not felt sorry. It's only now I realized what the problem was: my 'Idea' was to blame. In short, I came straight to the conclusion that, having in my mind some fixed, persistent, and strong idea with which I was frightfully preoccupied, I'd been forced by this very thing to retreat from the world, as it were, into a wilderness and everything that happened would simply slip by without involving the main thing. Even what I saw around me I would understand incorrectly. Apart from that, the main thing was that I always had an excuse. No matter how much I upset my mother at this time, or how shamefully I neglected my sister, I would always tell myself: 'Well, I have my "Idea" and everything else is nonsense.' If I were ever told off—and badly told off at that—I would go away feeling humiliated and later I'd suddenly say to myself: 'Oh, I may be a low-down bastard, but I've still got my "Idea" and they know nothing about that.' My 'Idea' comforted me in my shame and insignificance. But all the nastiness in my nature took refuge, as it were, behind my idea. It made everything easier, so to speak, but it also blurred everything for me. But such a vague understanding of events and things could, of course, even do harm to the idea itself, not to mention other things.

Now for the other story.

Marya Ivanovna had her name-day on 1 April last year. Some guests came in the evening, a very small number. Suddenly Agrafena rushed in out of breath and announced that there was an abandoned baby crying by the kitchen door and she didn't know what to do. The news took everyone by surprise and we all went there and saw a basket, and in the basket was a three- or four-week-old baby, crying. I picked up the basket and carried it into the kitchen and right away found a folded note which read: 'Kind friends, please help this little girl christened Arina. She and I will eternally raise up our tears to the altar on high and forever bless your name-day. People unknown to you.' At this point, Nikolay Semyonovich, for whom I had much respect, was a great disappointment to me. He made a very serious face and decided to dispatch the little girl immediately to a foundling home. I was deeply saddened. They lived very economically, but they had no children and Nikolay Semyonovich was always glad of this. I carefully raised little Arina from the basket and lifted her up by her tiny shoulders. There rose from the basket the pungent, sour smell one associates with a dirty baby. After some angry words with Nikolay Semyonovich, I suddenly announced to him that I would take responsibility for the little girl. He started to object with a certain sternness, notwithstanding his

101

gentle nature, and although it all ended with a laugh the plan to dispatch her to a foundling home remained in full force.

However, it worked out my way. In that same building, but in another wing, there lived a very poor carpenter, an elderly man and a drunkard. But his wife, a woman who was very far from old and in very good health, had just lost a baby of her own and, what is more, the only one born to her after eight years of childless marriage, also a little girl and, by a strange coincidence, also called Arina. I say 'by coincidence' because while we were quarrelling in the kitchen this woman, hearing of our find, rushed to have a look and when she learned that this baby was also called Arina she just doted on her. Her milk had not yet dried up, so she undid her dress and let the baby feed at her breast. I seized on her and begged her to take the baby and said I would give her a monthly allowance. She was frightened her husband wouldn't allow it, but she took the baby for that night. The next morning the husband said he'd allow it for eight roubles a month and then and there I counted out the first month's advance. He immediately spent the money on drink. Nikolay Semyonovich, all the while smiling oddly, agreed to guarantee to the carpenter on my behalf that I would pay the money—eight roubles each month—without fail. I had wanted to give Nikolay Semyonovich, as a guarantee of my own, the sixty roubles I had to hand, but he wouldn't take them; besides, he knew I had money and he had faith in me. With this delicacy of his he wiped the slate clean of our little quarrel. Marya Ivanovna said nothing, but was amazed that I should take on such a responsibility. I particularly valued their delicacy in not allowing themselves to make the least fun of me but, on the contrary, in taking the matter as seriously as it deserved.

Every day I ran over to Darya Rodivonovna's three times or so and after a week I gave her personally, without her husband knowing, an extra three roubles. I spent another three roubles on a little bedcover and some swaddling clothes. But after ten days little Arina suddenly fell ill. I got a doctor at once, he prescribed something, and we busied ourselves all night long torturing the poor little thing with his horrible medicine, but the next day he announced it was already too late and to all my pleas, which I think were more like reproaches, he declared with dignified condescension: 'I am not God.' The baby's little

102

tongue, lips, and mouth were all covered with fine white spots and towards evening she died, fixing on me her large, dark eyes as though she understood. I cannot understand why it never occurred to me to have a photograph taken of the little dead baby. Well, believe it or not, I didn't so much cry as literally howl that night, which I'd never let myself do before, and Marya Ivanovna had to come and comfort me—and again without either she or her husband making fun of me.

The carpenter made a little coffin. Marina lined the inside of it with ruche and put a pretty little pillow in it, and I bought some flowers and strewed them over the baby. That was how we buried my poor little sprite, whom, believe it or not, I cannot get out of my mind even now. However, a little later this almost completely unexpected episode made me think about things very deeply. Of course, little Arina didn't cost me much—all in all, what with the little coffin, the burial, the doctor, the flowers, and the payments to Darya Rodivonovna, about thirty roubles. I made up this money when I left for St Petersburg from the forty roubles Versilov sent me for the trip and from the sale of one or two things, so that all my 'capital' remained intact. 'But,' I thought, 'if I get distracted like this, I won't go far.' The episode concerning the student showed that my 'Idea' could distract me to the point of not seeing clearly and divert me from what was really going on around me. The story of little Arina taught the opposite—that no 'idea' had the power to distract (at least, not in my case) to the point where I could not stop dead before some overwhelming fact and sacrifice to it everything that I'd spent years labouring to achieve for my 'Idea'. Nevertheless, both conclusions were right.

CHAPTER VI

I

MY hopes were not realized fully—I didn't find them at home by themselves: Versilov may not have been there, but mother had Tatyana Pavlovna with her and she counted as a stranger. Half my goodwill instantly left me. It's surprising how quickly my feelings change in circumstances like that. A grain of sand or a hair out of place is enough to drive out all my goodwill and replace it with bad feelings. My bad feelings, to my regret, aren't driven out all that quickly, although I don't bear grudges. When I entered, it struck me that my mother instantly broke off what seemed to be a very lively conversation with Tatyana Pavlovna. My sister had only returned from work a moment or so before me and had not yet come out of her room.

The apartment consisted of three rooms. The one where they usually sat, the middle room or sitting-room, was fairly large and almost respectable. It contained soft, red-upholstered divans, which were, however, extremely worn (Versilov couldn't stand covers), some rugs, a few tables, and unnecessary side-tables. To the right was Versilov's room, small and narrow, with one window; it had a wretched writing-table strewn with unreadable books and discarded papers, and there stood in front of it an equally wretched upholstered armchair with a spring that stuck up and frequently made Versilov groan and swear. In this study of his he also used to have a bed made up on a soft and very tattered divan. He disliked this study and I think he didn't do anything in it, but preferred to sit around in the sitting-room for hours on end. To the left was exactly the same kind of room where my mother and sister slept. The sitting-room was entered from a corridor which ended in the kitchen where the cook Lukerya lived, and whenever she cooked she showed no mercy in the way she filled the whole apartment with a smell of burning fat. There were times when Versilov loudly cursed his life and his fate on account of these cooking smells, and in this alone I fully sympathized with him. I also hated these smells although they didn't penetrate to where I lived—on the floor above, in a little attic beneath the roof, which was reached by a very steep and creaky ladder. The only thing I had of note up there was a half-moon window, a dreadfully low ceiling, an oilskin-covered divan on which Lukerya regularly laid out a sheet for me at night and set down a pillow, and two other items of furniture—the simplest plank table and a wicker chair full of holes.

However, there were still some remains of a former comfortable life. There was still, for example, an extremely handsome porcelain lamp in the sitting-room, and on one wall hung a large and excellent engraving of the Sistine Madonna and facing it, on

104

the other wall, an expensive, large-size photograph of the bronze doors of the baptistry of the cathedral of Santa Maria in Florence. Also in this room, in one corner, hung a large icon case containing the ancient family icons, one of which (of all the saints) had a large gold and silver frame, the very one they had wanted to pawn, and the other (of the Holy Mother) a velvet surround embroidered in pearls. There was a lamp hanging in front of the icons which was lit at each religious festival. Versilov was indifferent to the icons so far as their meaning was concerned and, visibly restraining himself, merely frowned sometimes at the lamplight's bright reflection in the gilding, complaining mildly that it hurt his eyes, but he did not prevent my mother from lighting the lamp.

I usually entered the room in a surly silence, avoiding their eyes and sometimes without saying a word of greeting to anyone. I had always in the past come back earlier than this and they had given me my dinner upstairs. This time on coming in I said: 'Hello, mother,' which I had never done before, although, sort of ashamed of myself, I couldn't make myself look at her and took a seat in an opposite corner of the room. I was very tired, but I didn't give it a thought.

'This ignoramus of yours still comes into a room like an absolute lout, as he always did,' Tatyana Pavlovana hissed at me. She had always used insults before and it had become a habit between us.

'Hello, dear . . .' mother responded, instantly finding herself at a loss because I had greeted her. 'Supper's been ready a long time,' she added almost in confusion. 'The soup's probably not gone cold yet and I'll order the cutlets . . .' She was on the point of getting up and hurrying off to the kitchen, and for the first time in a whole month, perhaps, I felt ashamed that she should jump up so quickly on my account since, until then, I had been the one to give orders.

'I'm very grateful, mother, but I've already eaten. If I'm not disturbing you, I'll relax here.'

'Oh . . . of course . . . why not, do sit down . . .'

'Don't worry, mother, I'm not going to be rude to Andrey Petrovich any more,' I blurted out.

'Oh, good Lord, what generosity on his part!' cried Tatyana Pavlovna. 'Sonya, my darling, why on earth do you go on addressing him as if he's a real adult? I mean, who is he that he deserves such an honour, even from his own mother! Just look at the way you've gone all red in front of him, it's absolutely shameful!'

'I would find it very pleasant, mother, if you were to address me as a boy.'

'Oh, well, good . . . well, I will,' mother said hurriedly. 'I, er, I wasn't always . . . well, from now on I'll know.'

She had indeed gone red. Certainly there had were times when her face was extraordinarily attractive . . . Her face was uncomplicated, but by no means simple, slightly pale and anaemic. Her cheeks were very thin, even hollow, and a mass of tiny wrinkles had begun to gather on her temples, but there were none about the eyes and the eyes themselves, fairly large and open, always shone with a calm and contented light that had attracted me to her from the very first day. I also liked it that her face had nothing sad or pinched about it. On the contrary, her expression would even have been a happy one, if she hadn't been worked up so frequently, sometimes for no reason at all, taking fright and jumping up at the least thing or listening nervously to some new talk so long as she wasn't sure everything was all right as it had been before. For her 'everything was all right' meant literally 'as it had been before'. Everything was all right so long as nothing changed, so long as nothing new happened, even something happy! One might have thought that she had been frightened out of her wits as a child. Apart from her eyes I also liked the oval of her rather long face, and I think that, if only her cheek-bones had been a mite less broad, not even in her youth but even now she could have been called a beauty. Even now she was no more than 39, but grey hairs had already begun to break out conspicuously in her dark-brown hair.

Tatyana Pavlovna glanced at me with resolute disapproval.

'What a chubby cheeks he is! Fancy shaking all over on account of him! You're silly, Sofya! You're annoying me, that's what!'

'Oh, Tatyana Pavlovna, you mustn't get at him so much now! You're probably joking, aren't you?' mother added, having noticed what looked like a smile on Tatyana Pavlovna's face. Tatyana Pavlovna's insults sometimes couldn't be taken at their face value, but she smiled (if she smiled at all) only at mother,

106

because, of course, she was terribly fond of her kindly nature and had without doubt noted at that moment how pleased she was by my meekness.

'Of course, I can't fail to be aware of the way you hurl insults at some people, Tatyana Pavlovna, and precisely when I said "Hello, mother" as I came in, which is not something I'd done before,' I felt it necessary to remark to her at last.

'Just imagine,' she flared up instantly, 'he thinks he's a real hero doing that, doesn't he? So we've got to kneel before you, have we, because you've been polite for the first time in your life? Some politeness that is! Why do you always avoid our eyes when you come in? I know just the sort of tantrums you get up to with her! You could've said "Hello" to me as well, after all I knew you when you were a baby, I'm your godmother!'

It goes without saying that I didn't bother to answer her. Just at that moment my sister came into the room and I hurriedly turned to her:

'Liza, I saw Vasin today and he asked me about you. You met him, didn't you?'

'Yes, in Luga, last year,' she answered completely simply, taking a seat beside me and looking at me fondly. I don't know why, but I thought she would go all pink when I mentioned Vasin to her. My sister was blonde, with very fair hair quite unlike mother's or father's, but her eyes and the oval of her face were almost exactly the same as mother's. Her nose was very straight, small, and well proportioned. However, she had one peculiarity which mother did not have at all—small freckles on her face. There was little of Versilov about her, except for her narrow waist, her tallness, and something rather attractive in the way she walked. She did not look at all like me. We were poles apart.

'I knew his highness about three months,' Liza added.

'*Highness*—is that what you call him, Liza? You ought to say *him*! Forgive me for correcting you, but I'm annoyed that nobody seems to have done anything about your education.'

'To make a remark like that in your mother's presence is disgraceful!' burst out Tatyana Pavlovna. 'And you're wrong—her education wasn't neglected at all!'

'I'm not referring to mother!' I broke in sharply. 'You know, mother, that I look on Liza as a second you. You've made out of her someone so charming in her kindness and her character, just like you were probably, and like you are now, right up to the present time, and like you always will be . . . I was only referring to the surface gloss, to all the silly social airs and graces, necessary though they are. All I'm annoyed about is that Versilov, on hearing you talk about Vasin as "his highness" rather than simply "him", wouldn't have corrected you at all because he's so arrogant and indifferent to us. That's what makes me mad!'

'He himself's no more than a cub and yet he's teaching us how to behave! Don't you dare, sir, in your mother's presence talk about "Versilov" like that—and don't you do it in mine either, I can't stand it!' cried Tatyana Pavlovna in a flash of temper.

'Mother, I received my salary today, fifty roubles. Here it is, please take it!'

I went up to her and held out the money and she immediately panicked.

'Oh, I don't know whether I should!' she said as if she were frightened of even touching it.

I was bewildered.

'Please, mother, if you both consider me in the family as a son and a brother, then . . .'

'Oh, I'm sorry, Arkady, I know I ought to tell you something but I'm so frightened you'll . . .'

She said this with a shy and imploring smile. I was still bewildered and interrupted with:

'You know, mother, don't you, that Andrey Petrovich's court case with the Princes Sokolsky is going to be decided today?'

'Oh, of course I do!' she exclaimed, bringing the palms of her hands together in front of her with a look of alarm (it was her particular gesture).

'Today?' Tatyana Pavlovna was literally quivering. 'It couldn't be, he'd have said. Did he tell you?' she asked, turning to mother.

'Oh, no, he didn't say it was today. But I've been worried about it all week. I prayed he'd lose and it would all be over and done with and we'd be back where we were.'

'So he didn't even tell you, mother!' I cried. 'That's just like him! He's a perfect example of indifference and arrogance, didn't I tell you?'

'What's being decided, what is it? And who told you?' threw out Tatyana Pavlovna. 'Say something, for heaven's sake!'

'Look, here he is himself! He can tell you,' I announced, hearing his footsteps in the corridor and hurriedly taking a seat beside Liza.

'Brother, for God's sake spare mother's feelings and be patient with Andrey Petrovich,' my sister whispered to me.

'I will, I will, that's why I came back.' I squeezed her hand. Liza gave me a mistrustful look. She was right about that.

II

He came in looking self-satisfied, so much so he didn't find it necessary to hide his feelings. Recently he was usually accustomed to showing his feelings to us all without the slightest ceremony and not only when he was in a bad mood, but even when he was being silly, which people are frightened of doing. Still, he was fully aware that we'd understand everything down to the last detail. In the last year, as Tatyana Pavlovna put it, he'd 'sunk' in matters of dress, meaning he was always dressed decently, but in old clothes and without elegance. It is true that he was prepared to change his underwear only every other day, which even upset mother. He considered he was making a sacrifice in doing so and the entire group of women who were devoted to him saw something heroic in it. He always wore soft, black, wide-brimmed hats. When he took off his hat in the doorway, a whole mass of his very thick but grey hair literally sprang up on his head. I liked watching his hair when he took off his hat.

'Good evening. Everyone's here, I see. Even he is, is he? I thought I heard his voice as I came in. I imagine he's saying bad things about me, isn't he?'

One of the signs that he was in a good mood was that he started kidding me. Naturally, I didn't say anything. Lukerya came in with a whole armload of various bags of things and put them on the table.

'It's victory, Tatyana Pavlovna! The court case is won and the princes aren't likely to appeal. I've done it! I've just borrowed a thousand roubles. Sofya, put down your work, don't strain your eyes. Is Liza back yet?'

'Yes, father,' Liza answered affectionately. She always called him father. I couldn't make myself do that for anything.

'Are you tired?'

'Yes, I am.'

'Then stop work. Don't go tomorrow and give it up completely.'

'Father, that'd make things much worse.'

'I'm asking you to . . . I absolutely hate it when women work, Tatyana Pavlovna.'

'Why shouldn't they? As if women shouldn't work!'

'I know, I know, it's all marvellous and right and I'm in agreement with you. But I'm referring to needlework. Just imagine, I think it was one of the sickest or—better—one of the most unjust memories from my childhood. In the troubles memories of when I was 5 or 6 I remember most of all—with loathing, of course— a conclave of clever women at a round table, all stiff and severe, and the scissors, the material, the patterns, and the fashionable design. They'd pass their comments and draw out the dress, with a lot of slow and self-important noddings of heads and measuring and calculating and preparations for sewing. All the kindly people who were so fond of me suddenly became unapproachable. The instant I made a sound I'd be taken out. Even my poor nanny, holding my hand and indifferent to all my shouts and pesterings, would have eyes and ears only for what was going on, as if a bird from paradise had flown in. You see, it's the sternness of the clever faces and the self-importance before the sewing begins—that's what I find terribly hard to stand even now. Tatyana Pavlovna, you're terribly fond of needlework—you know what I mean! No matter how lordly it may seem, I much prefer a woman not to work at all. Don't take it to heart, Sofya—no, you mustn't! A woman exercises great authority in her own right, anyhow. In any case, you know that, Sofya, don't you? What's your opinion, Arkady Makarovich, you're probably against?'

'No, not at all,' I answered. 'That's a particularly good phrase—a woman exercises great authority in her own right—though I don't understand why you've linked it to work. You know yourself, it's impossible not to work when you haven't got any money.'

'But that's enough for the present,' and he turned to mother,

110

who brightened up instantly (when he'd spoken to me, she had been all in a tremble), 'at least for the immediate present I don't want to see any needlework, I'm asking you for my sake. You, Arkady, as a young man of our time, are probably a bit of a socialist. Well, believe it or not, my friend, it's your everlasting working man who's the one most given to idleness!'

'Relaxation, perhaps, but not idleness.'

'No, idleness, doing absolutely nothing—that's his ideal! I knew one everlasting working man, though he wasn't from the common people—he was a fairly cultivated chap and could generalize about things. All his life, maybe every day, he used to indulge in a pipe-dream about the utmost imaginable idleness, carrying his ideal to an absolute extreme—to endless independence, to an everlasting freedom of day-dreaming and idle contemplation. That's how it was right up to the moment he collapsed at work and they couldn't do a thing for him—he died in hospital. I am sometimes seriously prepared to conclude that all the stuff about the pleasures of work was invented by people with time on their hands—well-intentioned people, mind you. It was one of the "Genevan ideas" of the end of the last century.* Tatyana Pavlovna, I cut an advertisement out of the paper the day before yesterday, here it is . . .' He took a piece of paper out of his waistcoat pocket. 'It's yet another of those countless "students" who know classical languages and mathematics and are ready to go anywhere, live in a garret, do anything. Listen to this: "Schoolmistress prepares pupils for all scholastic institutions . . ."—all, mark you!—". . . and gives lessons in arithmetic." Only one line but an absolute classic! She prepares pupils for all scholastic institutions—of course, that includes arithmetic, doesn't it? No, arithmetic is for her a subject on its own. It's . . . it's a product of hunger pure and simple, the ultimate in need. The ineptitude is what's so touching—obviously she's never prepared herself to be a schoolmistress, so she's scarcely in any condition to teach anyone else. Still, come hell or high water, she'll hand over her last rouble to a newspaper and advertise that she prepares pupils for all scholastic institutions and, above and beyond that, gives lessons in arithmetic! *Per tutto mondo e in altri siti*, as they say in Italian. "In the whole world—and elsewhere."'

'Oh, Andrey Petrovich, she needs help! Where does she live?' cried Tatyana Pavlovna.

'There's such a lot of them!' He thrust the scrap of paper back in his pocket. 'Look, there are sweets here for you, Liza, and you, Tatyana Pavlovna. Sofya and I don't like sweet things. Maybe you'd like something, young man. I got it all at Eliseev's and Balle's.* We've spent too long "sitting around hungry", as Lukerya puts it.' (NB: not one of us had in fact sat around hungry.) 'There are grapes, sweets, Duchess pears, and strawberry tarts. I even got some excellent liqueur. Also nuts. It's a curious thing, but I've been fond of nuts ever since I was a child, Tatyana Pavlovna—and the most ordinary ones, you know. Liza takes after me. She's like a little squirrel, she also likes munching nuts. There's nothing more marvellous, Tatyana Pavlovna, than sometimes, when you're reminiscing about your childhood, imagining for a moment you're in a wood, in the undergrowth, going nut-picking . . . The days are almost autumnal but crystal clear, and it's sometimes so fresh you can lose yourself in the depths of it as you wander into the forest and there's the smell of leaves all round you . . . I see you're sympathizing, are you, Arkady Makarovich?'

'The first years of my childhood were also spent in the country.'

'I thought you were brought up in Moscow—if I'm not mistaken.'

'He was living with the Andronnikovs in Moscow when you went there. But until then he'd been living with your late lamented aunt, Varvara Stepanovna, in the country,' chimed in Tatyana Pavlovna.

'Sofya, here's some money. Keep it safely. Five thousand is promised shortly.

'Does that mean there's no hope for the princes?' asked Tatyana Pavlovna.

'None at all, Tatyana Pavlovna.'

'I've always sympathized with you and yours, Andrey Petrovich, and I've been a friend of the family, but though I don't know the princes, oh dear, I can't help feeling sorry for them. Don't be annoyed, Andrey Petrovich.'

'I don't intend to go shares, Tatyana Pavlovna.'

'Of course, you know what I think, Andrey Petrovich, that they should have not pursued their case if you'd proposed going halves with them at the start. Now, of course, it's too late. Still, I

112

daren't say for sure . . . I mean, the deceased would surely not have left them out of his will for certain.'

'He wouldn't have left them out but certainly left them everything, and he'd only have left me out if he'd known what he was up to and drawn up the will properly. But now the law's on my side and it's over. I can't go shares and I don't want to, Tatyana Pavlovna, and that's the end of the matter.'

He made this pronouncement even with some bitterness, which he rarely showed. Tatyana Pavlovna fell silent. Mother rather sadly lowered her eyes. Versilov knew she shared Tatyana Pavlovna's opinion.

It's what happened at Ems! I thought. The document which Kraft had supplied and was now in my pocket would have had an unhappy fate if it had fallen into his hands. I suddenly felt it all rested on my shoulders. This thought, along with everything else, of course, made me irritable.

'Arkady, I'd like you to dress better, my friend. You're not dressed badly, but in view of our prospects I could recommend you a good Frenchman, conscientious and with good taste.'

'I would ask you never again to say such a thing to me!' I suddenly snapped.

'Why not?'

'Of course, I don't find it degrading, but we're not likely to be on good terms, on the contrary, on bad terms, since very soon, tomorrow even, I'm going to stop going to the prince because I've got nothing at all to do there . . .'

'The fact that you go there and sit around there—that's doing something!'

'The very idea is degrading.'

'I don't understand. However, if you're as fussy as all that, then don't accept any money, just go anyway. You'll be a terrible disappointment to him. He's already quite attached to you, you know. Still, it's as you wish . . .'

He was evidently most upset.

'You say I shouldn't accept any money. Thanks to you, I did the worst possible thing today. You hadn't warned me, you see, and I demanded a month's salary from him.'

'So you've already done it! I confess, I thought you wouldn't. What a cunning lot you young people are nowadays! There's no such thing as a true young person nowadays, Tatyana Pavlovna.'

He was in a terrible mood. I was also in a terrible temper.

'I've got to settle with you! You've forced me to . . . Now I don't know what else there is to do!'

'All right, Sofya, give Arkady his sixty roubles at once. And you, my boy, don't take offence at such a rapid settling of accounts. I can see from your expression that you've got some plan in mind and you need capital for it—or something of the kind.'

'I don't know what my expression is, but I never expected mother to have told you about the money when I asked her not to!' I glanced at mother with flashing eyes. I was inexpressibly hurt.

'Arkady, darling, for God's sake forgive me, I just couldn't keep it to myself . . .'

'My boy, don't go away with the idea that she betrayed to me any of your secrets,' he said, turning to me. 'She just had the best of intentions. It was a case of a mother taking pride in her son's feelings. But, believe it or not, I would have guessed anyhow that you are a capitalist. All your secrets are written all over your honest face. He has an "idea", Tatyana Pavlovna. I told you.'

'That's enough about my honest face!' I snapped again. 'I know you can often see through things, though in other cases you can't see beyond your nose. I've been astonished how perceptive you can be. Well, yes, I do have an "Idea". That you've put it like this is pure chance, of course, but I don't mind admitting I have an "Idea". I'm not frightened to admit it and I'm not ashamed of it.'

'The main thing is not to be ashamed.'

'Still, I'll never tell you what it is.'

'You mean, you won't deign to tell me. You don't have to, my friend, I know essentially what it's all about. In any case, it's a case of:

Into desert regions I depart . . .*

'Tatyana Pavlovna, it's my idea that he wants . . . wants to become a Rothschild or something of the sort and retire into a stately magnificence! It goes without saying that he'll generously allow us all a pension—or perhaps he won't allow me one—but, in any case, we'll have been the only ones to see him. Like a new moon, he'll no sooner be seen than he's gone.'

I was shattered. Of course, it was all pure chance. He knew nothing about it and wasn't talking about it at all, except that he had mentioned Rothschild. But how could he have gauged my feelings so accurately about whether I should break with them all and go off on my own? He seemed to have guessed everything and wanted to smear the likely tragic outcome with his cynicism. He had a terribly wicked tongue, there was no doubt about that.

'Mother! Forgive my outburst, more particularly because it's impossible to hide anything from Andrey Petrovich!' I cried with a false laugh as I tried for a moment to turn it all into a joke.

'That's the best thing you could have done, my dear boy—turned it into a joke. You can't imagine how much can be gained by doing that, even if it's just for the sake of appearances. I say this in all seriousness. He always has the look, Tatyana Pavlovna, of someone with something so important on his mind he's even a bit ashamed of it.'

'Seriously, Andrey Petrovich, watch what you're saying.'

'You're right, my boy. But one's got to say a thing once and for all so as not to go on and on about it. You came to us from Moscow and were straightaway up in arms about everything—that's as much as we know about your intentions. On whether you came here with the intention of astonishing us somehow, naturally I can't say. But you've spent a whole month grousing at us—and meanwhile you've shown yourself to be intelligent and in that capacity you could have left all your grousing to those who haven't any better way of avenging themselves on people for being nonentities. You are always secretive, when your honest looks and red cheeks bear witness to the fact that you can look everyone straight in the eyes with complete openness. He's a hypochondriac, Tatyana Pavlovna. I can't understand why people are all such hypochrondiacs nowadays!'

'If you didn't even know where I grew up, how could you know why I'm a hypochondriac?'

'So that's it! You're offended because I forgot where you grew up!'

'Not at all! Don't put words in my mouth! Mother, Andrey Petrovich has just praised me for being able to make a joke of things. Come on, let's have a joke now we're all sitting here! If you like, I'll tell you a funny story about myself, shall I? More particularly since Andrey Petrovich knows nothing at all about what happened to me.'

I had reached boiling point. I knew we'd never again be all together as we were now and, what's more, once I'd left the house I'd never come back again and therefore, on the eve of leaving, I couldn't hold back. He had driven me to such an extreme.

'Of course, that'll be very charming of you, if it really is funny,' he remarked, gazing intently at me. 'You picked up some crude ways where you were brought up, my young friend, but still you're not all that bad. He's being very nice today, Tatyana Pavlovna. Oh, you've done splendidly in opening the bag!'

But Tatyana Pavlovna frowned. She did not even turn round at his remark and continued fussing with the bag and putting sweets and dainties out on plates. Mother also sat there completely bewildered, understanding everything, naturally, and anticipating that we were about to quarrel. My sister once more touched me on the elbow.

III

'I simply wanted to tell you all', I began in the most extrovert manner, 'about the way a father first met his darling son. It happened precisely "where I grew up".'

'My young friend, won't it be a bit of a bore? You know what Voltaire said: "*Tous les genres . . .*" All genres are good so long as they're not boring.'

'Don't look so grim, Andrey Petrovich—I'm not doing what you're thinking at all! I want everybody to laugh!'

'Well, then, as God is your witness, my boy! I know you're fond of us . . . and wouldn't want to spoil our evening,' he mumbled sort of affectedly and casually.

'Of course, you've guessed from my face that I'm fond of you, have you?'

'Yes, partly from your face.'

'Well, I've also guessed long ago from Tatyana Pavlovna's face that she's in love with me. Don't make such a beastly face at me, Tatyana Pavlovna! It'd be better to laugh! Go on, laugh!'

She suddenly turned briskly towards me and fixed me with a penetrating stare for several seconds.

'You watch it!' She shook her finger at me so seriously it couldn't refer only to my silly remark, but was a warning about something else, as much as to say: 'You're not thinking of starting something, are you?'

'Andrey Petrovich, don't you really remember how we met for the first time in our lives?'

'My God, my young friend, I've forgotten and I'm sincerely sorry. I remember only it was very long ago and happened somewhere or other . . .'

'Mother, don't you remember being in the country where I grew up, when I was 6 or 7, I think, and the main thing is, were you really in the country somewhere or did I just dream that that's where I first saw you? I meant to ask you about this a long time ago and kept on putting it off. Now the time's come.'

'Of course, Arkady, my darling, of course! I stayed with Varvara Stepanovna three times. I came first when you were just a year old, and the second time when you were 3 and then when you were just turned 6.'

'That's what I'd wanted to ask you about for a whole month.'

Mother had literally gone crimson from such an access of reminiscence and asked me with feeling:

'Arkady darling, do you remember *me* at all from that time?'

'I don't remember a thing and I know nothing about it, but your face remained in my heart for the rest of my life and, apart from that, the knowledge that you were my mother. To me that life in the country is as vague as a dream and I've even forgotten my nanny. I remember a bit about Varvara Stepanovna because she always used to bandage up her jaw. I remember there were enormous trees round the house, limes, I think, and then I remember very strong sunlight sometimes in the open windows, and a flower garden and a path, but I only have one clear recollection of you, mother, at the moment when I was taken to the church there and you lifted me up to receive the sacrament and kiss the chalice. It was summertime and a dove flew across below the cupola, from window to window . . .'

'Oh, my God, that's just what happened!' Mother threw up her arms. 'I remember that dove, too. You were just being held up and grew excited and cried: "Look, a dove, a dove!"'

117

'Your face, or some part of it, perhaps your expression, stayed in my memory, so that five years later, in Moscow, I recognized you at once, though nobody had told me you were my mother. But when I met Andrey Petrovich for the first time, I had just been taken away from the Andronnikovs. I'd spent five happy years quietly vegetating with them. I can remember their official apartment down to the smallest detail, and all the ladies and girls there who've now grown so much older, and Andronnikov himself and how he'd bring all the provisions from town in bags—the poultry, the fish, and the sucking pigs—and how at table, instead of his wife, who always stood on her dignity, he'd dole out the soup himself and how we'd all laugh at this, he more than the rest. Young ladies taught me French there, but most of all I loved the fables of Krylov,* learned many of them by heart and would each day repeat one to Andronnikov, going straight into his tiny little study, no matter whether he was occupied or not. Well, it was because of a fable I got to know you, Andrey Petrovich. I see you're beginning to remember.'

'I do recall something, my dear fellow, something about you reciting—was it a fable or a bit from *Woe from Wit** Still, what a memory you've got!'

'A memory! Sure I have! It's the only thing I've always remembered.'

'Good, good, my boy, you're even rousing my interest.'

He even smiled and immediately afterwards my mother and sister started smiling as well. An air of trustfulness was returning. But Tatyana Pavlovna, having put out the delicacies on the table and taken a seat in the corner, continued eyeing me with intense ill will.

'It so happened', I went on, 'that suddenly one fine day the friend of my childhood turned up, Tatyana Pavlovna, who has always turned up in my life unexpectedly, like some theatrical Goddess *ex machina*, and took me off in a carriage and brought me to a lordly mansion and into a sumptuous apartment. You were living at the Fanariotovs at the time, Andrey Petrovich, in the lady's empty house which she'd bought from you. She herself was abroad. I was still wearing little boys' short jackets. I suddenly found myself dressed up in a handsome blue suit and a fine shirt. Tatyana Pavlovna fussed over me the whole day long and bought me a mass of things. I walked backwards and forwards through the empty rooms and looked at myself in the mirrors. That's how it happened that the next morning, about ten o'clock, in mooching about I quite by chance found your study. I'd already caught sight of you the day before as I arrived, for an instant, on the outside steps. You were coming down the steps to get in a carriage and go off somewhere. At that time you'd arrived in Moscow alone, after an extraordinarily long absence and for a very short time, so you were in demand everywhere and hardly spent any time at home. Seeing me and Tatyana Pavlovna, you uttered a protracted "A-ah!" and didn't even stop.'

'He is describing it all very lovingly,' remarked Versilov, addressing Tatyana Pavlovna. She turned away and did not say anything.

'I can see you right now as you were then, good-looking and in the pink of health. You've managed to grow older and less handsome in the last nine years, forgive me for being so honest. Still, you were 37 then and I just gawped at you—at your amazing, almost completely black hair that had a dazzling sheen to it and not a streak of grey! At your moustache and sideburns that had a jeweller's perfection to them—I don't know how else to describe them! At your pale, smooth face, not as sickly pale as it is now, but like your daughter's, Anna Andreevna's, is now! I had the honour of seeing her yesterday. And what blazing, dark eyes and flashing teeth you had, especially when you smiled! You smiled broadly precisely when you saw me coming in. I wasn't very perceptive at that time and my heart was simply overjoyed by that smile. That morning you were in a dark-blue velvet jacket, a purplish-red scarf, and magnificent shirt decorated with Alençon lace, standing in front of a mirror with a notebook in your hand and declaiming Chatsky's final monologue, particularly his final cry:

"Summon me a carriage! Summon a carriage!"'

'Oh, my God,' exclaimed Versilov, 'he's absolutely right! I'd undertaken, despite being such a short time in Moscow—and because of Zhileiko's indisposition—to play the role of Chatsky at Aleksandra Petrovna Vitovtov's, in her private theatre.'

'Surely you couldn't have forgotten that!' teased Tatyana Pavlovna.

'He's just reminded me! And I confess that those few days in

Moscow were probably the happiest in my life! We were all so young then . . . and we all had such high hopes . . . It was when I was in Moscow then that I unexpectedly got to know so many people . . . But, go on, young man, you've done very well this time in remembering it all in such detail.'

'I stood there, looked at you, and suddenly cried out: "Oh, how good, a real Chatsky!" You suddenly turned to me and asked: "You don't know Chatsky, do you?" and sat down on a sofa and took a sip of coffee in the very best of spirits—I could have kissed you at that moment. Then I told you that at the Andronnikovs they did a great deal of reading and the young ladies knew many poems by heart and they would act out scenes from *Woe from Wit*, and every evening during that last week they'd been reading aloud from Turgenev's *Sketches*. But I said I liked Krylov's fables best of all and knew them by heart. You asked me to recite something and I recited "The Fussy Girl": "A girl there was who sought a suitor . . ."'

'That's right, that's right, I remember it all now!' cried Versilov. 'But, my dear chap, I can remember you clearly as well. You were such a charming little boy then, even a bright one! I swear to you, you've also gone downhill a lot in the last nine years!'

Everyone laughed at this, including Tatyana Pavlovna. Evidently Andrey Petrovich was paying me back in my own coin for my barbed remark about how old he looked. They were all in a good humour, and it was a good retort.

'As I recited you started smiling, but I hadn't got half-way before you stopped me, rang, and told the manservant to fetch Tatyana Pavlovna, who came rushing in at once with such a happy face that I, after seeing her the day before, hardly recognized her. In Tatyana Pavlovna's presence I again started on "The Fussy Girl" and finished it brilliantly, so that even Tatyana Pavlovna broke into a smile and you, Andrey Petrovich, you even shouted "Bravo!" and remarked enthusiastically that if I'd recited "The Grasshopper and the Ant" it wouldn't have been as surprising for a clever boy of my age, but I'd chosen this one:

> A girl there was who sought a suitor,
> And it's no sin to seek a suitor

"You hear how he says it!" you cried: 'And it's no sin to seek a suitor—just listen to him!' In short, you were delighted. Then you suddenly started talking to Tatyana Pavlovna in French and she instantly frowned and started objecting, even getting very worked up. But since it's impossible to contradict Andrey Petrovich if he's suddenly set his mind on something, Tatyana Pavlovna hurriedly led me away to her own room and once again washed my face and hands, changed my clothes, greased my hair, and even curled it. Later on Tatyana Pavlovna decked herself out quite sumptuously, so much so that I hadn't expected anything of the kind, and took me off in a carriage.

'I found myself in a theatre for the first time in my life, at Mrs Vitovtov's amateur theatricals. Candles, chandeliers, ladies, soldiers, generals, girls, the proscenium curtain, rows of chairs—I'd seen nothing like it before. Tatyana Pavlovna chose a most modest seat in a back row and settled me down beside her. Naturally there were other children like me but I hadn't got eyes for them; I was too busy waiting for the show to begin. When you came on stage, Andrey Petrovich, I was in an ecstasy, to the point of tears—I haven't any idea why. Why tears of ecstasy? It's the craziest thing for me to remember after all these nine years! I followed the comedy with a sinking heart. All I understood, of course, was that *she* had betrayed *him* and that he was being laughed at by silly people who weren't worth his little toe. When he made his speech at the ball I realized he was humiliated and insulted and that he was reproaching all those miserable people, but he, he was *great, great*! Of course, the fact that I knew the play already at the Andronnikovs helped, but it was your acting, Andrey Petrovich, that did it! I was seeing real acting for the first time! At the finale, when Chatsky shouts: "Summon me a carriage!" (and you shouted it superbly) I jumped up and along with the rest of the audience who had burst into applause I clapped my hands and cried out "Bravo!" as hard as I could.

'I vividly remember the way Tatyana Pavlovna gave me a pinch on the bottom as sharp as if she'd stuck a pin in me, but I didn't pay any attention! Of course, as soon as the play was over Tatyana Pavlovna took me home. 'You're not staying for the dancing, so because of you I can't stay!' you hissed at me, Tatyana Pavlovna, all the way in the carriage. I had delirious dreams all night and the next day, at ten o'clock, I went to the study but the door was shut tight. You had people with you and you were talking business with them. Then you suddenly went out for the whole day and didn't come back till late at night, so I didn't see you. What I wanted to say to you, I've forgotten, of course, and didn't even know then, but I was burning to see you as soon as possible. The very next day, at eight o'clock in the morning, you set off for Serpukhov. At that time you'd just sold your Tula estate to pay off creditors, but you still had a nice tasty lot of money, which is why you came to Moscow, which you'd not been able to visit before because you were owing so many people. And the only one of your creditors who'd not been agreeable to taking half of what he was owed instead of the whole lot, was that scoundrel from Serpukhov.

'Tatyana Pavlovna didn't even trouble to answer my persistent questions. "It's no concern of yours," she said. "But the day after tomorrow I'm taking you off to boarding school. Get ready for that, collect up your books, try packing them yourself, I'm not going to let you grow into a shirker, my good sir!" and so on and so forth, and that's how you went on banging away at me, Tatyana Pavlovna, for three whole days! It ended by my being carted off to boarding school, to Touchard's, me who was so innocent and in love with you, Andrey Petrovich, and so I think it was the silliest episode, that meeting of ours, but, believe it or not, I was still wanting to chase after you by running away from Touchard's six months later!'

'You've told it all marvellously and reminded me of it all so vividly!' cried Versilov ringingly. 'But what I'm chiefly struck by in what you've said is the wealth of odd details, about my debts, for instance. Without emphasizing the impropriety of all these details, I don't understand how you could even have got hold of them.'

'The details? How I got hold of them? I told you—all I've been doing in the last nine years is finding out details about you!'

'What an odd thing to say and what an odd way of passing the time!'

He turned away, lay back in his armchair and even yawned slightly—whether intentionally or not I don't know.

'Shall I go on about how I wanted to chase after you by running away from Touchard's?'

'Stop him, Andrey Petrovich! Get him out of here! Drive him away!' Tatyana Pavlovna snapped.

'I can't, Tatyana Pavlovna,' Versilov answered her grandly. 'Arkady's evidently got something on his mind and so we must allow him to finish. Well, let him, I say! Let him tell it and get it off his chest, that's the main thing. Go on with your new story, my boy. That's to say, I only call it new. Don't worry, I know how it ends.'

IV

'It's very simple—I was going to run away to you, or I wanted to. Tatyana Pavlovna, don't you remember that about two weeks after I'd gone there Touchard wrote you a letter? It turned up at Andronnikov's later. Touchard suddenly realized he wasn't charging enough and "with respect" informed you by letter that he considered it beneath him to keep a pupil of my background without additional payment.'

'*Mon cher*, you could've . . .'

'Oh, don't worry,' I interrupted, 'I haven't got much to say about Touchard! You replied to him when you'd already reached the country, Tatyana Pavlovna, two weeks later, and sternly refused. I remember how he came into our classroom all purple in the face. He was a very small and very tubby little Frenchman of about 45, a true Parisian, son of cobbler, but he'd been officially employed in Moscow since God knows when as a teacher of French and had even acquired entitlement to a rank, of which he was extraordinarily proud—a man of absolutely no culture at all. He had about six pupils. There was a relative of a Moscow senator among them, true, but we all lived there as part of his family, mostly under the authority of his wife, a very mannered lady, the daughter of a Russian official. In the two weeks I'd been there I'd been showing off terribly, boasting about my blue suit and my daddy, Andrey Petrovich, and their questions about why I was Dolgoruky and not Versilov didn't worry me at all, because I didn't know why myself.'

'Andrey Petrovich!' shouted Tatyana Pavlovna in an almost threatening voice. Mother, by contrast, followed everything I said very closely and she evidently wanted me to continue.

123

'*Ce* Touchard . . . I do recall now that he was a small, fidgety fellow,' pronounced Versilov, 'but he was recommended to me on the best authority . . .'

'*Ce* Touchard came in with the letter in his hand, strode up to our large oak table where all six of us were learning something by heart, seized me firmly by the shoulder, lifted me from my chair and told me to pick up my schoolbooks. "Your place isn't here, but there," he said, pointing to a cubby-hole of a room to the left of the hallway with a plain table, wicker chair, and an oilskin-covered divan just like I have up in my attic now. I went there in astonishment and very downcast because no one had ever treated me as rudely as that before. Half an hour later when Touchard left the classroom I began exchanging looks with the others and giggling. Of course, they were laughing at me, but I didn't realize that and thought we were laughing because we were enjoying ourselves. At this Touchard flew in, seized me by my hair and started pulling me about. "You mustn't sit with boys of good family! You've got no background at all and you're no better than one of the servants!" And he slapped me hard on my chubby red cheek. He took a liking to it and slapped me a second and a third time. I was terribly astonished and burst into tears. I sat there for a whole hour, my hands over my face, crying and crying. Something had happened that I didn't understand at all. I couldn't understand how someone like Touchard, who was a foreigner and not a bad man and had even been delighted by the liberation of the Russian serfs, could want to hit such a silly boy as me. Still, I was merely astonished, not offended. I hadn't yet learned how to take offence. I thought I'd just done something wrong, but when I'd put it right I'd be forgiven and we'd all be happy again and go and play out in the yard and get on as well as ever.'

'My boy, if only I'd known . . .' drawled Versilov with the casual smile of someone who is rather tired. 'But what a rotter that Touchard was! However, I'm still hopeful you'll somehow or other pull yourself together and eventually forgive us and we'll get on as well as ever.'

He yawned deliberately.

'But I'm not blaming you, not at all, and, believe me, I'm not complaining about Touchard!' I cried, slightly put out. 'Well, he kept on hitting me about for a couple of months or so. I remember that I always wanted to disarm him by rushing to kiss his hand, and I kissed his hand and still went on crying and crying. The others laughed at me and despised me because Touchard would sometimes treat me just like a servant and get me to hand him his clothes as he got dressed. My servility came to me instinctively at this point. I tried my best to oblige and not feel humiliated, because I didn't understand any of it, and I'm still surprised even now that I was stupid enough not to understand how different I was from the rest. True, my classmates taught me a good deal then; it was a good way of learning. Touchard finally ended up by preferring to stick his knee in my back rather than slap me on the face. After about six months he even started being kind to me—except about once a month he'd likely give me a slap just to show he hadn't forgotten. I also soon joined the other boys and was allowed out to play with them, but not once in the whole two and a half years did Touchard ever forget the social difference there was between us and, though not a great deal, he still treated me as a servant just, I think, to remind me.

'I'd have run away—I wanted to, that is—five months after the end of the first two months. All my life I've found it hard to make up my mind. When I got into bed and hid beneath the covers I'd always start thinking about you, Andrey Petrovich, about you and no one else. I don't know why this was. I even dreamed about you. The chief thing is I had this passionate hope you'd suddenly come in and I'd rush to you and you'd take me away with you to that study of yours and we'd go to the theatre again, and so on. The main thing is we'd never be apart—yes, that was the main thing! When it was morning and time to wake up, the boys' taunts and their contempt would start all over again. One of them used to start hitting me and making me get his boots for him. He would swear at me using the filthiest names, trying in particular to make clear to me where I came from, to the delight of all who heard. When Touchard himself eventually came in, I couldn't endure it any longer. I thought I'd never be forgiven the longer I stayed there—oh, yes, I'd begun to realize that I'd never be forgiven and that I really had done something wrong! And so I then decided to run away.

'I spent two months thinking about it and finally decided. It was September by that time. I waited until all the boys had left for the weekend and meanwhile carefully tied up all my essential belongings in a small bundle. I had two roubles. I wanted to wait until it was dark. Then I'll go down the stairs, I thought, and go out and be on my way. But where? I knew that Andronnikov had already gone to St Petersburg and I decided to look for the Fanariotov house on the Arbat. I'll spend the night somewhere, I thought, and in the morning I'll ask someone at the house where Andrey Petrovich is and, if he's not in Moscow, in which city or country he is. They'll be bound to tell me. I'll go away and then I'll ask someone else somewhere else what way to go and, if it's to some city or other, I'll go there, and so I'll go on from place to place. I'll keep on going. I thought I'd spend my nights sleeping under some bush or other and I'd only eat bread. My two roubles would keep me going on bread for a long time.

'On the Saturday, though, I didn't manage it. I had to leave it until the next day, Sunday, and as usual Touchard and his wife went away somewhere on Sunday. Only Agafya and I remained in the house. I remember I could hardly wait for it to grow dark and sat by the window of our classroom and stared at the dusty street and the little wooden houses and the occasional passer-by. Touchard's house was on the outskirts and from the windows one could see the way into town. Was that the way to the Arbat? I wondered. It was a very red sunset, the sky looked so cold and a brisk wind, just like today, blew dust everywhere. At last it grew dark. I knelt before the icon and said a prayer, only a very quick one because I was in such a hurry. I picked up my bundle and went on tiptoe down our creaking stairs, terrified that Agafya might hear me from the kitchen. The door was locked. I turned the key and suddenly right there was blackest night staring me in the face like something endlessly and frighteningly unknown. And the wind literally tore my cap off my head. I was on the point of going out when I heard the hoarse, drunken swearing of a passer-by on the other side of the street. I stopped, looked round, and calmly turned back, calmly went upstairs, calmly undressed, calmly undid my bundle, and lay down flat on my face, without a single thought and without a single tear. That's the very moment I realized that, above all, I was no better than a servant and—what's more—a cowardly one, and that's when my development began, real and proper!'

'And this is the very moment I see what you really are!' cried

Tatyana Pavlovna, suddenly jumping up so unexpectedly I wasn't prepared for it. 'You weren't just a servant-boy then, you're one now! You've got the soul of a servant! Andrey Petrovich should have apprenticed you to a bootmaker! He might have done you a bit of good that way, you'd have been taught a trade! Who could've asked or demanded any more of him on your behalf? Your father, Makar Ivanych, didn't so much ask as demand that you and his other children should never be raised above the servant class. No, you're not appreciating that he got you as far as university and that it's through him you've got any social status at all! So the little boys teased you, did they, and now you've sworn to avenge yourself on humanity! You're a brat, that's what you are!'

I admit I was shocked by this outburst. I stood up and stared at her for some moment, not knowing what to say.

'Tatyana Pavlovna really has said something new, you know!' I spoke firmly, turning at last to Versilov. 'You know, I was really such a servant-boy I wouldn't be satisfied by being apprenticed to a bootmaker! Even social status wouldn't be enough! What I wanted was the whole of Versilov, what I wanted was a father . . . That's what I demanded! That's bound to make me a servant-boy, isn't it? Mother, I've had it on my conscience for eight years how you came by yourself to see me at Touchard's and the way I received you then, but now's not the time to talk about it because Tatyana Pavlovna won't let me. Till tomorrow, perhaps, when we'll see each other again. Now, Tatyana Pavlovna, what if I'm such a servant-boy that I can't even allow someone with one wife to marry another? But, you know, that's what almost happened to Andrey Petrovich at Ems! Mother, if you don't want to remain with a husband who'll be marrying someone else tomorrow, then bear in mind you've got a son who promises always to remain a devoted son, remember it and let's be off! With the one proviso that it's him or me, all right? I don't want your answer right away. I know things like that can't be answered all at once . . .'

But I couldn't finish, firstly because I was worked up and had got confused. Mother went white and her voice failed her. She couldn't say a word. Tatyana Pavlovna said a great deal very loudly, so that I couldn't make head or tail of it, and she shoved me once or twice in the shoulder with her fist. I can only recall that she was shouting something about my words being 'made up, the maunderings of a shallow mind, all discombobulated!' Versilov sat there unsmiling, very still and solemn. I went up to my attic. The final glance accompanying me from the room was the reproachful glance of my sister. She sternly shook her head at me.

CHAPTER VII

I

I AM describing all these things without sparing my own feelings in order to recall everything clearly and reconstitute the original impression. Going up to my attic I had no idea whether I should be ashamed or proud of myself at having done my duty. If I had been the least bit more experienced I would have guessed that the slightest doubt could be taken as a bad sign. But something else took precedence. I don't understand why I was so glad, but I *was* glad, terribly glad, despite having my doubts and clearly realizing that downstairs I had made a mess of things. Even the fact that Tatyana Pavlovna had been so vicious to me simply amused me and made me laugh, but didn't irritate me at all. That was probably because I'd cast off my chains and felt myself free of them for the first time.

I also felt I'd spoilt my chances because it was even more difficult for me to see now how I could deal with the letter about the inheritance. They'd definitely assume now that I'd be trying to get my own back on Versilov. But downstairs I'd planned, during all the exchanges, that I'd put the letter about the inheritance to arbitration and I'd turn for judgement to Vasin, or if I couldn't get him, then to someone else and I already knew who. For just once, I thought, I'll go and see Vasin—but afterwards I'll vanish clear away for several months so far as everyone is concerned, particularly so far as Vasin is concerned. I'll just see my mother and sister occasionally perhaps. It was all pretty chaotic. I felt I'd done something, but not what I wanted and . . . and I had to be content with that. I repeat, for some reason I felt glad.

128

I'd planned to go to bed early in view of all the walking I'd have to do the next day. Apart from renting somewhere to live and moving there I'd made various decisions which I'd planned to fulfil somehow or other. But the evening wasn't destined to end without further odd things happening, and Versilov managed to astonish me quite remarkably. He had never been up into my attic and suddenly, after I'd only been there myself less than an hour, I heard his footsteps ascending the ladder. He called out to me to light his way. I held up a candle and, stretching out my hand, which he seized, I helped him clamber up.

'*Merci*, dear boy, I haven't been up here before, not even when I rented the place. I thought it'd be like this, but I didn't anticipate quite such a cubby-hole.' He stood in the middle of my attic looking round him curiously. 'But it's a coffin, an absolute coffin!'

It actually did have a resemblance to the interior of a large coffin and I was astonished at the way he'd hit on the right word first go. The attic space was narrow and long. The angle of the wall and roof was level with my shoulder and I could reach up to the ceiling with the palm of my hand. Versilov unconsciously kept himself bent to start with for fear of knocking his head on the ceiling. But he managed to avoid doing so and eventually sat down fairly calmly on my divan which had already been made ready for me to sleep on. As for me, I remained standing staring at him in the most profound astonishment.

'Your mother tells me that she didn't know whether or not to accept the money you had offered her for your month's keep. In view of this coffin, not only shouldn't she accept it, but we ought to compensate you out of our own funds! I'd never been up here . . . and I simply can't imagine how anyone can live here!'

'I've got used to it. What I can't get used to is seeing you up here after everything that happened downstairs.'

'Oh, yes, you were pretty rude downstairs . . . but I've also got special reasons for coming to see you, as I'll explain. Besides, there's nothing unusual about my coming to see you. Even what happened downstairs is also quite in the usual order of things. But just tell me one thing, for heaven's sake! What you were saying downstairs and had been preparing us for so solemnly and going on about, is that the sum total of what you intended to divulge and impart, and there's nothing else?'

'That's all. That is, let's assume that's all.'

'It's not much, my boy. I confess that, judging by your opening remarks and how you called on us to have a laugh, in short, seeing how keen you were to tell us things, I'd expected more.'

'But isn't it all the same to you?'

'I was talking about a sense of proportion. All your sound and fury wasn't worth it; it was out of proportion. To have kept quiet for a whole month, to have saved up so much to say and then, all of a sudden—nothing at all!'

'I wanted to spend a long time telling what I had to tell, but I'm ashamed of what I actually said. You can't put everything into words and some things are better not talked about at all. I've already said enough and you've just not wanted to understand it.'

'Ah, the way one sometimes suffers when one can't express oneself! It's a noble suffering, my boy, and is given only to a select few. A fool is always satisfied with what he's said and, what's more, always says more than necessary. They love to keep a lot in reserve.'

'Just like me downstairs. I also said more than necessary. I demanded "the whole of Versilov"—that's much more than I need. I don't need Versilov at all.'

'My boy, I see you want to make up for what you lost downstairs. You've obviously got a lot of bad conscience about it, and because having a bad conscience means we've immediately got to start attacking someone else, you don't want to miss the mark again in my case. I've come a bit too soon, before you've cooled down, and you're still a bit sensitive to criticism. But sit down, for heaven's sake. I've got something to tell you. Thank you.

'Judging by what you said to your mother downstairs as you went out, it's only too clear that the two of us have come to a parting of the ways, no matter what happens. I've come here to try and persuade you to do this as gently as possible and without any scandal, so as not to hurt and frighten your mother even more. The fact that I've come here myself has already cheered her up. She believes we can still sort it all out and everything'll go on as before. I think that if you and I were to laugh loudly once or twice while we're up here, that would give great pleasure to the simple hearts down below. They *are* simple hearts, but

130

they're also loving, sincerely and openly loving, so why shouldn't we appease them when we can? Well, that's the first thing. The second thing is: why do we have to part thirsting for vengeance, grinding our teeth, swearing oaths, and so on? Without any doubt we can't clasp each other in a warm embrace, but we can part, can't we, with mutual respect for each other. That's true, isn't it?'

'This is absolute nonsense! I promise to leave without making a fuss—that's all! So you're doing all this for mother's sake, are you? I don't think mother's peace of mind matters to you one jot and you're just saying it, that's all!'

'So you don't believe me?'

'You're talking to me as if I were a child!'

'My boy, I'm ready to ask your forgiveness a thousand times over—well, for all you hold against me, for all those years of your childhood and so on, but, *cher enfant*, what would be the good of it? You're so clever you yourself don't want to be put in such a stupid position. I'm not even referring to the fact that, even now, I'm not quite sure what you're reproaching me for. The fact that you weren't born a Versilov? Or perhaps that's not it? Bah! The way you're laughing and waving your arms about must mean that's not so, eh?'

'You can be sure not! You can be sure I wouldn't consider it any kind of honour to be called Versilov!'

'Forget about honour! You'd be bound to answer as a democrat. But if so, what are you blaming me for?'

'Tatyana Pavlovna expressed only a moment ago everything I wanted to know and couldn't understand before she said it—that you hadn't apprenticed me to a bootmaker, so I must be grateful for that! I just can't understand why I feel so ungrateful even now, even when I've been told the truth. Is it that your proud blood will out, Andrey Petrovich?'

'Probably not. And, besides, you must agree that all your attacks downstairs, instead of hitting me as they were meant to, were hard on your mother and not on anyone else. In any case, I don't think it's up to you to judge her. What's she ever done to you? What's more, my boy, explain to me why, for what purpose, did you spread it about at school and high school and all your life, to all and sundry, so I've heard, that you were illegitimate? I've heard you took special pleasure in doing it. Anyhow, it's all

131

nonsense and a filthy slander. You were legitimately Dolgoruky, the son of Makar Ivanych Dolgoruky, an honourable man of remarkable mind and character. If, though, you received any kind of further education, then it was thanks to your former estate owner, Versilov, but what of it? The main thing is, proclaiming your illegitimacy as you have done, which is in any case a slander, you have publicly declared to one and all your mother's secret and out of some sort of false pride dragged your mother's reputation through the mud for all to see. That, my boy, is a very ignoble thing to have done, more especially since your mother is not personally to blame for anything. She is the purest character imaginable, and if she's not called Mrs Versilov then it's simply because she is still married.'

'That's enough! I agree with you and have enough faith in your intelligence to hope you'll stop going on and on at me! You're fond of talking about keeping things in proportion. Then keep a sense of proportion about everything, even about your sudden love for my mother. Look, it'd be better if, having decided on coming to see me and spending a quarter of an hour or half an hour up here—I still don't really know why, but let's say it's for my mother's peace of mind, and, above all, the pleasure of having a talk with me after what happened downstairs—it'd be better if you told me something about my father, about this pilgrim, this Makar Ivanych. I've always wanted you in particular to tell me about him and I've been meaning to ask you for a long time. Since we're saying goodbye, perhaps for quite a while, I'd very much like to get an answer to the question—why is it that, in all of twenty years, you haven't been able to work upon my mother's prejudices sufficiently—and even now on my sister's—to eradicate by your civilizing influence the sinister remnants of her background? Oh, I'm not talking about her purity! Despite that, she's always been incomparably above you in a moral sense, forgive me for saying so, but . . . but it's just that she's dead, even if incomparably above you! It's only Versilov who lives, and all the others around him and everything connected with him are only allowed to flourish on condition they let all their strength and vital juices flow into him. But surely she had a life of her own once? You fell in love with something in her, didn't you? She was a real woman once, wasn't she?'

'My dear boy, if you really want to know, she never was,' he answered me, at once screwing his face up in the way he had always been used to doing for my benefit from the very beginning, which I knew so well and so infuriated me. To all appearances, he would seem the very soul of honesty, but, on closer scrutiny, he looked as if he were just kidding me, so there were times when I simply couldn't tell from his face what he was thinking. 'She never was at all! A Russian woman never is a real woman!'

'There are Polish women, aren't there, and Frenchwomen? Or Italian women, passionate ones—aren't they capable of enchanting upper-class civilized Russians like Versilov?'

'Well, I never thought I'd be meeting a Slavophile up here!' Versilov burst out laughing.

I remember the story he went on to tell word for word. He started speaking with great pleasure and evident satisfaction. I knew only too well he hadn't come to see me just for a chat, least of all to please mother, but had other ideas in mind.

II

'The entire twenty years your mother and I have lived together have passed in silence,' he began saying (exceedingly pompously and artificially). 'And all that happened between us happened in silence. The chief characteristic of our twenty-year association has been—not a word! I don't think we've even quarrelled. True, I've often been away and left her by herself, but it's always ended in my coming back. *Nous revenons toujours*—it's a man's basic characteristic, you know, the product of pure magnanimity. If marriage depended only on women, it would never survive. Humility, meekness, submissiveness, and at the same time firmness and strength, real strength—that's what makes up your mother's character. You should take note she's the best of all the women I've ever met on this earth. That she has strength I know, because I can bear witness to the way she feeds on her strength. When it comes to—I won't say convictions, because right convictions can't really come into it—but when it comes to what the peasantry call a conviction, something they regard as sacred, then she would simply undergo torture for its sake. Well, you can make up your mind whether I'm a torturer. That's why I preferred in almost every case not to say a word, and not only

133

because it was easier that way, and I confess I don't regret it. In this way everything worked out in the broadest, most human sense, so I don't even ascribe any special merit to myself in all this. However, I will say, in inverted commas, as it were, that I suspect she never believed I was all that humane and therefore was in a constant state of anxiety. Being so anxious, she could never let herself be affected by culture of any kind. They know how to do this, and we have no comprehension of it. In general they're better than we are at arranging their affairs. They can go on living in their own way in the most unnatural circumstances and remain true to themselves in places that are quite alien to them. We can't.'

'Who are *they*? I don't understand you.'

'The peasantry, the people, my boy. I'm talking about the people. They have demonstrated their great, living strength and historical breadth of perspective both morally and politically. But, to turn to our own affairs, I'll say this about your mother—she is not silent all the time. Your mother will sometimes say something, but she will speak so directly to the point you'll realize you've just been wasting your time talking to her, even though you may have spent five years gradually preparing her for it. She also makes the most unexpected retorts. Note, please, that I'm not calling her a fool. On the contrary, she has a mind of her own and a quite remarkable one. However, you probably don't accept that.'

'Why not? What I won't accept is that you really believe in her mind and are not pretending.'

'Really? You think I'm shamming, do you? My boy, I'll give you a certain amount of rope, seeing you're a spoiled son of mine, but this time let it stop right there!'

'Tell me about my father—the truth, if you can.'

'About Makar Ivanovich, you mean? Makar Ivanovich, as you already know, was an estate worker who sought, so to speak, after a certain fame and glory . . .'

'I bet you're envious of him right now!'

'On the contrary, my boy, on the contrary. If you want to know I'm very glad to find you in such a receptive state of mind. I swear to you that right now I'm in a highly repentant mood, at this precise moment, for the thousandth time perhaps, I'm helplessly contrite about everything that happened twenty years

134

ago. Still, as God is my witness, everything that happened then was utterly and completely accidental . . . Well, afterwards, too, the humane thing was done, in so far as it was in my power to do it and at least as I then conceived it to be. Oh, in those days we all had such a burning desire to do good, to serve civic aims, to pursue a higher idea. We were against rank and our hereditary rights and our estates and even pawn-shops—at least some of us were, I swear to you. There weren't very many of us, but we were great talkers and sometimes, I assure you, we were great doers.'

'Were you a great doer when you wept on his shoulder?'

'My boy, I agree with you in everything right from the start. But you heard about that very thing from me and I think this time you're abusing my simple honesty and my trustfulness. You ought to agree that weeping on his shoulder wasn't as bad as it may seem at first sight, particularly for those far-off times. We were only just getting our act together then. I was showing off, of course, but at the time I didn't know it. Have you never shown off in practice?'

'Downstairs I let myself go a bit and I felt very ashamed when I got up here that you'd think I'd been showing off. It's true that there are times when you feel quite sincere about something but make a whole production out of it. I swear to you now that I was being absolutely natural downstairs.'

'That's just how it was! You've put it in a nutshell by saying "you feel quite sincere about something but make a whole production out of it"! That's just what happened to me. I made a production out of it, but I wept quite sincerely. I won't dispute that Makar Ivanovich could have taken my weeping on his shoulder as a bad joke if he'd been a bit sharper in the uptake, but his honesty prevented him from seeing through me. I simply don't know whether he pitied me then or not. I remember I very much wanted him to . . .'

'You know,' I interrupted him, 'you're having a bit of a giggle saying that now. All the time you've been talking to me, this whole past month, you've been having a giggle. Why've you always done this when talking to me?'

'You really think that, do you?' he answered meekly. 'You're very touchy. Besides, even if I am having a giggle, you needn't worry, it's not at your expense or, at least, not only your expense.

135

But I'm not having a giggle now. Then I was—then I did everything I could, and not for my own good, believe me. We, the beautiful people of our time, in contrast to the simple masses, had no idea how to act for our own good. On the contrary, we blackened our reputations as much as possible, and I suspect this was considered at the time "the highest good we could do ourselves!" The present generation of progressives is much more hard-nosed than we were. I explained all this to Makar Ivanovich before there was any adultery—everything, with extraordinary directness. I now agree there was no need to explain much of this at all, certainly with such directness. Without mentioning the humane aspect of it, it would even have been more polite. But at the end of a dance have you ever tried stopping yourself from making that final show-off twirl? Maybe that's exactly what one means in fact by the demands of the lofty and beautiful—all my life I've never been able to decide!

'Still, that's much too deep a theme for the superficial matters we're concerned with, but I swear to you I sometimes die of shame nowadays when I think about it. I offered him three thousand roubles and I remember he said nothing while I did all the talking. Just imagine, I thought he was frightened of me—of my proprietorial rights, I mean—and I remember I did all I could to cheer him up. I tried persuading him without fear or favour to tell me everything he wanted, even including every possible criticism. As a guarantee I gave him my word that if he didn't accept my conditions—the three thousand, that is—plus freedom for his wife and himself and a ticket to go where he liked (without his wife, of course), then he should say so at once and I'd immediately give him his freedom, let him have his wife back, compensate them both—with the same three thousand—and then they wouldn't have to go away but I'd go away from them—to Italy, for three years, all on my own. *Mon ami*, you can be sure I wouldn't have taken Mademoiselle Sapozhkov with me to Italy. I was extraordinarily pure in my ideas at that time!

'So what happened? Makar knew only too well that I'd do what I said. But he continued saying nothing and it was only when I pressed him for a third time that he turned away, gave a wave of the hand, and went out, even with a certain lack of ceremony, I assure you, which surprised me a good deal at the time. At that instant I caught sight of myself in the mirror and

I'll never forget it. In general it's worst of all when people like that don't say anything, and he was a solemn character and I confess that I not only didn't trust him when I summoned him into my study, but I was terribly in awe of him because in that society there are characters—and a terrible lot of them too—who epitomize sheer anarchy, so to speak, and that's more frightening even than physical violence. I mean it literally. Oh, the risk I took, the risk! Well, I mean, what if he'd let everyone know about it, shouted it all out loud, this provincial Uriah—what would it have been like for an immature David like me, what on earth could I have done then?* You see, that's why I offered the three thousand beforehand. It was instinctive. But fortunately I was wrong. Makar Ivanovich was something else . . .'

'Tell me, had you committed adultery? You said just now you summoned the husband before the adultery, didn't you?'

'You see, it depends what you mean . . .'

'Right, so you had. You said just now you were wrong about him, that he was something else—what?'

'That's precisely what I don't know—even today I don't know. But he was something else, even something very special. I say that because, by the end of it, I felt three times worse than ever in his presence. The next day he agreed to go away, with nothing more said between us, but not forgetting the compensation I'd offered.'

'Did he take the money?'

'Indeed he did! And you know, my boy, on that point he even quite astonished me. Of course, I didn't have three thousand in my pocket, but I got hold of seven hundred and let him have them as a down payment. And then what do you think? He demanded the remaining two thousand three hundred from me in the form of a letter of credit made payable as security to a certain merchant. Then, after a couple of years, on the strength of that letter of credit, he took me to court and got the money out of me with interest, so he again astonished me, all the more so since he literally set about raising money to build a church—since when he's spent twenty years as a pilgrim. I don't know why a pilgrim needs so much money of his own—money's such a worldly thing. Of course, I offered the money quite sincerely at the time and in a first fine flush, so to speak, but later, after the passing of several minutes, I might naturally have had second thoughts ... and I might have counted on him at least being kind to me, or to *us*, her and me, and at least waiting a little. However, he didn't wait at all ...'

(I will add an essential footnote here: should it happen that mother survived Mr Versilov, she would have been left literally penniless in her old age if it weren't for Makar Ivanovich's three thousand roubles, which had long since doubled their value through interest and which he had left to her in their entirety, down to the last rouble, last year in his will. He had anticipated Versilov's fecklessness even then.)

'You once told me, didn't you, that Makar Ivanovich used to come and visit you and would always stay in mother's apartment?'

'Yes, my boy, he did, and I confess, to start with, I was terribly frightened of these visitations. In the whole twenty-year period he's only come six or seven times, and during his first visits, if I were at home, I'd try and hide. I didn't even understand at first what it meant, why he was there. But later, for several reasons, I realized it wasn't all that silly of him. Afterwards, by chance, I took it into my head to nose about and came out of hiding to take a look at him and, I assure you, received a highly original impression of him. It was on his third or fourth visit, when I was acting as an arbitrator after the Emancipation and trying, of course, as hard as I could to study my native Russia. I heard an extraordinary amount of new things from him. What's more, I came across in him what I'd never expected to find—a kind of placid good humour, a level-headedness and—more surprising still—something like sheer joy. No hint of *that* (*tu comprends?*) and a highly developed capacity for talking sensibly and very eloquently, without, that is, any of the silly pretentiousness of the lower classes which I admit, despite all my democratic feelings, I can't stand, and without any of that Russian mummerset which "real Russians" have to use in plays and novels. He also had very little to say about religion if you didn't bring up the subject yourself, but if you were interested he had some delightful stories to tell about monasteries and monastic life. But the main thing was his deference, that modest deference which is essential for the highest kind of equality and without which, to my mind, you'll never get to the top. It is here, through the absence of the least arrogance, that the truest form of dignity is achieved and you have a man who undoubtedly respects himself no matter what his position in the world may be and no matter what fate has to offer him. The capacity for respecting oneself no matter what one's position is is extraordinarily rare, at least as rare as a sense of true personal dignity. The older you get, the more you'll be aware of it. But what struck me most of all subsequently— subsequently,' added Versilov, 'rather than to start with—was that Makar had exceptional *gravitas* and, I assure you, exceptional good looks. True, he was old, but

Swarthy, tall and straight,*

unaffected and serious. I was even amazed at my poor Sofya for preferring *me* in those days. He was 50 then, but he was such a fine-looking fellow and I was such a lightweight by comparison. Still, I remember even then he was unforgivably grey-haired, and he must have been just as grey when he married her . . . I think that probably influenced her.'

Versilov had the nastiest kind of upper-class mannerism. For want of anything else, having uttered a few highly intelligent and beautifully expressed things, he would deliberately end with some sort of silliness, like the suggestion about Makar Ivanovich's grey hairs and their influence on mother. He would do this quite deliberately and probably with no idea why, simply out of the silliest upper-class habit. To hear him you would think he was talking very seriously, but really he was showing off for his own benefit or having a bit of fun.

III

I don't know why I suddenly felt such terrible loathing at that moment. It's generally with considerable dislike that I recall the remarks I made then. I suddenly stood up.

'You know,' I said, 'you said you'd come chiefly to let mother think we'd made peace with each other. It's been long enough for her to think that. Isn't it time you left me alone?'

He flushed slightly and rose to his feet, saying:

'My boy, you're hardly doing me justice. Still, I'll be on my way. I can't force you to be nice to me. Let me ask you one thing, though: do you really want to leave the prince?'

'Aha! I just knew you had an ulterior motive . . .'

'You mean you suspect that I came up here to persuade you to stay with the prince, because there's something in it for me? But, my dear boy, do you really think I got you to come all the way from Moscow simply because there was something in it for me? Oh, how touchy you are! On the contrary, I was wishing the best for you. And even now, you see, when my finances are in such good order, I would like it if, sometimes, you'd allow your mother and me to help you.'

'I dislike you, Versilov.'

'And even *Versilov*! By the way I very much regret I couldn't pass on my name to you, because essentially that's all I did wrong, isn't it? If I did any wrong at all? But you know yourself I couldn't marry someone who was already married.'

'Which is why you probably wanted to marry someone already married, isn't it?'

A slight tremor passed across his face.

'You're referring to Ems. Listen, Arkady, you came out with that downstairs, pointing at me right in front of your mother. You ought to know this—that's precisely where you're wrong! You know literally nothing about what happened to the late Lydia Akhmakov. You don't know how much part your mother played in it, despite not being there with me. And if I've ever seen a good woman, then it was at that time when I saw what your mother did. But enough of this. It's all still a secret. And you—you're saying God knows what based on what you've heard from a stranger!'

'It was the prince who told me just today that you were very fond of fledgling little girls.'

'The prince said that?'

'Yes. Listen, if you like I'll tell you precisely why you've come up here to see me, shall I? I've been sitting here all the time asking myself what the real reason for your visit was and now I think I've got it.'

He gave the impression of leaving but stopped and turned his head towards me expectantly.

'Not long ago I mentioned that Touchard's letter to Tatyana Pavlovna had turned up among Andronnikov's papers and that's where it was after his death—at Marya Ivanovna's in Moscow. I saw as I said it how your face twitched and I've just now guessed why, because your face twitched again just now. You suddenly hit upon the idea downstairs that if one letter was at Marya Ivanovna's, why shouldn't there be another there? After all, when Andronnikov died he might have left some very important letters—isn't that so?'

'And in coming to see you up here I wanted to get you to chatter about it?'

'You must know that well enough.'

He went very pale.

'It isn't all your own doing. There's a woman's hand in all this. And what loathing there is in what you've said, in all your crude guesswork!'

'A woman? I saw that woman this very day! Perhaps you want me to stay at the prince's in order to spy on her?'

'I see you'll go a long way in your new career! Is that what your *idea* is all about? Carry on, my dear boy, you've got an undoubted flair for detective work. Inborn talent ought to be perfected!'

He paused a moment to catch his breath.

'Watch out, Versilov! Don't turn me into your enemy!'

'My dear boy, in such circumstances one doesn't tell all, but keeps something to oneself. Let me have a bit of light, please. You can be my enemy if you like, but probably not to the extent of wanting me to break my neck! *Tiens, mon ami!* Just imagine,' he continued as he descended, 'all this past month I've assumed you're someone with a nice nature. You've so wanted to be alive, you're so greedy for life, three lives wouldn't be enough for you. It's written all over your face! Well, people like that are mostly nice-natured. But how wrong I've been!'

IV

I can't express the way my heart bled when I was left alone—it was as if I'd literally cut a pound of living flesh out of myself! Why I'd become so full of loathing and said such hurtful things to him—so forcefully and deliberately—I can't say now and I couldn't have said then. And how pale he went! Yet that very act of turning pale could have been an expression of the purest and most sincere feeling, of the deepest bitterness, but not of malice and hurt! It had always seemed to me that there were times when he was very fond of me. Why, oh why can't I believe that

141

even now, more especially since so much is clear as daylight now?

I'd become suddenly so full of loathing and literally driven him away very probably out of a sense that he'd come to me in the hope of learning whether or not there were any more of Andronnikov's letters remaining at Marya Ivanovna's. I knew he'd have to be looking for such letters. But who knows, maybe it was at that very moment I made an awful mistake! And who knows, perhaps with that mistake, I'd suggested to him the idea of Marya Ivanovna and the possibility that she had some letters?

Finally, there was another strange thing: he'd repeated word for word what I'd just said to Kraft about three lives not being enough for me—and in my very own words, that's the main thing! It could have been just a coincidence, but, still, how he seemed to know the very essence of my nature! What perception, what insight! But if he had such an understanding of that, why did he have no understanding whatever of something else? Surely he wasn't just pretending, wasn't incapable of guessing that it wasn't his Versilov lineage I needed, it wasn't my illegitimate birth I couldn't forgive him, it was Versilov himself I'd been wanting all my life, the whole man, my father, and this idea had entered into my very bloodstream? Was such a sensitive man so obtuse and crude? And if he wasn't, then why was he so infuriating, why was he pretending all the time?

CHAPTER VIII

I

THE next morning I tried to get up as early as possible. Usually we all got up about eight o'clock—mother, sister, and I, that is—while Versilov remained in bed till 9.30. Precisely at 8.30 mother would bring me coffee. But this time, without waiting for my coffee, I slipped out of the house just as it struck eight. Since the previous evening I had been working out a general plan of action for the whole day. I felt this plan contained, despite my passionate determination to put it to the test at once, far too much that was uncertain and ill-defined in its most important

142

aspects. That was why I spent almost the whole night in a kind of half-sleep and, literally as if I were delirious, had a great many dreams and hardly ever fell properly asleep. Despite that, I rose feeling more lively and fresher than ever. I had no particular wish to meet mother. I wouldn't be able to talk to her about anything except the well-worn matters and I was frightened of being distracted from what I aimed to do by some new and unexpected impression.

It was a cold morning and everything was covered in a raw, milky fog. I don't know why, but I always liked busy, early, St Petersburg mornings, in spite of the extraordinarily nasty appearance of everything, and the entire mass of people hurrying about their business, always self-centred and preoccupied, had for me, at eight o'clock in the morning, something particularly attractive about it. I would particularly enjoy as I hurried along either asking someone something or being asked something, because the question and the answer were always so brief, lucid, and to the point, given without stopping and almost invariably in a friendly spirit, and the readiness to answer questions was always greater then than at any other time of day. Inhabitants of St Petersburg become less communicative during the day and towards evening, a bit more ready to swear and jeer; it's quite different in the early morning, before the business of the day has started, at the soberest and most solemn time. This is something I've noticed.

I set off once more for the Petersburg side. Since I had to be back on the Fontanka at Vasin's place at twelve (the time he was most likely to be there), I hurried on without stopping although I would have done anything for a cup of coffee. What's more, I had to make sure of finding Efim Zverev at home. It was to him I was going once again and I was almost too late. He was just finishing his coffee and preparing to leave.

'What brings you here so often?' he asked without getting up.
'I'll tell you what.'

Every early morning, including a St Petersburg morning, has a sobering effect on a man's nature. Most fiery dreams of the night vanish completely with the cold morning light, and it has sometimes happened to me to remember on cold mornings with self-reproach and shame the dreams of the recent night and occasionally even my actions. But in passing, however, I'll remark that I consider St Petersburg mornings, apparently the most prosaic on earth, probably the most fantastic in the world. That is my personal view or—better—my personal impression, but I stick to it. On such a St Petersburg morning—so raw, damp, and foggy—I have always thought that the wild dreams of someone like Pushkin's Hermann in *The Queen of Spades* (a colossal character, an extraordinary and completely Petersburg type—a type of the Petersburg period!) must be strengthened and receive endorsement. A hundred times over amid such a fog I have had the strange but persistent notion: 'What if this fog were to disperse and rise up into the sky, wouldn't the whole rotten, sleazy city go up with it and vanish like smoke, and all that would remain would be the original Finnish marsh with, in the middle of it, for decoration perhaps, a bronze horseman on a snorting, rearing steed?' In short, I cannot express my feelings, because they're all fantasy, just poetry, after all, and therefore nonsense. Nevertheless, I've frequently been struck—and am still struck—by a completely senseless question: 'Here they are, you see, all rushing and hurrying on their way, but what if this were perhaps someone's dream, and there wasn't a single, true, genuine human being, not a single real action among them? If the person dreaming it all were to wake up, it would all suddenly vanish.' But I am digressing.

I will say to start with that there are ideas and plans in everybody's life which can seem so eccentric that they can be unfailingly regarded as mad at first glance. It was with one such fantastic idea that I went to Zverev that morning—precisely to Zverev because I didn't have anyone else in St Petersburg to whom I could turn on this occasion. But Efim was precisely the one person to whom, if I'd had any choice, I'd have turned to last with such a proposal. When I took a seat opposite him I even had the impression that, absolute embodiment of delirium and fever as I was, I was confronted by an absolute embodiment of the most prosaic golden mean. But on my side was an idea and genuine feeling, on his only the practical assumption that things never work out as they should.

In short, I explained to him briefly and clearly that, apart from him, I had no one in St Petersburg I could send as my second, since an exceptional matter of honour was involved; that he was an old friend and therefore had no right to refuse; and that I

wanted to challenge to a duel a Prince Sokolsky, a guards'
lieutenant, for having struck my father, Versilov, in the face, a
year ago, in Ems. I will add that Efim had a very detailed
knowledge of my family circumstances, my relations with Versilov, and almost everything that I knew about Versilov's background. I had told him things at various times, apart, that is,
from certain secrets.

He sat there and listened, bristling as he usually did like a
caged sparrow, silent and serious-looking, puffy in the face, with
his fair hair all ruffled. A fixed, mocking grin never left his lips.
This grin was all the more nasty because it was not assumed for
the occasion but was completely involuntary. It was obvious that
he really and truly considered himself at that moment a great
deal better than me in intelligence and character. I also suspected
that he despised me for what had happened yesterday at
Dergachev's. It was only to be expected. Efim was one of the
crowd, a true man-in-the-street, and all they ever worship is
success.

'Does Versilov know anything about this?' he asked.

'No, of course he doesn't.'

'Then what right have you to interfere in his affairs? That's
the first thing. And the second thing is, what do you want to
prove by doing this?'

I knew he would have objections and at once explained to him
that the whole thing wasn't as silly as he supposed. In the first
place, the impudent young puppy of a prince would be shown
that there are still some people who understand the meaning of
honour—and in our class of society, what's more. Secondly,
Versilov would be thoroughly shamed and taught a lesson.
Thirdly, and chiefly, even if Versilov had been right, according
to his own lights, in not challenging the prince to a duel and
deciding to put up with the insult, he would at least see that
there was someone capable of feeling his humiliation so strongly
that he would take it on himself and be prepared to lay down his
own life for his interests, despite the fact that he was ready to
part from Versilov for ever and ever . . .

'Stop it! Don't shout! Auntie doesn't like it! Tell me, isn't
Versilov engaged in a lawsuit with this very Prince Sokolsky over
an inheritance? In this case it'll be a completely new and original
way of winning by killing one's opponent in a duel!'

145

I made it clear to him quite candidly, *en toutes lettres*, that he was simply being silly and impudent and that if his mocking grin grew any larger this would merely indicate how self-regarding and ordinary he was and he couldn't assume that considerations about the court case hadn't been in my head as well right from the beginning and had only been worthy of conception in his capacious brain. I went on to explain to him that the court case was aleady won, that it wasn't being conducted against Prince Sokolsky but the Princes Sokolsky, and that if one prince was killed there would still be others around, but that, without doubt, the challenge would have to be postponed until after the appeal date (although the princes wouldn't appeal) simply for the sake of decency. Once the date was passed the duel could take place. I explained that I had come to him now, not because the duel was about to take place but because I had to be sure of things, because I didn't have a second and didn't know anyone here and would at least have time to find one if he refused. That was why I'd come to see him, I said.

'Well, then, you should have come and talked to me then, instead of coming all this way for nothing now!'

He rose and picked up his cap.

'Anyhow, will you do it?'

'No, of course I won't!'

'Why not?'

'I won't because, if I agree now, you'll be round here every day to see me until the appeal date. But chiefly because it's all nonsense, that's why. Why should I ruin my career because of you? What if this prince suddenly asks me: "Who sent you?" "Dolgoruky," I say. "What's Dolgoruky got to do with Versilov?" So I've got to explain your entire family tree, have I? He'll laugh his head off!'

'Then bash him in the face!'

'Oh, don't talk nonsense!'

'You're not frightened, are you? You're so big. At school you were stronger than any of us.'

'Of course I'm frightened. Anyhow a prince will only fight with an equal.'

'By upbringing I'm a gentleman, too ... and I have my rights and I'm his equal. He's the one who's not equal.'

'No, you're under age.'

146

'What d'you mean—under age?'

'You're under age. We're both under age. He's the grown-up.'

'You're a fool! For a year now I've been old enough to marry—so the law says!'

'Well, then, get married! But you're still a young bastard—just grow up a bit!'

Of course, I realized he'd been trying to have me on. There's no doubt this whole silly episode needn't have been told and it would even have been better if it had been left to die in obscurity. What's more, it was repugnant both in its triviality and its pointlessness, although it had fairly serious consequences.

But to punish myself even more, I'll tell it in full. Seeing that Efim was poking fun at me, I let myself jab him in the shoulder with my right hand or—better—with my right fist. At that he seized me by the shoulders and flung me down on my face—demonstrating, in fact, that at school he'd been the strongest of us all.

II

The reader will of course think that I was in a frightful state when I left Efim and yet he'd be wrong. I realized only too clearly that the whole thing had ended in typical school or high-school fashion, but the seriousness of the matter remained entirely intact. I had some coffee on Vasilevsky Island, having deliberately avoided yesterday's pub on the Petersburg side. Both that pub and its caged nightingale had become doubly hateful to me. I have this strange habit—I'm capable of hating places and things just like people. Yet there are, for me, several happy places in St Petersburg, places, I mean, where I've felt happy for some reason, and I treasure these places and visit them deliberately less frequently so that, when I am completely alone and unhappy, I can go there and feel sad and recall past happiness. As I had my coffee, I gave Efim his due for his common sense. Yes, he was more practical than me, but hardly more realistic. Realism which sees no further than the end of its nose is more dangerous than the most mindless fantasizing, because it is blind. But in doing justice to Efim (who at that moment was very likely thinking I was walking along the street swearing at him) I

147

was not conceding any of my convictions, as I haven't done right up to the present moment. I have seen some people who, at the first dousing in cold water, retreat not only from their actions but also from their ideas and themselves start jeering at everything they'd considered sacred—oh, how easily they can do it! Suppose Efim, even as regards the heart of the matter, was more correct than I was and I was sillier than everyone and just making a fool of myself, but there was still, at rock bottom, a point on which I knew I was right to insist, something which put right on my side and which they could never understand.

I arrived at Vasin's on the Fontanka, by Semyonovsky Bridge, promptly at midday but he wasn't home. He worked on Vasilevsky Island and was only home at set times, but usually always by twelve o'clock. However, because it was a holiday of some kind I supposed I'd be sure to find him there. Since I hadn't, I felt inclined to wait for him despite the fact that it was my first visit.

I thought about it like this: the letter about the inheritance was a matter of conscience and, in choosing Vasin as a judge in the matter, I was demonstrating the depth of my respect for him, which should of course be very flattering to him. It goes without saying that I was really very concerned about this letter and convinced of the need for third-party help. Still, I also suspected that I could get out of my difficulties without any outside assistance. Chiefly, I knew all that needed to be done was to hand over the letter in person to Versilov and let him do what he wanted with it—and that would be that. To set myself up as judge and jury in a matter of this sort would be quite wrong. By keeping myself out of it through handing the letter to Versilov without saying a word, I would immediately score top points and place myself morally above him because, in refusing, so far as I was concerned, all gains from the inheritance (because, as Versilov's son, some of the money would accrue to me, if not now, then later), I would be forever preserving for myself a higher moral attitude towards whatever Versilov did. And no one would be able to reproach me for destroying the princes' chances because the document in question had no decisive meaning in law. I mulled all this over in my mind and clarified it to myself while I sat in Vasin's empty room and it even suddenly occurred to me that in coming to Vasin so keen for his advice I'd really come with the sole aim of making him see what an extremely noble and selfless chap I was. I'd also be paying him back for my fawning on him yesterday.

When I realized this, I was extremely annoyed. Nevertheless, I didn't go, but remained, although I was certain my annoyance would increase with each five minutes that went by.

First of all, I found Vasin's room horrible. 'Show me your room and I'll know the sort of person you are' is true enough. Vasin lived in a furnished room rented from tenants who were evidently poor and scraped a living out of others as well as him. I am very familiar with these cramped little rooms, barely furnished at all but with pretensions to comfort. Invariably they contain a bargain-basement soft divan which it is dangerous to move, a wash-basin, and an iron bedstead surrounded by a screen. Vasin was obviously treated as the best and most dependable of the lodgers. Every landlady has such a lodger she likes best and takes special care of by dusting and sweeping his room better than the others, hanging a lithograph above the divan and providing some threadbare rug to go under the table. People who are fond of such crummy cleanliness and, more especially, the fawning respectfulness of their landlady seem pretty suspect to me. I was convinced that Vasin was flattered by the title of 'best lodger'. I don't know why, but I became gradually more and more incensed at the sight of the two tables piled high with books. Books, papers, ink—all were in the most disgustingly good order, an ideal state of things which met the landlady's and housemaid's view of how things should be arranged. There were plenty of books—not newspapers and journals, but real books—and evidently he was used to reading them and would, no doubt, sit down to read and set about writing with an extraordinarily self-important and punctilious air. I don't know why, but I much prefer a place where books are lying about haphazardly, where studying is not turned into an act of religious devotion. Very like this Vasin would be extremely polite to visitors, but very likely every gesture of his would say: 'You see, here I am spending a quiet half-hour with you but when you're gone I've really got work to do.' Very likely one could strike up an extremely interesting conversation with him and learn something new, but he'd really be thinking—'You see, here we are chatting, and I'm very interested in what you say, but when you're gone I'll get down to the most interesting thing of all . . .' Still, I didn't go. I remained sitting there. I eventually convinced myself that I didn't need his advice at all.

I sat there an hour or more, seated by the window on one of two wicker chairs placed by it. I was driven crazy by wasting so much time when I had to find somewhere to live by nightfall. I felt tempted to open one of the books out of boredom but didn't—the very idea of entertaining myself with one of his books redoubled my repugnance. For more than an hour the extraordinary silence continued all round me and then suddenly, somewhere very close, just beyond the door which was blocked by the divan, I couldn't help gradually hearing the sound of voices whispering louder and louder.

Two voices were talking, evidently women, but it was quite impossible to hear what they were saying. However, out of boredom I started listening. It was clear they were talking animatedly and passionately and not about anything as simple as cutting out dress patterns, because they were either conspiring together or quarrelling, or one voice would be persuading and begging while the other was disagreeing and objecting. I assumed they must have been other lodgers. I quickly got fed up and my ear grew accustomed to it, so that though I went on listening I did so mechanically and sometimes quite forgot I was listening, when suddenly something extraordinary occurred as if someone had sprung up from a chair with both feet or suddenly jumped up and started stamping. There was then the sound of a groan and a sudden cry—not even a cry, so much as a squeal, like an animal enraged and in pain, made by someone who didn't care whether others heard or not. I dashed to the door and opened it. Simultaneously another door opened at the end of the corridor— the landlady's as I learned later—and two inquisitive heads poked out. The cry, however, had no sooner ceased than the next door along the corridor suddenly opened and a young woman, so it seemed to me, rushed quickly out and ran down the stairs. Another, older, woman tried to stop her but couldn't and simply shrieked after her:

'Olya, Olya, where're you going? O-o-oh!'

But, seeing the other two doors open, she swiftly drew hers to, leaving only a chink through which she listened until the descending Olya's footsteps had finally ceased. I went back into

150

my room. Everything fell quiet. An occurrence, that's all, probably a silly one, and I stopped thinking about it.

About fifteen minutes later a loud, confident male voice resounded in the corridor directly outside Vasin's room. Someone turned the door-handle and opened the door sufficiently for me to see a tall man in the corridor who had also obviously caught sight of me and even looked me up and down, but who did not come into the room, preferring to keep his hand on the handle while talking to the landlady down the full length of the corridor. The landlady responded to him in a thin, delighted little voice, from which it could be gathered that she was long familiar with the visitor and respected and valued him both as an honoured guest and good company. The jovial chap shouted and joked, but it was all to do with Vasin not being there, that he couldn't find him anywhere, that it was the way the cookie always crumbled so far as he was concerned and he'd wait for him again here—all of which proved the acme of wit and humour for the landlady. At last the new arrival drew open the door with a flourish and came into the room.

He was well dressed, having obviously been to a 'gentleman's' tailor, but the last thing he really looked like was a gentleman despite evidently wanting to appear so. He was not so much self-confident as naturally cheeky, which is less offensive than the type which cultivates its impudence by practising in front of a mirror. His hair, dark-brown with traces of grey in it, his black eyebrows, large beard, and large eyes not only did not give him any particular character but had the precise effect of endowing him with a generally ordinary look like the rest of humanity. Fellows like him are always laughing and ready to laugh, but you never feel happy in their company. From laughing one moment he can be serious the next, from being serious he can be playful or giving suggestive winks, but always pointlessly, casually . . . There's no need to go on and on about him. I got to know him much better later on, so I have a clearer idea of him now than I had when he opened the door and came into the room. However, I would still find it hard to say anything exact and definitive about him because the main thing about people like him is their incompleteness, their vagueness and lack of definition.

Even before he had managed to sit down it occurred to me

that he must be Vasin's stepfather, a certain Mr Stebelkov, of whom I had heard something but so vaguely I couldn't remember what, except that it was something unpleasant. I knew that Vasin had spent a long time as an orphan under his guardianship, but had long since escaped from his tutelage and that both their aims and their interests were now different and they lived completely separate lives in every respect. I also remembered that this Stebelkov had a certain amount of capital and played the market as a speculator. In short, I may have known something more about him at one time, but I'd forgotten. He measured me with a glance, without troubling to greet me, placed his top hat down on the table in front of the divan, shoved the table away with his foot and did not so much sit as collapse straight down on to the divan (on which I had not dared sit), so that it creaked, crossed his legs and, lifting up the toe of his right-hand patent-leather shoe, started admiring it. Finally he turned to me and again measured me with his large and rather immobile eyes.

'Never can get hold of him!' He gave me a slight nod.

I said nothing.

'He's unpunctual! Got his own views about things. Are you from the Petersburg side?'

'You mean you've come from the Petersburg side, have you?' I asked in turn.

'No, I'm asking you.'

'I, er, yes, I've come from the Petersburg side. How did you know?'

'How? Well, hmm . . .' He winked but did not explain.

'That's to say, I don't live on the Petersburg side, but I was there and I've just come from there.'

He continued smiling significantly in a way which I intensely disliked and said nothing. His winking was just silly.

'Been at Mr Dergachev's?' he asked eventually.

'At what Dergachev's?' I had my eyes open wide in astonishment. He looked at me triumphantly. 'I don't know who you mean.'

'Hmm . . .'

'Have it your own way,' I answered. I found him obnoxious.

'Hmm . . . Well, sir, say you buy something in a shop, in the shop next door another purchaser buys something else, which is what, do you think? Money, sir, from a trader, who calls himself a money-lender, yessir . . . because money, you see, is also a commodity and a money-lender is also a trader . . . Do you get my meaning?'

'Yes, I get it.'

'A third purchaser comes by and, pointing to one of the shops, says, "That's a sound one" and pointing to another shop says, "That's not a sound one." What am I to make of this purchaser?'

'I haven't a clue.'

'No, sir, hang on, I'll give you an example. Man lives by good example, you know. I'm going down the Nevsky Prospect and I notice that on the other side of the street, walking along the pavement, is a gentleman whose character I'd like to define. Going on our separate sides we reach the turning into Sea Street and just by where the English shop is we reach a third passer-by who has been knocked down by a horse. Now take note of this: along comes a fourth gentleman who wants to define all three of us, including the chap knocked down by a horse, in terms of our solvency and soundness . . . You get my meaning?'

'Forgive me, with great difficulty.'

'All right, sir. It's as I thought. I'll change the subject. I'm at a spa in Germany, taking the waters, as I have done more than once—it doesn't matter where. I'm walking around the place and I see some English people. As you know, it's very hard to strike up an acquaintance with English people. But after a couple of months, having finished the course of treatment, we're up in the mountains, say, all climbing together armed with sharp walking sticks up some mountain or other—it doesn't matter which. At a turning by one of those rest-stops—as a matter of fact where the monks make Chartreuse—take note of that—I come across one of the locals standing by himself and watching us in silence. Say I want to ascertain whether he's sound and solvent, what do you think, can I turn to the crowd of English people with whom I'm walking solely because I hadn't known how to strike up a conversation with them when I'd been down at the spa?'

'I haven't a clue. Forgive me, I find it very hard to follow you.'

'You find it hard?'

'Yes, you're wearing me out.'

'Hmm . . .' He gave me a wink and made a gesture which was probably intended to indicate he'd got the better of me. Then very self-importantly and calmly he extracted from his pocket a newspaper, evidently just bought, unfolded it, and started to read the last page, apparently leaving me to my own devices. For five minutes he did not look at me.

'Brest-Graev haven't collapsed, have they?* No, they're still going! I know a good many that have collapsed, though.'

He looked at me very meaningfully.

'I know nothing about stocks and shares,' I said.

'You object, do you?'

'To what?'

'To money, my good sir.'

'I don't object to money, but . . . but I think there should be an idea first and then money.'

'Hang on, sir, you mean . . . er, everyone ought to have his own capital, so to speak . . .'

'To start with there should be some higher idea of society, and then one should think about money, but without there being some higher idea along with the money society will collapse.'

I don't know why I got so worked up. He looked at me rather glumly, as if he'd lost his way, but suddenly his face expanded into the happiest and slyest of smiles:

'What about Versilov, eh? What a killing he's made! Yesterday's court case, what?'

Quite suddenly and unexpectedly I saw he'd known for a long time who I was and perhaps a great deal else. I simply don't know why I suddenly went red and stared at him in the stupidest way, unable to take my eyes off him. He evidently thought he had scored a triumph and looked happily at me as if he had been extremely cunning in catching me out.

'Well, sir . . .' He raised both eyebrows '. . . just ask me anything, anything about Mr Versilov! What was I saying just now about soundness, eh? Eighteen months ago, if it hadn't been for that child, he might have pulled off a perfect deal, but he slipped up, yessir, he slipped up!'

'What child?'

'The baby who's being looked after somewhere, only he won't get anything out of it . . . since . . .'

'What baby? What're you talking about?'

'His baby, of course, his very own, sir, by Mademoiselle Lydia

Akhmakov ... Remember Pushkin's line "The charming girl grew fond of me ...".* Phosphorous matches, wasn't it?'

'What absolute bloody nonsense! He never had a child by Miss Akhmakov!'

'Really! So where've I been all the time? After all I'm both a doctor and an obstetrician, my good sir. The name's Stebelkov— you may have heard of me. True, I hadn't practised a long time even then, but I could still give practical advice on practical matters.'

'You were the obstetrician, you mean, when Miss Akhmakov gave birth?'

'No, sir, I wasn't. In the place out of town where it happened there was a Dr Granz, a fellow with a big family, and he got half a thaler for it—it's the way things are with doctors there, and, what's more, nobody knew about him, so he did it instead of me. Mind you, I suggested him, so that things should be kept hush-hush ... You get my meaning? But all I gave was a piece of quite practical advice in answer to Andrey Petrovich Versilov's question, his very confidential question, sir, man to man. But Andrey Petrovich was trying to catch two hares at once.'

I heard all this in absolute amazement.

'If you try and catch two hares at once, as the saying goes, you won't catch any. What I say is, though, that if exceptions go on repeating themselves they turn into their own rule. He chased after another hare—translated that means: he chased after another woman—and nothing came of it at all. Once you've got something, I say, hold on to it. But where he should have got a move on he didn't. Versilov—yes, he really is a "petticoat prophet",* as the young Prince Sokolsky described him so graphically to me at that very time. You should come to me, you know, if you want to know much about Versilov, you really should!'

He was evidently delighted at seeing my mouth wide open in astonishment. I had never before heard a word about any baby. And then, at that very moment, the door of the neighbouring room banged and someone went quickly into their room.

'Versilov is living by the Semyonovsky Barracks, on Mozhaisk Street, in Mrs Litvinov's house, No. 17, I've just looked it up!' shouted an angry female voice. We could hear every word. Stebelkov's brows shot up and he raised a finger above his head.

155

'Talk of the devil! We've just been mentioning him here and now he's cropping up next door as well . . . See, it's another of these constantly recurring exceptions! *Quand on parle d'une corde . . .*'

I was terribly astonished. I realized that the young woman who was shouting was very likely the same one who had recently run down the stairs in such excitement. But what on earth had Versilov got to do with things here?

Suddenly the former screech occurred again, wild and untamed, the yell of someone driven wild with anger at not being given something or being refused something. The only difference was that this time the yelling and shouting went on much longer. There were sounds of struggle and rapid, hurried words such as 'I don't want it! I don't want it! Give it me! Give it me at once!' and so on—I can't remember exactly what they were. Then, as before, someone dashed to the door and flung it open. Both the women were by then in the corridor, one of them trying, as before, to hold the other back. Stebelkov, having long since jumped up from the divan and delighted by the commotion, literally leapt to the door and at once flung himself towards the women in the corridor. Naturally, I also ran to the door. But his appearance in the corridor acted like a bucket of cold water. The women instantly vanished into their room and slammed the door behind them. Stebelkov was just on the point of springing after them but stopped, raised a finger, smiled, and took stock. On this occasion I saw something nasty, sinister, and malicious in the way he smiled.

Catching sight of the landlady, who had again taken up her position outside her door, he rapidly ran on tiptoe towards her down the corridor. After hobnobbing with her for a couple of minutes and finding out what he wanted, he returned decisively and self-importantly to the room, picked up his top hat, glanced in the mirror, smoothed back his hair and, with self-assured dignity and paying me not a scrap of attention, went up to the neighbouring door. For a moment or so he listened at it, putting his ear to it and winking triumphantly down the corridor at the landlady who wagged a finger at him and shook her head, as much as to say: 'Oh, you scamp you! Oh, you scamp!' Finally, assuming a resolute, but extremely posh air, even bowing slightly out of politeness, he tapped on the door with his knuckles. A voice was heard saying:

'Who's there?'

'May I speak to you on a very important matter?' declared Stebelkov loudly and self-importantly.

There was a delay, but then the door was opened just a little to start with, about a quarter of the way. Stebelkov immediately seized the door handle and stopped the door from being closed again. A conversation began, with Stebelkov starting to speak loudly and all the while edging his way into the room. I don't remember the exact words, but he talked about Versilov, saying he could let them know what they wanted and explain everything—'Just you ask me! Just you come and see me!'—and so on. They soon let him in.

I returned to the divan with the intention of eavesdropping but I could not make everything out and all I heard was frequent mention of Versilov's name. By the intonation of his voice I gathered that Stebelkov dominated the conversation, not speaking confidentially but authoritatively and with the sort of free-and-easy drawl he had used with me, employing phrases like 'You get my meaning, do you?' 'Now let's take a look at this!' and so on. However, with the women he must have been unusually ingratiating. Once or twice his loud laugh resounded and quite inappropriately, for sure, because along with his voice and sometimes defeating it could be heard both women's voices which did not express happiness at all, and predominately the voice of the young woman, the one who had recently shrieked so loudly. She did a lot of talking, in a nervous, hurried way, evidently divulging something and complaining, seeking to justify herself and receive justice in turn. But Stebelkov would not give way and raised his voice more and more and laughed more and more often—people like him never know how to listen to anyone else.

I soon left the divan, because I felt ashamed of continuing my eavesdropping, and transferred to my old place by the window on the wicker chair. I was sure that Vasin considered this man totally worthless, but if I were to express that very opinion of him he would at once stand on his dignity in support of him and declare in a primly edifying way that he was 'a practical man, one of today's businessmen, and one we can't judge from our abstract, general point of view'. At that moment, however, I remember I was undoubtedly waiting for something to happen. About ten minutes passed and suddenly, in the very middle of one resounding salvo of laughter, someone—just as before—jumped up from a chair and both women started shouting. Stebelkov jumped up as well and began saying things in a different tone of voice as if he were justifying himself and asking to be listened to. But they wouldn't listen to him. Angry cries of 'Get out! You shameless man, you no-good, get out!' In a word, it was clear that they wanted to be rid of him. I opened the door at the very moment he shot out into the corridor from next door, having literally, I think, been shoved on his way. Seeing me he suddenly cried out and pointed:

'Here he is, Versilov's son! If you don't believe me, here's his son, his very own son! Take a look!' And he seized me firmly by the shoulder. 'Here's his son!' he repeated, leading me towards the women and offering nothing more in the way of explanation.

The young woman was standing in the corridor and the older one just behind her in the doorway. All I can remember is that the younger one, the girl, wasn't bad looking, about 20 years old, but thin and sickly, with reddish hair and a face a little like my sister's. That likeness was a fleeting impression but it stuck in my memory, except that Liza had never been and, of course, never could be seized by such a frenzy of anger as this girl was. Her lips were pale, her bright, grey eyes literally flashed and she was shaking with indignation. I also remember that I found myself placed in an extremely silly and undignified position because due to this impudent Stebekov, I couldn't find a thing to say.

'What d'you mean, what son? If he's with you, then he's a no-good. If you're a son of Versilov,' she said, turning to me suddenly, 'then tell your father from me he's a no-good, an unworthy and shameless man and I don't want his money! Here, here, here, give him his money back at once!'

She had taken several banknotes hurriedly out of her pocket, but the older woman (her mother, as it turned out later) grabbed her by the arm:

'Olya, perhaps it's not true, perhaps he's not his son!'

Olya shot a rapid glance at her, realized she might be right, gave me a scornful look, and turned back into the room, but before slamming the door and while still in the doorway shouted frenziedly at Stebelkov:

'Get out!'

And she even stamped her foot. Then the door was slammed shut and a key was turned in the lock. Stebelkov, still holding me by the shoulder, raised one finger and, expanding his mouth into a long, thoughtful smile, fixed me with a querying look.

'I find your behaviour towards me comic and unworthy,' I muttered indignantly. But he wasn't listening, though he didn't take his eyes off me.

'It's to be *looked into*!' he announced thoughtfully.

'But you had the impudence to involve me, didn't you? Who *was* that? Who was the woman? Why did you seize me by the shoulder and present me like that?'

'Oh, to hell with 'em! Some girl who's lost her innocence—another of those frequently recurring exceptions, know what I mean?'

And he stuck his finger in my chest.

'And to hell with you!' I thrust his finger away.

But he suddenly, and quite unexpectedly, started chuckling softly, scarcely audibly, and went on chuckling happily for a while. At last he put on his hat and, with a rapidly changed, almost sombre look on his face, remarked with a frown:

'The landlady needs to be taught a lesson. She ought to get rid of them—and the sooner the better, otherwise they'll . . . Well, just you wait and see! Remember what I'm saying—just you wait and see! Oh, to hell with 'em!' He burst out laughing again suddenly. 'Will you be waiting till Grisha gets here?'

'No, I won't wait,' I answered decisively.

'Well, it's all one to me . . .'

And without a further word he turned, left the room, and went down the stairs, not even deigning to glance in the direction of the landlady who was obviously waiting for an explanation. I also picked up my hat and, asking the landlady to say that I, Dolgoruky, had been there, ran down the stairs.

I had simply been wasting my time. The moment I left I set about looking for somewhere to live, but I was in a distracted frame of mind, wandered about the streets for several hours and visited five or six rooms to rent but was sure I'd passed twenty others without noticing them. It was still more vexing to find that I hadn't imagined renting a room would be so difficult. There were many rooms just like Vasin's and even some that were a lot worse, but the rents were enormous, far more than I could afford. I asked straight out just for a corner to turn around in and they let me know scornfully that, in that case, I'd better just find 'the corner of a room' somewhere. Apart from that, there was everywhere such a mass of strange tenants with whom I could tell at a glance I wouldn't be able to live—would even have paid good money not to live with! Such as types in waistcoats, jacketless, with dishevelled beards, over-familiar and over-inquisitive. In one tiny room there were as many as ten men sitting over cards and drinking beer—and they offered me a room next door! In other places I gave such ridiculous answers to landlords' questions they looked at me in astonishment and in one case even lost their temper.

However, there is no point in describing all these futile things. I simply want to say that, having got terribly tired, I had something to eat in a cookhouse just as it was growing dark. I had finally decided that I would go at once to Versilov and hand over the letter about the inheritance (without offering any explanation), pack all my things in a suitcase and bundle up the rest and spend the night in a hotel. I knew that at the end of Obukhov Prospect, by the Arch of Triumph, there was somewhere I could get a room for thirty copecks. I decided to make that sacrifice so as not to spend another night under Versilov's roof. And then, as I walked past the Technology Institute, I suddenly decided for some reason to call on Tatyana Pavlovna who lived just opposite. The reason for calling on her was the letter about the inheritance, at least that was my pretext, but my overwhelming desire to see her had other reasons, of course, which I really can't be sure of even now. In my mind they had something vaguely to do with Stebelkov's talk of a 'baby' and 'exceptions becoming a general rule', etc. Whether or not I wanted to tell her something or show off or have a fight with her or even burst into tears I don't know, but all I did was climb up the steps to her apartment. I had been to her place only once before, shortly after arriving from Moscow, on an errand from mother and I remember that all I had done was visit and convey the message, leaving after a minute without even sitting down, and she had not asked me in.

I rang the bell and the door was opened instantly by a female cook and I was shown without a word into the apartment. I have to give all these details in order to explain the mad thing that happened which had such an enormous influence on what occurred subsequently. And, firstly, about the cook herself. She was a snub-nosed Finnish woman with a malicious tongue who despised her mistress, Tatyana Pavlovna, I think, while the latter was unable to part with her on the same principle that elderly maiden ladies are passionately devoted to pet dogs with wet noses and cats which sleep all the time. The Finn would either be malicious and rude or, after a quarrel, would be silent for weeks on end as a way of punishing her mistress. I must have hit on a silent day because to my question 'Is your mistress at home' (which I positively remember giving her) she said nothing and walked off in silence to the kitchen. Sure after this that her mistress was at home, I went into the sitting-room and, finding no one, started waiting, supposing that Tatyana Pavlovna would shortly be emerging from the bedroom, otherwise the cook would not have let me in. I did not sit down and waited there two or three minutes. It was almost completely dark and Tatyana Pavlovna's dark little apartment seemed to be made even more unwelcoming by the endless quantities of chintz hanging everywhere.

A word or two about this nasty little apartment, so as to give a better idea of the place where it all occurred. Tatyana Pavlovna, as a result of her stubborn and authoritarian character and her many years spent as mistress of an estate, could not make herself at home in ordinary rented rooms and used instead to hire this parody of an apartment simply in order to be her own mistress. The two rooms she had were just like a couple of canary cages set side by side, the one smaller than the other, on the third floor, with windows looking out on to a courtyard. Entering the tiny apartment you found yourself at once in a narrow little

161

corridor just over a metre wide, with, on your left, the above-mentioned canary cages, and, directly ahead of you down the corridor, the tiny little kitchen. The apartment had maybe the regulation cubic density just sufficient to provide enough air for twelve hours but hardly more than that. The little rooms had grotesquely low ceilings, but the silliest thing of all was that the windows, doors, and furniture were all hung with chintz, good French chintz, in little festoons, which made everything seem twice as dark and like the interior of a travelling carriage. In the little room where I was waiting it was still just possible to move about, although it was stuffed with furniture and not bad furniture at that. There were various little side-tables with marquetry work and bronze inlay, little boxes and even an elegant and expensive dressing-table. But the adjoining room, from which I expected to see her come, the bedroom, that is, thickly screened from this one by a curtain, turned out later to contain nothing but a bed. All these details are necessary to understand what a stupid thing I had done.

So I waited there in the certainty of being received, when the doorbell rang. I heard the cook make her slow way down the corridor and silently let people in as she had let me in before. They were two women and both were talking loudly, but imagine my astonishment when I gathered from their voices that one was Tatyana Pavlovna and the other the woman I was least of all prepared to meet now, particularly in such circumstances! I couldn't be mistaken—I had heard that resonant, strong, metallic voice only yesterday (true, only for a couple of minutes), but it had stuck in my memory. Yes, it was 'yesterday's woman', as I had described her to myself. What on earth could I do? I am not asking the reader this question, merely imagining to myself that very moment, and I wouldn't be able to explain even now how it came about that I suddenly dashed behind the curtain and found myself in Tatyana Pavlovna's bedroom. In short, I had scarcely had time to hide before they came in. Why I hid myself and did not go out to meet them, I don't know. Everything happened so unexpectedly and completely by chance.

Having dashed into the bedroom and tripped up against the bed, I at once noticed that there was a door from the bedroom into the kitchen, so it seemed I had a way of escaping but—horror of horrors!—the door was locked and there was no key.

162

In desperation I fell on to the bed. I had a clear picture of myself in a position of eavesdropping on what was said and, judging by the first phrases used in their talk and their tone of voice, I guessed it was of a secret and delicate nature. Of course, had I been a man of honest and noble character I would even at this point have stood up and gone out and said loudly: 'Just a moment, I'm here!' and, no matter how silly I might have seemed, I'd have then gone past them. But I didn't stand up and didn't go out. I didn't have the guts. I behaved like an abject coward.

'My dear, dear Katerina Nikolaevna, you're distressing me no end,' Tatyana Pavlovna was saying to her, 'do put it out of your mind once and for all, it's not like you to be like this. Wherever you are you radiate joy, and now suddenly . . . Look, you must go on trusting me. After all, you know I'm devoted to you. No less than I am to Andrey Petrovich, for whom I've never for a moment concealed my undying devotion . . . Just take my word for it, I swear to you—he hasn't got the document and it's quite possible no one has. What's more, he's just not capable of intriguing in such a way and it's wrong of you to suspect him of it. The two of you have simply made up this whole silly feud . . .'

'The document exists and he's capable of anything. I mean, I go there yesterday and who do I meet straight off? *Ce petit espion*, that little spy he's put there to keep watch on the prince.'

'Oh, *ce petit espion*! First of all, he's not a spy at all, because it was I, I who insisted he be found a place with the prince, otherwise he'd either have gone out of his mind in Moscow or starved to death. That's what the people there told us. But the main thing is that foul-mouthed little boy's a complete idiot, he'd never be any good as a spy!'

'All right, so he's an idiot, it doesn't stop him being a scoundrel. If I hadn't been so annoyed, I'd have died laughing at the way he went all white and fawned and scraped his feet and started blurting out French. But Marya Ivanovna had assured me in Moscow he was some kind of genius. The main thing I learned, judging from the look on Marya Ivanovna's face, was that the wretched letter had not been destroyed and was likely to be in a most dangerous place.'

'Oh, my dear, surely you told me yourself she had nothing at all!'

'That's what I said, yes, only maybe she's lying—she's really artful, she is, I can tell you! Before I went to Moscow I was still hopeful of there being no more papers, but once I got there, well . . .'

'Oh, my dear, it's not like that. They say she's kind and sensible and the dead man had a higher opinion of her than of all the rest of his relatives. True, I don't know her that well, but you ought to have used all your charms on her! It wouldn't have been a thing for you—after all, I'm an old woman and I'm crazy about you and I'm just about to give you a kiss . . . It wouldn't have been any trouble to you to win her over!'

'I did use all my charms, Tatyana Pavlovna, and tried this and that and even got her all in a tizz, but she's sly and she's very . . . Well, she's all of a piece, you know, she's got a character of her own, like all Moscow people . . . And would you believe it, she advised me to go and see someone living here, a man called Kraft, Andronnikov's former assistant, because she thought he knew something. I know a bit about this Kraft and even remember seeing him, but as soon as she told me about him I was sure it wasn't a question of her knowing nothing about it, but she was lying and knew everything.'

'But why, why on earth should she? And probably you can get all the information from him! This German, Kraft, isn't a gossip, he's the soul of honesty, as I recall—yes, go and ask him! Except I don't think he's in St Petersburg . . .'

'He came back yesterday and I've just been to his place . . . That's why I've come to you in such a state, just literally shaking all over, because I wanted to beg you, Tatyana Pavlovna, angel that you are, and because you know everyone, can you please find out what papers he has, because he's bound to have left papers behind him, and who they'll be going to now? Maybe they'll once again get into dangerous hands, you know. I came rushing here to ask your advice.'

'What papers are you talking about?' Tatyana Pavlovna seemed bewildered. 'Didn't you say you've just been to Kraft's?'

'I was, I was, only a moment ago, but he's shot himself! Just last night!'

I jumped up from the bed. I could endure it when they called me a spy and an idiot, and the longer their conversation went on the less likelihood there seemed of my appearing. That would have been unimaginable! I decided to put up with things, with my heart in my mouth, until Tatyana Pavlovna showed her guest out (so long as she didn't come into the bedroom for some reason) and then, when Miss Akhmakov had gone, and only then would I tussle with Tatyana Pavlovna . . . But suddenly, on hearing about Kraft and jumping up from the bed, I was seized by an absolute frenzy. Without so much as a thought, without calculating or imagining what the effect would be, I stepped forward, drew aside the screening curtain and found myself right in front of them.

It was still light enough for them to see me standing there pale and quivering. Both of them screamed. Well, who wouldn't have?

'Kraft?' I said, turning to Miss Akhmakov. 'He's shot himself? Yesterday? At sunset?'

'Where've you been? Where've you come from?' screeched Tatyana Pavlovna and literally stuck a claw into my shoulder. 'Have you been spying on us? Have you been eavesdropping?'

'What have I just been telling you?' said Katerina Nikolaevna getting up from the sofa and pointing at me.

I lost my cool.

'It's a bloody lie! It's bloody nonsense!' I broke in furiously. 'My God, you've just called me a spy! There's not only no point in spying, there's not even any point in living with people like you around! Here's a fine man and he's committed suicide— Kraft has shot himself, for an idea, for Hecuba . . . Besides, what's Hecuba to you? Life here is nothing but your intrigues, messing about with all your lies and deceits and plots—Just shut up!'

'Slap his face! Slap his face!' shrieked Tatyana Pavlovna, but because Katerina Nikolaevna looked at me steadily (I remember it all down to the last detail) but did not make a move, Tatyana Pavlovna in another instant would very likely have followed her own advice, had I not raised my hand to protect myself. This involuntary movement of mine made her think I was about to strike her.

'Well, come on then, hit me, hit me! Just show what a young bastard you really are! You're stronger than women, so don't pretend you aren't!'

'Shut up! That's enough of your bitching!' I shouted. 'I've never hit a woman in my life! You're utterly shameless, Tatyana

165

Pavlovna, in the way you've always despised me. Oh, you've always bossed everyone about without any sign of respect! As for you, Katerina Nikolaevna, you're probably laughing at the way I look. Well, God didn't give me the elegant figure of one of your adjutants! Still, I don't feel the need to kowtow to you, on the contrary I feel proud . . . But it doesn't matter what I say, I am simply not to blame! I was here quite by chance, Tatyana Pavlovna. The only one to blame is that Finnish cook of yours or—better—the way you keep her in your employment, because she didn't answer when I asked if you were here and just let me in. After that, you'll agree, to come jumping out of a lady's bedroom would seem so monstrous I decided it would be better to put up with your bitching in silence and not show myself! What are you laughing at now, Katerina Nikolaevna?'

'Get out! Get out of here!' shouted Tatyana Pavlovna, almost shoving me out. 'Don't take any notice of his chatter, Katerina Nikolaevna! I told you where he came from they thought he was out of his mind!'

'Out of my mind? Where I came from? Who? And where's that? Oh, shut up! Katerina Nikolaevna, I swear to you by all that's holy, this conversation and everything I've heard will remain just between ourselves . . . Am I to blame for overhearing your secrets? Anyhow, tomorrow I'm stopping work with your father, so you don't need to worry any more about that document you're looking for!'

'What's that? What document are you talking about?'

Katerina Nikolaevna was so worked up, she even went pale, or that's how it seemed to me. I realized I'd already said too much.

I quickly went out. Silently they followed me with their eyes, and their looks expressed astonishment in the highest degree. In short, I'd left them guessing.

CHAPTER IX

I

I RUSHED home and—strange to say—I was very satisfied with myself. Of course, no one talks to women like that, more especially women of that kind—or, to be honest, to that kind of woman, because I didn't count Tatyana Pavlovna. Perhaps one should never say face to face to that kind of woman 'Damn your bloody intrigues!' but I had done and was glad I had. Regardless of anything else, I was at least certain that by adopting such a tone I had rid myself of everything farcical in my situation.

But there was no point in thinking much about that. My head was fully occupied by Kraft. It wasn't that I'd given him all that much thought, but I was still shaken to the very roots of my being. Even so far as that ordinary human feeling of satisfaction at someone else's misfortune was concerned, as when someone breaks a leg, loses his honour, is abandoned by a loved one, and so on, even that ordinary feeling of ignoble satisfaction gave way in me completely to another, exceptionally wholesome feeling—to one of grief and regret for Kraft, though I don't know whether it was really regret so much as some extremely strong and warm-hearted feeling. And I was also very glad of that. It is astonishing how many irrelevant thoughts can flash through one's mind even when one is shaken by some colossal piece of news which should overwhelm all other feelings and drive out all irrelevant thoughts, particularly superficial ones. Yet they always come creeping back, particularly the superficial ones. I can still recall that I was gradually seized by a rather sensitive, nervous shivering which went on for several minutes and even throughout the entire time I was at home and engaged in talking to Versilov.

This talk occurred in strange and unusual circumstances. I have already mentioned that we lived in the separate wing of a building facing on to a courtyard. The apartment was designated No. 13. Even before going through the gates I heard a female voice asking loudly, impatiently, and irritably 'Where is No. 13?' I saw it was a woman just by the gates, she'd opened a door to a tiny little shop, but nobody appeared to answer her, or they'd

167

even driven her away, and she was descending the steps in a furious temper.

'Where on earth is the janitor?' she shouted, stamping her foot. I had recognized her from her voice as soon as I heard it.

'I am going to No. 13,' I said, approaching her. 'Who do you want to see?'

'I've spent a whole hour looking for the janitor, asking all and sundry and going upstairs and downstairs.'

'It's in the courtyard. Don't you recognize me?'

But she already had.

'You're looking for Versilov, I imagine. You've got matters to discuss with him and so have I,' I went on. 'I'm here to say goodbye to him for good and all. Let's go.'

'Are you his son?'

'It doesn't mean a thing. However, let's suppose I am his son, though I'm called Dolgoruky and I'm illegitimate. That gentleman has got a whole mass of illegitimate children. When honour and conscience demand it, even a native son leaves home. As it says in the Bible. What's more, he has come into an inheritance, but I don't want to have any part of it and I am going to make my way with the work of my own hands. When necessary, a fine man will even sacrifice his own life. Kraft has shot himself, Kraft has, for an idea, just imagine, a young man with everything to hope for . . . This way, this way! We're in the separate part here. In the Bible it says sons must leave their fathers and find their own nests . . . so long as an idea makes them . . . so long as there is an idea! The idea's the main thing, the idea's everything . . .'

I went on chattering in this fashion the whole way to our place. The reader no doubt realizes I'm not being very sparing to myself and, where necessary, I'm my own best recommendation for wanting to learn how to speak the truth. Versilov was at home. I entered without taking off my coat, as she did as well. She was terribly scantily dressed. Some sort of old rag intended to serve as a cloak or a mantilla was worn over a miserable dark dress and on her head she wore an old, battered sailor hat which did nothing to improve her appearance. When we entered the main room mother was sitting in her usual place busy with her needlework and my sister came out of her room to see who it was and remained standing in the doorway. Versilov was as usual doing nothing and stood up as we came in. He fixed his eyes on me with a stern, questioning look.

'Don't mind me,' I said hastily, dismissively waving my hand and stepping to one side. 'I met this lady by the gates. She was trying to find out where you lived and no one could tell her. I'm here simply on my own business which I'll be happy to explain afterwards . . .'

Versilov still went on studying me curiously.

'Allow me, please,' the girl began saying impatiently and Versilov turned to her. 'I've spent a long time wondering why you took it into your head to leave me money yesterday . . . and . . . well, here it is!' She almost shrieked this out, as she had done everything else, and flung the wad of banknotes on the table. 'I had to look you up in the list of addresses, otherwise I'd have brought it sooner! Listen, please!' She turned suddenly to mother, who had gone white. 'I don't want to insult you, you have an honest look, and perhaps this is even your daughter here. I don't know whether you're his wife, but you ought to know something—this gentleman has a habit of cutting out newspaper advertisements on which governesses and school teachers have spent their last pennies and then goes round to these unfortunate people seeking dishonourable ways of providing an income and bringing them to ruin with his money! I simply can't imagine why I should have taken his money yesterday! Probably because he looked so honest! No, not a word! You're a scoundrel, my good sir! Even if you came to me with the most honest intentions, I still don't want your charity! Not another word, not a word! Oh, I'm so glad I've shown you up for what you are right now, in front of your womenfolk, too! Damn you, sir!'

She quickly ran out, but in the doorway she turned back for an instant to shout:

'And I'm told you've come into an inheritance!'

At which she vanished like a ghost. I would remind the reader that this was the furious woman at Vasin's place. Versilov had been deeply shaken and stood there lost in thought, very mindful of something. At last he suddenly turned to me:

'You really haven't any idea who she is?'

'I saw her by chance a short while ago. She'd gone quite crazy in the corridor outside Vasin's room, screaming and cursing about you. But I didn't have a chance to talk to her and know nothing about her and have only just met her at the gates. It's yesterday's teacher who advertised about lessons in arithmetic, isn't it?'

'Yes, it's her. For once you try and do something good in your life and just look what happens! But why are you here?'

'Here's the letter,' I answered. 'I don't think I need explain. It came from Kraft and he got it from Andronnikov. It's self-explanatory. I will add that no one in the whole wide world knows about this letter now apart from myself, because Kraft, after he'd given it me yesterday and just after I'd left him, shot himself . . .'

While I said all this in a breathless haste he took the letter from me and, holding it in his outstretched left hand, followed me closely. When I mentioned Kraft's suicide, I studied his face particularly attentively to see what effect it would have. Yet it didn't make the slightest difference. He didn't so much as raise an eyebrow! Instead, seeing that I had stopped, he brought out his lorgnette, which he always had with him hanging by a black ribbon, lifted the letter to the candle and, after glancing at the signature, began studying it intently.

I cannot describe how insulted I felt by this high-and-mighty show of indifference. He should have known very well who Kraft was. In any case, it was hardly a very usual piece of news! Naturally I had also wanted to produce an effect by announcing it. Still, after hanging around for half a minute and knowing the letter was long, I turned round and went out. My case was already packed and all I had to do was tie a few other things up in a bundle. I thought of mother and how I'd avoided her. After ten minutes, by which time I'd done everything and was about to send for a cab, my sister came up into my little garret.

'Look, mother wants you to have this sixty roubles and wants again to apologize for telling Andrey Petrovich about them—oh, and another twenty roubles. You gave her fifty yesterday to pay for your keep, but she says she can't take more than thirty from you because she didn't spend anything like fifty on you, and so she's returning twenty.'

'Well, many thanks—if she really is telling the truth! Goodbye, sister dear, I'm leaving!'

'Where are you going now?'

'I'll find somewhere, just so I don't have to spent another night in this house. Tell mother I love her.'

'She knows that. She knows that you also love Andrey Petrovich. You ought to be ashamed about bringing that wretched girl here!'

'I swear to you I didn't. I simply met her at the gates.'

'No, you brought her.'

'I assure you . . .'

'Just think a moment, ask yourself the real reason why she came and you'll see that *you* were.'

'All I'm glad about is that I put Versilov to shame. Can you imagine it? He's had a baby by Lydia Akhmakov. But I can't think why I'm telling you this . . .'

'He has? A baby? Oh, it's not his! Where did you hear such nonsense?'

'Well, you ought to know.'

'Heavens, how couldn't I? Wasn't I looking after that very baby when I was in Luga? Listen, I've been aware for a long time you don't know anything about what's going on and yet you've been saying insulting things about Andrey Petrovich and mother as well!'

'If he's right, then I'll plead guilty and that'll be that and I won't love you any the less. Why are you blushing, Liza? And now more than ever! Well, all right, I'm still going to challenge that runt of a prince to a duel for slapping Versilov in the face at Ems. If Versilov did the right thing by Lydia Akhmakov, then that makes it all the worse!'

'Watch what you're saying, please!'

'Thank God the court case is now over . . . Now you've gone all white!'

'The prince won't accept your challenge.'

Pale with fright, Liza gave a wan smile.

'Then I'll publicly put him to shame. What's wrong with you, Liza?'

She had gone so pale she could not remain on her feet and sank down on to the divan.

'Liza!' came mother's voice from below.

She pulled herself together and stood up, smiling fondly.

'My dear brother, will you please give up all this nonsense or wait until you find out what it's all about. Because you know terribly little about it all.'

'I will remember, Liza, that you went pale when you heard I was going to fight a duel!'

'All right, remember that!'

She gave me another smile as she said goodbye and then she went downstairs.

I summoned a cabbie and with his help carried my things out of the apartment. None of the servants tried to stop me. I did not go and say goodbye to mother so as not to meet Versilov. When I was seated in the cab I suddenly had another thought.

'To the Fontanka, by Semyonovsky Bridge!' I ordered and set off again to see Vasin.

II

It had suddenly occurred to me that Vasin would already know about Kraft and would probably know a hundred times more than I did. This was precisely the case, as it turned out. Vasin at once gave me all the details in a perfunctory way, without much enthusiasm. I concluded he was tired, which indeed he was. He had been at Kraft's that morning. Kraft had shot himself with a revolver (the very one I'd seen) the previous evening when it was already dark. His diary indicated as much. The last entry had been made just before he shot himself and he had noted that he was writing in almost total darkness, hardly able to make out the letters. He hadn't wanted to light a candle for fear of causing a fire later.

'But I don't want to light it and then have to blow it out just before I blow out my own brains,' he had added strangely, almost as the last entry. He had started a kind of last-minute diary of entries the day before yesterday just after returning to St Petersburg and before he had made the visit to Dergachev. After I had been to see him he had made entries at fifteen-minute intervals and the final three or four entries had apparently been made at five-minute intervals. I expressed loud surprise that Vasin, having had the opportunity of spending a long time studying them (he had been given them to read), had not made a copy, the more so since they did not occupy more than a few sheets and they were all short—'At least the last side!' I said.

Vasin remarked with a smile that he had committed them to memory and, in any case, they were not systematic but just odd thoughts. I tried to convince him that this was valuable anyhow, but gave up and tried to get him to remember something or other and he did remember a few of the jottings occurring about an hour before the trigger was pulled, such as 'It's perishing cold' or that he'd thought of having a tot of vodka to warm himself up but then been put off by the thought that he might bleed more profusely as a result.

'Stuff like that, said Vasin.

'And you call that nonsense!' I cried.

'When did I say that? I just didn't copy them, that's all. And even if they're not nonsense, they're really pretty ordinary or—you know—natural, the sort of thing you'd expect in the circumstances . . .'

'But they were his last thoughts, his final thoughts!'

'Final thoughts can sometimes be extremely trivial. One suicide complained in his diary that at least one "higher thought" might have occurred to him at such an important moment but no, they were all trivial and ordinary.'

' "It's perishing cold"—was that an ordinary thought?'

'Are you thinking of his being cold or of bleeding profusely? It's a well-known fact that very many people who've got the guts to think about their imminent death, whether by their own hand or not, are very concerned about how they'll look, what their corpses will look like. In this sense Kraft was frightened of bleeding profusely.'

'I don't know whether it's a well-known fact or not,' I muttered, 'but I'm astonished you think it's natural. I mean, wasn't Kraft one of us not so long ago, sitting among us, talking, sharing our interests? Aren't you sorry for him at all?'

'Oh, of course I'm sorry for him! That's quite a different thing. But Kraft, in any case, made out his own death was the result of logical thinking. It turns out everything said about him yesterday at Dergachev's was right because he has left behind him a notebook setting out his case for assuming that the Russians are a second-class race of people, according to phrenology, craniology, and even mathematics, and that therefore there's not much point in staying alive if you're a Russian. If you like, the most obvious sign of character in this instance is that you can make any kind of logical case you like, but it doesn't always happen that you up and shoot yourself as a consequence.'

'At least you ought to admit it shows character.'

'Perhaps—and not only that,' remarked Vasin evasively, but it was clear he had had in mind the stupidity and weakness of the reasoning process. I was irritated by this.

'You yourself were talking yesterday about the importance of feelings, Vasin.'

'I'm not denying them now. But in view of the fact we're faced with, there seems to be something so grossly wrong about it that a sternly objective view of it must even exclude a feeling of compassion.'

'You know, I could have guessed yesterday from the look in your eyes that you would have something bad to say about Kraft and so as not to hear what it was I decided not to ask you. But now you've come out with it and I'm bound to agree with you. Still, I hate you for it! I'm sorry for Kraft!'

'You know we've gone a bit too far . . .'

'All right, all right,' I interrupted him, 'but at least what's comforting is that always, in cases like this, those who are still alive, in passing judgement on the deceased, can always say, "So he shot himself and he deserves all our pity and leniency, but we're still here, so there's not all that much to cry about, is there?"'

'Well, of course, if you look at it like that . . . Ah, I see you're joking! Jolly good! I always have some tea at this time and I'll just go and order it. You'll probably be joining me, eh?'

And he went out after having carefully eyed my suitcase and bundle.

I had really wanted to say something much more vicious, in vindication of Kraft, and I had succeeded up to a point, but it was curious that at first he had taken quite seriously what I had said about us still being here. The fact was that he was much more in the right than I was, even over the matter of feelings. I admitted this to myself without any sense of dissatisfaction, but I felt certain I didn't like him.

After the tea had been brought in, I explained to him that I was seeking hospitality from him only for one night and that, if that was impossible, he should say so and I would go and find a place in an inn. Then I gave my reasons, offering straight off the

174

simple fact that I had quarrelled for good and all with Versilov, without going into any detail about it. Vasin listened attentively but with no show of feeling. Generally speaking, he responded only to questions, although he did so readily and adequately. I did not mention the letter I had come to see him about earlier and I explained that visit by saying I had simply dropped in on him.

I had given my word to Versilov that, apart from myself, no one knew about that letter and I did not consider I had the right to mention it to all and sundry. For some reason I was particularly opposed to telling Vasin certain things. Certain things, but not others. I managed to tickle him with my account of what had occurred so recently in the corridor outside his room and about his female neighbours, ending with what had happened at Versilov's. He was particularly interested in what I had to say about Stebelkov. He asked me to repeat what Stebelkov had been saying about Dergachev and even pondered on it, but by the end of it he was grinning. It suddenly occurred to me at that instant that nothing could ever cause Vasin any trouble and, besides, when the idea first occurred to me, I remember that it seemed very flattering to him.

'Generally speaking I couldn't get very much out of what Mr Stebelkov said,' I concluded. 'He seems to jump from thing to thing . . . and there's something lightweight about him . . .'

Vasin at once looked serious.

'He really doesn't seem to have a way with words, but that's only how it appears at first glance. He's been known to make some very shrewd remarks. He's more of a businessman, more a man of affairs than a man of ideas. One's got to judge him from that point of view . . .'

He said just what I thought he would.

'However, he kicked up a terrible row with your female neighbours and God knows how that might have ended!'

About his female neighbours Vasin informed me that they had been living there about three weeks and they had come from somewhere in the provinces. Their room was extremely tiny, to all appearances they were very poor and they spent all their time sitting in their room and waiting for something. He did not know that the younger one had advertised in the newspapers as a teacher, but he had heard that Versilov had visited them. It had happened while he had been away and the landlady had told him. His neighbours kept themselves to themselves and even shunned the landlady. Quite recently he had noticed that things were not well with them, but there had been no scenes like today's.

I recall our discussion of these female neighbours because of what happened subsequently, but at the time dead silence reigned in their room beyond the door. Vasin took special interest in the fact that Stebelkov had considered it necessary to talk to the landlady about them and had repeated the words 'Just you wait and see!'

'And you'll see,' Vasin added, 'he didn't say that for nothing. He's very perceptive about that sort of thing.'

'You mean he was advising the landlady to get rid of them?'

'No, I'm not saying to get rid of them, but to beware of scandal. However, scandals will out, and they pass ... Let's leave it.'

He had nothing definite to offer over Versilov's visit.

'It could be anything. Maybe it was because he had money in his pocket. Still, it's more probable he was just offering charity. His sort would commonly do that or perhaps it's the way he's inclined.'

I told him that Stebelkov had chattered about a baby.

'In this case, Stebelkov is completely wrong,' Vasin declared emphatically and with special seriousness (I took particular mental note of this).

'Stebelkov,' he went on, 'sometimes puts too much faith in his practical common sense and jumps to conclusions compatible with his often very penetrating logic. Meanwhile, the actual occurrence can have a much more fantastic and unexpected complexion, bearing in mind those taking part in it. That's what happened here. Knowing about only part of it, he assumed Versilov was the ba' y's father, but he wasn't.'

I urged him on to speak and I learned to my great astonishment that the father was Prince Sergey Sokolsky. Lydia Akhmakov, whether due to her illness or her fantasizing, used sometimes to behave as if she were deranged. Even before meeting Versilov she had become infatuated with the prince and the prince 'had not been above accepting her love', as Vasin put it. The affair was over in a flash. They quarrelled, as was well known, and Lydia threw the prince out, 'which I think the latter was glad about' (Vasin's words).

'She was a very strange girl,' he added, 'and it's even very possible that she wasn't always completely in her right mind. But, going off to Paris, the prince had no idea of the state he had left her in and didn't know until it was all over, after his return. Versilov, who had become friends with her, proposed marriage, precisely owing to the circumstances I've described (which, it seems, even her parents didn't suspect until it was almost over). The girl, having fallen in love, was delighted by Versilov's proposal and, as she put it, "I didn't just see the sacrifice he was making," which, however, she valued highly. Of course, he knew how to do things,' added Vasin. 'The baby—a girl—was born a month or six weeks before time and was looked after somewhere in Germany, but was later brought back by Versilov and is now somewhere in Russia, perhaps in St Petersburg.'

'And what about the phosphorous matches?'

'I don't know anything about that,' Vasin concluded. 'Lydia Akhmakov died a couple of weeks after her confinement. What happened then I don't know. No sooner had he got back from Paris than the prince learned about the baby and I think he didn't believe at first it was his . . . In general the whole thing has been hushed up so far.'

'But damn that prince!' I shouted in disgust. 'What a thing to do to a sick girl!'

'She wasn't all that sick then . . . Anyhow, she threw him out! True, he may have been a bit hasty in the way he left his regiment.'

'Are you trying to justify the bastard?'

'No, but I'm not calling him that. There's a good deal more to it than just being a bastard. On the whole, it was a pretty ordinary affair.'

'Tell me something, Vasin—you knew him intimately, didn't you? I would particularly like to have your opinion of him, in view of something that concerns me very much.'

But at this point Vasin was very reluctant to answer. He had known the prince, but he deliberately avoided saying anything about the circumstances in which he got to know him. He went on to say that, in terms of his character, he was worthy of

177

considerable respect. 'He is full of honourable inclinations and very impressionable, but he has neither the intellect nor the will-power to give proper direction to his desires.' He was an uneducated man. The vast majority of ideas were beyond him, but he nevertheless flung himself at them regardless. For instance, he would buttonhole you and say: 'I'm a prince, a descendant of Ryurik, but why shouldn't I be a cobbler if I have to earn my daily bread and I'm not fitted for any other work? I'll hang out a sign—Cobbler Prince So-and-so. Noble that, eh?'

'Something's no sooner said than done—that's the chief thing about him,' added Vasin, 'and yet this has got nothing to do with strength of conviction but it's because he's so easily influenced. Then there are the inevitable regrets and he's ready to go off to an exactly opposite extreme. His whole life's been like that. In our time many people have put their foot in it that way,' Vasin concluded, 'precisely because they've been born in our time.'

I thought about this for a while.

'Is it true,' I asked, 'that he'd been drummed out of his regiment?'

'I don't know whether he was drummed out, but he left the regiment due to some unpleasantness. You're aware, aren't you, that last autumn, after he'd retired from his regiment, he spent two or three months in Luga?'

'I . . . I, er, know you were then in Luga.'

'Yes, I was there too. The prince also knew Lizaveta Makarovna.'

'Really? I didn't know that. I admit I haven't talked to my sister all that much. Surely,' I shouted, 'he was never received at home by my mother, was he?'

'Oh, no. It was a distant acquaintanceship, through third parties.'

'Didn't my sister say something about this baby? Wasn't the baby in Luga?'

'For a short while.'

'And where is it now?'

'Very probably in St Petersburg.'

'I'll never, never believe,' I cried in extraordinary excitement, 'that my mother had any part at all in this whole business with Lydia!'

'In this whole business, apart from all the side issues that I

178

don't want to go into, Versilov's role had nothing particularly reprehensible about it,' Vasin remarked with a condescending smile. I felt he was finding it tedious talking to me but he didn't want to show it.

'I'll never, never believe,' I cried again, 'that a woman could give up her husband to another woman! I simply won't believe it! I swear my mother had nothing to do with it!'

'I don't think she's ever denied this, has she?'

'I'd deny it on her behalf out of sheer pride!'

'For my part I entirely refuse to pass judgement in the matter,' declared Vasin flatly.

Actually Vasin, with all his cleverness, probably had no understanding of women, so that a whole range of ideas and emotions remained beyond his ken. I said nothing.

Vasin had temporary employment in a joint-stock company and I knew that he brought work home. He confessed, when I persisted in asking, that he had work to do—some accounts, in fact—and I begged him not to stand on ceremony with me. This seemed to please him, but before he got down to his work he made up a bed for me on the divan. He had begun by offering me his bed, but when I refused the offer he seemed happy with that as well. A pillow and blanket were obtained from the landlady. Vasin was extremely polite and considerate, but I didn't like seeing the way he fussed so much on my behalf. I had much preferred it when, three weeks or so ago, I had spent the night at Efim's on the Petersburg side. I remember he had then made up a bed for me on the divan surreptitiously so that his aunt shouldn't know, supposing for some reason that she would be annoyed if she knew he had friends coming to spend the night with him. We had a great joke putting a shirt down instead of a sheet and a folded coat instead of a pillow. I remember how Zverev had then snapped his fingers fondly over the divan and said to me:

'*Vous dormirez comme un petit roi.*'

Both his silly fooling about and the French phrase, which suited him about as much as a saddle on a cow, made it so that I slept at that idiot's place with exceptional enjoyment. So far as Vasin was concerned, I was extremely pleased when he finally sat down to work with his back to me. I lay on the divan and, watching his back, was lost in thought.

Indeed, there was a lot to think about. I had an obscure feeling of great unease and yet it had no content to it. But certain feelings stood out very clearly, although not one of them occupied me fully because there were so many of them. The whole lot sent out flashing signals in a disconnected and disorderly way, and I remember I personally had no desire at all to dwell on any one of them or put them in some sort of order. Even the thought of Kraft imperceptibly receded into the background.

My personal positon was what excited me most, that I had 'broken away' and had my case with me, was no longer at home and had begun something completely new. It was as if until this moment all my intentions and preparations had just been a joke and it was only 'now, suddenly' (as I put it to myself) 'and, chiefly, *this instant* everything had begun'. The thought stimulated and, despite all the obscure unease inside me, gladdened me. But ... but there were other feelings. One in particular sought to break free of the rest and take possession of me and, oddly, this feeling also proved stimulating as if it were summoning me to something terribly joyful. But it began with apprehension. I had been fearful for a long time, indeed ever since it happened, that in the heat of the moment and in my agitation I had said too much to Miss Akhmakov about the document.

'Yes,' I thought, 'I said too much, and very likely they'll guess something ... Hell! Of course they won't give me a moment's peace if they suspect something ... all right, so let them! Maybe they won't find me because I'll have disappeared! But if they do start chasing after me ...' And that's when I began remembering down to the last detail, and with growing enjoyment, how I had stood there in front of Katerina Nikolaevna and seen her bold but terribly surprised eyes gazing at me so intently. And, in going out, I had left her standing there astonished, and I remember thinking 'her eyes are not completely black, it's her eyelashes that are very black, that's why the eyes seem so dark ...'

And suddenly, I remember, I found it absolutely horrid thinking about it, and I felt angry and sick, both with them and with myself. I told myself to shut up and started thinking about something else. I suddenly thought: 'Why don't I feel the least bit of annoyance at Versilov for doing what he did with the girl next door?' For my own part, I was firmly convinced he had played the role of lover and he had come here to enjoy himself, but that didn't upset me at all. I didn't even think there was any other way of looking at what he had done, and though I was glad he'd been shown up, I didn't blame him. That wasn't what bothered me. What bothered me was that he had given me such a look of anger when I had come in with the lady from next door, a look I had never seen on his face before. 'At last,' I thought, as my heart missed a beat, 'he's actually looked at me *seriously*!' Oh, if I hadn't been fond of him I'd never have been overjoyed at his anger!

Finally I dozed and fell asleep. I remember in my sleep how Vasin, having completed his work, tidied up and, after studying me closely on the divan, got undressed and blew out the candle. It was getting on for one o'clock.

IV

Almost exactly two hours later I jumped up half-awake like a lunatic and sat up on my divan. Fearful cries, weeping, and commotion could be heard beyond the door to the neighbouring room. Our door was wide open and in the corridor, which already had a light in it, people were running about and shouting. I almost cried out to Vasin, but I guessed he wasn't in his bed. Not knowing where to find matches, I felt for my clothes and started hurriedly dressing in the dark. Evidently the landlady and perhaps other lodgers had rushed to the neighbouring room. One voice, that of the older woman from next door, broke into a howl, but yesterday's younger female voice, which I remembered only too well, was quite silent. I remember being struck particularly by this. Before I had finished dressing Vasin rushed into the room. In an instant, with hands accustomed to finding them, he had sought out the matches and given us light. He was in his underwear, in dressing-gown and slippers, and immediately started dressing.

'What's happened?' I cried out to him.

'An exceedingly unpleasant and troublesome business!' he answered almost angrily. 'That young lady from next door whom

181

you were telling me about has gone and hanged herself in her room.'

I literally gave a yell of anguish. I cannot convey how appalled I was!

We rushed out into the corridor. I admit I didn't dare go into the room next door and it was only later I saw the unfortunate girl when she had been taken down—true, only from a distance, covered in a sheet, from which the narrow soles of her shoes protruded. I never caught a glimpse of her face.

The mother was in a fearful state. Our landlady was with her, showing no great alarm. All the lodgers had gathered round. There were not all that many of them. They consisted of an elderly sailor, a man always given to complaining and demanding this and that, who was now, however, completely silent, and some visitors from Tver province, an old man and woman, husband and wife, fairly dignified people of some rank.

I refrain from describing the rest of that night, all the commotion and, later, the visits by officials. Right up to first light I was literally quivering all over and thought it my duty not to go back to bed, although I had nothing to do. Everyone had an extremely alert look, even a particularly cheerful one. Vasin even went out somewhere. The landlady turned out to be an estimable person, far better than I had supposed. I persuaded her that the mother should not be left alone with her daughter's corpse (this does me credit) and that she ought to be transferred to the landlady's room. The latter instantly agreed, and no matter how much the mother struggled and cried at being parted from the corpse she eventually went to the landlady, who immediately had the samovar got ready. After this the lodgers dispersed to their rooms and shut themselves in, but I did not go back to bed and spent a long time sitting with the landlady, who was glad to have an extra person there, especially someone who could tell her one or two things relevant to what had happened.

The samovar came in very useful, and the samovar is generally the most essential Russian thing to have by you at times of catastrophe and misfortune, particularly if they are really awful, really eccentric, and totally unexpected. The mother even had two cups of tea, only, of course, after great persuasion and almost under threat of force. Yet I can say in all sincerity that I have never seen more plain and inconsolable grief than I saw in that unfortunate person. After the initial bouts of weeping and hysterics, she even began to talk quite willingly, and I listened avidly to what she had to say. There are some unhappy people, particularly among women, who must be allowed to talk as much as possible in cases like this. Apart from that there are people too worn out by grief, so to speak, who have spent their whole life putting up with things, have endured an extraordinary amount both of huge sorrow and of constant grieving over life's trivia, whom nothing can surprise, no sudden catastrophes can alarm and, most of all, who even when confronted by the coffin of their nearest and dearest never forget a single one of the rules of ingratiating behaviour which they have had to acquire at such cost throughout their lives.

And I do not hold it against them. This is not a case of the vulgarity associated with egoism and any coarseness in their development. There is probably more gold in the hearts of such people than in the hearts of the supposedly noblest heroines, but a life-long habit of subservience, an instinct of self-preservation, long-term anxiety, and repression finally triumph. The poor suicide did not resemble her mother in this respect. In their looks, however, I think they were like each other, although the deceased had certainly not been bad-looking. The mother was herself not old, something under 50, fair like her daughter, but with sunken eyes and cheeks and with large, uneven, yellow teeth. Everything about her suggested a kind of yellowishness. The skin of her face and hands had a parchment look. Her darkish dress seemed to have gone quite yellow with wear and one fingernail, on the index finger of her right hand, had been carefully and meticulously covered in yellow wax, I have no idea why.

What the poor woman had to tell us was disconnected in places. I will tell it as I myself understood and can recall it.

V

They had come from Moscow. She had been widowed long since, but she described herself as a 'state counsellor's wife', her husband having been a civil servant, leaving practically nothing 'except a pension of two hundred roubles. And what's the good of two hundred roubles?' Anyhow, she had brought up Olya and put her through high school. 'And she's done so well, so well, she'd got a gold medal on leaving . . .' (At this point, I hardly need say, there was a flood of tears.)

Her late husband had lost his capital of almost four thousand roubles through a local St Petersburg merchant. Suddenly the merchant had made another fortune. 'I had documents, took advice, and was told I ought to pursue the matter and I'd be bound to get the money back . . . I did, and the merchant agreed at first. "Come and see me," he said. Olya and I came here a month ago. There wasn't much money, so we took the room here because it was smallest of all, but we could see it was an honest place and the worst thing for us inexperienced women was knowing we were at everyone's mercy. Well, we paid a month's rent, didn't we? And then we felt the pinch here in St Petersburg, what with the merchant flatly refusing. "I just don't want to know you," he said, and anyhow I knew the documents I had weren't right. So I was told I should go and see a well-known lawyer, a professor, not just an attorney, and he'd be sure to tell me what to do.

'I took our last fifteen roubles to him. He came out to see me and wouldn't listen to what I said but started saying: "All right, I see, I know, if your man wants to, he'll give it back, if he doesn't, he won't, but if you want to make a case of it you've got to be able to pay for it, so you'd much better leave things as they are," and he even quoted the Bible at me: "Agree with thine adversary quickly, whilst thou art with him in the way . . ." and he laughed as he said goodbye to me. So I lost my fifteen roubles!

'I came back to Olya and we sat opposite each other and I burst into tears. She doesn't cry, she's too proud. She just sits there looking angry. She was always like that all her life, even when she was little, never complaining, never crying, just sitting there looking angry. I didn't dare even watch her when she was like that. Believe it or not, I was frightened of her, really frightened, so I'd sometimes want to cry in front of her but didn't dare. I went to see that merchant for the last time and broke down in front of him and all he said was, "All right, all right" and didn't even listen to me. I've got to admit we were soon out of money because we didn't reckon on staying here long. I started pawning my clothes little by little, and then everything. Then she started giving up hers, down to the last

184

stitch, and I cry and cry, and she stamps her foot and jumps up and rushes off to this merchant. He's a widower and he says to her: "You come and see me at five o'clock the day after tomorrow and I'll have something for you." She comes back and she's happy. "Maybe he'll have something for us," she says. Well, I'm glad, but in my heart I think there's something up, yet I daren't ask her. In two days' time she comes back from the merchant all pale and shaking and throws herself on the bed and I knew what it was all about then but didn't dare ask her.

'What do you think? He offers her fifteen roubles, the villain, and says if he finds she's quite pure he'll offer her forty. He says it right to her face, no shame at all. And she says she flung herself at him then, and he fought her off and locked himself in his room.

'Well, I can tell you now in all honesty we couldn't afford to eat. So we sell her jacket lined with rabbit fur and she goes to the newspapers and puts in an advertisement saying she will teach all subjects and arithmetic as well and says, "Maybe it'll bring in thirty copecks." And, you know, after that I was horrified by her because she'd say nothing, just sit by the window hours on end staring at the roof of the house opposite and sometimes stamping her foot and crying out: "If only I could take in washing, dig a ditch, anything!"

'And we didn't know anyone here. We didn't have anyone to go and see. "What's going to become of us?" I ask myself. And I'm frightened to talk to her. One day she's been sleeping during the day, and she wakes up, opens her eyes, looks at me. I'm sitting on our trunk and I'm looking at her. She stands up without a word, comes over to me, gives me such a tight, tight hug and we can't help ourselves, we both burst into tears, and sit and cry together, and can't let go of each other. That was the first time she ever cried like that in her whole life. It's just then, when we're sitting, hugging each other, your Nastasya comes in and says there's some lady asking for us.

'It was just four days ago, that was. A lady comes in. We can see she's very well dressed and, though she speaks Russian, she sounds German. "Have you", she asks, "put an advertisement in the paper about giving lessons?" We welcome her, offer her a seat, she gives a charming laugh. "It's not for me," she says, "it's for a relative with small children. Come and see us and we can talk about it." And she gives an address by the Voznesensky Bridge, the number of the house, the number of the apartment. then she leaves. Olya goes off there that very day, just dashes off there—and in two hours she's back, all hysterical!

'She told afterwards how she'd gone and asked the porter where the place was and he looked at her and said: "What d'you want with that place, eh?" and given her such a strange look as though she'd maybe got it wrong. But she was always so strong-willed and impatient and would never put up with lots of questions and rudeness. "Up there!" he says and points a finger at the stairs and turns his back on her and goes back into his cubby-hole. So what d'you think, eh? She goes there and asks and straightaway women come rushing from all directions, shouting "Come in! Come in!" and there's only women there, all laughing and flinging themselves on her, all painted and made-up, all horrible-looking, and someone's playing a piano, and they drag her in. "I wanted to get away from them," she said, "but they wouldn't let me go!" And she goes faint and weak at the knees, but they won't let her go and try persuading her and open a bottle of port and give her some. And she jumps up and shouts and demands to be let out and dashes to the door, but they keep hold of it and she starts screaming. In comes the woman who'd been to see us, slaps Olya twice on the cheek, pushes her through the door, saying, "We don't want a bitch like you in a respectable house!" And another of them shouts at her on the stairs, "You slut, you come 'ere 'cos you ain't got nothin' to eat, but we don't like seeing sluts like you round 'ere!"

'All night she was in a fever and delirious and in the morning her eyes were glittering and she gets up and walks about and says, "I'll take her to court, I will!" and I don't say anything and I think to myself, what'll be the good of going to court? And she walks to and fro wringing her hands and crying, but her lips are shut tight, not moving an inch. And her whole face got a dark, angry look then and stayed like that to the very end. After three days she began to get over it and went quiet, as if she'd calmed down. That was when Mr Versilov came to see us, at four o'clock in the afternoon.

'And I'll tell you straight out, I can't understand even now why Olya, who was always so mistrustful, started listening to him almost from the very first word. What struck us most of all was the serious look he had, even a bit stern, and the quiet way he talked, courteously and all so politely—ever so, even respectfully—and there seemed to be nothing underhand about him. It just looked as if he had come out of the pureness of his heart. "I read your advertisement in the paper," he said, "but, my dear young lady, you wrote it wrongly and could even do yourself harm as a result." And he began to explain, though I didn't understand all he was saying about arithmetic and so on—anyhow, Olya goes red, I see, and livens up, listens, and talks easily (a really clever man, he is!) and I hear her thanking him. He asks her about things so courteously and it turns out he'd lived in Moscow a long time and knew the head teacher of the high school personally. "I'll be sure to find a place where you can give lessons," he says, "because I know a lot of people here and I can ask a lot of influential people, so that if you might want a permanent position, then something could be kept in mind . . . Forgive me, though," he says, "for asking a direct question—can I offer you any help now? It's not I who'll be doing you the favour," he says, "but you'll be doing it to me, if you'll allow me to be of assistance to you. Consider it a debt," he says, "and you can pay me back as soon as you obtain a position. Believe me, in all honesty, should I fall on hard times in the future and you, on the other hand, were fully provided for, then I'd be the first to approach you for help and even send you my wife and daughter as well . . ."

'I don't remember everything he said, it's just that I had tears in my eyes when I saw Olya's lips quiver in gratitude. "If I accept money," she told him, "it's because I trust a man of honesty and humanity, who could be my father . . ." She put it just like that, so brief, so dignified: "honesty", she said, "and humanity . . ." He stood up at that and said: "Certainly, certainly, I will find you lessons and a position. I'll start on it at once because you have all the qualifications . . ." I forgot to say that when he'd first come in he'd looked at all her high-school certificates. She'd shown them him and he'd tested her on various subjects. "Mother," she said afterwards, "he tested me, you know, and he's so clever! It's ages since I've talked to such a clever and educated man . . ." She glowed with happiness. The money lay there on the table and she said: "Take it, mother. When I get a place, the first thing I'll do is repay it as soon as possible and

187

prove we're as honest and respectable as he sees we are." Afterwards she said nothing and I saw her sighing. "You know, mother," she suddenly says, "if we'd been insensitive, perhaps we shouldn't have accepted it because we'd have been too proud, but we have accepted it now and by doing so we've shown how respectable we are, that we trust him completely as a respectable man, isn't that so?" And I didn't understand to start with what she meant and said: "Why shouldn't we accept charity from a benevolent and wealthy man if he's got a kind heart?" She frowned at me then. "No," she says, "mother, it's not his charity we need, it's his *humanity*! And it'd be even better not to take his money at all, mother. If he's promised to find a position for me, that's enough—even though we need the money." "Well," I say, "Olya, our needs are so great we can't refuse it!" I even laughed. Well, I was glad, you know, only she turned to me after an hour and said firmly: "Wait a bit before spending it." "Why?" "Just wait," she snaps and falls silent.

'She's silent all evening. I wake up between one and two in the morning and I hear her churning about on her bed. "Can't you sleep, mother?" she asks. "No, I can't," I say. "You know," she sayd, "he just wanted to humiliate me." "What do you mean?" "I mean what I say," she says. "He's a low-down bastard, that man is, and don't you dare spend any of his money!" I tried to answer her and even started crying then and there, in bed, and she just turned over to face the wall. "Shut up!" she says. "Let me get some sleep!"

In the morning I watch her walking to and fro and she's not herself. Believe it or not, I swear to you in God's name she wasn't in her right mind then! Ever since she'd been treated like that in that brothel she'd lost heart—and she'd become a bit touched. I looked at her that morning and had my doubts. I felt awful. I thought, I'm not going to contradict her in anything! "Mother," she says, "he never left his address, did he?" "Oh, you ought to be ashamed, Olya!" I say. "You yourself heard what he said yesterday, you yourself praised him, you were ready to shed tears of gratitude for him!"

'I'd no sooner said this than she screams at me and stamps her foot: "Oh, mother, you're a woman of really low-down feelings, because you were brought up under serfdom!" And, saying this, she seizes her hat and rushed out and I shout after

188

her, because I can't think where she's off to. And she's dashed off to the address office to find where Mr Versilov is living. She comes back and says: "This very day I'm going to take his money back to him and hurl it in his face! He just wanted to humiliate me like Safonov"—that's out merchant's name—"but Safonov was just a crude peasant while he was cunning as a Jesuit!"

'Then suddenly that man from yesterday knocked on our door. "I heard you talking about Versilov," he says. "I can tell you a thing or two." The moment she heard the name Versilov she flung herself at him in an absolute frenzy, talking away all the time, and I'm amazed how she, who normally doesn't say a thing, talks away like mad to this stranger. Her cheeks are burning red and her eyes all a-glitter! And he says: "It's the absolute truth, dear lady! Versilov", he says, "is like the notorious general they write about in the newspapers. They dress up in all their medals and call on all the governesses who advertise in the newspapers and find what they want. And if they don't get exactly what they want—you know what I mean—they have a sit-down and talk and spin a yarn and leave and they've had a bit of entertainment, you know what I mean.' And Olya even bursts out laughing at this, only in anger, and I see this gentleman take her hand and start drawing it towards him, saying: "Madam, I am a man of some capital and I could always find something for a beautiful young girl, but I'd rather simply kiss her charming little hand . . ." and I see him drawing her hand to his lips. At that she jumps up and I help her and we both throw him out!

'Then, late in the afternoon, Olya grabs the money, rushes out and when she comes back says: "I've got my own back on that beastly man!" "Oh," I say, "Olya, Olya, we've probably lost our last chances now you've been rude to someone really decent and helpful!" I burst into tears with vexation at her, I couldn't help it! She shouts at me: "I won't, I won't, I won't! If he were the most honest man in the world, I still wouldn't want his charity! I won't let anyone take pity on me!"

'I went to bed and I didn't have a single thought in my head. The times I'd seen that nail in the wall where the mirror was—never given it a moment's thought, I hadn't, never a moment's, not yesterday or before, and I'd never expected it of Olya . . . never! I usually sleep soundly and snore and the blood rushes to my head and sometimes to my heart, so I cry out and Olya has

189

to wake me up in the night and say: "Mother, you're sleeping so soundly I shan't be able to wake you up when I have to." And I say: "Oh, Olya, I sleep soundly, so soundly . . ." And so I must have fallen fast asleep last night and she must have waited for me to fall asleep and got up without being afraid of waking me. The belt that went round the trunk, a long one, had been lying about all month and just yesterday morning I'd thought I ought to tidy it away. And she must have knocked away the chair with her foot and put her skirt under it so it wouldn't make a noise. And I must have woken up a long, long time afterwards, maybe a whole hour or more, and I called out: "Olya, Olya!" And I suddenly had an inkling something was wrong and shouted at her. It was either that I couldn't hear her breathing from the bed, or perhaps I could sort of sense it was empty even in the darkness, only I jumped up and felt with my hand there was nothing on the bed and the pillow was cold. My heart literally stopped and I stood there not feeling a thing and not knowing what to do.

'She's gone out, I think to myself. I take a step, and I'm by the bed, and I look in the corner by the door and it's just as if she's looking at me out of the darkness and not moving. And I think, why's she stood on a chair? "Olya," I whisper, feeling scared. "Olya, do you hear me?" Only it suddenly dawns on me then and I take a step forward, thrust out both hands straight at her and take hold of her and she swings there in my arms and I seize her and she still swings and I understand everything and don't want to . . . I want to cry out and I can't . . . I think, Oh, my God! . . .

'Then I fell down flat on the floor and started howling . . .'

'Vasin,' I said about six that morning, 'if it wasn't for Stebelkov this might never have happened.'

'Who knows? It would probably have happened anyhow. In a case like this it's impossible to judge, it was ready to happen without him . . . True, Stebelkov sometimes . . .'

He did not finish and made an unpleasant face. At about seven he went off again—he seemed to be very busy. I was left entirely by myself. It was already daylight. My head spun slightly. I thought of Versilov: the mother's story had shown him in a completely different light. To think about it more comfortably for a while, I lay down on Vasin's bed just as I was, fully dressed and in my boots, with no intention at all of sleeping—and suddenly I fell asleep, not even aware it had happened. No one woke me and I slept almost four hours.

CHAPTER X

I

I WOKE at about half past ten and could not believe my eyes. On the divan where I had slept the previous night sat my mother and, beside her, our unfortunate neighbour, Olya's mother. They were holding each other by the hand, talking in whispers so as not to disturb me, and both were crying. I got up and at once rushed over to kiss mother. She literally broke into a radiant smile, kissed me back and made the sign of the cross over me three times with her right hand. We had no time to say a word to each other before the door was flung open and in came Versilov and Vasin. Mother at once stood up and led the neighbour out with her. Vasin offered me his hand, but Versilov did not say a word to me and seated himself in the armchair. He and mother had evidently been there some time. He was frowning and looked careworn.

'What I regret most of all,' he said in measured tones to Vasin, evidently continuing a conversation, 'is that I didn't manage to settle it yesterday evening, and I'm sure then that this dreadful thing wouldn't have happened! I had the time, too. It wasn't even eight o'clock. The moment she left our place yesterday I had it in mind to go after her and make her change her mind, but then this unexpected and urgent matter, which I could very well have put off until today—or for a week even—this annoying business got in the way and spoilt everything. It would work out like that!'

'You might not have been able to make her change her mind. No matter what you did, I think she'd just got too worked up,' Vasin let drop in passing.

'No, I'd have managed, I'm certain of it. And I even had the idea of sending Sofya Andreevna in place of me. It was just a thought, no more. Sofya Andreevna alone would have dissuaded her and the poor girl would still be alive. No, I'm never again going to start poking my nose in . . . well, with so-called good intentions . . . And that's the only time I've done it in my life! I thought, you know, I was still up with things and understood the young people of today. Yes, well, our older generation grows old before it grows mature. Besides, there are an awful lot of people alive today who think of themselves as the younger generation out of habit, because that's what they were only yesterday, only they haven't noticed how out of touch they are!'

'It's a case of misunderstanding, and only too clearly so,' said Vasin reasonably. 'Her mother says that after being humiliated in that brothel she seemed to lose her reason. Add to that her initial humiliation at the hands of the merchant, and it could all have happened just as well at any time previously and is in no way specially characteristic, in my opinion, of the youth of today.'

'It's a little impatient, the youth of today, apart, of course, from not understanding reality fully, which is true of any youth at any time, but is particularly true of today's . . . Tell me, what was Mr Stebelkov up to in all this?'

'Mr Stebelkov,' I butted in suddenly, 'is the cause of it all. If it hadn't been for him, nothing would have happened. He poured oil on the flames.'

Versilov heard what I said, but did not look at me. Vasin frowned.

'I also reproach myself over one silly circumstance,' Versilov went on unhurriedly and measuring his words as before. 'I think I allowed myself, through a bad habit of mine, to adopt a certain light-heartedness and frivolousness towards her—in short, I was insufficiently sharp, dry, and serious, three qualities which, I think, are held in particularly high regard by today's younger generation. What I mean is that I gave her grounds for thinking I was some sort of womanizer.'

'Completely opposite!' I butted in again sharply. 'Her mother specially insisted that you produced an excellent impression through being so serious, even stern, and so sincere—those were her very own words! The dead woman herself praised you in that sense after you'd left.'

'R-really?' mumbled Versilov, finally glancing at me for an

instant. 'Take a look at this scrap of paper, it's essential to the business.' He stretched towards Vasin with a small piece of paper. He took it and, noticing that I was looking at it inquisitively, gave it to me to read. It was a note of two lines dashed off in pencil and probably in the dark:

'*Mummy darling, forgive me, I'm curtailing my début in life, your disappointing Olya.*'

'It was only found this morning,' Vasin explained.

'What a strange note!' I exclaimed in astonishment.

'What's strange about it?' asked Vasin.

'You don't use funny expressions at a time like that, do you?' Vasin gave me a questioning look.

'And the fun's so strange,' I continued. 'It's sort of chummy, high-school language. I mean, who'd write at such a moment to her poor mother—and she loved her mother, it seems—"I'm curtailing my début in life"!'

'Why shouldn't one write that?'

'I don't think this has got anything to do with being funny,' remarked Versilov finally. 'The phrase is inappropriate, of course, and has the wrong tone and might well have arisen in high school or in some chummy way of speaking, as you said, or in the gutter press, but the poor dead girl used it in her dreadful note completely straightforwardly and seriously.'

'That can't be so. She graduated from high school and was a silver medallist.'

'Being a silver medallist doesn't mean a thing. Nowadays many graduate with that.'

'You're again down on young people,' Vasin remarked with a smile.

'Not at all,' Versilov answered, standing up and picking up his hat. 'If today's younger generation is not all that literary, then it undoubtedly possesses other attributes.' Then he added with unusual seriousness: 'In any case, I said "many", not "all"—for example, I don't accuse you of being poorly developed in a literary sense and you're still a young man.'

'Yes, Vasin couldn't even see anything wrong with using the funny word *début*!' I couldn't refrain from saying.

Without a word Versilov extended his hand to Vasin and the latter also picked up his cap to leave along with him and cried

193

out to me: 'Be seeing you!' Versilov left without noticing me. I also had no time to lose if I were going to find a place for myself—something that was now more necessary than ever!

Mother was not with the landlady. She had gone out and had taken Olya's mother with her. I went out on to the street in a particularly lively frame of mind. Some big, new feeling had been born within me. What's more, it was as if everything conspired to be on my side. I was unusually lucky and soon found a place that was perfectly suitable. I'll have something to say about that later, but now I'll finish with the main thing.

It was shortly after two when I returned again to Vasin for my case and once again found him at home. On seeing me he cried out with a happy and sincere look on his face:

'How glad I am you've found me here, because I was just going out! I can tell you a fact which I think will be very interesting to you.'

'I'm sure you can!' I cried.

'Hey, you're looking pretty cheerful! Say, did you know anything about a letter which Kraft had in his possession and reached Versilov yesterday, relating directly to the court case he'd just won? In the letter the testator expressed his wishes in a sense contrary to yesterday's court decision. The letter was written a long time ago. To put it briefly, I don't know precisely what it was all about, but maybe you know something?'

'Sure. The day before yesterday Kraft took me to his place— you know, right after what happened at Dergachev's—in order to give me the letter and yesterday I gave it to Versilov.'

'Really? I thought so. Just imagine, the business Versilov was talking about just now which prevented him from coming here yesterday evening to talk to the girl—that was a direct result of the letter. Yesterday evening Versilov went straight off to the Sokolsky lawyer, gave him the letter, and renounced his entire right to the inheritance he had won. The renunciation is now being put into a legal form. Versilov is not making a gift, but he is making legal acknowledgement of the princes' full entitlement.'

I was struck dumb, but I was overjoyed. I had really been completely convinced that Versilov would destroy the letter despite what I had said to Kraft about it being an ignoble thing to do and though I had repeated it to myself in the pub and had come here to St Petersburg, as I'd told myself, to 'see someone decent, not him'—but more so because, deep down, in the very pit of my stomach, I'd considered the only thing to do was to get rid of the document. I'd considered it the most ordinary thing to do. If I'd held Versilov to blame afterwards, then I'd have done so deliberately to make a show of it, in order, that is, to demonstrate my superiority to him. But having now heard what a great thing he had done, I was utterly, sincerely overjoyed and roundly rejected my cynicism and indifference with real shame and repentance and at that moment, realizing Versilov was way, way above me in a moral sense, I almost fell upon Vasin and kissed him.

'What a man! What a man! Who else would have done that?' I cried in an absolute ecstasy.

'I agree with you that a great many people wouldn't have done that . . . True, it's an extraordinarily selfless thing to do . . .'

'*But*? Finish what you wanted to say, Vasin. But what?'

'Yes, of course, there's a "but". In my opinion, Versilov did it a bit too quickly and not all that straightforwardly.' Vasin gave a smile.

'Not all that straightforwardly?'

'Yes. He's made what you might call a "pedestal" to stand on. Because, in any case, one could do the very same thing without letting oneself down. If not half, then undoubtedly a part of the inheritance could still go to Versilov, even if one took the most finicky view of the business, since the document has no decisive significance and he has already won the court case. The counsel for the other side is of that opinion—I've just been speaking to him. The gesture would have been no less laudable, but solely out of an access of pride it has turned out otherwise. The main thing is that Mr Versilov got excited and was in too much of a hurry. After all, he himself said only a moment ago he could have put it off for a whole week . . .'

'You know, Vasin, I've got to agree with you but . . . but I love it better the way I see it, I like it much better that way!'

'Well, it's a matter of taste. You yourself asked me. I wouldn't have said anything otherwise.'

'Even if he has set himself up on a pedestal, that's no bad thing,' I went on. 'A pedestal's just a pedestal, but it's valuable in its own right. In this case his pedestal is the ideals he has, and it can't be a bad thing for anyone to have ideals nowadays. Even if they are a bit deformed, so long as they exist—that's what matters! And I'm sure you think so, too, Vasin, my dear chap, my dear friend! Of course, I know I'm rattling on, but you know what I mean—that's why you're Vasin! In any case, I'm going to hug and kiss you!'

'Out of sheer joy?'

'Out of a great joy! Because, as the Bible says, I am one who was dead and now liveth, was lost and is found! Vasin, I'm just a shit and not worthy of you. I admit I'm sometimes quite different, nobler and profounder. The day before yesterday I praised you to your face—and I only did it because I'd been crushed and humiliated—so I've absolutely loathed you for the past two days! I promised myself that night I'd never come and see you, and I only came yesterday morning out of sheer malice—yes, *malice*! I sat here in your chair and criticized your room, and you, and your books, and your landlady, and tried to really hate you and loathe you . . .'

'There's no need to tell me . . .'

'Yesterday evening, supposing from something you said you knew nothing about women, I was glad I could get you for that. Just now, when I got you with the word "début", I was again glad, just because I'd praised you to your face . . .'

'Hey, that's enough!' shouted Vasin at last (he was still smiling and showed no surprise at what I was saying). 'Anyhow, it's always happening and to almost everyone, it's even the very first thing that happens. But no one admits it, and there's no need to, because it all passes, in any case. Nothing comes of it.'

'Surely not everyone? You mean everyone's like this? And you can say this quite calmly? You couldn't live if that's what you really thought!'

'So you think "The lie that pulls the wool over our eyes | Means more to me than hosts of lowly truths"*—is that it?'

'That's absolutely right!' I cried. 'Those two lines contain a sacred truth!'

'I don't know about that. I'm not going to undertake to decide whether those two lines are right or not. As is always the case, the truth very likely lies somewhere in between—I mean, in one case it's a sacred truth, in another it's a lie. I only know one thing for sure: the idea will remain one of the chief points of

196

contention between people for a long time to come. In any case, I see you now want to be on your way. All right, be on your way. Exercise is good for you. But today I've just had a mass of things to do—and right now you're making me late!'

'All right, I'm on my way! Just one more thing!' I cried, seizing my case. 'If I wanted to hug you just now, then it was only because, when I came in, you told me what you did with such sincere pleasure and were really delighted I'd found you here—and this, mind you, after the silly business about the word "début"! Your sincere pleasure at once got me on your side. Well, goodbye, goodbye, I'll try to bother you as little as possible from now on. I know you'll be exceptionally pleased about that. I can even see it in your eyes. It'll even be to our mutual advantage. . .'

Chattering away like that and almost choking from the happy drivel I was talking, I hauled out my case and set off with it to the new lodging. Most of all I was frightfully glad that Versilov had been so annoyed with me recently and hadn't even wanted to talk to me or look at me. Having deposited my case, I at once dashed off to see my old friend, the prince. I admit that the last couple of days without seeing him had even been a bit tedious for me. Anyow, he had very likely already heard what Versilov had done.

II

I knew he'd be overjoyed to see me and I'd even have gone to see him that day if there hadn't been news about Versilov. All that had frightened me from going there yesterday and more recently was the thought I might meet Katerina Nikolaevna. But now I wasn't frightened of anything.

He joyfully embraced me.

'You've heard about Versilov, haven't you?' I started off with the main thing.

'*Cher enfant*, my dear boy, it's superbly high-minded, superbly noble—in short, it even shook Kilyan rigid!' (Kilyan was the clerk who worked downstairs.) 'It's not a very sensible thing for him to do, but it's brilliant, absolutely heroic! Ideals of that kind can't be overvalued!'

'Isn't that right! We've always agreed about that!'

197

'My dear boy, we've always seen eye to eye. Where've you been? I'd been wanting to come and see you but I didn't know where to find you. Because I couldn't go and call on Versilov . . . Although now, after all this . . . You know, my boy, I think it's this sort of thing, this feature of his character, that's undoubtedly made him such a success with women . . .'

'That reminds me, I've got something for you. Yesterday the silliest of idiots, while telling me all sorts of unpleasant things about Versilov, called him "a petticoat prophet"—what a thing to say! I thought you'd like that.'

'"Petticoat prophet"! *Mais . . . c'est charmant!* Ha-ha! It fits him—or rather it doesn't at all! But it's good—no, it's not good at all! Still . . .'

'It doesn't matter, just consider it a kind of *bon mot.*'

'It's a marvellous *bon mot*, and you know it means something very profound. As an idea it's absolutely right! That's to say, believe it or not . . . I'll let you into one tiny, tiny secret. You remember that girl called Olimpiada? Would you believe it, she's got a bit of a crush on Versilov, to the point, I think, when she even hopes . . .'

'Hopes! Does she, indeed! She can take that!' I cried, sticking two fingers in the air.

'*Mon cher*, keep your voice down! That's how it is. You may be quite right, of course. But, dear boy, don't you remember what happened the last time Katerina Nikolaevna was here? You were rocked back on your heels . . . I thought you were out for the count! I rushed to your aid!'

'Please, not about that now! I was simply overcome because of something . . .'

'You've gone red!'

'All right, so you've got to rub it in! You know she and Versilov are at daggers drawn—well, it was all to do with that. That's why I was so upset. Let's leave it for the time being!'

'Let's leave it be, leave it be, I'm only too glad to . . . It's just that I feel terribly, terribly in the wrong over her, and even—remember?—the things I said to her then . . . Right, let's forget it, dear boy. I have an inkling, only too clear an inkling, she'll be changing her mind about you . . . Ah, here's Prince Seryozha!'

A handsome young officer came in. I devoured him with my eyes because I had never seen him before in my life. I say he was handsome, since everyone described him as that, but there was something not entirely attractive about his young and handsome face. It was something I noted as an impression left by that first instant of seeing him and it always remained with me. He had a rather dry look about him, a man of splendid stature and dark-brown hair, with a fresh face of slightly yellowish complexion and a general air of decisiveness. His beautiful dark eyes looked a trifle severe even when he was completely calm. But the general air of decisiveness tended to put one off because one couldn't help feeling it cost him all too little. However, I don't know quite how to put it. Of course, his expression was capable of changing suddenly from being severe to being surprisingly affable, meek, and gentle and, chiefly, with undoubted sincerity in the changeability. It was this sincerity which was so attractive. I will mention something else, too. Despite the affability and sincerity, his faced never looked entirely happy. Even when the prince laughed with all his heart, you always had the feeling that there was never any real lightness and gaiety in his heart ... However, it's terribly hard to describe a face. I have no talent for it at all.

The old prince immediately rushed to introduce me in his usual silly way.

'This is my young friend, Arkady Andreevich'—once again he made the mistake of calling me Andreevich—'Dolgoruky.'

The young prince instantly turned to me with a doubly polite expression on his face, but it was obvious my name meant nothing to him.

'A relative of Andrey Petrovich,' muttered the irritating old prince—and how irritating old men can sometimes be with their little habits! The young prince guessed who I was at once.

'Ah, I've heard about you!' he said hurriedly. 'I had the very great pleasure of meeting your sister, Lizaveta Makarovna, in Luga last year ... She talked about you.'

I was even taken by surprise at the way his face glowed with sincere pleasure.

'Allow me, prince,' I said, absolutely babbling out the words as I drew both hands behind me, 'I must say in all sincerity—and I am glad I am saying this in the presence of my good friend, the old prince—that I had wanted to meet you, and not all that long ago, only yesterday, but for a completely different purpose.

I am saying this straight out so as not to spare your astonishment. In short, I had wanted to challenge you to a duel for the insult which you did to Versilov eighteen months ago in Ems. And though, of course, you might not have accepted my challenge, because I am merely recently out of high school and under age, I would still have made the challenge, no matter whether you accepted it or whatever what you did . . . and I confess I would do the same right now.'

The old prince told me later that I had managed to say this with the utmost dignity. Sincere misgivings appeared on the prince's face.

'You have not given me any time to speak for myself,' he answered with impressive composure. 'If I addressed you just now so warmly, the reason was my present, true feelings for Andrey Petrovich. I am sorry that I cannot inform you of all the circumstances at present, but I can assure you on my honour that I have long felt the deepest regret for my behaviour in Ems. On returning to St Petersburg I was determined to give Andrey Petrovich every satisfaction—that is to say, to ask his forgiveness in a literal sense, straight out, in whatever way he wished. Higher and much more influential matters have caused me to change my mind. The fact that we were involved in a lawsuit did not affect my decision at all. His behaviour towards me yesterday has shaken me to the core and—believe me—I still haven't completely recovered. And now I have to inform you of this— I've just come here to see the old prince and give him the extraordinary news that only three hours ago, at exactly the same time as the renunciation was being legally drafted, Andrey Petrovich sent me someone authorized to say that he was offering a challenge, a formal challenge to a duel, in connection with what happened at Ems . . .'

'He's actually challenged you?' I shouted and felt that my eyes were burning and I was red in the face.

'Yes, he has. I have just accepted the challenge, but I decided before meeting him to send him a letter explaining my attitude to what I had done and expressing all my remorse at my mistake—because that's all it was, a mistake—an unfortunate and fateful mistake! I will mention to you that my position in the regiment forced me to take the risk of sending such a letter and landing myself in deep water with my brother officers . . . you understand what I mean, I think, don't you? But, even so, I was determined, and only failed to get the letter to him because an hour later I received another note from him asking me to forgive him for troubling me, to forget about the duel, and adding that he regretted his 'momentary lapse into small-minded egoism'—his very words. So he has made things a lot easier for me over the letter. I haven't yet sent it and have come here precisely to have a word about it with the prince . . . You must believe me when I say I have suffered perhaps more than anyone from pangs of conscience . . . Is that enough to be going on with, Arkady Makarovich? Will you do me the honour of believing in my complete sincerity?'

I was completely overwhelmed. I saw an indisputable straightforwardness in him which I had never for a moment suspected. I had not expected anything of the kind. I muttered something in reply and held out both hands to him. He shook them joyfully with both of his. He then took the prince aside and spoke to him for about five minutes in his bedroom.

'If you would like to give me particular pleasure,' he addressed me loudly and openly on returning, 'come along with me now and I will show you the letter I am sending to Andrey Petrovich and the one he sent me.'

I agreed with the utmost warmth. The old prince was agitated as he said goodbye to me and also summoned me into his bedroom for a moment.

'*Mon ami*, how glad I am, how very glad! We'll talk about it all later. I just wanted to say there are a couple of letters there in my briefcase—one needs to be delivered with a personal explanation, the other's for the bank and also needs explaining . . .'

What it meant was that he was entrusting me with two urgent tasks demanding unusual effort and attention. I had to go round to these places, hand the letters over in person, sign for them, and so on.

'Oh, you old fox, you!' I cried, taking the letters. 'I swear this is all nonsense, and there's nothing in any of this at all, but you've simply invented something for me to do to prove to me I am in your service and not taking your money for nothing!'

'*Mon enfant*, I swear you are wrong. These *are* two very urgent matters . . . *Cher enfant*,' he cried, quite overcome himself, 'my

201

dear young fellow!' He placed both hands on my head. 'Here's my blessing on you and your life! Let's always be as pure in heart as we are this day ... always as kind and beautiful as possible ... Let us always love the beautiful in all its many forms ... Well, *enfin* ... *enfin rendons grace* ... *et je te benis*!'

He could not bring himself to finish and started snivelling over me. I admit I almost started crying myself. At least I embraced the eccentric old chap with genuine and sincere pleasure. We covered each other with kisses.

III

Prince Seryozha (Prince Sergey Petrovich, as I shall call him from now on) took me to his apartment in his fancy carriage and the first thing that struck me about the apartment was its magnificence. That is to say, it wasn't exactly magnificent, but one of the kind owned by 'people of the right sort'—tall, large well-lit rooms (I saw only two of them; the others were closed), and furniture with Versailles or Renaissance pretensions, but soft, comfortable, plentiful, and, broadly speaking, lavish; also plenty of carpets, carved wood, and statuettes.

The princes were reputed to have absolutely nothing at all. However, I had heard it said that this prince used to put on a show wherever he could—here, in Moscow, in his former regiment, in Paris—and was even a bit of a gambler and a man with many debts. Whereas I had nothing at all except my crumpled jacket, covered in fluff as well because I had slept in it, and a shirt I had not changed for three days. Although my jacket was not yet in an appalling state, once inside the prince's apartment I was reminded of Versilov's remark that I ought to have a new suit.

'Can you imagine it? On account of a girl who committed suicide I slept the whole night in what I'm wearing,' I remarked, looking hot and bothered, and because he at once expressed interest I told him about it briefly. But he was obviously most of all concerned about his letter.

What I chiefly found strange was that he had not only not smiled but he had not even shown the slightest inclination to do so when I had declared not so long ago that I wanted to challenge him to a duel. Although I could have cut short his laughter had I wanted to, it was strange behaviour from a person of his sort. We sat down opposite each other in the middle of the room at a large writing-table and he handed me a fair copy of his letter to Versilov.

It was written in very similar vein to the way he had spoken at the old prince's, and it had even been written with a certain passion. I simply did not know how to accept this apparent sincerity of his and all his readiness to do the right thing, but I began wondering why indeed I shouldn't believe in it. Whatever sort of man he was, and no matter what was said about him, he could still be someone with good intentions. I also took a look at the seven-line note from Versilov withdrawing his challenge. Although he did refer in it to his 'small-minded egoism', the note as a whole was distinguished by a kind of haughtiness or— better—an air of negligence over the whole business. I did not mention this.

'How do you regard this withdrawal?' I asked. 'Do you consider his behaviour cowardly?'

'Of course not,' smiled the prince, but his smile was a very serious one, and in general he became more and more preoccupied. 'I know only too well he is a man of courage. He has, of course, his own view of things . . . his own set of ideas . . .'

'Certainly he has!' I interrupted. 'Someone I know called Vasin says his behaviour over the letter and his renunciation of the inheritance show he wants to set himself up on a pedestal. In my opinion, things like that aren't done just for show but are basic and intrinsic to a person.'

'I know Mr Vasin very well,' remarked the prince.

'Oh, yes, you must have seen him in Luga.'

We suddenly glanced at each other and I remember I blushed very slightly. He, at least, broke off the conversation. For my own part, I had been very keen to continue it. The thought of yesterday's encounter tempted me to ask him several questions, except I didn't know where to begin. In general I was a bit unsure of myself. I was awed by his astonishing urbanity, his politeness and his free-and-easy manner—awed, in short, by the surface brilliance of his tone which people like him seem to acquire virtually in the cradle. Yet I had noticed he had made a couple of grammatical howlers in his letter, and in general when I meet people of his sort I never kowtow but become increasingly sharp, which is perhaps sometimes bad behaviour. In the present case I was particularly helped by the thought that I was covered in fluff, so I was even inclined to say to hell with it all and be familiar . . . I noticed the prince eyeing me very intently from time to time.

'Tell me, prince,' I burst out suddenly, 'don't you find it funny that such a novice as I am should want to challenge you to a duel—and for an insult to someone else, what's more?'

'One can be very insulted by an insult to one's father. No, I don't find it funny.'

'I think it must seem frightfully funny—from someone else's point of view, of course, not my own. The more so since my name's Dolgoruky, not Versilov. If you're not being truthful with me or somehow want to soften the blow for reasons of social propriety, then how do I know you're not deceiving me in everything else?'

'No, I don't find it funny,' he repeated terribly seriously. 'Surely you can feel your father's blood in your veins, can't you? True, you're still very young, because . . . I'm not sure, but I think someone under 21 cannot fight a duel and the rules say one cannot accept a challenge from someone of that age . . . But, if you like, there can only be one serious objection, and it's this: if you are issuing your challenge without the knowledge of the injured party on whose behalf you are doing it, aren't you in some way showing your personal lack of respect for him?'

Our conversation was suddenly interrupted by the arrival of a servant with an announcement. On seeing him the prince, who had apparently been waiting for him, stood up without finishing and walked briskly over to him, so that the announcement was made in a low voice and I heard none of it.

'Excuse me,' the prince addressed me. 'I'll be back in a moment.'

And he went out.

I was left on my own. I walked to and fro about the room and started thinking. I found it strange that I both liked and disliked him a great deal. There was something about him I couldn't define, but it was something repugnant. 'If he doesn't laugh at me even the teeniest bit, then he's undoubtedly terribly sincere. But,' I thought in the oddest way, 'if he *had* laughed at me, I'd probably have thought him a lot cleverer!'

I went to the writing-table and again read his letter to Versilov. I grew so interested in it, I even forgot about the time and when I came to my senses I suddenly noticed the prince's 'moment' had turned into a whole quarter of an hour. I was a bit upset by this. After walking up and down again, I finally seized my hat and decided, I remember, to leave the room to go and find a servant who could fetch the prince, so that when he came my farewells could be conveyed with the assurance that I had things to attend to and was unable to wait. I thought this would be the politest thing to do because I couldn't help being tormented by the notion that, in leaving me alone for so long, he was being inconsiderate.

Both closed doors to the room came at both ends of the same wall. Forgetting which door we had come in by, but more because I wasn't paying proper attention, I opened one of them and suddenly, in a long, narrow room, caught sight of my sister Liza sitting on a divan. There was no one there apart from her and she was obviously waiting for someone. But before I could even be surprised at the sight I heard the voice of the prince in loud conversation with someone as he returned to the study. I quickly closed the door and the prince, entering through the other door, noticed nothing. I remember that he started apologizing and then mentioned someone called Anna Fyodorovna. But I was so confused and shaken I could hardly make head or tail of anything and simply babbled out something about having to go home and insisted on leaving quickly. The well-bred prince could of course do no more than study my behaviour with some curiosity. He accompanied me to the front door, talking all the time, but I did not respond and did not look at him.

IV

Going out on to the street, I turned left and walked nowhere in particular. My head was full of disjointed thoughts. I strolled on and had gone a good many paces, I think—fifty or so—when I suddenly felt a tap on my shoulder. I turned round and saw Liza. She had caught up with me and had tapped me with her umbrella. There was something terribly happy and also a wee bit sly in her glowing features.

'I'm delighted you've come this way, otherwise I wouldn't have seen you today!' She was trying to catch her breath after walking fast.

'You're terribly out of breath!'

'I was hurrying to catch up with you.'

'Liza, didn't I see you just now?'

'Where?'

'At the prince's—at Prince Sokolsky's.'

'No, it wasn't me, you didn't see me there.'

I said nothing and we walked a dozen steps in silence. Bursting out laughing, Liza said:

'It was me, me, of course it was me! Look, you saw me, you looked straight at me and I looked straight at you, so why do you ask? Oh, you're a funny boy! You know, I desperately wanted to laugh when you looked straight at me because you had such a terribly funny look on your face!'

She roared with laughter. I felt all the pain had gone from my heart.

'Tell me what you were doing there.'

'I was at Anna Fydorovna's.'

'Who's Anna Fyodorovna?'

'Anna Fyodorovna Stolbeev. When we lived in Luga, I used to spend days at a time with her. She always liked mother to visit her and she even used to come and see us. But she hardly visited anyone else there. She's a distant relative of Andrey Petrovich. She is also related to the Princes Sokolsky. She's a sort of grandma to the prince.'

'You mean she lives with him?'

'No, the prince lives with her.'

'So whose apartment is it?'

'It's hers, she's taken it for the whole year. The prince has only just arrived and is staying with her. She herself's only back in St Petersburg four days.'

'I see. You know something, Liza, I couldn't care less about her or her apartment . . .'

'No, she's a lovely person.'

'Maybe she is! Maybe butter wouldn't melt in her mouth! What matters is *we*'re the loveliest of all! Look how beautiful it is today! Look how beautiful you are today, Liza! But you're still dreadfully childish . . .'

'Arkady, tell me about that girl, the one who came yesterday.'

206

'Oh, that's such a pity, Liza, such an awful pity!'

'Yes, an awful pity! What a thing to happen! You know, it even makes me feel wrong that we're walking along here so happily and her soul is now flitting about in the dark, in some infinite gloom, a soul that's transgressed and full of resentment ... Arkady, who's to blame for what she did? Oh, it's horrible! Do you ever think about that darkness? I'm frightened of dying and I know it's wrong to be! I hate the dark. Give me the sun every time! Mother says it's wrong to be frightened ... Arkady, how well do you know mother?'

'Far too little, Liza, far too little.'

'What a marvellous person she is! You really ought to get to know her. She's someone you've got to take care to understand.'

'Yes, it's just like not knowing you, and now I know everything. I've discovered it all in a flash. Liza, even though you may be frightened of death, you're definitely proud and bold and courageous. Far better than me, far better! I'm terribly fond of you, Liza. Oh, my dear Liza, let death come when it has to, but now it's time to live! We can be sorry for that poor, unfortunate girl, but let's give life our blessing, shall we? Shall we? I have my own "Idea"—you know that, don't you? Liza, you know, don't you, that Versilov's renounced his inheritance?'

'Of course! Mother and I were overjoyed.'

'You don't really know me, Liza, and you don't really know what that man has meant to me ...'

'What's there to know? I know all about it.'

'All about it? Well, maybe! You're clever. You're cleverer than Vasin. You and mother have both got such sharp, perceptive eyes, such understanding ones ... I don't mean eyes, I mean the way you look at people ... I'm talking nonsense, I'm bad at all sorts of things, Liza!'

'You need taking in hand, that's all!'

'Please take me in hand, Liza. Oh, it's lovely to see you today! Have you any idea at all how pretty you are? I've never really looked in your eyes before ... Now's the first time I've seen them properly ... Where did you get them from today, Liza? Where did you buy them? How much were they? Liza, I've never had a real friend, and I know my Idea's nonsense, but I know it's not nonsense being with you ... Let's be real friends, shall we? Do you understand what I mean?'

'I understand very well.'

'You know, without any conditions, without any contract, simply being friends!'

'Yes, simply being friends, simply that—except on one condition that if we ever accuse each other of anything, if we ever fall out over something, if we ever say bad things to each other or behave badly, even if we forget everything else, then we'll never forget today and this very moment! We must give ourselves our word. We must promise we'll always remember how we walked arm in arm today and laughed and felt so happy . . . Do you agree?'

'Yes, Liza, yes, and I swear I will. But, Liza, you know it's just as if I've never heard you say anything before . . . Do you read many books?'

'So now he asks! Yesterday was the first time, when I made a slip over a word, that you deigned to pay me any attention, my good sir, my Mister Brainy!'

'Why on earth didn't you say something first if I was such a young fool?'

'I kept on waiting for you to grow up. I saw right through you from the start, Arkady Makarovich, and I just thought to myself: "He'll come round in the end, he'll end by coming round." Well, I thought it best to leave you the honour of taking the first step. "No," I thought, "just you come to me now!"'

'Oh, what a coquette you are! Liza, tell me straight out—did you laugh at me a lot over the past month?'

'Oh, you're terribly funny, you're really quite comic, Arkady! You know, I probably liked you most of all over this month because you're such an odd person. But in many ways your oddness is bad and you mustn't be proud of it. You know something—who do you think also laughed at you? Mother—mother and me, we both did. "Isn't he odd?" we'd whisper. "He's just quite crazy!" And you'd be sitting there thinking we were frightened to death of you!'

'Liza, what do you think about Versilov?'

'I think a great deal of him. But now's not the time to talk about him. We won't say anything about him today—agreed?'

'I agree absolutely! Yes, you're terribly clever, Liza! You're a whole lot cleverer than me. Liza, in a while, when I'm through with all this, then maybe I'll tell you something . . .'

'What are you frowning for?'

'No, I wasn't frowning, it was just that I . . . Look, Liza, it'll be better if I come straight out with it. It's in my make-up that I don't like people touching on certain private feelings I find ticklish . . . or, rather, if certain feelings are often brought to the surface for people to admire, then I feel ashamed—do you know what I mean? So I just prefer to frown and say nothing. You're clever, you know what I mean.'

'Yes. What's more, I'm just the same. I know just what you mean. Mother's just like that, too.'

'Oh, Liza, you ought to go on living on this earth just as long, as long as you can! What do you say to that?'

'I don't say anything.'

'What are you looking at?'

'You're the one who's doing the looking, too! I look at you and I love you.'

I took her almost right home and gave her my new address. When we parted, I kissed her for the first time in my life.

V

And that would have been all very well, but there was one thing that wasn't. An idea had been weighing me down ever since the previous night and I couldn't get it out of my mind. It concerned the fact that when I had met that unfortunate girl at our gates the previous evening I had told her that I was myself leaving home, leaving the family nest, that people leave the wicked behind and make their own nests for themselves and that Versilov had many illegitimate children. Such words about a father from his son must have confirmed all her suspicions about Versilov and the fact that he had humiliated her. I had been putting the blame on Stebelkov when perhaps I was the one who had poured oil on the flames . . .

But then, that morning, although I'd begun to be tormented by the idea, it still seemed to me nonsense. 'It could have all come to the boil without me,' I thought from time to time. 'It doesn't matter, it'll pass! I'll get over it! I'll get the better of it by doing some good deed! I've still got fifty years ahead of me!'

But the idea still weighed me down.

PART II

CHAPTER I

I

I WILL skip on almost a couple of months. The reader need not be worried. Everything will become clear from the ensuing narrative.

I particularly emphasize 15 November—a day I remember only too well for many reasons. Firstly, because no one who had seen me two months before would have recognized me—at least, not judging by my outward appearance, although I might have been recognized but not understood. The first thing was that I was dressed like a real dandy. The conscientious Frenchman with taste who had been recommended to me by Versilov not only made me a new suit, but was already rejected by me in favour of other first-class tailors and I even had an account with them. I also had an account at a well-known restaurant, but I was still a bit unsure of myself there and used to pay right away in cash although I knew this was not the done thing and that I was letting myself down by doing so.

On the Nevsky I had made friends with a French hairdresser and when I went to get my hair done he told me all sorts of stories. I admit I practised my French on him. Although I knew French, and even knew it rather well, I was still uneasy about using it in polite society. My accent, what is more, was far from being really Parisian. I had a servant called Matvey, a dare-devil expert at driving a carriage who was at my beck and call whenever I needed him. He had a light-bay stallion of a trotter (I cannot stand greys).

Besides, not everything was as it should be. It was 15 November and winter had arrived three days before and my fur coat was an old raccoon one, a cast-off of Versilov's not worth more than twenty-five roubles. I had to get a new one but my pockets were empty and, apart from that, I had to save up some money for the evening that day no matter what happened. Otherwise I'd be 'completely done for!'—the very words I used of myself at the time. Oh, what a young bastard I really was! Where on earth had all the money, the carriage and dare-devil driver, the accounts at fashionable restaurants—where had it all come from? How could I have forgotten everything and changed

213

so much? It was disgraceful! Reader, I am now about to tell you the story of my shame and disgrace. Nothing in my life can ever be more shameful than these memories of mine!

I speak like a judge and I know I am guilty. In the vortex of events which swallowed me up at the time, though I was alone, without a guide and counsellor, I still knew how low I had sunk, I swear it, and was therefore fully to blame. And throughout those couple of months I was almost happy ... Why 'almost'? No, I was too happy for words! And even so far as being aware of any disgrace (glimpsed a good many times, for sure, and making me literally shudder) even that awareness—can you believe it?—redoubled my intoxication by making me think, 'All right, so I'll go right to the bottom, or no, I won't, I'll get out of it—I've been born under a lucky star!' I felt I was walking over the frailest of plank bridges above a precipice, with no handrails, and even enjoying it. I even enjoyed looking right down into the precipice. It was risky and that's what I liked.

And my Idea? My Idea could come later; it could wait. Everything that happened was simply a temporary diversion. Why shouldn't I enjoy myself? I asked myself. But that's just what was wrong with my Idea, I repeat. It allowed for too many diversions. If it had been less firm and radical, I might, perhaps, have been fearful of being diverted from it.

Meanwhile, I still had my little lodging, but I did not live there. My case was there, my knapsack and other things, but my main residence was at Prince Sergey Sokolsky's. That's where I lived and slept and spent whole weeks on end ... I'll tell how that came about in a moment. Meanwhile, a word or two about my own little place.

It was dear to me because Versilov had himself come to see me there first thing after our row, and later he came many times. I repeat that this was a time of frightful shame to me, but also of enormous happiness. Yes, it was a time of success and a time for smiles. Why on earth did I have so many glooms before? I used to ask myself in moments of elation. What was the point of remembering all my old hurts, my grim and solitary childhood, the dreams I nursed under my bedcover, the vows I made, the calculations—and even my Idea? Those were things I had invented for myself, something I had made up, and it had turned out that the real world was not like that at all. Here I was feeling light-hearted and joyous. I had Versilov as my father, Prince Seryozha as my friend, and there was something else, too . . .

But we'll leave that until later. Alas, everything was apparently being done in the name of love, magnanimity, and honour, but turned out later to be hideous, brazen, and dishonest.

That's enough for now.

II

He came to see me for the first time on the third day after our rift. I was not there and he had to wait. When I entered my tiny room, even though I had been expecting him for three days, I was overwhelmed and could scarcely see where I was going. My heart best so fast I even had to stop in the doorway. Fortunately he was sitting with my landlord who, to ensure no guest of his would be bored, had found it necessary to make his acquaintance at once and start busily telling him something. He was a civil servant of about 40 years of age, very pock-marked, very poor, burdened with a consumptive wife and a sick child. He was a man of extraordinarily affable and mild character who was also fairly sensitive. I was glad to find him there because he guaranteed I would have something to say to Versilov. I knew, knew quite seriously, throughout the three days, that Versilov would make the first move and come of his own accord, exactly as I wanted, because nothing in the world would have made me go to him first, and not out of bloody-mindedness but out of love for him, out of love mixed with envy—I don't know how to express it. (Generally speaking, the reader will not find me one for flowery language.) But although I had been awaiting his arrival for three days and had hardly ever ceased trying to imagine how he would look as he entered, I still couldn't imagine, no matter how hard I tried, what we might find to talk about on the spur of the moment after all that had happened.

'Ah, there you are!' He offered me his hand in a friendly way without getting up. 'Sit down and join us. Pyotr Ippolitovich is telling the extremely interesting story of that stone near the Pavlovsky Barracks . . . or wherever it is . . .'

'Yes, I know it,' I answered, taking a seat next to them. They were sitting at the table. The whole room was only about three metres square. I drew in a deep breath.

215

A glint of dissatisfaction shone in Versilov's eye for a moment because I imagine he had his doubts about me and thought I might be on the point of making a scene. Then he calmed down.

'Do start from the beginning again, Pyotr Ippolitovich.'

They were already on first-name terms.

'It all happened, sir, under the late tsar,'* Pyotr Ippolitovich said to me nervously and with a certain painful striving for effect. 'You must know what I mean by the stone—that stupid thing right in the middle of the street and getting in everyone's way. The tsar went that way frequently and each time there it was . . . At long last the sovereign got fed up with it and rightly so, too, because it was a huge thing, stood like a mountain in the middle of the street. 'Get rid of it!' he ordered. Well, they all knew what he meant when he said 'Get rid of it!' You remember what the late tsar was like, don't you? But how to get rid of the stone— that was the problem. They all lost their heads. The city council and chiefly one of the bigwigs—I don't remember who—was responsible. This bigwig heard people saying it would cost at least fifteen thousand roubles to get rid of it, and in silver money, too (because under the late tsar they only used silver roubles, not paper money). 'Fifteen thousand roubles—absolutely crazy!' he said. To start with Englishmen suggested laying rails to it and carting it away with steam. But what the hell would that cost? We didn't have any railways then, except the one out to Tsarskoe Selo . . .'*

'It could be sawn up, couldn't it?' I said, beginning to frown with annoyance. I was terribly annoyed and ashamed at all this going on in front of Versilov. But he was listening with evident pleasure. I realized he was glad to have the land-lord there because I could see he was also ill at ease in my presence and I remember I even found this rather touching.

'That's right, that's just what they chose to do! It was precisely Montferrant, the architect of St Isaac's,*who talked of cutting it up and carting it away. Yessir, but what d'you think that would have cost?'

'Nothing. You just cut it up and cart it away.'

'No, just hang on a bit—you'd need to bring up an engine for that, and a steam one, sir, and then where do you dump all the stuff? A mountain like that? You wouldn't get away with less than ten or twelve thousand, you know . . .'

'Please listen a moment, Pyotr Ippolitovich, this is all non-sense, you know that. It wasn't like that at all . . .'

But at that moment Versilov winked at me, and in that wink I saw such tactful fellow-feeling for the landlord, even pity for him, I was utterly delighted and burst out laughing.

'Well, all right, all right,' said the delighted landlord who had not noticed the wink and was terribly worried, like all story-tellers, that he might be asked questions, 'except that up comes some local fellow, a young chap, you know, a Russian with a little wedge-shaped beard in a long caftan and a bit drunk—except no, sir, he wasn't drunk, not drunk, sir, no. He just stands there, this fellow does, while the Englishmen and Montferrant confer and the responsible bigwig drives up in a carriage and listens to what they've got to say and gets annoyed at the way they can't make up their minds. And all of a sudden he sees this fellow standing at some distance with a kind of, you know, false smile on his face—not a false smile, no, sort of . . .'

'Mocking?' suggested Versilov cautiously.

'Mocking, yessir, a little bit mocking, except it's a good, kind, Russian smile, you know what I mean, and, well, that's what annoys the bigwig, and he says: "Hey, you there, with the beard, what're you hanging about here for? Who are you?" And the fellow says, "I'm looking at the lump of stone, Your Grace." I think that's what he says—"Your Grace"—because he was someone or other like Prince Suvorov, you know, the one famous in Italy, a descendant of his . . . No, it wasn't Suvorov, I just can't recall who it was, but, you know, he was a Your Grace, you know, a pure Russian kind of man, a Russian type, a patriot, with a Russian heart of gold. Well, he said to the fellow on the off chance: "You think you can get rid of it, eh? What're you grinning at?" "At the Englishmen mostly, Your Grace," the fellow says, "'cos they'll be asking such a high price, sir, because the Russians've got fat purses and they've got nothing to eat back home. For a hundred roubles, Your Grace, we'll get rid of that lump of stone by tomorrow evening." Well, you can imagine the effect of that. The Englishmen, naturally enough, want to get their teeth into him and Montferrant just laughs. Except that the most gracious high-and-mighty so-and-so, the Russian heart of gold, says: "Give you a hundred roubles! You can't really get rid of it, can you?" "We'll have it done by tomorrow evening, Your

217

Grace." "How are you going to do it?" "That's our secret, sir—no offence intended, Your Grace." He speaks, you know, quite plainly. Your Grace likes it. "Give him what he asks," he says. Well, that's how they left it. So what do you think he did?'

The landlord stopped and surveyed us with his jovial gaze.

'I've no idea,' smiled Versilov, while I frowned.

'This is what he did, sir,' said the landlord triumphantly, as if he had done it himself. "He hired peasants with spades, just ordinary Russian peasants, and set about digging a huge hole just beside the stone. They went on digging all night and made a gigantic hole, just about the size of the stone, only a little deeper, and when they'd done this he ordered them to start digging cautiously right under the stone. Well, naturally, the more they dug underneath the less there was for the stone to rest on and it began to topple, and so, with a great hurrah, they pushed it from the other side—the stone went plop into the hole! Then they covered it over, rolled the soil flat, laid paving—and it was smooth, the stone had gone!'

'Well I never!' said Versilov.

'The people came running, such a crowd. The Englishmen had got wind of what was happening and were furious. Montferrant rode up and said it was too primitively done, too simple. But that's the whole point, it *was* simple, and you fools, you hadn't sussed it out! So I'll tell you the man in charge, the official, he was astonished, hugged the chap who'd done it, kissed him and asked him where he was from. "From Yaroslav Province, your excellency, by trade I'm a tailor, but in the summer we come to the capital to sell fruit." Well, the authorities heard about it and gave him a medal to hang round his neck and he walked about with it round his neck and got dead drunk—you know what they say, a Russian can't do things by halves! That's why foreigners go on getting the better of us—yessir, indeed!'

'Of course the way the Russians think . . .' Versilov began.

At this point the story-teller had the good luck to be summoned by his sick wife and dashed off, otherwise I wouldn't have been able to restrain myself. Versilov gave a laugh.

'My dear boy, he had been entertaining me a whole hour before you came. That stone . . . of all such stories, it's the most idiotic patriotic whimsy, but how could I stop him? He was simply melting with pleasure. That apart, though, I think the

218

stone's still there, if I'm not mistaken, and not put in a hole at all . . .'

'Oh, my God,' I cried, 'that's absolutely true! How could he dare tell a story like that?'

'Why get so worked up? I think you're taking it far too seriously. Don't. He's actually got mixed up. I heard something of the same kind about a stone when I was a child, only it wasn't *that* story and it wasn't *that* stone. I mean to say—when he said "the authorities heard about it" he was in seventh heaven. People like him have to tell stories like that. They've got masses of them to tell—you know, they're sort of incontinent with them. They've never had any schooling, don't know anything except how to play cards and prattle about this and that, and yet there's this desire to talk about something great and universal, something poetic . . . Who is he, this Pyotr Ippolitovich?'*

'Poorest of the poor, and even down on his luck.'

'Well, then, it's very likely he doesn't even play cards! I repeat that, in telling this nonsense, he is satisfying his love for mankind, since, after all, he had wanted to cheer us up. His patriotism is satisfied at the same time. The same is true of that story about that Russian manufacturer to whom the English paid a million roubles not to put any trademark on his goods . . .'

'Oh, my God, I've heard that story.'

'Who hasn't? The fellow telling you knows that only too well, but he still tells it, *deliberately* pretending you've never heard it before. The vision which appeared to the Swedish king—I think that's a bit out of date now, but when I was young it was passed around in mysterious whispers just like the story that at the beginning of the century someone knelt down in the senate in front of all the senators.* There was a lot about General Bashutsky and the stolen monument. And people are terribly fond of scandal at court—you know, the one about the minister, Chernyshev,* under the last tsar and how he, as a 70-year-old, made himself up to look as if he were 30 and how astonished the late tsar was to see him at parties . . .'

'I've heard that, too.'

'Of course, everyone has. All these stories are the height of impropriety, but it's a type of scandalmongering that goes much deeper and is far more widespread than we think. The wish to tell lies with the aim of pleasing one's neighbour can even occur

219

in the most respectable society, because we all suffer from the same intemperance in our hearts. The only difference is that our stories are of a different kind—we only talk about America or somewhere—and how we love it, even people in the government! I admit I myself belong to this improper type and have done all my life . . .'

'I've told that one about Chernyshev several times.'

'You have?'

'Apart from me, there's another lodger here, an official, also pock-marked, an old man, but he's a terrible stickler for facts and as soon as Pyotr Ippolitovich starts off he begins interrupting and contradicting him. It's reached such a point that our landlord'll do anything for him just to get him to listen.'

'That's another type of scandalous talk and perhaps it's even worse than the first. The first is madly enthusiastic—you know: "All right, so make it all up and just see how well it works out!" The second is all malicious nit-picking: "I won't let you get away with it—where did such-and-such happen, when, in what year?" In a word, it's heartless. My dear boy, there's nothing wrong with letting someone tell a few fibs now and then. Even a whole lot. In the firt place, it shows how tactful you are and, secondly, it'll let you tell a few of your own—two enormous advantages straight off. Devil take it! or *Que diable!*, as they say, one's got to be in love and charity with one's neighbour . . . But it's time I was going. You've got a nice place here,' he added, rising from his chair. 'I'll tell Sofya Andreevna and your sister that I dropped by and found you in the best of health. Goodbye, dear boy!'

That wasn't the end, was it? I'd not been needing anything like that at all. I'd been expecting him to talk about something else, the *main thing*, although I fully understood that it couldn't be otherwise.

I accompanied him downstairs with a candle. The landlord tried to waylay us but, without Versilov knowing, I grabbed him by the arm and gave him a ferocious shove. He glanced at me in astonishment and instantly made himself scarce.

'Oh, these staircases . . .' drawled Versilov, spinning the words out so as to say something and evidently frightened I might butt in '. . . oh, these staircases—I'm not used to them and you're on the third floor, but I'll find my way . . . Don't worry, dear boy. Don't you catch cold.'

But I stayed with him. We went down the second flight.

'I've been expecting to see you for the past three days.'

The words burst from me suddenly as if of their own accord. I was out of breath.

'Thank you, dear boy.'

'I knew you'd be bound to come.'

'And I knew you knew I'd be bound to come. Thank you, dear boy.'

He fell silent. We had already reached the front door and I was still behind him. He opened the door and the inrush of wind extinguished my candle. At that point I suddenly seized him by the hand. It was completely dark. He gave a shudder but did not speak. I put my lips to his hand and suddenly started hungrily kissing it, at first a few times and then time and time again.

'My dear boy, what on earth makes you so fond of me?' he asked, but in a quite different voice. His voice shook and had a completely new ring to it, as if someone else had said the words.

I tried to say something in return but could not and ran back upstairs. He stayed where he was and it was only as I reached my room that I heard the outer door below being opened and then banging shut. Slipping past the landlord, who had again popped out, I entered my room, turned the key in the latch and, without lighting a candle, flung myself on my bed, pressed my face into my pillow and burst into tears. It was the first time I had cried since being at Touchard's! The sobs broke from me with such force and yet I was so happy . . .

Oh, I can't describe it! I've put it all down on paper now without a scrap of shame because it probably felt good despite all its absurdity.

III

But he really got it in the neck from me for that! I became frightfully bossy. That scene was never again mentioned between us. On the contrary, we met a couple of days later as if nothing had happened. What's more, I was almost rude to him that second time and he was also very caustic with me. It again took place at my lodging. I was still reluctant to take the initiative and visit him, no matter how much I wanted to see mother.

The whole time—throughout those two months, I mean—we

always talked about the most abstract subjects. And it astonishes me that we did precisely that, talking all the time about abstract matters—of common human interest, of course, and things that needed talking about very much—but not of immediate concern to ourselves. In the mean time a great deal—a very great deal— of immediate concern to ourselves needed defining and clarifying, and even urgently, but we said not a word about it. I even said nothing about mother and Liza and . . . well, nothing, too, about myself and my past. Whether this was from shame or youthful stupidity I do not know. I suppose it was from stupidity because it was easy enough to skip the feeling of shame. I was frightfully bossy with him and more than once really got on a high horse with him, even against my better judgement, because it all came bursting out and I could not restrain myself.

His own tone was, as before, tinged with a certain delicate mockery, although it was always exceptionally fond no matter what was said. I was also struck by the fact that he much preferred coming to me, so that I finally visited mother terribly rarely, once a week only, no more, particularly in recent times when I lost my head for good and all. He would only come in the evenings and sit down and chat. He was also very fond of chatting with my landlord—and this infuriated me coming from someone like him. It also occurred to me that he probably preferred seeing him to seeing me. But I knew for sure that he had other acquaintances. In the recent past he had renewed many of his connections in polite society which had been abandoned by him over the past year. Yet I think he was not particularly enchanted by them and renewed many of them only in an official sense, preferring to call on me instead. I was sometimes very touched that, on entering each evening, he almost always showed signs of diffidence, opening the door and always glancing in my eyes with a strangely anxious look to start with, as if to say: 'I'm not disturbing you, am I? If I am, just say the word and I'll go.' He sometimes even said as much. On one occasion, for instance, just lately, he came in when I was already fully dressed in a new suit which had just come from the tailor and when I was about to leave to go to 'Prince Seryozha', in order to go off somewhere (where—I'll explain later). After coming in, he sat down, probably not having noticed I was on the point of going out. He showed signs of being exceptionally

222

absent-minded at times. He started talking about the landlord and I flew into a rage:

'Oh, damn the bloody landlord!'

'My dear boy!' He suddenly jumped up. 'Yes, I see you're on your way out and I'm in your way. Please forgive me.'

And he hurried to be off in all humility. It was just such humility shown to me by such a man, by such a worldly and independent man who had so much of his own, that instantly revived in my heart all my fondness for him and all my faith in him. But if he had really loved me, why hadn't he stopped me then as I hurtled towards shame and disgrace? If he had said one word, I might have desisted. Or maybe not. But he saw it all with his own eyes—the playing at being a dandy, the showing off, my coachman Matvey (I even wanted to offer him a lift, but he wouldn't take it, and that happened more than once)—and he saw with his own eyes the way I let money pour through my fingers, and yet he never said a word, not a word, and didn't even seem to be interested! This has always surprised me and still does. And I, naturally, never stood on ceremony with him in the least at that time and was quite open about everything, although of course I also never said a word in explanation. He never asked and I never spoke about it.

However, there were a few times when we talked about essentials. I asked him once at the start, shortly after he had refused the inheritance, what he proposed to live on.

'I'll get by, dear boy,' he uttered with extraordinary composure.

Now I know that half of even Tatyana Pavlovna's tiny capital, amounting to some five thousand roubles, was expended on Versilov in the last couple of years.

Another time we talked about mother.

'Dear boy,' he said, suddenly sad, 'I often told Sofya Andreyevna at the start of our relationship—at both the start and in the middle and at the end—"Darling, I'm difficult to live with and I'll go on being difficult, but so long as you're here I'll never feel sorry; but if you were to die, I know that would be my death warrant!"'

I remember that evening he was particularly frank.

'If only I'd been a characterless nonentity I'd have suffered from knowing this! But no, that wasn't so. I knew, after all, I was limitlessly strong—and why. Do you know why? Precisely

223

through that straightforward power of being able to adjust to anything, which is so characteristic of all intelligent Russians of our generation. You can't destroy me, can't get rid of me, can't even take me by surprise. I'm as indestructible as a mongrel dog. I can be completely at home feeling two quite contrary emotions at one and the same time—and not of course because I want to. I know this is dishonest, for the chief reason that it's far, far too reasonable. I'm almost 50 and I'm still not sure whether it's a good thing or a bad thing to have lived so long. Of course, I love to be alive, and yet that's beside the point. For someone like me to love life is . . . is despicable. Recently something new has begun and the Krafts of this world haven't been able to live with it, they've shot themselves. But it's obvious the Krafts of this world are silly, whereas we're clever—or so one supposes. But one can't draw any parallels here, and the question remains open. Is the world, though, only for people like us? Very likely the answer is yes, but it's a far too joyless thought. Still . . . still, the question must remain open.'

He spoke with sadness in his voice, but I had no idea whether he was sincere or not. He had some sort of skeleton in the cupboard which he could never leave well alone.

IV

I overwhelmed him with questions at that time, literally flung myself on him like a starving man hungry for bread. He always gave me ready and direct answers, but in the end always resorted to the most commonplace aphorisms so that, in essence, nothing could be properly thrashed out. Yet these were questions which had troubled me all my life and, I admit quite openly, I had put off answering them in Moscow precisely because I had been waiting to discuss them with him in St Petersburg. I even told him so. He didn't laugh at me. On the contrary, he squeezed my hand. I could get almost nothing out of him about politics and social questions, but it was these questions, bearing in mind my Idea, which most troubled me. As regards people like Dergachev, I once extracted from him the remark that they 'were beneath criticism', but at the same time he added oddly that 'I reserve the right not to attribute any significance to what I've just said.' As regards the way the states of the present day and the world as we know it will end and how society could be rejuvenated, he was silent a frightfully long time, but I finally wheedled a few words from him on one occasion:

'I think all this will work itself out in an exceptionally ordinary way. Put quite simply, all states, no matter how balanced their budgets and how small their deficits, will end up one fine morning—*un beau matin*, as they say—in total confusion and not wanting to pay anyone anything, so that they can one and all be renewed through universal bankruptcy. In the mean time, the entire conservative element in the world will be opposed to this, because they're the shareholders and creditors, after all, and won't want to have everyone bankrupt. That'll be followed, naturally, by a general process of oxidization, as it were. Jews will take over and a Jewish kingdom will be established. All those who've never owned shares, indeed who've never owned anything at all, all the beggars, that's to say, naturally won't want to be part of this general oxidization. There'll be a fearful struggle and, after seventy and seven defeats, the beggars'll wipe the floor with the shareholders, take over their shares, and take their place, becoming shareholders themselves, of course. Maybe they'll have some new message for mankind, maybe they won't. Most likely they'll end up bankrupt too. I can't go any further, dear boy, in foretelling what'll change the face of the world. However, you can always take a look at the Apocalypse of St John . . .'

'Has everything got to be materialistic? Will the world as we know it come to an end simply because of money?'

'Oh, I chose to talk only about one corner of the picture, of course, but that corner is linked to everything else by unbreakable bonds, so to speak.'

'So what's to be done about it?'

'Oh, my God, you shouldn't jump the gun! None of it'll happen all that soon. Generally speaking, the best thing is to do nothing at all. At least you can then have a quiet conscience at not being part of it.'

'That's enough of that! Get to the point! I want to know what I should *do*, how I should *live*!'

'What you should *do*, dear boy? Be honest, don't tell lies, don't covet thy neighbour's house—in short, read the ten commandments in the Old Testament. It's all written down there.'

225

'Enough! Stop it! That's all such old stuff—and it's just so many words. I want to know what to *do*!'

'Well, if you're very, very bored, try falling in love with someone or something or simply getting involved.'

'You're just making a joke of it! And anyhow, what can I do on my own with all your ten commandments?'

'All you have to do is obey them, despite all your queries and doubts, and you'll be a great man.'

'Not known to a soul!'

'There is nothing that will not be revealed eventually.'

'Oh, you're simply joking!'

'All right, then, if you're taking it all to heart so much, the best thing is to try and gain a specialization as soon as possible, specialize in construction work or in the law and then, being occupied with something real and serious, you'll be content with that and forget about all this nonsense.'

I had nothing to say to that. Well, I mean, what on earth could one make of it? And yet, after each of our conversations like that, I became more excited than ever. What's more, I saw clearly there always remained something mysterious about him and this drew me to him more and more closely.

'Listen,' I interrupted him on one occasion, 'I've always suspected that you say all the things you do simply out of malice and pain but that secretly, in your real self, you're fanatically devoted to some higher ideal and are simply concealing it or ashamed of admitting it.'

'Thank you, dear boy.'

'Listen, there's nothing higher than being useful. Tell me how, at this very moment, I can be most useful. I know it's not up to you to decide this, but I'm simply asking your opinion. Whatever you say, however you put it, that's what I'll do, I swear! Okay, so what is the Great Idea?'

'Well, turning stones into bread, that's one.'

'That can't be the greatest thing a man can do, surely? No, that's just pointing the way. You're not telling me that is the greatest thing a man can do, are you?'

'It's a very great one, dear, a very great one, but not the greatest. It's a great one, but of secondary importance and only great at any given moment because a man'll eat his fill and then forget about it. Right away he'll start saying, "Well, I've had

226

enough to eat, so what can I *do* now?" That's the question that remains eternally unanswered.'

'You once talked to me about the "Geneva ideas". I don't understand what these "Geneva ideas" are.'

'The "Geneva ideas" concern the idea of virtue without Christ, dear boy, the ideas of the present day or—better—the idea dominating the whole of present-day civilization.* In short, it's one of those long stories which are very boring, and it'd be a lot better if we talked about something else and even better if we didn't talk at all.'

'You're always passing over things in silence!'

'Dear boy, just bear in mind that silence is a good thing, it is safe and it is golden.'

'Golden?'

'Of course. Silence is always golden, and the silent man is always more precious than the talker.'

'So talking as you and I are is tantamount to saying nothing at all! To hell with being golden and—most of all—to hell with the profit element in it!'

'Dear boy,' he said to me suddenly, slightly altering his tone, even speaking with feeling and particular insistence, 'dear boy, I have no wish at all to entice you with some vision of bourgeois virtue in place of your own ideals, and I am not insisting that happiness is better than being boldly heroic. On the contrary, being boldly heroic is higher than any happiness, and only a capacity for such heroism comprises real happiness. So let that be clear between us. I respect you precisely because you have been able, in this miserably sour time of ours, to nurture in your soul an idea of your own (don't worry, I haven't forgotten about it). But you've still got to keep a sense of proportion, because you're now at the point of wanting to make a big noise in life, set the world alight, blow it all up, set yourself up above Russia, fill the sky like a thunder cloud, leaving everyone full of fear and wonder while you go off and take refuge in the United States of America! You know perfectly well you've got something like that in your soul, so I consider it necessary to warn you because, dear boy, I am really very fond of you.'

What on earth could I make of that? I could make out his concern for me and my material welfare. In this he was like any father with worldly, but kindly, feelings. But did I need any of

227

this when I was concerned with ideas for which any decent father would have sent his son to possible death, as Horatius in antiquity sent his sons to die for the idea of Rome?*

I often raised questions of religion with him, but here he was vaguer than ever. To the question: what should I do about religion? he answered in the stupidest way as if he were talking to a child:

'One must believe in God, dear boy.'

'Well, what if I don't believe in any of it?' I shouted in annoyance.

'Splendid, dear boy.'

'What do you mean by splendid?'

'Dear boy, that's the most excellent sign, even the most hopeful one, because our Russian atheist, always supposing he is really an atheist and clever enough to be one, is the very best man in the world and always inclined to show God favours because he is undoubtedly kind, and he is kind because he is overflowing with satisfaction at being an atheist. Our atheists are eminently respectable people and reliable in the highest degree, the backbone of the country, so to speak . . .'

That was something, of course, but I didn't want that. He only came out with everything on one occasion, but so strangely I was greatly astonished, particularly in view of his interest in Roman Catholicism and his zealotry, about which I'd heard so much.

'Dear boy,' he said to me once, not in my room but out on the street after a long conversation. I was walking beside him. 'Dear boy, to love people as they are is impossible. And yet one must. And so you've got to be kind to them, suppressing your feelings, pinching your nose and closing your eyes—especially closing your eyes. You've got to put up with their evil-doing, if possible without getting angry, conscious all the time of being a man yourself. Naturally, you're in a position to be stern with them if you're privileged to be a little more clever than the common run. People are despicable and are fond of loving out of fear. Don't give in to such love and never stop despising it. Somewhere in the Koran Allah orders the prophet to look upon the "disobedient" as mice, to be kind to them and pass them by—it's a bit arrogant, but it's right.* You've got to learn how to despise them even when they're good, because more often than not they'll be bloody awful. Dear boy, I say this based on knowing myself!

Anyone who is the faintest bit intelligent cannot live without despising himself—and it doesn't matter whether he's honest or not. It is impossible to love one's neighbour and not despise him. In my opinion, it is physically impossible for a man to love his neighbour. From the very start there's been a kind of verbal confusion at work here. The words "love of humanity" should be understood as only applying to the image of humanity one has created for oneself in one's own soul—in other words, you have created yourself and so you love yourself—but it has never existed in reality and never will.'

'Never will?'

'Dear boy, I agree it might seem a bit silly, but it's not my fault. Because I wasn't consulted when the world was created, I reserve the right to have my own opinion on the matter.'

'Then I don't understand how you can be called a Christian after this,' I cried, 'or a zealot, or a preacher!'

'Who calls me that?'

I told him. He listened very attentively, but that was the end of our conversation.

I simply cannot remember the pretext for this conversation, which I remember so well. But he even came close to losing his temper, which almost never happened in his case. He had spoken passionately and in great seriousness, as if he had not been talking to me. But I still couldn't believe in him. How could he talk seriously to someone like me about such things?

CHAPTER II

I

ON that very morning, 15 November, I found him at Prince Seryozha's. I was the one who had brought them together, although even without my intervention they had a fair number of points of contact (I refer to what had happened abroad and so on). Apart from that, the prince had given him his word to let him have at least one third of the inheritance, which amounted to twenty thousand roubles or so. I remember I found it terribly strange at the time that he was only offering a third and not half.

229

But I kept quiet. The prince had made the promise to share the inheritance of his own accord. Versilov had not so much as breathed a word and had sought nothing. The prince himself had come up with the offer and Versilov had let it be made without saying anything and had not referred to it afterwards and even gave no sign that he remembered the promise being made. I will add that the prince was utterly charmed by him to start with, particularly by his conversation, and went into raptures over him and even told me so several times. He even used to exclaim to me when we were by ourselves and when he was almost in despair at himself that he was 'so uneducated, going about everything the wrong way!' Oh, we were such friends then! Versilov and I tried all the time to find only good things to say about the prince and defend his inadequacies, though he saw them only too clearly himself. But Versilov used to hold his tongue or smile.

'If he has inadequacies,' I once remarked to Versilov, 'then he has at least as many good points as bad!'

'My God, you're really flattering him!' he laughed.

'Flattering?' I didn't understand what he meant.

'As many good points! You're turning him into a saintly relic if you say he's got as many good points as bad!'

Of course, that was not his real opinion. He generally avoided saying anything about the prince at that time, much as he generally avoided talking about essentials. But he particularly said nothing about the prince. I suspected he used to call on the prince without me and that they had a special relationship of their own, but I made allowances for this. I was also not envious about the way he talked to him more seriously than to me, more positively, so to speak, and made fewer jokes. I was so happy at the time I even approved of this. I forgave the fact that the prince was a bit limited and liked an exact use of words, while even failing to understand certain kinds of witticism. And yet recently he had begun to emancipate himself. His feelings towards Versilov changed. Being sensitive to such things, Versilov naturally noticed.

I must also give warning that the prince had changed his attitude towards me, even too obviously. There remained only certain dead forms of our initial, almost fiery friendship. Meanwhile, I still went on visiting him. I could hardly fail to, having been drawn in so deeply. Oh, how inept I was at that time! And was it simply having such a stupid heart that brought me to such ineptitude and humiliation? I used to take money from him and thought I ought to. But no, it wasn't that. I knew at the time I didn't need to, but I simply didn't give it much thought. I didn't visit him for money, although I needed it desperately. I knew I didn't visit him for his money, but each day I realized I was sponging on him. But I wasn't in my right mind and, apart from that, my heart was full of something completely different. It was singing, singing!

When I entered the room at about eleven in the morning, I found Versilov already finishing a long tirade about something. The prince was listening, pacing about the room, while Versilov was seated. The prince seemed in a state of some excitement. Versilov could almost always arouse such excitement in him. The prince was unusually impressionable, to the point of naïvety, which often made me look down on him. But, I repeat, lately I had detected a certain malicious snarling in him. He stopped on seeing me and it was as if he winced. I knew how to explain shades of dissatisfaction on his face that morning, but I had not expected him to wince. I knew there had been an accumulation of various troubles for him, but the nasty thing was I only knew a tenth part of them. The rest of them at that time were a well-kept secret. So it was pretty nasty and silly of me that I frequently pretended to offer him comfort and give advice and even condescended to make fun of his feebleness in losing his temper 'because of such trifles'. He had a habit of saying nothing, but it was impossible for him not to loathe me at times like that because I was in much too false a position and yet did not even suspect it. Oh, let God be my witness that I never suspected the chief thing!

However, he politely offered me his hand. Versilov gave a nod without interrupting what he was saying. I flung myself on a divan and stretched out. How I used to behave in those days, the things I used to do! I even showed off in front of his friends, treating them as my own ... Oh, if only I could change it all now, I'd have done things so differently!

A couple of words, before I forget: the prince was still in the same apartment at that time and occupied almost the whole of it, after Madame Stolbeev, its owner, had been there only a month and once again left.

They were talking about the nobility. I have to say that this was a subject which sometimes greatly excited the prince, despite his view of what was progressive, and I even suspect that much of what went wrong in his life derived from it. Being poor and yet treasuring his princely status, out of a false sense of pride he was continuously spending money and running into debt. Versilov pointed out to him a number of times that this was not what his princely status entailed and tried to make him adopt a loftier view of his role, but the prince ended by taking offence at being told what to do. Evidently something of the kind had been happening that morning, though I did not arrive at the beginning. Versilov's words struck me as retrograde to start with, but he improved later on.

'The word "honour" means duty,' he was saying (I am giving only the gist of what he said as far as I can remember it). 'When a state is dominated by a ruling class, then that country is strong. A ruling class always has its own code of honour, which can be incorrect, but almost always serves to bind together and strengthen a country. Morally useful, it is more useful politically. The rest, all those not belonging to the ruling class, have to put up with it and to ensure their compliance they are all given equal rights. That's what's happened in our case and it's worked well. But all the evidence shows that everywhere to date—in Europe, that is—it is the case that equal rights have caused a reduction in the sense of honour and, therefore, in the sense of duty. Egoism has taken the place of the former unifying idea and everything has disintegrated into a matter of freedom of the individual. Those who have achieved such freedom while having no integrating idea have ultimately lost all contact with anything higher, so much so that they have even ceased defending their own freedom. But the Russian type of nobility has never resembled the European. Our nobility even now, having lost its rights, could still remain an upper class as a defender of honour, learning, science, and a higher ideal and, most important, without turning into a separate caste, which would be the death of the ideal. On the contrary, the gates to that class have been open long ago. Now is the time to open them once and for all. Let every noble achievement in the field of honour, of learning, and of valour give every single one of us the right to join the top rank of people. In this way the entire class could turn itself into a gathering of the best people in a true and literal sense, and not in the former sense of being a privileged caste. In this new or— better—renewed form the class could still maintain its position.'

The prince snarled:

'What sort of a nobility would that be? You're advocating some sort of Masonic lodge, not a nobility.'

I have to repeat that the prince was terribly badly educated. I even turned away in annoyance on my divan, even though I did not entirely agree with Versilov. He was only too aware of the prince's snarling.

'I don't know what you mean when you talk about a Masonic lodge,' he responded, 'but if even a Russian prince renounces such an idea, then it means its time is not yet ripe. The idea of honour and enlightenment as guarantees for anyone wanting to join this class, no longer with restricted entry but continually renewing itself, is, of course, utopian, but why should it be impossible? If the notion is alive at least in a few heads, then it means it hasn't perished yet, but remains alight like a beacon shining in the darkness.'

'You love using terms like "higher idea", "Great Idea", "integrating idea", and so on. I'd like to know exactly what you mean by the term "Great Idea"?'

'I really don't know how to answer you, my dear prince,' said Versilov with a delicate grin. 'If I admit to you that I don't know how to describe it to myself, then that would be nearer the truth. The Great Idea is more often than not a feeling which sometimes remains too long undefined. I simply know that it was always the thing from which living life flowed—not, that is, life as something intellectualized and made up but, on the contrary, life as essentially interesting and joyous. So that the higher idea from which it flows is absolutely essential—to everyone's annoyance, of course.'

233

'Why to everyone's annoyance?'

'Because it's boring to have to live with ideas and always much happier without them.'

The prince took a pill.

'And what's this living life you're talking about?' He was evidently in a foul mood.

'I also don't know, prince. I simply know that it has to be something terribly simple, the most commonplace and obvious of things, the most day-to-day and minute-by-minute thing imaginable, and so simple that we could never believe it was as simple as that and, naturally, have spent many thousands of years passing it by without noticing it and knowing anything about it.'

'I simply mean that your idea for the nobility is also a negation of the nobility,'said the prince.

'Well, if you like to put it that way, then we've probably never had a nobility at all.'

'It's all terribly obscure and unclear. If one says something, in my opinion one ought to elaborate on it . . .'

The prince frowned and glanced at a wall clock. Versilov stood up and picked up his hat.

'Elaborate?' he said. 'No, it's better not to elaborate. In any case, it's my way of doing things—talking without elaborating. And that's the truth. And it's a strange thing, you know, but if I begin elaborating on an idea in which I believe it almost always ends up with my ceasing to believe in what I am saying. I am frightened of doing the same thing now. Goodbye, dear prince. When I'm with you I always chatter away at unforgivable length.'

He went out. The prince politely said goodbye to him, but I felt hurt and annoyed.

'Your feathers ruffled, are they?' he shot at me without giving me a glance as he passed me on the way back to his writing-desk.

'My feathers are ruffled,' I began with a tremor in my voice, 'because of finding such a strange change in your tone towards me and even towards Versilov . . . Of course, Versilov may have started off with some reactionary remarks but he got better later on and . . . and, er, his words may have contained a thought of some profundity, but you simply didn't understand it . . .'

'I simply don't want people telling me what to do and treating me like a child!' he shot at me almost angrily.

'Prince, words like that . . .'

'Please, no theatricals, if you don't mind. I know what I'm doing is mean and dishonest, that I'm a wastrel, a gambler, perhaps even a thief—yes, a thief, because it's the family's money I'm losing—but I don't want to have people passing judgement on me. I don't want it and I won't have it. I'll be my own judge. And why all the double-talk? If he had wanted to tell me off, then he could have said so straight out and not engaged in such a lot of obscure palaver. But in order to tell me what to do, he's got to earn the right, he's got to be honest himself . . .'

'In the first place, I wasn't in on the beginning of your conversation and, secondly, may I ask in what way Versilov was being dishonest?'

'That's enough. Please. Yesterday you asked for three hundred roubles, here they are.'

He laid the money down on the desk in front of me and sat down himself in an armchair, nervously leaned back and flung one leg over the other. I was so confused I was stunned.

'I really don't know,' I mumbled. 'Though I did ask you, and though I really need the money right now, in view of your tone . . .'

'Leave my tone out of it. If I have spoken sharply, then forgive me. I assure you I'm not concerned with that. Listen to what I've got to say. I've received a letter from Moscow. My brother Sasha, still a child, died, as you know, four days ago. My father, as you also know, has been paralysed for two years and now they say he is worse, can't utter words, and doesn't recognize anyone. They are delighted with the inheritance and want to take him abroad. But the doctor writes to say he probably won't live more than a couple of weeks. So it'll mean my mother and sister and I, we'll be the only ones remaining, and now I'll be almost all alone . . . Well, I mean, I *am* all alone . . . The inheritance . . . The inheritance—oh, it would have been better if it had never come at all! But this is what I had wanted to tell you. I promised Andrey Petrovich a minimum of twenty thousand. But meanwhile, as you can imagine, it's been impossible to deal with the formalities. I haven't even . . . we haven't . . . that's to say, my father hasn't even been granted legal rights to the estate. Meantime, over the last three weeks, I've lost such a lot of money and that scoundrel Stebelkov is charging such high interest . . . I've just given you almost the last money there is . . .'

'Oh, prince, if so . . .'

'I'm not referring to that, no. Stebelkov will be bringing some money today for sure and that'll be enough to be going on with, but devil take that man! I asked him to let me have ten thousand, so I'd at least be able to give Andrey Petrovich that much. My promise to give him a third is driving me crazy. I gave my word and I must keep it. And, I swear to you, I'm desperate to free myself from my commitments on that side. They really are a terrible burden, unbearable! The whole friendship with him is getting too much for me—I mean I can't look Andrey Petrovich straight in the eyes any more . . . Why's he doing this to me?'

'What's he doing to you, prince?' I stood in front of him in astonishment. 'Has he been dropping hints?'

'Oh, no, and I appreciate that, but I've been dropping hints to myself. And I'm being sucked in more and more . . . It's that Stebelkov . . .'

'Listen, prince, take it easy, please! I see the more you go on about it, the more worked up you get, and the whole thing could be nothing more than a mirage. Oh, I know I'm involved myself quite unforgivably and dishonestly! But it's only temporary, you know. As soon as I've won back the money what'll it be then? I'll be owing you two thousand five hundred roubles, including this three hundred—that's right, isn't it?'

'I don't think I've asked you for it,' said the prince, suddenly scowling.

'You say you need ten thousand for Versilov. If I take your money now, then this money must come out of the twenty thousand you owe him. I won't take it otherwise. But . . . but I'll let you have this back in any case. You surely don't think Versilov visits you for the money.'

'I would prefer it if he did,' muttered the prince rather oddly.

'You talked about a friendship getting too much for you. If you're referring to your friendship with Versilov and myself, then, by God, I find that insulting! And you ask why he doesn't do as he teaches—well, that's your own logic! In the first place, that's not strictly logical, because, even if he weren't who he is, he would still be able to profess the truth. And finally, what's the word "profess" got to do with it? You talk of him as a prophet.

Tell me, wasn't it you who nicknamed him a "petticoat prophet" when you were in Germany?'

'No, I didn't.'

'Stebelkov told me you did.'

'He was lying. I'm not all that good at making up funny nicknames. But if somebody professes honesty, then he ought to be honest himself—that's my logic and if it's incorrect then I don't give a damn. That's how I want it to be and that's how it will be. And no one, *no one* comes into my house and passes judgement on me and treats me like a child! Enough!' he shouted, waving his hand to make me stop. 'And that's an end to it!'

The door opened and Stebelkov came in.

III

He was exactly the same, just as smartly dressed, sticking his chest out in the same way, looking one stupidly straight in the eyes and trying to give the impression he was clever and very full of himself. But on this occasion, on entering, he was oddly inquisitive. There was something especially cautious and penetrating in his glance, as if he was trying to guess something from our expressions. In a moment, though, he was as composed as ever, and a self-confident smile shone on his lips, that sort of brazenly solicitous smile which I found inexpressibly shifty.

I had been aware for a long time that he had been pestering the prince. He had visited once or twice while I was there. I, also, had had dealings with him during the past month, but this time I had reason to be slightly surprised at his arrival.

'Just a moment,' the prince said to him without greeting him and, turning his back on him, started getting papers and accounts out of his desk. As for me, I had been thoroughly offended by the prince's last words. The reference to Versilov's dishonesty had been so obvious—and so astonishing!—that it deserved some kind of radical explanation. But this would be impossible with Stebelkov there. I once more spread myself out on the divan and opened a book that was lying there.

'Belinsky, Part Two! This is something new! Do you want to improve yourself?' I called out to the prince and I think it must have sounded very artificial. He was very preoccupied and in a hurry, but on hearing my words he suddenly turned to me.

'Please put that book down!' he said sharply.

This went beyond all bounds—and mainly because Stebelkov was there! Quite deliberately Stebelkov gave a clever-clever, shifty grin and surreptitiously included me in a nod towards the prince. I turned away from the idiot and decided not to restrain myself:

'Don't be annoyed, prince. I am giving way in favour of the one who's boss here and meanwhile I won't say another word . . .'

'I'm the boss here, am I?' chimed in Stebelkov, happily pointing at himself.

'Yes. You're the boss here and you know it.'

'No, sir, allow me to say I am always number two. I am *the* number two in the world. There is a number one man and there is a number two. The number one does, and the number two takes. Which means number two becomes number one, and number one number two. Is that so or not?'

'That may be so, only, as usual, I don't understand you.'

'Allow me to explain. There was a revolution in France and everyone was put to death. Along came Napoleon and seized everything. The revolution was number one and Napoleon number two. But it ended up by Napoleon being number one and the revolution being number two. Is that so or not?'

I will mention, among other things, that I saw in the fact of his talking to me about the French revolution evidence of his former attempt to be clever with me, something that had much amused me, since he still seemed to regard me as some sort of revolutionary and at each meeting with me appeared to consider it necessary to talk about things of that kind.

'Let's go,' said the prince and they both went off into another room. Left alone, I came to the decision to hand back the three hundred roubles as soon as Stebelkov had left. I needed the money desperately, but that was my decision.

They were there for about ten minutes without making a sound and then suddenly started talking loudly. Both of them talked loudly, but the prince suddenly started shouting as if in great annoyance, rising to a state of frenzy. He could sometimes be extremely short-tempered, so that even I deferred to him. But at that moment a footman entered with an announcement. I indicated where they were and instant silence ensued. The prince came out of the room briskly with a concerned expression, but smiling. The footman ran off and in half a minute a guest came in to see the prince.

His guest was a man of importance, arrayed in aiguillettes and a monogram, no more than 30 years of age, of upper-class and rather stern appearance. I must warn the reader that Prince Sergey Petrovich still did not belong to St Petersburg high society in a real sense, despite his passionate wish to be part of it—I knew about this wish, of course—and therefore he was terribly appreciative of such a visit. It was an acquaintanceship, as I knew, which had only just begun after great efforts had been made by the prince to initiate it. His guest was now repaying a visit but had unfortunately caught his host at an inopportune moment. I noticed with what an anxious and lost look the prince glanced at Stebelkov. But Stebelkov received the look as if it meant nothing and, without in the least thinking of making himself scarce, sat down grandly on a divan and began running his hand through his hair, probably as a sign of his lack of involvement. He even put on such a self-important expression he was, in short, quite impossible.

So far as I was concerned, I naturally knew how to behave in polite society and did not, of course, want anyone to be ashamed of me, but imagine my astonishment when I found the same lost, pitiful, and disapproving look of the prince's directed at me as well. He appeared to be ashamed of both of us and lumped me together with Stebelkov. This realization drove me crazy. I stretched out even more arrogantly on the divan and began flicking through the book as if the whole thing were no concern of mine. Stebelkov, on the other hand, leaned forward and began listening to their conversation, probably assuming it was courteous and polite to do so. The guest glanced at him more than once, as he did at me as well.

They were discussing family news. The gentleman had at one time been acquainted with the prince's mother who came from a well-known family. So far as I could make out, the guest, despite his courteousness and apparent straightforwardness of tone, was very much on his dignity and, of course, thought so much of himself that a visit from him could be considered a great honour to whomsoever it was made. If the prince had been alone, without us being present, that is, I am sure he would have been more dignified and resourceful. As it was, a special trembling of his lips as he smiled a bit too fondly and a certain odd vagueness of manner gave him away.

They had scarcely been seated five minutes when another guest was suddenly announced, and naturally he had to be of a compromising kind. I knew him well and had heard a lot about him, although he did not know me at all. He was very young—well, about 23—extremely well turned out, from a good home and very good-looking, but undoubtedly mixed up in bad society. The previous year he had been serving in one of the best cavalry guards' regiments, but had been obliged to retire and everyone knew why. His parents had even advertised in the newspapers to the effect that they would not be responsible for his debts, but he had continued his fast living, obtaining money at 10 per cent interest while passionately frequenting gaming clubs and squandering money on a French lady of some repute. The fact was that a week previously he had succeeded in winning twelve thousand in an evening and was now triumphant. He was on a friendly footing with the prince because they frequently went gambling together. But the prince now visibly shuddered on seeing him, as I noticed from where I was. This boy had a reputation for making himself at home wherever he was, talking loudly, gaily, and unrestrainedly about anything that came into his head, and of course it would never have occurred to him that our host was in such awe of his important guest because of his social position.

On entering he interrupted their conversation and instantly began talking about the previous evening's gambling before he had even sat down.

'I think you were there as well,' he announced almost as the first thing he said, mistaking the important guest for one of his own circle but crying out the instant he looked closer:

'Ah, forgive me, I thought you were also one of those there yesterday!'

'Aleksey Vladimirovich Darzan, Ippolit Aleksandrovich Nashchokin.'

The prince hurriedly introduced them. The boy certainly had things to recommend him, in the sense of having a good family name, but the prince did not think to introduce us and we continued to sit in our respective corners. I had no wish at all to turn my head in their direction, but Stebelkov, on seeing the boy, started grinning delightedly and evidently threatened to start talking. I began to find the whole scene quite entertaining.

'I came across you frequently at Countess Verigin's last year,' said Darzan.

'I remember you, but I think you were then in the army,' Nashchokin responded warmly.

'Yes, I was in the army, but thanks to ... Ah, Stebelkov's here, is he? What's he doing here? Precisely thanks to the likes of him I'm no longer in the army.' He pointed at Stebelkov and roared with laughter. Stebelkov laughed delightedly in turn, probably taking the other's laugh for a pleasantry. The prince reddened and quickly turned to Nashchokin with a question, while Darzan, going over to Stebelkov, started saying something to him very vigorously but under his breath.

'I think when you were abroad you knew Katerina Nikolaevna Akhmakov very well, didn't you?' his guest asked the prince.

'Oh, yes, I did.'

'I think we'll soon have some news of her. They say she's getting married to Baron Björing.'

'Quite true!' cried Darzan.

'Do you know this for sure?' the prince asked Nashchokin with obvious concern and giving particular emphasis to his question.

'It's what I was told. People are talking about it. But I can't be sure.'

'Oh, it's for sure!' Darzan returned to their group. 'Dubasov told me yesterday. He's always the first to know news of that kind. The prince ought to know surely ...'

Nashchokin waited until Darzan had finished and then again said to the prince:

'She very rarely goes out nowadays.'

'In the last month her father's been unwell,' the prince remarked rather drily.

'A lady, I think, notorious for her escapades!' Darzan spluttered suddenly.

I raised my head and sat up straight.

'I have the pleasure of knowing Katerina Nikolaevna personally and I consider it my duty to assure you that all these scandalous rumours are nothing but shameful lies . . . er, lies thought up by those who've, er, been around her and not, er, had any luck.'

I broke off stupidly at that point, continuing to sit up straight and look at them. They all turned in my direction, but Stebelkov began sniggering and Darzan also grinned in astonishment.

'Arkady Makarovich Dolgoruky,' said the prince, introducing me to Darzan.

'Oh, you must believe me, *prince*,' Darzan said, addressing me frankly and jovially, 'I'm not speaking for myself. If there have been rumours, then I've not been the one to spread them.'

'Oh, I wasn't referring to you!' I said quickly, but Stebelkov had burst out laughing unforgivably loudly and precisely, as it turned out later, because Darzan had called me 'prince'. My diabolical surname had again mucked everything up. Even now I go red at the thought that—out of shame, of course—I didn't say out loud right then and there that a silly mistake had been made and I was simply Dolgoruky. It was the first time in my life I hadn't done so. Darzan stared at me in some bewilderment and at Stebelkov, who was still laughing.

'Oh, yes, I meant to ask you, who was that pretty girl with the turned-up nose and fair hair I met on the stairs?' he suddenly asked the prince.

'I've no idea,' the latter answered immediately, going red.

'Who would know but you?' Darzan laughed.

'Well, it might have been, er . . .' the prince stammered.

'It was his sister, Lizaveta Makarovna!' Stebelkov declared, pointing at me. 'I myself have just seen her . . .'

'Ah, in that case,' the prince said, but this time with an unusually serious and authoritative look on his face, 'it must have been Lizaveta Makarovna, who knows Anna Fyodorovna Stolbeev, who owns where I'm staying now. She had probably been calling on Darya Onisimovna, who is also a close friend of Anna Fyodorovna and to whom the house was left when she went away . . .'

That is exactly how it was. Darya Onisimovna was poor Olya's mother, whose story I've already told and to whom Tatyana Pavlovna Prutkov had offered a place to stay here in the Stolbeev house. I was only too well aware that Liza used to call on Anna Fyodorovna and from time to time visited the poor Darya

Onisimovna, of whom we were all very fond. But at that moment, after the prince's extraordinarily businesslike announcement and particularly after Stebelkov's stupid remark, and perhaps because I had just been addressed as prince, I suddenly blushed crimson. Luckily at that very moment Nashchokin got up to go. He offered his hand to Darzan. The instant I was alone with Stebelkov he nodded significantly in the direction of Darzan who was standing with his back to him in the doorway. I shook my fist at Stebelkov.

Darzan left the next moment after arranging to meet the prince next day at a rendezvous, presumably in the gaming house. As he went out he shouted something at Stebelkov and gave me a slight bow. The instant he had gone, Stebelkov jumped up and stood in the middle of the room with one finger raised, saying:

'That young gent played the following trick last week. He issued an IOU, but he had forged it in the name of Averyanov. The IOU exists in that form, only of course not accepted! That's a criminal act. In the sum of eight thousand.'

'And the IOU is very likely in your possession?' I gave him a ferocious look.

'I have a bank, I have a *mont de piété*, not IOUs. You've heard about the *mont de piété* in Paris, haven't you?* Bread and good works for the poor. I have a *mont de piété* . . .'

The prince stopped him rudely and angrily: 'What are you doing here? Who said you could stay here?'

'Ah!' Stebelkov blinked his eyes rapidly. 'Something's the matter, is it?'

'Yes, yes, yes, something is!' shouted the prince and stamped his foot. 'I've said it is!'

'Well, in that case, so be it. Except it's not so . . .'

He turned sharply round and, with bent spine and lowered head, suddenly left the room. The prince shouted at him when he was in the doorway:

'I am not frightened of you in the least, you know!'

He was very worked up and was on the point of sitting down but, seeing me, remained standing. His glance seemed to say: 'Why the hell are you still here?'

'Prince, I . . .' I started saying.

'I've no time, Arkady Makarovich. I must be off.'

'Just a moment, prince. I've got something very important to say. First of all, take back your three hundred.'

'What's all this about?'

He was on his way, but he stopped.

'It's about what's just happened . . . and what you said about Versilov, that he was dishonest, and your tone for the rest of the time. In short, I can't take it.'

'You've been *taking* my money a whole month.'

He suddenly sat down in his armchair. I stood by his desk and fingered the volume of Belinsky with one hand and held my hat in the other.

'There were other feelings then, prince . . . And, anyhow, I'd never have taken as much as all that . . . The gambling . . . In short, I can't!'

'You've simply not covered yourself in glory all that much today and you're furious, that's all. Please leave that book alone!'

'What do you mean—not covered myself in glory? It was you who put me on the same level as Stebelkov in front of your guests!'

'O-o-o, we're really getting to the bottom of it!' He gave a sour grin. 'And you got all hot and bothered, didn't you, because Darzan called you a prince.'

He laughed spitefully. I burst out with:

'I don't even understand why you're a prince and I wouldn't want your title if you gave it me for free!'

'I know what you are! How funny you were, speaking out for Miss Akhmakov! Leave that book alone!'

'What's that mean?' It was my turn to shout.

'LEAVE THE BOOK ALONE!' he screamed suddenly, drawing himself up straight in his armchair in such a ferocious way he seemed about to spring at me.

'This is more than I can stand,' I said and quickly left the room. But I had scarcely reached the end of the hall when he shouted to me from the door of his study:

'Arkady Makarovich, come back here! Come back here! Come back here this instant!'

I paid no attention and went on walking. With rapid strides he caught up with me, seized me by the arm, and dragged me into his study—and I put up no resistance!

'Take the money!' he said, pale with emotion, holding out the

244

three hundred roubles. 'You must take it! Otherwise we'll . . . You must take it!'

'Prince, how can I?'

'Well, if you like, I'll say I'm sorry, shall I? Well, I'm sorry, so please forgive me!'

'Prince, I've always loved you, and if you've loved me, too . . .'

'Yes, I've loved you, too! Now take it . . .'

I took the money. His lips quivered.

'I realize, prince, you're furious over that rascal, but I won't take the money unless we kiss and make up as we have done after previous tiffs . . .'

Saying this, I was also quivering.

'Well, what a sentimentalist you are!' muttered the prince, smiling in embarrassment, but he leaned forward and kissed me. I gave a shudder. At the moment of the kiss I read such disgust in his face.

'At least he brought you some money, didn't he?'

'Oh, it doesn't matter.'

'I could get some for you . . .'

'Yes, he brought some, he brought some . . .'

'Prince, we were friends . . . And Versilov, you know, is . . .'

'Yes, yes, it's all right!'

'And when all's said and done I really don't know about this three hundred . . .' I held the money in my hand.

'Go on, take it, take it!' He was again smiling, but his smile had something very unkind in it.

I took the money.

CHAPTER III

I

I took it because I loved him. To anyone who doubts this I will say that at least at the moment I took the money I was absolutely certain that, if I wanted, I could get it from another source. So it could be I took it not out of necessity but out of politeness, so as not to offend him. Anyhow, that's how I put it to myself at the time! But I still felt very bad about things as I left him because I had seen an extraordinary change in his attitude towards me that morning. He had never used that tone before. And as for Versilov, he was in open revolt against him! Stebelkov had, of course, caused him considerable annoyance for some reason, but it had all begun long before Stebelkov. I will say it again: the change from the way things had been at the start had been noticeable throughout the last few days, but not in the same degree, not to this extent—that's the main thing.

It could have been that the silly piece of news about Baron Björing was the cause . . . I was also in a high state of emotion, but the thing was that I had a gleam in my eye about something quite different and I let so much pass unnoticed in a light-hearted way because I wanted to overlook it, wanted to drive everything gloomy away and set my face towards the gleaming future . . .

It was not yet one o'clock. Leaving the prince's place, I set off directly with Matvey to—guess where?—to Stebelkov! The point is that he had just astonished me not so much by visiting the prince (he had promised to do that) as by his winking at me in his silly way concerning a matter which I had not expected at all. Yesterday evening I had received from him through the city mail a fairly enigmatic communication in which he begged me to be at his place today, at two o'clock, when he would be able to inform me 'of some unexpected matters'. And yet just now, at the prince's, he had given no hint of this. What on earth kind of secrets could there be between me and Stebelkov? The very idea was comic. But in view of what had just happened, I was a bit worried as I travelled towards him. I had, of course, asked him for a loan of some money on one occasion a couple of weeks ago and he was ready to give it, but it came to nothing and I had not taken the money, since he had then made some obscure remark, as he usually did, and I had assumed he wanted to propose special conditions of some kind. Because I had looked down my nose at him every time I met him at the prince's, I arrogantly rejected any thought of special conditions and walked out on him even though he rushed after me to the front door as I was leaving. I then borrowed from the prince.

Stebelkov lived in a place of his own, and he lived very comfortably. He had an apartment of four beautiful rooms, good furniture, male and female staff, and a housekeeper, who was, however, rather elderly. I entered in a rage.

'See here, my good sir,' I began the moment I was inside, 'what's this communication mean? I won't have letters being exchanged between you and me. And why didn't you say straight out just now at the prince's what you wanted? I was at your disposal.'

'And why did you say nothing about it just now? Why didn't you ask?' He spread his mouth in a most self-satisfied smile.

'Because it's not I who needs you, but you who needs me!' I cried out, suddenly incensed.

'Then why have you come here if that's so?' He almost leapt with joy as he said this. I turned away that instant and was just about to go out when he seized me by the shoulder.

'No, no, I was simply having a joke. It's an important matter, you'll see.'

I sat down. I confess I was curious. We were seated at the end of a large writing desk, facing each other. He smiled in his clever-clever way and raised a finger.

'Please,' I once more shouted in anger, 'no clever stuff and no fingers raised! And most of all, no allegories and stuff like that, but get straight down to business! Otherwise I'll leave!'

'You're . . . a stuck-up bastard!' he declared with a stupid tone of reproach in his voice, rocking forward in his chair and knitting all the furrows on his forehead.

'So I have to be when I'm with you!'

'You've . . . just today you've accepted three hundred roubles from the prince, haven't you? I've got money. Mine's better.'

'How do you know I've accepted three hundred?' I was absolutely astonished. 'Did he tell you about it?'

'He told me. Don't worry, it just cropped up, he mentioned it, but not deliberately. He told me, that's all. But you needn't have accepted it. True or untrue?'

'I've heard you charge impossible rates of interest.'

'I have a *mont de piété* but I don't fleece people. I only make arrangements for friends and I don't lend to others. For other people I have a *mont de piété* . . .'

This so-called *mont de piété* was a very ordinary pawnbroking business run in someone else's name, in another apartment, and very profitable.

'I give large sums to friends.'

'Is the prince one of your friends?'

'In a manner of speaking. But ... but he will go on about things. And he shouldn't dare go on about things.'

'You've got him in your clutches, have you? Does he owe you a lot?'

'He owes me a lot.'

'He'll pay you. He's due to come into an inheritance.'

'It won't be his. He owes the money and something else. The inheritance won't amount to much. I'll let you have the money without charging interest.'

'As a *friend*, you mean? What have I done to deserve this?' I asked with a laugh.

'You'll deserve it.' He once more turned his whole body towards me and raised a finger.

'No raised finger, Stebelkov! Otherwise I'll go!'

'Listen ... he can get married to Anna Andreevna!' And he screwed up his left eye in a devilish wink.

'You listen to me, Stebelkov—what you're saying is scandalous! How can you dare mention the name of Anna Andreevna?'

'Don't lose your temper.'

'I can only take so much of what you're saying because I can clearly see you're up to something and I'd like to know what it is. Maybe I can only take so much of this, Stebelkov, eh?'

'Don't lose your temper and don't get on your high horse! Calm down a bit and listen. You can get back again on your high horse afterwards. You know about Anna Andreevna, don't you? You know the prince might marry her, don't you?'

'I've heard about this, of course, and I know all about it, but I've never spoken to the prince about it. I simply know it was an idea emanating from the old Prince Sokolsky, who is now unwell, but I've never said anything about it and had nothing to do with it. In saying all this to you, in an effort to explain things, I want to ask you, firstly, why you've been talking to me about it and, secondly, whether the prince has talked to *you* about such things.'

'No, he hasn't. He doesn't like talking to me, but I talk to him and he doesn't like listening. He started shouting this morning.'

'Well, well! One up to him!'

'The old man, the old Prince Sokolsky, will give Anna

Andreevna a large dowry. She's in his good books. Then the young Prince Sokolsky can give me all my money back. And he can also repay a debt not involving money. For sure he'll be able to! But at present he's no means of doing so.'

'So why do you need me?'

'For the sake of the main question. You're familiar with things there. You're familiar with everything there. You could find out everything, couldn't you?'

'Devil take it! Find out what?'

'Whether the prince wants to, whether Anna Andreevna wants to, whether the old prince wants it. You can find out for sure.'

'You're daring to suggest I become your spy—and for money!' I cried, jumping up in disgust.

'Don't get on your high horse! Just calm down a bit! Give me five minutes.'

He again made me sit down. He was evidently unperturbed by my objections and protests, but I was now determined to hear him out.

'I've got to know quickly because . . . because it'll soon be too late. Did you see how he took a pill the moment that officer mentioned Miss Akhmakov and the Baron?'

I felt definitely humiliated by having to listen to more of this, but my curiosity was utterly won over.

'Listen,' I said emphatically, 'you're a shit! If I sit here and listen to what you've got to say about such people . . . and even give you some answers, it's not at all because I think you've any right to. All I can see here is something underhand. Anyhow, in the first place, what hopes can the prince entertain about Katerina Nikolaevna?'

'None, but he's crazy about her.'

'That's a lie!'

'He's crazy. Now he's had to pass on Miss Akhmakov—he lost out there—and all he's got is Anna Andreevna. I'll give you two thousand—no interest and no IOU.' So saying, he leaned back decisively and self-importantly in his chair and gazed at me with his eyes screwed up. I gazed straight back at him. 'You're wearing a suit from Millionaires' Row. You're in need of money, cash, and mine is better than his. I'll let you have more than two thousand . . .'

'What on earth for, devil take it?'

I stamped my foot. He leaned towards me and said meaningfully:

'So you don't interfere.'

'I wouldn't in any case!' I shouted.

'I know you can keep quiet. That's good.'

'I don't need your approval. For my own part I very much want it myself, but I consider it's no business of mine and it would even be indecent of me.'

'You see, you see—indecent!' He raised his finger.

'See what?'

'It's indecent—oh, hell!' And he suddenly burst out laughing. 'I understand, I understand perfectly what you find indecent about it, but . . . but you won't interfere, will you?' He gave me a wink.

There was something so insolent, even mocking and nasty in his winking. It was precisely because he supposed I had something really nasty in me and counted on that. This was obvious, but I couldn't understand what it was.

'Anna Andreevna, my young sir, is also a sister of yours, I think,' he said, full of innuendo.

'Don't you dare talk about that! Don't dare talk about Anna Andreevna at all!'

'Okay, cool it! No high horse! Just listen a moment—he'll get the money and he'll repay everyone,' said Stebelkov weightily. '*Everyone*, get it?'

'So you think I've taken his money?'

'Haven't you done that just now?'

'I've taken my own.'

'How do you mean?'

'It's Versilov's money. He owes Versilov twenty thousand.'

'So he owes Versilov, not you.'

'Versilov's my father.'

'No, you're a Dolgoruky, not a Versilov.'

'It's the same thing!'

Actually that's what I thought then. I knew it wasn't the same thing, I wasn't that stupid, but out of 'politeness' that's the way I thought of it.

'Anyhow, that's enough!' I shouted. 'I literally don't understand a damn thing. And how dare you involve me in all this nonsense!'

'Are you sure you really don't understand? Do you really mean that or don't you?' asked Stebelkov slowly, looking at me closely and with a kind of mistrustful smile.

'I swear to you—I don't understand!'

'I am telling you he can pay everyone back, *everyone*, provided you don't interfere and don't try to dissuade him . . .'

'You must be out of your mind! What are you going on about *everyone* for? Will he even pay Versilov, that's what I want to know.'

'You're not the only one, nor's Versilov—there's others. And Anna Andreevna is just as much of a sister to you *as is Lizaveta Makarovna*!'

I sat and stared at him. Suddenly there was a flash of pity for me discernible in his horrible eyes.

'Don't understand it then, so much the better! It's a good thing, a very good thing, you don't understand it. It's truly praiseworthy if you really don't . . .'

I got completely mad at that.

'Get out of here with all your nonsense, you're plain crazy!' I shouted and picked up my hat.

'It's not nonsense! So you're going, are you? You'll be back!'

'No, I won't!' I shot at him from the doorway.

'You'll be back—and then there'll be something else to talk about. We'll talk about the main thing. Remember—two thousand!'

II

He produced such a dirty and confused impression on me that, on leaving him, I even tried to put him out of my mind by literally spitting him out. The idea that the prince should have talked to him about me and the money pierced me to the quick like a sharp pin. 'I'll win and give it all back today!' I decided.

No matter how silly and obscure in his speech Stebelkov was, I saw him clearly enough as an absolute rascal and, chiefly, I saw he had to be up to some trickery. Except that I had no way of knowing then what the tricks were and this was the chief reason for my being so chicken-hearted and blind! I looked anxiously at my watch but it wasn't yet two o'clock. I still had time for another visit, otherwise I knew I'd go crazy with worry before it was three.

I drove to Anna Andreevna Versilov, my sister. I had become acquainted with her at the old prince's some while ago, before he had fallen ill. The thought that I had not seen him for three or four days troubled me, but it was compensated for precisely by Anna Andreevna's assurance that the prince had become extraordinarily attached to her and had even taken to calling her his guardian angel. Besides, the idea of marrying her off to Sergey Petrovich had actually been born in the old man's head and he had even mentioned it to me more than once—confidentially, of course. I had passed it on to Versilov, having noted, as on previous occasions, that although Versilov was usually so indifferent to all essentials he always took a particular interest whenever I told him about my meetings with Anna Andreevna. Versilov had remarked to me that Anna Andreevna was far too clever and could find her way in tricky matters of that sort without advice from others. True, Stebelkov was right that the old man would give her a good dowry, but how could he himself dare to count on something from it? The prince had only just shouted out to him that he wasn't frightened of him. Had Stebelkov perhaps been talking to him about Anna Andreevna in his study? In his place, I could imagine how infuriated I would have been.

I had been to see Anna Andreevna fairly frequently recently. But the same strange thing had always happened. It had always been the case that she had told me when to be there, and had even been expecting me, but as soon as I arrived she would invariably give the impression that I had come unexpectedly and at the wrong moment. I had noted this habit of hers, yet I still felt drawn to her.

She lived with Madame Fanariotov, her grandmother, as a ward (Versilov provided nothing towards her upkeep), but not in the way that wards are usually described as living in the houses of titled ladies, like the ward Pushkin describes as living with the old countess in *The Queen of Spades*. Anna Andreevna behaved more like a countess in her own right. She lived in the house quite separately, that is to say on the same floor and in the same apartment as the Fanariotovs, but in separate rooms, so that during my comings and goings I never, for instance, met a single one of them. She enjoyed the right of having anyone she liked to visit and spent her time just as she wished. In fact, she was already 22. In the past year she had almost given up appearing in society, although Madame Fanariotov showed no meanness in providing for her granddaughter, of whom, I gathered, she was very fond. On the contrary, what I liked about Anna Andreevna was that I always found her wearing such modest dresses and always busy with something, with a book in her hand or a piece of work. She had a convent, almost nun-like look about her and I liked it. She was a girl of few words, but always spoke weightily when she did and was terribly good at listening, which I was never any good at.

When I told her that, despite having no feature in common, she reminded me very much of Versilov, she always used to blush slightly. She would blush often and very quickly, but always only very slightly, and I very much enjoyed this peculiarity of hers. When I was with her I never used the name Versilov but unvariably referred to Andrey Petrovich, and this was done entirely spontaneously. I was even very much aware that in general among the Fanariotovs they were rather ashamed of Versilov. However, I was particularly aware of it in Anna Andreevna's case, although I don't know whether I should have used the word 'ashamed'. It was something equivalent, though. I would frequently talk to her about Prince Sergey Petrovich, and she would listen intently to me and, I thought, take an interest in what I had to say. But it always happened that I would say things and she would never ask me anything about them. I never dared raise the question of her marrying him, although I often wanted to because the idea quite appealed to me. But there was a terrible number of things I never dared talk about when I was with her, and yet I was terribly happy being with her. I was also very pleased that she was educated and read a great deal, and even read worthwhile books. She read a great deal more than I did.

She herself took the initiative in asking me to come and see her the first time. I understood at that time that she was probably counting on sometimes getting something out of me. Oh, in those days lots of people could have got a lot out of me! 'But so what,' I thought, 'she doesn't want me to visit her just for that!' In a word, I was even glad I could be of use to her and . . . and whenever I was with her I always thought to myself, Here's my sister sitting beside me, though we never mentioned our relationship, never so much as hinted at it, as if it didn't exist at all. When I was with her I thought it quite senseless to talk about it and, true, when I looked at her I sometimes had the silly thought that perhaps she knew nothing at all about our relationship, judging by the way she behaved in my presence.

III

When I entered I suddenly found Liza with her. This almost astonished me. I knew very well that they had met previously over the business of the 'baby'. About this whole fantastic business of the proud and prudish Anna Andreevna seeing this baby and meeting Liza there I'll maybe tell all sometime, if I have the space. But I had still never anticipated that Anna Andreevna would invite Liza to come and see her. This is what pleasantly astonished me. Naturally, giving no sign of it, I took a seat beside her, having greeted Anna Andreevna and shaken hands warmly with Liza. Both were busy with serious women's business. On the table and on their knees lay one of Anna Andreevna's expensive outdoor dresses, but an old one, already worn three times, that is to say, which she wanted to alter. Liza was a great expert at that sort of thing and she had taste, so a kind of council of wise women was taking place. I remembered what Versilov had said about this and burst out laughing. I was generally radiating goodwill.

'You are in a very good mood today and that is very pleasant,' announced Anna Andreevna, enunciating her words solemnly and one by one. She had a full and resonant contralto voice, but she always spoke calmly and quietly, always slightly lowering her long eyelashes and with a fleeting smile illuminating her pale face.

'Liza knows how unpleasant I am when I'm in a bad mood,' I said happily.

'Perhaps Anna knows that, too,' needled Liza playfully. The dear girl! If only I'd known what she was thinking then!

'What are you doing today?' Anna Andreevna asked. (I will mention that she had herself asked me to visit her today.)

'Right now I am sitting here and asking myself why I always find it pleasanter when you're reading a book rather than dressmaking. No, believe me, dressmaking doesn't suit you. In this respect, I go along with Andrey Petrovich.'

'Have you still not yet made up your mind to go to university?'

'I am only too thankful that you do not forget our conversations. It must mean you sometimes think about me. But, er, as for university, I've not yet conceived an opinion, and in any case I have ideas of my own.'

'That's to say, he's got a secret,' remarked Liza.

'Spare me your jokes, Liza. A clever chap said recently that throughout the last twenty years of our progressive movement we've demonstrated one thing above all—how appallingly uneducated we are! Of course, this was said about our universities.'

'Well, that's what father said. You repeat his ideas terribly often,' remarked Liza.

'Liza, it's just as if you didn't think I had a mind of my own.'

'In a time like ours it's useful to listen to what clever people say and bear it in mind,' said Anna Andreevna, as if backing me up slightly.

'Exactly, Anna Andreevna,' I warmly agreed. 'Someone at the present moment who doesn't think about the state of Russia is not a true citizen! Perhaps I take a strange view of Russia. I think we lived through the Tartar invasion and two centuries of slavery because both of these things were to our taste. Now we've been given our freedom, we've got to live through that, too. Do you think we can? Do you think it'll be to our taste, eh? That's the question.'

Liza glanced rapidly at Anna Andreevna, but the latter lowered her head instantly and began searching about for something. I noticed that Liza was holding herself in as hard as she could, but suddenly our eyes accidentally met and she burst out laughing. I flared up at once:

'Liza, you're incomprehensible!'

'Sorry!' she said suddenly, not laughing any more and almost with sadness. 'Forgive me, I don't know what's got into me . . .'

And indeed her voice trembled on the brink of tears. I felt awfully ashamed. I seized her hand and kissed it.

'You are a very kind man,' Anna Andreevna remarked to me softly when she saw me kiss Liza's hand.

'I'm most of all glad, Liza, that today I find you in a laughing mood,' I said. 'Believe me, Anna Andreevna, recently every time I've met her she's given me such a strange look, as much as to say: "What, you haven't discovered anything yet? Is everything all right?" It really has been something like that with her.'

Anna Andreevna gave her a slow, piercing look and Liza lowered her eyes. I could see they knew each other a lot better and more closely than I had supposed when I came in, and this pleased me.

'You said just now I was kind. You can't believe, Anna Andreevna, how much I am changed for the better by being here and how pleasant it is to be with you,' I said with real feeling.

'I am very glad to hear you say that right now,' she answered, giving me a significant look. I must say that she had never spoken to me about my disorderly life and the morass I was sinking into, although I knew she not only knew all about it but had even asked other people about it. This was by way of being the first hint of her knowledge and my heart felt all the more drawn to her.

'What about our sick patient?' I asked.

'Oh, he's a lot better. He's up and walking about, and yesterday he went out for a drive. Haven't you been to call on him today? He's very keen to see you.'

'I'm sorry, I feel guilty about it. But now you're visiting him so often you've taken my place. He's terribly fickle and he's substituted you for me.'

She made a very serious face, so it may well have been that she found my joke trivial.

'I've just been at Prince Sergey Petrovich's,' I mumbled, 'and I . . . By the way, Liza, didn't you go and see Darya Onisimovna just now?'

'Yes,' she murmured rather shortly, not raising her head. 'And I think you go and see the old, sick prince every day, don't you?' she asked rather suddenly, perhaps because she was looking for something to say.

'Yes, I set off on my way, except I don't go and see him,' I laughed. 'I go in and then I turn to the left . . .'

'Even the prince has noticed that you're seeing a great deal of

Katerina Nikolaevna. He said so yesterday and laughed,' said Anna Andreevna.

'Laughed at what?'

'He was joking—you know what I mean. He said that, just to be awkward, as it were, a young and beautiful woman always produces an impression of dissatisfaction and anger on a young man of your age . . .' And Anna Andreevna suddenly roared with laughter.

'Listen—that was terribly perceptive of him!' I shouted. 'Are you sure it wasn't you said it, not him?'

'Why should I? No, it was he who said it.'

'Well, if this beautiful woman pays such attention to him, no matter how much of a nonentity he is, spending all his time standing in a corner and seething with anger at being a mere *bastard*, and if she suddenly prefers him to the crowd of admirers surrounding her, what then?' I asked suddenly with the boldest and most challenging look on my face. My heart had begun beating like crazy.

'You'll be on your knees in front of her!' said Liza, laughing.

'On my knees?' I cried. 'No, I won't. Not me. If a woman gets in my way, then she'll have to tag along behind. People aren't going to get in my way for nothing . . .'

Liza told me a long while later that she remembered I uttered these words terribly strangely and seriously and with a kind of thoughtfulness, but they sounded so funny one couldn't help laughing. Indeed, Anna Andreevna once more burst out laughing.

'All right, laugh at me!' I cried exultantly, because I was greatly enjoying this talk and the way it was going. 'You really please me! I love the way you laugh, Anna Andreevna! You've got this way of saying nothing and then suddenly laughing, all in a moment, so you can't even tell from your face what you're thinking. I knew a woman in Moscow like that—not closely, just by observing her—she was almost as beautiful as you are, but she didn't have your way of laughing and her face, just as attractive as yours, lost all its attractiveness when she laughed. With you it's terribly attractive, precisely because you know how . . . I've wanted to say this to you for a long time.'

When I said I knew someone 'almost as beautiful as you', I was having her on. I tried to make it seem I had said this quite spontaneously. 'Spontaneous' compliments, I knew, were always much more appreciated by women than highly polished ones. And no matter how much Anna Andreevna blushed, I knew she was pleased. I had invented that woman; I didn't know any woman in Moscow. I had said it simply in order to flatter Anna Andreevna and make her happy.

'One might really imagine,' she said with a charming smile, 'that recently you had been under the influence of a beautiful woman.'

I felt literally airborne and wanted to confess something to them, but held back.

'Besides, it was not all that long ago you were saying quite nasty things about Katerina Nikolaevna.'

'If I ever expressed myself unfavourably . . .' My eyes flashed '. . . then the reason for it was the monstrous slander that she was an enemy of Andrey Petrovich, and the slander that he was supposedly in love with her and had proposed to her—and other such nonsense! This idea was just as monstrous as the further slander that, during the lifetime of her husband, she had promised Sergey Petrovich to marry him when she was widowed and had then not kept her word. But I know at first hand this wasn't so. It was just a joke. I have first-hand knowledge of this. One time when she was abroad, at a light-hearted moment, she actually told the prince: 'Maybe, in the future . . .' But what was that if it wasn't just a joke? I know only too well that the prince ascribes no value to the promise . . . and intends doing nothing about it!' I added. Suddenly I had a brainwave. 'I think he has quite other ideas,' I inserted slyly. 'I've just heard Nashchokin say in his presence that Katerina Nikolaevna is going to marry Baron Björing. I assure you he took the news as well as possible, you've got to believe me.'

'Nashchokin was there?' asked Anna Andreevna suddenly, her voice heavy with surprise.

'Yes. I think he's one of those respectable people . . .'

'And Nashchokin talked about a marriage with Björing?' Anna Andreevna suddenly showed herself very interested.

'Not about marriage as such, but about the possibility, as a rumour. He said there was a rumour about it going the rounds in society. So far as I'm concerned, I'm sure it's nonsense.'

258

Anna Andreevna thought a moment and then bent over her sewing.

'I love Prince Sergey Petrovich,' I added suddenly with great fervour. 'He has his faults, undoubtedly, as I've told you, particularly a certain one-sidedness ... But they also show he has real nobility of spirit, don't you think? We almost quarrelled today over his conviction that if you talk about being noble, you should be noble yourself, otherwise you'd just be telling lies. Well, is that logical or not? Anyhow, it's evidence of his high standards of honesty, of his sense of duty and justice, isn't it? ... Oh, my God, what time is it?' I suddenly cried, seeing by chance the clock above the fireplace.

'Ten to three,' she said calmly, glancing at the clock. Throughout what I had been saying about the prince she had listened to me with her head bent, a charming, knowing little grin on her face, because she knew exactly why I was praising him. Liza listened with her head bent over her work and had dropped out of the conversation for a while.

I leapt to my feet as if scalded.

'Are you late for something?'

'Yes ... No ... Oh, I'm late, but I'll be going in a moment. Just one word, Anna Andreevna,' I began in great excitement. 'I've got to tell you right away! I want to confess to you that I've several times literally worshipped your kindness and the delicacy with which you've invited me here. Knowing you has had a very strong effect on me. When I'm here in your room I feel somehow cleaner in my soul and I always leave you feeling better than I am. That's the truth. When I'm sitting with you, it's not only that I cannot talk about bad things but I can't even have bad thoughts. They vanish away when I'm with you. If I do have a casual bad thought when I'm with you I instantly feel ashamed of it and blush and go red in my soul, if you know what I mean. And it's also been very pleasant for me, you know, to find my sister with you today ... It's evidence of such nobility of spirit on your part, of such a beautiful relationship ... In a word, you've behaved in such a *brotherly* way, if you'll permit me to break the ice by saying so, that I ...'

While I was speaking she had risen and grown redder and redder. But suddenly she took fright at something, some point which could not be jumped over, and quickly interrupted me:

'Believe me, I fully appreciate how you feel. I've understood it without having it all put into words . . . and for a long time . . .'

She stopped in embarrassment, pressing me by the hand. Suddenly Liza inconspicuously tugged at my sleeve. I said goodbye and went out, but in the next room Liza caught up with me.

IV

'Liza, why did you tug my sleeve?' I asked.

'She's nasty, she's cunning, she's not worth it . . . She has you here so as to wheedle things out of you,' she said in a rapid, vicious whisper. I had never seen such a look on her face before.

'Liza, in God's name, she's a charming girl!'

'Well, in that case I'm the nasty one.'

'What do you mean?'

'I'm very bad. Perhaps she's a very charming girl and I'm bad. Now that's enough of that, let's forget it. Listen, mother is asking you for something she "daren't ask about herself", as she put it. Arkady darling, do stop gambling, I beg you—and mother begs too . . .'

'Liza, I know that myself, but . . . I know it's pitifully feeble of me, but . . . but it's only a lot of nonsense, nothing else! Look, like a fool, I'm in debt and I want to win so as to pay the money back. I can win now because I used to play without thinking, just for the fun of it, like a fool, but now I'll be in a state over every single rouble . . . I just won't be me if I don't win! I'm not addicted. It's not the main thing, just a passing fad, I assure you. I am too strong not to stop when I want to. I'll get back the money and then I'll be yours for ever and ever, and you can tell mother I'll never leave you . . .'

'That three hundred you got just now must mean a lot to you!'

'How do you know about that?' I shuddered.

'Darya Onisimovna heard it all . . .'

But at that moment Liza suddenly shoved me behind a curtain and we found ourselves in the space of a bay window. I had not realized what was happening until I heard a familiar voice and the clink of spurs and guessed who it was by his tread.

'Prince Seryozha,' I whispered.

'Yes,' she whispered.

'Why are you so frightened?'

'Because I don't want him to find me here . . .'

'*Tiens*, as they say. Well I never! He's not making a pass at you, is he? I asked, smiling. 'If he is, I'll give him one. Where are you going?'

'Let's go, just you and me.'

'Have you already said goodbye to her?'

'Yes. My coat's in the hall.'

We went out. On the stairs I was struck by a thought:

'You know, Liza, he might have come to propose to her!'

'N-no . . . he won't be proposing,' she said slowly and firmly in a quiet voice.

'You don't know that, Liza. Though I've just had a quarrel with him—if you haven't already been told all about it—but, for heaven's sake, I still love him sincerely and wish him success. We've just made up. When we're happy, we're so good for each other . . . Look, he has a mass of fine impulses . . . and he has humanitarian feelings . . . at least the rudiments . . . And in the hands of such a strong-minded and clever girl as Miss Versilov he'd really improve and be happy. It's just a pity there's no time . . . Let's drive part of the way and I can tell you a bit about it!'

'No, you go off, you're not going my way. Will you be coming to dinner?'

'Yes, yes, as I promised. Listen carefully, Liza. There's one type—an absolutely loathsome creature, well, Stebelkov, if you know who I mean . . . he's got a terrible grip on his affairs . . . through IOUs, you know . . . Well, anyhow, he's got him in his claws and squeezed him so tight, and the prince is so humiliated by it that both of them can't see any way out except by his proposing marriage to Anna Andreevna. She really ought to be warned. Still, that's nonsense, she herself can put his affairs to rights afterwards. Will she refuse him—what do you think?'

'Goodbye, there's no time for that,' Liza said, breaking away, and in her passing glance I suddenly saw such loathing that I cried out in fright there and then:

'Liza dear, what's wrong?'

'I'm not angry at you. Just don't you go gambling . . .'

'Oh, so you're worried about that. I won't.'

'You said just now "When we're happy . . ." That means you're very happy now, are you?'

261

'Blissfully, Liza, blissfully! My God, it's already after three! 'Bye! Oh, Liza dear, one thing—should one make a woman wait? Is it allowed?'

'When you've arranged a date with her, you mean?' Liza gave a faint, rather ghastly, unsteady smile.

'Give me your hand for good luck.'

'For good luck? My hand? Never!'

And she turned briskly away. The main thing was she had meant it by the way she shouted. I jumped into my sledge.

Yes, all right, 'bliss' was the main reason why I was as blind as a mole and saw and understood nothing beyond my own nose!

CHAPTER IV

I

NOW I'm even frightened to tell it all. It was some while ago, but even now it still seems to me like a mirage. How could such a woman arrange a date with such a rotten young bastard as I was then? It must have seemed like that at first glance! When, after leaving Liza, I rushed away, my heart was beating just as fast and I thought I had gone out of my mind because the very idea of such a *date* seemed to me such obvious nonsense there was no way I could believe in it. And yet I didn't doubt it for a moment. It was even a case of the sillier it seemed, the more I believed.

The fact that it was gone three o'clock worried me. 'If I've got this date,' I thought, 'what am I doing being late for it?' Other silly questions flashed through my mind, such as: 'What's better now, boldness or diffidence?' But this was all surface stuff, because the chief thing was in my heart and that I couldn't define. Yesterday I'd been told: 'I'll be at Tatyana Pavlovna's at three o'clock tomorrow' and that was that. But, first of all, when I'd been to see her I'd always seen her alone and she'd been able to say whatever she liked and there'd been none of this going to Tatyana Pavlovna's. So why this date at Tatyana Pavlovna's now? And then there was the question about whether Tatyana Pavlovna would be there or not. If it was a date, then Tatyana

Pavlovna wouldn't be there. But how could this be arranged without Tatyana Pavlovna knowing about it? Did that mean Tatyana Pavlovna was in on it? The idea struck me as crazy and somehow unwholesome, almost vulgar.

And, finally, she might simply have wanted to be at Tatyana Pavlovna's and told me about it yesterday without intending anything and I had just been imagining things. What's more, it had been said so casually, lightly, calmly, and at the end of a very boring visit, because all the time I had been with her yesterday I had been at my wits' end, sitting there and rattling on about this and that and not knowing what to say, getting terribly worked up and shy, while she, as it turned out, had been preparing to go out somewhere and was visibly pleased when I stood up to leave. All these thoughts crowded into my head. At last I decided I would go there, ring, and, when the cook opened the door, ask if Tatyana Pavlovna was at home. If she wasn't, it would mean the date was on. But I never doubted it, never!

I ran up the steps and on the stairs, before her door, all my fears vanished and I thought, 'Well, the sooner it's over, the better!' The cook opened the door and in her horrid, phlegmatic way announced nasally that Tatyana Pavlovna was not at home. I intended asking whether there might not be someone else waiting to see her, but didn't, thinking it would be better if I saw for myself, and, muttering to the cook that I would wait, I threw off my fur coat and opened the door into the sitting-room.

Katerina Nikolaevna was sitting by the window 'waiting,' as she put it.

'Isn't she here?' she suddenly asked me with concern and annoyance the instant she saw me. Both her voice and her face were so unlike what I had expected that I literally froze in the doorway.

'Who isn't?' I stammered.

'Tatyana Pavlovna! I asked you yesterday to tell her I'd be here at three o'clock, didn't I?'

'I . . . I haven't seen her at all.'

'You mean you forgot?'

I collapsed in a chair as if shot in the heart. So that's how it was! Everything was as clear as twice two is four while I'd—I'd stubbornly gone on believing what I wanted to.

'I just don't remember you asking me. And I don't think you

263

did. You simply said you'd be here at three.' I muttered this impatiently and did not look at her.

'Ah!' she suddenly gave a cry. 'If you forgot to tell her, but knew I'd be here, why have you come here?'

I raised my head. Her face betrayed neither mockery nor anger, but only her bright, happy smile and a certain forced playfulness of expression—her habitual expression, as a matter of fact—and one that was almost childish, as if her whole face were saying: 'See, I've caught you out! Now what are you going to say?'

I had no wish to answer and again lowered my eyes. The silence lasted about half a minute.

'Have you just come from father's?' she suddenly asked.

'I've just been seeing Anna Andreevna and I haven't been at Prince Nikolay Ivanovich's at all—as you well know,' I added.

'Did something happen to you at Anna Andreevna's?'

'You mean I've now got this mad look? No, I had the mad look before I went to Anna Andreevna's.'

'Didn't you come to your senses when you were there?'

'No, I didn't. By the way, I've heard you're getting married to Baron Björing.'

'Did she tell you?' She suddenly showed great interest.

'No, it was I who told her. I'd just heard Nashchokin tell Prince Sergey Petrovich.'

I still refrained from raising my eyes. To look at her would mean being engulfed in light and joy and happiness and I did not want to be happy. I had been stung to my heart with annoyance and that very instant I had made an enormous decision. It was then I suddenly started talking, though I scarcely remember what I said. I sighed and somehow rattled on, but I had a bold look about me. My heart beat fast. I talked about nothing very relevant but I probably made sense. At first she listened with a calm, patient smile that never once left her face, but little by little surprise and then even fear could be discerned in her steady gaze. The smile remained there, but even it wavered slightly.

'What's wrong?' I asked suddenly, seeing her shudder.

'I'm frightened of you,' she answered me almost in alarm.

'Why don't you leave? Tatyana Pavlovna's not here now and you know she won't be, so why don't you get up and go?'

'I wanted to wait for her, but now . . . actually I'll . . .'

She started rising.

'No, no, sit down,' I said, stopping her. 'You see, there you are, shivering again and smiling apprehensively. You're always smiling. There, look, you've smiled right now . . .'

'Are you delirious?'

'Yes.'

'I'm frightened,' she whispered again.

'Of what?'

'That you'll start knocking the wall down . . .' She gave another smile, but she was now in fact genuinely alarmed.

'I can't stand your smile!'

Once more I started talking. My words made me airborne. Something continually spurred me on. I had never, never talked to her like this, but always been too shy of her. I was terribly shy of her now, but I still went on talking. I remember I started saying something about her looks.

'I can't stand your smile any more!' I screamed out suddenly. 'Why was it that when I was still in Moscow I imagined you were threatening and grand and always making waspish, upper-class remarks? Yes, in Moscow. Marya Ivanovna and I used to talk about you there and wonder what you must be like . . . Do you remember Marya Ivanovna? You went to see her. When I came here by train, I spent the whole night dreaming about you. When I got here I spent a whole month before you arrived gazing at your portrait in your father's study and not making any sense of it. Your expression is one of childish playfulness and always so uncomplicated—so there you have it! I was terribly struck by this the whole time I was visiting you. Oh, of course, you know how to look arrogant and crush people with a glance. I remember the way you looked at me at your father's when you'd just got back from Moscow . . . I saw you then, but if someone had asked me after I'd left the house what you looked like I wouldn't have been able to say. I couldn't even have said how tall you were. I'd no sooner seen you than I lost the power of sight. Your portrait isn't like you at all. Your eyes aren't dark but light, and it's only because of your long eyelashes that they seem dark. You've got a full figure and you're of medium height, but you've got the full, light plumpness of a healthy country girl. Yes, and you've got a country girl's face, the face of a country beauty—don't be

265

offended, it's pretty, more than pretty, it's a round, red-cheeked, clear-skinned, bold, laughing and . . . and unassuming face! Yes, really unassuming. The unassuming face of Katerina Nikolaevna Akhmakov! Unassuming and wholesome, I swear! More than wholesome, it's childish—that's what your face is! I was always amazed and used to ask myself, is that woman really her? I now know you're very clever, but to start with I thought you were a bit simple. You've got a cheerful mind, but without any pretensions . . . I also like the way you're always smiling. To me that's pure delight! I also like your calmness, your quietness, and the way you always say words so smoothly and calmly and almost languidly—I love the way you're always so languid! I think even if a bridge collapsed under you you'd still go on talking in the same languid way . . . I imagined you as the height of arrogance and high-flown feelings, but we've spent the last couple of months talking together like students . . . I never imagined you had that kind of forehead. It's a bit low, like a statue's, but white and soft as marble beneath your luxuriant hair. You have a high bosom, you walk so lightly, you have extraordinary beauty and no trace of arrogance. You know, I believe in you now! I hadn't before!'

She listened to this crazy tirade with large, wide-open eyes. She saw I was quivering. Now and then she raised a gloved hand in a charming, apprehensive gesture designed to stop me, but each time she let it drop back in confusion and fear. Sometimes she even visibly flinched. Two or three times a smile was on the point of lighting up her face, and at one time she blushed a deep red, but finally she definitely looked frightened and went pale. The instant I finished she stretched out her hand tentatively and in a pleading, albeit smooth, voice said:

'You can't say things like that . . . You're just not allowed to . . .'

And suddenly she stood up, unhurriedly picking up her scarf and sable muff.

'Are you going?' I cried.

'I am definitely frightened of you . . . You are misusing . . .' She spoke in a pitying and reproachful drawl.

'Listen a moment—I'm not going to start knocking the wall down.'

'You've already started!' she couldn't help saying and smiled.

266

'I don't even know whether you'll let me get by you.' And I think she was genuinely frightened I wouldn't.

'I will myself open the door for you and you can go. But I want you to know I have taken an enormous decision. And if you want to shed light into the dark places of my soul, then come back, sit down, and listen to a few short words. But if you don't want to, then please go and I will open the door for you!'

She glanced at me and sat down.

'Another girl would have walked out indignantly, but you've sat down!' I cried in sheer delight.

'You never let yourself say things like that before.'

'I was always too shy before. This time I came here not knowing what I would say. Do you think I don't feel shy right now? Well, I do. But I've just taken an enormous decision and I've got the feeling I'll go through with it. It's just that, when I took the decision, I went mad and started talking like that . . . Listen, I just want to ask this. Do you think I'm spying on you or not? Answer me!'

Her face coloured quickly.

'Don't answer right away, Katerina Nikolaevna, but listen to what I've got to say and then tell me the whole truth.'

At that moment I broke free of the earth's pull and flew off into outer space.

II

'A couple of months ago I stood here behind the curtain—you know the one I mean—and heard you talking to Tatyana Pavlovna about a letter. I jumped out into the open and, quite beside myself, blurted something out. You realized at once that I knew something . . . You couldn't fail to . . . You had been looking for an important document and were very anxious about it . . . Just a moment, Katerina Nikolaevna, let me go on. I can tell you your anxieties were well founded. The document exists—that is, it did exist, and I saw it. It was your letter to Andronnikov, wasn't it?'

'You saw that letter?' she asked in a rush of confusion and excitement. 'Where?'

'I saw it . . . I saw it at Kraft's, the man who shot himself.'

'Really and truly? You saw it with your own eyes? What happened to it.'

'Kraft tore it up.'

'When you were there? You saw him do it?'

'When I was there. He must have torn it up just before his death ... After all, I didn't know he was going to shoot himself ...'

'So it's destroyed, thank God!' she said slowly, sighed and crossed herself.

I was not lying to her. That is to say, I told a lie in the sense that I had had the document and not Kraft, but that was only a detail, and I had not lied over the main thing because the moment I spoke I made myself promise to burn the letter that evening. I swear that if I had had it in my pocket at that moment I would have taken it out and handed it to her. But I didn't have it; it was in my lodgings. However, I might not have handed it over, because it would have made me very ashamed to have had to confess to her that I had had it all along and kept it and not disclosed the fact. It didn't matter now: I would burn it when I got home in any case and so would not have lied! I swear I had a clear conscience at that moment.

'If that's how it was,' I went on, almost beside myself, 'then tell me why you wanted me to come and see you, why you were so nice to me—was it because you thought I knew about the document? Just one moment, Katerina Nikolaevna, don't say anything, let me finish. All the time I was seeing you I suspected you were only being nice to me in order to wheedle that letter out of me and get me to confess ... Wait just a moment. I suspected you, but I couldn't help feeling bad. I couldn't bear your duplicity because ... because I found you were the noblest of human beings! I am telling you straight to your face—I was your enemy, but I found you the noblest of human beings! I was completely overwhelmed by you. But the duplicity, or the suspicion of it, nagged at me ... Now the time's come for everything to be decided, everything to be explained. But don't say anything yet, just listen to the way I see everything right now, this very minute. I am telling you straight to your face that, if there was any duplicity, I won't be angry—I mean, I won't be offended, because it would be quite natural, I realize that. What would be unnatural and wrong about it? You were very worried

268

about a document, you suspected someone knew something about it, so you were very keen that someone should say something about it . . . There's nothing bad in that, nothing at all. I am being quite sincere. But you've still got to say something to me now, you've still got to confess—sorry about using a word like that! I must have the truth, for some reason I must! So, tell me—have you been so nice to me in order to wheedle that document out of me, have you, Katerina Nikolaevna?'

I spoke as if I were in free fall through space and my forehead was red hot. She listened to me without any alarm, her face expressing her feeling for me, but she had her unassuming look as if she were ashamed of herself.

'Yes, in order to wheedle it out of you,' she said slowly, in a low voice. 'I'm sorry, I'm guilty,' she added suddenly, raising her hands towards me slightly. I had not expected this. I had expected anything from her save the two words 'I'm guilty'—even from her, whom I knew so well.

'You say "I'm guilty"! Just like that—"I'm guilty"!' I shouted.

'Oh, I've been aware a long time how guilty I am in your case. I'm even glad it's all out in the open now . . .'

'A long time? Why didn't you say something before?'

'I didn't know how to,' she smiled. Then she added with another smile: 'I mean I did know how to but I had a guilty conscience . . . because at first I really was being nice to you, as you put it, in order to get what I wanted, but afterwards I felt revolted . . . I hated all the pretence, I assure you!' she said bitterly. 'And all the fuss and bother, too!'

'Why, oh why didn't you ask straight out? You could have said: "You know about the letter, why go on pretending?" And I'd have told you everything straight out.'

'Yes, well, I was a bit frightened of you. I admit I didn't trust you. That's the truth. If I was pretending, so were you,' she added with a grin.

'Yes, yes, I wasn't worth it!' I cried out, absolutely devastated. 'Oh, if only you knew all the depths of my degradation!'

'Depths, indeed! I know how you like to exaggerate!' She gave me a quiet smile. 'That letter,' she added, 'was the saddest and silliest thing I did in my life. The knowledge I'd written it was a constant reproach to me. Under the influence of circumstances and various fears I cast doubt on the sanity of my dear, generous father. Knowing that the letter could fall . . . could fall into the hands of wicked people, and having every reason to think so . . .' she spoke heatedly at this point '. . . I was worried they might make use of it and show it to daddy. It could have had a very great effect on him . . . in his state of mind and his health . . . and he could have broken with me . . . Yes,' she added, looking me straight in the eyes and probably having read something in my glance, 'yes, I was also frightened about what might happen to me. I was frightened that . . . as a result of his illness . . . he could cut me out of his will. That feeling also entered in, but I was probably in the wrong about that, because he's such a good, kind man he'd have forgiven me of course. So that's the whole thing. That I've behaved this way to you wasn't necessary,' she concluded, again looking guilty. 'You've made me feel thoroughly ashamed of myself.'

'No, you've got nothing to be ashamed of!' I cried.

'I had really been counting on your . . . on your hot-headedness, I admit that,' she murmured, looking down.

'Katerina Nikolaevna! Who, tell me, who is making you admit all these things out loud to me like this?' I shouted as if I were drunk. 'Wouldn't it have been worth your while to stand here in front of me and in a few well-chosen words prove to me in the most delicate fashion, as sure as two and two is four, that although something had happened, nevertheless nothing had happened—you know, in the way they usually know how to manipulate the truth in high society? After all, I'm crude and silly, I'd have believed you at once, I'd have believed whatever you said! After all, it wouldn't have cost you anything, would it? You're not really afraid of me, are you? How could you willingly humiliate yourself in front of an upstart, a mere boy like me?'

'At least I've not humiliated myself in front of you over this!' she said with extraordinary dignity, having evidently misunderstood what I was exclaiming about.

'Oh, on the contrary, on the contrary! That's just what I've been saying!'

'Oh, it was all so bad and frivolous on my part!' she cried, raising her hand to her face and trying to hide herself. 'I was so ashamed yesterday and not myself when you were with me. The whole truth is,' she added, 'that my circumstances have now all combined to make it essential I know exactly what happened to that unfortunate letter, otherwise I'd have forgotten about it . . . And it wasn't at all because of that I liked you to visit me,' she added suddenly.

My heart jumped.

'Of course not,' she smiled in her delicate way, 'of course not! I . . . You put it very well just now, Arkady Makarovich, when you said we often talked like a couple of students. I assure you I'm sometimes extremely bored with people, particularly after being abroad and all our family troubles . . . I hardly go out anywhere now, and it's not simply out of laziness. I often want to travel into the country. I would reread my favourite books, which I've laid aside for so long and haven't found time for. I've told you about this. Remember how you laughed at my reading two Russian papers a day?'

'I didn't laugh because of that.'

'Of course you didn't, because you were just as involved, and I'd long ago admitted that I was a Russian and loved Russia. You remember the way we only read "the facts" as you called them.' She smiled. 'Though you're very often a bit odd, you were sometimes so lively you always knew exactly how to put things and interest yourself in what interested me. When you're behaving like a student, you really are very charming and original. I think other roles don't suit you,' she added with a sly, enchanting grin. 'You remember how we sometimes spent whole hours talking only about statistics, counting them and adding them up in our concern for how many schools we had and the direction our education was going in. We counted up the number of murders and criminal trials and compared them with the so-called good news . . . We wanted to find out where it was all leading and what would happen to us in the end. I thought you had genuine sincerity. In our high society no one talks with women like that. Last week I mentioned Bismarck to Prince So-and-so because I was very interested in the problem and didn't know how to decide things for myself and—just imagine—he sat down next to me and began to tell me all about it, even in some detail, but all the time with a certain irony and the, to me, insufferable condescension with which "great men" address us women if we're concerning ourselves with what *isn't our business* . . . Remember how we nearly had a row over Bismarck? You were trying to prove to me that your idea of things was "a lot

271

cleaner" than Bismarck's,' she laughed suddenly. 'I've only met two men in my life who've talked to me completely seriously—my late husband, who was a very, very clever and hon-our-able man . . .' she spoke the word with great feeling '. . . and you know who . . .'

'Versilov!' I cried. I had been hanging on her every word.

'Yes. I used to love listening to him. Perhaps I became in the end, er, a bit too candid, but it was then he didn't believe me!'

'He didn't believe you?'

'After all, no one's ever believed me.'

'But Versilov! Versilov!'

'It wasn't simply that he didn't believe me,' she said, lowering her eyes and giving a strange smile, 'but he considered I was a mass of vices.'

'Of which you didn't have a single one!'

'No, I have some.'

'Versilov didn't like you because he didn't understand you,' I said and my eyes flashed.

Her face worked. 'Let's leave it. Don't ever talk to me about . . . about that man!' she added hotly and with emphatic insistence. 'But that's enough. I have to go.' She stood up to leave. 'Well, do you forgive me or not?' she asked, looking me straight in the face.

'I . . . forgive . . . you! Listen, Katerina Nikolaevna—and don't be angry! Are you really getting married?'

'It's not completely decided,' she said in confusion and apparently with some apprehension.

'Is he a good man? Forgive me for asking.'

'Yes, very good . . .'

'Don't say anything more! Don't bother to answer me! I know such questions from me aren't permitted! I only wanted to know whether he was worthy or not, but I'll find out for myself.'

'Oh, just listen to him!' she cried in fright.

'All right, all right, I won't. I'll let that pass . . . But this is what I'd like to say—God grant you every happiness, whatever happiness you like, because . . . because you've given me such happiness now, during this past hour! You're now engraved forever on my heart. I have acquired a priceless treasure—the idea of your perfection. I had suspected you of greed and cunning and coquettishness and was miserable because I couldn't reconcile you with this idea . . . And recently I've been thinking about it night and day and suddenly it's all clear as daylight! Coming here, I thought I would leave you feeling I'd confronted the cunning of the Jesuits and the proverbial snake in the grass, but I found honesty and splendour and the earnestness of a student! You're laughing, are you? Well laugh away! You know you're a saint, so you can't laugh at what's sacred . . .'

'Oh, no, I was simply laughing at the dreadful words you use! Well, I mean, what is "a snake in the grass"?' she laughed.

'You blurted out something priceless today,' I continued enthusiastically. 'How could you have said you "counted on my hot-headedness"? So you're a saint and even admit it, because you've imagined you're somehow guilty and want some kind of martyrdom . . . Though there was no guilt whatever in fact, because even if there was, in your case everything's sacred! But still you needn't have said that, not those words, not that expression! Even such abnormal purity of heart simply shows your true wholesomeness, your respect for me, your belief in me!' I cried out disjointedly. 'Oh, don't blush! Don't blush! Who on earth could slander you by saying you were a passionate woman? Oh, forgive me, I can see I've hurt you! Forgive a crazy 19-year-old for saying something like that! Anyhow, do words matter now? Isn't all this beyond mere words? Versilov once said that Othello didn't kill Desdemona and then himself because he was jealous, but because he had been deprived of his ideal! I can understand that, because this very day I've had my ideal returned to me!'

'You're way out of line! I'm not worth that!' she declared with feeling. 'Remember what I once said about your eyes?' she asked jokingly.

'You mean, that I didn't have eyes, but a couple of microscopes and I magnify every fly into a camel! No, ma'am, I'm not seeing any camel right now! Are you off?'

She was standing in the middle of the room with her muff and shawl in her hand.

'No, I'm waiting for you to leave and I'll go out after that. I want to drop a line to Tatyana Pavlovna.'

'I'm leaving right away. But let me just say again—be happy, by yourself or with whoever you choose! As for me, all I need is an ideal!'

'Dear, kind Arkady Makarovich, believe me, about you I . . . About you my father always says: "the dear, kind boy!" Believe me, I'll always remember what you had to say about a poor boy left with strangers and his lonely dreams . . . I know only too well how it must have affected you . . . But now you and I are like students,' she added, with a pleading and shamefaced smile, pressing my hand. 'But we can't see each other as we used to—you understand that, don't you?'

'Why can't we?'

'We can't, not for a long time. It's my fault. I can see it's impossible now. We'll sometimes meet at daddy's . . .'

I wanted to shout out: 'You're frightened of the hot-headedness of my feelings, is that it? You don't trust me?' but she suddenly became so self-conscious I didn't say a word.

'Tell me . . .' She stopped me suddenly right by the doors. 'You really did see it—the letter. . . being torn up? You remember actually seeing it? How did you know it was the letter to Andronnikov?'

'Kraft told me what it was about and even showed it to me . . . Goodbye! When I used to visit you in your room I was so shy of you, and when you went out I would be ready to fling myself on the floor and kiss the spot where you'd been standing!' I blurted out unaccountably, not knowing why, and dashed out without looking at her.

I rushed home. I was overwhelmed by excitement. Everything flashed through my mind like a whirlwind and my heart was full to bursting. As I approached the place where mother lived, I recalled Liza's ingratitude to Anna Andreevna, the cruel and fantastic things she had just said, and suddenly my heart sank. Why are they all so hard-hearted? And what's wrong with Liza? I thought as I stepped out of the sleigh.

I sent Matvey away and ordered him to come and pick me up at my lodgings at nine.

CHAPTER V

I

I WAS late for dinner, but they had not yet sat down and were waiting for me. Perhaps because I had dinner with them so rarely certain special additions had been made, such as sardines for starters, and so on. But to my surprise and dismay I found all of them preoccupied and frowning. Liza scarcely managed to smile on seeing me, mother was visibly upset, and Versilov smiled, but only with an effort. Has there been a quarrel? I thought. However, to start with things were all right. Versilov did no more than frown a little at a soup with dumplings and only started really making faces when meatballs were served.

'I only have to give due warning that I can't stand certain food for it to appear the next day,' he declared in annoyance.

'We can't think up something new all the time, Andrey Petrovich, can we? One simply can't think up new things,' said mother timidly.

'Your mother is the exact opposite of some of our newspapers, which imagine that only the new is good,' quipped Versilov, trying to be playful and ingratiating but only succeeding in alarming mother even more, since she could not make head or tail of the way she was being compared to newspapers and stared round in bewilderment. At that moment Tatyana Pavlovna came in and, saying she had already had dinner, sat down beside mother on the divan.

So far I had failed to gain this lady's approval. On the contrary, she had begun attacking me worse than ever on every conceivable thing. Her dissatisfaction had become particularly marked recently. She could not bear the sight of my dandyish style of dress and Liza had told me that she almost had a fit when she learned I had hired a dare-devil driver. I ended by avoiding her. Two months ago, after the handing back of the inheritance, I had called on her in the hope of talking about what Versilov had done but encountered not the slightest sympathy from her. On the contrary, she had been awfully vexed that the whole of it had been handed back and not just half. She had remarked to me then in her sharp way:

'I bet you're certain that he returned the money and wanted that duel solely in order to put himself to rights in the opinion of someone called Arkady Makarovich!'

And she was almost right: I *had* felt something of the kind at that time.

I realized the instant she came in that she would be certain to attack me. I was even fairly sure she had come precisely for this reason and so I suddenly became unusually casual in my attitude. It cost me nothing, because I was still, since my recent visit, in a glowing state of high excitement. I will mention once and for all that casualness was never my thing, it didn't suit me and always left me with egg on my face. That is what happened this time. I instantly put my foot in it. Without the least malice and purely out of frivolity, seeing that Liza looked terribly bored, I suddenly blurted out without thinking:

'Every time I've had dinner here, Liza, you have invariably looked bored!'

'I've got a headache,' Liza answered.

'Oh, my God,' cried Tatyana Pavlovna, instantly picking up the thread, 'so the poor girl's ill, is she? Arkady Makarovich has deigned to come to dinner and she ought to be dancing and having fun!'

'You are definitely the bane of my life, Tatyana Pavlovna! I'll never come here again if you're here!' In genuine annoyance I slapped my palm down on the table. Mother shuddered and Versilov gave me a strange look. I suddenly burst out laughing and asked their forgiveness.

'Tatyana Pavlovna, I take back what I said about you being the bane of my life.' I turned to her, still quite casual.

'Oh, no,' she shot back, 'I'm much more flattered to think I'm your bane than the other way round, you can be sure!'

'My dear boy, one must learn to put up with the minor misfortunes in life,' murmured Versilov, smiling. 'Without misfortunes life wouldn't be worth living.'

'You know, you're sometimes an awful reactionary!' I exclaimed, giving a nervous laugh.

'My dear boy, to hell with that!'

'No, why to hell with it? Why shouldn't you tell someone straight to his face he's an ass if he is one?'

'Are you referring to yourself? In the first place, I don't want to judge people and I can't.'

'Why don't you want to, why can't you?'

'I'm too lazy and it goes against the grain. A clever woman once told me that I had no right to judge others because "I didn't know how to suffer" and in order to judge others one has to earn the right by suffering. A bit far-fetched, but in reference to me it was probably correct, so I willingly acquiesced in that judgement.'

'It was Tatyana Pavlovna said it, wasn't it!' I exclaimed.

'How did you guess?' Versilov glanced at me in some astonishment.

'From Tatyana Pavlovna's face. I saw the way it twitched.'

I had guessed quite by accident. It had been said by Tatyana Pavlovna, as it turned out later, the previous day during a heated discussion. I must reiterate that, generally speaking, with all my own joyousness and expansiveness I had appeared among them at the wrong time, because each one of them had their own worries and very onerous ones at that.

'I don't understand any of it because it's so abstract. It's characteristic. You're terribly fond of being abstract, Andrey Petrovich. It's an egoistical characteristic. Only egoists like abstractions.'

'That's well put, but don't go too far.'

'One moment, though, let me ask,' I went on expansively, 'what's it mean—"earn the right by suffering"? An honest man is the one to judge—that's what I think.'

'You won't find a lot of judges in that case.'

'I already know one.'

'Who's that?'

'He's sitting right here and talking to me.'

Versilov gave a strange little laugh, bent to my ear and, taking me by the shoulder, whispered:

'Everything he's said is a lie.'

I still don't know what he meant by this, but evidently at that moment he was in a state of extreme agitation (as a result of some news just received, as I gathered later). But the phrase 'Everything he's said is a lie' was so unexpected and spoken so seriously and with such a strange, solemn expression that I gave a nervous shudder, almost felt frightened, and looked anxiously at him, but he hurriedly laughed it off.

'Well, thank heavens!' cried mother, alarmed by his whispering in my ear. 'I'd thought . . . Arkady, darling, don't be angry with us. There'll always be clever people besides us, but who will there be to love you if we don't have each other?'

'The love of relatives is immoral, mother, because it isn't earned. Love's got to be earned.'

'You haven't earned it yet, but here you're loved for free.'

Everyone suddenly laughed.

'Well, mother, you didn't intend to shoot but you still hit the bull's-eye!' I cried, also bursting out laughing.

'And you actually believe, do you, you've got something to be loved for?' said Tatyana Pavlovna, again on the attack. 'It's not that they love you for nothing, but they love you through loathing!'

'Not true!' I cried gaily. 'Who do you think told me today I was loved?'

'He was laughing at you when he said it!' suddenly broke in Tatyana Pavlovna with a kind of unnatural malice, just as if she had expected to hear me say such words. 'Anyone of any delicacy, particularly a woman, would get polluted simply by contact with all the filth inside you. Your hair's neatly parted, you wear a nice shirt, you've got a suit made by a French tailor, but it's just a cover for filth! Who's decked you out, who feeds you, who gives you money to gamble at roulette? Just think, who are you sponging on so shamelessly?'

Mother went so red I had never seen such a look of shame on her face before. I was completely shattered.

'If I spend money, then I spend my own and don't need to account to anyone!' I shot back, going red in the face.

'What do you mean by your own? What money of your own?'

'So it's not mine, it's Andrey Petrovich's. He won't say no . . . I took the money from the prince on account of what he owed Andrey Petrovich . . .'

'My dear boy,' Versilov suddenly said firmly, 'none of that money's mine.'

That remark had a terrible meaning for me. I had shot my bolt. Oh, it goes without saying, in view of my paradoxical and reckless mood at that time, I could have offered some high and

278

mighty outburst in rebuttal, or some ringing retort, or something of the kind, but suddenly I noticed in Liza's frowning face a sort of malicious look of reproach, an expression I found unjust, almost mocking, and a devil got into me.

'I think, my dear,' I said, turning to her instantly, 'you're often visiting Darya Onisimovna in the prince's apartment, aren't you? Perhaps you'd be good enough to let him have back the three hundred roubles for which you've been pillorying me today!'

I took out the money and handed it to her. Whether believable or not, these crass words were said at that moment without any real purpose, without the slightest allusion to anything. In fact, there couldn't be any allusion because at that moment I simply did not know a thing. Perhaps I simply wanted to annoy her by saying something that was comparatively terribly innocent such as: someone like you, my dear girl, who's always poking her nose into other people's business, wouldn't you like to, if you really want to interefere, meet the prince yourself, a young man, a St Petersburg officer, and hand him the money in person 'if you're so keen to get involved in young men's affairs!' But imagine my astonishment when my mother suddenly stood up and, raising one threatening finger, shrieked out:

'Don't you dare! Don't you dare!'

I could never have imagined her doing such a thing and I myself jumped up not so much in alarm as with a painful wound in my heart at having suddenly realized I had said something dreadful. But mother could not make herself stay. Covering her face with her hands, she walked quickly from the room. Without so much as a glance in my direction, Liza followed her out. For a full half-minute Tatyana Pavlovna surveyed me in silence.

'Surely you didn't really want to talk such nonsense?' she exclaimed wonderingly, looking at me with the deepest astonishment, but, without waiting for me to answer, ran out after them. Versilov, with a disagreeable, almost malicious look, rose from the table and picked up his hat in the corner.

'I assume you're not all that silly, but simply innocent,' he mumbled at me sarcastically. 'If they come back, tell them not to wait for me for dessert. I'm going out for a short walk.'

I remained alone. At first I felt strange, then hurt, and finally I could clearly see I was in the wrong. However, I did not know why, but only sensed that I was. I sat by the window and waited.

After ten minutes I also picked up my hat and went up the ladder to my former attic room. I knew they would be there, mother and Liza, that is, but Tatyana Pavlovna had already gone. That was where I found them both, sitting on my divan and whispering about something. When I appeared they stopped their whispering. To my surprise, they were not angry. Mother, at least, smiled at me.

'Mother, I'm in the wrong,' I began.

'Oh, it's nothing,' she interrupted. 'So long as you love each other and never quarrel, God will send you happiness.'

'Mother, he's never been horrible to me, I'm telling you!' said Liza emphatically and with feeling.

'If it hadn't been for Tatyana Pavlovna, nothing would have happened!' I cried. 'She's evil!'

'Do you see, mother? Do you hear what he says?' Liza pointed at me.

'This is what I'll tell you both,' I declared. 'If there's anything beastly in the world, then I am, but everything else is lovely!'

'Arkady, darling, don't be angry, but if only you'd stop . . .'

'Stop? You mean my gambling? I will, mother. Today'll be the last time, particularly after what Andrey Petrovich announced about none of the money being his. You can't believe how ashamed I was . . . Oh, I must have it out with him . . . Mother, dear mother, last time I was here I said something silly . . . I lied . . . I do sincerely believe, I was only showing off then, I do love Christ very much . . .'

We had actually talked about this last time and mother had been very annoyed and upset. Listening to me now, she smiled at me as if I were a small child:

'Christ, Arkady darling, will forgive everything—both your own blasphemous words and far worse than yours. Christ is our father, Christ is never wanting and his light shines out to us in the darkest depths . . .'

I said goodbye to them and went out, thinking about my chances of seeing Versilov that day. I had a great desire to talk to him and had not been able to recently. I had a strong suspicion he would be waiting at my lodging. I walked there. After being warmer it had begun to freeze a little and it was very pleasant to have a walk.

I was living next to Voznesensky Bridge in the couryard of a large building. Just as I was going through the gates I bumped into Versilov as he was leaving.

'As is my habit, I strolled as far as your lodging and even waited for you at Pyotr Ippolitovich's, but got bored. They're always so quarrelsome there, and today the wife's even gone to lie down and is crying. I glanced in and came away.'

For some reason I felt annoyed.

'You're always coming just to see me. Haven't you got anyone else to see in the whole of St Petersburg apart from me and Pyotr Ippolitovich?'

'My dear boy . . . it doesn't mean a thing.'

'Where are you going now?'

'No, I won't go back to your room. If you like, we can go for a walk. It's a lovely evening.'

'If, instead of talking about abstract matters, you'd talked to me man-to-man and, for example, dropped a hint about my damned gambling, I wouldn't perhaps have been dragged in like a fool,' I said suddenly.

'You're regretting it, are you? That's good,' he responded, hissing the words slightly. 'I always suspected that for you gambling was not the chief thing but just a temporary distraction . . . You're right, dear boy, gambling is bloody silly, and—what's more—you can lose a lot.'

'You can lose other people's money.'

'Have you lost other people's?'

'I've lost yours. I borrowed from the prince what he owed you. Of course, it was terribly silly and foolish of me—to treat your money as mine, I mean, but I wanted to win it all back.'

'I must warn you again, dear boy, that none of it's my money. I know that young man's in difficulties of his own and I don't count on him for anything despite all his promises.'

'In that case I'm in a doubly bad situation—and it's comic! Why should he let me have the money and why should I take it after this?'

'That's your business . . . Are you really sure there's not the slightest reason for you to take money from him, eh?'

'Apart from comradeship . . .'

'No, aside from that, I mean? Is there nothing at all which would make it possible for you to take money from him? Well, for one or another consideration?'

'What consideration? I don't understand.'

'It's all the better you don't, and I admit, dear boy, I was sure of it. *Brisons-là, mon cher*, let's forget about it! And do try to stop your gambling.'

'If only you'd said that before! You tell me now as if you're sort of saying it under your breath!'

'If I'd said it earlier, then we'd simply have quarrelled and you wouldn't have wanted me to come and see you in the evenings. And you should know, dear boy, that all warnings and good advice are merely intrusions into other people's consciences. I've done enough of jumping into other people's consciences and have only been hit and snubbed for it. Of course, I don't give a damn about being hit and snubbed, but the main thing is you'll get nowhere with this sort of manœuvre, because no one'll listen to you no matter how involved you get and you'll be disliked by one and all.'

'I'm glad we've started talking about real things. I want to ask you about something else, have been wanting to a long time, but it's somehow not been possible to talk to you. It's good that we're out on the street. Do you remember that evening two months ago when we were sitting in my coffin of a room, that attic room, and I started questioning you about mother and Makar Ivanovich—do you remember how *frank* I was then? How could you have let a mere boy like me talk like that about his mother? What's more, you didn't say a word to stop me but sort of opened up yourself and made me franker still!'

'My dear boy, I find it only too pleasant to hear you expressing feelings of that kind. Yes, I remember it very well. I was actually waiting to see you go red, and if I did pile it on a bit it was probably just in order to drive you to the limit . . .'

'So all you did was make a fool of me and pollute the fount of purity in my heart! Oh, I can see I'm just a mere boy who can't tell from one minute to the next what's good and what's bad! If you'd shown me then just a bit of the way, I'd have guessed how to go and got on the right path! But all you did then was make me mad!'

'*Cher enfant*, I always had the feeling that you and I would somehow get to know each other. The blush has come to your cheeks of its own accord now, without any help from me, and I swear that's a lot better for you . . . My dear boy, I see you've recently picked up a lot. Is it from enjoying the society of that princeling?'

'Don't be nice, I can't stand that. Don't leave me with the strong suspicion you're being nice out of a kind of Jesuitical disregard for the truth, just in order to go on pleasing me. Recently, you see, I have been seeing some ladies. Did you know I was very well received, for example, at Anna Andreevna's?'

'I knew that from her, dear boy. Yes, she is extremely charming and clever. *Mais brisons-là, mon cher.* Today I feel strangely upset—maybe it's depression, eh? I attribute it to haemorrhoids. What happened at home? Nothing at all? I imagine you made it up there and there were hugs all round, eh? *Cela va sans dire.* It makes me miserable sometimes going back there, even after the muddiest walk. Sometimes I make a long detour in the rain in order not to have to return to the bosom of the family—God, it's so boring, so boring!'

'Mother . . .'

'Your mother is the most perfect and delightful creature, *mais* . . . To put it briefly, I'm probably not worthy of them. By the way, wasn't there something wrong with them today? In the last few days they've all been so . . . so . . . You know I always try to ignore these things, but today something's been happening. Did you notice?'

'I don't know anything and wouldn't even have noticed anything if it hadn't been for that damned Tatyana Pavlovna, who simply cannot resist getting her teeth into me. You're right: something *is* wrong. Just now I found Liza at Anna Andreevna's. Even there she was a bit . . . she even astonished me with something she said. Did you know she went to Anna Andreevna's?'

'Yes, dear boy, I did. When were you at Anna Andreevna's, at what time exactly? I have a reason for asking.'

'Between two and three. And imagine, as I was leaving, the prince arrived . . .'

I told him all about my visit down to the last detail. He listened in silence, made no mention of the possibility of the prince courting Anna Andreevna and in response to my excited praise for Anna Andreevna herself again mumbled that she was 'charming'.

'I succeeded in astonishing her a great deal today by giving her the news—hot from the oven, as it were—that Katerina Nikolaevna Akhmakov was going to marry Baron Björing,' I said explosively, just as if the news had burst out of me.

'Are you sure? I mean, she told me that very same news just before midday, much earlier, that is, than you could have astonished her.'

'You mean?' I literally stood stock still. 'How could she have known? But what am I saying? Of course, she could have known it before I told her, but she gave the impression of hearing it from me for the very first time! Still, what am I going on about? Long live broadmindedness! You've got to let people be as broad as they're long, eh? There I was, blurting everything out, and she was tight as a clam . . . All right, that's how it was. Still, she's a most charming person with a most excellent character!'

'Oh, no doubt of it! Each to his own! And what's oddest of all is that these excellent characters sometimes have a special way of knowing exactly how to catch you out. Just think, Anna Andreevna suddenly turned on me this morning and asked: "Do you love Katerina Nikolaevna Akhmakov or not?"'

'What a crazy, unbelievable question!' I cried, again quite staggered. Things even went dark before my eyes. I had never discussed this with him, and here he was himself mentioning it . . . 'So what made her ask it?'

'Nothing, my boy, nothing. She clammed shut again worse than ever, and the main thing is I never allowed even the slightest hint of it in our conversation, nor did she . . . However, you say you know her, so you can imagine whether it's her sort of question. Do you know why?'

'I'm as astonished as you are. Curiosity, perhaps—or maybe she was joking?'

'Oh, on the contrary, it was asked in all seriousness, and it wasn't just a question so much as a demand and obviously made for the most extreme and categorical reasons. Will you be seeing her? Can you find out why? I would ask her myself, only you see . . .'

'But the likelihood, that's the chief thing—the likelihood of you proposing to Katerina Nikolaevna! Forgive me, I'm still a bit stunned! I've never, never talked to you about something like this . . .'

'And a good thing, too, my dear boy!'

'Your past associations and relationships are, you know, something we shouldn't talk about and it would even be silly of me to do so, but recently, just over the last few days, I've wondered to myself several times, what if he had been in love with this woman, if only for an instant? Oh, you'd never have made such a terrible mistake over her as what actually happened! And I know what happened—your mutual hostility and your revulsion, so to speak, against one another, I've heard all about it! I even knew about it in Moscow! But what stands out more than anything is the fact of that intense revulsion, intense dislike, *hatred* even, and suddenly Anna Andreevna asks you if you love her! How could she have got things so wrong? It's absolutely crazy! I tell you, she was having a joke, she must have been!'

'But I note, dear boy . . .' There was suddenly something nervous and emotional in his voice, even heartfelt, which was very rare in his case '. . . I note you yourself are talking about this rather too heatedly. You said just now you have been seeing certain ladies. Of course, it's not for me to ask who, but could "this woman", as you put it, be on the list of recent acquaintances of yours?'

'This woman . . .' My voice suddenly shook. 'Listen, Andrey Petrovich, this woman is what you were just talking to the prince about, she is "living life"—remember? You said that this "living life" is something so direct and simple, something looking you so straight in the face that it's precisely because of this directness and clarity it's impossible to believe it's precisely what we've been looking for so hard all our lives . . . But you see, having this view, you come across an ideal woman and all you can see in such perfection, in this ideal, is "a mass of vices"! So there!'

The reader can judge how excited I was.

'"A mass of vices", indeed! Oh, I know where you got that from!' cried Versilov. 'If the point has been reached where you're told that, then oughtn't you to be congratulated? It means you've reached a state of such intimacy that you're probably to be congratulated on a degree of modesty and discretion rare in a young man.'

His voice was alive with a kindly and friendly laughter. There

285

was something very evocative and delightful in his words and in the bright look on his face, as far as I could see in the dark. He was in a state of surprising elation. I was caught up in it.

'Modesty! Discretion! Oh, no, no!' I exclaimed, blushing and simultaneously squeezing his hand which I had somehow managed to grab and, without noticing, not released. 'Not that at all! I've got nothing to be congratulated on and nothing could ever, ever happen,' I cried, catching my breath and taking off, literally wanting to fly in my enjoyment, 'you know, except, maybe, just this once, just one little time! You see, dad, my marvellous father—you'll let me call you dad, won't you—it's not just between a father and son, but there isn't anyone you can talk to about your relations with a woman, even the purest kind of relations! The purer they are, the worse it is! It's forbidden, it's indecent—confidences are impossible! But if there's nothing, nothing at all, then you can talk about it, can't you?'

'The heart has its own rules.'

'Let me ask you an immodest, very immodest question— you've known women, you've had affairs, haven't you? I'm not asking for details, just, you know, in general!' I had blushed red and was gulping with excitement.

'Sure, I sowed my wild oats.'

'So take a case like this—you can explain it to me, being a more experienced man. Suddenly a woman says when she says goodbye, a bit casually, looking away, "I'll be at such-and-such a place at three o'clock tomorrow afternoon"—let's say it's at Tatyana Pavlovna's!'

I had cut loose again and was now in full flight. My heart thumped and practically stopped. I even almost stopped talking, almost couldn't speak. He listened terribly closely.

'And so the next day I'm at Tatyana Pavlovna's at three o'clock, and I go in and I think to myself, if that cook of hers— you know, her housekeeper—if she opens the door and I ask her if Tatyana Pavlovna's at home and she says she's not, but she's got a lady visitor waiting for her, what on earth am I supposed to think? Well, what do you think?'

'Quite simply, that you've got a date. So you had one, eh? It was today, was it?'

'Oh, no, no, no, it wasn't like that! It happened, but it wasn't a date as such, and I'm saying this to start with, so as not to seem a bastard, but . . .'

'My dear boy, this begins to sound so intriguing I suggest . . .'

'Ten, twenty-five copecks—that's what I used to give to beggars! On the off chance! Just a few copecks, sir, is all I'm asking! A former lieutenant, sir! Just asking for a few copecks, sir!'

A tall figure barred our way suddenly. Perhaps he really was a retired lieutenant. The oddest thing about him was that he was extremely well dressed for his profession and yet there he was holding out his hand.

III

This wretched little episode of the begging lieutenant is something I do not want to leave out because it reminds me of Versilov, the whole man, along with all the minutest details surrounding what was, for him, a moment of fateful significance.

'If you, my good man, do not give way, I will call the police!' suddenly cried out Versilov in an unnaturally high voice, stopping in front of the lieutenant.

I would never have imagined that such anger could be shown by such a philosophical man over such a trifle. And, what's more, just when we had reached what was for him the most interesting point in our conversation, as he had himself declared.

'So what about just five, eh?' shouted the lieutenant rudely, waving his hand. 'Hasn't any bastard got a five? You scoundrels! You bastards! There you are wearin' beaver and yet makin' a national issue out of a measly five copecks!'

'Officer!' shouted Versilov.

But there was no need to shout. A policeman was standing on the corner and had heard the lieutenant swearing.

'I ask you to bear witness to this insulting behaviour and take the man into custody,' said Versilov.

'Hey, I don't care, you got nothing against me! Most of all, you'll show you got no brains!'

'Don't let him go, officer, and come with us,' Versilov insisted.

'Hell, you're not taking him to the station, are you?' I whispered.

'Certainly I am, dear boy. This irresponsible behaviour on our streets is becoming unendurable to the point of ugliness, and if only each citizen did his duty it would turn out more useful for everyone. *C'est comique, mais c'est ce que nous ferons.* Comic though it is, it's what we've got to do.'

The lieutenant expressed himself extremely heatedly for a hundred yards or so, made a show of boldness and courage and claimed 'You can't do this!' and 'It's just five copecks!' and so on. But finally he began whispering something to the policeman. The police officer, a man of good sense and evidently hostile to street disturbances, was, I think, on his side, but only to a certain degree. He responded to his questions with muttered remarks about it being 'too late now' and 'It's a police matter' and 'If you were to apologize and the gentleman were to accept it, then maybe . . .'

'Well, please listen, sir, where are we goin', eh? I'm asking you—where are we goin' and what's the point of it, eh?' the lieutenant shouted loudly. 'If someone who's fallen on hard times is ready to apologize, if you want him to be humiliated, well, look, we're not in a drawing-room now, are we, we're out in the street, dammit! This apology's good enough for the street!'

Versilov stopped and suddenly roared with laughter. I was even beginning to think that he had set up this whole thing just for a joke, but it wasn't so.

'I forgive you completely, Mr Lieutenant, and assure you you're a man of considerable ability. Behave like that in a drawing-room—your behaviour'll soon be quite good enough even for a drawing-room, and so here are a couple of ten-copeck bits, have a drink and a bite to eat. Forgive me, officer, for bothering you. I'd have offered you something for what you've done, only you're on such a good footing as it is . . . Dear boy,' he turned to me, 'there's an eating-place here, the pits really, but one can get some tea there and I'd like to suggest . . . Yes, there it is, let's go.'

I repeat that I had never before seen him in such an excited state, even though his face looked happy and glowed with pleasure. But I noticed that as he took a couple of coins out of his purse to give to the lieutenant his hands were shaking and his fingers would not obey him, so that he had to ask me to do it for him. I can never forget that.

He led me to a tiny dive down some steps near one of the canals. There were only a few people. A creaking, out-of-tune barrel-organ was being played and the place smelled of greasy napkins. We took our seats in a corner.

'You've probably got no idea, have you, but sometimes out of pure boredom—out of a terrible spiritual boredom—I like coming to various filthy dives like this. The surroundings, that hiccoughing aria from *Lucia*, the waiters looking indecently grubby in their Russian outfits, the smell of tobacco, the shouts from the billiard-room, all of it's so mundane and prosaic it almost borders on the fantastic. Well, dear boy, isn't it? I think that son of Mars stopped us in just the right place . . . Ah, here's our tea! I love having tea here . . . Imagine, Pyotr Ippolitovich, your landlord, was just now trying to convince that other pock-marked tenant there that in the last century, in the English parliament, a commission of lawyers was set up to look into the trial of Jesus when he was brought before the high priest and Pilate in order to discover how it would have been conducted according to the laws of the time, and everything was done with the utmost solemnity, with defence counsel and prosecuting counsel and so on. Well, it turned out the jury had to bring in a verdict of guilty! The astonishing thing was that that idiot of a lodger started arguing and swearing, lost his temper, and announced that he'd be leaving tomorrow. The landlord's wife burst into tears because it would mean loss of income . . . *Mais passons*. Let's leave that. Dives like this sometimes have nightingales. Have you heard the story they tell in Moscow? Like the sort of thing your landlord tells. Well, there's a nightingale singing away in a Moscow dive and in comes a merchant who likes everything the way he wants it. "How much is that nightingale?" he asks. "A hundred roubles." "Right, cook it and serve it." They cooked it and served it. "All right, so cut me off ten copecks' worth." I told it to Pyotr Ippolitovich but he wouldn't believe me and even got ratty . . .'

He said a great deal else. I quote this as an example. He endlessly interrupted me the moment I opened my mouth to tell my story and began talking some completely irrelevant nonsense. He talked excitedly and happily and laughed at God knows what and even giggled, which I had never seen him do before. He gulped down one glass of tea and poured himself another. Now

289

I know why, but at the time he seemed just like a man who has received an intriguing, precious, long-awaited letter, who keeps it in front of him and deliberately does not open it but, on the contrary, turns it round and round, studies the envelope and the seal, goes off into another room, postpones, in short, the most interesting moment knowing it will never go away, simply to relish the greater fullness of the pleasure.

It goes without saying that I told him everything, everything from the very beginning, and it probably took about an hour. There was no other way, because I had been dying to speak about it for a long time. I began with our very first meeting at the old prince's, on her arrival from Moscow. Then I described how things had progressed. I did not leave anything out and couldn't because he continuously egged me on, anticipated my words, prompted me. At moments it seemed to me that something fantastic was happening, as though he had been sitting there somewhere or standing behind doors on each occasion during the last two months, seeming to know beforehand every gesture I made and every feeling I had. I felt overwhelming pleasure in confessing it all to him because I saw such emotional gentleness in him, such profound psychological sensitivity, and such an astonishing capacity for anticipating what I wanted to say. He listened as lovingly as a woman. Chiefly, he knew how to do it without making me feel ashamed. Sometimes he would suddenly stop me at some detail, frequently repeating nervously: 'Don't forget the details, that's the main thing. The smaller a thing is, the more important it sometimes is.' He interrupted me several times in this way.

Oh, it goes without saying that I began by being condescending to her, by looking down on her, but I quickly came down to earth. I told him in all sincerity how I was ready to fling myself on the floor and kiss the spot where she had been standing. Most marvellous and brightest of all was his ability to understand to perfection how someone could 'suffer absolute terror over a document' and yet remain the pure and irreproachable person that she had revealed herself as being that day. He understood to perfection my use of the word 'student' to describe her. But as I was drawing to the end of my account I noticed that his kindly smile began to be overtaken from time to time by something exceedingly impatient in his look, something rather distracted and sharp. When I got as far as the 'document', I asked myself whether I should tell him the whole truth and didn't, despite all my excitement. I note this down here as something I will remember all my life. I explained it to him as I had explained it to her, by referring to Kraft. His eyes were burning. A strange furrow formed on his brow, a very sombre one.

'You're quite sure, my boy, about the letter, are you? That Kraft set light to it with a candle? You're not wrong about that?'

'No, I'm not wrong,' I asserted.

'The fact of the matter is that that piece of evidence is exceedingly important for her and if it were in your hands today, this very day you could . . .' But he did not go on to say what I could do. 'So it isn't in your hands now?'

Inwardly I gave a shudder, but not outwardly. Outwardly I did not give myself away at all. I did not even blink. But I still found the question hard to take.

'Not in my hands—what do you mean? Not in my hands *now*? How can it be if Kraft burned it?'

'You're sure?' He directed at me a fiery, fixed, extremely memorable look. However, he was smiling, but all the kindliness, all the former fond femininity in his look, suddenly vanished. It was replaced by something indefinite and distracted. He had become more and more distracted. If he had been more self-possessed then, as he had been before, he would never have asked me about the document. He did ask very likely because he was himself in a frenzy. Yet I say this only now, though at that time I did not pick up all that quickly on the way he had changed. I was still in full flight and my heart was still full of the same old music. But my story was finished and I looked at him.

'Astonishing!' he said suddenly when I had finally finished. 'Very odd, my friend! You say you were there between three and four and Tatyana Pavlovna wasn't at home?'

'Between three and half-past four.'

'Well, believe it or not, I called on Tatyana Pavlovna at just about 3.30 and she was there in her kitchen. I practically always go in the back way.'

'She was there in her kitchen?' I shouted, recoiling from his words in amazement.

'Yes. And she said she couldn't receive me then. I was there a couple of minutes. I had gone to ask her to come to dinner.'

'Maybe she'd just got back from somewhere?'

'I don't know. No, of course she hadn't! She was in her ordinary housecoat. It was just on 3.30.'

'And Tatyana Pavlovna didn't say I was there?'

'No, she didn't tell me you were there. Otherwise I'd have known and wouldn't have asked.'

'Listen, this is very important . . .'

'Yes, though it depends which way you look at it. You've gone quite pale, my dear boy! Anyhow, what's so important?'

'I've been treated like a mere child!'

'It was simply a matter of being "frightened of your hot-headedness", as she herself put it. Well, she had Tatyana Pavlovna there to call on.'

'God, what a dirty trick! Listen, she let me say all those things in the presence of a third party, in the presence of Tatyana Pavlovna, and so that woman overheard everything I've said just now! That's . . . that's terrible even to imagine!'

'*C'est selon, mon cher.*' It all depends, dear boy. Only just now you mentioned the need for "broadmindedness" in your view of women. "Long live broadmindedness!" you said.'

'If I were Othello and you were Iago, then you couldn't have done it better . . . All right, so I'm laughing! There can't be any Othello because the rest of the relationship isn't there. So all I can do is laugh! Why not? I still have faith in what's infinitely greater than me and I've not lost sight of my ideal! If it's one of her jokes, then I forgive her. To play a joke on a silly boy like me—all right, let her! Anyhow, I didn't pretend I was anything else, but a student's what she was and what she is, and that's what she'll be heart and soul and it's what she'll always be! So that's that! Listen, do you think I should go to her right now to find out the truth, or not?'

I had said I was laughing, but there were tears in my eyes.

'Yes, go there, dear boy, if you like.'

'I feel all polluted inside at having told you everything. Don't be angry, dad, but I'm telling you again you can't talk about women to a third person. He'll never understand. An angel wouldn't even understand. If you respect a woman at all, don't tell anyone. If you respect yourself, don't tell anyone. Right now I don't respect myself. Goodbye. I can't forgive myself . . .'

'Please, my dear boy, you're exaggerating. You yourself said there was nothing to it.'

We went out on to the embankment beside the canal and said goodbye.

'Why is it you never give me a proper kiss, a heartfelt, childish kiss, the way a son should kiss a father?' he said with a strange quivering in his voice.

I kissed him passionately.

'Dear boy, try always to be as pure in heart as you are now.'

I had never kissed him before in my life. I could never have imagined he wanted me to.

CHAPTER VI

I

'SO go there!' I told myself, hurrying home. 'At once. I'll very likely find her at home alone or with someone—it doesn't matter, I can ask to speak to her. She'll receive me. She'll be surprised, but she will. If she doesn't, I'll insist and say it's absolutely essential. She'll think it's got something to do with the document and she'll receive me. And I'll find out all about Tatyana. And then what, eh? If I'm wrong, then I deserve whatever she does to me, but if I'm right and she's in the wrong, then that'll be the end of everything! In any case, it'll be the end of everything! What have I got to lose? Nothing! Go there! Go!'

And yet I'll never forget, and I'll even take pride in remembering, that I did *not* go! No one will ever know this, it will die with me, but it's enough that I know it and that at such a moment I was capable of doing something so noble! 'I am tempted but I shall pass by on the other side,' I told myself after thinking it over. A so-called fact may have scared me, but I haven't believed it and I haven't lost my faith in her purity! So why go—what's there to find out about? Why should she have to believe in me in the way I believe in her, in my 'purity', and not be alarmed by

293

my 'hot-headedness' and not call on Tatyana if she wanted? I haven't deserved that much so far as she's concerned. Supposing she doesn't know I deserve it, that I haven't succumbed to 'temptations', that I haven't believed any of the rumours about her, well, I will know and I will be able to respect myself. Respect my own feelings. Oh, yes, she let me say all those things with Tatyana present, she let Tatyana be there, knew she was sitting there and eavesdropping (because that woman couldn't *not* eavesdrop), knew she'd laugh at me—oh, it was dreadful, dreadful! But ... but what if it couldn't have been avoided? What could she have done in a situation like that and how could she be blamed for it? After all, I'd lied to her about Kraft, I'd deceived her, too, because I couldn't avoid it and had told a white lie regardless!

'Oh, my God,' I suddenly exclaimed, going painfully red, 'when I think what I've just been doing! Haven't I just shown her up in front of that Tatyana woman? Haven't I just told Versilov all about it? Still, what am I saying? There's one difference. All I was doing was talking about that document. In all essentials, I was only telling Versilov about that document. There wasn't anything else to tell him about and couldn't have been. Wasn't I the first one to tell him and cry out "there couldn't have been?" He's an understanding man. Hmm ... What hatred there must still be in his heart for that woman! And what a scene there must have been between them then! And why? Out of sheer vanity, of course! *Versilov is not capable of any feeling except sheer vanity.*'

Well, this last thought just popped up at the time and I didn't even notice it. One after another these were the thoughts that rushed through my head at the time and I had a quite clear conscience—I didn't pretend, didn't deceive myself. And if there was something I overlooked at the time, then it was simply through lack of thought and not out of any Jesuitical urge to conceal things.

I went back to my lodgings in a terribly excited and—I have no idea why—a terribly happy, if utterly confused, frame of mind. I was fearful of analysing my feelings and tried as much as possible to stop worrying. The moment I arrived I went to see the landlord's wife. It turned out there had really been a terrible row between her and her husband. She was a very consumptive woman, kindly, perhaps, but, like all consumptives, extremely capricious. I immediately began to calm things down by going and seeing their tenant, the foul-mouthed, pock-marked fool, an extremely self-important official called Chervyakov who worked in a bank, whom I personally greatly disliked but with whom I lived on fairly good terms because I frequently joined with him in the vulgar business of making fun of our landlord, Pyotr Ippolitovich. I at once dissuaded him from leaving, though he would never in fact have reached that decision on his own. The matter concluded with my being able to put an end to the fears of the landlady's wife and setting to rights the pillow beneath her head. 'Pyotr Ippolitovich never knows how to do it properly,' she remarked maliciously. I then busied myself in the kitchen making mustard poultices and preparing a couple for her very expertly with my own hands. Poor Pyotr Ippolitovich merely stared at me enviously, but I did not let him touch them and was literally rewarded with tears of gratitude from her. And then I remember I suddenly got fed up with it all, realizing I hadn't been looking after the sick woman out of the goodness of my heart but for some quite different reason.

I had been nervously waiting for Matvey because that evening I had decided to try my luck for the last time and . . . and, luck apart, had been feeling a terrible need to gamble. Anything else would have been intolerable. If I'd had nowhere else to go, I'd probably have gone to see her. Matvey was about to arrive, when the door suddenly opened and I had a quite unexpected guest, Darya Onisimovna. I frowned in astonishment. She knew where I lived because she had once called on me with a message from mother. I offered her a seat and gave her a questioning look. She did not say anything, simply looked me straight in the eyes and forced herself to smile.

'You haven't come from Liza, have you?' it occurred to me to ask.

'No, sir, I'm just visiting.'

I warned that I would be going out soon, but she again answered that she was 'just visiting' and would be going out herself soon. For some reason I suddenly felt sorry for her. I will mention that she had received a great deal of help from all of us, from mother and particularly from Tatyana Pavlovna, but, having arranged for her to live at Madame Stolbeev's, we had all tended to forget about her apart from Liza who visited her frequently. I think she was the real cause of this because she had such a capacity for self-effacement and reserve despite all her obsequiousness and ingratiating smiles. Personally I disliked those smiles of hers and the fact that she always so obviously composed her looks, and I even thought on one occasion that she had not spent very long grieving over her poor Olya. But this time I somehow felt sorry for her.

And then suddenly, without saying a word, she bent down and, flinging both arms forward, seized me round the waist and rested her face on my knees. She seized hold of my hand with, I thought, the intention of kissing it, but she pressed it to her eyes and hot tears poured down on it. She shuddered all over from her sobbing but she cried without a sound. My heart melted even though I was also rather annoyed. But she embraced me quite trustingly, not at all frightened of my being angry, despite the fact that only a moment before she had been giving me such cringing and servile smiles. I started begging her to be calm.

'Sir, dear, dear young sir, I'm at my wits' end. As soon as it gets dark I can't stand it. It gets dark and I can't stand it, I feel forced to go into the street, into all the murk. It's my imagining makes me, that's the chief thing. I imagine that maybe I'll just go out and suddenly I'll meet her there on the street. I'll be out walking and I'll see her there. I mean, there'll be people out walking and I'll deliberately walk behind them because I'll think to myself: It's her, it's Olya, surely, isn't it? Again and again I think like that. Till I'm just driven silly and just bump into people—oh, it's sickening! I act like I'm drunk, you know, being bumped and pushed and having people swear at me. I keep it all to myself and don't go and see anyone. And when I do it's just more sickening still. I was passing by here where you live and I thought: "I'll go and call on him. He's kinder than all of them. And he was there when it happened." Dear young sir, forgive me, a silly, useless woman. I'll be off now.'

She suddenly stood up and was about to hurry off, but Matvey arrived at that moment. I took her with me and on the way dropped her at Madame Stolbeev's apartment.

Recently I had been going to Zerschikov's to play roulette.*
Before that I had gone to three other places, always with the
prince, who had 'introduced' me. At one place it had been
principally faro and they had played for very high stakes. But I
did not like it there. I saw it was all right there if you had big
money and, besides, too many beginners went there and gilded
high-society youths who were on the make. That is what the
prince liked. He liked to gamble, but he also liked the company
of these rowdies. I noticed that, on the evenings we went there,
although we sometimes entered together, he would manage to
leave me on my own in the course of the evening and never
introduced me to any of his cronies. I would look completely out
of place and it sometimes even got to the point that I attracted
attention for this reason. At the gambling table one sometimes
had to say something to someone, but there was one occasion
when I tried the next day, in those very rooms, to exchange bows
with one young milord, with whom I had not only talked but also
laughed the night before when we'd been sitting next to each
other, and had even guessed a couple of cards for him, and he
completely ignored me—worse, he pretended to look through
me and strolled by me grinning.

So I gave up going there and developed a passion for another
dive (there's no other name for it). They played roulette, on a
pretty small scale, for low stakes, and it was run by a kept woman
who was never there. The atmosphere was terribly free and easy,
though officers and rich merchants frequented it, but everything
was a bit squalid, which tended, however, to attract many people.
Apart from that, I was often lucky there. But I also gave that up
after a disgusting incident which occurred at the height of a
game and ended in a fight between two of the players and started
going to Zershchikov's, to whom the prince had also introduced
me. He was a retired army captain, and the tone of his evenings
was quite bearable, military, annoyingly punctilious in observ-
ance of all forms of honour, businesslike, and to the point. For
example, no pranksters were allowed in, nor were any of the fast
set. That apart, the stakes were no joke. Both faro and roulette
were played. Before that very evening, 15 November, I had been
there only a couple of times and I think that Zershchikov already

knew me by face, but I knew no one else there. As luck would have it, the prince turned up with Darzan that evening about midnight after playing faro with the society rowdies I had abandoned. So that evening I was a stranger in a strange crowd.

If I have a reader who has already read everything I have so far written about my adventures, there is no doubt he would have no difficulty in understanding that I am definitely not suited to society of any kind. The main thing is that I do not know how to conduct myself in society. Whenever I enter somewhere full of people I always feel that I am being electrocuted by people's looks. I begin to feel my flesh literally creep even in places like theatres, not to mention private houses. At all roulette games and gatherings of that sort I simply have no idea how to behave. I either sit there and reproach myself for being excessively soft and polite, or I suddenly spring to my feet and do something rude. Yet scoundrels of every kind know how to conduct themselves with astonishing decorum by comparison with me— and this is what's been maddening me most of all, so that I have been losing my composure more and more. I will say straight out that not only now, but even then, that whole society, including the winning of money, if one is to be quite frank—everything became a trial and a torment. Very definitely a torment. I used to get an extraordinary thrill from it, but it was a thrill from the pain of it. I thought all of it—the people, that is, the gambling and, chiefly, my being there—all of it was bloody horrible. 'The moment I've won I'll say to hell with the whole thing!' I told myself each time I went to sleep at dawn after a night's gambling spree.

And then there was the business of winning, which had nothing to do with my love of money. That's to say, I am not going to repeat the old cliché, usual in such explanations, that I gambled, so to speak, only for the sake of the game, for the sake of the feelings, the love of the risk, the thrill of it, and so on, but not in the least for the profit. No, I needed the money badly, and although it wasn't my chosen path, not my Idea, one way or another I still decided to try it, to experiment with this path to wealth. I was reinforced in this by one strong argument: 'If you have worked out that you can certainly become a millionaire provided you have a sufficiently strong character—and, after all, you have subjected your character to various tests—then show

298

how you get on in this respect, since you're likely, aren't you, to need more character for roulette than for your Idea?' I repeated this over and over to myself.

Since I still hold fast to the conviction that, in a game of chance, having a cool head, keeping all one's faculties of mind and calculation sensitively aware, it is impossible not to overcome the vagaries of blind chance and eventually win through, I was naturally at that time growing more and more annoyed at seeing how I was constantly playing my character false and being distracted all the time by this and that just like a small boy. 'I'm someone who's learned to put up with hunger, but I can't get the better of this silly nonsense!' It drove me crazy. In addition there was an awareness that I had within me, no matter how comic and downtrodden I might seem, a great fund of strength which could make the whole lot of them change their minds about me. This awareness—something I had had virtually all the time during the humiliations of my childhood years—was at that time my sole source of life, the light of my life and my dignity as a human being, my defence and my comfort, otherwise I would probably have killed myself as a child. So how could I not feel annoyed with myself in view of the miserable creature I turned into at the gambling table?

That is why I could not give up gambling. I can see all that clearly now. Apart from this main thing, it was my shallow self-esteem that suffered most, because I always felt humiliated in front of the prince if I lost, and in front of Versilov, although he never deigned to mention it, and in front of everyone, even in front of Tatyana. That's what I thought and felt at the time. Finally, I'll confess something else: I was by then already corrupted. I could not give up my seven-course meals in restaurants, my coachman, my visits to the English store, the gossip of my French hairdresser, all that sort of thing. I was aware of all this at the time, but simply dismissed it with a wave of the hand. Now, as I write, I blush for my sins.

III

Having come by myself and finding myself in an unfamiliar crowd, I took a seat at one corner of the table and started making small bets and spent a couple of hours doing this without stirring from my place. During these two hours my play went in dribs and drabs—neither one thing or another. I missed some great chances, tried not to get worked up, tried to take everything calmly and surely. It ended by my neither winning nor losing. Out of three hundred roubles I had lost some ten to fifteen. This miserable result infuriated me and, what's more, an extremely dirty and unpleasant trick was played on me.

I know that thieves sometimes turn up at roulette games—not street thieves but thieves among the gamblers. I am sure, for example, that the famous gambler Aferdov is a thief. Even now he pops up all over town. I recently came across him driving about with a couple of his own ponies, yet he's a thief because he has stolen from me. I'll leave that story till later. Only a kind of prelude to it occurred this particular evening. I had been sitting throughout the two hours at the corner of the table and beside me, to my left, had been a rotten little dandified fellow, a yid, I think. Besides, he had connections, even wrote and published a bit. At the very end of a game I suddenly won twenty roubles. There were two red banknotes lying on the table in front of me and suddenly I saw this yid reach out and calmly take one of them. I was just about to stop him but he, with the most impudent expression on his face and without raising his voice in the least, suddenly announced to me that they were his winnings, that he had just staked that much and won. He even refused to discuss the matter and turned away.

Inevitably at that moment I was in quite the silliest frame of mind. I had been preoccupied with a big thought of my own and, telling him to go to hell, stood up abruptly and walked away, leaving him a present of the banknote without even wanting to dispute it. What's more, it would have been hard to get into a hassle with the impudent little thief because time would have been lost and play was still continuing.

That was my big mistake, which was reflected in what happened subsequently. Three or four players next to us noticed our tiff and, seeing how easily I acquiesced, probably assumed I was of the same kind. It was exactly midnight. I went into an adjoining room, had a thought, came up with another plan and, returning, exchanged my banknotes for five-rouble demi-imperial gold coins. I ended up with just over forty of them. I divided them into ten piles and decided to put ten stakes of four coins

300

one after another on zero. If I win, I thought, my luck's in; if I don't, so much the better: I'll never gamble again. I will mention that during the whole two hours of play zero had never come up, so eventually no one staked anything on it.

I staked my money standing up, without a word, frowning and gritting my teeth. At the third spin Zershchikov called out zero, which had not come up all day. I was counted out a hundred and forty gold coins as my winnings. I still had seven stakes to play and I continued, with everything beginning to spin and dance around me.

'Come over here!' I shouted across the table to one player whom I had recently been sitting next to, a grey-haired man with a moustache, with a purple face, and dressed in a frock-coat, who had spent several hours placing small bets with inexpressible patience and losing again and again. 'Come over here! This is where the luck is!'

'Are you talking to me?' he cried with a sort of threatening astonishment from the end of the table.

'Yes, you. You'll lose your last penny if you stay there!'

'It's none of your business and I'd ask you not interfere!'

But I could not contain myself. An elderly officer was sitting opposite me. Glancing at my winnings, he remarked to his neighbour:

'Odd about the zero. No, I won't bet on that.'

'Bet on it, Colonel!' I cried, placing my stake.

'I would ask you to leave me alone and spare me your advice, sir,' he said to me sharply. 'You are being very noisy.'

'I am giving you good advice. Well, then, would you like to bet me on zero coming up again? I bet you ten gold coins—see?'

And I staked ten of my demi-imperials.

'A bet of ten in gold? That I can do,' he muttered drily and sternly. 'I bet you zero won't come up.'

'Ten louis d'or, Colonel.'

'What ten louis d'or?'

'Ten demi-imperials, Colonel, or, to put it grandly—louis d'or.'

'Just you call them demi-imperials and don't make jokes with me!'

Of course, I had no hope of winning the bet. It was thirty to one against that zero would come up. But I had made the bet,

301

firstly, because I was showing off and, secondly, because I somehow wanted to attract everyone's attention. I saw only too clearly that no one liked me and took particular pleasure in letting me know it. The roulette wheel began spinning—and imagine the general astonishment when suddenly zero came up again! There was a general outcry.

The splendour of winning completely clouded my senses. A hundred and forty gold demi-imperials were again counted out to me. Zershchikov asked me if I would like to receive part of the winnings in notes, but I mumbled something at him because I literally could not give him a calm, considered answer. My head was going round and my legs were wobbly. I suddenly felt that I terribly wanted to take more risks. Apart from that, I wanted to *do* something, to make a bet and pay someone several thousand. Mechanically I scooped up my heap of banknotes and coins in my palm and had no time to count them. At that very moment I noticed that the prince and Darzan were just behind me. They had just come from their game of faro, at which, so I learned later, they had lost their very last penny.

'Ah, Darzan,' I shouted at him, 'this is where the luck is! Bet on zero!'

'I've lost everything, haven't got a penny,' he answered drily. The prince seemed deliberately not to notice me or know me.

'Here's some money!' I cried, pointing at my pile of gold coins. 'How much do you want?'

'Damn that!' exclaimed Darzan, going red in the face. 'I don't remember asking you for money.'

'He's calling to you.' Zershchikov tugged at my sleeve.

The Colonel who had lost ten demi-imperials in his bet had called me several times and was on the point of swearing at me.

'Please take your winnings!' he shouted, purple with anger. 'I don't have to stand over you. But you'll probably claim later that you didn't receive them. Count them up!'

'I believe you, Colonel, there's no need to count them. All I ask, please, is that you don't rave and shout at me.' And I gathered his little heap of gold coins in my hand.

'My good sir, I beg of you, reserve your raptures for someone else, not for me!' the Colonel cried sharply. 'I don't consort with swine like you!'

'It's odd that someone like that—a mere boy—should be allowed in here,' hushed voices remarked.

But I paid no attention to them, I staked regardless and not again on zero. I bet a whole pile of notes on the first eighteen numbers.

'Let's go, Darzan,' the prince's voice said behind me.

'Are you going home?' I asked, turning round. 'Wait for me, we'll leave together. I'm through here.'

My stake won and it was a big win.

'That's it!' I cried and began gathering my winnings with trembling hands and pouring the gold coins into my pockets without counting them and idiotically shuffling together the banknotes which I wanted to stuff into my side pocket. Suddenly the beringed, puffy hand of Aferdov, who had been sitting to my right and also placing high stakes, came down on three of my hundred-rouble banknotes and covered them with its palm.

'Allow me, sir, to point out those are not yours,' he rapped out sternly, emphasizing each word, but in a fairly soft voice.

That was precisely the prelude to what, in a few days, was destined to have such consequences. Even now I can honestly swear that these three hundred-rouble notes were mine, but my bad luck would have it that, though even then I was sure they were mine, there remained one tenth part which made me doubt and for an honourable man that's everything—and I am an honourable man. The chief thing was that at the time I did not know for certain that Aferdov was a thief. I did not even know his name at that time, so that I could actually believe I was mistaken and the three hundred-rouble notes were not part of my winnings. I did not bother to count my pile of money but simply grabbed hold of it, while Aferdov had a pile of money in front of him next to mine, but counted out in neat piles. Aferdov, moreover, was known there; he was considered wealthy and people treated him with respect. All this influenced me and once again I did not protest. It was a terrible mistake! The worst thing was that I was in a state of high excitement.

'I am extremely sorry that I am not sure, but I think they're actually mine,' I said, my lips quivering in annoyance. The words at once caused an uproar.

'To say something like that you must be *sure* and you've just said you're *not* sure,' said Aferdov in an unendurably haughty way.

'Who is this person? How can this sort of thing be allowed?' were questions that resounded on all sides.

'It's not the first time it's happened to him. The same thing happened between him and Rechberg over a ten-rouble note!' some vile voice cried out beside me.

'All right, that's enough!' I shouted. 'I'm not protesting, take it! The prince . . . Where are the prince and Darzan? Have they left? Gentlemen, did you see where the prince and Darzan went?' And, seizing all my money, literally unable to stuff a few of the gold coins into my pockets and holding them in my fists, I dashed off after the prince and Darzan. I think the reader will see that I am not sparing myself and am remembering myself exactly as I was then, down to the last beastly detail, so as to explain what happened afterwards.

The prince and Darzan had already descended the stairs without paying any attention to my calling and shouting. I caught up with them, but stopped for an instant in front of the doorman and thrust three gold coins into his hand for some reason. He glanced at me in bewilderment and didn't even thank me. But I couldn't care less, and if Matvey had been there I'd probably have doled out a whole fistful of coins to him. I think that's just what I wanted to do, but on dashing outside I remembered I'd sent him home. At that moment the prince's trotter was led up and he took his seat in his sleigh.

'I'm coming with you, prince!' I cried, seizing hold of the travelling rug and waving it about to signal I was getting into the sleigh with him, but suddenly Darzan dashed past me and jumped into the sleigh and the coachman, seizing the rug from me, began tucking his passengers in.

'What the hell!' I shouted frantically. It looked as if I had simply been holding up the travelling rug for Darzan as if I were just a footman.

'Off home!' shouted the prince.

'Stop!' I roared, holding on to the sleigh, but the horse jerked forwards and I tumbled into the snow. I even had the impression they laughed. Jumping to my feet, I instantly summoned an approaching cab and dashed after the prince, urging on the wretched nag every moment of the way.

304

As if on purpose the wretched horse went unnaturally slowly even though I promised the driver a whole rouble. The driver simply whipped his horse and of course gave it a rouble's worth of a beating. My heart sank. I struck up a conversation with the driver, but I could hardly even pronounce my words and muttered a lot of nonsense. It was in this state that I dashed into the prince's apartment. He had only just returned. He had dropped off Darzan on the way and was alone. Pale and angry, he paced about his study. I will repeat: he had lost an awful lot of money that night. He gave me a bewildered, offhand glance.

'You again!' he said, frowning.

'Let's have it out once and for all, sir!' I cried, fighting for breath. 'How dare you treat me like that?'

He gave me a querying look.

'If you were taking Darzan, they you could have said so, but instead you set the horse going and I . . .'

'Oh, yes, I think you fell in the snow!' And he laughed in my face.

'You can get challenged to a duel for that, so we'll start by settling our accounts . . .'

And with a shaking hand I started taking out my money and laying it in little piles, in handfuls and packets on a divan, on a little marble table, and even on an open book. Some coins even fell on the carpet.

'Ah, I see you've won, eh? I can tell from your tone . . .'

He had never spoken to me so cheekily before. I was extremely pale.

'Here it is . . . I don't know how much, it'll have to be counted. I owe you up to three thousand . . . or how much? Is it more or less than that?'

'I don't think I've ever wanted you to pay me back.'

'I want, sir, to pay you back and you know perfectly well why. I know there's a thousand in notes in this packet—look!' And I started counting out the money with shaking hands, but gave up. 'Anyhow, I know there's a thousand here. Well, look, I'll keep this thousand, and all the rest, these piles here, you take to cover what I owe, part of what I owe. I think there's up to two thousand there or maybe more!'

'So you'll still be keeping a thousand for yourself, eh?' The prince showed his teeth in a grin.

'Do you want it? In that case I'd like to . . . I'd thought you wouldn't mind . . . But if you want it, here it is . . .'

'No, I don't need it.' He turned away from me contemptuously and once more started pacing about the room. 'Devil take it! What's got into you to start giving me money?' He faced me suddenly with a terribly challenging look.

'I'm giving it to you to settle accouounts!' I yelled at him in turn.

'Get out of my sight—you and your endless words and gestures!' he cried at me suddenly, stamping his foot in a rage. 'I've long wanted to be rid of both of you, you and your Versilov!'

'You're out of your mind!' I shouted. He did indeed look mad.

'The two of you have driven me crazy with your high-flown phrases—always phrases, phrases, phrases! And about honour—I ask you! I've long wanted to get rid of you! I'm glad, really glad, the time's come! I thought I was in honour bound and blushed at having to receive the two of you! But now I don't consider myself bound by anything if you want to know! Your Versilov's kept on urging me to have a go at Miss Akhmakov and ruin her reputation . . . Don't you dare talk to me about honour after that! Because you're not men of honour, either of you . . . Weren't you ashamed when you took my money?'

I felt things go dark before my eyes.

'I took it from you as a friend,' I began saying terribly quietly. 'You yourself offered it and I believed your friendship meant something . . .'

'I'm not your friend! I didn't give it you because of that, and you yourself know why.'

'I took it against what was owed to Versilov. Of course, that was silly, but I . . .'

'You couldn't do that without his permission and I couldn't give it you without it. I gave you my own money. You knew that and you took it. I had to put up with a hateful farce in my own house!'

'What do I know? What farce? Why did you give me money?'

'*Pous vos beaux yeux, mon cousin!* Because of your beautiful eyes, dear coz!' He laughed right in my face.

306

'To hell with that!' I shouted. 'Here, take it all! Here's the other thousand as well! Now we're quits and tomorrow . . .'

And I flung the packet of banknotes at him that I had been intending to keep for myself. They hit his waistcoat and fell to the floor. Quickly, in three giant strides, he came right up to me.

'Are you trying to tell me,' he said in a fury, giving the words emphasis by pausing between them, 'that after taking my money for a whole month you had no idea your sister was pregnant by me?'

'What? Oh, my God!' I cried, and suddenly my legs gave way and I collapsed on the divan. He told me afterwards I had literally gone white as a sheet. I was out of my mind. I remember that we looked each other in the face without saying a word. A kind of fright showed in his features. He suddenly leaned down, took me by the shoulders and started lifting me up. I remember only too well his fixed smile. It contained mistrust and surprise. He had really not supposed that his words would have such an effect because he was convinced of my guilt.

It ended with my fainting, but only for a moment. I came to, got to my feet, looked at him and considered things—and suddenly the full truth dawned on my long-dormant mind! If I'd been told earlier and someone had asked me what I'd do to him, I'd certainly have answered that I'd have torn him limb from limb. But it all turned out quite differently and not the way I wanted at all. I suddenly covered my face with both hands and burst into bitter, helpless tears. Just like that! Suddenly the young man had become a little boy. Half of me, I mean, was still a little boy. I fell on the divan and gulped out:

'Oh, Liza! Liza! Poor, unfortunate girl!'

The prince was suddenly completely convinced. 'Oh, my God, I've wronged you!' he cried in profound anguish. 'Oh, the dreadful things I thought about you in my suspiciousness . . . Forgive me, Arkady Makarovich!'

I suddenly jumped up meaning to say something to him, stopped in front of him but, without a word, ran out of the room and out of the apartment. I made my way home on foot and scarcely remember a thing about it. I flung myself on to my bed, my face in my pillow, and lay there in the darkness thinking and thinking. At moments like that thoughts are never strictly logical.

My mind and imagination had been torn to shreds and I remember I even began wondering about something completely unrelated, God knows what it was. But the grief and misfortune suddenly once more returned full of pain and heartache and I again wrung my hands and exclaimed 'Liza! Liza!' and started crying again. I don't remember how I fell asleep, but I slept soundly and sweetly.

CHAPTER VII

I

I AWOKE about eight, instantly locked my door, sat down by the window, and started thinking. I stayed there until ten. The maidservant knocked on my door twice but I sent her away. Finally, when it was already eleven, there was another knock. I was on the point of shouting out again, but it was Liza. The maidservant came in with her, bringing me coffee and preparing to light the stove. I could not send her away and the whole time Fyokla was laying the sticks and getting the fire alight I walked up and down my little room, taking huge strides, without initiating a conversation and even trying not to look at Liza. The maidservant took an unconscionably long time over what she was doing and quite deliberately, as all servants do when they know they are preventing people from talking. Liza sat down in the chair by the window and watched me.

'Your coffee'll get cold,' she said suddenly.

I glanced at her. She showed no sign of embarrassment and was completely composed. She even had a smile on her lips.

'That's women for you!' I couldn't help saying and shrugged. At last the maidservant had the stove lit and started tidying up, but I sent her packing and locked the door behind her.

'Tell me, please, why have you again locked the door?' Liza asked.

I stood in front of her.

'Liza, I just couldn't think you'd deceive me like this!' I exclaimed suddenly, not even thinking I would begin this way and without any tears this time, but an almost angry feeling suddenly pierced my heart quite unexpectedly. Liza blushed but said nothing and merely went on looking me straight in the eyes.

'Stop, Liza, stop, don't say anything—oh, I've been such a fool! Or have I? Everything came to a head only yesterday and before that how could I have known about it? From the way you often went to see that Stolbeev woman and Darya Onisimovna? But to me, Liza, you were always so sunny. How could anything like that ever enter my thoughts? Remember how I came across you two months ago in *his* apartment and how we walked along together in the sunshine and were so happy together . . . it was going on then, was it? Was it?'

She gave an affirmative nod of the head.

'So you were deceiving me even then! It wasn't that I was being a fool, Liza, it was my egoism, not my foolishness that was the reason, my heart's egoism and—perhaps my certainty of your saintliness. Oh, I've always been sure you were infinitely superior to me—and now look what's happened! Finally, yesterday, in the course of the whole day I didn't manage to guess despite all the hints . . . Anyhow I had other things on my mind yesterday!'

It was at that point I suddenly remembered Katerina Nikolaevna and once more something pierced my heart like a painfully sharp pin and I went red. Naturally, I couldn't be kind at such a moment.

'Why are you so busy justifying yourself? Arkady, I think you're trying hard to justify yourself—why?' Liza asked quietly and meekly, but in a very firm and assured voice.

'What do you mean—why? What should I be doing now? That's what I might ask! But you ask: "Why?" I don't know what I ought to do. I don't know how brothers behave in these circumstances. I know they ought to force a shotgun marriage. I will behave like an honourable man! But I don't know how honourable men ought to behave in a case like this! Why? Because we're not upper class and he's a prince and he's making a career for himself and he can't be bothered with people like us who are honest and honourable. You and I, we're—I'm not even your brother—we're illegitimate, people with no family name, children of a serf. Do princes marry serfs? Oh, bloody hell! And, to top it all, you just sit there and look at me in astonishment!'

'I believe you're very hurt,' said Liza, again going red, 'but you're rushing to conclusions and making it painful for yourself.'

'Rushing to conclusions? So you think I've not been slow enough! How can you, Liza, how can you say that to me?' I was finally quite carried away in my indignation. 'The shame I've had to put up with! And how much that prince must despise me! Oh, it's all clear to me now, the picture's right there in front of me! He must have imagined that I'd known for a long time about your connection with him, but I'd kept quiet and even given myself airs and graces and boasted to myself of being so "honourable"—that's what he must have thought about me! And all the time I was taking his money because of my sister, because of my sister's shame! That's what he must have found so sickening, and I know exactly how he feels. Day after day to go on seeing and receiving such a bastard because he's her brother, and he talking all the time about being honourable . . . it would freeze any heart, even a heart like his! And you let all this happen, you never warned me! He despised me so much he even talked about me to Stebelkov and told me himself yesterday he wanted to drive both me and Versilov out of his house! I ask you—Stebelkov even talked about Anna Andreevna being as much of a sister to me as Lizaveta Makarovna and claimed his money was better! And I . . . I lazed about impudently on the prince's sofas and pretended to be his equal to his friends, devil take them! And you let all this happen! Maybe even Darzan knew all about it, judging at least by his tone yesterday evening . . . Everyone, everyone knew about it except me!'

'No one knows anything, he's said nothing to any of his friends and *couldn't* say anything,' Liza interrupted. 'As for that Stebelkov, all I know is that Stebelkov's got his knife into him and that Stebelkov could only make so many guesses . . . But I've talked to him about you several times, and he has believed me completely when I've said you knew nothing, so I really don't know why all this came up between you yesterday.'

'Oh, at least I was quits with him yesterday—and that was a load off my heart! Liza, does mother know? Of course she must, that's why she was up in arms against me yesterday . . . Oh, Liza, why are you so certain you're right in everything and don't blame yourself just one little bit? I don't know how people judge things

310

nowadays and what your thoughts are regarding me and mother, your brother and your father . . . Does Versilov know?'

'Mother's not said anything to him. He doesn't ask. Really and truly he doesn't like asking.'

'He knows and doesn't want to know, that's just like him! Well, all right, so you make fun of your brother, your fool of a brother, when he talks about a shotgun marriage, but mother, what about her? Haven't you thought, Liza, what a shameful thing it is for mother? I was thinking about it all night. Mother's first thought right now is: "It's all because I sinned, so it's a case of like mother, like daughter."'

'Oh, what a cruel, wicked thing to say!' cried Liza with tears bursting from her eyes. She stood up and rushed to the door.

'Stop! Stop!' I seized hold of her, put her back in her chair, sat down next to her and did not let go of her.

'It's just as I thought it would be when I was on my way here. You'd be sure to insist I was in the wrong. So I'm in the wrong. It was out of pride I kept silent just now and didn't say anything, but I'm much more sorry for you and mother than I am for myself . . .'

She could not say any more and suddenly broke down in tears.

'That's enough, Liza, don't, don't go on. I'm not going to judge you. Liza, what about mother? Has she known a long time?'

'I think she's known it a long time, but I only told her myself a short while ago when *this* happened,' she said quietly, lowering her eyes.

'And what did she say?'

'She said: "Put up with it!"' said Liza even more quietly.

'Oh, Liza—"Put up with it!" Oh, God forbid you shouldn't do something to yourself!'

'I won't do anything,' she answered firmly and again raised her eyes to mine. 'You don't have to worry,' she added. 'It's not like that.'

'Liza, my dear, all I can see is that I know nothing at all, but despite that I've just realized how much I love you. There's one thing, though, I don't understand. Everything's clear to me, Liza, except for one thing. Why did you fall in love with him? How could you fall in love with someone like that? That's what I want to know!'

'And is that what really kept you awake at night?' Liza asked, smiling calmly.

'Stop, Liza. It was a silly question and you're laughing. Laugh if you like, but surely it's impossible not to be astonished—you and *him*, you're such opposites! I know him well, he's sombre and nervy, very kind, perhaps—I'll grant him that—but by contrast inclined in the highest degree to see the evil in everything to start with—just as I do, of course! He is passionately devoted to everything noble, I grant you, but only, I think, as an ideal. Oh, he's given to being repentant, all his life he's endlessly cursing himself and then repenting, but he never gets any better—much like me, I suppose. Thousands of prejudices and false ideas—and no real thoughts at all! He's looking for something great to sacrifice himself to and all the time mucks about with trivia. Forgive me, Liza—I'm being a fool in saying this, because I'm insulting you, I know . . .'

'Your portrait would be a true one,' Liza smiled, 'but you've been much too hard on him on my account and so there's nothing true about it. He mistrusted you from the start and you couldn't see him whole either, but with me ever since meeting him in Luga . . . even since then he's been seeing only me. Oh, yes, he's nervy and neurotic and without me he'd have gone out of his mind. And if he were to leave me, he'd either go out of his mind or shoot himself. I think he's understood this and knows it.' Liza added this thoughtfully, as if talking to herself. 'Yes, he's weak all the time, but weak people like him are sometimes capable of doing something extraordinarily strong . . . You said something odd about a shotgun marriage. There's no need for anything like that. I know what'll happen. I'm not chasing after him, he's chasing after me. Mother cries and says: "If you marry him, you'll be unhappy, because he'll stop loving you." I don't believe it. I'll probably be unhappy, but he won't stop loving me. That's not why I've not agreed all this time, but for another reason. For a couple of months now I've said no, but today I said yes, I'll marry you. Arkady dear, yesterday, you know, he . . .' Her eyes shone and she suddenly put both arms round my neck '. . . he went to Anna Andreevna and told her straight out, in all sincerity, he couldn't love her . . . Yes, he made everything clear, and now that idea's over and done with! He was never really party to that idea, it was all Prince Nikolay Ivanovich's dream, backed up by his tormentors, Stebelkov and someone else . . . That's why I said yes to him today. Darling Arkady, he very much wants to see you, and don't you take offence after what happened yesterday. He's not very well today and is spending the whole day at home. He really is unwell, Arkady. Don't get the idea he's pretending. He deliberately sent for me and begged me to tell you he "needs" you, he's got lots to tell you and he feels awkward about coming here to your lodgings. Well, good-bye for now! Oh, Arkady, I feel ashamed to say it, but I came here terribly frightened you didn't love me any more and kept on crossing myself the whole way, but you—you're so kind, so nice! I'll never forget this! I'm going to see mother now. You'll try and like him, won't you, just a bit?'

I embraced her passionately and said:

'Liza, I think you're a really strong character. Yes, I can really believe you're not chasing after him but he's chasing after you, except that . . .'

'Except for that question "Why did you fall in love with him", eh?' she broke in, suddenly laughing playfully as she did usually and mimicking the way I had asked the question. And at the same time, just as I do when I say the same thing, she raised her index finger in front of her eyes. We exchanged kisses, but when she left I felt a return of the old heartache.

II

I will note here, simply for my own purposes, that there were moments after Liza left when the most unexpected thoughts swarmed into my head and I was even very glad of them. 'Well,' I thought, 'I'll do what I can. But what's it to me? It can happen to everyone more or less like that. What's it matter that it's happened to Liza? Is it the so-called "honour of the family" I've got to save?' I give an idea how foul my thoughts were just to show what a feeble understanding I had of good and evil. It was only my feelings that saved me. I knew that Liza was unhappy, and so was mother, and I knew this through my feelings whenever I thought about them, and so I had the feeling that what had happened had to be bad.

I must now warn that the events from that day to the catastrophe of my illness occurred with such speed that I am

313

myself astonished, on recalling them now, that I managed to survive them and was not crushed by fate. They rendered my mind and even my feelings so powerless that if, towards the end, I had not been able to help myself and had committed a crime (and a crime was only narrowly avoided), then the jury would very likely have acquitted me. But I will try to describe everything in logical sequence, although I must warn that there was little order to my thoughts at that time. The events burst upon me like a hurricane and my thoughts spun round in my mind like dry autumn leaves. Because I was so full of other people's ideas, where could I get any of my own from when decisions had to be made? I had no one to guide me.

I decided to go to the prince that evening in order to discuss everything in complete freedom and stayed at home till then. But towards evening I received by city mail another note from Stebelkov, three lines in length, insisting and giving the 'most convincing' reasons for seeing him the next morning at eleven 'on the most pressing matters, and you will see for yourself how pressing'. After a moment's thought I decided to act as circumstances might demand, because the following day was still a long way off.

It was already eight by then and I would have gone out, but I had been expecting Versilov. There was a great deal I wanted to say to him and my heart was literally burning. But Versilov showed no sign of coming and did not come. I felt it was impossible for me to go and see mother and Liza, and I had the strong feeling that Versilov had not been there all day. I went out on foot and the thought occurred to me that I ought to take a look in yesterday's 'dive' by the canal. As it happened, Versilov was sitting where he had sat the previous day.

'I thought you'd come here,' he said, glancing at me strangely and giving me a strange smile. It was not a kindly smile and I had not seen one like that on his face for a long while.

I sat down at his table and told him to start with all the facts about the prince and Liza and the previous day's scene with the prince after playing roulette, not forgetting my own winnings. He listened very attentively and questioned me about the prince's decision to marry Liza.

'*Pauvre enfant*, poor child, she's not likely to get much from

314

that. But it'll probably never happen . . . though he's quite capable . . .'

'Tell me as a friend—did you know about this, did you see it coming?'

'My boy, how could I? It's all a matter of someone else's feelings and someone else's conscience, albeit that poor girl's. I repeat to you what I said before—I've had enough of jumping into other people's consciences. It's a most uncomfortable procedure! I won't refuse help in time of misfortune, in so far as I'm able to and if I can make out what's wrong. And you, dear boy, you never suspected anything?'

'How could you,' I cried, flaring up, 'how could you, even if you'd had the faintest suspicion that I knew about Liza's connection with the prince and seeing that I was accepting money from the prince at the same time, how could you talk to me, sit with me, offer your hand to me—*me*, whom you must have considered an absolute bastard, because I bet you must have suspected I knew everything and was knowingly accepting money from the prince because of my sister?'

'Again it's a matter of conscience,' he grinned. 'And how do you know,' he added distinctly, with a feeling I could only guess at, 'how do you know I wasn't frightened, as you were yesterday on another occasion, of losing my "ideal" and, instead of my passionate and honest boy, finding a scoundrel? Being wary, I put off the evil day. Why not presuppose that instead of laziness or double-dealing I was guided by something more innocent, if silly, but nobler? *Que diable!* Devil take it, I'm all too often silly and petty! What use would you be to me if you were the same? Persuasion and correction would be morally wrong in such circumstances. You'd have lost all your value in my eyes, even though you'd be a reformed character . . .'

'Are you sorry for Liza, really sorry?'

'Very sorry, dear boy. Where on earth do you get the idea I'm so unfeeling? On the contrary, I'll try as hard as I can . . . Well, tell me about yourself, how are *your* affairs?'

'Forget my affairs. *I* haven't got any affairs now. Listen, why do you doubt he'll get married? He was at Anna Andreevna's yesterday and definitely put an end . . . well, gave up that silly idea . . . the one Nikolay Ivanovich had of marrying them off. He positively refused.'

315

'Really? When did this happen? And who did you hear this from?' he inquired with interest. I told him everything I knew.

'Hm . . .' He spoke thoughtfully and as if he were turning things over in his mind. 'It must have happened just about an hour . . . just about an hour before that other frank exchange. Hm . . . Well, of course, the same thing could have happened there . . . although I know that so far nothing has been said or done on either side in that case . . . Of course, a couple of words are enough for a frank exchange. But here's something for you.' He suddenly grinned in an odd way. 'I'll intrigue you right now with an exceptionally interesting piece of news. If your prince had proposed to Anna Andreevna yesterday—which, between ourselves, *entre nous soit dit*, I'd have done everything to stop, bearing Liza in mind—then Anna Andreevna would certainly and in any case have refused him outright. I think you're very fond of Anna Andreevna, aren't you? You respect her and care for her, don't you? That's very nice of you, so you'll probably be very pleased for her. She is getting married, my boy, and judging by her character I think she will certainly go ahead with it and I—well, of course, I give her my blessing.'

'She's getting married! Who's she marrying?' I cried out, absolutely astonished.

'Just you guess. No, I won't keep you in suspense. She's marrying Nikolay Ivanovich, your dear old prince.'

I gaped at him.

'She's been toying with the idea for a long time and looking at it artistically, as it were, from every angle,' he went on, speaking in a languid drawl that emphasized each word. 'I suppose it must have happened just about an hour after Prince Sergey's visit. He would have dashed up just at that moment, wouldn't he! She simple went to Prince Nikolay Ivanovich and proposed to him.'

'What do you mean—"proposed to him"? You mean he proposed to her.'

'Not him, no! No, *she* did. Anyhow, he's over the moon! I gather he just sits there in amazement that it had never occurred to him. I hear he's even indisposed—very likely from sheer excitement!'

'Listen a moment, you're making so light of it I can hardly believe a word . . . How could she propose to him? What did she say?'

'I assure you, dear boy, I am sincerely pleased,' he answered, suddenly adopting a surprisingly serious look. 'He is old, of course, but he can get married according to all prevailing laws and customs, while she . . . here again it's a matter of someone else's conscience, as I've just repeated to you, dear boy. Besides, she is only too capable of having her own view of things and making up her own mind. But as for the details and the words she actually used, about that I can't say anything, my dear boy. Of course she knew what to say, just as you and I would and without making anything up. The best thing of all is that there's been no scandal; in society's eyes everything's just right, it's *très comme il faut*. Of course, it's only too obvious she wanted a place for herself in society, but she deserves one, after all. It's all a completely social thing, dear boy. She must have made her proposal elegantly, magnificently. She's a stern type of girl, dear boy, a female monk, as you once called her, or a "quiet girl" as I've long referred to her. She's almost one of his protégées, you know, and can testify to his kindness. She assured me a long while back that she "respected him so much and cared for him so much and felt such pity and sympathy for him", and so on and so forth, so that I was even partly prepared for what's happened. I was told all this this morning, on her behalf and at her wish, by my son and her brother, Andrey Andreevich, who I think you don't know and who I see regularly every six months. He gives his respectful approval to what she's doing.'

'So it's already been announced, has it? My God, I'm amazed!'

'No, no, it's not announced as yet . . . I don't know when it'll be. In general I'm completely on the sidelines. But it's all true.'

'But now there's Katerina Nikolaevna . . . What do you think, Björing won't like that, will he?'

'I have no idea, personally, what he'll find to dislike. But, believe me, Anna Andreevna is in this sense respectable in the highest degree. And Anna Andreevna's got her head screwed on! She asked me just yesterday morning whether I was in love with the widow Akhmakov. Remember, I told you yesterday, with some amazement. What she meant was: won't it be impossible for her to marry the father if I marry his daughter? Do you understand now?'

'Well I never!' I cried. 'You don't really mean that Anna

317

Andreevna could suppose that . . . that you might want to marry Katerina Nikolaevna?'

'It seems so, dear boy, but anyhow . . . but anyhow I think it's time you were on your way. I have a headache, you see. I'll ask them to play *Lucia* for me. I adore the sheer pomposity of boredom, but I've already told you about that . . . I'm repeating myself unforgivably. Anyhow, I'll probably be going myself. I love you, dear boy, but goodbye. Whenever I have a headache or toothache I long to be alone.'

A furrow of pain appeared on his brow. I am certain now that he had a headache then, a particularly painful headache.

'Till tomorrow,' I said.

'What's tomorrow and what'll be happening tomorrow?' He smiled sarcastically.

'I'll come to you or you to me.'

'No, I won't come to you, but you'll come rushing to me . . .'

There was a thoroughly nasty look on his face, but I did not give him another thought because I was thinking: how extraordinary! What a remarkable occurrence!

III

The prince really was unwell and was sitting at home with a damp towel wrapped round his head. He had been waiting anxiously for me. Yet it was not just his head that ached, his whole being was morally sick. I must repeat the warning that, throughout this final period, and right up to the moment of catastrophe, I was destined to come across people who were so worked up they were almost deranged, so that I could hardly fail to be infected by them. I confess I arrived full of bad feeling towards him and very ashamed that I had burst into tears in front of him the previous evening. Also, I had been so misled over Liza that I could not help feeling I had been a complete fool. In short, when I entered his room I felt extremely highly strung. But everything false and artificial quickly vanished between us. I must do him the justice of saying that as soon as his nerviness waned and dispersed he gave himself up utterly to feelings which expressed themselves in an almost childlike fondness, trustfulness, and love. He gave me a tearful kiss and at once launched into what he had to say. Yes, I really was very necessary to him because, in what he had to say and in the flow of his ideas, everything was extraordinarily chaotic.

He announced to me quite firmly that he intended to marry Liza, and as soon as possible. 'The fact that she's not of the nobility, believe me, has not concerned me for a second,' he told me. 'My grandfather married a serf girl, a singer in a neighbouring landowner's private theatre. Of course, my family entertained various hopes regarding me, but they now have to give way and there will be no fights. I want to make a final break with eveything right now! It'll all be different, all be new! I've no idea why your sister's fallen in love with me. But without her, of course, I probably wouldn't be able to go on living. I swear to you from the bottom of my heart that I now regard our meeting in Luga as an act of Providence. I think she fell in love with me because of what she called "the boundlessness of my downfall" . . . You understand that, don't you, Arkady Makarovich?'

'Perfectly!' I said with absolute conviction. I was sitting in an armchair at the table while he walked about the room.

'I must tell you the whole story of our meeting without concealing a thing. It all began with an innermost secret of mine which she alone knew, because she was the only person I trusted. And no one else knows it to this day. I had arrived in Luga in a state of despair and stayed with Madame Stolbeev, I don't know why, perhaps because I wanted to be completely by myself. I had only just left my regiment. I had joined it on returning from abroad after my meeting with Andrey Petrovich. I had money in those days and I used to squander it quite openly. But my brother officers disliked me, although I tried not to offend any of them. I will say candidly that I've never really been liked. There was a second lieutenant there, a chap called Stepanov, exceptionally empty-headed, I confess, worthless and even a bit hangdog, with nothing remarkable about him. However, he was unquestionably honest. He attached himself to me and I was on friendly terms with him. He used to spend days on end sitting in a corner of my room without saying a word, but with a certain dignity and without interrupting what I was doing.

'On one occasion I told him a story that was going the rounds, with a lot of embellishments, of course, about the colonel's daughter not being exactly indifferent to me, and so the colonel looked on me as a prospective son-in-law and would do anything

I wanted . . . Anyhow, I'll spare you the details, but the whole thing developed into a very complicated and particularly nasty piece of gossip. It emanated not from Stepanov but from my orderly who had overheard what I said and remembered one joke which compromised the young lady. This orderly of mine when cross-examined by fellow officers after the scandal broke blamed it on Stepanov. Stepanov was placed in a position of not being able to deny what he had heard because it was a matter of honour. Because I had been blatantly lying for two-thirds of the story the officers were outraged and the commander of the regiment, having gathered us all together, was obliged to seek an explanation. In front of everyone Stepanov was asked if he had heard it or not. There and then he told the truth. Well, what did I do then, I, a prince with a thousand-year lineage? I denied it and told Stepanov to his face he was lying, and I did it courteously, in the sense, that is, that he had "misunderstood my meaning" and so on . . . I'll again spare you the details, but the advantage of my position was that, since Stepanov had spent so much time in my company, I could represent the whole business without too much difficulty as a case of him being in cahoots with my orderly for his own profit. Stepanov merely looked at me in silence and shrugged. I remember that look and I'll never forget it. He at once put in his resignation . . . But what do you think happened then?

'All the officers to a man, without a single exception, paid him a visit and persuaded him to withdraw. In a couple of weeks I had resigned myself. I was not expelled, I was not invited to go, I pleaded family reasons for my departure. That's the way it ended. At first I didn't care less and even felt annoyed with them. I stayed in Luga and got to know Lizaveta Makarovna, but after about a month I was looking for my revolver and having thoughts about death. I take a sombre view of things, Arkady Makarovich. I drafted a letter to the commander of the regiment and my fellow officers in which I acknowledged my lying to the full and fully rehabilitated Stepanov's honour. Having written the letter, I confronted myself with the task of deciding whether "to send it and live or send it and die". I could never have decided by myself. Chance, blind chance, following a rapid and unusual conversation with Lizaveta Makarovna, suddenly made us close friends. Up until then she had merely been coming to

320

see Madame Stolbeev. We had been introduced, exchanged greetings, and even a few words. Suddenly I told her everything. It was then she offered me a helping hand.'

'What did she decide?'

'I didn't send the letter. She decided against it. Her argument was that if I sent the letter, then of course I'd be doing something noble and magnanimous and sufficient to wipe away all the disgrace and even more, but would I be able to survive it? Her opinion was that no one would be able to survive that because all future prospects would have been ruined and there would be no hope of renewing my life. And, what's more, though Stepanov might have suffered, he had, after all, been fully vindicated by his brother officers. A paradox, in a word. But she kept me going and I let her have her own way completely.'

'She decided just like a Jesuit, not like a woman!' I cried. 'She was already in love with you!'

'That's what gave me renewed life. I vowed I would change myself, transform my life and deserve respect in my own eyes and in hers, and—and you see how it's all ended! It's ended with you and me going off playing roulette and faro and my not being able to withstand all the temptations of the inheritance, the pleasure of a career, all the people I met, the betting on horses . . . I have given Liza hell—I'm utterly ashamed!'

He wiped his temple with his hand and strode about the room.

'Arkady Makarovich, we've both been afflicted by a fate common to all Russians—you've not known what to do and I've not known what to do. The moment a Russian slips ever so slightly out of the rut of habit and convention he hasn't got the faintest idea what to do. When he's in his rut everything's plain as day: he's got his income, rank, place in society, carriage, visits to friends, his job, and his wife—but the moment that . . . So what am I? A leaf blown about by the wind! I do not know what to do! For two months now I have been trying to stay in my rut, I've loved my rut, I've been drawn to it. You can't imagine the real depths to which I've sunk! I've been in love with Liza, sincerely in love with her—and at the same time I've been thinking about Miss Akhmakov!'

'What?' I cried out, literally in pain. 'No, it can't be true! Anyhow, prince, what were you saying yesterday about Versilov urging you to ruin her reputation?'

'Maybe I exaggerated and I'm as guilty in my suspiciousness towards him as I am towards you. Forget about that. Do you imagine that the whole time—maybe even since Luga—I haven't yearned for some high ideal in life? I swear to you it's never left me, it's been constantly in the forefront of my thoughts without ever losing any of its beauty in my feeling for it. I remember the vow I made to Lizaveta Makarovna to renew my life. Yesterday Andrey Petrovich, talking about the Russian nobility, had nothing new to tell me, I assure you. My own ideal is firmly fixed—it is a few dozen acres of land, only a few, because there's almost nothing left from my inheritance, and then a final, absolutely final break with society, career, etc., followed by a cottage, a family, and I myself a ploughman or something of the kind. Oh, there's nothing new in that so far as my background is concerned! My uncle used to till the soil with his own hands, so did my grandfather. We're just princes of a thousand-year lineage and as aristocratic as the Rohans,* but we're still paupers. And that's what I would say to my children: "Always remember that you're a Russian 'nobleman, that the sacred blood of Russian princes flows in your veins, but don't ever be ashamed that your father ploughed the land, because he did it *like a prince*!" I wouldn't leave them anything apart from a bit of land, but I'd consider it my duty to give them a higher education. Oh, Liza was such a help! Liza, children, physical work—oh, we dreamed about it, she and I, right here, in these very rooms! And yet at the same time my thoughts were on Miss Akhmakov, not loving the lady at all, and on the possibility of an affluent, society marriage! And it was only after the news brought yesterday by Nashchokin—about that Björing—that I decided to go and see Anna Andreevna.'

'Surely you went to her to say no, didn't you? I think that was an honourable thing to do, wasn't it?'

'Do you really think so?' He stopped right in front of me. 'No, you still don't know what I'm really like! Or . . . or perhaps there's something here I don't know myself, because it's not a matter of my true nature. I am genuinely fond of you, Arkady Makarovich, and yet I've been seriously misleading you throughout these last two months and I'd like you, as Liza's brother, to know the whole truth: I went to see Anna Andreevna to propose to her, not to say no.'

'How can that be? Liza said . . .'

'I was lying to Liza.'

'Allow me, then, to ask—you made a formal proposal of marriage and Anna Andreevna turned you down, did she? Was that how it was? Details are of the utmost importance to me, prince.'

'No, I didn't make any proposal, simply because I didn't manage to. She herself anticipated me—not in so many words, of course, but gave me to understand as *delicately* as possible, in all-too-lucid, all-too-transparent terms, that the idea was impossible.'

'You mean, it didn't matter you didn't propose and your pride hasn't suffered!'

'How can you think like that! There's my own conscience, and there's Liza, whom I've misled . . . and would have abandoned, isn't there? There's the vow I gave to myself and all my ancestors—to be born again and atone for all my past errors! Don't say anything to her about this, I beg you! Perhaps this was the one thing she wouldn't be able to forgive me! I've been ill since yesterday, because I think the chief thing is it's all over now—the last of the Sokolsky line of princes will be sent to Siberia! Poor Liza! I've been waiting for you all day, Arkady Makarovich, to reveal to you, as Liza's brother, what she herself doesn't know. I am a criminal. I am implicated in the forgery of railway shares.'*

'What the hell! What do you mean—Siberia?' I was on my feet, gazing at him in horror. His face wore a look of the most profound, gloomy, helpless sorrow.

'Sit down,' he said and himself sat down in the armchair opposite 'First of all, you should know this. A bit over a year ago, the summer I was in Ems with Lydia Akhmakov and Katerina Nikolaevna, and then in Paris, at the very time I left for a couple of months in Paris, I was short of money. At that very moment Stebelkov turned up. Besides, I'd known him before. He gave me some money and promised me more, but asked for my help in return. He needed to find an artist, a draughtsman, an engraver, a lithographer, and suchlike, a chemist and technician—for a particular purpose, mind. He talked fairly openly about his purpose from the start. Well, he knew my character, didn't he? The whole thing just made me laugh. The point was that, ever since my schooldays I'd known someone who was now a Russian *émigré* and lived in Hamburg, though he wasn't Russian by birth. In Russia he'd been involved in forging documents. This was the chap Stebelkov counted on, but he needed an introduction and he turned to me. I gave him a couple of lines of introduction and forgot about it. Later we kept on meeting and I received as much as three thousand roubles from him. Then I literally forgot about the whole thing. Back here I kept on taking money from him against IOUs and he kept on dancing attendance on me, and suddenly yesterday I learned from him for the first time that I was a criminal.'

'When yesterday?'

'When he and I were shouting at each other in my study before Nashchokin's arrival. For the first time he dared to speak to me quite openly about Anna Andreevna. I raised my hand to strike him, but he suddenly stood up and announced that he and I were in it together and that I ought to remember I was his accomplice and I was just as much of a scoundrel as he was. If those weren't his exact words, then that was what he meant.'

'What nonsense! Surely he was imagining it?'

'No, he wasn't. He came to see me today and explained things in more detail. The shares have been around for quite a while and more are likely, but some have already begun to turn up as forgeries. Of course, I'm not directly involved but "After all, you did give me that letter of introduction"—that's how Stebelkov put it.'

'Did you, or did you not, know why he wanted it?'

'I knew,' the prince answered quietly and lowered his eyes. 'That's to say, you see, I both knew and didn't know. I laughed, I was happy. I didn't give it a thought, the more so since I hadn't any need for forged shares and wasn't intending to forge them myself. But, still, there were those three thousand roubles he'd given me and he didn't even ask for them back and I'd let it happen. Besides, maybe I *was* a forger? I could hardly have failed to know, not being exactly of little importance. I knew about it, but was glad and had been of help to criminal types—for money! So I must be a forger, you see!'

'Oh, you're exaggerating! You may not be blameless, but you're exaggerating!'

'The main thing is that there's a certain Zhibelsky involved, a young chap connected with the law, some kind of lawyer's assistant. He got mixed up in the share business by acting as go-between between me and the gentleman in Hamburg over a lot of nonsense, and I didn't even know why because there was no mention of shares at all . . . Still, he kept two notes in my handwriting, each of only a couple of lines, and yet they could also be evidence. It's only today I've realized this. According to Stebelkov, this Zhibelsky's the real obstacle. He's stolen something, government funds, I think, and intends to steal more and then emigrate. So he needs eight thousand roubles, no less, to help him emigrate. My part of the inheritance is enough to pay off Stebelkov, but Stebelkov says Zhibelsky's got to be paid off as well. Briefly it means I've got to give up my part of the inheritance, plus another ten thousand roubles—that's their last word. Then they'll return the two notes in my handwriting. Clearly they're both in this together.'

'What utter stupidity! If they inform on you, they'll give themselves away! They're not going to inform.'

'I understand that. They're not threatening to inform. They are simply saying: "We're not going to inform, but if the whole thing comes to light, well, then . . ." That's all they're saying, but I think that's enough! It's not a case of having those notes in my pocket no matter what happens, but to be associated with those scoundrels, to be everlastingly thought of as friends of theirs! That would be false to Russia, to my children, to Liza, and my own conscience!'

'Does Liza know about this?'

'No, she doesn't know everything. In her state she wouldn't get over it. Nowadays whenever I wear my regimental uniform and meet a soldier of the regiment I wonder all the time how I could dare wear it.'

'Listen,' I cried suddenly, 'there's no point in any more talk! There's only one thing you can do—go to Prince Nikolay Ivanovich, get ten thousand from him, ask for it but don't say why, then summon those two scoundrels, have it out with them and buy back your notes—and that'll be that! The whole thing'll be over and done with and you can go off and plough the land! Enough of fantasies, try trusting life!'

'I'd been thinking about that,' he said firmly. 'I've spent the whole day trying to decide and now I have decided. I was simply waiting for you. Now I'll be off. You know, I've never in my life taken a penny from Prince Nikolay Ivanovich. He's been kind to our family and even, you know, shown an interest, but I personally, I've never taken money from him. But now I have decided . . . Our Sokolsky line is older, you know, than Prince Nikolay Ivanovich's. They're a junior line, even secondary and a bit dubious . . . Our ancestors feuded. At the beginning of the Petrine reforms my great-great-grandfather, also called Peter, was a schismatic and went off to live in the forests of Kostroma. That Prince Peter was married twice, both times to a girl who wasn't from the aristocracy . . . That's when the other line of Sokolskys started, but I . . . What on earth was I talking about?'

He was very tired and could hardly string two words together.

'Don't worry.' I stood up, seizing my hat. 'Lie down and have a rest, that's the first thing. Prince Nikolay Ivanovich certainly won't refuse you, particularly now he's so overjoyed. You've heard about that, haven't you? No? I've heard the strangest thing—he's going to get married. It's secret, but not of course from you.'

And I told him everything, standing there with my hat in my hand. He knew nothing. He quickly acquainted himself with the details, mainly about the time and place and the degree of authenticity. Of course, I did not hide the fact that it had happened immediately after his visit to Anna Andreevna the previous day. I cannot describe the unhealthy impression the news had on him. His face was contorted by a crooked grimace of a smile that made his lips twitch. Eventually he went dreadfully pale and became lost in thought, his eyes lowered. I suddenly saw only too clearly how badly his self-esteem had been hurt by Anna Andreevna's rejection yesterday. Perhaps, in his unhealthy state, he saw only too clearly the comic and humiliating role he had played before a girl whose agreement, as it now turned out, he had calmly taken for granted the whole time. And finally, perhaps, he recognized he had done the dirty on Liza—and all to no avail! It is curious who these society dandies think they are and the grounds they have for respecting each other. After all, the prince could well have supposed that Anna Andreevna knew about his association with Liza—with her own sister, in effect— and if she didn't know, then very likely would know in due course; and yet he harboured no doubts about her!

'And can you really imagine . . .' arrogantly and aggressively he suddenly flung a glance at me '. . . that I, I could now go, after being given such news, to Prince Nikolay Ivanovich and ask him for money? He is engaged to be married to a girl who has only just turned me down—what scum I'd be, what a creep! No, it's all over now, and if help from the old man was my last hope, then that hope's gone as well!'

In my heart of hearts I agreed with him. But the reality had to be looked at rather more broadly. The old prince was a man, wasn't he, a future bridegroom? A number of ideas occurred to me. Even apart from that, I had already decided to go and see the old prince the next day. Now, though, I tried to make the poor young prince take a less harsh view of things and have a rest. 'If you sleep on it, things'll seem brighter, just you wait and see!' He shook my hand warmly but we did not kiss. I promised to call on him the following evening, saying, 'We'll talk and talk, there'll be so much to talk about!' He smiled morbidly at these words.

CHAPTER VIII

I

ALL that night I dreamed of roulette and gambling and gold and winnings. I was totting up sums of money the whole time, whether at a gambling table or making a stake and taking a chance, and all night long this bore down on me like a nightmare. I will truthfully admit that throughout the previous day, notwithstanding all the unusual things that happened to me, I kept on thinking about my win at Zershchikov's. I tried to suppress the memory, but could not get over it and shuddered every time I thought about it. The win gnawed at my heart. Was I really a born gambler? At least I was sure I was born with the qualities of a gambler. Even now, as I write this, there are moments when I love to think about gambling. I sometimes spend whole hours sitting quietly working things out in my mind and dreaming how it would be if I staked my money and took my winnings. Yes, I have many 'qualities' secreted inside me and my spirit is a restless one.

At ten o'clock I intended to go on foot to see Stebelkov. I sent Matvey home the moment he appeared. As I sipped my morning coffee I tried to think things out. I was feeling content for some reason. An instant's reflection told me I was content chiefly because 'I'll be visiting Prince Nikolay Ivanovich today'. But that day was to prove fateful and full of the unexpected and began with a surprise.

Just on ten o'clock the door of my room was flung open and in flew Tatyana Pavlovna. I could have expected anything save a visit from her and jumped up in alarm. Her expression was ferocious and her movements disordered and, if she'd been asked, she probably wouldn't have been able to say why she had come to me in such a rush. I must say in advance that she had ony just received an exceptionally bad piece of news and was still suffering from the shock of it. And the piece of news involved me as well. However, she stayed in my room only half a minute— or, say, a full minute, but no longer. She literally tore into me.

'So there you are!' She stood in front of me, all bent double looking at me. 'Oh, you puppy-dog, you! What on earth have you done? You still have no idea? He just drinks his coffee! Oh, you chatterbox, you, you little windbag, you paper Casanova, you . . . They thrash boys like you, thrash them, thrash them!'

'Tatyana Pavlovna, what's happened? What is it? Is it mother?'

'You'll find out soon enough!' she shouted threateningly and ran out of the room; and that was that. I would have dashed after her, of course, but I was deterred by an idea—or not an idea so much as a kind of dark foreboding that the expression 'paper Casanova' was the nub of her insults. Needless to say, I could not guess what it meant on my own, but I quickly went out with the idea of dealing with Stebelkov as soon as possible so that I could then go and see Prince Nikolay Ivanovich. My instinctive thought was: 'That's where the key to it all is!'

It was astonishing, but Stebelkov already knew all about Anna Andreevna and even down to the details. I will not describe everything he said and did, but he was in a high state of excitement, indeed in a frenzy of excitement over the 'artistry of the deed'.

'That's a lady for you, sir! No, sir, really what a woman!' he exclaimed. 'No, sir, it's not our way. We sit around doing nothing, but she really wanted to taste the very wellsprings of life—and she did! Oh, she's . . . she's like a classical statue! A classical statue of Minerva, is what she is, except she's alive now and wearing modern-day clothes!'

I asked him to get down to business. As I had guessed, it all boiled down to trying to persuade the prince to go and seek ultimate help from Prince Nikolay Ivanovich. 'Otherwise it'll probably be very, very bad for him and through no wish of mine—eh, is that so or not?'

He looked me closely in the eyes but I don't think he supposed I knew any more than I did the previous day. Nor could he, because it goes without saying that I did not breathe a word about the shares. We had only been talking a short while when he immediately began offering me money—'a considerable amount, sir, considerable, if only you can get the prince to go and ask for the money. It's very, very urgent—that's what it's all about!'

I had no wish to argue with him or dispute things as I had done the previous day and got up to leave, throwing out the remark that I'd try. But suddenly he took me completely by surprise. I had already started going towards the door when he suddenly seized me fondly round the waist and began saying the most incomprehensible things.

I will omit the details and will not describe the thread of what was said for fear of being boring. The essence was that he asked me to introduce him to Mr Dergachev, because he knew I was a visitor at his house.

For an instant I did not say a word, trying as hard as I could not to give myself away by anything I did. Then I answered at once that I was not well acquainted with him and, if I'd been there, then it was only once by accident.

'But if you were *allowed in* that once, you can go again, can't you?'

I asked him directly, but very coldly, why he wanted such help. Even now I cannot understand the naïvety of some people who are no fools, men of business, as Vasin defined them. He explained to me quite openly that he suspected 'something forbidden was going on there at Dergachev's, something strictly forbidden, and if I investigated it I could do myself a bit of good'. And, smiling, he winked at me with his left eye.

I gave no definite answer, but promised to think it over and then left in a hurry. Things had got more complex and so I dashed off to see Vasin, finding him at home luckily.

'Oh, so it's you as well!' he said mysteriously on seeing me.

Without picking up on what he said, I came straight to the point and told him why I was there. He was evidently astonished, although he never lost his composure. He asked about everything in detail.

'Isn't it quite possible you misunderstood him?'

'No, I understood it correctly. The meaning was quite obvious.'

'In any case, I am extremely grateful to you,' he added sincerely. 'Yes, in fact if everything was like that, he assumed you wouldn't be able to turn down his offer of money.'

'He knows my position only too well, what's more. I've been gambling and behaving badly, Vasin.'

'So I've heard.'

'The oddest thing of all to me is how he knows you go there,' I risked saying.

'He knows only too well', Vasin answered quite simply, 'that I'm not there for any purpose. And all the young ones who go there are no more than a lot of talkers. Besides, you can remember that better than any of us.'

It occurred to me he mistrusted me in some way.

'In any case, I am extremely grateful to you.'

'I've heard that Mr Stebelkov's affairs are in a bit of a mess, aren't they?' I ventured to ask. 'At least I've heard something about some shares . . .'

'What shares?'

I mentioned the shares deliberately, but not, of course, in order to tell him about the prince's secret. I simply wanted to offer a hint and see from his face and his eyes whether he knew anything about the shares. I got what I wanted. Through an almost indistinguishable and momentary change of expression I guessed that he probably knew something. I did not answer his question 'What shares?' and said nothing, and he, curiously enough, said no more about them.

'How is Lizaveta Makarovna's health?' he inquired with interest.

'She is well. My sister always speaks of you most respectfully . . .'

Pleasure shone in his eyes. I had long ago guessed he was not indifferent to Liza.

'Prince Sergey Petrovich came to see me a few days ago,' he said suddenly.

'When?' I cried.

'Four days ago.'

'Not yesterday?'

'No, not yesterday.' He gave me a querying look. 'I'll tell you about it in greater detail later, but now I think I ought to warn you,' Vasin went on mysteriously, 'that he seemed to me to be in an abnormal state—emotionally and even mentally. However, I've just had another visitor,' he said with a sudden smile, 'just before you, and was also forced to conclude he was not exactly normal either.'

'You mean the prince has just been here?'

'No, not the prince, I wasn't referring to him. Andrey Petrovich Versilov has just been here and . . . You knew nothing about it? Has something odd happened to him?'

'Maybe something has, but what happened when he came here?' I asked frantically.

'Of course, I ought to keep it secret . . . But then you and I are talking about such odd, all-too-secret things anyhow.' He smiled again. 'Still, Andrey Petrovich didn't ask me to keep it to myself. You're his son, and because I know how you feel about him I think this time I might be doing a good thing if I gave you due warning. Just imagine, he came to ask me that if, in a few days' time—very soon, that is—he was obliged to fight a duel, would I agree to be his second. It goes without saying that I turned him down flat.'

I was flabbergasted. This was the most disturbing thing I had heard. Something had evidently come up, something had happened, there had been some occurrence of which I didn't know a thing! I remember in a flash how Versilov had said yesterday: 'No, I won't come to you, but you'll come rushing to me . . .' I dashed off to see Prince Nikolay Ivanovich, feeling even more

331

strongly I'd find the clue to it all there. In saying goodbye, Vasin once more said how grateful he was.

The old prince was sitting in front of the fire, a rug over his legs. He met me with an interrogatory look, as if he were surprised to see me, although he had been sending word for me to visit him almost daily. Still, he greeted me warmly but gave rather casual and terribly absent-minded replies to my first questions. From time to time he seemed to collect his thoughts and gaze at me fixedly, as if he had forgotten, and was trying to recall, something that should undoubtedly have related to me. I told him straight out that I had heard all about it and was very glad. A kind and welcoming smile at once sprang to his lips and he grew animated. His caution and mistrust vanished in an instant as if he had literally put them out of his mind. And of course he had.

'My dear friend, I just knew you'd be the first to come. You know, only yesterday I thought in regard to you "Who'll be overjoyed? *He* will!" Well, maybe no one else, but that doesn't matter. People'll wag their malicious tongues but it won't amount to much ... *Cher enfant*, it's all so uplifting and delightful ... But then you know her only too well. Anna Andreevna has a high, high opinion of you. She's ... she's a stern and delightful person, a person with a face like those you find on English keepsakes. She's got a face like the most charming English engraving imaginable ... I had a whole collection of engravings like that a couple of years ago ... I've always, always intended to do this, always, I'm just astonished I never thought of it.'

'As far as I can remember, you always singled out Anna Andreevna for special affection.'

'My friend, we don't want to harm a soul. Life with one's friends, with relatives, with those dear to one is real paradise. All people are poets ... In short, ever since prehistoric times this has been recognized. You know, we'll start with summer in Soden and then in Bad Gastein. But why is it you've not been here for such a long time, my friend? What's been wrong with you? I've been expecting you. And such a lot has happened, hasn't it, since then? It's a pity I get so worked up. As soon as I'm alone, I get worked up. That's why I find it impossible to stay alone, isn't that so? It's clear as twice two is four. I realized that from the very first words she said. Oh, my dear friend, she said only a couple of words but they were . . . they were like the finest poetry! You're her brother, aren't you—or almost her brother, eh? My dear chap, it's no wonder I am so fond of you! I swear I had an inkling of all this. I once kissed her sweet little hand and started crying.'

He took out a handkerchief as if ready to cry again. He was deeply moved and was, I think, in one of the worst 'states of mind' of any I could remember since knowing him. Usually, indeed almost always, he was far fresher and livelier.

'I'd have forgiven everyone, my friend,' he went babbling on. 'I want to forgive everyone and I've not quarrelled with anyone for ages. Art, *la poésie dans la vie*, poetry in life itself, a very present help in trouble and she herself, one of biblical beauty. *Quelle charmante personne, a? Les chants de Salomon . . . non, ce n'est pas Salomon, c'est David qui mettait une jeune belle dans son lit pour se chauffer dans sa vieillesse. Enfin David, Salomon,** it's all mixed up in my head—such a terrible muddle! Every single thing, *cher enfant*, can be both magnificent and, at the same time, laughable. *Cette jeune belle de la vieillesse de David—c'est tout un poeme*, it's pure poetry, but Paul de Kock* would have made something pornographic of it and we'd all have laughed. Paul de Kock has no sense of proportion and no taste, but he's got talent . . . Katerina Nikolaevna is all smiles . . . I said we won't get in anyone's way. We've started on our romance and so we ought to be allowed to get on with it. So maybe it's just a dream, but they mustn't take our dream away from us.'

'What do you mean, prince—a dream?'

'Dream? What's that about a dream? Well, maybe it is, but at least let us die from it.'

'Oh, prince, what's death got to do with it? You must live, now's the time for life, nothing else!'

'Isn't that what I'm saying? I'm saying the very same thing. I haven't the faintest idea why life is so short. Of course, it's to prevent boredom, because life's a work of art from the Creator Himself with the finished and irreproachable form of a Pushkin poem. Brevity is the first condition of all true art. But the ones who aren't bored can always have the chance of living longer.'

'Tell me, prince, has it already been announced?'

'No, dear boy, certainly not. We were all agreed on that. It's only in the family, a family matter. So far I've only told Katerina Nikolaevna because I consider I owed it to her. Oh, Katerina Nikolaevna is an angel, a perfect angel!'

'Yes, she is!'

'Yes? You're saying "Yes"? I thought you and she were enemies. Besides, she asked me not to receive you any more. Just think, when you came in I suddenly forgot that.'

'What are you saying?' I jumped up. 'Why? When?'

(My premonition had not deceived me. I'd had the feeling ever since Tatyana Pavlovna came bursting in on me.)

'Yesterday, dear boy, yesterday. I can't even understand how you could have come straight in here, because orders had been given. How did you?'

'I simply came in.'

'Quite the likeliest thing. If you'd tried to get in the back way you'd certainly have been caught. But because you simply came straight in they let you through. Simplicity, *mon cher*, is really the most artful form of deceit.'

'I don't understand. You mean, you'd decided not to receive me?'

'No, dear boy, I said I was on the sidelines . . . That is to say, I gave my complete consent. You can be sure, my dear boy, that I'm very, very fond of you. But Katerina Nikolaevna was far, far too insistent in her demands . . . Ah, here she is!'

At that moment Katerina Nikolaevna suddenly appeared in the doorway. She was dressed for going out and, as was customary with her, had come into her father's room to kiss him goodbye. On seeing me, she stopped, looked confused, quickly turned round, and went out.

'*Voilà!*' cried the prince, stunned by her behaviour and terribly upset.

'It's a misunderstanding!' I cried. 'Just a moment! I . . . I'll be back in a moment, prince!'

And I ran out after Katerina Nikolaevna.

Everything that followed happened so quickly I not only could not keep my wits about me, I also could not even prepare myself. If I'd been able to prepare myself I would, of course, have behaved differently! But I became as lost as a small boy. I dashed in the direction of her rooms, but a footman told me *en route* she had already left and was on her way to her carriage. I flung myself headlong towards the main staircase. Katerina Nikolaevna was going downstairs, dressed in a fur coat, and beside her walked—or, better, led her—a tall, elegant officer, in uniform, without a greatcoat but wearing a sword. A footman followed with the greatcoat. This was the baron, a colonel, a man of about 35, a dandified sort of officer, dry as dust, with a slightly long face, sandy whiskers, and even sandy eyelashes. Although his face was not at all handsome, he had sharp and provocative features. I describe him rapidly, as I saw him at that moment. I had never seen him before. I ran down the stairs behind them without my hat and coat. Katerina Nikolaevna was the first to notice me and quickly whispered something to him. He turned his head, but instantly gave a nod to a manservant and the doorman. The manservant took a step towards me just by the front door, but I brushed him aside and dashed out on to the entrance steps. Björing was seeing Katerina Nikolaevna into her carriage.

'Katerina Nikolaevna! Katerina Nikolaevna!' I shouted out idiotically (Oh, like a fool, like an idiot! Oh, I recall it all, especially standing there without a hat like a fool!)

Björing turned to the manservant once more in a fury and shouted something loudly. They were words I did not catch. I felt someone seize hold of my elbow. At that moment the carriage began to move. I again gave a shout and dashed towards it. I saw Katerina Nikolaevna glance out of the carriage window in what looked like great anxiety. But in my rush towards it I suddenly, without thinking, bumped into Björing and stepped very painfully on his foot. He let out a slight cry, gritted his teeth, and, seizing me firmly by the shoulder, flung me angrily from him, so that I was shoved back three or four steps. At that instant he was handed his greatcoat, flung it over him, took his seat in his sleigh and from there once again yelled at me threateningly, pointing me out to the footmen and doorman. They seized hold of me and restrained me. One manservant threw my coat over my shoulders, another presented me with my hat, and I cannot for the life of me remember what they said. They said something to me and I stood and listened to them without understanding a word. But all at once I turned my back on them and ran off.

Unaware what I was doing, continually bumping into people, I ran to Tatyana Pavlovna's apartment without even thinking of taking a cab. Björing had shoved me about right there in front of her! Of course I had trodden on his foot and he had instinctively pushed me away as someone who had trodden on a corn (and maybe that's just what I had done!). But she had seen it, just as she had seen the servants seize me, and it had all happened right there before her very eyes! When I reached Tatyana Pavlovna's I couldn't say a word to start with and my jaw quivered as if I were in a high fever. And I was! What's more, I was in tears! Oh, the humiliation!

'Ah! What? So you've been thrown out! A good thing! A good thing!' exclaimed Tatyana Pavlovna. Without a word I dropped on to the divan and gazed at her.

'What's the matter with him?' She looked me over intently. 'There, now, have a drink of water! Go on, drink it! So what've you been up to over there?'

I muttered that I had been thrown out and Björing had given me a shove in full view of the street.

'Can you take something in or not? Just you read this, then, and have a gloat.' And, reaching for a note on the table, she handed it to me and waited for my reaction. I instantly recognized Versilov's handwriting. It was a brief note to Katerina Niko-laevna. I shuddered, and that very moment my full awareness of things returned to me. Here are the contents of the awful, ugly, silly, villainous note, word for word:

Dear Katerina Nikolaevna,

No matter how degenerate you may be by nature and through your own devising, I still thought you could restrain your passions and at least not inflict them on children. But you've stooped to that as well. I would like you to know that a certain document of interest to you was not burnt to ashes in a candle flame and was never in Kraft's possession, so there's nothing for you there. Please do not try seducing a certain young person. Spare him, he is not yet adult, is scarcely more than a boy, undeveloped both intellectually and physically—what's he to you? I am taking an interest in him and that is why I have risked writing to you, although I have no hope of success. I have the honour to warn you that I am also sending a copy of this to Baron Björing.

A. Versilov

336

I went pale as I read it, but then I lost my temper and my lips quivered with rage.

'He's writing about me! That's what I told him the day before yesterday!' I shouted in a fury.

'So you did tell him!' Tatyana Pavlovna tore the note out of my hand.

'But . . . that wasn't at all, not at all what I said! Oh, my God, what can she think of me now? But he's out of his mind, surely? He must be mad . . . I saw him yesterday. When was the letter sent?'

'Yesterday afternoon. It came yesterday evening and she herself passed it on to me today.'

'But I myself saw him yesterday. He must be out of his mind! Versilov couldn't have written that! That was written by a madman! Who could write like that to a woman?'

'That's just what madmen write in a fury when they're driven deaf and blind by jealousy and malice and the blood in their veins has turned to gall . . . You still have no idea what he's really like! He'll get a right drubbing now, he'll be beaten to a pulp! He's really done for himself! It'd be better if he laid his head on the rails of the Nikolaevsk line one of these nights! He'd lose it then right enough if he can't bear to keep it any longer! What on earth made you tell him? What could've made you tease him like that? Did you want to show off?'

'But there's such loathing, such absolute hatred in it!' I struck my head with my hand. 'And why? Why? To a woman, too! What's she done to him? What sort of relations have they had, that letters like that can be written?'

'Ab-so-lute hatred!' taunted Tatyana Pavlovna in furious mockery of me.

Once more I went red. I had suddenly realized something completely new. I stared at her questioningly as hard as I could.

'Get out of here!' she hissed at me, turning smartly away and waving her hand dismissively. 'I've had enough of the lot of you! Now that's enough! The whole lot of you can go to hell! The only one I'm sorry for is your mother . . .'

Naturally, I dashed off to see Versilov. The bloody deceit of the man! The crafty devil!

Versilov was not alone. I will explain. Yesterday, having sent off that letter to Katerina Nikolaevna and having actually—God alone knows why—sent a copy to Baron Björing, he had naturally today been awaiting the consequences and had taken precautionary measures. That morning he had transferred mother and Liza (who, as I later learned, having returned home that morning, had fallen ill and was lying in bed) upstairs, into my 'coffin' of an attic, and the rooms downstairs, particularly our 'drawing-room', had been vigorously swept and cleaned. And as actually happened at two o'clock in the afternoon, he had been called on by a certain Baron R., a military man, a colonel, about 40 years of age, German by extraction, tall, boring as hell, physically very strong to all appearances, sandy-haired just like Baron Björing, and fairly broad-shoudered. He was one of those Baron R.s of whom there are dozens in the Russian army, all of them men who give themselves the most affected baronial airs but have no money at all, live only on their pay and are the most out-and-out front-line blimps. I did not arrive to hear the start of their exchanges, but both were very animated. It could hardly be otherwise. Versilov was seated on the divan in front of the table and the baron in an armchair beside it. Versilov was pale but spoke with precision and restraint while the baron blustered loudly and, evidently preferring curt gestures, curbed himself, but looked stern, condescending, and even contemptuous, though a bit astonished as well. On catching sight of me he frowned, but Versilov appeared almost delighted by my arrival:

'Welcome, dear boy. Baron, this is the very young person referred to in my note and, believe me, he will not get in the way, but may even prove useful.' The baron looked me over contemptuously. 'Dear boy,' added Versilov, addressing me, 'I am even glad you are here, but I would ask you to take a seat in the corner until the baron and I are finished. Don't worry, baron, he will just sit quietly in the corner.'

I could not care less, because I had already made up my mind and, besides, the whole thing was such a shock to me. Without a word I took a seat in the corner, tucked away as far as possible, and sat there without stirring until the confrontation was over.

'I repeat to you, baron,' said Versilov, enunciating each word ringingly, 'that I consider Katerina Nikolaevna Akhmakov, to whom I wrote that unworthy and hurtful note, not only the noblest person imaginable but also the summit of all that is humanly perfect!'

'Such a reversal of your words, as I have already remarked, looks awfully like an affirmation of them,' growled the baron. 'Your words were decidedly disrespectful.'

'Yet the best thing would be if you accepted them precisely as they are meant. You see, there are times when I have attacks and, er, various disorders, and I am even receiving treatment for them, and it so happened that on one of these occasions . . .'

'That sort of explanation cuts no ice at all. I have told you over and over that you are continuing to remain stubbornly in error, perhaps deliberately so. I warned you at the start that the entire question as regards the lady—that is to say, your letter to the widow of General Akhmakov—must be left to one side during our present discussion. Yet you keep on going back to it. Baron Björing asked me and entrusted me to clarify only what concerns him personally—that is to say, your impudent inclusion of a copy of your letter and your postscript to the effect that you are prepared to answer for it however and whenever is convenient.'

'But I think the last point is clear and needs no amplification.'

'I understand that. I've heard what you say. You're not even apologizing, but simply going on insisting that "you are prepared to answer for it however and whenever is convenient". But you won't get away as cheaply as that. So I now consider I have the right, in view of the meaning which you persist in attributing to your words, to express myself to you completely frankly. That is to say, I have come to the conclusion that Baron Björing should have nothing whatever to do with you . . . on a basis of equality.'

'Such a decision is, of course, one of the most advantageous so far as your friend, Baron Björing, is concerned, and I confess you have not surprised me in the least. I expected as much.'

I will mention, as a footnote, that it was only too obvious to me from his first words and looks that Versilov was seeking a quarrel with this irascible baron by provoking and teasing him, and was perhaps testing his patience to the limit. The baron bristled.

339

'I have been told that you can be witty, but wit is not the same thing as intelligence.'

'An extraordinarily profound observation, Colonel.'

'I am not asking for any praise from you!' cried the baron. 'And I didn't come here to pass the time of day! Please listen carefully. Baron Björing was in considerable doubt after receiving your letter, because it smacked of a lunatic asylum. And, of course, means could then be found of, er, restraining you, so to speak. But an exception was made in your case and certain information was obtained about you. It turned out that, though you used to belong to good society and had once served in a guards' regiment, you had been socially ostracized and had a more than dubious reputation. However, despite that, I came here in order to see for myself, and what I find above all is that you still permit yourself to play with words and are ready to admit that you are subject to various attacks. Anyhow, enough of that! Baron Björing's social position and reputation cannot be made to suffer in this matter ... In short, my good sir, I am empowered to inform you that if there is any repetition or anything similar happens, means will immediately be found to deal with you—very swift and sure means, I can assure you. We are not living in a jungle but in a well-run country!'

'You're sure of that, are you, my good Baron R.?'

'To hell with that!' The baron suddenly got to his feet. 'You're provoking me to prove to you that I am not your *good Baron R.*!'

'Ah, I must warn you again—' Versilov had also stood up '—that my wife and daughter are within earshot—and I must ask you not to speak so loudly, because your shouts will reach them.'

'Your wife is ... Dammit, if I've been sitting here talking to you, it's been purely with the aim of elucidating this whole nasty business!' The baron went on angry as ever and without lowering his voice. 'Enough!' he shouted in a rage. 'You're not only banished from the company of decent people, you're also a maniac, a really crazy maniac, as people have said you are! You're not worth bothering with and I am telling you that certain measures will be taken today and you will be summoned to a certain place where they know how to treat madmen ... and then you'll be got rid of, out of this town!'

He left the room taking large, rapid strides. Versilov did not see him out. He stood there and looked at me lost in thought,

340

apparently without seeing me. Suddenly he smiled, shook his head and, picking up his hat, also strode in the direction of the door. I seized him by the arm.

'Oh, so it's you! You heard all that, did you?' He stopped right in front of me.

'How could you have done a thing like that? How could you be so nasty and spiteful? How could you be so crafty?'

He looked intently at me and the smile on his lips expanded to the point where he burst out laughing.

'After all, *I*'ve been humiliated—right before her very eyes! He gave me a shove—right before her eyes!' I shouted out beside myself with anger.

'Really? Oh, you poor boy, I'm so sorry! So they've been nasty to you, have they!'

'You're laughing at me, making fun of me! To you it's a joke!'

He quickly tore his arm free of my hand, put on his hat and, laughing real laughter now, left the room. Why should I rush after him then, eh? I understood it all now. In one instant I'd lost everything. Suddenly I caught sight of mother. She had come down from the attic and was looking nervously round.

'Has he gone?'

I silently embraced her and she hugged me as tight as she could.

'Mother, darling mother, how can you stay here? Come with me now, I'll look after you, I'll work myself to the bone to look after you and Liza . . . Give them all up, the whole lot, and come away with me. We'll be by ourselves. Mother, do you remember how you came to see me at the Touchard school and I didn't want to recognize you?'

'I remember, my dear, that I've spent my whole life feeling guilty that I was your mother and I didn't know you.'

'He's the really guilty one, mother. He's to blame for everything. He never loved us.'

'Oh, he loved us.'

'Come away, mother.'

'Where could I go if I wasn't sure he was happy?'

'Where's Liza?'

'She's lying down. She came home and felt so poorly. I'm frightened. Why are people so angry with him? What'll happen now? Where's he gone? Why was that officer threatening him?'

341

'Nothing'll happen to him, mother, nothing ever does. Nothing'll ever happen to him and nothing ever can. He's just that sort of man! Here's Tatyana Pavlovna. Ask her if you don't believe me!' (Tatyana Pavlovna suddenly entered the room.) 'Goodbye, mother! I'll be back in a moment and when I do come back, I'll once again ask you just the same thing . . .'

I dashed out. I couldn't face anyone, not just Tatyana Pavlovna, and mother bothered me so much. I wanted to be alone, quite alone.

V

But I had hardly crossed the street when I felt I couldn't go on walking about bumping senselessly into people, alien and indifferent to them. Yet where could I go? Who needed me? And what did I want now? I went automatically to Prince Sergey Petrovich's without giving him a thought. He was not at home. I told Pyotr, his manservant, that I'd wait in his study (as I had done so many times before). His study was a very large room with a very tall ceiling, crammed full of furniture. I made my way to the darkest corner, sat down on the divan and, leaning my elbows on a table, supported my head with both hands. Yes, the question facing me was 'What do I want now?' If I was quite capable of formulating that question then, the last thing I could do was answer it.

But I was incapable of thinking straight, let alone of asking questions. I have already given due warning that, towards the end of these days, I was 'crushed by events'—and sitting there as I was then everything spun round chaotically in my mind. From time to time various things occurred to me:

'All right, so I've overlooked everything about him and not understood a thing. He has just laughed straight in my face—but he wasn't laughing at me, it was all to do with Björing, not me. The day before yesterday over dinner he knew everything and was gloomy. He seized on the silly confession I made in that "dive" and distorted it all, regardless of the truth—anyhow, what's the truth to him? He doesn't believe a word of what he wrote to her. All he wanted to do was insult her, stupidly insult her, not even knowing why, on any old pretext, and I gave him the pretext! It's the act of a mad dog! Does he now want to kill

342

Björing? Why? Only his heart knows the answer to that! I don't know what's in his heart . . . No, no, I have no idea right now. Is he passionate in loving her or passionate in hating her? I don't know. Does he? When I told mother nothing can ever happen to him, what did I mean? Have I lost him or not?'

'. . . She saw me being shoved . . . Did she also laugh? I'd have laughed! I was a spy, a spy being beaten up!'

'What did it mean . . .' Another thing suddenly occurred to me '. . . what did it mean when he mentioned in that beastly letter of his that the document was not burnt but still exists?'

'Oh, he won't kill Björing? Right now he's probably sitting in that dive listening to *Lucia*! Or maybe, after listening to *Lucia*, he *will* go and kill Björing! Björing shoved me, he almost hit me! Did he really hit me? Björing would not even deign to fight Versilov, so he's unlikely to fight me. Maybe I ought to kill him tomorrow with a revolver after waiting for him out on the street . . .'

I thought of this quite mechanically without dwelling on it at all. There were times when I imagined the door would open and in would come Katerina Nikolaevna and give me her hand and we would both burst out laughing . . . Oh, it's my charming student! she would say. This was my fantasy as well as my wish even when it began to get quite dark in the room.

'Yes, it wasn't all that long ago, was it, that I was standing in her room, saying goodbye to her, and she gave me her hand and laughed? How could it happen that in such a short time there could be such a distance between us? How simple it would be to go to her and have everything out with her right now, this very minute—oh, so simple, so simple! My God, suddenly there's a quite new world! Yes, a quite, quite new world! Liza and the prince—they're part of the old world . . . Which is where I am right now at the prince's. And mother, how could she go on living with him in the old way? I could, I could do everything, but could she? What'll happen now?'

And there whirled through my sick brain the images of Liza, Anna Andreevna, Stebelkov, the prince, Aferdov, and all the rest, but without leaving any trace. My thoughts became all the more formless and elusive and I was glad when I managed to have a single thought and catch hold of it.

'I've got my idea!' I suddenly realized. 'Or have I? Haven't I

343

just been telling myself I've got an idea? My idea is gloom and isolation and can I now really creep back into that former gloom of mine? Oh, my God, I didn't burn that document after all! I literally forgot to burn it the day before yesterday! I'll go back and set light to it with a candle flame—yes, exactly, with a candle flame! Except I don't know if I'm thinking straight . . .'

It had long been quite dark and Pyotr brought in some candles. He stopped in front of me and asked if I had eaten anything. I simply waved my hand. Still, after a while he brought me some tea and I thirstily gulped down a large cupful. Then I asked what the time was. It was 8.30. I was not even surprised I had been sitting there five hours.

'I came in to see you three times,' said Pyotr, 'but I thought you were asleep.'

I hadn't remembered him coming in. I don't know why, but I suddenly took fright at the thought that I had been asleep and started walking about the room so as not to go to sleep again. Finally, my head began aching very badly. Promptly at nine the prince came in and I was surprised that I had been waiting for him. I had forgotten about him completely.

'You're here and I've just been to your place looking for you,' he told me. His face was gloomy and stern, with no trace of a smile. His eyes contained one fixed idea.

'I've spent the whole day looking for help and I've used up every avenue.' He spoke very concentratedly. 'Everything's come to nothing and the outlook's terrible . . .' (NB: he had *not* been to see Prince Nikolay Ivanovich.) 'I saw Zhibelsky, he's an impossible man. The thing is, you see, you've got to have the money to start with and then we'll see what we can do. But if you haven't got the money, well, then . . . I've decided today not to think about it. If we can only get some money today, then we'll see what happens tomorrow. Your winnings of a couple of nights ago are still untouched down to the last copeck. It's just three roubles short of three thousand. After substracting what you owe there'll be three hundred and forty roubles. You take them, and another seven hundred to make up a thousand, and I'll take the remaining two thousand. We'll sit down at Zershchikov's at different ends of the table and try and win ten thousand—maybe we will, maybe we won't . . . In any case, it's the only thing left to us.'

344

He gave me a fatalistic look.

'Yes, yes!' I cried at once, as if given a new lease of life. 'Let's go! That's just why I've been waiting for you . . .'

I must mention that never for an instant throughout all the time I had been there had I thought about roulette.

'But isn't it pretty low-down? Isn't it a mean thing to do?' the prince asked suddenly.

'It's what roulette's for! That's what it's all about!' I cried. 'It's all about money! You and I are saints. Björing's already sold himself. Anna Andreevna has, too, and as for Versilov—have you heard he's a maniac? That's what he is—a maniac, a maniac!'

'Are you all right, Arkady Makarovich? You've got a strange look in your eyes.'

'You'd like to go without me, would you? No, I won't desert you now. Not after I've been dreaming about roulette the whole night long. Let's go, let's be off!' I cried repeatedly as if I had just found the answer to everything.

'All right, let's go, although you seem to be in a fever and there . . .'

He did not finish what he was saying. He had an awfully serious look on his face. We were already on our way out.

'You know,' he said suddenly, coming to a stop in the doorway, 'there is another way out apart from roulette, isn't there?'

'What?'

'The princely way!'

'What's that?'

'You'll find out later. All you ought to know is that I'm unworthy of it because I've left it too late. Let's go, but just you remember what I've said! We'll take the servants' entrance . . . And don't I just know—consciously, wilfully—that right now I'm behaving no better than a lackey in doing what I'm doing!'

VI

I flew off to play roulette as if all hope of saving myself, all possibility of escape was concentrated in that, and yet, as I have already said, until the prince's arrival I had not given it a thought. What's more, I went off to play not for myself, but using the prince's money on the prince's behalf. I cannot rationalize what drew me there, but I was drawn there irresistibly. Oh, never had the people there, their faces, the croupiers, the shouts of the gamblers, the entire nasty astmosphere of Zershchikov's place, never had it all seemed to me so repugnant, so sordid, so crude and sad as it did that time! I can remember only too well the anguish and sadness which seized hold of my heart from time to time during the period spent at the table. So why didn't I leave? Why did I go on with it, as if I had taken on myself the entire responsibility for the course of play, the sacrifice, the feat itself? I will say only this: I can hardly speak of myself then as being in my right mind. And yet I never played so intelligently as I did that evening. I was silent and concentrated, terribly attentive and calculating. I was patient and miserly and at the same time decisive when I had to be. I settled myself again by zero, that is to say again between Zershchikov and Aferdov, who was always seated to Zershchikov's right. I did not like being there, but I was determined to stake on zero and all the other seats near zero were taken. We played for an hour or more. Eventually I saw from where I was sitting that the prince had suddenly risen and, looking pale, had moved towards us and was standing directly across the table from me. He had lost everything and was watching my play in silence, probably not understanding it and not even thinking about it. At that time I had just started winning and Zershchikov was counting out my winnings. Suddenly Aferdov calmly, right before my eyes and quite brazenly, appropriated to his own pile of money one of the hundred-rouble notes which had been counted out to me. I cried out and seized him by the arm. At that moment something totally unexpected happened to me. I literally lost control of myself. It was as if all the horrors and insults of that day had become concentrated in this moment, in the appropriation of this hundred-rouble note! As if everything that had become accumulated and bottled up in me was waiting for this moment to explode!

'He's a thief! He's just stolen my hundred-rouble note!' I exclaimed, beside myself, glaring round me.

I will not describe the ensuing commotion. Such a thing was completely unknown. At Zershchikov's everyone behaved correctly and his gambling was famed for it. But I had lost control of myself. Amid the shouts and cries Zershchikov's voice was suddenly heard saying:

'Well, the money's not here and it *was* lying here! Four hundred roubles!'

Simultaneously something else had happened. Right under Zershchikov's nose four hundred roubles' worth of notes had disappeared from his bank. He pointed to where they had just been and the place turned out to be right beside me, right next to where my own money was, much closer, that is, to me than to Aferdov.

'He's the thief! He's stolen them! Search him!' I cried, pointing at Aferdov.

'This is entirely due', resounded a loud and authoritative voice amid the general shouting, 'to letting anybody you like in here. People are being let in without any recommendation. Who brought him here? Who is he?'

'Dolgoruky someone.'

'Prince Dolgoruky?'

'Prince Sokolsky brought him!' someone shouted.

'Listen, prince!' I yelled frantically at him across the table. 'They think I'm a thief when I've just had money stolen from me! Tell them, tell them about me!'

At this point the worst thing of the whole day happened, even the worst thing in my entire life: *the prince refused*. I saw him shrug his shoulders and in response to a torrent of questions say crisply and clearly:

'I am not answering for anyone. Please leave me alone.'

Meanwhile, Aferdov stood up and loudly demanded that he should be searched. He was busy turning out his own pockets. But his demand was answered by shouts of 'No, no, we know who the thief is!' and two footmen seized hold of me and held me by my arms from behind.

'I will not let you search me, I won't allow it!' I yelled, trying to break free.

But I was led away into a side room and there, before a crowd of people, I was searched down to the last fold of my clothes. I shouted and struggled the whole time.

'He's got rid of it! We must search the floor!' someone decided.

'No point in that now!'

'He could have thrown it under the table!'

'There'll be no trace now!'

They led me out, but in the doorway I managed to shout in a senseless fury, so that the whole room heard it:

'Roulette is forbidden by the police! Today I'll inform on the whole lot of you!'

I was taken downstairs, given my coat, and shown the door to the street.

CHAPTER IX

I

THE day ended in catastrophe, but the night still remained and this is what I remember of it.

I think it was about one o'clock when I found myself out on the street. The night was clear, calm, and frosty. I went almost at a run, in a frightful hurry, but not in the direction of home. 'Why go home?' I told myself. 'Can there be somewhere called home at the moment? People are alive when they're at home and tomorrow I'll wake up in order to go on living—but that's impossible now, isn't it? Life is over, I can't go on living now.' And so I wandered about the streets, having no idea where I was going and not even knowing where I wanted to go. I felt very hot and from time to time undid my heavy racoon coat. It seemed to me at that moment nothing I did could have any purpose. And I had the weird feeling that everything around me, even the air I was breathing, belonged to another planet, as if I had suddenly found myself on the moon. Everything—the city, the passers-by, the pavement along which I ran—was *not mine*. There's Palace Square, I thought, there's St Isaac's, but they've got nothing to do with me! They're strangers to me, they're suddenly *not mine* any more! What I've got is mother and Liza—or have I? What do mother and Liza mean to me now? Everything's finished, it's all over and done with, except for one thing: I'm branded a thief—always and forever a thief!

'How can I prove I'm not a thief? Surely that's impossible now, isn't it? So do I go off to America? What'll I prove by doing that? Versilov'll be the first to believe I stole the money! My "Idea"—well, what about it? What's it worth now? In fifty, in a

348

hundred years' time I might be about the place and there would always be someone to say, pointing at me: "There he goes, the thief! He began his so-called *Idea* by stealing money while playing roulette . . ."'

Was I filled with resentment? I don't know, maybe I was. Strangely enough, it's always been characteristic of me, perhaps ever since earliest childhood, that if anyone ever did me wrong, and did so utterly and completely, totally humiliating me, then I always felt an insatiable urge to submit passively to my humiliation and even go some way towards satisfying the desires of my persecutor by saying: 'All right, so you've humiliated me, now I'll humiliate myself even more, just you see!' Touchard used to beat me and try to show I was a snivelling bastard, not a senator's son, and I immediately took on the role of a snivelling bastard. I not only danced attendance on him by helping him dress, I would myself pick up a brush and set about brushing every last speck of dust off his clothes, entirely without him asking me or ordering me, and would sometimes rush after him with a brush in a fervour of snivelling servility in order to get rid of some speck from his frock-coat, so much so that he would sometimes stop me and say: 'That's enough, Arkady, enough!' He would come home and take off his coat, and I would brush it, fold it carefully, and cover it with a chequered silk handkerchief. I knew the other boys laughed at me and despised me for this, I knew it only too well, but to me what really mattered was that, if someone wanted me to be a snivelling bastard, then I'd be one, or if they wanted me to be a wimp, I'd be a wimp! I could keep up such passive hatred and deep-down loathing for years. So what? At Zershchikov's I had shouted out for everyone to hear, in a complete frenzy: 'I'll inform on the lot of you! Roulette is banned by the police!' And here, I swear, there was something of the same thing. I had been humiliated, searched, declared a thief, utterly crushed. All right, so you've found me out, I'm not only a thief, I'm an informer as well! Recalling it all now, that's how I explain it all, but I wasn't into analysing it at the time. I shouted that out then without intending to, not even knowing for a second I would. The shout just came out of its own accord—proof of that *characteristic* of mine!

While I ran about the place, I was beginning to get delirious, but I remember very clearly I acted quite consciously. Meantime,

I can say quite firmly that a whole series of ideas and assumptions were impossible for me then. I even felt about myself in those minutes that 'I can have some thoughts, but I can't have others'. Just as some things I decided, although clearly knowing what I was doing, could not have had the slightest logic about them. Moreover, I can remember very well that there were moments when I was fully aware of the silliness of some decisions and yet could at the same time set about quite consciously implementing them. Yes, a crime could have been committed that night and it was only by accident it never occurred.

Suddenly I remembered what Tatyana Pavlovna had said about Versilov: 'He ought to lay his head on a rail of the Nikolaevsky line—that'd get rid of it!' For a moment that idea possessed my thoughts, but I instantly rejected it, thinking in anguish: 'So I put my head on a rail and die, but they'll still say tomorrow he did it out of shame because he'd stolen the money—no, no way!' And at that moment, I remember, I suddenly had an instant of frightful resentment, the idea shooting into my mind: 'So what? You can't justify yourself, no way, and you can't start a new life, so you'd better give in, be a snivelling bastard, be a shit, be a louse, be an informer, be a real informer, but meanwhile get things ready on the sly—and then suddenly Bang! Blow the whole lot sky-high! Exterminate the lot, the whole lot, the guilty and the innocent! Then they'll suddenly realize it was the chap they called a thief . . . After that you can kill yourself!'

I don't remember how I got into an alley-way not far from the Horseguards Boulevard. This alley-way had high stone walls on both sides—the rear walls to backyards. Behind the wall on the left I saw a large heap of firewood all stacked as if in a timber yard and rising a metre or more above the wall. I suddenly stopped and had a thought. There were some wax matches in my pocket in a little silver matchbox. I will say again I was fully aware of what I thought of doing at that moment, and that's how I remember it right now—but I don't know why I wanted to do it, I haven't the faintest idea. I just remember I suddenly wanted to do it. It'd be easy to get in there, I reasoned, and, sure enough, within a couple of steps I found a gate in the wall which had certainly been shut tight for months on end. Suppose I get on the bottom rung of the gate, I thought, by grabbing the top of the gate I could get on to the wall, and nobody'd see me, there's nobody about, not a sound to be heard! If I sit on top of the wall I could easily set light to the firewood without even dropping to ground level because the wood's almost touching the wall. It'll burn all the fiercer because it's cold, so all I have to do is grab hold of a birch log ... Hey, there's no need even for that! All I have to do is sit on the wall, pull the bark off a piece of birch, light it with a match and thrust it in the firewood—boy, there'll be a blaze! Then I'll jump down and walk away. There'll be no need to run, it'll be a while before it's noticed ...

Those were my thoughts—and suddenly I came to a decision. I experienced an extraordinary rush of joy and pleasure as I started climbing. I was very good at climbing—gymnastics had been my speciality at school—but I was wearing galoshes and that made things more difficult. However, I managed to grab hold of a higher rung and lift myself up and put out my other hand to get hold of the top of the gate when I suddenly lost my balance and fell to the ground. I suppose I must have struck the back of my head on falling to the ground and lay there senseless for maybe a couple of minutes. Regaining consciousness, I automatically pulled my fur coat round me because I suddenly felt intolerably cold and, still unsure what I was doing, crawled into the corner of the gates and crouched there, bent and shivering, in the recess made by the gates and the jutting wall. My thoughts were all mixed up and I probably very quickly fell into a daze. As if I am dreaming it now I remember my ears were suddenly filled with the massive, heavy clangour of a bell and I was delighted to hear it ringing.

II

The bell rang firmly and precisely once every two or three seconds, but it was not so much an alarm bell as a pleasant, smooth ringing sound and I suddenly knew I recognized it. It was the bell of St Nicholas's, the red-painted church across the road from Touchard's, an ancient Moscow church* which had been built, I remembered, in the reign of Aleksey Mikhailovich and was elaborately decorated, many-domed, and 'pillared' and I was reminded it was only just the end of Holy Week and in the garden of Touchard's house green little leaves would be newly

351

out on the slender birches. A bright, early-evening sun poured its slanting rays into our classroom, but in my little tiny room to the left of the door, where Touchard had put me to be away from 'the sons of Counts and Senators', I had a guest. Yes, I, illegitimate as I was, I had a guest—the first one since I had been at Touchard's. I had recognized her the moment she came in—it was mother, though I had not seen her once since the time she took me to the village church and the dove had flown beneath the cupola. We sat down, the two of us, and I kept on staring at her in an odd way. A great many years later I learned that, abandoned by Versilov who had suddenly gone abroad, she had come to Moscow *on her own*, using her own sparse money, almost without telling those charged with looking after her, simply in order to see me. It was also odd that, after coming in and talking to Touchard, she did not say a word to me about being my mother. She sat beside me and I even remember being surprised she had so little to say. She had a bundle with her and she undid it. It contained six oranges, a few gingerbread biscuits, and two ordinary French loaves. I took offence at the French loaves and announced with a hurt look that we had very good 'eats' at the school and each day we were given a whole white French roll with our tea.

'It doesn't matter, dearest. In my simple way I thought you'd maybe not get fed all that well at school, so don't be offended, my darling.'

'Antonina Vasilevna' (Touchard's wife) 'will be offended. The other boys'll make fun of me . . .'

'Take them, do, and maybe have them to eat, won't you?'

'Please, just don't . . .'

I never even touched the presents. The oranges and gingerbread lay in front of me on the desk and I sat there with my eyes lowered, but with a great look of personal dignity. Who knows, perhaps I had also had a strong desire not to hide from her that her visit would shame me before the other boys. Or maybe just to show her enough of my feelings to make her understand, so to speak: 'You see, you're making me ashamed and you can't even see it!' At that very time, of course, I was running about after Touchard, brushing off every speck of dust! I could just imagine everything I'd have to endure from the other boys the moment she left, and perhaps from Touchard as well. I felt no kindness whatever towards her in my heart. I looked askance at her dark, worn, old-fashioned clothes, her rather coarse, working-class hands, her crude-looking shoes, and her terribly thin face. Deep furrows already seamed her temples, although Antonina Vasilevna remarked to me later on that evening, after she had gone: 'Your mother was very likely very good-looking at one time.'

So we sat there and suddenly Agafya came in with a tray on which there was a cup of coffee. It was after dinner and the Touchards always had coffee in their sitting-room at that time of the evening. But mother said thank you, no she wouldn't. As I learned later, she never took coffee because it gave her palpitations. The thing was that the Touchards, for their part, evidently considered her visit and the granting of permission to see me an extraordinary concession, so that the offer of coffee to mother constituted, so to speak, the acme of humanitarianism which, relatively speaking, did extraordinary honour to their civilized feelings and European ideas. And mother seemed deliberately to have rejected it.

I was summoned to see Touchard and he ordered me to get all my schoolbooks and exercise books and show them to mother 'so she can see how much you have managed to acquire at my establishment'. There and then Antonina Vasilevna, pursing her lips, hissed at me in a jeering, mocking stage-whisper:

'So your mother did not like our coffee, it seems.'

I collected my exercise books and carried them to mother past the huddle of 'sons of Counts and Senators' in the classroom who were all watching mother and me. I was pleased, you see, to fulfil Touchard's instructions literally to the letter. Methodically I started opening my exercise books and explaining: 'Here are French grammar lessons, here are dictations, here are the uses of the auxiliary verbs *avoir* and *être*, here is geography, here is a list of the main cities of Europe and all parts of the world' and so on, and so forth. I took half an hour or more to explain everything in a small, level voice, with eyes lowered, like a well-brought-up little boy. I knew mother understood none of it and perhaps did not even know how to write, but I enjoyed what I was doing. I was unable to tire her. She listened to everything without interrupting me, showing unusual attentiveness and even awe, so that in the end I myself got bored and stopped. However, her expression was sad and her face seemed full of pity.

Finally she rose to leave. Suddenly Touchard entered and with an idiotically self-important look asked her whether she was satisfied with her son's progress. Mother began mumbling something disconnected and thanked him. Antonina Vasilevna came in as well. Mother began beseeching them both 'Please, do not to abandon the orphan boy, because that's now what he is, do be good to him . . .'—and with tears in her eyes she bowed to both of them, to each one individually, giving a deep bow as the lower classes are used to bowing to their lords and masters when they are asking for a favour. The Touchards had not expected anything like this and Antonina Vasilevna was evidently mollified and, of course, at once changed her opinion about the cup of coffee. With even greater self-importance Touchard answered genteelly that he made no difference between the boys, they were all his children and he was like a father to them and I was treated almost exactly the same as the sons of Counts and Senators and this deserved to be appreciated, and so on, and so forth. Mother simply went on bowing, but finally became embarrassed and turned to me with tears glittering in her eyes and said:

'Goodbye, my darling!'

And she gave me a kiss—that is to say, I allowed her to kiss me. She obviously wanted to kiss me again and again and embrace me and hug me, but whether she was embarrassed to do so in front of them, or felt miserable about doing it for some other reason, or guessed that I would be ashamed of her doing it, she hurriedly turned to go, after bowing once again to the Touchards. I stood stock still.

'*Mais suivez donc votre mère,*' said Antonina Vasilevna. '*Il n'a pas de cœur, cet enfant.*'

Touchard responded by giving a shrug, as much as to say: 'It's no wonder, in that case, I treat him like a lackey.'

I dashed after mother. We went out on to the porch steps. I knew they'd all be watching from a window. Mother turned towards the church and crossed herself with a flourish three times, her lips quivering, and the clangorous bell resounded loudly and evenly from the bell-tower. She turned to me and

354

was unable to restrain herself any longer. She placed both hands on my head and burst into tears.

'Mummy, that's enough, please ... It's embarrassing ... Can't you see, they're watching us from the window ...'

She threw her head back and said in a rush:

'Well, the Good Lord ... the Good Lord be with you ... Angels of God watch over you, and the Mother of God, and St Nicholas the beloved ... Oh, dear God, dear God!' she repeated over and over in a great hurry, making the sign of the cross over me the whole time and trying to make as many signs as possible. 'Oh, my darling, my dear boy! Oh, my darling, just one moment ...'

She hurriedly thrust her hand in her pocket and took out a small blue, chequered handkerchief with a small, tight bundle tied in one corner and tried to undo the bundle and failed.

'There, take it as it is, it's a clean hankie, and you'll find four little coins in it. Maybe they'll come in useful. Forgive me, darling, I couldn't manage any more ... Sorry, my darling.'

I took the little handkerchief, although I wanted to say something about being very well supplied by Mr Touchard and Antonina Vasilevna and not needing anything, but I refrained and took the handkerchief.

She again made the sign of the cross, again muttered a short prayer and then suddenly ... and then quite suddenly she bowed to me just as she had bowed to the Touchards upstairs in their room, a long, slow, deep bow which I shall never forget as long as I live! I literally shook all over and I don't know why. Whether she wanted to acknowledge by this deep bow the guilt she felt towards me—which was what I thought once very much later—I do not know. But at the time it only made me all the more embarrassed because I told myself they were all watching me from an upstairs window and, anyhow, Lambert would very likely start hitting me again before long.

Finally she left. The sons of Counts and Senators had already consumed the oranges and gingerbread before I got back, and Lambert immediately grabbed the four coins, which were spent on cakes and chocolates at a confectioner's and I wasn't even offered a thing.

A whole six months passed and a windy, rainy October set in. I had forgotten about mother. Oh, it was then that resentment, real resentment entered my heart and filled it to the brim! Although I was still brushing Touchard's clothes as I had done, I now hated him with all my heart and more and more each day. And it was then, one melancholy evening at dusk, I started rummaging in my box and suddenly came across her small blue cotton handkerchief tucked away in a corner. It had been lying there ever since I stuck it there. I took it out and looked at it. One corner of it still showed signs of the former knot and the clear imprint of the little round coins. However, I put it back in its place and closed the box. It was the eve of a church festival and the bell was ringing for the all-night service. The other boys had already dispersed to their various homes after dinner, but on this occasion Lambert was also staying at school for Sunday. I have no idea why he hadn't been sent for as well. Though he continued to hit me as he always had done, he also had a great deal to tell me and he needed me. We talked the whole evening about Le Page pistols* which neither he nor I had ever seen, about Circassian swords and how they could cut people down, about the fun it would be to form a gang of robbers and, eventually, Lambert turned to his favourite filthy topics, which he loved talking about and which I surprised myself by loving to listen to.

This time I suddenly couldn't stand it and told him I had a headache. At ten o'clock we went to bed. I burrowed down under the bedcover and took the little blue handkerchief out from beneath my pillow. An hour or so before I had got it from my box for some reason and as soon as our beds were made I had stuffed it under the pillow. I immediately pressed it to my face and started kissing it. 'Mummy, mummy,' I whispered as I remembered and my whole chest contracted in a vice-like pain. I could close my eyes and see her face with the quivering lips as she crossed herself before the church and then made the sign of the cross over me and I said 'It's embarrassing, they're watching.' 'Mummy, darling mummy,' I whispered, 'you've come to see me only once in my life . . . Mummy, where are you now, my visitor from long ago? Do you still remember your poor little boy you once came to see? . . . Come and see me at least once again now, if only in a dream, so I can tell you how I love you, so I can hug you and kiss your dear blue eyes and tell you I am not ashamed of you at all now, that I loved you then and my heart longed for you and yet I just sat there like a lackey. Mummy, you'll never know how much I loved you then! Mummy, where are you now, can you hear me? Mummy, do you remember that little dove in the village church?'

'Oh, hell! The way he goes on!' grumbled Lambert from his bed. 'Stop it! I tell you. I can't sleep!' He jumped out of bed, dashed over to me and started trying to pull the bedcover off me, but I had burrowed down into it and held on to it as firmly as I could.

'You're blubbering! Why are you blubbering, you fool! This'll make you!' And he hit me, hit me painfully with his fist in my back and my side and hit me harder and harder, and. . .

And suddenly I opened my eyes . . .

It was already growing quite light and needles of frost were glittering on the snow and on the wall. I was sitting hunched up, scarcely alive, frozen stiff in my fur coat, and someone was standing over me, trying to wake me by shouting loudly and kicking me in the side with the toe of his right shoe. Half rising to my feet, I saw a man standing in front of me in an expensive bearskin coat and sable cap, with jet-black eyes and fashionable sideburns black as tar, a hooked nose, white teeth bared at me in a grin, and a pink and white mask of a face. He was leaning very closely towards me and frosty steam flew from his mouth at every breath he took:

'You're frozen stiff, you drunken cretin, you fool! You'll die like a dog! Get up! Get up!'

'Lambert!' I shouted.

'Who are you?'

'Dolgoruky!'

'The devil take it! What Dolgoruky?'

'*Simply* Dolgoruky! . . . Touchard . . . The one you stuck a fork into in that pub!'

'Ha-a-a!' he cried gutturally, smiling a long, slow smile of recognition (after all he could hardly have forgotten me!) 'Ha! So it's you, is it! You!'

He lifted me up and put me on my feet. I could scarcely stand upright and scarcely move and he led me along, holding me by the arm. He kept on glancing in my eyes as if wondering about me and calling me to mind and listening to me as hard as he could, and I chattered away, also as hard as I could, ceaselessly,

357

without stopping, and I was so glad, so glad I was able to talk to someone, and glad it was Lambert. Whether he appeared to me as a kind of saviour, or whether I threw myself on his mercy at such a moment because I took him to be someone from another world, I do not know—I gave it no thought then—but I threw myself at him without a thought. What I said to him then I don't recall at all, and I could scarcely have made any sense, could scarcely have spoken the words clearly, but he listened very attentively. He summoned the first cab that came by and within a few minutes I was sitting in the warm, in his room.

III

Everyone, no matter who he might be, has some memory of something that has happened to him that he considers, or is inclined to consider, fanastic, unusual, out of the ordinary, almost miraculous, whether it be a dream, an encounter, a piece of fortune-telling, a presentiment, or something of the kind. Right up to the present time I am inclined to regard my meeting with Lambert as even a bit prophetic, judging at least from the circumstances and consequences of the meeting. Besides, it all occurred—at least from one point of view—totally naturally, since he was simply returning from a night-time activity (I will explain later what it was) half-drunk, and in the alley-way, stopping by the gate for a moment, caught sight of me. He had only been in St Petersburg a few days.

The room in which I found myself was small, a very unimpressively furnished example of the average kind of furnished room. Lambert himself, however, was splendidly and opulently turned out. Two trunks stood on the floor, only half-unpacked. One corner was shielded by a screen hiding the bed.

'Alphonsine!' Lambert called out.

'*Présente*,' cried a quavering female voice with a Parisian accent from behind the screen, and in no more than a couple of moments Mademoiselle Alphonsine jumped out at us, evidently straight out of bed and hastily dressed in a little jacket—a very odd-looking creature, tall and dry as a stick, a girlish brunette with a long waist and a long face, darting eyes and sunken cheeks, in short a terribly run-down creature!

'Be quick about it!' (I am translating, because he spoke to her

358

in French.) 'The samovar must be ready by now. Get some hot water, red wine, and sugar and a glass and bring it here quick as you can! My friend is chilled to the bone—he slept the whole night out in the snow!'

'*Malheureux!*' she exclaimed, flinging her arms wide theatrically.

'Now, now!' Lambert reprimanded, as if she were a pet dog, threatening her with his finger. She instantly abandoned her theatrical gestures and dashed off to do what he asked.

He studied me carefully and felt me, took my pulse, ran his fingers over my forehead and temples. 'Strange you didn't freeze to death,' he grumbled. 'Still, I suppose, with your fur coat over your head, you'd have been in a kind of furry rabbit-hole . . .'

A glass of hot toddy appeared. I gulped it down greedily and it enlivened me at once. Once again I started chattering. Propped up in a corner on a divan I talked and talked, sipping the drink as I did so, but what I said and how I said it I still have almost no idea. For whole moments, even for whole periods, I quite forgot what I was saying. I will emphasize that whether he understood anything from my stories I do not know, but of one thing I was later clear and it was this: he managed to understand enough to reach the conclusion that it would pay him not to neglect this meeting with me . . . I will explain in due course what he might have had in mind.

I was not only terribly animated, but there were times, I think, when I was overjoyed. I remember the sun suddenly pouring into the room when the shutters were opened and the stove starting to crackle as someone lit it—who and how I don't remember. Just as memorable was a tiny black lap-dog which Mademoiselle Alphonsine held in her arms, coquettishly pressing it to her bosom. This lap-dog, I remember, I found extremely entertaining, so much so that I would stop my chatter and once or twice tried to stroke it, but Lambert waved his hand and Alphonsine and her lap-dog instantly took cover behind the screen.

He himself was very silent as he sat opposite me and, leaning forcefully towards me, listened to what I had to say. From time to time he smiled his long, slow smile, bared his teeth in a grin, and screwed up his eyes as if making an effort to understand and hazard a guess or two. All I can remember clearly is that when I

359

told him about the so-called 'document' I could not express myself properly and made little sense, and I saw only too clearly from his face that he couldn't understand me but very much wanted to, so that he even risked stopping me with a question, which was dangerous, because as soon as I was interrupted I lost the thread of my story and forgot what I was talking about. How long we sat there and talked, I do not know and cannot even imagine. He suddenly stood up and summoned Alphonsine.

'He must have time to rest. Maybe he'll need a doctor. Do whatever he asks . . . *vous comprenez, ma fille? Vous avez l'argent*, you understand, don't you, and you've got some money . . . You haven't? Here's some then!' He gave her a ten-rouble note. He started whispering to her, repeating over and over: '*Vous comprenez! Vous comprenez!*' wagging his finger and frowning fiercely. I could see she was terribly frightened of him.

'I'll be back and you'd better get some sleep.' He smiled at me and picked up his cap.

'*Mais vous n'avez pas dormi du tout, Maurice!*'* cried Alphonsine pathetically.

'*Taisez-vous, je dormirai après.*'* And he went out.

'*Sauvée!*' she whispered with great feeling, demonstratively dismissing him as he left. '*Monsieur, monsieur!*' she declaimed at once, adopting a pose in the middle of the room, '*jamais homme ne fut si cruel, si Bismark, que cet être, qui regarde une femme comme une saleté de hasard. Une femme, qu'est-ce que ça dans notre époque? "Tue-la!"—voilà le dernier mot de l'Académie française! . . .*'*

I screwed up my eyes to look at her, because I seemed to be seeing double, seeing two Alphonsines, and then I suddenly realized she was crying, and I shivered and wondered if she had been talking to me for a considerable time and I had been asleep or unconscious. She was saying:

'—. . . *Hélas! de quoi m'aurait servi de le découvrir plutôt—et n'aurais-je pas autant gagné à tenir ma honte cachée toute ma vie? Peut-être, n'est-il pas honnête à une demoiselle de s'expliquer si librement devant monsieur, mais enfin je vous avoue que s'il m'était permis de vouloir quelque chose, oh, ce serait de lui plonger au cœur mon couteau, mais en détournant les yeux, de peur que son regard exécrable ne fît trembler mon bras et ne glaçât mon courage! Il a assassiné ce pope russe, monsieur, il lui arracha sa barbe rousse pour la vendre à un artiste en cheveux au pont des Maréchaux, tout prés de la*

Maison de monsieur Andrieux—hautes nouveautés, articles de Paris, linge, chemises, vous savez, n'est-ce pas? . . . Oh, monsieur, quand l'amitié rassemble à table épouse, enfants, sœurs, amis, quand une vive allégresse enflamme mon cœur, je vous le demande, monsieur: est-il bonheur préférable à celui dont tout jouit? Mais il rit, monsieur, ce monstre exécrable et inconcevable et si ce n'était pas par l'entremise de monsieur Andrieux, jamais, oh, jamais je ne serais . . . Mais, quoi, monsieur, qu'avez, vous, monsieur?

She flung herself at me. I think I had a fit of the shivers and I may also have fainted. I cannot describe the oppressive and sickly effect this half-mad creature had on me. Maybe she imagined she was intended to entertain me. At least she did not leave me alone for a moment. She may have been on the stage at one time because she was terribly given to declaiming, flitting about the place, and ceaselessly talking, while I had long since fallen silent. All I could gather from what she said was that she had been closely connected with some House of Mr Andrieux—'*la Maison de monsieur Andrieux—hautes nouveautés, articles de Paris, etc.*'—and may even have come from this *Maison*, but had been forever parted from it *par ce monstre furieux et inconcevable* and all this comprised the tragedy of her life . . . She shed tears, but I thought it was only a matter of form and she was not really crying at all. There were moments when I imagined she would suddenly fall apart like a skeleton. She had a way of pronouncing words in a kind of crushed, quavering voice, so that when she said the word *préférable*, for instance, she pronounced it *préfé-a-able* and the vowel *a* sounded like the bleating of a sheep. Once I could scarcely believe my eyes when I saw her do a pirouette in the middle of the room, but she was not dancing so much as relating the pirouette to what she was saying and impersonating someone. Suddenly she pounced on a small, old, out-of-tune piano, opened it, started strumming on the keys and singing . . . I think I must have been unconscious for ten minutes or more and had fallen asleep, but the lap-dog whined and I woke up. Consciousness suddenly returned to me fully and I saw everything clear as daylight. I jumped up in horror.

'Lambert, I'm at Lambert's!' I thought and, seizing hold of my cap, rushed to get my fur coat.

'*Où allez-vous, monsieur?*' cried the sharp-eyed Alphonsine.

'I want to go, I want to get out! Let me go, don't stop me!'

'*Oui, monsieur!*' chimed in Alphonsine and dashed to open the door into the corridor. '*Mais ce n'est pas loin, monsieur, c'est pas loin du tout, ça ne vaut pas la peine de mettre votre chouba, c'est ici prés, monsieur!*'* she shrieked for the whole corridor to hear. Having dashed out, I turned right.

'*Par ici, monsieur, c'est par ici!*' she shouted at the top of her voice, clutching my fur coat with her long, bony fingers and pointing to the left along the corridor to somewhere I didn't want to go. I tore myself free and ran towards the doors at the top of the stairs.

'*Il s'en va, il s'en va!*' cried Alphonsine in her cracked voice as she raced after me. '*Mais il me tuera, monsieur, il me tuera!*'*

But I had already dashed down the stairs and, despite the fact that she even dashed down the stairs after me, managed to open the front door, rush out into the street, and summon the first cabbie in sight. I gave mother's address . . .

IV

But consciousness, having returned for a moment, quickly vanished. I can still remember being taken there and led into mother's house, but once there I almost immediately fell into a complete unconsciousness. The next day, as I was told later (and I also have some recollection of it), I was again lucid for an instant. I can remember being in Versilov's room, on his divan. I remember the faces of Versilov, mother, and Liza and I remember particularly Versilov saying something to me about Zershchikov and the prince and showing me some letter and trying to calm me. They later said that I kept on asking horrified questions about someone called Lambert and claiming that I heard a lapdog barking. But such a gleam of lucid consciousness soon faded. Towards evening of that second day I was at the height of my fever. But I will anticipate events and explain what happened.

The evening I had dashed from Zershchikov's gambling place and after everything had calmed down, Zershchikov, on resuming play, suddenly announced loudly that there had been a grave mistake: the lost money, the four hundred roubles, had turned up in another pile of money and the bank was completely intact. At this point the prince, who had remained behind, approached Zershchikov and insisted that he should make a public declaration of my innocence and, what is more, offer me his apologies in the form of a letter. Zershchikov, for his part, found this demand worthy of respect and gave his word before all present that he would send me a letter of explanation and apology the next day. The prince gave him Versilov's address, and the very next day, in fact, Versilov received personally from Zershchikov a letter addressed to me containing more than 1,300 roubles of mine which I had forgotten about at the roulette table. In this manner the Zershchikov business was settled. The joyous news did a great deal to help my recovery once I regained consciousness.

The prince, on returning from gambling, wrote two letters that night—one to me and one to his former regiment where the affair of second lieutenant Stepanov had occurred. He sent both letters the next morning. He then wrote a report for the authorities and, with this report in his hand, presented himself early in the morning before the commander of his regiment and announced to him, in his own words, that he was 'a criminal, implicated in the forgery of shares, and wished to give himself up and be brought before a court of law'. He then handed over the report, in which everything was stated in writing. He was arrested.

Below is the letter he wrote me that night, word for word:

Inestimable Arkady Makarovich,

Having tried the lackey's way out, I have lost the right even so much as to assuage my soul with the thought that I might and I have finally decided to do the right thing. I am guilty in the eyes of my country and my own family line and, being the last in the line, I will personally inflict on myself my own punishment. I cannot understand how I could have seized on the base idea of self-preservation and have dreamed for a while of buying myself off with money. In that case I would have remained, in my own conscience, a criminal for all time. Those people, even had they returned to me those compromising papers, would have left me nothing in life to live for. The fate awaiting me would be to have gone on living with them and to have been one of them for the rest of my life! I could not accept such a fate and finally found in myself enough strength of will—or, perhaps, simple desperation—to act as I am doing now.

I have written a letter to my former colleagues in my former regiment and exonerated Stepanov. In no way can such an act be one of

363

exculpation. It is no more than the last will and testament of someone who is about to die. It should be thought of in that way.

'Please forgive me for disowning you at the gambling place. It was because at that time I was unsure of you. Now that I am already numbered among the dead, I can make such a confession . . . from the next world.

'Poor Liza! She has known nothing about this decision. I hope she won't blame me but will think it over on her own. I could not justify myself and even find the words to explain things to her. You should know, Arkady Makarovich, that yesterday morning, when she came to see me for the last time, I revealed to her how I had deceived her and confessed that I had been to see Anna Andreevna with the intention of proposing to her. I could not have had this on my conscience in the light of my final decision, seeing how much she loved me, and I disclosed everything to her. She forgave me, forgave everything, but I did not believe her. It could not have been real forgiveness. In her place I could not have forgiven.

Remember me a little.

Your unhappy last prince *Sokolsky*.

I lay unconscious exactly nine days.

PART III

CHAPTER I

I

NOW —about something else entirely.

I keep on announcing it's all about something else, or someone else, and yet I go on writing only about myself. What's more, I have declared a thousand times I have no desire whatever to write about myself. This was my firm intention when I began writing because I understood only too well that in no way was I needed by the reader. I was describing, and wanted to describe, other people, not myself, and if I am constantly turning up again and again, then this is simply a sorry state of affairs there is no way of getting round, no matter how much I might like to. What chiefly worries me is that, in describing my personal adventures with such zest, I might be giving grounds for thinking that I am the same now as I was then. The reader will recall, none the less, that I have more than once exclaimed: 'Oh, if only one could have changed what happened and made a completely fresh start!' I could not have made such an exclamation if I had not now changed radically and become a completely different person. That must be only too obvious. Just imagine, then, how bored I must be by all these apologies and prefatory remarks I am having to insert the whole time right in the middle of these notes of mine!

To business.

After lying unconscious for nine days I came to in a reborn but unreformed state. Besides, my rebirth was a silly thing if understood in a broad sense and maybe if it happened now it wouldn't be so silly. My idea—my impulse, that is to say—was once more centred (as it had been a thousand times) on leaving home, on going away for good, not as I had done previously when I had set myself the task of thinking about it a thousand times and done nothing about it. I had no desire to avenge myself on anyone, and I say this quite honestly, although I felt myself scorned by one and all. I was ready to go without recrimination, without harsh words, but I wanted my own personal strength, real strength, independent of any of them and of the whole world—to think I wanted that, I, who had come so close to being reconciled with everything in the world! I note down this dream I had then not as a fully-formed thought but as an irresistible sensation belonging to that time. I did not want to formulate it fully while I was still lying in bed. Sick and feeble, lying in Versilov's room, which had been set aside for me, I was painfully aware of the low state of my strength. I felt I was a piece of straw lying on the bed, not a man, and not only because I was ill—and that was the shameful part of it! And then from the very depths of my being a sense of protest began to arise in full force, and I was consumed by infinitely exaggerated feelings of arrogance and defiance. I do not remember a single time in my life when I was filled with more arrogant feelings than during the first days of my recovery, when, that is, I lay on my bed like a piece of straw.

But in the mean time I kept quiet and even resolved not to think about anything! I kept on searching their faces, trying to assess from them what I ought to do. It was equally clear that they had no wish to question me or appear inquisitive and talked to me purely about extraneous matters. This simultaneously pleased and annoyed me, but I can't explain why. I saw Liza less often than mother, although she came to see me every day, even twice a day. From snatches of conversation and judging from the looks on their faces I gathered that Liza had an awful lot of things to see to and on account of this was often away from home, because the very idea that she had so much to see to involved me in feeling ashamed in some way. Still, all these were merely sick, purely physiological sensations which are not worth describing. Tatyana Pavlovna also came to see me almost daily and, though in no sense affectionate towards me, at least did not scold me as she had done previously—something which made me so furious I simply told her: 'Tatyana Pavlovna, when you're not scolding me, you're a right old bore.' 'In that case, I won't come and see you!' she shot back and left. I was glad to be rid of one of them.

Worst of all I tried mother's patience and nagged her all the time. I developed a frightful appetite and grumbled a great deal about the late arrival of meals (though they were never late). Mother had no idea how to do her best for me. Once she brought me some soup and as usual started feeding me herself and I grumbled the whole time. And I was suddenly angry at myself for grumbling so much because, as I told myself: 'Probably she's the only person I really love and yet I nag her all the time.' But I couldn't help feeling spiteful, and suddenly out of spite I burst into tears and she, poor thing, thinking I was crying out of tenderness, bent towards me and started kissing me. I gritted my teeth and put up with it and at that moment actually hated her. But really I always loved mother, even then, and never hated her at all. It was a case, as it always is, of hurting first the one you love most.

The person I really hated in those first days of my recovery was the doctor. The doctor was a young man with a presumptuous look on his face who spoke sharply and even rather rudely. Everyone in the world of science likes to give the impression he has just the day before come up with something remarkable, when in fact nothing remarkable has happened at all. That's what your average, mediocre 'man in the street' is always like. I put up with it for a while, but finally lost my temper and announced to him in the presence of the entire family that he was fussing about for nothing, that I would get quite well without him, that he, while giving the appearance of being realistic and up to date, was actually a mass of prejudices and quite unable to appreciate that medicine never cured anyone and, finally, that in all likelihood he was boorish and uneducated 'like all technicians and specialists nowadays who have recently become so stuck up'. The doctor was extremely offended (thereby proving the sort of man he was), but still went on visiting. I eventually told Versilov that if the doctor didn't stop his visits I'd say something ten times more unpleasant. Versilov simply remarked that it would be impossible to say something twice as unpleasant, let alone ten times. I was delighted by that remark.

What a man he was, though! I am speaking of Versilov. He—and he alone—had been the cause of it all and yet he was the one I was least angry with at the time. It was not just his way of treating me which won me over. I think that we both had the feeling at that time that we owed each other a great many explanations—and precisely for that reason it was a lot better not to say a thing. It is extremely pleasant when life presents you with situations like that to have someone intelligent to deal with! I have already described in Part II of my account, running ahead of myself, as it were, how he told me very succinctly and clearly

369

about the letter from the prince (already under arrest), about Zershchikov, about the words said on my behalf, etc., etc. Because I was determined to keep quiet, I asked him, in the driest manner possible, only one or two brief questions and he gave me clear, precise answers, entirely devoid of superfluous words and—best of all—devoid of all unnecessary feeling. At that time I was terrified of unnecessary feeling.

Of Lambert I did not say a word, but the reader will have guessed, of course, that I thought about him all too often. In my delirium I mentioned him several times, but on regaining consciousness and studying them closely I soon realized Lambert still remained a secret and they knew nothing about him, including Versilov. I was overjoyed at the time and my fear subsided, but I was wrong, as I found out later to my surprise. He visited several times during the course of my illness, but Versilov said nothing to me about it and I concluded that, in Lambert's opinion, I had already sunk without trace. Nevertheless, I often thought about him. What's more, I thought about him not only without animosity, not only out of curiosity, but even out of sympathy, as if anticipating from this quarter something new and profitable in keeping with the new feelings and plans I was already hatching. In short, I resolved to think carefully about Lambert the moment I started thinking properly again. I will add one strange thing: I had entirely forgotten where he lived and the street where it all happened. I could remember the room, Alphonsine, the lap-dog, and the corridor and could have drawn it all straightaway, but where it all happened, in which street and which building, I had completely forgotten. Odder still, I became aware of this only three of four days after my full recovery, long after I had begun worrying about Lambert.

So these were my first feelings on regaining consciousness. I have not known how to mention the main things. In fact, all the main things were probably at that very time becoming crystallized and defined in my heart. After all, I was not spending my entire time grumbling and being vexed over the fact that I did not get my soup on time! Oh, I remember how miserable I used to feel then and how I sometimes felt such intense yearning, particularly when I was left by myself for long periods. They, of course, quite deliberately soon realized how tiresome I found them and how much their fussing irritated me, and they started leaving me alone more and more—an unduly zealous display of sensitivity and concern on their part!

On the fourth day of my recovery I was lying in bed at three o'clock in the afternoon and no one was with me. The day was bright and I knew that at four o'clock, when the sun began sinking, a brilliant, slanting ray from it would fall directly on the corner of my wall and illuminate the place like a spotlight. I knew this from what had happened on previous days and the fact that this would be certain to occur in an hour's time, and chiefly the fact I knew it would happen as surely as twice two is four, absolutely infuriated me. With a shudder I turned my whole body round and suddenly, in the profound silence of the room, clearly heard the words: 'Lord Jesus Christ, have mercy upon us.' The words were spoken in a half-whisper and followed by a profound, full-chested sigh, and then once again everything became completely silent. I quickly raised my head.

I had already noticed on the previous evening and even earlier that something unusual was occurring in the three rooms on the ground floor. In the little room on the other side of the living-room where mother and Liza had been there was now someone else. I had already heard a few sounds, both day and night, but only for the briefest instants, and then complete silence had at once returned, lasting for several hours, and I had paid no more attention. I had thought the previous day it must have been Versilov, all the more since he had soon come in to see me, although I knew for certain from what they had said that while I was ill Versilov had moved to another apartment and that was where he slept at night. So far as mother and Liza were concerned I knew that both of them (for my peace of mind, or so I thought) had moved upstairs into my former 'coffin' in the attic and I had even wondered how the two of them could find room to live up there. And now it suddenly transpired that their former room was occupied by someone else and it was not Versilov at all. With an ease which I did not suppose I had (in view of my total lack of strength until then), I lowered my feet over the side of the bed, pushed them into slippers, threw on a grey, lambskin dressing-gown lying nearby (a sacrifice made on

371

my behalf by Versilov), and set off across our living-room in the direction of mother's former bedroom. What I saw there utterly astounded me. I had never supposed anything of the kind and I stopped stone-dead in the doorway.

Sitting there was an exceedingly elderly, grey-haired man, with an extremely white beard, and he had obviously been sitting there a long time. He was not seated on the bed, but on mother's little stool with his back against the bed. Yet he held himself so straight I do not think he needed anything to lean against, although it was clear he was not in good health. He wore over his shirt a fur-lined short sheepskin jacket, his knees covered by mother's plaid and his feet in slippers. One could tell he was tall and broad-shouldered, of very sturdy appearance despite his illness, although rather pale and thin, with an elongated face and extremely thick but not very long hair. I thought he was about 70 years old. Beside him on a little table, within arm's reach, were two or three books and a pair of silver-rimmed spectacles. Although I had had no idea I would be meeting him, I guessed immediately who he was and simply could not imagine how he had spent so long almost next door to me without my hearing a sound.

On seeing me, he did not move a muscle, but gazed at me intently and in silence, just as I did at him, with the one difference that I stared at him with immeasurable surprise and he at me with none at all. On the contrary, after surveying me from head to foot during five or ten seconds of silence, he suddenly smiled and even gave a quiet, barely audible laugh, and, though the laugh was quickly over, bright, joyous remnants of it lingered on his face, chiefly in his eyes—very blue, radiant, large eyes, though shaded by sunken lids made puffy with age and surrounded by countless tiny wrinkles. It was his laugh that had the greatest effect on me.

I think that, in the majority of cases, whenever someone laughs he looks disgusting. More often than not people's laughter reveals something common and vulgar about them, something demeaning to the person laughing, although that person almost always has no idea of the effect he is creating. Just as he does not know, as on the whole nobody knows, what he must look like when he is asleep. One person's face looks intelligent when he's asleep, another—even an intelligent person's—becomes stupid

372

and consequently laughable. I do not know why. I simply want to say that someone laughing, like someone asleep, mostly has no idea what he looks like. The vast majority of people have no idea how to laugh. In any case, there's nothing to be learnt: laughter is a gift, you can't fake it. You can only do something about it by re-educating yourself, making yourself better and conquering the evil instincts within you. Then it is very likely your laugh will also change for the better. Some people give themselves away completely by their laugh and you're suddenly aware exactly what they're like. Even indisputably clever laughter can sometimes be repugnant. Laughter demands sincerity above all, and where do you find sincerity in people? Laughter demands lack of malice, but people's laughter is usually malicious. Sincere and good-natured laughter is a sign of enjoyment, but where is there enjoyment in people nowadays, and do people nowadays even know how to enjoy themselves? (Versilov's remark, this: all I've done is recall it.) The way a man enjoys himself is a man's most outstanding feature, along with his arms and his legs. You may spend a long time trying to make someone out, but as soon as that person breaks into sincere laughter the whole of his character can be grasped instantly. Only someone highly developed in the happiest way knows how to enjoy himself convivially—openly, that is, and whole-heartedly. I am not talking about intellectual development, but about the nature of a person as a whole, his character. Consequently, if you seek to study someone and know who he really is, take a close look at him not when he is silent or talking or crying or even when he is excited by the noblest of ideas, but take a good look at him when he laughs. If a man has a good laugh, it means he is a good man. Take note of all the shades of his laughter. For example it is essential that a man's laugh should never seem silly, no matter how light-heartedly he may be enjoying himself. If you notice the slightest hint of silliness in someone's laughter, it undoubtedly means he is of limited intelligence, even though he may have been doing nothing save spill out ideas the whole time. Even if his laugh may not be silly, if the man himself, when he laughs, suddenly seems to you just a bit silly, then you can be sure he has no real personal dignity in him, at least not in the full meaning of the word. Or, finally, though a laugh may be convivial, if it starts seeming common and vulgar to you for some reason, you can be sure that person is common and vulgar, and all the nobility and high-mindedness you may have noticed in him earlier was either deliberately counterfeit or unconsciously appropriated from others, and he will inevitably change for the worse, will sell out to Mammon, and he will cast aside all his noble ideals without regret as merely the pastimes and peccadilloes of youth.

I have inserted this long tirade about laughter quite deliberately, even at the risk of spoiling the flow of my story, because I regard it as one of the most serious conclusions I have drawn from life. And I particularly recommend it to all girls who are engaged to be married but still view the man of their choice with some concern and mistrust and have not made up their minds completely. And I urge them not to laugh at me, miserable bastard that I am, when I poke myself with my moralizings into the business of marriage, about which I know nothing at all. But all I know is that laughter is the surest test of someone's true nature. Take a child, for example. Children know how to laugh absolutely perfectly, which is why they are quite enchanting. A crying child I find quite repulsive, but a child laughing and enjoying himself is like a ray of light from paradise, a glimpse of the future when humanity will eventually become as pure and uncomplicated as a child. And it was something childlike and unbelievably attractive that flashed for a moment in the fleeting laugh of the old man. I at once went up to him.

III

'Sit down by me here. It's likely your legs aren't strong yet.'

He accompanied his warm invitation with a gesture indicating I should sit by him, all the time continuing to fix his radiant look on my face. I sat down next to him and said:

'I know you, you're Makar Ivanovich.'

'Quite right, dear boy. It's fine you're up. You're young, it's fine for you. The old face the grave, but the young face life.'

'Are you sick?'

'I am, my friend. My feet are the worst. They brought me here, but the moment I sit down, you see, they swell up. They've been like this since last Thursday, when the temperatures came . . .' He was referring to the frost. 'I used to put ointment on them, you see. The year before last, Lichten, the doctor,

Edmund Karlych, in Moscow, prescribed it, and the ointment helped, it helped a lot. But it's not helping now. And my chest's all blocked up. Since yesterday my back's been bad, too, as if a pack of dogs are gnawing at it . . . Can't sleep at night.'

'How is it you've not made a sound since being here?' I interrupted. He gave me a look, as if thinking of something.

'Just don't you wake your mother,' he added, seeming suddenly to have thought of it. 'She was up the whole night seeing to things, and not a sound out of her, just as quiet as a fly. But I know she's having a lie-down now. Oh, it's no good being a sick old man!' he sighed. 'It seems like it's only the soul's clinging on to life, and keeps hold of it, and rejoices at the light of day. It seems like, if one was given one's life to start all over again, one's soul would have no fear. Though maybe that's a sinful thought.'

'Why sinful?'

'It's a dream, a thought like that. An old man must pass away with dignity and grace. Another thing, too, if you meet death with a great outcry and discontent, it's a mighty great sin, that. But if you've loved life out of a joyous spirit, then I think God'll forgive you, even if you're old and pious. It's hard for a man to know regarding sin what's sinful and what isn't. There's a secret here which is too much for the mind of man. A man who's old and pious must be content at all times, and he must die in the full flower of his mind blessedly and gracefully, full of days, sighing for his final hour and joyful in his going as the ear of wheat is for the threshing floor and acting out the secret within it.'

'You talk about the secret. What's this "acting out the secret within it" mean?' I asked and glanced round towards the door. I was glad we were alone and all around there was an imperturbable silence. The sun shone brightly in the window just before setting. He spoke rather high-falutingly and vaguely, but very sincerely and in a state of high excitement, just as if he were indeed glad I had come to see him. But I noted in him an undoubtedly feverish condition, even a strong one. I had also felt unwell, also feverish, the moment I entered his room.

'What's the secret? Everything's the secret, my friend. It's all God's secret. Every tree, every blade of grass has the secret concealed within it. Whether it's the song of a little bird, or the stars shining in their myriads in the firmament of the night—it's

375

all a secret, all the same one. And the greatest secret of all is what awaits the soul of man in the next world. That's for sure, my friend!'

'I don't know in what sense you're using the word ... Of course, I don't say this to annoy you and, believe me, I do believe in God, but all these secrets have long ago been understood rationally, and what's not been understood so far will be understood, absolutely certainly, and perhaps in a very short while. Botany knows perfectly well how a tree grows, physiology and anatomy know why a bird sings, or will know soon, and as for the stars, they've not only all been counted, but every movement they make has been calculated with the minutest accuracy, so that one can predict, even a thousand years ahead, minute by minute, the appearance of some comet or other ... and now even the composition of the furthest stars has become known. Take a microscope—it's a magnifying glass that can magnify things a million times over and look through it at a drop of water and you'll see a whole new world there, a whole world of living organisms, and yet at one time that was a secret, but now it's all been revealed.'

'I've heard about that, dear boy, heard it more than once from people. What's there to say—it's a great thing, a marvellous thing, and all granted to man by the will of God. It's not for nothing God breathed into man the breath of life and told him to "live and learn".'

'Granted, those are commonplaces. You're not an enemy of science, are you, a clerical? That's to say, I don't know if you can grasp ...'

'No, dear boy, since I was little I have honoured science, and though I am not myself informed about it, I do not complain, since if I do not know it, someone else does. That is maybe so much the better, because it is each to his own. Because, my dear friend, science is not for everyone. All men have ambition, each one wants to startle the whole world, and I'd likely be the worst of the lot if I could. But seeing now as I am very disabled, how could I even pretend to when I know nothing at all? You are young and sharp-witted, and these are your assets, so you must learn. You should study and study, so that whenever you come across a godless man or one intent on making mischief you can answer back and he cannot confuse your immature thoughts by hurling his wild words at you. And that magnifying glass you mentioned, I saw one not so long ago.'

He took in a deep breath and sighed. There was no doubt that I had given him extraordinary pleasure by coming. His longing to talk was part of his sick condition. Apart from that, I am sure I am right in saying he looked at me at times with unusual feeling, even with love, since he continually laid his palm down tenderly on my hand and stroked my shoulder ... But I must confess, too, there were moments when he forgot about me completely, as if he were sitting there by himself, and, though he went on talking as eagerly as ever, he spoke only into the air.

'There is, my friend,' he went on, 'a man of great intellect in the Gennadian monastery.* He is a man of noble birth, with the rank of lieutenant colonel, and he has great wealth. When he lived in the world, he did not wish to assume the obligations of marriage. He has now shut himself off from the world for almost ten years, enjoying all the while his calm and silent retreat and letting his feelings rest from all worldly vanities. He observes all the rules of the monastery, but he does not wish to become a monk. And he has so many books, my friend, I have never seen a man with so many—he himself told me they were worth as much as eight thousand roubles! He is called Pyotr Valeryanych. At different times he has taught me a great deal and I have been extremely fond of listening to him. I once asked him: 'Why is it, sir, that you, with your great intellect and after living in monastic obedience ten years and in perfect subjugation of your will— why do you not accept the honest vows of a monk in order to become even more perfect?' And he said to me: 'Old man, you talk about my intellect, but maybe it's my intellect that has control of me and I still cannot curb it. And you talk about my obedience, but maybe I have long since lost any sense of who I really am. And what was that you were saying about the subjugation of my will? You see, I could renounce all my money this minute, and my rank, and all the trappings of my career in the cavalry, but a pipe of tobacco, which I have been struggling to give up for ten years now, that I couldn't renounce! What sort of a monk would I make in that case, and how can you praise me for subjugating my will?' And I was astonished at such humility.

'Well, last year, on the feast day of St Peter and St Paul at the end of June, I paid another visit to that monastery—it was the

377

Good Lord led me there—and I saw that very thing there in his cell, a microscope, ordered from abroad for a lot of money. 'Just a moment, old man,' he says, 'I'll show you something surprising you've never before seen in your life. You see that drop of water, pure as a tear, well, just you have a look and see what's inside it, and you'll see that men who know the way things work will soon have sought out all God's secrets and there won't be a single one left for us.' That's what he said and I remembered it.

'I had looked into a microscope like that thirty-five years before, one belonging to Aleksandr Vladimirovich Malgasov, our master, an uncle of Andrey Petrovich on his mother's side, whose estate passed to Andrey Petrovich when he died. He was an important gentleman, a general, and he kept a large pack of hounds and for many years I was his master of hounds. It was then he also came out with a microscope which he'd brought with him and he ordered all the servants to come up one by one, both men and women, and look in it and see a flea and a louse and the top of a needle and a hair and a drop of water. And the fun there was then! They were frightened to come forward, frightened of the master, they were—he was a man with a temper. Some didn't know how to look into it, they'd screw up their eyes and not see a thing. Others took fright and screamed, and the head man, Savin Makarov, he covered his face with both hands and shouted they could do what they liked with him, he wouldn't go and have a look! Oh, what a lot of silly laughter there was! Well, I didn't let on to Pyotr Valeryanych I'd looked into one of 'em more'n thirty-five years before, seeing it gave him such great pleasure, and I started oo-ing and ah-ing. He let me look a while and then he asked: "Well, old man, what do you say now?" And I bowed to him and answered: "The Lord said, Let there be light, and there was light." And he suddenly said: "Are you, sure it wasn't Let there be darkness?" And he spoke so oddly, not even giving a grin. I was astonished at him then, and he even seemed really angry and didn't say another thing.'

'It's all quite simple—your Pyotr Valeryanovych eats the monastery victuals and makes his devotions, but he doesn't believe in God, and you happened to be there at that particular moment, that's all,' I said. 'What's more, it's pretty comic of someone who's probably seen a microscope ten times already to

378

go crazy about it the next time he sees it! How nervy and impressionable! It comes of being in a monastery!'

'He is a pure man, a man of lofty intellect,' the old man uttered impressively, 'and he is no atheist. He is a man of many thoughts and he has a restless heart. There are many men like that nowadays among the upper class and the learned. And I will tell you something else as well: he is engaged in punishing himself. You should care for people like that, not deride them, and remember them in your prayers before you go to bed at night, because people like that are seeking God. Do you say your prayers before going to bed?'

'No, I regard it as an empty ritual. But I've got to confess I like your Pyotr Valeryanovych—at least he's not made of straw, he's a real man not unlike someone we both know.'

The old man only took note of the first thing I had said.

'You should say your prayers, my friend. It is a good thing to do and uplifts the heart, both before going to sleep and awakening from sleep and when wakened in the night. I will tell you something. One summer, in the month of July, we hurried on our way to celebrate the festival at the monastery of the Mother of God. The closer we got to it, the more people there were, and finally there were almost two hundred people all on their way to kiss the sacred, well-preserved relics of the two great miracle-working saints Aniky and Grigory. We spent the night out in the open, my friend, and I awoke early when the others were all asleep and the sun had not yet risen above the trees. I gave a bow, my friend, and then gazed around me and gave a great sigh, for the beauty everywhere was beyond words. It was all peaceful, the very air had a light feel. The grass was growing—and I thought, Grow, dear grass of the Lord! And there was a bird singing—and I thought, Sing, dear bird of God! And there was a child crying in its mother's arms—and I thought, God be with you, little one, grow and be happy, my little man! And that was the very first time in my life I took account of the thoughts within me . . . And again I bowed down and fell asleep in perfect peace. Oh, my dear boy, it is good to be alive on this earth! If I get better, I will be off again in the spring. And if it is all a secret, it's all the better for being that, because the heart is full of fear and trembling before it, and such fear uplifts the heart to proclaim: "All is yours, dear God, and I, too, would be received within you!" Do not fret, my young friend. It is even more beautiful for being a secret,' he added with deep feeling.

'"It is even more beautiful for being a secret ..." I'll remember that. You express yourself terribly vaguely but I know what you mean. What astonishes me is that you know and understand a great deal more than you are able to express. It's as if you're in a high fever ...'

I blurted out these words on seeing his feverish eyes and pale face. But I think he did not hear me.

'You know, don't you, my young friend,' he began again, continuing as before, 'there's a limit to the length of time a man is remembered on this earth. The limit is set at a hundred years. For a hundred years his children can still remember him, or grandchildren can still remember his face, but then, though his memory may still continue, it will only be by word of mouth, in people's minds, because all those who may have seen his face when he was alive will have passed away. And his grave in the graveyard will become overgrown, the white gravestone will disintegrate and everyone will forget him, even his heirs and successors, they will even forget his very name, because only a few remain alive in the memory of men—and so be it! Let them all forget, my dear ones, but you—*you* I will love from beyond the grave. Little ones, I will hear your happy voices and I will hear your feet on the graves of your forefathers on the appointed day! Live out your span in the sunlight and be joyful! I will pray to God for you and in your dreams I will come to you! Whatever happens, love outlasts death!'

The main thing was that I was in as much of a fever as he was. Instead of going away or persuading him to calm down or maybe putting him on the bed, because he was virtually delirious, I suddenly seized him by the hand and, bending over him and squeezing his hand, uttered in an agitated whisper, my heart brimming with tears:

'I'm so glad you're here! You're probably the one I've been waiting for! I don't like any of them here because none of them have real nobility ... I won't be like them ... I don't know where I'll go ... I'll go away with you ...'

Happily, at that moment mother suddenly came in, otherwise

I don't know what I might have said. She entered looking worried at having only just woken up, with a medicine bottle and tablespoon in her hands. On seeing us, she cried out:

'Just as I thought! I missed the time for giving you your quinine and now you're feverish! I overslept, Makar Ivanovich, my darling!'

I stood up and went out. She gave him his medicine and put him to bed. I also went back to bed, but in a state of great excitement. I was utterly consumed with curiosity and thought very hard about this encounter. What I expected from it at the time I do not know. Of course, my thoughts were all at sixes and sevens, and it was not really ideas so much as scraps of ideas that flashed through my mind. I lay with my face to the wall and suddenly noticed in the corner that bright spotlight caused by the setting sun which had infuriated me so recently. And I remember that my whole spirit seemed to spring to life and a new light flooded into my heart. I remember that sweet moment and never want to forget it. It was simply an instant filled with new hope and new strength . . .

I was on the way to recovery then, and it may be that such abrupt changes were an inevitable consequence of the state of my nerves. But I still believe even now in the brightness of such hope—and it is this I now want to place on record and remember. Of course, I knew even then surely enough that I would not go on a pilgrimage with Makar Ivanovich and that I did not know what exactly this new striving was, but there was one thing I had said, even though I was in a fever: 'None of them have real nobility!' Of course, I thought frenziedly, *that's* what I'll look for from now on—*real nobility*! They haven't got it and that's why I'll go away from here!

Something rustled and I turned over. Mother was standing there bending over me and peering into my eyes with a look of meek concern. I suddenly seized her by the hand.

'Mother, why didn't you tell me about our dear guest?' I asked suddenly, hardly expecting I would ask something like that. All the concern instantly vanished from her face and was replaced by a momentary joy, but she did not answer me save to say:

'Don't you forget Liza. You're forgetting Liza.'

She spoke the words in a rush, went red, and made an attempt to dash away, because she was frightened to death of showing her feelings and, in this sense, was just like me, diffident and awkward. What is more, of course, she did not want to start discussing Makar Ivanovich with me. It was enough for us just to exchange glances on that score. But I, the one who loathed all show of feeling, I, it was, who kept firm hold of her hand. I looked her lovingly in the eyes, laughing quietly and tenderly, and with my free hand stroked her sweet face and her sunken cheeks. She bent down and pressed her forehead to mine.

'Christ be with you,' she said all of a sudden, bowing low, her face radiant. 'Get better. I'm relying on you. He is sick, very sick . . . It is God's will . . . Oh, what have I said, oh, it can't be . . .'

She left the room. All her life, in fear and trembling, in true piety, she had greatly honoured her lawful husband, the holy pilgrim Makar Ivanovich, who out of the goodness of his heart had forgiven her once and for all.

CHAPTER II

I

BUT mother was wrong, I had not 'forgotten' Liza. Sensitive as she was, she had noted a cooling between brother and sister, but it had been not so much a matter of dislike as of envy. I will explain briefly, in view of what happened later.

From the moment of the prince's arrest poor Liza had given herself such a haughty air, a sort of inaccessible aloofness which, was almost unbearable. But everyone at home knew the truth and realized how much she was suffering, and if, at first, I grumbled and frowned at the way she was behaving towards us, then it was solely due to my petty irritability, made ten times worse by my illness—or that's what I think now. I never for a moment stopped loving Liza, but, on the contrary, loved her all the more, simply not wishing to make the first move, aware, besides, that no way would she ever make it herself.

The fact was that, as soon as everything became known about the prince immediately after his arrest, Liza made it her primary duty to adopt a position regarding us and anyone else in which she would not even permit it to be thought that she could be pitied or comforted, or the conduct of the prince might be justified. To the contrary, in an effort to avoid all discussion and any controversy, she all the while gave the impression of being proud of what her unfortunate fiancé had done, as if it were a superior form of heroism. She seemed to be saying to everyone (mind you, without actually saying a word): 'Is there no one among you who wouldn't have done the same, wouldn't have given yourselves up out of a sense of honesty and duty? Has none of you such a pure and sensitive conscience? And as for what he did, have none of you anything bad on your conscience? The only difference is that you all hide it, but this man would rather ruin himself than remain unworthy in his own eyes.' Every gesture she made seemed to be saying this. I cannot be sure, but I think I would have behaved in the same way if I had been in her position. I cannot be sure, also, whether these were really the things she said to herself. I suspect they weren't. With the other—lucid—half of her mind she must have seen through all the fatuousness of her 'hero'. Because everyone must be in agreement now that this man—unfortunate and yet high-minded after his fashion—was at the same time completely fatuous. Even her very haughtiness and her devil-may-care attitude towards us, her constant suspicion that we might have other ideas about him, gave partial grounds for assuming that, in the secret places of her heart, she might indeed be ready to make a different judgement on her unfortunate friend. But I hasten to add for my own part that, in my view, she was half-way right and it was even more forgivable in her case that she should waver in her final assessment. I confess personally, from the bottom of my heart, that right up to now, when everything is over and done with, I have no idea at all how to reach a final evaluation of this unfortunate man who has posed us all such a problem.

Nevertheless, a kind of mini-hell developed in our house as a result of her. Liza, who had loved so strongly, must have suffered a great deal. It was in character for her to prefer to suffer in silence. Hers was a character like mine, wilful and proud, and I have always thought, both now and at the time, that she fell in love with the prince out of wilfulness, precisely because he had no character of his own and completely subordinated himself to her from the very first moment and the very first word spoken between them. This can occur in the heart of its own accord without any preliminaries, but love of the strong for the weak can sometimes be incomparably stronger and more tormenting than love between equals, because you inevitably take upon yourself the responsibility for the weaker partner. At least, that's how I look at it. All of us, from the very start, surrounded her with the most loving care, particularly mother; but she did not soften, did not respond to the love offered her and seemed to reject any form of help. To start with, she used to talk to mother, but as each day passed she became more sparing with her words and sharper and even crueller. She used to discuss things with Versilov at the beginning, but soon chose Vasin as an adviser and helper, as I learned later to my astonishment. She used to go and see Vasin daily and would daily attend the court hearings. She spent her time calling on the prince's commanding officer, his lawyers, and the prosecutor, so much so that, towards the end, she was sometimes away from home for days at a time. She made daily—sometimes twice-daily—visits to the prince who was held in prison in the section reserved for the nobility, but these meetings, as I was later fully convinced, were extremely hard for Liza to bear. Though how can a third party have any idea what goes on between two people who are in love? What I do know is that the prince constantly caused her very deep hurt—why, though? Oddly enough, because he was madly jealous! However, I will have more to say about that later. But I will add one thing: it would be hard to know which of them was the more hurtful. Putting on such a haughty air about her hero for our benefit, Liza probably behaved quite differently towards him when they were face to face. I suspect this quite firmly on the basis of certain evidence which I will also have something to say about later.

Thus, so far as my own feeilngs about Liza and our mutual attitudes were concerned, everything was superficially such a show of envy and falsehood on both sides, and yet we never loved one another more deeply than we did then. I will add that, ever since Makar Ivanovich's arrival and her initial excitement and curiosity, Liza had for some reason begun to treat him negligently and even condescendingly. She seemed quite deliberately not to pay him any attention at all.

Having given myself a promise not to say a word, as I explained in the previous chapter, I thought—of course, in theory, ideally, so to speak—I would keep my word. Oh, with Versilov, for example, I would sooner have talked about zoology or Roman emperors than about *her*, for instance, or about that most important of lines in his letter to her where he mentioned that the document had not been burnt, but was extant and would turn up—a line I began thinking about the instant I came to my senses and began to recover from my fever. But, alas, on first putting this into practice, even almost before the first steps were taken, I realized the extent to which it was difficult, not to say impossible, to keep to such an intention, because the very next day after my encounter with Makar Ivanovich I was frightfully upset by something quite unexpected.

II

I was upset by the unexpected visit of Nastasya Yegorovna or 'Darya', Olya's mother. I had heard from mother that she had come to see me more than once during my illness and she was very concerned about my health. Whether this 'good woman', as mother always called her, had come especially to see me, or was simply calling on mother through some prior arrangement, I did not ask. In order to entertain me, mother always used to discourse on domestic matters when she came to give me my soup (when I was still not strong enough to feed myself) and each time I stubbornly tried to give the impression I was little interested in all her news, and so refrained from asking any detailed questions about Nastasya Yegorovna, even to the point of not saying a word.

It was around eleven o'clock. I had been about to get out of bed and move to the armchair by the table when she came in. I deliberately stayed where I was, in bed. Mother was very busy with something upstairs and did not come down on her arrival, so that we suddenly found ourselves alone. She sat down opposite me in a chair against the wall, smiling and saying nothing. I had anticipated she would say nothing. In fact, her arrival had a most irritating effect on me. I did not even give her a nod and just stared at her straight in the eyes, but she simply looked back at me in the same way.

'Aren't you bored being by yourself in the apartment now that the prince isn't there?' I asked suddenly, losing patience.

'I am not in the apartment any longer, sir. Through Anna Andreevna I now look after the baby.'

'Whose baby?'

'Andrey Petrovich's,' she said in a confidential whisper, glancing round at the door.

'Surely Tatyana Pavlovna's there . . .'

'Both Tatyana Pavlovna and Anna Andreevna, they're both there, sir, and Lizaveta Makarovna, as well, and your own dear mother—they're all there, sir. They all do their bit. Tatyana Pavlovna and Anna Andreevna are great friends now, sir.'

That was news! She grew very animated as she talked. I looked at her with loathing.

'You've perked up a lot since you last came to see me.'

'Oh, yes, sir.'

'I think you've put on weight, haven't you?'

She gave me a strange look: 'I've got very fond, very fond of her, sir.'

'Of whom?'

'Anna Andreevna—very fond, sir. Such a fine young lady and so clever . . .'

'Well, well. How is she getting on now?'

'She's very calm, sir, very . . .'

'She was always very calm.'

'That she was, sir.'

'If you've come here to gossip,' I cried out suddenly, losing patience, 'then you'd better know I'm not getting mixed up in anything! I've decided to give it all up, give up everyone! Whatever happens, I'll be going away!'

I stopped at that, realizing what I was saying. It seemed degrading to tell her all my new plans. She had listened to me without surprise or excitement, but a short silence still followed. Suddenly she stood up, went to the door, and glanced into the next room. After convincing herself there was no one there and we were alone, she came back as if nothing had happened and sat down where she had been sitting previously.

'A lot of good that's done you!' I laughed suddenly.

'You'll be leaving that room with the civil servants, will you, sir?' she asked suddenly, bending a little towards me and lowering her voice as if it were the main reason she had come to see me.

386

'My room? Maybe. Perhaps I will . . . How do I know what I'll do?'

'Your landlords are very anxious. Both he and his wife want to know. Andrey Petrovich assured them you'd be going back.'

'Why do you want to know?'

'Anna Andreevna also wanted to know. She was very glad to hear you'd be staying.'

'How does she know I'll be staying?' I wanted to add: 'And what's it to her?' but refrained from asking out of arrogance.

'And Mr Lambert also told them the same thing.'

'Wha-a-at?'

'Mr Lambert, sir. The gentleman also told Andrey Petrovich you'd be staying for sure, and he's also confirmed it to Anna Andreevna.'

This news shook me rigid. Wonders'll never cease! So Lambert already knew Versilov, he had wormed his way in there—and, what's more, he had wormed his way into Anna Andreevna's good graces as well! I went hot all over, but said nothing. A terrible wave of sheer arrogance engulfed me. If it wasn't arrogance, I don't know what it was. Yet instantly I seemed to tell myself: 'If I ask so much as a word in explanation, then I know I'll be drawn into that world again and I'll never be able to break with it!' My heart boiled with resentment. I was determined not to say a word and I lay there motionless. She also fell silent for a whole minute.

'How is Prince Nikolai Ivanovich?' I asked suddenly, as if I had gone out of my mind. I asked the question deliberately, in order to change the subject, and once again, quite accidentally, put a leading question, just like a madman returning to the very place from which he had only recently been quivering to escape.

'He is in Tsarskoe Selo, sir. He was a bit poorly, and in the town the fevers started coming back, so everyone advised him to move to Tsarskoe, to his very own house there, for the sake of the good clean air there, sir.'

I said nothing.

'Anna Andreevna and General Akhmakov's widow pay him a visit every three days. They go there together by carriage, sir.'

Anna Andreevna and General Akhmakov's widow—that's to say, *her*—are close friends! They go there together by carriage! I was at a loss for words.

'They've become so close, sir, and Anna Andreevna speaks so well of Katerina Nikolaevna . . .'

I remained at a loss.

'And Katerina Nikolaevna is again making a hit in society, at one occasion after another! She shines like a star. They do say everyone's doting on her at court . . . but she's given up Mr Björing, there'll be no wedding. That's what everyone's been saying . . . ever since once particular moment.'

Ever since Versilov's letter, that is. I was literally shaking, but I did not say a word.

'Anna Andreevna is so sorry for Prince Sergey Petrovich, and so is Katerina Nikolaevna, too, sir, and everyone says he'll be proved innocent and Mr Stebelkov'll be condemned . . .'

I glanced at her resentfully. She stood up and suddenly bent down towards me.

'Anna Andreevna particularly asked me to find out how you were,' she said in the quietest of whispers, 'and is very keen you should go and see her the moment you start going out. Goodbye, sir. Get well quickly, sir, and I'll tell her . . .'

She went out. I sat up in bed. A cold sweat stood out on my forehead, yet I felt no fright. The incomprehensible and ugly news about Lambert and his activities, for instance, did not fill me with any horror, judging at least by the possibly unaccountable fear with which, when I was ill and in the first days of recovery, I recalled my meeting with him that night. On the contrary, in that initial troubled moment when I sat bolt upright in the bed after she had gone, I did not even pause for a moment to think of Lambert but was literally gripped by what had been said about *her*, about the rift with Björing, her good fortune in society, the social occasions, her success, her 'stardom' . . . 'She shines like a star.' Nastasya Yegorovna's words echoed in my mind. And I was suddenly aware I was not strong enough to escape from the whirlpool, although I had managed to hold my tongue and not shower Nastasya Yegorovna with questions after all the fantastic things she said! An uncontrollable hunger for that life, *their* life, gripped me . . . and another kind of sensual hunger as well, which I felt to the point of sheer joy and sheer torment. My thoughts were all in a whirl and I let them whirl. 'To hell with reason!' was what I felt. 'Yet mother didn't say a word to me about Lambert coming,' I thought disconnectedly.

388

'Versilov probably told her not to. Well, I'd rather die than ask Versilov about Lambert!' 'Versilov . . .' the thought flashed into my mind again, 'Versilov and Lambert—that's really something! Bully for Versilov! He terrified that German, Björing, with that letter, libelled her and, as they say, *la calomnie—il en reste toujours quelque chose*, some mud always sticks after calumny, and that courtly German took fright at any whiff of scandal—ha-ha! That taught her a lesson! And Lambert—has Lambert also wormed his way in with her? Of course he has! Why shouldn't she and he get together?'

At that point I suddenly gave up thinking all this nonsense and in despair let my head fall on the pillow.

'No, it won't be like that!' I cried out, suddenly filled with determination, and jumped out of bed, put on my slippers and dressing-gown and went straight to Makar Ivanovich's room, as if that was where I would find an escape from all enchantments, where I would find salvation and an anchor to which I could hold firm.

That was in fact what I probably felt at that moment with my whole heart. Why otherwise would I suddenly, irresistibly, have jumped up and dashed to Makar Ivanovich in such a state?

III

But in Makar Ivanovich's room I quite unexpectedly found people—mother and the doctor. Because I had been absolutely sure I would find the old man by himself as I had done the day before, I stopped dumbfounded in the doorway. Yet I had scarcely time to frown before I was joined by Versilov, followed quickly by Liza. It meant that everyone was for some reason gathering in Makar Ivanovich's room just when they weren't needed!

'I came to find out how you were,' I said, going straight up to Makar Ivanovich.

'Thank you, dear boy, I was waiting for you. I knew you'd be coming. I was thinking about you last night.'

He looked me fondly in the eyes and I could see he loved me just that much more than the others, but I also couldn't help noticing that, though his face was full of joy, the illness had enjoyed some success during the night. The doctor had only just

389

finished giving him a very serious examination. I learned later that this doctor (the very same one with whom I had quarrelled and who had been looking after Makar Ivanovich since his arrival) was very attentive to his patient and—I am not versed in their medical jargon—had diagnosed several complications. As I could see at first glance, Makar Ivanovich was on extremely friendly terms with him. I took exception to this at that moment, but then at that moment I was in a bad mood.

'So how is our dear invalid today, Aleksandr Semyonovich?' enquired Versilov.

If I had not been in such a disturbed state, my first concern would have been to have followed very closely the relations between Versilov and the old man, something I had been thinking about the day before. What most of all struck me at that moment was the extraordinarily soft and pleasant look on Versilov's face. There was something completely sincere in it. I think I noticed long ago that Versilov's face usually became surprisingly beautiful whenever he was being open and honest.

'We will quarrel all the time,' the doctor answered.

'With Makar Ivanovich? I don't believe it! You can't quarrel with him!'

'He won't listen to me. He won't sleep at night . . .'

'Stop it now, Aleksandr Semyonovich, that's enough of scolding me!' cried Makar Ivanovich with a laugh. 'Well, Andrey Petrovich, sir, what has happened to our lady of the manor? She,' he added, pointing at mother, 'has spent the entire morning clucking and worrying.'

'Oh, Andrey Petrovich,' mother exclaimed with real concern, 'tell us at once, don't beat about the bush—what's the verdict?'

'It went against her.'

'Ah!' cried mother.

'Don't worry, it's not Siberia! A fine of fifteen roubles! It was a farce!'

He sat down and so did the doctor. They had been talking about Tatyana Pavlovna, and I knew nothing about it. I sat down on Makar Ivanovich's left and Liza sat opposite me to the right. She evidently had some sadness of her own which she had come to see mother about. Her face showed concern and irritation. We exchanged looks at that moment and it suddenly struck me we were both in disgrace and I ought to make the first move. My heart softened towards her at that moment. Meanwhile, Versilov began speaking about the morning's events. It turned out that that very morning Tatyana Pavlovna had been involved in a court case with her cook. The whole thing was quite ridiculous. I have already mentioned that the malicious Finnish woman sometimes, to get her own back, maintained complete silence for weeks on end, not saying a word in response to any of her mistress's questions. I have also mentioned Tatyana Pavlovna's weakness for her in putting up with everything from her and not wanting to dismiss her for good. All these psychological caprices by elderly maiden ladies and their mistresses are only worthy of scorn, in my eyes, and do not deserve to be taken seriously, and if I mention the matter here it is solely because this cook-housekeeper is destined to play a certain significant and fateful role in my ensuing narrative. And so, losing patience with this stubborn Finnish woman, who had not spoken to her for several days, Tatyana Pavlovna suddenly struck her—something which had never happened before. The Finnish woman did not utter a single sound at the time, but that day she made contact with a retired midshipman called Osetrov who lived in some corner off the back stairs of their apartment and scraped a living by offering his services in various ways and, naturally, by organizing court cases for people like the cook. It ended by Tatyana Pavlovna being taken to court, and Versilov was called upon for some reason to appear as a witness.

Versilov told it all exceptionally hilariously, jokily acting out the parts of Tatyana Pavlovna and the midshipman and the cook so well that even mother burst out laughing. The cook declared from the very start that she only wanted her mistress fined, 'otherwise if my mistress goes to prison, who'll I be able to cook for?' Tatyana Pavlovna replied to all the judge's questions with great haughtiness, without even deigning to justify herself. On the contrary, she ended by saying: 'I hit her and I'll do it again!' at which she was immediately fined three roubles for contempt of court. The midshipman, an exceptionally thin, gangling young fellow, embarked on a long speech in defence of his client, but came a cropper and sent the whole court into fits of laughter. The case was soon over and Tatyana Pavlovna was ordered to pay to Marie, the injured party, the sum of fifteen roubles. She took out her purse there and then and began handing out the money, at which point the midshipman immediately came up and held out his hand, but Tatyana Pavlovna literally struck it away and turned to Marie.

'Enough's enough, mistress dear, don't trouble yourself! Add it on to the account! I'll deal with this myself!'

'Just look what a gangling creature you've employed!' said Tatyana Pavlovna, pointing at the midshipman, quite delighted that Marie was now talking to her.

'Oh, isn't he just!' Marie answered slyly. 'Well, mistress, was it cutlets and peas you asked for today? I didn't quite catch what you said because I was in such a hurry to get here.'

'Oh, no, with cabbage, Marie, and please don't burn it like you did yesterday.'

'I'll do my very best today, madame. Please give me your hand.'

And she kissed her mistress's hand as a sign that peace was restored between them. The court-room was in fits.

'What a woman she is!' cried mother, shaking her head, delighted with what she heard and with the way Andrey Petrovich told it, but glancing covertly and anxiously at Liza.

'A lady of character, ever since she was little!' cried Makar Ivanovich with a grin.

'Idle and intemperate!' was the doctor's verdict.

'So I'm a lady of character, am I, and idle and intemperate?' said Tatyana Pavlovna suddenly coming into the room and looking very pleased with herself. 'Aleksandr Semyonovich, you shouldn't talk such nonsense! Ever since you were a boy of 10 you've never known me idle for a moment, and you spent a whole year trying to cure me of being so bilious and "intemperate" as you call it and you couldn't, so you ought to be ashamed! You can stop making fun of me. Thank you, Andrey Petrovich, for taking the trouble to come to court. So, dear Makar, how are you? I only came to see you, not this one here.'

She indicated me, but at once gave me a friendly tap on the shoulder. I had never before seen her in such a good mood.

'Well?' she asked finally, turning to the doctor and frowning anxiously.

'You can see, he won't lie down and sitting up like that simply wears him out.'

'I only want to sit up just a little, just when there are people here,' muttered Makar Ivanovich with the pleading look of a small child.

'Yes, we all love doing that. We all love chatting, with people round us. I know what you mean, Makar dear,' said Tatyana Pavlovna.

'He's on to me, just like that!' said the old man, smiling again and turning to the doctor. 'You won't let me say a word! Let me say just you hold on a bit, I'll lie down, I heard what you said, but what we say is: "If you lie abed, it's likely you'll be dead"—and that's . . . that's what it'll be like for me, my friend, over the hill.'

'As I thought! Peasant superstition: "I'll lie abed," the saying goes, "and sure enough I'll be dead"—it's what the peasants often fear and so they prefer to face illness on their feet rather than spend time lying in a hospital. But as for you, Makar Ivanovich, it's a simple case of wanderlust—you're all for doing your own thing, being off on the high road, that's what your illness is all about. You've lost the habit of living in one place. You're a so-called pilgrim, aren't you? Well, among our peasants the idea of being a tramp has become a passion. I've noticed this frequently. Our peasant people are predominantly vagabonds.'

'So you think Makar's a tramp, do you?' cried Tatyana Pavlovna.

'Oh, I didn't mean it like that! I was using the word in a general sense. But there are religious vagabonds and, even if they're men of God, they're still tramps! In a decent, honourable sense of the word . . . but it still means they're tramps. I mean, from the medical point of view . . .'

'I assure you . . .' I turned to the doctor suddenly, '. . . you and I, we're more like tramps, and all the rest of us here, but not this old man, who we've got a lot to learn from, because he has something firm in life to hold on to, but we, no matter who we are, have nothing firm in life to hold on to . . . Still, you probably can't understand that.'

I obviously spoke sharply, but I came with that intention. I was not in my right mind and I really do not know why I remained sitting there.

'What are you on about?' Tatyana Pavlovna eyed me suspiciously. 'So what do you think about him, Makar Ivanovich?' she asked, pointing at me.

393

'God be praised, he's really clever,' said the old man with a serious look on his face.

But at the word 'clever' they practically all burst out laughing. I bristled. The doctor laughed most of all. The worst thing was that I knew nothing then about their intentions. Three days previously Versilov, the doctor and Tatyana Pavlovna had all agreed to do everything possible to distract mother from dwelling on her forebodings and fears about Makar Ivanovich, whose condition was a great deal more serious and hopeless than I suspected. That was why they all made jokes and tried to laugh as much as possible. It was only the doctor who was stupid and had no idea how to make a joke of things. That accounted for what happened. If I had been in on their plan, I would not have done what I did. Liza also knew nothing about it.

I sat there listening out of one ear while they chatted and laughed, but my head was full of what Nastasya Yegorovna had told me and I could not get out on my mind the sight of her sitting there and looking at me and then getting up and peering into the next room. At last they all suddenly laughed at once because Tatyana Pavlovna—I have no idea why—suddenly called the doctor an atheist. 'Oh, all you doctors, you're all atheists!' she cried.

'Makar Ivanovich,' the doctor shouted, pretending that he had been insulted and sought justice, 'am I an atheist or not?'

'You, an atheist? No, you're not an atheist,' answered the old man with dignity, gazing intently at him. 'No, thank God,' he shook his head, 'you're a happy man!'

'You mean a man who's happy can't be an atheist?' the doctor noted ironically.

'That's a thought,' remarked Versilov, but quite seriously.

'It's a powerful thought!' I exclaimed despite myself, struck by the idea. The doctor glanced round him questioningly.

'I was frightened at first of learned men, of professors,' Makar Ivanovich began saying, looking down slightly. Probably they had been talking about professors earlier. 'I did not dare face up to them because I was awfully afraid of being influenced by their atheism. I reasoned that my soul within me was the only one I had. If I destroyed it, I would never find another. But then I took heart and reasoned that these learned people weren't gods, after all, they were just like you and me, humble servants like

394

ourselves. And I had a great curiosity to know what atheism was. Only then, my friend, that very curiosity itself vanished away.'

He fell silent, but had every intention of continuing, smiling in the same calm and dignified way. There is a kind of openness and honesty which trusts one and all without ever being aware of mockery. Such people are always limited because they are always prepared to lay bare the most precious things in their heart to the first person they meet. But in Makar Ivanovich there was something else, I think. Something else motivated him, not openness and honesty pure and simple. There was the hint of a propagandist about him. I was pleased to catch sight of a sly little grin in the way he looked at the doctor and maybe Versilov as well. The topic was obviously a continuation of previous discussions earlier in the week, but unfortunately the same fateful remarks cropped up which had so electrified me the day before and led me to do something I still regret.

'A man who is an atheist', the old man went on in his concentrated way, 'is probably someone I would be afraid of even now. Except, my friend, Aleksandr Semyonovich, I have never yet come across real atheists, I have only come across people who are vain—that is the best thing to call them. People like that are all sorts. There's no knowing what sort they are— large, small, silly, clever, even simple, working people—but it's all vanity. They spend their whole lives reading and thinking, sating themselves with book-learning, but they themselves remain just as bewildered as ever and cannot solve a thing. Some have gone this way and that and lost sight of themselves. Others have become hard as stone, though they still have dreams in their hearts. Others have no feelings, no thoughts at all and are just content to snigger. Yet others have merely chosen what they think are pretty posies from books, but are themselves vain and indecisive. I repeat—they all have a great boredom. The small men of this world are in sore need, they have no bread, cannot feed their children, sleep rough, yet their hearts are joyous and light. They swear and sin, and yet their hearts are light. But the great of this world eat and drink well and have heaps of gold, but are filled with a great boredom. Some have studied all there is to know, yet still they yearn for more. I always think the greater a man's mind, the greater his boredom. And here's another thing: people have taught things since the beginning of the world, but what good thing have they taught that could make the world the most beautiful, the happiest, the most joyous place in which to live? And I will say this, too: they have no true nobility and do not even want it. They have all come to ruin and yet each one praises his ruined state and gives no thought to the one and only truth of God; and yet to live without God is nothing but torment. And it transpires we curse the one thing that may light the way for us and do not know it. For you must know it is impossible to be a man and not bow down and worship. A man cannot tolerate himself, no man can. And if he rejects God, then he will bow down before an idol—a wooden one or a gold one or one made of ideas. They are become idolaters, not atheists— that's what they should be called. And why shouldn't there be atheists, eh? There *are* people who are out-and-out atheists, save that they are much more terrible than the others, because they come to us with the word of God on their lips. I have heard about them many times, but I have never come across them. There are people like that, my friend, and I think there must be.'

'There are, Makar Ivanovich,' Versilov suddenly affirmed, 'and there must be people like that!'

'There certainly are and must be people like that!' I couldn't help exclaiming too, and heatedly, though I do not know why. I had been caught by Versilov's tone and captivated by the idea that 'there must be people like that'. The topic had come as a complete surprise to me. But at that moment another complete surprise occurred.

IV

It was an extremely bright, sunny day. On the doctor's orders, the blind in Makar Ivanovich's room was usually not raised all day, but the upper part of the window had a curtain, not a blind, and was therefore not covered because the old man had been worried about not seeing the sun at all when the blind had been drawn previously. And at that very moment as we sat there a ray of sunlight suddenly shone directly on Makar Ivanovich's face. While he had been speaking he had not worried about it to start with but had automatically leaned his head to one side, because the bright light seriously affected his weak eyes. Mother, standing beside him, had glanced several times anxiously at the window. The simplest thing would have been to put something over the window, but, so as not to interfere with what he was saying, she tried to move the little bench on which Makar Ivanovich was sitting just a little. Only three or four inches were needed. She several times bent down and took hold of the bench but with Makar Ivanovich's weight on it she could not move it. Feeling she was trying to do something, Makar Ivanovich tried instinctively to lift himself up while still busy speaking but his legs refused to respond. Mother, however, still went on trying to push and pull and finally the whole thing quite exasperated Liza. I remember noticing her furious, bright-eyed glances but I did not know at first what caused them and had in addition been preoccupied with what was being said. And then I suddenly heard her almost screech at Makar Ivanovich:

'Get up a bit! You can see mother finds it hard!'

The old man gave her a quick glance, saw at once what was meant, and instantly tried to rise, but couldn't. He only managed to lift himself a couple of inches and then fell back on the bench.

'I can't, my dear,' he answered Liza rather pitifully, gazing at her in a submissively crestfallen way.

'You can spout a whole book but you can't budge an inch, eh?'

'Liza!' shouted Tatyana Pavlovna. Makar Ivanovich again made a great effort.

'Get your crutch! It's lying beside you, use it to get up!' cried Liza in the same sharp way.

'Right you are!' said the old man and hurriedly picked up his crutch.

'He just needs lifting up!' said Versilov as he rose to his feet. The doctor had also made a move, as had Tatyana Pavlovna, but before they could come to his aid Makar Ivanovich, leaning with all his might on his crutch, suddenly raised himself and stood looking round in triumph.

'And I did it!' he said almost proudly, with a happy grin. 'Thank you, Liza dear, for reminding me. I'd been thinking my old legs wouldn't be able to do it at all . . .'

But he had scarcely been on his feet any time at all and had not managed to say anything when the crutch, on which he had been putting his full weight, slipped along the carpet and, since his old legs could hardly hold him, he crashed to the floor. I remember it was sickening to watch. Everyone cried out and rushed to help him up, but, thank heavens, nothing had been broken. Both his knees had struck the floor heavily and loudly, but he had managed to put out his right hand to break his fall. He was lifted up and placed on the bed. He went very pale, not so much from shock as from the way he was shaking (the doctor, incidentally, having diagnosed in him heart disease in addition to everything else). Mother was beside herself with fear. And suddenly Makar Ivanovich, still pale, his body quivering and not fully recovered, turned to Liza and told her in a quiet, gentle voice:

'No, my dear, you can see my old legs wouldn't!'

I cannot express exactly what I felt then. The fact was that the old man's words had no complaint or reproach in them. On the contrary, it was obvious he had not noticed anything malicious in what Liza said and he had taken her screeching at him as quite justified, as if he deserved such a scolding. All this had a terrible effect on Liza. The moment he fell down she had jumped up like the rest of us and stood there half-dead and, of course, full of pain at being the cause of it all, but on hearing those words she suddenly, almost in an instant, blushed red with shame and remorse.

'That's enough!' commanded Tatyana Pavlovna. 'We've had enough talk! It's time we went our separate ways. No good'll come of it when a doctor initiates so much talk!'

'Precisely,' said Aleksandr Semyonovich, who was busying himself with the sick man. 'I'm to blame, Tatyana Pavlovna. He must have rest!'

But Tatyana Pavlovna had stopped paying attention. For as long as half a minute she studied Liza in intent silence.

'Come here, Liza. I'm an old fool, but you can kiss me if you like,' she said unexpectedly.

She did kiss her, I don't know why, but that is just as it should have been, so much so that I almost dashed to give Tatyana Pavlovna a kiss as well. Precisely what Liza did not need was to be crushed by reproaches; the new and fine feeling sure to be born in her deserved congratulations and a joyous welcome. But instead of showing such feelings, I suddenly stood up and began saying in firm, ringing tones:

'Makar Ivanovich, you've again used the expression "real

nobility" and I've been worried sick by it ever since yesterday . . . and my whole life I've been worried sick by it, only I did not know what it was. This coincidence of words seems to me a matter of fate, almost miraculous . . . I want to say this right now in your presence . . .'

But I was stopped that instant. I repeat that I did not know about their agreement concerning mother and Makar Ivanovich. Judging, I suppose, by what I had done before, they considered me capable of all manner of scandalous things.

'Take him away! Get him out of here!' screamed Tatyana Pavlovna furiously. Mother began shaking. Makar Ivanovich, seeing the general panic, panicked as well.

'That's enough, Arkady!' cried Versilov sternly.

'For me, ladies and gentlemen,' I said in an even louder voice, 'for me to see you all here alongside someone as feeble as a child . . .' I pointed at Makar '. . . is an absolute disgrace! There's only one saint among you, and that's mother, but she's . . .'

'You're terrifying him!' the doctor insisted.

'I know I'm all men's enemy,' I muttered (or something of the kind), but, glancing round me, I looked challengingly at Versilov.

'Arkady!' he again cried. 'We had a scene just like this once before. I beg you—don't do it again!'

I cannot convey the forcefulness with which he said this. His features expressed the fullest, most sincere, and extraordinary sadness. Most surprising of all was the way in which he looked so guilty. I was now the judge and he was the criminal. All this drove me crazy.

'Yes,' I shouted back at him, 'there was a scene like this, when I buried Versilov, tore him out of my heart! But then came a resurrection from the dead, and now, now . . . There won't be any new dawn! But you'll all see what I'm capable of! You've no idea what I can prove!'

Saying this, I dashed back to my room. Versilov ran after me.

V

I had a relapse. A very strong attack of the fever occurred and by that night I was delirious. But I was not delirious all the time. There were countless dreams, a whole series of them, of which one dream, or a fragment of it, stuck in my memory. I will

399

describe it without offering any explanations. It was prophetic and I cannot overlook it.

I suddenly found myself, my heart proud and mightily determined, in a large, high-ceilinged room, but it was not at Tatyana Pavlovna's. I remember the room very well (I mention this now, though I am anticipating things). Despite being by myself, I constantly felt, in fear and trepidation, I was not alone, that I was expected, and someone was watching me. I felt there were people on the other side of doors waiting for me to do something. It was an unbearable feeling, this wanting simply to be alone. And then suddenly *she* came in. She looked shyly at me, obviously terribly frightened and looking constantly into my eyes. I was standing there, *holding the document, the letter, in my hand*! She tried enticing me with smiles and making up to me. I was sorry for her, but I also began to feel repelled. Suddenly she covered her face with her hands. I flung the document down on a table with utter contempt and shouted: 'Don't beg! I don't need anything from you! I'm getting my own back on you for all the nasty things you've said by showing utter contempt!' And I left the room, choking with pride. But in the dark of the doorway Lambert seized hold of me. '*C-crétin! C-crétin!*' he whispered, holding me as hard as he could by the arm. 'She's got to open a girls' school on Vasilevsky Island!' (In order, that is, to feed herself, if her father, knowing about my document, cut her off without a penny. I put down Lambert's words just as I remembered them from my dream.)

'Arkady Makarovich is looking for true nobility!' came Anna Andreevna's little voice from somewhere nearby on the stairs. Her words sounded unbearably mocking, not approving. I went back into the room with Lambert. But on seeing Lambert *she* suddenly burst out laughing. My first reaction was one of such terrible horror that I stopped and could not go near her. I stared at her unbelievingly, because it was just as if she had suddenly torn a mask from her face. The features were generally the same, but it was as if each feature separately had become distorted by a blatant impudence. 'Time to pay up, dear lady!' shouted Lambert, and they both laughed louder than ever, and my heart died at the thought that this shameless hussy was the very same woman whose single glance had once made my heart brimful of good feelings!

'Look what they're capable of for money, these stuck-up ladies in their so-called high society!' exclaimed Lambert. But the shameless hussy was not even embarrassed by that; she was laughing at the look of horror on my face. Oh, she was ready to do it for money, I could see that . . . and yet what was happening to me? I was no longer feeling either pity or loathing. I was shaking as never before, seized by a new and inexpressible feeling which I had never known before and was as strong as the whole world . . . Oh, I was powerless now to leave! Oh, I loved the shamelessness of it! I seized her by the hands and the touch of her hands made me cringe in torment and I pressed my lips to her impudent, crimson, quivering lips that shouted my name and gave peals of laughter!

Oh, to hell with the recollection! I curse that dream! I swear before I had that beastly dream I had never had any such shameful thought in my head! I had not even day-dreamed about anything like that (although I had kept the 'document' sewn up in my pocket and had sometimes given the odd grin when I touched it). Where on earth had all this come from? It was all due to the spider lurking in my soul! It meant that the whole thing had come into existence long ago and had lain concealed in my corrupt heart, lain concealed in my libido, but my heart had not wanted to admit it openly and my mind had not been able to assimilate it consciously. But the dream mirrored and laid bare what had been in my heart, in complete detail, in the most graphic and prophetic form. Was *this* what I wanted to show them as *proof* when I dashed from Makar Ivanovich's room?

That's enough for the time being! The dream was one of the strangest experiences of my life.

CHAPTER III

I

THREE days later I got out of bed in the morning and suddenly felt as I stood up that I would not go to bed again. I felt I was close to full recovery. Perhaps there is no need to give such details, but several days then followed which have remained in my memory as tranquil and happy although nothing particular happened—and that is rare enough in these reminiscences of mine. My inner, spiritual condition need not be described. If the reader knew what it had been really like, he would not have believed it. Everything is better left to be explained by the facts. For the time being I will just say one thing: the reader should remember that I have *the soul of a spider*! And this is the soul of someone who wanted to escape from his family and the world at large in the name of 'true nobility'! My lust for such nobility was extreme and that is, of course, as it should be, but how it was to be reconciled with God knows what other kinds of lust—for me that's a mystery. And it always has been a mystery. I have marvelled thousands of times at a man's capacity (I think of a Russian's capacity above all) to nurse in his heart the highest of ideals alongside the greatest lasciviousness and to do so quite innocently. Whether there is a special breadth of spirit in Russians which will take them a long way, or simply sheer lustfulness, is the big question!

But let's leave that. Somehow or other a kind of calm descended. I had simply come to the realization that I had to get better as soon as possible no matter what happened, in order to resume what I had been doing, and therefore I decided to observe the rules of hygiene and the doctor's instructions (no matter who he was) and, with extraordinary good sense (the fruit of my breadth of spirit!), to postpone all idea of rebelling until the day I went out—until I was fully recovered that is. How all my tranquillity and enjoyment of calm were to be reconciled with the deliciously tormenting and excited beating of my heart in anticipation of my rebellion I do not now, but I again attribute it all to my 'breadth of spirit'! But I felt none of my recent impatience. I put off everything, no longer trembling at what might happen, as I had done recently, but, like a rich man, feeling confident of my resources and my strength. The sense of the overweaning and challenging character of the fate awaiting me grew more and more obvious, and partly, I presume, because I was really recovering and my strength was rapidly returning. And it is precisely those last few days of real, final recovery that I remember now with the greatest pleasure.

Oh, they forgave me everything, all my outrageous remarks, that is! And these were the very people whom I had called an absolute disgrace! This is what I love about people. It's what I call the way the heart thinks. At least, it attracted me at once—up to a point, of course. Versilov and I, for instance, went on discussing things as the best of friends, but only up to a point. The moment we became too expansive (and it happened) we instantly held back, both of us, as if slightly ashamed of something. There are cases when a victor has to feel ashamed of winning, precisely because this opponent is defeated. I was obviously the winner in this case, and I felt ashamed.

That morning—when, that is, I got out of bed after my relapse—he came in to see me and it was then I learned for the first time about their general agreement concerning mother and Makar Ivanovich. At the same time he remarked that, though the old man was better, the doctor could not be positive about his recovery. With all my heart I gave him a promise to be more careful in future. As Versilov was telling me all this I noted for the very first time how very sincere was his own concern for the old man—a great deal more than I would have expected from someone like him. He regarded the old man as someone particularly dear to him personally, and not simply dear to him because of mother. This caught my attention at once, almost with surprise, and I confess that, without Versilov, I would have failed to see and appreciate a great deal in the old man, someone who has remained one of the firmest and most original memories locked in my heart.

Versilov was a bit apprehensive about my attitude to Makar Ivanovich, being mistrustful, that is to say, of my mental attitude and my tact and yet becoming very satisfied later when he saw that I could sometimes understand how to behave towards someone holding completely opposed opinions and viewpoints—in short, that I knew, when necessary, how to be conciliatory and broadminded. I also confess (without, I think, demeaning myself) that I found in this man of the people something completely new to me concerning other people's feelings and attitudes, something unknown to me, something much more lucid and rewarding than I had realized before. Nevertheless, there were times when I simply blew my top over some of the out-and-out superstitious nonsense in which he believed with the most outrageous imperturbability and complacency. But in this case his lack of education was of course to blame. His spiritual state was well-ordered enough, so much so, even, that I have never some across anyone better ordered in this respect.

II

What attracted me about him most of all, as I have already mentioned, was his extraordinary purity of heart and the absence of the least self-importance. One could sense in him a heart almost untainted by sin. There was 'joy' in his heart, and 'true nobility' too. He was very fond of the word 'joy' and used it often. True, he was now and then affected by a kind of morbid elation, a kind of sickly sweetness in his emotions—partly, I assume, because he never, strictly speaking, ceased to escape the effects of the fever, but it never affected his true nobility. He was a man of contrasts. Side by side with an astonishing straightforwardness that sometimes (often to my annoyance) entirely failed to notice when people were being ironical, there was also a sensitivity allied to cunning which emerged most of all in his polemics. He loved polemics, but sometimes only in his own way. It was obvious he had derived a great deal from travelling through Russia and picked up much in conversing with people, but, I repeat, he was most of all fond of uplifting feelings and everything that tended to uplift and edify and was himself very fond of stories of that kind. In fact, he loved being a story-teller. I heard a great many stories connected with his own travels as well as legends from the lives of religious zealots in ancient times. I am not an expert in such things, but I think he concocted a good many of these legends, having heard them mostly by word of mouth from uneducated peasants. It was simply impossible to credit certain things. But along with obvious fabrications or simply so much falsehood there always shone through them a certain astonishing wholeness and unity full of folksy emotion that was always edifying. I remember, for example, one long account—'The Saintly Life of Mary of Egypt'. Till that moment I knew nothing at all about such 'lives of saints'. I have to say straight out that it was almost impossible to listen to them without having tears in one's eyes, and not tears of edification simply but of a strangely heightened feeling, as if one could actually feel something as hot and extraordinary as the white-hot, sandy desert full of lions through which the saint wandered. Still, I do not want to talk about this, because I am no expert.

Apart from the feeling of uplift and edification, what I liked in him were the sometimes extraordinarily original opinions he had on certain very contentious aspects of contemporary reality. For instance, he used to tell a recent story about a soldier returning from service, of which he claimed to be almost an eyewitness. This soldier returned home to peasant life from military service and he disliked the peasants and they disliked him. He went off the rails, drank, and robbed someone somewhere. There was no strong evidence, but they seized him and took him to court. The lawyer defending him made his case—there was no evidence and that was that. Then suddenly the defendant, after listening and listening, stood up and interrupted the lawyer with: 'No, just you stop all this talk!' and went on to tell his story down to the last detail, confessing tearfully to everything and expressing bitter remorse. The jury withdrew to consider its verdict and then suddenly came back to announce: 'Not guilty'. Everybody shouted and rejoiced, but the soldier stood there rooted to the spot unable to understand a thing. He did not understand a word the president of the court said to him in admonition as he released him. Even when again free, the soldier still could not believe it. He started fretting, plunged in thought, unable to eat or drink or talk to people and on the fifth day he hanged himself.* 'That's what it's like to live with a sin on your conscience!' Makar Ivanovich concluded.

The story is, of course, unimportant, and there are masses of such things reported in our papers nowadays, but what I liked was his tone in telling it and the way he used certain words with a new meaning. For instance, in telling how the soldier was disliked by the other peasants when he returned to his village, Makar Ivanovich talked about the soldier as a 'polluted peasant'. And talking about the lawyer who had almost won the case, he described him as a 'hired conscience'. He used these two expressions without labouring them, unaware what he was doing, and yet these two expressions contained a whole, special view of the two matters, if not, of course, attributable to the peasantry as a whole, then attributable to Makar Ivanovich as his very own and not derivative at all. Such folksy sayings are sometimes marvellous in their originality!

'Makar Ivanovich, what is your view of suicide?' I asked in this connection.

'Suicide is the greatest sin of all,' he answered with a sigh, 'but only God may be the judge of it, because He alone can know everything, the limit and extent of it all. It is for us to pray earnestly for such sinners. Every time one hears of such a sin, on going to sleep one should pray tenderly for the soul of the sinner, if only as a sigh to God on the sinner's behalf, even as if you did not know about it at all—so much more profitable, then, will be the prayer on the sinner's behalf.'

'But will my prayer help him if he is already condemned?'

'Who knows? Oh, there are many, many unbelievers and they deafen ignorant people with their unbelief! Don't you listen to them, because they do not know where they are going. A prayer for a condemned man from one of the living is sure to reach God. So what can be done about the man who has no one to pray for him? When you kneel to pray before going to sleep, always add at the end: "Lord Jesus Christ, forgive all those for whom there is no one to say prayers." A prayer like that can be very pleasing and beneficial in the sight of the Lord! And for all sinners who are still alive "Lord God, Who holdest all destinies in Your hands, save all who have not confessed their faults" is also a good prayer.'

I promised him I would pray, feeling that in making such a promise I was giving him great pleasure. And his face really did radiate joy. But I hasten to add that in cases like this he never condescended to me, as if he were an elder condescending to some junior. On the contrary, he very often wanted to hear what I had to say and would even give way to me on certain topics on the assumption that, though he was dealing with a 'young'un' as he used to say grandly (knowing full well it should be 'youngster', not 'young'un'), but aware that this 'young'un' was much better educated than he was. He loved, for example, to talk very often about living in a wilderness as a hermit and he put the life of a hermit far above that of a pilgrim. I fiercely objected to this, emphasizing the egoism of people who threw up the world and the use they could be to humanity solely for the egotistical idea of their own salvation. To start with he appeared not to understand and I really believe he didn't. He insisted on defending the life of a hermit:

'Of course, to begin with you'd be sorry for yourself—that is, when you first settled in the wilderness—but afterwards you would rejoice all the more day by day, and then you would come to see the face of God!'

Then I painted for him a full picture of the useful work done by scientists and doctors and others friends of humanity in the world at large and made him thoroughly enthusiastic, because he himself started excitedly egging me on with remarks like: 'God bless you, dear boy, what you think is honest and true!' But when I was finished, he could not bring himself to agree completely:

'So be it,' he sighed deeply, 'but how many people are there like that who could hold out and not be distracted? Though money is not a god, it is a demi-god and a great tempter of men. And there's the female sex, too, and self-regard and envy. Men might easily forget their great cause and occupy themselves with trivia. Could that happen in a wilderness? Alone in a wilderness a man can gather strength to undertake any task. Oh, my friend, what is there in this world?' he exclaimed with great feeling. 'Isn't it all just a dream? Take sand and sow it in a rocky place. When your sand grows up yellow on that rocky place, then and then only will your dream come true! That's a saying we have among us. As Christ said: 'Go and give up your riches and become a servant to all.' And you will become countless times richer than you ever were, because it's not by what you eat, by fine clothes, by pride and envy that you will be made happy, but by love multiplied over and over in countless ways. You will receive no small riches then—not a hundred thousand, not a million, but the whole world! Now we gather things to us and are never sated, and we expend things extravagantly without thought, but then there will be neither orphans, nor beggars, because all will be mine, all will be of my own family, I will have obtained all people, I will have bought them all down to the last one! Nowadays it is no rare thing for the richest and most important to be indifferent to the number of their days and not even to know how to invent a new way of passing the time. But in the time to come hours and days will multiply a thousand times and you will not want to miss a single minute and you will experience each one with joy in your heart. Then you will obtain true wisdom not merely from books, but from being face to face

407

with God. And the earth will shine brighter than the sun, and there will be neither sadness, nor lamentation, but only a paradise beyond all price . . .'

It was precisely such high flown visionary words that had extraordinary appeal for Versilov, I think. On this occasion, he was also in the room.

'Makar Ivanovich,' I broke in suddenly, immeasurably excited (I can remember the evening clearly), 'you're preaching communism, out-and-out communism, if there is such a thing!'

And because he knew absolutely nothing about communism and was only now hearing the word for the first time, I began there and then explaining to him everything I knew on the subject. I confess I did not know much, and nothing consistent, and even now I am quite inexpert; but, no matter, I outlined what I knew with the greatest fervour. To this very day I remember with pleasure the extraordinary effect I had on the old man. It was not so much an effect as something approaching an earthquake. At which point he became terribly interested in historical details, in where, how, who did what, who said what. I have noticed, by the way, this is characteristic of the simple peasantry—they're dissatisfied by general ideas if they're really interested in something and always start demanding to know everything down to the finest detail. I got mixed up over the details and, because Versilov was there, I was a bit tongue-tied and grew more heated than ever. It ended with Makar Ivanovich adopting a look of edification and saying 'Yes, yes' to every word and evidently not understanding what I said and losing his way. I was annoyed, but Versilov suddenly interrupted our talk by standing up and announcing it was time for bed. We had been at it for some time and it was late.

When he looked in on me in my room a few minutes later, I at once asked him what he thought of Makar Ivanovich. Versilov grinned happily (not on account of my mistakes in explaining communism—he did not even refer to them). I have to repeat what I have said about him being very attached to Makar Ivanovich. I often noticed a very attractive smile on his face whenever he listened to the old man. However, his grin did not prevent him from being critical.

'Makar Ivanovich is first and foremost not a true peasant, but a house servant,' he said very readily, 'a former house servant, a former serving man, born of serving people. Servants in manorial houses used to share a great deal of the private lives of their masters and mistresses in the past, both in a spiritual and an intellectual sense. Take note that Makar Ivanovich has so far been chiefly interested in things that have happened in the upper classes. You have no idea how interested he is in what has been happening in Russia recently. Did you know he was great on politics? He needs no prompting to tell you who will be at war with whom and whether or not we will be at war too. In the past I have sent him into second heaven with discussions on that topic. He has the greatest respect for science and loves astronomy most of all. At the same time he has worked up for himself a set of ideas so much his own there is no shifting him. He has convictions that are firm and lucid enough—and quite genuine. Despite his complete lack of education he can suddenly astonish you by his unexpected knowledge of certain ideas which you would never suppose he had. He sings the praises of a hermit's calling, but he would never be a hermit, nor a monk, because he is above all a "tramp" as the doctor kindly called him—and about which there was no need for you to get angry, by the way. Finally, well, he's a bit of an artist with words, but not all of them are his own. He limps a bit when it comes to logical exposition and he is inclined to be very abstract. He is inclined to outpourings of sentiment, but in a completely folksy way—or better—outpourings of that uplifting, edifying kind which our simple peasantry bring to their religious feeling. I will not say anything about his purity of heart and loving forgiveness. It is not for you and me to start talking about that . . .'

III

To complete my characterization of Makar Ivanovich I will recount some of the stories he had to tell, particularly those drawn from people's private lives. The character of these stories was strange or, to be more accurate, what they lacked was any kind of general character at all. No general direction, nothing edifying could be extracted from them, beyond the fact that they were all more or less uplifting. But some were not uplifting at all—they were even quite funny, even quite mischievous at the expense of various monks who had gone astray, so that it was hardly in his best interests to tell them. I pointed this out to him, but he did not know what I meant. Sometimes it was difficult to imagine what made him tell such stories, so that I was occasionally amazed at such garrulousness and ascribed it in part to his being old and sick.

'He is not as he used to be,' Versilov once whispered to me. 'He wasn't like this before. He will die soon, much sooner than we think, so we must be ready for it.'

I have forgotten to say that we arranged evening sessions of a sort. Apart from mother, who never left Makar Ivanovich's side, Versilov used to come regularly to his little room for such sessions. I always used to come because I had nowhere else to go. Towards the end Liza almost always dropped in, though later than anyone else, and she almost always sat there saying nothing. Tatyana Pavlovna used to come, and occasionally the doctor was there as well. It turned out suddenly that I got on with the doctor—not very well, but a least there were none of the former rows. I liked the simple straightforwardness, as it were, which I had discerned in him and the way he was so attached to our family, so that I eventually decided to forgive him his high-handed medical manner and, above all, taught him to wash his hands and clean his nails even if he was incapable of changing his underclothes. I declared straight to his face that this had nothing to do with being dandified and fashionably elegant, but that bodily hygiene was natural for a doctor and I convinced him of it. Finally, Lukerya used often to come from the kitchen and stand in the doorway and listen to Makar Ivanovich's stories. One time Versilov asked her to come in and join us. I was pleased by this, but after that she stopped coming altogether. Each to his own!

I will give one of the stories, for no special reason, just because it has stuck in my memory. It is a story about a merchant, and I think similar stories happen in our cities and towns by the thousand if only one knew where to look. Readers may wish to skip it, more especially since I tell it the way it was told.

"Tis a wondrous thing I tell now, of what happened in our town of Afimevsk. There lived there a merchant by the name of Slaughterer, Maxim Ivanovich, and there was no richer man in the whole region. He built a cotton mill and had several hundred workers, and he thought a mighty lot of himself. And it has to be said that everything used to depend on a sign from him, the authorities put no obstacles in his way and the archimandrite was grateful for his zeal as a believer since he spent much on the monastery and, when he was depressed, expended much anxiety over his own soul and was greatly concerned about the life to come. He was a widower and childless. Concerning his wife there had been a rumour he had done for her in the first year of marriage, since he had always liked to be free with his fists. Except that had been a long while back and he had never wanted to marry again. He also had a weakness for drink and in his cups he would run naked about the town shouting at the top of his voice. Maybe it wasn't much of a place, but that was still shameful behaviour. When he'd sober up, he'd be furious, condemning that, ordering this, and it'd all be just as he said. He paid his people arbitrarily. He'd get out the abacus and put on his glasses. "How much do I owe you, Foma?" "I've had nothin' since Christmas, Maxim Ivanovich, sir, and I bin owed thirty-nine roubles." "Oh, what a lot o' money! That's too much for you. You don't deserve all that much. It won't look right, so I'll take off ten. You can have twenty-nine roubles." And the man wouldn't say a word. No one dared contradict; they all held their tongues.

'"I know," he used to say, "how much they deserve to get paid. You can't treat the people round here any other way. They're a depraved lot. Without me they'd all have died of hunger, no matter how many there were of them. I'll say it again and again—the locals are a thieving lot. They no sooner see something than they want to get their hands on it! They're not real men at all. Take your local chap—he's no more'n a drunkard. Give him some money and he's off down the pub and he'll drink it all away till he's not got a stitch on and comes out stark naked! What's more, he's a low-down bastard, your local

411

chap is—sitting out in front of the pub and going on about: 'Oh, mother dear, why'd you ever bring such a wretched drunk like me into the world? Oh, it'd have been better if you'd crushed me at birth!' Is that sort of person a man? He's an animal, not a man! First thing is he's got to learn how to behave, then he can have his money. I know when to give him it."

'That's how Maxim Ivanovich used to talk about the people of Afimevsk. Maybe he was harsh on them, but there was some truth in it: they were a poor, weak lot with no staying power.

'There was another merchant living in the town and he died. He was a young fellow, light-headed, wasted all his money, and had nothing left. In his last year he thrashed about like a fish out of water and yet he learned no better. He never got on with Maxim Ivanovich and was roundly in debt to him. At the very end he laid a curse on Maxim Ivanovich. And he died leaving behind a young widow and five children. For a poor widow to be left alone after her husband dies is to be a bird deprived of its nest, which is bad enough, but to have five young ones and nothing to feed them with is worse, since Maxim Ivanovich seized their last property, their wooden house, to cover the debts. And she lined them all up outside the church door—the eldest a boy, 8 years old, the others all girls with a year between them, the eldest 4 and the youngest still a babe in arms. When the service was finished, Maxim Ivanovich came out and all the little girls knelt down in front of him—she had taught them to do this and hold out their hands palm upwards while she, holding the fifth child in her arms, bowed down low before him for all to see and said: "Maxim Ivanovich, good master, have pity on poor orphans, do not take away their last crust, do not drive us from our home!" And they all started crying there and then as she had taught them. She had reckoned that before all the people he would take pride in forgiving them and would give back the house for the orphans' sake, but it turned out otherwise.

'Maxim Ivanovich stood there and said: "You're a young widow, you need a husband and shouldn't be crying about your orphans. Anyhow, on his death-bed your late husband laid a curse on me . . ."

'And he strode off and didn't give up the house, telling himself he wasn't going to imitate any sillinesses (he meant: give in to any sillinesses), because if he'd shown charity then, she'd only have come asking for more and there'd be more gossip, as if there wasn't enough already! And there was gossip already that he had sent word to the young widow ten years before when she was a girl (she had been very beautiful) and offered a lot of money for her favours, forgetting it was a sin as great as violating the sanctity of the church. Nothing came of it then. But he fornicated all round the town and through the entire province and lost all sense of proportion over it.

'So the mother and her little ones wailed and he turned 'em out of their house. It wasn't just malice made him, because sometimes a man just doesn't know what makes him do things. Well, at first she got some help from people and she went out to find work. But there wasn't any way of earning a living apart from the mill and all she could do there was scrub floors, weed the garden, see to the bath-house, all with the babe in arms to look after while the four others ran about in the road in nothing but their little shirts. When she had lined them up outside the church, they all had proper shoes on and proper clothes like proper merchants' children, but now they ran about barefoot. Everyone knows how children wear out their clothes. Well, the children didn't mind—the sun was shining, they enjoyed themselves, like little birds they were fearless and their little voices rang out sweet as harness bells. But the widow thought: "When winter comes, how'll I clothe you? Oh, if only God were to take you to Him in due time!" Only it happened before winter came. In our region there's a kind of children's cough, a whooping cough, and it passes from one child to another. First the baby girl caught it, then the others fell ill, all four girls were carried away one after another that autumn. True, one of them was crushed by a horse on the road. So what d'you think she did? She buried them and wailed over them. One time she'd cursed at having so many children, but now God had taken them and she was full of sorrow. Such is a mother's heart!

'The only one remaining was the oldest, the boy, and she doted on him in fear and trembling. He was delicate and feeble and had a face as lovely as a girl's. She took him to the mill, to his godfather who was a manager there, while she herself got a job as a nanny in the house of an official. One day the boy was running about in the yard of the mill and suddenly Maxim Ivanovich drove up in a two-horse carriage a bit the worse for drink. The boy tripped over some stairs and ran slap-bang into him as he was getting out of the carriage, both hands landing in Maxim Ivanovich's stomach. He seized the boy by the hair and shouted: "What the hell's this mean? Get some twigs! I want the boy beaten right here and now in front of me!" The boy was frightened out of his life. They started beating him and he screamed. "So you're screaming, are you? Beat him till he stops!" No matter how much they beat him, he didn't stop screaming until he was nearly dead. Then they stopped, frightened he'd stopped breathing and was lying senseless. Later they said it hadn't been much of a beating and the boy'd simply been very timid. Maxim Ivanovich got a real fright. "Whose boy is he?" he asked. When they told him, he said: "Good heavens! Take him to his mother! What's he doing running about here at the mill?" For a couple of days he said nothing and then he asked: "How's the boy?" And the boy was bad, he was ill, lying in the corner in his mother's room, and she'd had to give up her work in the official's house because he'd caught pneumonia. "Good heavens!" he declared. "How come? If he'd been badly beaten, well, fair enough, but only a little strength was used. I've had others beaten and there's been none of this nonsense!" What he'd been frightened of was the mother making a complaint and so he put a proud face on it and said nothing; and she didn't dare lay a complaint, having nowhere to complain to. And he sent her fifteen roubles and a doctor on his own initiative, not because he was frightened of anything but just out of consideration. And then the time came for him to get drunk and he was drunk for three whole weeks.

'The winter passed and on Easter Sunday Maxim Ivanovich once again asked: "How's the boy?" All winter he had never asked a word about him. He was told: "He's better, living with his mother, and she goes out to work during the day." And there and then Maxim Ivanovich drove over to see the widow. He did not enter the house, but stayed in his carriage and summoned her to the gates. "See here, honest widow," he said, "I want to be a true benefactor to your son and do the best I can for him. I'll take him into my very own house from this moment forward. And even if he is not pleasing in my sight, I'll still leave him some of my money. And if he pleases me in all things, then I will leave him all I have on my death, making him my son and heir,

414

on the one condition that you yourself only come to my house on feast-days. If you find this all right, bring him tomorrow morning, because he shouldn't spend all his time playing childish games." And so saying he drove off, leaving the mother senseless with amazement. The people who'd heard him say these things told her: "When your boy grows up, he'll likely blame you for denying him the chance." She cried over him all night, but in the morning she took her child to him. And the boy was more dead than alive.

'Maxim Ivanovich dressed him up as a little milord and hired a teacher and from that moment set him to reading books. And it reached the point that he never let him out of his sight and was with him all the time. The moment the boy yawned, he'd shout: "Back to your book! Study! I want to make a man of you!" The boy was poorly; ever since the beating he'd been coughing. Maxim Ivanovich cried out in astonishment: "Isn't life good enough for him here? With his mother he ran about barefoot, had only crusts to eat, so why's he more poorly now?" The teacher answered: "Every boy needs playtime, he mustn't be learning all the time. He needs exercise," and he made Maxim Ivanovich see reason.

'Maxim Ivanovich thought: "You're speaking the truth, you are." And the teacher was one Pyotr Stepanovich, heaven bless him, something of a Holy Fool. He drank an awful lot, so much so he lost every post he had and lived on charity in the town, yet he was a man of great intellect and sound in his knowledge. "I shouldn't be here," he used to say, "I should be a university professor, but here I'm up to my neck in filth and 'my own clothes do abhor me'."* And Maxim Ivanovich sat down and shouted at the boy: "Play!" and the boy was too terrified even to draw breath. The point was reached when the boy couldn't even stand his voice and just shook like a leaf. And Maxim Ivanovich was yet more astonished: "It's no good any which way! I've picked him out of the gutter and given him good clothes. He's got good leather shoes and an embroidered shirt and I treat him like a general's son, so why doesn't he like me? Why's he dumb as a wolf cub, eh?" And though people had long since stopped being amazed at Maxim Ivanovich, they still couldn't help being surprised at the way he'd lost control of himself and become so worked up about a little lad and couldn't leave off. "So long as

I've a breath in my body," he'd say, "I'll get the better of him. His father laid a curse on me on his death-bed after the last rites and it's his father's character the boy's got!" And yet he never beat him (he was frightened because of that first time). He just terrified him anyhow. Terrified him without laying a finger on him.

'And then something happened. He left the room once and the boy put down his book and jumped on a chair because he had earlier thrown his ball up on the sideboard. As he was reaching for it, his sleeve caught on a porcelain lamp on the sideboard and it crashed down in smithereens on the floor and the noise could be heard throughout the house; it was an expensive piece of Saxon porcelain. Maxim Ivanovich heard the crash from a couple of rooms away and let out a yell. The boy dashed out of the house in terror the first way he could, on to the terrace, through the garden and by the back gate on to the river bank. That's where there was a boulevard with old willows. It was a lovely spot. He ran right down to the water's edge. People saw him stretch out his arms at the ferry landing and come to a dead stop, as if horrified by the sight of the water. It was wide there and the river flowed fast and barges went by. On the far bank were shops, a square, and a church with gold cupolas shining bright. At that very moment Colonel Fersing's wife and daughter (his infantry regiment was stationed in the town) came hurrying down to catch the ferry. The daughter, also a child of 8, in a pretty white dress, saw the boy and laughed. She was carrying a small bag and in the bag was a hedgehog. "Mummy," she said, "let's let him have a look at my hedgehog." "No," said the Colonel's wife, "he seems to be frightened by something. You're such a good-looking boy, why are you so frightened, eh? (She claimed later this is what she said.) How good-looking you are and how well dressed! Whose boy are you?" And because he had never seen a hedgehog before, he came up and looked at it and his fright slipped his mind—that's what happens when you're a child! "What's that?" he asked. "It's a hedgehog," the little girl said. "We've just bought it from a peasant. He found it in the wood." "What's a hedgehog?" he asked and laughed and tried touching it with his finger. But the hedgehog put out its spines and the little girl laughed at the boy. "We're going to take it home and teach it things," she said.

416

"Oh," he said, "please give it to me!" And he asked her so nicely, but he had no sooner spoken than suddenly Maxim Ivanovich's voice bellowed from above: "There he is! Get hold of him!" (He was so mad he had dashed after the boy without his hat on.) The boy, remembering what had happened, gave a shriek, rushed to the water's edge, pressed both little fists to his breast, looked up to heaven (they all saw him do this!)—and then went splash into the water! Well, there were shouts, people sprang off the ferry and tried to fish him out, but the water carried him away, the river flowed fast, and by the time they had pulled him out he had swallowed too much and was dead. He had a weak chest and couldn't stand the water—how could he be expected to? And no one in those parts could remember such a little boy giving up his life like that. It was a sin against the Lord! What would his little soul have to tell God in the next world?

'From that moment on Maxim Ivanovich fell to thinking about that very thing. And he changed so much you couldn't recognize him. He was bowed down with the sorrow of it. He started drinking, drank much, then gave it up. Nothing helped. He stopped going to the mill, stopped listening to people. They'd say things to him and he'd say nothing back or just wave his hand. A couple of months passed like that and then he started talking to himself. He'd walk about talking to himself. One time there was a fire in Vaskov, a nearby settlement of wooden houses, and nine houses were burnt down. Maxim Ivanovich drove to have a look. Those who had lost their homes crowded round him wailing and he promised to help and gave orders to that effect, but afterwards he summoned the man in charge and changed his mind, saying: "There's no need to give them anything," but gave no reason. "The Lord God," he announced, "has suffered me to become a monster for all men to deride, and so be it! Like the wind," he said, "my reputation has been carried hither and yon!"

'The archimandrite himself came to see him. He was a strict elder and had brought harmony to the life of the monastery. "What are you up to?" he asked him sternly. "This is what," said Maxim Ivanovich. He opened the bible and showed him the place:

'"But whoso shall offend one of these little ones which believe in me, it were better for him that a millstone were hanged about his neck and that he were drowned in the depth of the sea" (Matthew 18:6).

'"Yes," said the archimandrite, "even if it does not relate directly to your case, it touches on it. When a man loses his sense of proportion, that man will be lost. And you have been puffed up with pride."

'Maxim Ivanovich sat there as if turned to stone. The archimandrite studied him closely.

'"Listen," he said, "and mark well. It is said: 'The words of the despairing fly off on the wind.' And remember this, too, that even the angels of God are imperfect, and only our Lord God Jesus Christ is perfect and without sin, for it is Him the angels serve. You did not wish for the death of the little one, but you were simply unwise in what you did. Only what I find strange is that you seem so little troubled by far worse things you have done—by the people you have made homeless, and let rot and perish just as if you had killed them. Isn't that so? And didn't all his sisters die, all four little girls, long before this and almost before your very eyes? Why has this little boy upset you so? Am I to suppose you've forgotten not so much to pity but even to think about all the others? Why has the fate of this little one struck such terror in you when you're not really all that much to blame?"

'"He comes to me in my dreams," declared Maxim Ivanovich.

'"And what of that?"

'But he would divulge no more and sat there silent. The archimandrite marvelled and then drove away, knowing there was no more he could do.

'And Maxim Ivanovich sent for the teacher, Pyotr Stepanovich. They had not seen each other since the event.

'"Do you remember me?" he asked.

'"Yes," the other said.

'"You painted pictures with oil paints in the tavern, didn't you, and you copied the bishop's portrait? Can you do one for me?"

'"I can do anything," said the teacher. "I've got all sorts of talents and I can do anything."

'"Paint me, then, the largest picture you can, to fill up a whole wall, and start with the river, the way down to it and the ferry

418

and all the folk who were there at the time. The colonel's wife and the little girl must be in it, too, and the little hedgehog. And the other bank must be in the picture, too, with the church and the square and the shops and the cab rank—paint it all as it was. And by the ferry landing you must put the boy, just where he was above the river, and you must make sure his two little fists are pressed to his chest—that's essential. And you must show how the heavens on the other side from him, above the church, open up and are filled with angels flying to greet him. Can you do that or not?"

'"I can do anything."

'"If it hadn't been for the fact you remember his face, I could send for the best painter in Moscow, or even from London. If there's no likeness, or only a small one, I'll give you fifty roubles, but if you get a good likeness I'll give you two hundred. Remember, his eyes must be blue . . . And be sure you make it a really big picture."

'Preparations were made and Pyotr set about painting, but suddenly he upped and came to Maxim Ivanovich:

'"No, I can't paint it that way."

'"Why not?"

'"Because that sin, suicide, is the greatest of all sins. How can angels fly to greet him after such a sin?"

'"But surely he was just a boy, he didn't know what sin was."

'"No, he wasn't just a boy, he was a little lad of 8 when it happened. He'd have to answer for his sin just a bit."

'Maxim Ivanovich was more horrified than ever.

'"But this is what I thought," said Pyotr Stepanovich. "I won't show the heavens opening and there'll be no angels, but I'll show a shaft of light coming down from heaven towards him, just that one bright shaft of light. That'll have to do."

'So that's how it was. And I saw the picture when it was done, and the shaft of light, and the river—it was the length of a wall and all blue. And the little lad was there with both hands pressed to his chest, and the little girl, and the hedgehog—he'd got them all in. But Maxim Ivanovich wouldn't let anyone see it and locked it in his study away from prying eyes. Townspeople were dying to see it, but he had them driven away. There was a great deal of talk. It went to Pyotr Stepanovich's head. "I can do anything," he said. "I ought to be employed at the tsar's court in

St Petersburg." He was the nicest chap imaginable, but he loved singing his own praises. And Fate finally caught up with him. As soon as he had his two hundred roubles he started drinking and showing everyone his money, boasting all the time. And one of the townees with whom he'd been drinking killed him that night when he was drunk and stole his money. It all came out the next morning.

'Yet it all ended in a way people there still remember. Suddenly Maxim Ivanovich drove over to see that very same widow. She was renting a corner off a local woman in a hut on the edge of town. This time he walked into the yard and stood in front of her and bowed down to the ground. Ever since the tragedy she'd been unwell and could scarcely move. "My dear," says he loudly, "honest widow, take me, monster that I am, as your wedded husband, and come and live with me!" The widow stared at him more dead than alive. "I'd like," says he, "for us to have a boy, and if we do, then your boy'll forgive the two of us, both you and me. That is what your boy has commanded." She could see he wasn't in his right mind but all worked up and yet she'd had enough.

'"That's nonsense," she told him. "You're just mean, that's all. Because you've been so mean I've lost all my little ones. I can't stand the sight of you, let alone accept the idea of suffering unendurably as your wife."

'Maxim Ivanovich drove away, but he didn't give up. The whole town buzzed with the extraordinary news. And Maxim Ivanovich sent for matchmakers. He sent for two provincial aunts of his, shopkeeper types. They weren't really his aunts, though related, decent people, you know, and they started trying to persuade her, buttering her up, you know, and hanging around her hut. Then he sent women from the town, merchants' wives, the priest's wife, the wives of officials, and the whole town surrounded her, trying to persuade her. And she was fed up with it all. "If my dear dead children could be brought back," she says, "well and good, but what's the point now? And think of the sin I'd be committing against them if I did!"

'The archimandrite came and gave her an earful: "You could make a new man of him," he said. She was horrified at that. And people started being surprised by her for turning down the chance of happiness. And this is how Maxim Ivanovich finally subdued her:

'"Say what you like," he said, "the boy took his own life, and he weren't no little boy any more, he were a lad what maybe couldn't receive communion straight off but had to answer for what he did. If you consent to be my wife I'll make a great promise—I'll build a new church to his eternal memory."

'She could not hold out against that and agreed. So they got married.

'And everyone was astonished. From the very first day they started living in great harmony, without any hypocrisy, jealously observing their conjugal rights and abiding spiritually as one in their two bodies. And that winter she conceived and they visited various churches and awaited God's wrath with fear and trembling. They stayed at three monasteries and heard the utterance of prophecies. He had the promised church built and built a hospital and almshouse in the town. He set aside money for widows and orphans. And he was mindful of all he had offended against in the past and sought to make restitution. He handed out money endlessly, so much so that his wife and the archimandrite had to stay his hand, because, as they said, "enough is enough". Maxim Ivanovich deferred to them, and yet he would say: "I didn't let Foma have what I owed him that time." And so Foma'd get paid, and Foma'd even break down in tears, saying: "I, you know, I ... I'm so grateful for so much and I'll never stop praying to God, never, never ..." Everyone was affected by what had happened, and it is true, you know, what they say, that men will always live according to a good example. And they were a kindly people living there.

'The wife took upon herself the running of the mill and she did it in ways they remember to this day. He still drank, but she would watch over him during his binges and afterwards wean him from them. His talk became dignified and correct and even his voice changed. He showed limitless compassion for all, even for animals. Seeing from his window a peasant beating his horse over the head, he instantly sent out for the horse to be bought for twice what it was worth. And he received the gift of tears, for whoever spoke to him would begin to feel tears coming to his eyes. When his wife's time was due, the Lord harkened to their

421

prayers and sent them a son, and Maxim Ivanovich, for the first time since the tragedy, had a bright and smiling face and gave away much money to charity, forgave many debts, and invited the entire town to the baptism. He issued the invitation and the very next day came out of his room black as night. His wife saw something had happened and brought the new-born babe to him. "My lad has forgiven us," he said, "and harkened to our tears and prayers on his behalf." They had not mentioned this matter to each other for a whole year, but had kept it to themselves. And now Maxim Ivanovich looked at her black as night. "Wait," he said. "He hasn't come to me in a dream for a whole year, but last night he did." Afterwards she would always remember: "For the first time after those strange words," she would say, "a terrible fear entered my heart."

'And his dream about the young lad did really mean something. No sooner had Maxim Ivanovich spoken than at that very moment the new-born babe suddenly took sick. And he sickened for eight days and each day they prayed unceasingly and doctors were summoned and they got the leading doctor in all Moscow to come by rail. The doctor arrived, lost his temper, saying: "I'm the leading doctor and the whole of Moscow is waiting for me," prescribed drops and left. He was paid eight hundred roubles for his trip. But towards evening the baby died.

'And then what do you think? Maxim Ivanovich surrendered all his property to his beloved wife, all his capital, all the legal titles, did it all correctly and according to the law, and then he stood in front of her and bowed down to the ground, saying: "Release me, O wife beyond price, so that I may save my soul while I still can. Should I not succeed, then I will never return. I have been hard and cruel and oppressive in my life, but I think that, for the anguish and wanderings that await me, the Good Lord will not leave me unrewarded, because to give up all I have now is no small cross and no small anguish to bear." And his wife broke down in tears, saying: "You're all I have on earth now, who else should I stay for? Over the past year I have accumulated much love in my heart." And for a whole month the whole town begged him not to go, beseeched him and set watch over him. But he did not heed them and left secretly one night and never came back. And I have heard it said that even to this day he is still engaged on his pilgrimages, enduring much, and yet each year his dear wife hears word of him . . .'

CHAPTER IV

I

I NOW come to the final catastrophe which brings these notes of mine to a climax. But in order to continue them I have to jump forward and explain something about which I knew nothing at the time and only became completely clear to me much later when everything was over. Otherwise I will not be able to make things clear, since I would have to write in riddles. And so I will offer a simple and direct explanation, sacrificing any so-called artistry, and I will do it as if I had not written it, without having my heart in it, like an *entrefilet* or newspaper entry.

The point is that my boyhood friend Lambert can be described, without beating about the bush, as belonging to a gang of small-time blackmailers who collaborated for purposes of what is now called extortion in terms of the law. The gang to which Lambert belonged had its origins in Moscow and had been involved in a fair number of rackets there (as was later partially revealed). I heard later that, for a time in Moscow, they had an extraordinarily experienced, intelligent, older man for a leader. They undertook their operations both as a gang and in groups. They conducted, apart from the seamiest and dirtiest little crimes (of which reports have, however, appeared in the press), fairly complex and even quite cunning operations under the guidance of their boss. I knew about a number of them, but I won't give any details. I will only say that their principal method of operation was to discover the secrets of those who were sometimes fairly highly placed and the most honest of men. They would then approach these people and threaten to reveal compromising documents (which were sometimes not in their possession) and demand money for their silence. There are things that are neither wrong nor at all criminal, but their revelation can frighten even quite respectable and solid citizens.

For the most part they relate to family secrets. In order to give some idea how cleverly their boss sometimes acted, I will recount one episode without giving any details and in only a couple of lines.

In a highly respectable home there occurred something both wrong and criminal: the wife of a well-known and respected man had a covert, amorous affair with a rich young officer. The gang got wind of it and decided to let the young man know straightaway that they would inform the husband. They had no proof of any kind, the young man knew this and they did not hide the fact from him. But the clever and cunning thing about their method of operation in this case was their calculation that the husband, once informed, even without any proof, would behave exactly—and take exactly the same steps—as he would have done if he had been offered mathematically certain proof of misconduct. They relied on their knowledge of the man's character and his family circumstances. The chief thing was that a young man belonging to the gang came from a very respectable background and managed to get hold of information beforehand. They extorted a very tidy sum from the lover without any danger to themselves because the victim sought secrecy at all costs.

Although Lambert took part in such things, he did not really belong to the Moscow gang. Having acquired the taste for it, he started off in a small way working on his own. I have to say at the start that he was not entirely cut out for it. He was very clever and calculating, but he was hot-tempered and, above all, ingenuous or—better—naïve, meaning he had no knowledge either of people or of society. For example, I think he did not realize the significance of the role played by the Moscow boss and supposed it would be easy to organize and direct such operations. Finally, he supposed that everyone was as much of a bastard as he was. That is to say, once having got the idea into his head that so-and-so was frightened for such-and-such a reason, he never doubted that the man would be frightened. It was an axiom. I don't know how to put it exactly. I will explain later on the basis of facts, but, in my opinion, he was just rather crude and it wasn't that he didn't believe in feelings of kindliness and decency but he very likely had no understanding of them at all.

He came to St Petersburg because he had long thought of St

424

Petersburg as offering more scope for him than Moscow and because in Moscow he had been taken for a ride and someone was after him for the worst of intentions so far as he was concerned. On arriving in St Petersburg he was at once in touch with a former colleague, but the field was limited and the pickings poor. He got to know more people, but nothing much came of it. 'The people here are rubbish, just a lot of kids,' he once told me. And then one fine morning at dawn he suddenly came across me frozen stiff by that fence and felt he was on the track of, as he put it, 'bloody rich business'.

It was all due to the way I had babbled while I was thawing out in his room. Oh, boy, had I been delirious then! But from what I said it still became clear that, of all the indignities I had suffered on that fateful day, I remembered most of all—and took most to heart—only the insults inflicted by Björing and by *her*. Otherwise I wouldn't have babbled just about that but about what happened at Zershchikov's, for example. Anyhow that was merely the first thing I babbled about, as I learned later from Lambert himself. I was in an excited state, what's more, and looked upon both Lambert and Alphonsine as my liberators and saviours that terrible morning. When later, during my recovery, I wondered as I lay in bed what Lambert could have found out from my babbling and the extent to which I have given myself away, I had never for a moment suspected he could have learned so much. Oh, of course, judging by the gnawings of my conscience, I even then suspected I had blurted out too much, but, I repeat, I never supposed it had been as much as that! I had also hoped and counted on the likelihood that I'd not been able to say things all that clearly, which was as I remembered it, but it turned out I had enunciated everything a lot more clearly than I had hopefully supposed. The main thing was that all this was revealed a long time afterwards. That was what really did for me.

From my delirium, my babbling, my chatter, my excitement and so on he learned, firstly, almost all the names of the people involved and even some of their addresses. Secondly, he formed a fairly good idea of who these people were (the old prince, his daughter, Björing, Anna Andreevna, and even Versilov). Thirdly, he learned that I felt humiliated and was threatening to get my own back. And finally, fourthly, most important of all, he learned of the existence of a certain mysterious, hidden document, a letter, which, once shown to the half-mad old prince and read by him, would inform him that his very own daughter considered him mad and had already taken legal advice on how to have him put away and as a result of which he would either go insane once and for all or drive her from his house and cut her off without a penny or marry Mademoiselle Versilov, whom he had wanted to marry but not been allowed to. In short, Lambert had discovered a great deal. Undoubtedly a lot remained obscure, but the prospective extortionist had clearly picked up a trail. The moment I ran away from Alphonsine, he immediately found out my address (not at all hard: he merely had to look for the name Versilov in the official address lists). Afterwards he quickly made the necessary enquiries from which he learned that all the people I had babbled about actually existed. Then he proceeded directly to take the first step.

The main thing was that a *document* existed and I had it in my possession, and this document was of great value, as Lambert did not doubt. Here I will omit one circumstance which can be described later in the right place, but all I can say now is that this circumstance had an essential role in convincing Lambert that the document existed and, most of all, that it was valuable. (It was a circumstance of real gravity, I must emphasize, which I couldn't imagine not only then, but even right at the very end of the story I have to tell, when everything suddenly collapsed and became clear as daylight.) So, sure of the main thing, he went first of all to see Anna Andreevna.

I still have difficulty understanding how someone like Lambert could have wormed his way into the confidence of such an unapproachable and superior person as Anna Andreevna and sucked up to her. True, he took some information with him, but so what? True, he was well dressed, spoke Parisian French, and had a French name, but surely Anna Andreevna could have seen instantly what a scoundrel he was? Or did she suppose it was precisely a scoundrel like him she needed at such a time? Could it have been that?

I never discovered the details of their meeting, but later imagined it many times to myself. Very likely Lambert from the start pretended to her that he had known me since boyhood and was doing his best to help a close and dear friend. But at that very first encounter he would have hinted very clearly that I had the 'document' in my possession, that it was a secret and he alone knew it and that with the help of the document I was going to avenge myself on Katerina Nikolaevna and so on and so forth. The chief thing is that he would have made clear, as exactly as he could, the significance and the value of this piece of paper. As for Anna Andreevna, she would be in the position of being unable to ignore news of this kind, unable to disregard it and unable not to take the bait offered, since for her it was a matter of her very own survival. At that very moment her prospective husband had been taken away and confined at Tsarskoe and she, after all, had been put under observation as well. And suddenly *this* crops up, suddenly it's not a matter of a lot of women whispering in each other's ears, not a matter of tearful complaints, no longer so much slander and gossip, but a letter, a manuscript, mathematical proof of his daughter's evil intentions and of all those who had taken money from him. The time had come for him to save himself, to escape from them, to come to her, to Anna Andreevna, and to be married to her, even at the eleventh hour; otherwise he would be committed to a lunatic asylum!

Or maybe Lambert didn't hide anything from the girl and just announced straight off: 'Mademoiselle, either you remain an old maid or you become a princess and inherit millions—there's this document, I'll steal it from the young bastard and let you have it ... for an IOU for thirty thousand!' I think that's how it was. Oh, he thought everyone was a scoundrel like him! I repeat what I've already said: he had a scoundrel's ingenuousness, a scoundrel's innocence ...

Whatever way it was, it could very well be that Anna Andreevna, confronted by this, was not in the least put out and knew perfectly well how to conduct herself in the face of an opportunist like him offering his sort of spiel—and all because of her natural 'breadth'. Mind you, she might have blushed a little to start with, but then have gathered her wits about her and heard him out. And I can just imagine this unapproachable, proud, really fine girl, a girl with a mind of her own, going hand in hand with Lambert ... yes, precisely because she had a mind of her own! A Russian mind, of dimensions like that, just craves for breadth, especially if it's a woman's and in that sort of fix!

Now I'll summarize: on the day and hour that I first went out after my illness Lambert had the following two things in mind (I now know this for sure): firstly, to obtain an IOU from Anna Andreevna in a sum of not less than thirty thousand roubles for the document, then help her to frighten the prince, spirit him away, and have him suddenly marry her—anyhow, something like that. A plan had been prepared on those lines and all they were waiting for was my help, meaning the document itself.

His second plan was to do the dirty on Anna Andreevna, ditch her, and sell the document to Katerina Nikolaevna, if that were more profitable. Björing also came into his calculations at this point. But he had so far not approached her and was only keeping an eye on her. He was also waiting for me.

Oh, he certainly needed me—not me myself but the document! He had hatched two plans regarding me. The first was that, if there were no other way, he would act jointly with me and give me a half-cut after having subdued me beforehand both morally and physically. But he was much more in favour of a second plan. It consisted of fooling me, kid that I was, and stealing the document from me, even by brute force. This was the one he really liked and dreamed of. I repeat: there was one circumstance which left him with scarcely any doubt at all about the success of this second plan, but, as I've already said, I'll explain that later. In any case, he was waiting for me impatiently because everything depended on me, every next step and decision.

And I must give him his due: he bided his time despite all his hot-headedness. He did not come and see me at home while I was ill; he only came once and saw Versilov. He did not trouble me or frighten me and maintained a completely independent stance towards me until the very day and hour I first went out. As to whether I might hand over the document to someone else, or tell someone about it, or destroy it, he was quite unruffled. He could have concluded from the way I spoke that I myself wanted to keep it secret and was frightened of anyone knowing about it. Nor did he doubt that I would go to him, and to no one else, the moment I was better because Nastasya Yegorovna had been used to coming to see me partly at his bidding and he knew that my curiosity and apprehensions had already been aroused, so that I would be bound to go and see him. Moreover, he had

428

done everything he could to ensure he knew when I would be going out for the first time, so that I wouldn't have been able to escape him even if I had wanted to . . .

But if Lambert was waiting for me, then Anna Andreevna was probably waiting for me even more. I will have to admit that Lambert might have been partially in the right in wanting to ditch her, and it wasn't her fault. Despite their undoubted collaboration (what form it took, I don't know, but I had no doubt about it), Anna Andreevna had not been entirely frank with him right up to the last moment. She had not revealed all. She had hinted at a readiness to agree and make promises, but had only hinted. She probably heard everything he planned in great detail but only gave it her silent approval. I have firm evidence for saying this and the reason for it was that she *was waiting for me*. She much preferred to deal with me than with the scoundrel Lambert—and that's a fact! I realized that, but her mistake was letting Lambert realize it too. It would have done him no good at all if she had bypassed him, lured the document away from me, and come to an agreement with me. What's more, he was certain by then he had a real deal. Someone else in his place might not have been so daring, might have doubted, but Lambert was young, headstrong, thirsting impatiently for his profit, with little knowledge of people and undoubtedly prepared to believe they were all scoundrels. Someone like that doesn't waver, especially after having elicited all the most important data from Anna Andreevna.

One last and most important thing: did Versilov know anything about it at that time and did he play any part, however remotely, in any of Lambert's plans? No, no, and again no, especially not *then*, although perhaps some hints were dropped . . . But that's enough, I am running on too far ahead.

Well, what about me? Did I know anything and what did I in fact know by the time I first went out? At the start of this *entrefilet* I said I knew nothing, that I learned about it all much later when everything was finished. That is true, but is it the whole truth? No, it's not. I undoubtedly knew something about it, even too much, but how? Let the reader bear in mind that *dream*! If I could have dreamt that, if it could have burst out of my heart in precisely that form, then it means I knew an awful lot—did not actually know, that is, but had a *premonition* of what I have just

429

explained and did not know for sure until 'everything was finished'. So I did not know for sure, but my heart throbbed with premonitions and evil spirits possessed my dreams.

So I found myself drawn to that very man, fully aware of the sort of man he was and having a premonition even of the details of it all! And why was I drawn? Look at it this way: now, at the very moment I am writing this, it seems I knew everything then in every detail about why I was drawn to him, when I really knew nothing at all. Perhaps the reader will understand this. But now—to business, fact by fact.

II

It began with the fact that a couple of days before I went out at last Liza came home one evening in a state of considerable alarm. She had been terribly humiliated; and actually something quite intolerable had happened to her.

I have already mentioned her relationship with Vasin. She had gone to see him not only to show us she did not need us, but also because she really did appreciate him. They had become acquainted in Luga and I had always felt Vasin was not indifferent to her. In the misfortune which had overtaken her she would naturally seek advice from the sort of firm, calm, and invariably elevated intellect which she ascribed to Vasin. More-over, women are never the best judges of men's minds, especially if the man appeals to them, and they gladly accept paradoxical remarks as conclusive if they correspond to their own wishes. In Vasin what Liza liked was his sympathy for her position and, as it seemed to her at the start, his sympathy for the prince as well. Suspecting how he felt towards her, she could hardly fail to appreciate in him the sympathy he showed for his rival. The prince himself, to whom she confided the fact that she would sometimes go and talk things over with Vasin, received the news extraordinarily badly from the very start and became jealous. Liza took offence at this and deliberately went on seeing Vasin. The prince did not mention it, but was plunged in gloom. Liza herself confessed to me (much later on) that she had soon stopped liking Vasin. He was always so calm, and this perpetual calmness, which she had found so attractive to start with, later seemed repugnant to her. On the face of it he had been

430

businesslike and actually given her some good advice, but all the advice seemed deliberately quite unworkable. He sometimes passed judgements in too supercilious a way and without trying to hide it from her—something that became increasingly the case—and she attributed it to his inevitable and growing indifference to her position. On one occasion she thanked him for always being so well disposed to me and talking to me as an equal, although he was intellectually so superior to me (she was in fact repeating to him what I had said about him). He had answered:

'It's not like that or for that reason. It's because I do not think he's any different from the rest. I do not consider him either sillier than the clever or wickeder than the good. I treat them all the same because, in my eyes, they are all the same.'

'You mean you don't see any differences?'

'Oh, of course, people vary one from another, but there are no differences in my eyes because people's differences don't concern me. For me all are equal and everything's equal, so I'm equally kind to everyone.'

'Don't you find it a bit boring?'

'No. I am always quite satisfied.'

'And don't you ever long for something?'

'Of course I do, but not a lot. I need very little, not a rouble more than necessary. I couldn't care less if I were arrayed all in gold or just as I am. Gold would add nothing to Vasin's value. You couldn't tempt my palate. Could high positions and honours take the place of what I am right now?'

Liza assured me in all honesty that this was exactly what he said. Still, one shouldn't be too hard on him, bearing in mind the circumstances.

Gradually Liza came to the conclusion that he was also supercilious about the prince, perhaps because, for him, all were equal and 'there are no differences', and certainly not out of sympathy for her. But at last he clearly began to abandon his high and mighty manner and started not only criticizing the prince but also referring to him in terms of ironical dislike. This infuriated Liza, yet Vasin still persisted. The main thing was that he always expressed himself so gently, even displaying little real dissatisfaction in his criticisms and demonstrating the utter unworthiness of her hero simply by being quite logical. Mind

431

you, even the logic contained a degree of irony. Finally, he almost thrust in her face what he called the 'irrationality' of her love, all the stubborn, forced character of it.

'Your feelings have led you astray,' he announced, 'and errors of that kind, once recognized, definitely need to be corrected.'

This is what happened that day. Liza stood up in disgust, ready to go. And what do you think this intelligent man did then? With a look of the utmost dignity and even with a certain degree of feeling he asked for her hand in marriage. Liza called him a fool to his face and stalked out.

To suggest a woman betray her unfortunate fiancé because he is 'unworthy' of her and then, worst of all, propose marriage to her when she is already pregnant by the fiancé—why, that's just the way these people think! I call it being dreadfully theoretical and showing complete ignorance of life due to extreme smugness. And, what is more, Liza saw through him completely and knew he was proud of what he had done, even though he knew about her pregnancy. She rushed off to see the prince shedding tears of indignation, only for him to outdo even Vasin. It would have seemed he would have been convinced after what she had to say that there was no need for him to be jealous any more. But he went crazy. Mind you, jealous people are like that! He made a frightful scene and said such hurtful things to her that she was almost on the point of breaking off all relations with him.

However, she came home still maintaining some self-control, but couldn't stop confessing to mother what had happened. Oh, that evening they got together again just as they had been before and the ice between them was broken! Naturally, both of them burst into tears, embraced as they had always done, and Liza clearly felt better, though she was very gloomy. She spent the whole evening with Makar Ivanovich not saying a word but without leaving the room. She listened attentively to what he was saying. Ever since the episode with the bench she had been extraordinarily and rather diffidently respectful towards him, although she still remained far from talkative.

But on that occasion Makar Ivanovich unexpectedly turned the conversation in a surprising direction. In the morning Versilov and the doctor had been frowning as they discussed his health. That's one thing I ought to mention. I also ought to mention that for several days we had been preparing to celebrate mother's birthday, due in five days' time, and had often talked about it. In view of this, Makar Ivanovich had given himself over to reminiscences and remembered mother as a little girl when she could 'barely stand up on her little legs'.

'I hardly ever let her out of my arms,' the old man recalled. 'Sometimes I'd try teaching her to walk, you know, and I'd stand her in a corner three steps away and I'd call her to me and she'd come waddling across the room to me, and she'd not be frightened, she'd laugh and run right up to me and throw her arms round my neck. Then I'd tell you fairy stories, Sofya Andreevna. You were a great one for fairy stories. You'd sit on my knees listening for hours on end. People'd say: "Look how fond she is of Makar!" Then I'd take you into the forest and put you by a bush of raspberries and I'd whittle a little whistle for you out of some wood. We'd wander all over and then I'd carry you back home in my arms. You'd be fast asleep, just a babe in arms. One time you thought you saw a wolf and ran to me all trembling, but there wasn't any wolf at all.'

'I remember that,' said mother.

'Really?'

'I remember a great deal. My very first memory in life is of seeing your love and kindness for me.' She spoke in a voice full of feeling and suddenly went red.

Makar Ivanovich waited a moment before saying:

'Forgive me, dear children, I must leave you. The lesson of my life is nearing its end now. In my old age I have discovered solace from all sorrows. Thank you, my dear ones.'

'That's enough, Makar Ivanovich, my dear chap!' cried Versilov in some alarm. 'The doctor's only just told me you're much, much better . . .'

Mother was listening in a state of fright.

'Well, what does he know, your Aleksandr Semyonych, eh?' said Makar Ivanovich with a smile. 'He's a nice enough chap, but no more. Enough's enough, my friends. Or do you think I'm frightened of dying? I had the feeling today, after morning prayers, right here in my heart, that I'd never leave this place again. A voice had spoken. Well, if that's so, then God's name be praised! Still, I just want to have my fill of looking at you all. Job, of the Old Testament, who had suffered much, comforted

433

himself by looking at his new children, but did he forget the old ones, could he forget them? No, that was impossible! It's simply that, with the years, sadness becomes mixed with joy and is transformed into tears of light. So it is in the world that every soul is led into temptation and every soul is comforted. I wanted, my children, to say one small thing,' he went on with a calm, beautiful smile I will never forget and suddenly turned to me: 'You, dear boy, jealously watch over the holy church and, should you in due time receive the summons, then die for it. But wait, have no fear, it will not be right now!' he said with a grin. 'Maybe now you never give it a thought, but maybe later you will. Only just remember this: if you are minded to do such a blessed deed, then do it for God and not out of envy! Hold firm to whatever you do and never give in through any frailty of spirit. Do what must be done step by step, neither rushing in nor dashing from side to side. Well, that's all I want to say to you. Just learn to say your prayers day by day without fail—I just wanted you to remind yourself. To you, Andrey Petrovich, my good sir, I also had something to say, but God will seek out your heart without my help. We have long since ceased, you and I, to talk about the matter, ever since the time the arrow of fate pierced deep into my heart. Now I am leaving I just wanted to remind you . . . what you promised then . . .'

He almost whispered these final words with his head bowed.

'Makar Ivanovich!' said Versilov in embarrassment and rose from his chair.

'No, no, please don't be embarrassed! It was just a reminder . . . I am the one who is most to blame before God in this matter, for, though you were my lord and master, I should not have permitted this sin of weakness to occur. For that reason you, also, Sofya, must not agitate your soul too much, for your sin was all my fault, and you, I think, scarcely knew your own mind then, nor did you along with her, my dear sir . . .' He smiled with lips quivering from some kind of pain. 'Though I could have taught you sense with a rod, my wife, and should have done, I took pity on you when you fell at my feet in tears and hid nothing from me—and even kissed my feet. I don't recall this to reproach you, my beloved, but simply to remind Andrey Petrovich—because you yourself, sir, are mindful of the promise you made as a member of the Russian nobility—that in the laying on of hands in marriage all is put in order . . . I say this, noble sir, in the presence of the children . . .'

He was extraordinarily emotional and looked at Versilov as if he expected him to say something affirmative. I emphasize that all this was so unexpected I sat there without moving a finger. Versilov was obviously no less touched than he was, because he went up to mother without a word and embraced her, and mother in her turn, also in complete silence, went up to Makar Ivanovich and bowed right down at his feet.

In short, it was a terribly moving moment. The only people in the room were ourselves. Tatyana Pavlovna was not present. Liza drew herself up straight where she was sitting and listened to it all in silence. Then she suddenly stood up and said firmly to Makar Ivanovich:

'Give me your blessing, Makar Ivanovich. I have to undergo a great ordeal. My fate is being decided tomorrow. Please say a prayer for me today.'

And she strode out of the room.

I know that Makar Ivanovich had already heard all about her troubles from mother. But that evening was the first time I had seen Versilov and mother side by side as equals. Previously all I had ever seen beside him was his female slave. There was an awful amount I still did not know—or care to notice—about this man on whom I had already passed my own judgement, so that I returned to my room in a highly confused state. It has to be said that this was the moment when all my bewildered feelings about him suddenly came together. He had never seemed to me more of a mystery or an enigma than he did at that moment.

But that is precisely what I am writing about. Everything will be made clear in due course.

As I lay down to sleep I thought: 'So it turns out he gave Makar Ivanovich his word as a member of the Russian nobility that he would marry mother in the event of her being widowed. He did not say a word about that when he talked to me about Makar Ivanovich before.'

The next day Liza was not at home and, on returning fairly late, went straight to Makar Ivanovich. I had not wanted to go there so as not to disturb them. but having discovered that mother and Versilov were there as well I did go in. Liza was sitting beside her old man and crying on his shoulder and he, sad-faced, silently stroked her hair.

Versilov explained to me (later in my room) that the prince had stuck to his guns and insisted on marrying Liza at the first opportunity, even before the judgement in the court case. Liza found it hard to make up her mind, although she almost had no right not to. In any case, Makar Ivanovich had issued an order that she should get married. It goes without saying that everything should have happened naturally and she should have got married entirely of her own accord without having any doubts or orders issued, but at that very moment she had been so hurt by the very man she loved and so humiliated in her own eyes by the very love she felt for him that she found it hard to make up her mind. Apart, though, from the sense of humiliation there was another circumstance which I couldn't have suspected.

'You've heard, haven't you, that the group of young people from the Petersburg side were all arrested yesterday?' Versilov suddenly said.

'What? The Dergachev group?' I exclaimed.

'Yes. And Vasin, too.'

I was astonished, particularly about Vasin.

'Surely he wasn't mixed up in that, was he? My God, what'll happen to them now? And just when Liza's put all the blame on Vasin! What do you think'll happen to them? Stebelkov's in on this! I bet he is!'

'Let's leave that,' said Versilov, giving me a strange look (the kind of look one gives to someone who has no understanding or inkling). 'Who knows what was going on there and what'll happen to them. I don't want to talk about that. I heard you wanted to go out tomorrow. Will you be calling in on Prince Sergey Petrovich?'

'Yes, first thing. Though I admit it'll be difficult. Is there something you want me to tell you?'

'No, nothing. I'll be seeing him myself. I am so sorry for Liza. What sort of advice can Makar Ivanovich give her? He has no real understanding of people or of life in general. What's more, dear boy,' (he had not called me that for a long time) 'there are also some other young people—and one of them's your old friend Lambert . . . I think they're all the greatest scoundrels,

436

the lot of them! I just wanted to warn you. Still, it's all up to you, of course, and I haven't any right . . .'

'Andrey Petrovich!' I seized him by the hand without thinking and almost in a kind of ecstasy, as I tend to do often (it was almost dark by that time). 'Andrey Petrovich, I didn't say a word—you saw that, didn't you?—I haven't said anything so far, and you know why? So as to avoid your secrets. I don't want to know anything about them. I'm a coward, you see. I'm frightened your secrets'll finally tear you out of my heart for good and I don't want that. So if that's the case, why do you want to know mine? Just don't bother about where I go! Agreed?'

'You're right. But not another word, I beg you!' he said and went out of my room.

In that way, despite everything, an explanation of sorts occurred. But he merely added to the excitement I felt over the new step in my life I was taking the next day, so I spent the whole night continually waking up. Still, I felt good.

III

The next day I did leave the house, though only by ten in the morning, and trying at all costs not to make a sound, without saying goodbye or anything. I slipped out, so to speak. I don't know why I did this, but I know if mother had seen me leaving and tried talking to me I would have sworn at her. When I was out on the street and breathing in the cold street air, I literally shuddered from a very powerful sensation which was almost animalistic and which I would have called *carnivorous*. Why and where I was going was completely unclear to me and yet was like a lusting after flesh. I felt simultaneously frightened and excited.

'Will I make a killing today or won't I?' I asked myself jauntily although I knew only too well that once I'd taken today's step it would be decisive and unalterable for the rest of my life. But it is no good talking in riddles.

I went straight to the prison to see the prince. Three days earlier I had obtained a note from Tatyana Pavlovna to show to the prison overseer and it worked like a charm. I have no idea whether he was a good man and I think it's irrelevant, but he permitted me to see the prince and arranged for the meeting to

437

take place in his room, kindly handing it over to us. The room was just a room, an ordinary enough room in the apartment of a prison official, and I see no need to describe it. So the prince and I were left on our own.

He arrived kitted out in a kind of uniform but in the cleanest of shirts, wearing a dandyish tie, looking washed and well groomed but frightfully emaciated and jaundiced. I even noticed this jaundiced look in his eyes. In short, he had changed so much I was quite stunned on seeing him.

'How you've changed!' I cried.

'It's nothing! Please sit down, my dear chap.' He indicated an armchair in a rather foppish way and himself sat down opposite. 'Let's get down to business. You see, my dear Aleksey Makarovich . . .'

'Arkady,' I corrected him.

'What? Oh, yes. Well, anyhow, no matter. Yes, of course,' he recollected himself suddenly, 'I'm sorry, my dear chap. Let's get down to business . . .'

To put it briefly, he was in a frightful hurry to get on with what he wanted to say. He was entirely consumed, literally from head to toe, by some extremely important idea that he set about defining and explaining to me. He talked an enormous amount and he talked fast, clarifying his remarks forcibly and under pressure with accompanying gestures, but for the first few minutes I simply did not understand a thing.

'To put it briefly' (he had used that very expression a dozen times already), 'to put it briefly,' he concluded, 'if I alarmed you, Arkady Makarovich, by summoning you so insistently via Liza yesterday as if I were on fire or something, still the essence of the decision must be final and quite out of the ordinary, so we . . .'

'Prince,' I broke in, 'you summoned me yesterday? Liza said nothing to me about it.'

'What?' he cried, stopping suddenly in extraordinary bewilderment, even almost in a fright.

'She said absolutely nothing about it to me. She came home yesterday evening so upset she did not manage to speak to me at all.'

The prince jumped up.

'Surely you can't be right, Arkady Makarovich! In that case, it's . . . it's . . .'

438

'But what's it matter? Why are you so worked up? She simply forgot, or something of the kind . . .'

He sat down, but was clearly stunned. It seemed that the news of Liza's failure to tell me anything was simply crushing. Suddenly he started talking rapidly and waving his arms, but it was again terribly hard to understand what he meant.

'Stop!' he declared immediately, pausing and holding up a finger. 'Stop, it is . . . it is . . . if I'm not mistaken . . . it is certain matters, sir!' he muttered with a maniacal smile. 'And it means that . . .'

'It doesn't mean anything at all,' I interrupted. 'And I don't understand why something so trivial is bothering you so much . . . Oh, prince, ever since that very night—do you remember?'

'What? Since what night?' he cried capriciously, obviously vexed at my interruption.

'At Zershchikov's, the last time we saw each other, just before you wrote your letter. You were in a terrible state of excitement then, but there's such a difference between that time and now that I'm appalled at you . . . Or don't you remember anything?'

'Oh, yes,' he declared in the voice of a man-about-town, as if he had suddenly recalled it, 'oh, yes, that evening! I heard about you . . . Well, how is your health now and how do you feel, Arkady Makarovich? However, let's get down to business. You see, I am myself pursuing three aims, I have three tasks before me, and I . . .'

He once more began talking rapidly about his 'business'. I finally realized I had in front of me someone who at least needed a towel soaked in vinegar pressed to his head if not a vein opened. All his jumbled chatter was naturally concerned with his trial and its outcome, about the way his regimental commander had visited him and tried to advise him against something, but the prince had refused; about some note he had sent somewhere; about the prosecutor; about the probability of him being stripped of his rights and being exiled somewhere in the north of Russia; about the possibility of doing some colonizing and serving his time in Tashkent; about teaching his son (his future son by Liza) something or other and passing it on to him 'right out in the sticks, in Archangel, in Kholmogory'.*

439

'If I wanted your opinion, Arkady Makarovich, it was because, believe you me, I so cherish a feeling . . . If only you knew, if you knew, Arkady Makarovich, my dear chap, my very own brother, what Liza means to me now, what she has meant to me throughout all this time!' he cried out suddenly, seizing his head with both hands.

'Sergey Petrovich, surely you're not going to ruin her life by taking her away with you? To Kholmogory!'

The words suddenly burst out of me. Liza's fate in giving up her life for this maniac was suddenly clear to me for the first time. He glanced at me, stood up once more, took one step, turned round, and again sat down still clutching his head.

'I keep on dreaming of spiders!' he said suddenly.

'You're in state of terrible nerves and I'd advise you, prince, to lie down and call the doctor at once.'

'No, I'll do that later. The business I asked you here for is to explain to you about the wedding. The wedding, you know, will take place in the church here, as I've already told you. Permission has already been given and they've already been urging me to . . . As for Liza, what I . . .'

'Prince, please be kind to Liza!' I cried. 'Don't hurt her—at least not now! Don't go on being jealous!'

'What?'

He screamed out the word, looking at me with bugging, staring eyes and his whole face distorted by a long, idiotically querying smile. It was obvious that the words about not being jealous had come as a terrible shock.

'Forgive me, prince, I didn't mean it. Oh, just recently, prince, I've got to know an old man, my so-called father . . . Oh, if only you could meet him, you'd be so much calmer. Liza also values him highly.'

'Ah, yes, Liza—ah, yes, so he's your father, is he? Or . . . pardon, mon cher, there was something . . . I recall she said something . . . about an old man. I'm sure of it, quite sure. I also used to know an old man . . . Mais passons, enough of that, the main thing is, so as to clarify all essentials, is that we must . . .'

I stood up to leave. It hurt me to go on watching him.

'I do not understand!' he uttered sternly and solemnly on seeing me stand up.

440

'It hurts me to watch you,' I said.

'Arkady Makarovich, one more thing!' He seized me suddenly by the shoulders with a quite different look on his face and made me sit down again in the armchair. 'You've heard about them? You know who I mean.' He leaned towards me.

'Ah, you mean Degachev. I'm sure Stebelkov's in on that!' I cried out despite myself.

'Yes, it's Stebelkov and—you know something?'

He broke off and once again stared at me with the same bugging eyes and the same long, quivering, idiotically querying smile spreading ever more broadly on his lips. His face gradually went pale. Something suddenly dawned on me. I remembered the look Versilov had given me when he told me about Vasin's arrest.

'Oh, surely it wasn't you!' I cried in a fright.

'You see, Arkady Makarovich, I summoned you so as to explain . . . I wanted to . . .' He spoke in a rapid whisper.

'It was you informed against Vasin!' I shouted.

'No. You see, there was this manuscript. Vasin gave it to Liza at the last moment . . . to look after. She left it here for me to look at and then, the next day, they quarrelled . . .'

'You handed over the manuscript to the authorities!'

'Arkady Makarovich! Arkady Makarovich!'

'So it was you,' I cried, jumping up and singing out the words in ringing tones, 'you, without any prompting, for no other reason than that the unfortunate Vasin was *your rival*, purely out of jealousy, you handed over *a manuscript that had been given to Liza*—you handed it over to whom? To whom? To the prosecutor?'

But he had no time to answer, and indeed couldn't have, because he stood there in front of me like a dummy with the same sickly smile and staring look. Suddenly the door opened and Liza came in. She almost collapsed on the spot at seeing the two of us together.

'You here? You?' she cried, her face suddenly distorted as she seized me by the hands. 'So you *know*, do you?'

She could already tell from my face that I *knew*. I held her to me irresistibly and ever so firmly. And then only, for the first time, did I realize to the full what an inescapable and endless misery, with no hope of alleviation, weighed down eternally upon the destiny of this girl who was such a willing martyr to such suffering.

'How on earth can you talk to me now?' she cried, tearing herself away from me. 'How can you? Why're you here? Just look at him! Look at him! You can't judge him, can you?'

Limitless suffering and compassion shone in her face as she pointed at her unfortunate fiancé. He sat in the armchair with his hands over his face. And she was right. He looked just like a man suffering from delirium tremens and not responsible for his actions, and maybe that is how he had been for three days already. That very morning he was taken off to hospital and towards evening he was diagnosed as having brain fever.

IV

Leaving Liza with the prince, at about one o'clock I took a cab round to my former room. I forgot to mention that it was a raw day, overcast, with a thaw beginning and a warm breeze that could have upset the nerves of an elephant. My landlord was overjoyed to see me and made a great fuss, dashing about all over the place, something I cannot stand at times like that. I spoke fairly drily and went straight to my room, but he followed and, though he did not dare ask anything, curiosity literally flashed from his eyes and he looked, what's more, as if he had every right to be inquisitive. I had to behave politely for my own good, but although it was only too essential to find out something (and I knew what it would be) I could not make myself ask him. I enquired merely about his wife's health and we went in to see her. She was solicitous in her greeting, but she adopted an extraordinarily businesslike and uncommunicative look which reassured me a little. In short, I discovered an enormous amount on that occasion.

Of course, Lambert had been, but later he had made a couple of visits and looked at all the rooms, saying he would perhaps rent one. Nastasya Yegorovna had also made several visits, God knows why. 'She has been very inquisitive,' the landlord remarked, but I did not indulge him by asking what she was being inquisitive about. In general I did not ask anything, but left him to do the talking and gave the impression of rooting

442

about in my trunk (where practically nothing at all remained). But the annoying thing was that he also played at being mysterious and, seeing that I was refraining from asking questions, considered it his duty to resort to a kind of shorthand, almost to speaking in riddles.

'There was also a young lady,' he added, giving me a strange look.

'What young lady?'

'Anna Andreevna. She came twice. She got to know my wife. She was very charming, very pleasant. One cannot rate someone like that too highly, Arkady Makarovich . . .' And, on saying this, he took a step towards me as if he were very keen I should understand something.

'Twice?' I said in astonishment.

'The second time with her brother.'

Lambert, I thought.

'No, sir, it wasn't Mr Lambert,' he added immediately just as if he had read my thoughts, 'it was her brother, the young Mr Versilov. A Kammerjunker,* isn't he?'

I was extremely put out. He gazed at me, smiling terribly fondly.

'Oh, and there was someone else asked after you—that mademoiselle, the French lady, Alphonsine de Verdun. Oh, she's such a beautiful singer and declaims verse so beautifully! She'd been off that day seeing Prince Nikolay Ivanovich at Tsarskoe all secret-like, saying she wanted to sell him a little black dog, very rare, no bigger'n her little fist . . .'

I asked him to leave me alone, complaining I had a headache. He consented at once before I could finish what I was saying, not only without taking the least offence but almost with pleasure, mysteriously waving his hand and giving the impression of saying, 'I understand, sir, I understand,' though that was not what he actually said, but he left the room on tiptoe and took great pleasure in doing so. Some people can be as annoying as hell.

I sat there by myself thinking things over for an hour and a half—not so much thinking things over, however, as trying to work things out. Though I was put out by what I had heard, I wasn't in the least surprised. I had even been expecting something worse, something far more outlandish. 'Maybe they've

443

actually got things going,' I thought. I had been certain for a long time, while still at home, that they had things wound up and ready to go. 'All they're lacking is me,' I thought with a certain irritating and yet pleasant satisfaction. That they had been waiting for me as hard as they could and had tried to set something up in my room was as clear as daylight. 'The old prince's marriage, was that it? Only will I allow it, gentlemen? That's the question.' I concluded in haughty self-congratulation.

Once I start on this again, I thought, I'll be drawn into the whirlpool like a piece of flotsam. Am I really free now or not? Can I go home this very evening to mother and tell myself, as I have done these last few days, that I am my own man?

That was the essence of all the questions I posed to myself or—better—the thing that made my heart beat faster during the hour and a half I spent on my bed in the corner, my elbows on my knees and the palms of my hands supporting my head. But I knew, I knew then and there, that all these questions were utter nonsense and that it was *she*, she alone, who really attracted me! Yes, at last it's out, I've committed it to paper! Because even right now, as I am writing this a year later, I still don't know what name to give the feeling I had then!

Oh, I was sorry for Liza, but in my heart I had the most genuine aching pain! I thought maybe that very feeling of pain could lay to rest and extinguish, if only just for a time, the *carnivorous* (again that word crops up), the sheer *lusting of the flesh* which I felt. But I was driven on by limitless curiosity, by a sort of fear, by some feeling or other—I don't know what feeling exactly, but I know now and I already knew then it wasn't a good feeling. Maybe I was really trying to fall at *her* feet, and maybe I wanted to make her endure all sorts of torments, and maybe I wanted to prove to her something 'the sooner, the better'. But no pain and no compassion for Liza could stop me.

'Well,' I thought, 'can I stand up now and go home ... to Makar Ivanovich? Surely, it's just not possible to go and see them, find out about everything from them and then suddenly leave them forever, as if I were to pass harmlessly between Scylla and Charybdis?'

By three o'clock, having collected myself together and realizing I was almost too late, I dashed out, caught a cab, and flew off to see Anna Andreevna.

CHAPTER V

I

As soon as I was announced, Anna Andreevna abandoned her sewing and came out into her ante-room to meet me, something she had never done before. She stretched out both hands to me and quickly blushed. Silently she led me into her own room, sat down to her needlework once again, and settled me down beside her, but she did not start sewing and kept on eyeing me with the same fierce fondness without saying a word.

'You sent Nastasya Yegorovna to see me, didn't you?' I began straight off, slightly oppressed by her all-too-showy fondness, although I liked it.

Suddenly she started speaking without answering: 'I heard about it all, I know all about it. Oh, what a terrible night it must have been! What you must have gone through! Is it really true you were found unconscious lying out in the frost?'

'Lambert . . . he must've told you,' I muttered, reddening.

'It was from him I learned about everything then, but I was waiting to hear from you. Oh, he came to me in such a fright! At your house, where you were lying ill, they didn't want to let him in—it was odd, that. Mind you, I don't know why, but he told me all about that night. He told me you'd scarcely come to your senses when you mentioned me and said how devoted you were to me . . . I was touched to tears, Arkady Makarovich, and I don't even know why I deserved such fondness on your part, the more so in view of the state you were in! Tell me, is Mr Lambert really a boyhood friend?'

'Yes, but I admit on that occasion I was careless and perhaps blurted out a bit too much to him.'

'Oh, I'd have learned about that dirty, horrible intrigue without his help! I've always, always felt they'd bring you to this. Tell me, is it true Björing dared raise his hand against you?'

She spoke as if it was solely due to Björing and *her* that I ended up lying under the fence. It dawned on me she was right, but I flared up:

'If he had raised his hand against me, he wouldn't have got

445

away with it and I wouldn't be sitting here now in front of you unavenged!'

I spoke heatedly. The main thing was, I thought, that she wanted to annoy me for some reason and turn me against someone (it was quite obvious who); and yet I fell for it.

'If you are saying you'd always felt I'd be brought to *this*, then I think from Katerina Nikolaevna's point of view it was just a misunderstanding—though it's true she was all too quick to let her kindness be replaced by this misunderstanding . . .'

'You're right—all too quick!' chimed in Anna Andreevna with enthusiastic fellow-feeling. 'If only you knew what's going on now! Of course, Arkady Makarovich, you'll find it hard now to understand the delicacy of my position,' she observed, blushing and lowering her head. 'Since that morning when we last saw each other, I have taken a step which not everyone would be as capable of understanding and appreciating as a man like you would, with your as yet unsullied mind and your loving, unspoiled, freshly receptive heart. You can be sure, my friend, that I am quite capable of appreciating your devotion to me and I will repay it with eternal gratitude. In society, of course, they'll stone me and are preparing to do so. But even if they were right, from their own beastly point of view, who among them would dare to throw the first stone? Since childhood I have been abandoned by my father. We Versilovs—an ancient Russian family line of high standing—we are just rogues and free-loaders and I live off other people. Wouldn't it be natural for me to turn to the man who has taken the place of my father since I was a little girl and whose charity I have been receiving for so many years? God alone can see and judge my feeling for him and I won't allow society to pass judgement on what I have done! What's more, when there's the most wicked and sinister intrigue being hatched and a trustful, big-hearted father is about to be ruined by his very own daughter, can one just look away? No, even though I may ruin my own reputation, I will save him! I am already simply to be a nanny to him, stand guard over him, be his nurse, but I am not going to allow some cold, calculating, society scheme to get the better of him!'

She spoke with unusual passion, which may have been partly put on but was still sincere, because it was obvious to what extent she had become drawn into the whole business. Oh, I felt sure

446

she was lying (although quite sincerely, because one can still lie sincerely) and that she was now a wicked woman! But it is an astonishing thing about women: the look of uprightness, the lofty formality, the air of social superiority and inaccessibility and haughty propriety, all of it can fool one completely, and I started agreeing with her—so long, that is, as I sat there with her! At least, I decided not to contradict her! Oh, men are the absolute moral slaves of women, especially if they are big-hearted! A woman like that could convince a big-hearted man of anything!'

'She and Lambert—my God!' I thought, staring at her in bewilderment.

However, I will tell all. Even now I cannot blame her. God alone could see what her feelings really were, and a human being, what's more, is such a complex piece of machinery there are occasions when you can't make them out, particularly if the human being is a woman.

'Anna Andreevna, what precisely do you expect me to do?' I asked, but with a fair degree of firmness.

'What? What do you mean by asking that, Arkady Makarovich?'

'I thought, in view of everything . . . in view of certain other considerations,' I tried to explain, finding myself getting muddled, 'that you'd sent to me because you were expecting something from me. What precisely?'

Without answering, she instantly started talking about something else, just as passionately and rapidly:

'But I cannot, I'm too proud, to embark on explanations, to engage in deals with unknowns like Mr Lambert! I was waiting for you, not Lambert. My position is quite extreme, it's terrible, Arkady Makarovich! I have to be so cunning, surrounded by the scheming of that woman, and I can't bear it. I have almost been reduced myself to intriguing and I have been waiting for you as my saviour. I can't be blamed for looking greedily round me for at least someone who is friendly, someone who could even on a night like that, even frozen stiff, mention me and repeat my name over and over again—that man, of course, must be really devoted to me. That's what I've been thinking all this time and that's why I've placed my hope in you.'

She looked me straight in the eye with an impatient, querying look. And once again I did not have the guts to disabuse her and

447

explain straightaway that Lambert had deceived her and I had never told him I was particularly devoted to her and had never repeated her name 'over and over again'. As a result, by my silence I confirmed Lambert's lie, as it were. Oh, she herself, I am sure, understood only too well that Lambert had exaggerated and even lied to her simply in order to have a plausible pretext for coming to see her and establishing contact with her. If she had really looked into my eyes as someone who was sure of the genuineness of my words and of my devotion, then she would have known, of course, that I would not have dared deny them out of delicacy, so to speak, and on account of my youth. However, whether I was right or wrong in this guesswork I don't know. Maybe I'm just rotten to the core.

'My brother will stand up for me,' she said suddenly and heatedly, seeing that I would not respond.

'I was told you and he had been to my room,' I muttered in confusion.

'After all poor Prince Nikolay Ivanovich has practically nowhere to go now to get away from all the scheming or—better—from his very own daughter, apart, I mean, from your room, the room of a friend. At least he can still count on you as a friend! And if you want to do something for him, do this if you can, if you've got a big enough heart and the courage . . . finally, if *you can do anything at all*! Oh, it's not for me, not for me, it's for an unfortunate old man who was the only one to love you with real sincerity, whose heart is as devoted to you as if you were his own son and yearns for you even now! I am not expecting anything for myself, even from you . . . when my very own father has played such a dirty, such a foul trick on me!'

'I think Andrey Petrovich . . .' I began.

'Andrey Petrovich,' she interrupted with a sour smile, 'Andrey Petrovich, in answer to my direct question, gave me his word he never had any intentions at all towards Katerina Nikolaevna, which I fully believed when I did what I did. Yet it turns out he said nothing only until he heard something about a certain Mr Björing!'

'That's not the case!' I cried. 'There was a time when I believed he loved that woman, but it's not the case. Even if it were, he doesn't have to worry now—now that that gentleman's given up.'

448

'What gentleman?'

'Björing.'

'Who told you he'd given up? Maybe that gentleman was never better placed than now!' She gave a caustic laugh. I even felt her glance was mocking.

'Nastasya Yegorovna told me,' I mumbled in a confusion I had no way of concealing and which she noticed only too clearly.

'Nastasya Yegorovna is a very nice person, and of course I can't stop her being fond of me, but she has no means of knowing what is no concern of hers.'

My heart sank. Since she had counted on being able to make me indignant, I literally burned with indignation, but not towards Katerina Nikolaevna, only towards Anna Andreevna herself. I stood up.

'As an honourable man, I must warn you, Anna Andreevna, that your expectations regarding me could . . . could turn out to be fruitless in the highest degree . . .'

'I expect that you will stand up for me.' She looked at me fair and square. 'For me, someone who has been abandoned by one and all . . . for your sister, if that's what you want, Arkady Makarovich!'

In another moment she would have burst into tears.

'Well, you'd better not expect anything, because there won't be any "maybe"s about it,' I muttered with an inexpressibly heavy heart.

'How am I meant to understand that?' she asked. She seemed a bit too frightened.

'Because I'll be leaving the lot of you, for good and all! *Basta*, as the Italians say!' I suddenly shouted almost in a fury. 'And as for the so-called *document*, I'll tear it to pieces! Goodbye!'

I bowed to her and left without another word, at the same time hardly daring to look her in the face. But I had only just gone downstairs when Nastasya Yegorovna caught up with me holding a half-sheet of letter paper folded in two. Where Nastasya Yegorovna had come from and where she had been sitting while I was talking to Anna Andreevna, I have no idea. She did not say anything, but simply handed over the sheet of paper and ran back upstairs.

I unfolded the paper. It contained Lambert's address, carefully written out and obviously got ready some days before. I suddenly remembered that when Nastasya Yegorovna had come to see me I had said I didn't know where Lambert lived, but in a sense of not knowing and not wanting to know. Yet by that time I already knew Lambert's address via Liza, whom I had asked to find out from the public address lists. What Anna Andreevna had just done now struck me as proof, even cynical proof, that, despite my refusal to help her, she was directing me to go to Lambert as if she didn't believe a word I said. It was now only too clear to me she knew all about the 'document'—and from whom if not from Lambert, to whom she was now sending me to do a deal?

'The whole lot of them definitely take me for a mere kid without any will of my own or character and they think they can do what they like with me!' I thought indignantly.

II

Nevertheless I still went to Lambert. How else could I get the better of my curiosity as it was then? It turned out that Lambert lived a good distance away, in Hare Lane near the Summer Gardens, in the same apartment as before, but when I ran away from him I had taken so little notice of the way and the distance that, having got his address from Liza four days earlier, I had been astonished and had scarcely believed he lived there. Outside the main doors on the third floor, as I was still climbing the stairs, I caught sight of two young men and I thought they must have rung the bell before me and were waiting for someone to answer. As I came up, they both turned and looked at me closely with their backs to the doors. I frowned, thinking there were other lodgers they were waiting for, because it would have been very unpleasant to find that someone was with Lambert. Trying not to look at them, I reached out to the bell.

'*Attendez!*' one of them shouted at me.

'Please wait one moment,' said the other young man in a resonant, softish voice, drawling the words slightly. 'Do you mind if we finish what we're doing and then all ring together?'

I stopped abruptly. They were both very young men of about 20 or 22. They were doing something rather odd in front of the doors and, surprised, I tried to look closer. The one who had shouted '*Attendez!*' was extremely tall, six feet and more, thin and gaunt, but very muscular, with a very small head for his height and a strange, rather comically morose expression on his slightly pock-marked but far from stupid, even pleasant face. His eyes had an abnormally intent look and shone with excessive and completely unnecessary determination. He was very poorly dressed in an old cotton-wool quilted greatcoat with a small, badly worn racoon collar, obviously second-hand and too short for him, and in horrible boots, looking almost peasant-like, and a frightfully battered top hat that looked old and rusty. He was thoroughly grubby with his dirty, ungloved hands and his fingernails in mourning. By contrast, his companion was dressed very smartly, judging by his light mink overcoat, elegant head-gear, and the bright, fresh gloves on his small, delicate fingers. He was about my height, but with an extraordinarily charming expression on his fresh-looking, youthful features.

The tall chap had removed his tie, a completely tattered and greasy remnant hardly more than a tape, and the good-looking boy, having taken a new, recently bought, black tie from his pocket, was about to put it round the tall one's neck while the latter, with a terribly serious face, was stretching out his very long neck to receive it, having pushed his greatcoat down from his shoulders.

'No, it won't do, not with such a dirty shirt,' said the one doing the dressing. 'Not only won't it have the right effect, it'll look even grubbier. I told you to wear a collar. I can't do it. Can you?' He suddenly turned to me as he asked this.

'What?'

'You know, tie his tie. You see it's got to be done so that his grubby shirt can't be seen, otherwise the whole effect'll be spoiled. I've just bought him a tie at Phillipe's barber shop, for a rouble.'

'That's the rouble you spent, is it?' muttered the tall one.

'Yes, that's the one. I haven't got a copeck now. You can't, eh? Then we'll have to ask little Alphonsine.'

'Are you going to Lambert?' the tall one suddenly asked me sharply.

'Yes,' I answered with no less determination, looking him straight in the eyes.

'Are you Dolgorowky?' he asked in the same tone of voice.

'No, I'm not Korovkin,' I answered just as sharply, having misheard.

451

'Are you Dolgorowky?!' the tall one almost shouted, repeating his question and advancing on me threateningly. His companion burst out laughing.

'He is saying Dolgorowky and not Korovkin,' he explained. 'You know how the French in the *Journal des Débats* often get Russian names wrong . . .'

'In the *Indépendance*,' the tall one bleated.

'OK, so it's in the *Indépendance*! For example, they write Dolgoruky as Dolgorowky, I've seen that myself, and Valonyev always come out as Count Wallonieff.'

'Doboyny!' screamed the tall one.

'Yes, that's another one. I read it out and we both laughed. It was about some Russian Madame Duboyny while abroad . . . We don't have to talk about all that now, do we?' He turned suddenly to the tall one.

'Forgive me, are you Mr Dolgoruky?'

'Yes, I am Dolgoruky. Why do you want to know?'

The tall one suddenly whispered something to the good-looking boy, who frowned and made a gesture of disapproval. But the tall one suddenly turned to me.

'*Monsieur le prince, vous n'avez pas de rouble d'argent pour nous, pas deux, mais un seul, voulez-vous?*'

'Oh, that is really horrible of you!' cried the boy.

'*Nous vous rendons,*' said the tall one, pronouncing the French words crudely and awkwardly.*

'Oh, he's such a cynic, you know,' the boy said laughingly to me, 'and you'd think he doesn't speak French at all well, wouldn't you? He speaks it like a native of Paris and simply loves poking fun at Russians who are terribly keen to talk French among themselves in society and don't know how to . . .'

'*Dans les wagons,*' explained the tall one.

'Oh, sure, they do it in trains! What a bore you are! There's no need to explain things. You just love playing the fool.'

I took out a rouble and offered it to the tall one.

'*Nous vous rendons,*' he said, took it and, suddenly turning round, his expression completely immobile and serious, began kicking the door with the toe of his enormous boot and yet without any trace of irritation.

'Oh, you're going to have another row with Lambert!' the boy remarked anxiously. 'It'd be better if you rang!'

I rang, but the tall one went on hacking away with his boot.

'*Ach, sacré . . .*' came Lambert's voice from the other side and he quickly opened the doors. '*Dites donc, voulez-vous que je vous casse la tête, mon ami!*' he shouted at the tall one.

'*Mon ami, voilà Dolgorowky, l'autre mon ami,*'* the tall one announced solemnly, looking fixedly at a Lambert who had gone quite red with anger. The latter, on seeing me, though, was instantly transformed.

'Oh, it's you, Arkady! At long last! How are you feeling? Are you well?'

He seized my hands and pressed them firmly. In short, he was in a state of such sincere elation that, for an instant, I was terribly impressed by him and could even have liked him.

'It's to you I've come first!'

'Alphonsine!' Lambert called.

She immediately sprang out from behind the screens.

'*Le voilà!*'

'*C'est lui!*' cried Alphonsine, throwing her arms wide and hurling herself at me for an embrace, but Lambert came between us.

'No, no, no, down!' he shouted at her as if she were a dog. 'You see, Arkady, a few of the lads had arranged to go out to a Tartar restaurant today. I don't want to let you out of my sight, so come with us. We'll have dinner. I'll send this lot packing right away and we can have a talk. Please come in, come in! We'll be going in a moment, if you can just wait a moment . . .'

I entered and stood in the middle of the room looking round me and refreshing my memory. Lambert started quickly changing behind the screens. The tall one and his companion came in behind us despite what Lambert had said. We all stood in a group.

'*Mademoiselle Alphonsine, voulez-vous me baiser?*' bellowed the tall one.*

'*Mademoiselle Alphonsine,*' said the younger one, stepping forward and showing her the necktie, but she rushed furiously at both of them.

'*Ah, le petit vilain!*' she screamed at the younger one. '*Ne m'approchez pas, ne me salissez pas, et vous, le grand dadais, je vous flanque à la porte tous les deux, savez-vous celà!*'*

The younger one, despite her contemptuous and negligent

rejection of him as if she were frightened of being dirtied by him (which made no sense to me because he was so good-looking and appeared so well dressed when he removed his fur coat)— the younger one still persisted in asking her to tie the tie round the tall one's neck and to fix on one of Lambert's clean collars beforehand. She was on the point of hitting them indignantly at this suggestion when Lambert, having heard it, called out to her from behind the screens to stop and do what they asked, otherwise 'we'll never get rid of them', as he put it, and Alphonsine picked up a collar in a flash and started tying a tie round the tall one's neck without any sign of her former resentment. The tall one stretched out his neck for her just as he done outside on the stairs.

'*Mademoiselle Alphonsine, avez-vous vendue votre bologne?*' he asked.*

'*Qu'est que ça, ma bologne?*'

The younger one explained that '*ma bologne*' meant her little dog.

'*Tiens, quel est ce baragouin?*'

'*Je parle comme une dame russe sur les eaux minérales,*' remarked *le grand dadais*, still with his neck outstretched.

'*Qu'est que ça qu'une dame russe sur les eaux minérales et . . . où est donc votre jolie montre, que Lambert vous a donné?*' She asked this suddenly of the younger one.*

'What's that? Once again no watch?' Lambert cried out irritably from behind the screens.

'We ate it!' bellowed *le grand dadais*.

'I sold it for eight roubles. It wasn't gold, as you claimed, but gold-plated silver. They're on sale in all the shops now for no more than sixteen roubles,' the younger one answered Lambert, trying to justify himself.

'There's got to be no more of this!' Lambert went on more irritably than ever. 'I don't buy you nice clothes, my young friend, and give you nice things so that you can waste money on your tall friend . . . What's the necktie cost you've just bought?'

'Only a rouble. It's not your money. He didn't have a tie and he needs a hat.'

'Nonsense!' cried Lambert, really angry. 'I gave him enough money to buy a hat and he's spent it on oysters and champagne!

454

He stinks! He's a mess! You can't take him anywhere! How can I take him out to a restaurant?'

'By cab!' bellowed the *dadais*. '*Nous avons un rouble d'argent que nous avons prêté chez notre nouvel ami.*'*

'Don't give them a thing, Arkady!' Lambert cried again.

'If you don't mind, Lambert, I'm demanding ten roubles from you right now!' the boy exclaimed angrily, going quite red in the face and looking almost twice as handsome. 'And don't you ever say anything like that to Dolgoruky! I demand ten roubles from you, in order to give one back to Dolgoruky and with the rest to buy Andreev a hat—you can see for yourself he needs one!'

Lambert came out from behind the screens.

'Here's three paper roubles and that'll be your lot till Tuesday and don't you dare . . .'

Le grand dadais seized the money from him.

'Dolorowky, here's your rouble, *nous vous rendons avec beaucoup de grâce*. Pete, let's go!' he cried to his companion and suddenly, holding up the two remaining rouble notes and waving them about with his eyes fixed on Lambert, shouted at the top of his voice:

'*Ohé, Lambert! Où est Lambert! As-tu vu Lambert?*'

'Don't you dare!' screamed Lambert in the most frightful rage. I realized this was all to do with something that had happened previously I knew nothing about and I watched in astonishment. But the tall one was not in the least intimidated by Lambert's anger. On the contrary, he shouted: '*Ohé, Lambert!*' and so on even more strongly and, with this ringing shout, they went out on to the stairs. Lambert would have driven them away, but he turned back.

'Oh, I'd soon enough give 'em one in the neck! They cost more'n they're worth . . . Arkady, let's be off! I'm late. There's a chap waiting for me there . . . I need to see him. He's a shit like they all are! Bloody shits! Bloody shits!' he screamed once more, almost grinding his teeth, but suddenly he pulled himself together. 'Arkady, I'm so, so glad you've come. Alphonsine, not a step outside the house! Come on, let's go.'

A dare-devil cabbie was waiting for us outside. We took our seats, but throughout the journey he could not subdue his annoyance at the two young men. I was amazed it was taken so seriously and that they had not only shown so little respect for Lambert but he had even appeared frightened of them. To me, who had had the impression inculcated into me since boyood, it had always seemed that people ought to be frightened of Lambert, so that, despite all my independence of spirit, at that moment I also couldn't help feeling afraid of him.

'I tell you it's all a load of bloody shit!' Lambert went on. 'Can you believe it—that tall one, the bastard, made a fool of me only three days ago in front of decent people! He stood there in front of me and shouted, "*Ohé, Lambert!*" just like that. Right in front of them! They all laughed because they knew I'd have to give them money to stop it! Just imagine that! I gave them money. Oh, they're shits! Can you believe it—he was an officer cadet in a regiment, educated, mind you, and then he got kicked out! He's been well brought up, from a good home—just imagine! He's got ideas, he could've . . . oh, hell! He's as strong as Hercules. He's got his uses—in a small way. But you can see— he doesn't wash his hands. I recommended him to one person, an elderly, titled lady, saying he was full of remorse, had a bad conscience, and wanted to kill himself. He went to see her, sat down, and . . . started whistling! And that other one, the good-looking one, he's a general's son. His family's ashamed of him. I saved him from going to court, I rescued him—and now look how he pays me back! There's not a decent one among them. They'll get it in the neck all right!'

'They knew my name. Did you tell them about me?'

'That was silly of me. Please, during dinner, sit there and watch out . . . There'll be one awful crook there. He's a really dreadful crook and as cunning as hell! They're all bastards here! There's not a single decent man among them! Well, when we're finished, then we'll . . . What d'you like to eat? It doesn't matter, they have good food there. I'll be paying, don't worry. It's nice that you're well dressed. I could let you have some money. Come and see me whenever you like. Just imagine, I gave them dinner here, good solid food every day. The watch he sold—that's the second time he's done that! That small one, Trishatov—you saw how Alphonsine couldn't even bear to look at him and wouldn't let him come near me—he suddenly says right here in the restaurant, with officers present, "I'd like pheasant." I gave him his pheasant! Oh, I'll get my own back, you'll see!'

456

'Do you remember, Lambert, how we drove to a tavern in Moscow and you stuck a fork into me and you had five hundred roubles with you?'

'Yes, I remember! Hell, of course I do! I like you . . . Just you remember that! No one else does, maybe, but I do! I'm the only one, just you remember . . . That chap who's coming here, he's pock-marked and he's the most devious bloody crook imaginable. Don't say anything if he starts talking and if he starts asking questions, tell him some nonsense or just keep mum . . .'

In his excitement he at least refrained from asking me anything during the journey. I even felt rather insulted he was so sure of me and did not even suspect I could be guilty of mistrust. It seemed to me he had the silly idea he could order me about as he always had done. It's a sign how badly brought up he is, I thought as I entered the restaurant.

III

I had previously been to that very restaurant on Sea Street during the drunken and debauched phase in my life and therefore the impression left by the rooms and the waiters who recognized at a glance I was a former customer and, finally, the impression created by the questionable company of Lambert's friends in which I found myself and to which I appeared inseparably to belong and, most of all, the dark foreboding that I was wilfully letting myself in for something unpleasant and would undoubtedly end up badly—all this suddenly pierced me to the quick. There was a moment when I was on the point of leaving, but the instant passed and I stayed.

The pock-marked acquaintance Lambert was so afraid of was already there. He was a little man with one of those silly, businessman's faces I have hated ever since boyood, about 45, of medium height, with greying hair, clean-shaven to the point of obscenity, and with small, carefully coiffured sideburns looking like small sausages on either side of an extraordinarily smooth and evil face. Of course, as is usual with all such mediocrities, he was boring, pompous, taciturn, and, for some reason, super-cilious. He eyed me closely but did not say a word and Lambert was silly enough, as he sat us down, not to introduce us, so that the man took me for one of Lambert's criminal fraternity. With the other two (who joined us almost immediately) he also had no conversation during the entire meal, but it was obvious he knew them well. He conversed only with Lambert, almost in a whisper, and it was Lambert who did most of the talking while the pock-marked chap did no more than deliver himself of curt, angry, and peremptory remarks. He maintained a haughty air, was sharp-tongued and sarcastic whereas Lambert, by contrast, was in a state of great excitement as he evidently tried to persuade the man to take part in some project of his.

At one point I reached out for a bottle of red wine and the pock-marked man suddenly picked up a bottle of sherry and offered it to me, not having said a word until then.

'Try this,' he said, holding out the bottle.

Suddenly I realized he must know everything about me—my past life, my name, and perhaps also the reasons for Lambert's interest in me. The idea that he should have taken me for someone who was working for Lambert once again made me wild, and Lambert's own face expressed the gravest and most idiotic concern the moment the man spoke to me. He took note of this and started to laugh.

Clearly, I thought, Lambert is dependent on the whole lot, and I loathed him at that moment with all my heart. Thus, although we were all sitting at the same table through the meal, we were divided into two groups: Lambert and the pock-marked man by the window, facing each other, and I next to the greasy, smelly Andreev with Trishatov opposite me. Lambert wanted the meal over quickly and continually urged the waiter to hurry. When the champagne was served, he suddenly held out his glass to me.

'To your health!' he said interrupting what he was saying to the pock-marked man.

'Will you allow me to join in?' said the good-looking Trishatov, stretching across the table with his glass. Before the arrival of the champagne he had been very pensive and silent. The *dadais* had not said a word, but had munched away silently.

'With pleasure,' I answered. We clinked glasses and drank.

'I'm not going to drink to your health,' the *dadais* said suddenly, turning to me, 'not because I wish you dead but because I don't think you should drink any more here today.' He spoke sombrely and portentously. 'Three glasses are enough for you. I've noticed', he went on, laying his hand out on the table for all to see, 'you've been looking at my dirty fist. I don't wash it and in its unwashed state I hire it out to Lambert to do his dirty work in knocking other people's heads together whenever things get tricky for him.' And, on saying this, he suddenly struck his fist on the table with such force all the plates and glasses jumped about.

Apart from ourselves there were four other tables in the restaurant with diners, all either officers or various gentlemen of dignified appearance. It was a fashionable place. There was instant silence and they all looked at us in our corner. I think we had already attracted a certain attention. Lambert went scarlet.

'Ah, he's at it again! I think I asked you to behave yourself, Nikolay Semyonovich,' he whispered at Andreev in a fury.

The latter gave him a long, slow look: 'I don't want my new friend Dolgorowky to drink a lot of wine here today.'

Lambert looked even more furious. The pock-marked man listened to it all in silence but with evident pleasure. Andreev's prank had taken his fancy. I alone failed to understand why I shouldn't have any more wine.

'He only does it to get more money! You'll get seven roubles after the meal, do you hear! Only just let us have our meal in peace without another scene!' Lambert hissed at him.

'Ho-ho!' bellowed the *dadais* triumphantly. This delighted the pock-marked man and he started giggling wickedly.

'Listen, don't get very . . .' Trishatov told his friend anxiously and almost compassionately, evidently wanting to restrain him. Andreev fell silent, but not for long. It wasn't what he had in mind.

Half-a-dozen steps from us were two diners sitting at a table engaged in lively conversation. They were both middle-aged men of eccentric appearance. One was tall and very stout, the other also very stout but small. They were talking in Polish about what was currently happening in Paris. The *dadais* had for some while been listening to them and giving them curious glances. The small Polish gentleman clearly seemed to him a figure of fun and he took an instant dislike to him on the example of all jaundiced and liverish people with whom this can happen suddenly without the least cause. Suddenly the small Polish gentleman uttered the name of the deputy Madier de Mangeot, but, as with a great many Poles, he pronounced it in the Polish fashion with the accent on the penultimate syllable and it came out not as Madier de Mangeot, but as Mádier de Mángeot.* That was all the *dadais* needed. He turned towards the two Poles, drew himself up straight, and suddenly, speaking distinctly and loudly as if he were posing a question, cried:

'Mádier de Mángeot?'

The Poles looked at him in fury.

'What do you want?' shouted the large stout Polish gentleman in Russian. The *dadais* paused before speaking.

'Mádier de Mángeot?' he repeated once more for the whole room to hear, without offering any explanation, just as he had suddenly approached me outside Lambert's room asking: 'Dolgorowky?' The Poles jumped to their feet as Lambert himself jumped up and pounced on Andreev, but, abandoning him, dashed to the Poles and began abjectly apologizing.

'They have clowns here, absolute clowns!' the small Pole repeated scornfully over and over as he went red as a beetroot with indignation. 'There'll be no point in coming here soon!'

The whole restaurant was in a turmoil with shouting and much laughter.

'Please leave! Come on, let's go!' muttered Lambert at his wits' end, trying somehow or other to get Andreev to leave the room. The latter, having peered searchingly at Lambert and reckoning he would now get his money, agreed to follow him out. Very probably he had used similar shameless tactics in the past for extracting money from Lambert. Trishatov was on the point of going after them, but glanced in my direction and stayed.

'Oh, how beastly!' he said, covering his eyes with his delicate little fingers.

'Very beastly, my dear sir,' muttered the pock-marked man under his breath, looking absolutely furious by now.

Meanwhile Lambert had returned, his face almost drained of colour, and began whispering something to him, gesticulating animatedly. The pock-marked one meantime ordered the waiter to serve coffee, listened offhandedly to the whisperings, and showed every sign of wanting to leave. The whole thing had been no more than a schoolboy prank. Trishatov brought his cup of coffee and sat down next to me.

'I'm very fond of him,' he began, speaking so openly it was as

460

if he had always been used to talking to me about such things. 'You can't believe how unfortunate Andreev is. He drank away his sister's dowry—indeed he drank away everything they had in that one year he was in the army and I can see he's suffering for it now. It's out of despair he doesn't wash. He's got terribly strange ideas. He'll suddenly tell you that honest men and crooks are one and the same and there's no difference. Then he'll say there's no need to do good or bad or it's one and the same, you can do good and bad, but best of all is to lie about in the same clothes for a whole month doing nothing but drinking and eating and sleeping. You'd hardly believe he's putting it on. You know I even think he's been playing up just now so as to be done with Lambert! He was talking about it yesterday. You wouldn't credit it but sometimes at night or when he's been sleeping a long time he starts crying, and when he cries, you know, he has his own way of crying, like nobody else—he starts howling, howling terribly, and that makes it sound all the worse, and he's so big and strong and suddenly there he is—just howling and howling! What a poor chap, eh? I've wanted to save him, but I, myself, I'm hopeless, I'm just a little boy lost, you wouldn't believe how rotten I am! Would you let me into your house, Dolgoruky, if I came to see you?'

'Oh, certainly. I even rather like you.'

'You do! Why? Well, thanks. Listen, we'll have another glass. What am I saying, though? You'd be better not to drink. He was right when he said you oughtn't to drink any more.' He winked meaningfully at me suddenly. 'Still, I will. I've got nothing to worry about now and I just can't stop myself, believe it or not. You see, you've just got to tell me not to eat out in restaurants any more and it's the one thing I'll really want to do. Oh, we sincerely want to be honest, I assure you, but we go on putting it off. "And the years go by, all the best years!" as the poet says.* What I'm terribly afraid is he'll hang himself. He'll go and do it without telling anyone. He's that sort of person. People are always hanging themselves nowadays. I don't know why. Perhaps there are a lot of people like us. For example, I cannot live without having a lot of money. It's more important for me to have a lot of money than just money for necessities. Listen, do you like music? I love it. I'll play you something when I come and see you. I can play the piano really well and studied it a long

461

time. I was serious about it. If I composed an opera, I'd choose Faust as my subject. I'm very fond of it. I go on creating the scene in the cathedral—just in my head, in my imagination, that's all. There's this Gothic cathedral, on the inside, and a choir singing a hymn and then in comes Gretchen, and you know from what the choir's singing that it's the fifteenth century. Gretchen sings a lament, a recitative, quiet but painful and heart-rending and the choir intones sombrely, sternly, dispassionately: "*Dies irae, dies illa!*"

'And suddenly the voice of the devil is heard singing his song. He is invisible, only his song is heard, rising up together with the hymns, almost part of them but still quite different—somehow or other I've got to get this right. The song is a long one, it goes on and on—it must be a tenor voice, absolutely must! It begins quietly, softly, with the words: "Do you remember, Gretchen, how when you were still innocent, still a child, you used to come to this cathedral with your mother and say your prayers from the old prayer book?" But the singing will grow stronger, more passionate, more strident, rising to higher notes resonant with tears and unending, tireless lamentation and, finally, despair as the voice declares: "There is no forgiveness, Gretchen, no forgiveness for you here!" Gretchen tries to pray, but all that is torn from her breast are cries—convulsive cries, you know, born of her tears—and the song of Satan goes on rising and penetrates ever deepr and more sharply into her soul and, rising still higher, suddenly ends with what is almost a shout: "All is over, you are accursed!"

'Gretchen falls on her knees, clasping her hands before her. Then comes her prayer, something very short, a semi-recitative, but simple, unadorned, something in the highest degree medieval, four lines, that's all—Stradelli* does it in just a few notes—and on the last note she collapses in a faint! Great confusion. She is lifted up and they begin carrying her off and suddenly the choir thunders forth, in a kind of thunderclap of voices, inspired, triumphant, overwhelming, something like our own "Angels uplift our Lord on high!" and everything is shaken to its foundations and ends in an ecstatic, exultant, universal shout of "Hosannah!" that resounds, as it were, through the universe and she is carried slowly off-stage as the curtain falls! You know, if I could, I'd do something like that! Now, though, I can't do a

462

thing. I just dream about it. I dream about it all the time. My whole life's been turned into a dream. I even dream about it at night. Dolgoruky, have you read Dickens's *The Old Curiosity Shop?*'

'Yes. What about it?'

'Do you remember . . . Just a moment, I'll have another glass . . . Do you remember the part near the end when that mad old man and the charming 13-year-old girl, his niece, after all their fantastic adventures, settle near some medieval Gothic cathedral somewhere in a remote part of England and the girl finds work for herself showing visitors round . . . And there's this moment as the sun goes down and the girl is standing outside the church drenched in the sun's last rays. She stands there and watches the sunset with a calm, pensive awareness in her childish soul, in a soul astonished by it as if it were some kind of enigma, because the two things do comprise an enigma—the sun as the idea of God and the cathedral as the idea of man—that's true, isn't it? Oh, I can't express it, except that God loves such first ideas of children . . . And there beside her on the steps is this mad old man, her grandfather, gazing at her fixedly . . . You know, there's nothing at all special about this picture Dickens paints for us, nothing at all, but you can never forget it, and it's been remembered all over Europe—why? Because it's beautiful! Because it's innocent!* Oh, I don't know what I mean, except it's marvellous! At school I read novels all the time. You know, I've got a sister at home, just a year older than me . . . Oh, but it's all sold up now, there's no home left! We used to sit on the terrace, under our old lime trees, and read that novel, and the sun used to go down and suddenly we'd stop reading and tell each other we'd also be kind people, we'd also be beautiful . . . I was getting ready to go to university . . . Oh, Dolgoruky, we all have our memories, don't we?'

And suddenly, letting his pretty head fall on my shoulder, he burst into tears. I felt terribly, terribly sorry for him. True, he had drunk a great deal of wine, but he had talked to me so sincerely, with such feeling, as if I were his brother . . . Suddenly, at that moment, a shout came from the street and strong fingertaps on the window (they were plate-glass, the windows on the ground floor, so one could tap on them from street level). It was Andreev.

'*Ohé, Lambert! Où est Lambert? As-tu vu Lambert?*' came his wild cry from the street.

'Oh, he's still there! Didn't he go away?' exclaimed my young friend, jumping up.

'The bill!' Lambert hissed at the waiter. His hands even shook with anger as he started counting out the money, but the pock-marked man did not allow him to pay for him.

'Why not? I was the one who invited you and you accepted my invitation, didn't you?'

'No, permit me . . .' The pock-marked man brought out his wallet and, totting up what he owed, paid separately.

'You're insulting me, Semyon Sidorych!'

'That's how I want it, sir!' snapped Semyon Sidorych and, picking up his hat, left the room without saying goodbye to anyone.

Lambert flung the money down for the waiter and he hurried out after him, forgetting about me in his confusion. Trishatov and I followed out after him. Andreev was standing solid as a signpost at the entrance waiting for Trishatov.

'Bastard!' Lambert could not refrain from shouting.

'Ho-ho!' Andreev shouted at him and with one swipe of his arm knocked his round hat off his head and it went rolling along the pavement. An undignified Lambert rushed to pick it up.

'*Vingt cinq roubles!*' cried Andreev, showing Trishatov the twenty-five-rouble note he had got from Lambert.

'That's enough!' Trishatov shouted at him. 'Why do you always make such a row? And why did you get twenty-five out of him? It should have been only seven.'

'Why? He promised dinner just for us, with Athenian beauties, but instead of women he served up that pock-marked man and, apart from that, I didn't have enough to eat and did at least eighteen roubles' worth of freezing out here in the street! That leaves seven roubles, which makes exactly twenty-five!'

'Go to hell, both of you!' yelled Lambert. 'I'll give the both of you what for, I'll bash in your ugly snouts . . .'

'Lambert, I'll give you what for, I'll bash in your ugly snout!' shouted Andreev. '*Adieu, mon prince*, and don't drink any more wine! Pete, my boy, quick march! *Ohé Lambert! Où est Lambert! As-tu vu Lambert?*' he roared out for the last time, walking off with huge strides.

464

'Can I come and see you? Can I?' Trishatov muttered at me in a great hurry as he rushed after his friend.

I was left alone with Lambert.

'Well, let's be off!' he said, finding some difficulty in catching his breath and even seeming a bit disorientated.

'Where to? I haven't got anywhere to go with you!' I shouted challengingly.

'Nowhere to go?' he said in a flustered, anxious way and then came to his senses. 'I've just been waiting for the moment when we can be alone!'

'So where to?' I confess I had a certain ringing in my head after three glasses of wine and two of sherry.

'In here—look!'

'You can see what it says—Fresh Oysters. And it smells foul . . .'

'That's because you've just had dinner. It's a Milyutin shop.* We won't have any oysters but I'll buy you some champagne . . .'

'I don't want any! You just want to get me drunk.'

'That's what they were saying. They were having you on. You don't want to believe those bastards!'

'Trishatov wasn't a bastard. Anyhow I know how to look after myself! I'll show you!'

'So you have a character of your own, have you?'

'Yes, I have a character of my own, a bigger one than yours, because you'll sell out to the first person who comes along. It was shameful the way you were so servile in apologizing to those Poles. What I'd like to know is, how many times have you been beaten up in places like that?'

'*Crétin*, we've got to talk, you and I!' he cried with the sort of impatience and loathing that seemed to say: You're as bad as the other two, aren't you? 'Are you frightened, is that it? Are you my friend or not?'

'I'm not your friend, and you're a crook. Let's go, simply so I can prove to you I'm not frightened of you! Oh, what a dreadful smell! It's like bad cheese! It's foul!'

CHAPTER VI

I

I HAVE to remind the reader that I had a ringing in my head. If it had not been for that, I would have spoken and behaved differently. Oysters were indeed available for eating in a back room of the shop and we took our seats at a little table covered with a foul-smelling, filthy table-cloth. Lambert ordered champagne. A glass full of cold wine the colour of gold was set in front of me and winked at me seductively. But I was in no mood for it.

'Look, Lambert, the main thing is I don't like the way you think you can boss me about now as you did at Touchard's when you yourself are being bossed about by everyone round here.'

'*Crétin!* Let's drink a toast!'

'You're not even trying, are you! You might at least try to pretend you don't want to get me drunk!'

'Don't talk nonsense, you're drunk already! Have some more and you'll be a lot happier! Pick up your glass, go on!'

'What's it got to do with 'picking up' my glass? I'm going and that's that.'

And I actually stood up. He was furious.

'It's Trishatov doing all that whispering about me in your ear! I saw you whispering! You're a cretin to believe all that. Alphonsine won't even let him near her. He's filth. I can tell you a thing or two about him.'

'You've already said that. For you everything's just Alphonsine. You're terribly narrow.'

'Narrow?' He was puzzled. 'They'll be off to the pock-marked man now, that's what! That's why I've got rid of them. They've got no loyalty. That pock-marked man's a crook and he'll corrupt them. I always insisted they behaved honourably.'

I sat down, picked up the glass automatically, and drank a mouthful.

'In education I'm way above you,' I said. But he was too glad I had rejoined him to notice and at once poured out more wine for me. 'But be honest, you're frightened of them, aren't you?' I went on, putting the knife in (and right then I was better at doing that than he was). 'Andreev knocked your hat off and you gave him twenty-five roubles for it!'

'I gave the money, but he'll pay me back. They're kicking up rough, but I'll do the dirty on them . . .'

'That pock-marked man gets you very worried. You know something, I think I'm all you've got left. You've pinned all your hopes on me—isn't that right?'

'Yes, Arkady, my boy, that's right—you're the one friend I've got left. You've got it absolutely right!' He slapped me on the shoulder.

There was nothing to be done with someone as thick as that. He was completely immature and took mockery for approval.

'You could help me out of a lot of difficulties if you'd be a good friend, Arkady,' he went on, gazing fondly at me.

'How?'

'You know how. Without me you're just a fool and bound to stay one, but I could get you thirty thousand and we'd split it fifty-fifty. You know how. Just take a look at yourself! You've got nothing now—no name, no status! Suddenly you'd be rich, and with money like that you'd be able to start on a real career for yourself!'

I was simply astonished at his way of putting it. I had made up my mind he would try a cunning approach, but here he was starting straight off talking to me just like a child. I decided to listen to what he had to say out of sheer broadmindedness— and, of course, out of terrible curiosity to know what he'd say.

'Look, Lambert, you won't understand this, but I'm ready to listen to you because I'm broadminded,' I announced firmly and again knocked back some wine. He replenished my glass.

'It's like this, Arkady—if someone like Björing had dared to swear at me and strike me in full view of a lady whom I worshipped I don't know what I might have done! But you just accepted it. I think you're disgusting. You're trash!'

'How dare you say Björing hit me!' I cried, going red. 'I hit him, he didn't hit me!'

'No, it was he hit you, not you him.'

'Rubbish! I stamped on his foot!'

'He knocked you aside and ordered his servants to drag you

467

away . . . and she sat there and saw it all from the carriage and laughed at you. She knows you have no real father and can be treated like dirt.'

'I don't know, Lambert, why we're having this schoolboy talk. I'm ashamed of it. You're doing it just to irritate me, and so crudely and brazenly, as if I were just a 16-year-old kid! You're in league with Anna Andreevna!' I screamed, quivering with anger and automatically having another drink.

'Anna Andreevna's a cow! She's having you on and me on and everyone else! I have waited for you because you'll be better at dealing with the other one . . .'

'What other one?'

'Madame Akhmakov. I know it all. You yourself told me she's frightened of that letter you have . . .'

'What letter? . . . It's all rubbish! . . . Have you seen her?' I muttered in confusion.

'I've seen her. She's very good-looking. *Très belle.* You've got taste.'

'I know you've seen her. But you haven't dared talk to her and I'd prefer you not to talk about her at all.'

'You're still a kid, that's what you are, and she makes fun of you, that's what! We had one fine lady like that in Moscow. Oh, she was stuck up! But the way she trembled when we threatened to tell everything and gave in at once! We took both—know what I mean? Money and the other thing. Now she's once again the inaccessible society lady—boy, you can't believe what a high-flyer she is, and what a carriage she's got, but if you'd just seen what went on in that back room of hers! You haven't lived if you've no idea what they get up to in their back rooms . . .'

'I have wondered,' I couldn't help muttering.

'They're corrupt to the tips of their fingers. You don't know what they're capable of! Alphonsine lived in a house like that and she loathed it.'

'I have thought about it,' I repeated.

'But *you* get knocked about and you don't do a thing . . .'

'Lambert, you're a bastard, a bloody bastard!' I screamed at him, suddenly aware what he meant and starting to tremble. 'I had a dream, you were standing there and Anna Andreevna . . . Oh, you're a bloody bastard! Did you really think I'd be as low as that? I dreamt it, so I literally knew you'd say something like

468

that. And, anyhow, it can't be as simple as all that if you're telling me all about it straight off!'

'Temper! Temper! Tee-hee-hee!' drawled Lambert, laughing and gloating. 'Well, Arkady, my friend, I know all I need to know. This is what I've been waiting for! Listen, you're in love with her and you want to get your own back on Björing—that's all I wanted to know. I suspected as much all the time I've been waiting for you. *Ceçi pose, çela change la question.* And so much the better, because she's in love with you. So get married, that's the best thing. Don't delay. You've got no choice. It's your surest bet. And, Arkady, don't forget, you've got a friend, it's me. You can saddle me up and rely on me. I'm the friend that'll help you and get you married. I'll move heaven and earth for you, Arkady, my boy! All you've got to do is give your old friend a measly little thirty thousand for all his efforts, eh? I'll help you, don't doubt it. I know all the ins and outs in affairs like this, and you'll get all the dowry and you'll be a rich man with good career prospects!'

Although my head was spinning, I stared at Lambert in astonishment. He was serious—not serious as a person, that is, but serious about the possibility of marrying me off. I saw that clearly, and he himself believed in it and even took up the idea enthusiastically. Naturally, I also saw he was getting me into his trap, manipulating me like a little boy (no doubt I saw this at the time too), but the idea of marrying her had got so under my skin that, though I was astonished how Lambert could believe in something so fantastic, I myself strove simultaneously to believe in it without for a moment losing sight of the fact that it could never possibly happen. Somehow all this blended together.

'That's just not possible, surely?' I gasped out.

'Why not? You show her the document, she gets in a panic and marries you so as not to lose the money.'

I was determined not to stop Lambert in his squalid schemes, because until then he had outlined them to me so frankly that he did not even suspect I could suddenly turn nasty. But I murmured something about not wanting a forced marriage. 'I don't want any force. How could you be so foul to suggest I would?'

'Hold your horses! She'd be the one to go for it! She'd be frightened, not you, and she'd go for it. She'd do it because she's in love with you,' Lambert conceded limply.

469

'Nonsense. You're having me on! How can you know she's in love with me?'

'There's no doubt. I know. Anna Andreevna says it too. Seriously, I'm telling you the truth: Anna Andreevna says the same thing. And in a moment, when you come to my place, I'll tell you something and you'll see she loves you. Alphonsine went out to Tsarskoe and there she learned about it as well . . .'

'What could she have found out there?'

'Come back with me. She can tell you herself and you'll be pleased to hear it. You're no worse than anyone else, are you? You're good-looking, well-educated . . .'

'Yes, I'm well-educated,' I muttered, hardly able to draw breath. My heart was pounding and not, of course, solely from the wine.

'You're good-looking. You're well-dressed.'

'Yes, I'm well-dressed.'

'And you're kind-hearted . . .'

'Yes, I'm kind-hearted.'

'So why shouldn't she agree? Björing won't want her without a dowry, but you could deprive her of the money—that's what she's afraid of. You marry her and you get your own back on Björing. After all, you yourself told me that night I rescued you from the frost that she was in love with you.'

'I said that? No, I didn't.'

'Yes, you did.'

'I was delirious. Did I really tell you about the document then?'

'Yes, you said you had the letter. That made me think—if he really has the letter, mightn't he lose what was rightfully his?'

'That's all fantasy and I'm not silly enough to believe it,' I muttered. 'Firstly, there's the age difference and, secondly, I've got no status.'

'It'll work out. It's bound to when there's so much money at stake. I'll fix it. What's more, she's in love with you. The old prince is very well disposed to you, you know, and through him you'll have the right connections. As for you not having any status, that means nothing nowadays because you'll have money—and you'll go on and on and in ten years you'll be such a millionaire all Russia will tremble at your name, so what'll be the point of having a title then? In Austria you can buy a baronetcy,

470

you know. So, once you're married, take her in hand. You've got to show 'em who's master. When a woman falls in love, she likes to be treated with a firm hand. Women like men with strong characters. Once you've given her a fright with that letter, just you show her how strong you are from that moment on. She'll say: "Oh, he may be young, but he's a man of real character."'

I sat there in a stupor. I would never have had such a silly conversation with anyone else. But there was something sickly and voluptuous about it that made me want to prolong it. What's more, Lambert was so silly and crude it didn't seem shameful.

'No, Lambert, you know something,' I suddenly said. 'Like it or not, this is a whole heap of rubbish. I've talked to you because we're friends and have nothing to hide. But I'd never have talked such absolute garbage with anyone else. Anyhow, the main thing is, why are you so sure she loves me? It's all right, what you've just said about money, but you know nothing about high society, you know. It's all dependent on the most patriarchal, the most familial relationships, so to speak, which means that as long as she knows nothing about my capabilities and what I might achieve in life she'll still be ashamed to show her feelings. But I won't hide from you, Lambert, that there really is one thing which offers hope. You see, she might marry me out of gratitude, because I would save her from the hatred of one particular man. And she's afraid of him, this particular man.'

'Ah, you're talking about your father, are you? Why, is he very fond of her?' Lambert suddenly showed intense curiosity.

'Of course not!' I cried. 'What a frightful person you are, and so stupid, Lambert! If he were in love with her, why should I want to marry her? I mean, a father and son after the same woman, that's disgusting! He loves my mother, her and no one else, and I've seen how he kisses her, and though I did myself think he was in love with Katerina Nikolaevna I now see clearly he could have loved her at one time but now he's been hating her for quite a while and would like to get his own back and she's really afraid of that because, I'm telling you, Lambert, he can be an absolute horror when he sets out to get his own back. He goes almost crazy. When he starts hating her, he'll stop at nothing. It's like hostilities used to be in the old days when principles were really at stake. Nowadays real principles don't matter a toss. Nowadays it's not a question of principles, it's just

471

private interests that matter. Oh, Lambert, you don't understand a thing because you can't see beyond your own nose! I talk to you about principles and you don't understand a thing! You're just terribly ignorant. Remember how you used to hit me? Well, I'm stronger than you now, did you know that?'

'Arkady, my boy, come back to my place! We'll spend the evening there and drink a bottle and Alphonsine'll sing and play on her guitar.'

'No. Listen, Lambert, I have my "Idea". If it doesn't work out and I don't get married, I'll turn to my "Idea". You haven't got an Idea.'

'All right, all right, you can tell me about it. Let's go.'

'No, I won't!' I stood up. 'I don't want to and I won't! I'll come and see you, but you're a crook. Maybe I'll give you thirty thousand, but I'll still be above you morally, I'll still be cleaner than you ... I can see you're out to get the better of me in everything. But I forbid you even to think about her, because she's worth more than all the others put together and your plans are such garbage I'm surprised at you, Lambert! Say I want to get married—that's another matter, but I won't need capital for that, I despise capital! I wouldn't take it if she offered me her capital on her bended knee ... Getting married—that's different. You were right about being firm with them. To love, love passionately, with all the selflessness of a man, of which a woman isn't capable, but also to play the despot—that's good. Because you know what, Lambert—women love despotism. Yes, you know women, Lambert. But you're astonishingly silly about everything else. And you know something, Lambert, you're not as foul as you think you are. You're just simple. I like you. Oh, Lambert, why are you such a bloody idiot? If you weren't we might get on well! You know, though, that Trishatov—he's a nice person.'

I blurted out all these last disconnected statements when I was already out on the street. Oh, I am recalling all these details so that the reader can see that, along with all my enthusiasms and oaths and promises to be better and make true nobility my goal, I could very easily have sunk at that moment into life's excrement! And I swear that if I were not entirely sure now that I am no longer the same person and have since beaten out for myself

472

a new character on the practical anvil of life, I would not have confessed this to the reader.

We left the shop and Lambert supported me by lightly putting his arm round me. Suddenly I glanced at him and saw almost exactly the same expression of intent, searching, terribly attentive, and extreme sobriety in his eyes as I had seen on the morning I had been frozen stiff and he had led me off towards a cab, his arm round me in the same way, and listened so carefully, with both eyes and ears, to my blurted, disconnected chatter. People who are drunk, but not drunk and incapable, can suddenly have instants of such complete sobriety.

'No way will I go to your place!' I pronounced firmly and clearly, giving him a mocking look and removing his arm.

'Come on, stop it! I'll get Alphonsine to make some tea.'

He was terribly sure I wouldn't escape from him. He hugged me to him and held me close as if I were something he had captured, and I was, of course, essential to him, particularly on that evening and being in such a state! The explanation will come later.

'No way!' I repeated. 'Cabbie!'

That moment up came a sleigh and I jumped into it.

'Where're you going? Hey, you!' screamed Lambert in a frightful panic, seizing me by my fur coat.

'Don't you dare!' I shouted. 'Leave me alone!' And at that moment the cabbie set his sleigh going and the fur coat was torn from Lambert's hands.

'You'll be coming regardless!' he screamed at me angrily.

'I'll come if I want to! It's my choice!' I called to him, looking back from the sleigh.

II

He did not pursue me because there happened to be no other cabbie about and I managed to slip out of sight. I travelled as far as the Haymarket and there alighted and sent the cabbie off. I was terribly keen to walk for a bit. I felt neither tired nor especially drunk, only very alert, as if from an access of strength, an unusual sense of readiness for anything and countless pleasant thoughts swarming in my head.

473

My heart beat strongly and solidly. I could hear each beat. And everything seemed delightful to me, everything seemed so airy and light. Walking past the sentry boxes in the Haymarket I felt a terrible urge to go up to the sentry and kiss him. It was a period of thaw, the square was smelly and full of black snow, but I was still delighted by it.

'I am now in Obukhov Prospect,' I thought, 'and in a moment I will turn left and go as far as the Semyonovsky Barracks and make a detour and it'll be lovely, absolutely lovely. My fur coat is open—so why isn't someone snatching it off me, where have all the muggers gone? They say the Haymarket's full of them. All right, let 'em snatch it! What's it to me? It's just property and "*La propriété—c'est le vol*". Anyhow, what nonsense that is and how lovely everything looks! It's lovely because it's thawing. What's the use of frost? Nobody needs it! It's just lovely to talk nonsense. What was that I said to Lambert about principles? I said there were no real principles nowadays and only private concerns mattered. I was lying, lying through my teeth! Deliberately, to make my point. A bit shameful, that, but it doesn't matter, I'll get by. Don't be ashamed of yourself, Arkady Makarovich, don't give yourself a bad time. Arkady Makarovich, I like you. I like you very much indeed, my young friend. It's just a pity you're such a . . . such a little idiot . . . and . . . and . . . Oh hell!'

I suddenly came to a stop and my whole heart was plunged into a state of rapture.

'God, what had he just said? He said she was in love with me. Oh, he's just a scoundrel, he said a whole load of rubbish simply to get me to spend the night with him! But maybe it wasn't rubbish. He said Anna Andreevna had also thought so . . . Nonsense! Nastasya Yegorovna was just spinning him a yarn— she has a finger in everything! And why didn't I drive off to his place? I'd have learned everything then. So! He's got a plan worked out, I could tell all that down to the last detail! It was the dream! Well done, Mr Lambert, except you're talking rubbish and it'll never happen. But maybe it will! Maybe it will! He can't really marry me off, can he? Maybe, maybe. He's naïve and he believes in it. He's stupid and he's daring like all business people. Stupidity and daring, once they're combined, are a great force. Admit it, Arkady Makarovich, you used to be frightened of Lambert! What do honest people mean to him? The serious way he says there's not a single honest man round here! And you yourself—who are you? Well, I'm honest! Scoundrels need honest men, don't they? In double-dealing they're more necessary than ever! Bully for you, Arkady Makarovich, that with your complete innocence you've finally reached that conclusion. Good God, though, is it really true? Can he get me married off?'

I once more stopped in my tracks. I must at this point confess to one stupid thing (because it is long since over and done with), I must confess that I had wanted to get married long ago—that is to say, I hadn't really wanted to and it would never have happened (and it *will* never happen, I give my word on that), but I had often before that dreamed how good it would be to be married—I thought about it terribly, terribly often, particularly before going to sleep at night. It began when I was 16. There was a boy in high school of my own age, Lavrovsky, such a nice, quiet, good-looking boy, though not outstanding in any other way. I had hardly ever spoken to him. One time we sat down beside each other and he was very thoughtful and suddenly said to me: 'Oh, Dolgoruky, what do you think, wouldn't it be nice to be married now? When if not now, eh? Now's the very best time—but it's absolutely impossible!' And he said it all so openly. And suddenly I agreed with him with all my heart, because I had thought the same thing. For several days we met and talked all about it, as our very own secret, and about nothing else. Then, I don't know why, we didn't see each other and stopped talking. That's when I began dreaming about it. There'd be no point, of course, in mentioning this if it weren't that I wanted to show how far back things can go . . .

I set off walking again, all the time day-dreaming: 'You see, there's only one serious objection. Oh, of course, the tiny difference in age won't be an obstacle, but what will be is the fact that she's an aristocrat and I'm just plain Dolgoruky! This is bloody awful—I mean, to think of Versilov, if he married mother, asking the government for permission to make me his legal son . . . on account of his services as a father, so to speak . . . I mean he did serve the government, because he did offer his services, he was an arbitrator . . . Oh, hell, how bloody awful!'

I suddenly spat this out and suddenly stopped in my tracks for a third time, feeling utterly crushed. All the painful sense of humiliation at realizing I could want such a shameful thing as a change of surname through being made legitimate, all the betrayal of my entire childhood—almost in an instant all this destroyed my earlier good humour and all my joy was blown away like smoke.

'No, I'll never mention this to anyone,' I thought, going terribly red. 'It's because I'm so humiliated I'm, well, I'm . . . in love and behaving stupidly. No, if Lambert's right about anything it's about the fact that all the foolish fuss and bother isn't necessary at all nowadays, but nowadays the chief thing is the man himself and his money. That's to say, not his money but his power. With all the capital she'll bring me I'll be able to hurl myself into my Idea and in ten years the whole of Russia'll tremble at my name and I'll get my own back on the whole lot. And there'll be no need to stand on ceremony with her, Lambert's quite right about that as well. She'll lose her nerve and take what's coming. In the simplest, crummiest way she'll agree and take what's coming. "You've no idea, no idea at all . . ."' I was reminded of Lambert's words '". . . what goes on in those back rooms!" And it's true,' I insisted to myself, 'Lambert's right about everything, a thousand times more correct than me or Versilov or all the idealists! He's a realist! She'll see I have a strong character and she'll say, "He's a man of character!" Lambert's an out-and-out scoundrel and all he wants is to get thirty thousand roubles off me and yet he's the only real friend I've got. There isn't any other kind of friendship and can't be! That's just the invention of a lot of impractical people. And I won't even be humiliating her, will I? No way! All women are like that, they can't exist without being a bit underhand! That's why a man's got to be in charge of her, because she's created to be submissive. A woman is all vice and enticement, a man all nobility and selflessness. That's how it'll always be. And the fact that I intend to make use of the so-called "document"—that doesn't mean a thing. That doesn't cast doubt on my nobility or my selflessness. Schillers in a pure state don't exist. They're an invention. If the aim's a truly fine one, it doesn't matter if you pick up a bit of dirt on the way! It'll all be lost in the wash; it'll all be ironed out. Right now it's all a matter of being broadminded, a matter of life itself, just the truth of life, as people say in our day and age!'

Oh, I'll say it again, please forgive me for recounting all this

476

drunken babble down to the last detail! Of course, it's only the essential core of what I was thinking, but I think I used those very words at the time. I had to recount them because I sat down to write these notes in order to be my own judge and jury. And what are the grounds for judging me if not that? Can there anything more serious in life than that? It wasn't the wine talking. *In vino veritas.*

Day-dreaming as I was, and being so absorbed in it, I had not noticed that I had finally reached home, the apartment, that is, where mother lived. I had not even noticed that I had stepped inside, but it was only as I reached our tiny hallway that I suddenly realized something extraordinary had happened. The rooms were filled with raised voices, people shouting and mother crying. In the doorway I was almost knocked off my feet by Lukerya who had come dashing from Makar Ivanovich's room towards the kitchen. I threw off my coat and went to Makar Ivanovich's because that was where everyone was.

Versilov and mother were standing there. Mother was in his arms and he pressed her to him. Makar Ivanovich was seated as usual on his little bench but in a kind of collapsed state of weakness, so that Liza was trying to hold him by the shoulders to prevent him from falling. It was clear he was leaning so far he would soon fall. I deliberately stepped closer, shuddered, and realized the old man was dead.

He had only just died a moment or so before my arrival. Ten minutes before he had been feeling normal. Only Liza had been with him then. She had been sitting in his room and telling him about her misery and he had stroked her head as he had the previous day. Suddenly (so Liza said) he had started shaking all over, had tried to get up and cry for help and without a word had started to fall on his left side. 'A heart attack!' was Versilov's verdict. Liza shouted loud enough for the whole house to hear and they had all rushed in—and it had all been just a moment before my arrival.

'Arkady,' cried Versilov, 'go and get Tatyana Pavlovna! She's bound to be home. Ask her to come at once. Take a cab. Quick as you can, please!'

I have a clear recollection how his eyes glittered. I did not see any sign of tears or pure pity on his face. It was only mother, Liza, and Lukerya who were in tears. On the contrary, I remember very well being struck by the extraordinary look of arousal on his face, amounting almost to excitement. I ran off to get Tatyana Pavlovna.

There was not far to go. I did not take a cab but ran the whole way without stopping. I was mentally confused and even also a bit excited. I realized something unique had happened. When I rang the bell to Tatyana Pavlovna's apartment, my drunkenness had vanished completely, down to the last drop, along with all the garbage I had been thinking.

The Finnish cook opened the door, shouted: 'Not at home!' and started shutting it.

'What d'you mean, not at home?' I forced my way into the hallway. 'That can't be right! Makar Ivanovich is dead!'

'Wha-a-at?' shrieked Tatyana Pavlovna's voice from the other side of her sitting-room door.

'He's dead! Makar Ivanovich is dead! Andrey Petrovich asks you to come at once!'

'Rubbish!' The key was turned in the lock, but the door opened only an inch. A voice said: 'So go on, tell me about it!'

'I don't know myself what happened, but I'd just got back and he was dead. Andrey Petrovich said it was a heart attack.'

'I'll come right away, this minute. Go and say I'll be coming. Go on, go on! What are you stopping for?'

But I had clearly seen through the partly opened door that someone had suddenly come from behind the curtain dividing Tatyana Pavlovna's bedroom from her sitting-room and was standing in the middle of the room behind Tatyana Pavlovna. Automatically and instinctively I seized the handle and would not let the door shut.

'Arkady Makarovich! Is it true he's dead?' resounded a familiar, calm, smooth, metallic voice which literally made my heart all at once quiver; and there seemed to be something in the question which pierced and excited *her* heart as well.

'If that's how it is,' cried Tatyana Pavlovna, suddenly throwing the door open, 'then you sort things out between you any way you like! It's up to you!'

She dashed headlong from the room, pulling on a scarf and fur jacket as she went, and rushed down the stairs. We were left by ourselves. I threw off my fur coat, stepped into the room and closed the door behind me. She stood there in front of me as

478

she had done at our other meeting, with a bright face and a bright look in her eyes, and, as she had done then, she held out her hands to me. I was so shaken I literally fell at her feet.

III

I've no idea why, but I began crying. I cannot remember how she managed to sit me down beside her. I can only remember, in a priceless recollection I have, how we sat there side by side, hand in hand, and talked busily, she asking me all about the old man and his death and I answering her, so that it might have been thought I was crying for Makar Ivanovich, when it was really the height of silliness on my part and I knew she would never have supposed me capable of such completely infantile behaviour. At last I suddenly broke down and felt ashamed. I assume now that I cried then solely from excitement and I think she was aware of this, so that I am quite calm now about remembering this.

It suddenly seemed very odd to me that she should be asking all these questions about Makar Ivanovich.

'Surely you never knew him, did you?' I asked in astonishment.

'Long ago. I never met him, but he also played a part in my life. I used to hear a lot about him at one time from the man I'm frightened of. You know who I mean.'

'All I know now is that "the man", as you call him, was much closer to your heart than you wanted to admit before,' I said, not knowing myself what I meant by this but frowning reproachfully.

'Did you say he'd just been kissing your mother and hugging her? You saw him doing this?' She went on asking me this without having heard what I said.

'Yes, I did. Believe me, it was all utterly sincere and open!' I was quick to assure her, seeing how pleased she was.

'Thank God!' She crossed herself. 'Now he is free. That marvellous old man did nothing but keep his life in bondage. With his death the idea of duty can revive in him again . . . and his sense of dignity, as it used to. Oh, that's what he is most of all—big-hearted. He'll be able to calm your mother's heart, whom he loves more than anyone on earth, and then he'll calm his own—not before time, thank God!'

'Is he very precious to you?'

'Yes, but not in the sense he would like or you're asking.'

'Are you frightened now for yourself or of him?' I asked suddenly.

'Oh, it's so difficult to know. Let's leave that.'

'Of course, we'll leave it. It's just that I knew nothing about this, about far too much, perhaps. But suppose you're right and everything'll be new from now on, then the first one to be renewed will be me. In my thoughts, Katerina Nikolaevna, I'm way below you, and maybe only an hour ago I also did something mean and nasty against you, but, you know, I am sitting here beside you now and I don't feel any pangs of conscience. Because all that's vanished and everything's new from now on, and that man who was planning something mean and nasty against you only an hour ago is someone I don't know and don't want to know!'

'Wake up!' She gave a smile. 'You're talking as if you're delirious.'

'And can I really judge myself beside you?' I went on. 'Whether I'm good or bad, you're still like the sun, unattainable ... Tell me, how could you want to see me after all that's happened? Especially if you only knew what had occurred only an hour ago—and my dream and all!'

'Probably I know everything.' She smiled calmly. 'You wanted to get your own back on me, you swore to ruin me. Yet you'd very likely have killed or beaten up anyone who so much as dared to say anything bad about me!'

Oh, she was smiling and poking fun at me then! But it was only due to her extreme goodness, because her entire heart at that moment, as I guessed later, was full of her own enormous worries and of such a strong and powerful feeling that she could only talk to me and respond to my silly, irritating questions by treating me as a little boy who would go on nagging and needed to be told something to be made to shut up. I suddenly realized this and felt ashamed I hadn't shut up.

'No,' I cried, unable to control my feelings, 'no, I wouldn't have killed anyone who said something bad about you, I'd have helped him!'

'Oh, for God's sake, there's no need, none at all, to tell me things like that!'

480

She stretched out her hand to stop me, even with a look of suffering on her face, but I had already jumped up and stood in front of her with the intention of telling her everything and, if I had done, none of what happened later would have happened, because it would certainly have ended with my confessing everything and returning her the document. But she suddenly burst out laughing:

'Nothing, no details! I know all the things you've done wrong. I bet you've wanted to marry me, or something like that, and just been plotting with one of your helpers, one of your former schoolfriends . . . Ah, I see I'm right!' she cried, peering seriously into my face.

'How . . . how did you know?' I muttered like an idiot, absolutely appalled.

'You see, I'm right! But enough of that! I forgive you, only don't say any more about it!' She again gave a wave of her hand, evidently impatient. 'I'm a dreamer myself, and if only you just knew the lengths I go to in my dreams sometimes when I really let myself go! Anyhow enough of that, you're putting me off! I'm very glad Tatyana Pavlovna's gone. I wanted very much to see you and with her here we wouldn't have been able to talk as we are doing now. I think I'm to blame for what happened that time, aren't I? That's true, isn't it?'

'You? But that time I betrayed you to *him*—what you must have thought of me! I've been thinking about this the whole time, day after day, every moment of the day ever since, thinking it, feeling it over and over.' (And this was no lie.)

'There wasn't any need, I understood only too well why it happened. It was simply that you blurted out to him then, in sheer joy, that you were in love with me and that I . . . well, that I didn't object. It was because you were 20 years old. You love him more than anyone in the world, don't you, and you want him to be your friend, your ideal? I understood that only too well, but it was already too late. Oh, yes, I was to blame for what happened, because I should have asked you to come and see me then and should have reassured you, but I was in a bad mood and told them to say I wasn't at home! That's why there was that scene at the entrance and then that night. You know, just like you, I spent the whole time wondering how I could see you

481

without anyone knowing, only I didn't know how to arrange it. And do you know what I was most frightened of? That you'd believe the things he said about me.'

'Never!' I cried.

'I value the times we met before. It's the boy in you I find precious and even perhaps your very innocence . . . After all, I'm a very serious person. I'm the most serious and concerned kind of modern woman, you should know that . . . Ha-ha-ha! We'll talk about that later, but now I'm not quite myself, I'm all excited and . . . and I think I may be a bit hysterical. But at long last, at long last, *he*'ll now give me a chance to live my own life!'

This declaration broke from her unintentionally. I realized this at once and did not want to show I did, but I began quivering all over.

'She knows I've forgiven him!' she suddenly cried out once more as if to herself.

'You mean you could forgive him that letter? And how on earth could he know you'd forgiven him?' I exclaimed, no longer holding back.

'How? Oh, he knows,' she answered, but as if she had forgotten about me and was still talking to herself. 'He's come to his senses now. Anyhow, how could he fail to know I've forgiven him when he knows my heart inside out? After all, he knows I'm a bit like him.'

'You are?'

'Yes, and he knows it. Oh, I'm not a passionate woman, I'm calm and collected. But, like him, I'd also like everyone to be good . . . After all, he must have had some reason for falling in love with me.'

'Then why did he say you have every known vice?'

'He simply said that for fun. He has another secret of his own. Don't you agree it was a terribly funny letter he wrote?'

'Funny?!' (I was all ears and I suppose she was genuinely a bit hysterical and saying it all not for my benefit, perhaps, but I couldn't refrain from asking.)

'Funny, yes, and I'd have laughed if I . . . if I hadn't been so frightened. Still, I'm not really a coward, you mustn't think that, but I didn't sleep for a whole night after I got that letter. It was written in such bad blood . . . And what is there left after you've had a letter like that? I love life, I'm terribly frightened for my life, I'm just terribly feeble about it . . . Oh, listen!' She suddenly shot the words at me. 'Please go and see him! He's by himself now and he can't be there the whole time and he's bound to have gone out somewhere. Find him just as soon as you can, as soon as you can, run after him, show him what a loving son you are, prove to him you're a nice, kind boy, my very own student, whom I . . . Oh, God be with you! I don't love anyone, which is so much the better, but I give everyone my good wishes, everyone, and him first of all, and he ought to know about this . . . just as soon as possible, I'd love that!'

She stood up and suddenly disappeared behind the curtain. At that moment her face shone with tears—tears of hysteria remaining from her laughter. I was left by myself, in a state of high excitement and confusion. I positively had no idea what to attribute her outburst to and I had never suspected her capable of it. I felt something squeezed tight in my heart.

I remained there five minutes, then ten minutes. The profound silence suddenly astonished me. I decided take a look through the door and call someone. In answer to my voice Marya appeared and announced with the utmost composure that the young lady had long ago put on her clothes and gone down the back stairs.

CHAPTER VII

I

THAT was all I needed. I seized my fur coat and, throwing it over my shoulders as I went, dashed out of the house, thinking: 'She's ordered me to find him but where'll that be?'

Apart from anything else, I was struck by the question: 'Why does she think that something has now come up and *he* will now leave her in peace? Of course, because he will now marry mother, but what about her? Is she delighted he will marry mother or, on the contrary, saddened by it? Is that why she was so hysterical? Why can't I make up my mind?'

I give these thoughts literally as they occurred to me then in order to remember them, because they're important. This was to prove a memorable evening. And, believe it or not, that's what it should be called, because I had scarcely taken a hundred steps in the direction of mother's house when I bumped into the very person I was looking for. He seized me by the shoulder and stopped me.

'So it's you!' he exclaimed good-humouredly but, at the same time, in the greatest surprise. 'Imagine, I've just been to your room,' he said quickly, 'looking for you and asking about you. You're just the person I want to see, the only one in the whole universe! Your landlord told me an awful rigmarole. But you weren't there and I left without even remembering to leave word that you should get in touch. And now what? I was just strolling along absolutely certain fate wouldn't send you to me now when I most needed you and here you are, the first person I meet! Let's go to my place. You've never been to my place before.'

In short, we had both been looking for each other and the same thing had happened to each of us. We set off in a great hurry. On the way he muttered a few short remarks about leaving mother with Tatyana Pavlovna, and so on, and so forth. He led the way, holding me by the arm. He did not live far away and we soon reached his place. I had in fact never been there. It was a small apartment of three rooms which he had rented (or, more truthfully, Tatyana Pavlovna had rented) solely for the so-called 'babe in arms'. Tatyana Pavlovna had always looked after the apartment even before this and the baby had been settled here with its nurse (who was now Nastasya Yegorovna), but a room had been kept for Versilov, namely the principal one, at the entrance, a fairly spacious and comfortable, well-furnished room much like a study designed for reading and writing. Indeed, the table, cupboard, and shelves were full of books (there were almost none at mother's). There were also sheets of paper covered with writing and letters tied up in packets—in a word, it had a thoroughly lived-in look, and I know Versilov had formerly been used to moving in (though not very often) and spending weeks at a time here.

The first thing that caught my attention was a portrait of mother hanging above the writing-desk in a magnificent frame carved from rare wood—it was a photograph, done abroad of course and, judging by its unusual size, very expensive. I had never heard or known anything about this photograph before and what struck me most of all was the extraordinary likeness caught by the photograph, a spiritual likeness, so to speak, as if it were a real portrait from the hand of an artist and not a machine-made replica. As soon as I entered I stood stock still in front of it.

'It's her, isn't it? It's her?' Versilov suddenly repeated over my shoulder.

He meant: 'Doesn't it look like her?' I glanced behind me and was amazed by the look on his face. It was a little pale, but the fierce, intent look in his eyes glowed with happiness and strength. I had never seen such a look on his face before.

'I didn't know you loved mother so much!' I came out with suddenly in my excitement.

He gave a blissful smile, although there was also something compassionate or—better—something humane, something loftier reflected in it ... I can't express it properly. But I think highly developed people can never have happy faces in a triumphalist, victorious sense. Without saying a word to me in response, he took the portrait from where it was hanging with both hands, brought it close to him, kissed it, and then calmly replaced it on the wall.

'You know,' he said, 'photographs are only very rarely good likenesses, and one knows why. It's because the original, I mean each one of us, is only very rarely a good likeness of himself. Only at rare moments does a human face express its chief feature, its most characteristic idea. An artist can study a face and gauge its main idea, though at the moment he copies it it might not be on the face at all. A photograph captures a person as he is at one moment, and it's very likely that Napoleon at such a moment could appear stupid and Bismarck kindly. In this particular portrait the sun deliberately seemed to catch Sonya at the moment when her chief feature was visible, her shy, timid love and her rather challenging. fearful chastity. Oh, how pleased she was when she was finally convinced I really wanted to have a portrait of her! This photograph was not taken long ago and she was younger and better looking then and yet she still had those sunken cheeks, those wrinkles on her temples and that timid shyness in her eyes which has grown more marked with the years. You may not be able to believe it, dear boy, but now I can hardly think of her with a different face and yet there was a time when she was young and charming! Russian woman lose their looks very quickly, their beauty is gone in a flash, and it's not because of any ethnographic characteristics of their type but because they know how to love so devotedly. A Russian woman gives her all when she falls in love—her immediate life, her destiny, her present and future because she can't economize, can't think of putting anything by and her beauty quickly goes into whoever she loves. Those sunken cheeks are the beauty that has gone into me, into giving me a bit of pleasure. You're pleased that I love your mother and didn't even believe, perhaps, that I loved her, eh? Yes, dear boy, I loved her very much, yet I've caused her nothing but grief . . . Here's another portrait. Take a look at it.'

He picked it up from the table and gave it to me. It was also a photograph, very much smaller, in a delicate oval wooden frame—the face of a girl, thin and consumptive yet, despite that, beautiful, a pensive face and at the same time oddly devoid of ideas. The features were regular, of a type cosseted over many generations, but leaving an unhealthy impression, as if it were a case of a person suddenly seized by some fixed idea which was tormenting for the very reason that it was beyond the power of that person to comprehend it.

'It's . . . it's the girl you wanted to marry, the one who died of consumption, *her* stepdaughter, isn't it?' I said a little unsurely.

'Yes, I wanted to marry her, she did die of consumption, and it is *her* stepdaughter. I knew you'd know all the, er, gossip. The point is, apart from gossip, you probably don't know anything. Leave the portrait alone, there's a good chap. It's a poor mad girl and that's all.'

'Was she quite mad?'

'Either that or just an idiot. I think she was mad. She had a baby by Prince Sergey Petrovich, not out of love, but because she was crazy. It's one of the meanest things Sergey Petrovich ever did. The baby's here now, in the other room, and I've long wanted to let you see it. Prince Sergey Petrovich never dared come here and see it. That was the bargain we struck when we were abroad. I took charge of the baby, with your mother's permission. It was also with your mother's permission that I intended to marry the . . . the poor, unfortunate girl.'

'Surely she wouldn't have given it?' I said fiercely.

'Oh, yes she would! She'd have been jealous if it had been a woman, but this wasn't a woman.'

'Maybe for everyone else, but not for mother! I just don't believe mother wouldn't have been jealous!' I cried.

'And you'd be right. I realized that much when it was all over, when she gave her permission, that's to say. Let's leave it. The matter wasn't settled even with Lydia's death, and probably wouldn't have been had she lived, but even now I won't let mother see the baby. It's just one of those things. My dear boy, I've so long wanted to see you here. I've long dreamed of having you here. Have you any idea how long? Two whole years.'

He glanced at me sincerely and frankly, with heartfelt devotion. I seized him by the hand:

'Why so long? Why didn't you invite me long ago? If only you knew what's happened . . . and wouldn't have happened if you'd only asked me long ago!'

At that moment the samovar was brought in, and Nastasya Yegorovna brought in the baby, who was asleep.

'Just take a look!' said Versilov. 'I love the baby and made a point of asking it should be brought in now so you could take a look. All right, Nastasya Yegorovna, you can take him away again. Do sit down near the samovar, dear boy. I will try to imagine that you and I have always lived together and are inseparable enough to sit down together each evening. Let me look at you. Sit so I can see your face. How I love it, your face! I used to imagine your face and how you looked even when I was still waiting for you to come from Moscow! You were asking why I hadn't invited you here long ago. Give me a moment and maybe you'll understand.'

'Surely it's not just the old man's death that makes you talk like this now, is it? It's strange if it is . . .'

But even if this is what I said I still looked at him with love. We were talking like two friends, in the fullest and noblest sense of the word. He had brought me here to explain something to me, tell me something, justify himself to me, but before a word needed to be said everything was already clarified and justified. No matter what I might hear from him now, the right result had been achieved and we were both happy to know this and we looked at each other in precisely that way.

'It wasn't just the old man's death,' he answered, 'not just his death . . . Something else had just now struck the right note. May God bless this very moment and our life together, from now on and forever! Dear boy, let's have a talk. I've all the time been thrashing about, indulging myself, wanting to talk just about the one thing and shooting off into a thousand irrelevant details. It always happens like that when one's heart is full. But let's have a talk. The time has come . . . I've long been in love with you, dear boy . . .'

He leaned himself back in his armchair and once more surveyed me.

'How strange that sounds! How strange it is hearing you say it!' I repeated, breathless from excitement.

And then I remember that the usual furrow suddenly appeared on his face, a furrow seemingly combining sorrow and mockery and so familiar to me. He pulled himself together and with some effort began speaking.

II

'It's like this, Arkady—if I'd invited you here earlier, what would I have had to say to you? That question contains my whole answer.'

'You mean you're now mother's husband and my father but then you'd have been . . . You didn't know what to say to me on account of the social position, is that it?'

'That wasn't the only thing, dear boy, I couldn't talk about. I'd have had to have said nothing about lots of things. Much even so silly and humiliating it would have been like having to conjure it out of sight—yes, like a conjuror in a fairground sideshow! I mean, how could we have understood each other earlier, when it was only today I began to understand myself—only today, at five o'clock in the afternoon, exactly a couple of hours before Makar Ivanovich died! You're giving me an unpleasantly bewildered look, aren't you? Don't worry, I'll explain. But what I've just said is absolutely true—all my life has been so full of travels and quandaries and suddenly there's been a solution to them all on such-and-such a date at five o'clock in the afternoon! It makes you sick, doesn't it. Not so long ago I'd have taken it as a bloody insult!'

I really was listening to it all with painful bewilderment. The furrow on Versilov's face was now more marked than ever and it was something I hadn't wanted to see that evening after what had already been said. Suddenly I exclaimed:

'My God! You received something from her, was that it? At five o'clock today?'

He glanced at me intently and was evidently astonished at my exclamation, and perhaps also that I had said: 'from her'.

'You'll learn all about it,' he said with a thoughtful smile. 'And of course, so far as necessary, I won't hide anything from you, because that's why I brought you here. But let's leave all that for the time being. You see, my boy, I've long been aware there are children who've been consumed by thoughts of their family from childhood on and feel deeply offended by the lack of true nobility in their fathers and in their circumstances. During my own schooldays I noticed such deeply thoughtful children and I decided then it was all due to the fact that they'd become envious too soon for their own good. Still, I was myself one of them . . . Forgive me, dear boy, my thoughts are all muddled. I simply wanted to say how constantly worried I was here on your behalf almost the whole time. I always imagined you one of those small but lonely boys who was very conscious of being particularly gifted. I also, like you, was never fond of my classmates. It's a bad thing when boys are left to their own devices and dreams if they have a passionate, too precocious, and almost vengeful thirst for true nobility—and I mean precisely that: "vengeful". But enough of that, dear boy, I've again strayed from the point . . . Even before I began to love you I would imagine to myself you and your isolated, untutored day-dreaming . . . Enough, enough, I've even forgotten what I was going to say! Still, it all needed saying. But what on earth could I have said to you earlier? Now I see you looking at me and I know it's my *son* looking at me— and yet just yesterday I couldn't be sure I'd ever sit down like today and talk to my own boy!'

He had really become very distracted and, at the same time, very touched by something.

'I don't need day-dreams any more, I have you now! I'll be going with you!' I cried, giving myself to him heart and soul.

'With me? But all my wanderings have stopped this very day! You're too late, dear boy! Today has seen the finale and the curtain has come down. It's been a long final act. It began a very long time ago—when I last went abroad. I threw up everything then. It was then I broke with your mother—you've got to know this, dear boy—and I told her. You must know this. I explained to her then I was going away for good and she wouldn't see me again. The worst thing was I forgot to leave her any money. And I didn't give you a moment's thought. I left with the intention of remaining in Europe, dear boy, and never returning. I was emigrating.'

'To see Herzen, you mean? To take part in overseas propaganda?* I imagine you've spent your whole life taking part in various plots, haven't you?' I cried, unable to contain myself.

'No, my boy, I never took part in any plot. But I saw your eyes shine when you said it. I love these exclamations of yours, dear boy! No, I left simply out of nostalgia, a sudden nostalgia. It was the nostalgia only felt by a Russian nobleman—true, I can't put it any better than that! A nobility nostalgia and nothing else.'

'Was it to do with serfdom . . . the emancipation of the peasantry?' I gasped.

'Serfdom? You think I was nostalgic for the return of serfdom? That I couldn't stand the idea of the Emancipation? Oh, no, dear boy, it was *we*, after all, who were the liberators. I was emigrating without ill feeling at all. I had only just been an arbitrator and done the best I could for the peasants. I'd done it all selflessly and I didn't even leave because I'd received so little recognition for my liberalism. We none of us—people like me, I mean—got anything out of it. I left in a spirit of pride rather than regret and, believe you me, very far from thinking that the time had come for me to end up my life simply cobbling shoes! *Je suis gentilhomme avant tout et je mourrai gentilhomme!* I am a gentleman and I'll die a gentleman. But I still felt sad. In Russia there are perhaps about a thousand people of my sort. Certainly maybe no more, but that's quite enough to ensure the survival of an idea. Dear boy, we are bearers of an idea! . . . I am talking, my dear chap, in the strange hope you'll understand this whole rigmarole of mine. I brought you here on a heartfelt whim because, you see, I've long dreamed of telling you something—you and no one else! Still . . . still . . .'

'No, go on!' I cried. 'I can see how sincerely you mean it! What was it—did Europe revive you then? And what was this "nobility nostalgia" you mentioned? Forgive me, dad, I just don't get it!'

'Did Europe revive me? No, I went there to bury it!'

'Bury it?' I cried in astonishment.

He gave a smile.

'Arkady, my friend, I was moved in spirit and my soul was restless. I will never forget my first impressions of Europe at that time. I had lived in Europe before, but this time it was special and I had never gone there before in such a spirit of joylessness and sadness . . . and yet with such love. I will tell you one of my first memories, a dream I had then, a real dream. It occurred while I was still in Germany. I had just left Dresden and in my confusion I did not get off at the station where I should have changed trains and found myself on a branch line. I was told to get off the train immediately. It was three o'clock in the afternoon, the day was bright and I was in a small German town. I was shown the way to the hotel. The next train did not arrive until eleven at night, so I just had to wait. I was even quite happy about this because I wasn't in a hurry. I was just wandering from place to place, dear boy, just wandering. The hotel was small and worthless, but surrounded by greenery and flower-beds as is always the case in Germany. I was given a small room and, because I'd spent the whole night travelling, I fell asleep after having had lunch, at about four o'clock.

'I dreamt a completely unexpected dream because I had never had one like it before. In Dresden, in the art gallery, there is a picture by Claude Lorraine, described in the catalogue as *Acis and Galatea* but I always gave it the title *The Golden Age* for some reason.* I had seen it before and noticed it again this time, three days before. It was this picture I dreamed about, though not as a picture but as if it were a kind of myth. I don't really know what the dream was about. It was just as it was in the picture—somewhere in a Grecian archipelago as it must have been three thousand years ago with gently lapping, blue waves and islands and cliffs and colourful coastline, a magical panorama in the distance with an inviting sunset—words can't really convey it. It was a reminder of the cradle of European humanity, and that very idea filled my heart with a loving fellow feeling. Here was humanity's paradise on earth, the place where gods would come down from heaven and become as one with men ... Oh, here lived a beautiful people! They would rise and go to sleep happy and innocent. The woods and meadows would ring with their songs and happy cries. A great abundance of untapped energy would go on love and simple, unpretentious joys. The sun would pour down its heat and light upon them, delighting in the sight of its beautiful children ...

'A wonderful dream, humanity's visionary error of judgement! The Golden Age was the most implausible dream of all, but one for which people would give up their lives and all their strength, for which prophets would die and be killed, without which nations had no desire to live and yet couldn't bear to die! And it was all this I experienced in my dream. The cliffs and the sea and the oblique rays of the setting sun—I could see them all even after I had woken up and opened my eyes which were literally wet with tears. I remember I was elated. A sensation of happiness such as I had never known before filled my heart till it ached. It was a love for all humanity. By that time it was already evening. In the window of my little room, through the green leaves of the flowers on the window-sill, there broke a cluster of slanting rays and they doused me with light. And then you see, dear boy, the setting sun of the first day of European humanity which I had seen in my dream was instantly transformed for me when I woke up into the setting sun of the last day of European humanity!

'It was a time when the tolling of a funeral bell could be heard particularly loudly all over Europe. I am not only referring to the war and the Tuileries.* Regardless of that I knew everything would pass away, the whole face of the old European world, sooner or later. But as a Russian European I could not admit it. Yes, it was just when the Tuileries had been burned down ... Oh, don't worry, I knew it was "logical" and understood only too well how irresistible the current ideas were, but as a representative of the highest Russian culture and thought I could not admit it, because Russian thought is concerned with reconciling ideas. And who was there in the whole world at that time capable of thinking like that? I was travelling quite by myself. I am not talking personally about myself, I am talking about Russian thought in general. Invective and logic were all that mattered there. The French were simply being French, the Germans

492

German and with far greater intensity than ever before in history. No Frenchman had ever done more to damage France or German more to damage Germany than at that time! There wasn't a single European left at such a moment! I alone among all the fire-bugs could have told them to their faces that firing the Tuileries was a mistake. I alone among all the conservative reactionaries could have told those bent on revenge that what happened at the Tuileries, though a crime, was still logical. And that was because, my boy, as a Russian, I was *the only European* in Europe at that time. I am not talking about myself, I am talking about Russian thought. I was wandering, dear boy, travelling by myself and I knew for sure I had to hold my tongue and just go on travelling. But I still felt sad. I cannot, my boy, give up my respect for my own Russian nobility. I think you're laughing, aren't you?'

'No, I'm not laughing,' I said in a voice full of emotion. 'I am not laughing at all! You have shaken me to the core with your vision of a golden age and—don't worry—I think I'm beginning to understand you. But what pleases me most of all is your respect for who you are. I want to be the first to tell you so. I'd never expected that of you!'

'I've already told you I like the way you make such exclamations,' he said, smiling again at my naïve remark and, after rising from his chair, began walking to and fro about the room without noticing he was doing so. I also stood up. He went on talking in his strange way, but saying things of the greatest intellectual profundity.

III

'Yes, my boy, I say again, I cannot give up my respect for my own Russian nobility. Over the centuries we have created a higher cultural type, hitherto unseen elsewhere and unique throughout the world—a type concerned for the universal suffering of all men. It is a Russian type, but because it is contained within the higher cultural layer of the Russian people I have the honour to belong to it. It preserves within it the future of Russia. Maybe there are only a thousand of us—perhaps more, perhaps less—but so far Russia has only existed in order to produce these thousand people. It will be said that's far too few. There will be complaints that far too many centuries and far too many millions of lives have been sacrificed to produce these thousand people. In my opinion, it's not too few.'

I listened with fierce intensity. There was emerging a conviction and a sense of direction for a whole life. The 'thousand people' he referred to made him stand out in such sharp relief! I felt that his expansiveness towards me was due to some external shock he had received. He was speaking to me so fervently, evidently out of love for me, but the reason why he had started so suddenly and had wanted to speak only to me remained a mystery.

'I was emigrating,' he went on, 'and I left no regrets behind me. I had done everything I could for Russia so long as I was there and, having left, I still went on serving her, except in a broader sense. But, serving her in that way, I did a great deal more for her than if I had been simply a Russian, in the way that a Frenchman of those days was simply a Frenchman, or a German a German. This is something they haven't yet grasped in Europe. Europe has created noble types of Frenchman, Englishman, and German, but it has hardly any idea what its future type of man will be. And I don't think it wants to have any idea. Quite understandably, because they're not really free, whereas we are. I was the only man in Europe, with all my Russian capacity for nostalgia, who was truly free at that time.

'Take note, my friend, of this odd thing: every Frenchman can serve not only France, but even humanity as well, solely on condition that he remains first and foremost French. The same is true of an Englishman and a German. Only a Russian, even in our time—a good deal sooner, that is, than any final estimates will be made—has acquired the capacity to become first and foremost Russian the more European he becomes. This is our most fundamental national difference from all others, and it is ours as it is no one else's. In France I am a Frenchman, with a German I am a German, with an ancient Greek a Greek, and yet I am first and foremost Russian. In this way I am being truly Russian and serve the cause of Russia first and foremost, because I am exhibiting her principal idea. I am a pioneer of this idea. I emigrated from Russia then, but did I stop serving my country? No, I went on being of service. Maybe I did nothing in Europe, maybe I went there simply to go travelling (and I knew that was all I was doing), but all that mattered was that I went travelling there aware that I epitomized an idea.

'I took with me my Russian nostalgia. Oh, it wasn't just the bloodshed of those times that appalled me, and not even the Tuileries, but all the consequences! They're bound to go on fighting among themselves because they're still far too German and far too French and they haven't yet stopped playing out their roles. I never cease to regret the damage done. Europe is just as dear to a Russian as is Russia, because every stone is precious and priceless. Europe has been just as much of a fatherland to us as Russia. Oh, more so! No one can love Russia more than I do, but I never reproached myself for feeling that Venice, Rome, and Paris, and all the treasures of their science and art, all their history, were more precious than Russia. Oh, for Russians all those old foreign stones, all the wonders of a divine ancient world, all the relics of holy miracles are precious, and even more precious to us than to those who live there! They are now occupied by other ideas and other feelings and they have ceased to cherish their old stones ... All the conservatives over there are concerned with is struggling to survive, and the arsonists and bomb-throwers merely demand their right to something to eat. It is only Russia that lives not for itself, but for an idea, and you must agree, my friend, it's a significant fact that for almost a hundred years now Russia has really not been living for herself at all, but solely for Europe! And the people of Europe? Oh, they are doomed to experience terrible torments before they attain the Kingdom of God!'

I admit I listened in great confusion. The tone of his voice even alarmed me, although I couldn't help being struck by his ideas. I was painfully frightened of any falseness. Suddenly I remarked to him in a stern voice:

'You've just mentioned "the Kingdom of God". Didn't I hear you'd preached a belief in God then and worn chains?'

'Forget about my chains!' he smiled. 'That's another matter. I didn't preach anything then, but I felt sorry for their God, that's true. Atheism had been announced then ... by one group only, but—no matter—they were the front runners. The important thing was that it was the first real step in that direction. Again it was part of their logic, and yet every logic has some anguish in it. I was of a different culture and my heart wouldn't allow it. I couldn't stand the ingratitude which they showed in abandoning their ideas, all their mocking whistles and mud-slinging. The jackboot mentality of the process frightened me. Still, reality always resounds with jackboots, even when men are most obviously striving towards an ideal, and I of course should have known this. But I was still a man of a different type. I had freedom of choice and they didn't—and I grieved, I grieved for them, I grieved for their old ideas and I probably shed real tears—and I mean that literally!

'You believed in God as strongly as all that?' I asked doubtfully.

'My friend, that question's probably irrelevant. Let's suppose I didn't believe all that much, but I could still feel nostalgic about the ideas. I could never imagine to myself times when men could live without God, even whether it were possible to do so. My heart was always decisively against the possibility. But maybe for a time it could be possible . . . I didn't have any doubts that such a time would come, but I always envisaged a different picture . . .'

'What?'

True, he had already declared he was happy, and there was a great deal of strong feeling in his words—that's how I interpreted much of what he said then. Without doubt, I can't, out of respect for the man, bring myself to put down on paper everything we talked about then, but I will offer a few outlines of the strange picture which I managed to elicit from him. The main thing is that I was troubled all the time by the references to 'chains' and I wanted to understand what they meant, which is why I persisted. Some of the fantastic and extraordinarily strange ideas which he talked about have remained locked in my heart forever.

'I envisaged, dear boy,' he began with a thoughtful smile, 'that the battles were over and the struggle had come to an end. After all the curses, mud-slinging, and jeers a hush had fallen and people found themselves *alone*, which is what they wanted. All their former great ideas had been abandoned. The great well-spring of strength which had previously nurtured and warmed them was on the wane, like that majestically inviting sun in Claude Lorraine's painting, but now it was the last day of the human race. And people suddenly realized that they had been left entirely on their own and they instantly experienced a great sense of being orphaned. You know, my dear boy, I could never imagine that people could be stupid and ungrateful. Those orphaned people would immediately cleave to each other more closely and lovingly. They would seize each other by the hand on the understanding that they were now all they had. The great idea of immortality would have gone for good and would have to be replaced, and all the great abundance of earlier love for what had been immortality would have become directed by men towards nature, towards the world, towards people and every blade of grass. They would come to love the earth and life with an irrepressible love and to that very extent they would gradually become aware of their transience and finiteness and feel a particular love for it quite unlike their former love. They would begin noticing and discovering in nature phenomena and mysteries which they had not supposed to exist before, because they would be looking at nature with new eyes, with the eyes of a lover beholding his beloved. They would awaken from sleep and rush to kiss each other, hurrying to love and embrace, knowing that their days were short and it was all that remained to them. They would work for each other's welfare, and everyone would give all he had to others and in doing so would be happy. Every child would know and feel that everyone on earth was like a father and mother to him. Suppose tomorrow is my last day, everyone would think as he watched the setting sun, then it doesn't matter, I'll die, but all the others will remain, and their children after them—and the idea that others would remain, loving each other just the same and trembling for one another, would take the place of the idea of meeting beyond the grave. Oh, they would be in such a hurry to love one another in order to extinguish the great sorrow in their hearts! They would be proud and bold on their account but grow shy and bashful in their relations with each other. Each one would be concerned for the life and happiness of everyone else. They would grow tender towards each other and not be ashamed of it, as people are nowadays, and they would caress each other fondly like children. On meeting, they would look at each other with profound and significant looks, and their eyes would have a mixture of love and sadness in them . . .

'Dear boy,' he suddenly interrupted hmself with a smile, 'the whole thing's a fantasy, even one that's quite unbelievable! But I have all too often imagined it to myself because I couldn't have lived my whole life without it and without thinking about it. I am not talking about a belief of mine. My faith is not great. I am a deist, a philosophical deist, I suppose, like the rest of the thousand people I mentioned ... but the remarkable thing is that I always completed what I envisaged with a vision, as did Heine in his "Christ on the Baltic".* I could not get by without it, could not fail to imagine Him in the last resort among the orphaned people. He would come to them and stretch out his arms to them and say: 'How could you have forgotten Him?' And there and then the scales would fall from their eyes and there would burst forth a great, exalted hymn to the new and final resurrection ...

'Let's leave that now, my friend. As for my wearing "chains", that was nonsense. Don't worry about them! But there's one other thing. You know that in what I say I am usually sober and restrained. If I have been so eloquent now, it's due ... due to various emotions ... and because I've been talking to you. I would never have spoken to anyone else in this way. I add this just to reassure you.'

But I was deeply touched. There was none of the falseness which I had feared, and I was particularly pleased that it was clear to me he had really felt such feelings and suffered and really and truly loved a great deal—I treasured that above all. I told him so with enthusiasm.

'But you know,' I added suddenly, 'I think that despite all the nostalgia and anguish you felt you must have been extraordinarily happy at that time, weren't you?'

He broke into happy laughter.

'You're full of apt remarks today!' he said. 'Well, yes, I was happy. With a nostalgia like mine could I ever have been unhappy? No one is ever freer or happier than one of those thousand Russian Europeans when wandering abroad! I say this in all seriousness and not at all lightly. Apart from my nostalgia I would not want any other happiness. In this sense I have always been happy, my boy, all my life. It was out of just such happiness I fell in love with your mother then for the first time in my life.'

'What do you mean—the first time in your life?'

'Just that. In my melancholy wandering and nostalgia I suddenly felt myself in love with her as never before and at once sent for her.'

498

'Oh, tell me about it, tell me about mother!'

'Yes, that's why I asked you here—and you know something?' he smiled delightedly. 'I was fearful you'd have forgiven what happened to your mother on account of my relations with Herzen or some plot or other . . .'

CHAPTER VIII

I

BECAUSE we spent the whole evening talking, until it was already night-time, I will not give everything that was said but only the part that finally explained one enigmatic point in his life.

I will begin by saying I have no doubt he loved my mother, and if he abandoned her and wanted to be free of her by going abroad, then it was of course because he had grown far too bored or something of the kind, something that can happen to all of us, but is always hard to explain. Once abroad, though after a considerable time had elapsed, he suddenly fell in love with her again by proxy, in his own mind, that is, and sent for her. Probably people'll say this was just self-indulgence, but I'll say something different. In my opinion, this involved the most serious thing that can happen in a man's life, notwithstanding the apparent self-indulgence which I also grant was there. But I swear I have no doubt about the European nostalgia of his and I set it not only on the same level as, but incomparably higher than, today's practical concern for the building of railways. I recognize his love for humanity as the most sincere and profound emotion, without any hocus-pocus, and his love for my mother as something quite indisputable, although, perhaps, a trifle fantastic. Once abroad, in his 'happy state of nostalgia' and, I must add, in the strictest, monkish solitude (I received this piece of information later from Tatyana Pavlovna), he suddenly remembered my mother—particularly her 'sunken cheeks'— and at once sent for her.

'My friend,' he burst out with meanwhile, 'I instantly realized that my service to an idea did not in the least free me, as a moral and rational human being, from the duty to make at least one person happy in a practical sense during the course of my life!'

'Surely a bookish idea like that couldn't have been the cause of it all?' I asked in astonishment.

'It's not a bookish idea. Or maybe it is. Anyhow, it all amounted to the same thing. I loved your mother, after all, sincerely and truly, not bookishly. Had I not, I wouldn't have sent for her, I'd "have done the right thing by" whatever German man or woman came along, if I'd had a mind to. It's essential to do the right thing by at least one human being in your life, not only practically speaking but in fact. I would make that an axiom for any mature person. In the same way I would make it a rule for every peasant to plant one tree in his life in view of the deforestation taking place in Russia. Still, maybe one tree in his life's not enough, it ought to be a tree a year. A mature person of a higher type, in pursuing a higher ideal, can sometimes be deflected from essentials and become comic, capricious, and cold, even just plain stupid, I would say, and not only in the practical side of life but even in his theories. Thus, the duty to be practical and do the right thing by at least one human being should in fact put everything right and refresh the soul of any philanthropist. As a theory it's ludicrous. But once put into practice and made habitual, it shouldn't be at all silly. I experienced it for myself. No sooner had I begun developing the idea of a new precept—to start with, I admit, just for fun—than I suddenly began to understand the full extent of the love I cherished for your mother.

'Until then I hadn't realized I loved her. While I'd been living with her, I'd simply taken pleasure in her so long as she'd been pretty, but after that I'd pleased myself. It was only in Germany I realized I loved her. It all began with her sunken cheeks, which I could never recall—and sometimes couldn't even bear to look at—without feeling an ache in my heart, a real, physical ache. There are certain painful memories, my dear boy, which can cause real pain. Everyone has them, but people are inclined to forget. Yet it happens that they suddenly recall them, or even just some feature, some part of them, and afterwards they can never get away from them. I began recalling thousands of details of my life with Sonya. Eventually they came flooding in of their own accord and became a real torture to me while I waited for her to arrive. What tortured me worst of all was the memory of her eternal subservience to me and the way she had always considered herself so far beneath me in every respect—just imagine it!—even physically. She had been so ashamed and gone so red when I sometimes looked at her hands and fingers, which in her case were not at all aristocratic-looking. And it wasn't just her fingers she was ashamed of, it was her whole person, notwithstanding the fact that I loved her beauty. She was always intensely bashful and shy with me, but the bad thing was that there was always a degree of fear in this bashfulness. In short, by comparison with me she considered herself worthless and even close to indecent.

'True, occasionally, at the beginning, I sometimes used to think she still regarded me as her lord and master and was frightened of me for that reason, but it wasn't that at all. Besides, I swear, she knew better than anyone what my inadequacies were, and in the whole of my life I have never known a woman with such a sensitive and responsive heart. Oh, how miserable she was when I demanded, just when she was at her prettiest, that she should dress up! It was not just injured self-esteem in her case, it was another sense of hurt in that she realized she could never be a lady to the manner born and in a strange dress she would simply look silly. As a woman, she had no wish to appear silly in the way she dressed and realized that each woman ought to have *her own* way of dressing, something which hundreds and thousands of women, who merely dress to be fashionable, will never understand. It was not mocking glances she really feared! But what makes me particularly sad is the memory of the deeply astonished looks which I used to find directed at me all the time we were together. They expressed a full awareness of her destiny and the sort of future she could expect, so that I used to feel oppressed by them, although, I confess, I never used to discuss things with her and treated it all with lordly disdain. And—you know something—she was not always as apprehensive and wild-eyed as she is now. And even now it sometimes happens she will suddenly be as high-spirited and good-looking as a 20-year-old. And in those days, when she was young, she sometimes much enjoyed lively chatter and convivial laugher—with girls her own age, of course, and women about the house. And the way she used to shudder if I suddenly caught her laughing sometimes, how quickly she'd go red and give me frightened looks!

'Once, shortly before I went abroad, almost—that is—on the eve of disowning her, I went into her room and found her alone at her table, with no work, lost in deep thought, one elbow resting on the table-top. She hardly ever used to sit down without having some work to occupy her. By that time I had long given up showing any affection for her. I managed to go up to her very quietly, on tiptoe, and suddenly embrace and kiss her. She jumped up instantly. I shall never forget the delight, the happiness in her face. And suddenly it all changed to a quick blushing and her eyes flashed. Do you know what I read in that flashing look? "You're just giving me charity, that's all!" She burst into hysterical tears on the grounds that I'd taken her by surprise, but it made me think. Memories like that are terribly hard to bear, my friend. It's like the way great writers sometimes have such *painful* scenes, scenes you remember all your life with anguish, like Othello's last speech in Shakespeare's play, like Eugene Onegin at the feet of Tatyana, like the meeting of the runaway convict with the child, the little girl, by the well on a cold night in Victor Hugo's *Les Misèrables*.* Your heart is pierced and the wound remains forever. Oh, how I waited for Sonya to arrive and longed to hug her to me! Crazy with impatience, I dreamed of a whole new programme of life. I dreamed of gradually and methodically expending effort on destroying in her heart the constant fear she had for me and on making her rethink her personal worth and all the ways in which she was even higher than me. Oh, I knew only too well even then that I had always begun loving your mother just as soon as we were apart and always suddenly grew cold towards her as soon as we were together again. But it wasn't like that in this case.'

I was astonished and the question 'What did *she* think?' flashed through my mind.

'Well,' I asked cautiously, 'how did you meet up with mother then?'

'Then? I never met up with her at all then. She got only as far as Königsberg and stayed there, while I was on the Rhine. I did not go to her and sent word for her to stay there and wait. We didn't see each other until later, oh, much later, when I went to her to ask permission to get married . . .'

502

At this point I will describe the nub of the matter, as far, that is, as I was able to grasp it, because he began telling me things in a disconnected way. His speech suddenly became ten times more disconnected and muddled as soon as he reached this point.

He had met Katerina Nikolaevna by chance just at the time he was waiting for mother, at the height of his impatience. They had all been on the Rhine at that time, taking the waters. Katerina Nikolaevna's husband was almost at death's door—at least he was already condemned to death by his doctors. She had made a great impression on him at their first meeting and had enchanted him. It was an act of destiny. The strange thing is that, in noting it down as I recall it now, I do not remember that he ever used the word 'love' or described himself as being 'in love'. I only remember the word 'destiny'.

And, of course, destiny is what it was. He didn't *want* her, he 'didn't want to fall in love'. I don't know whether I can convey this clearly. It was simply that his whole heart was in turmoil over the fact that such a thing could have happened. All freedom of choice within him was destroyed at one stroke by this meeting and he found himself in thrall to a woman who had been no concern of his. He had not wanted to be such a slave of passion. I will say straight out now that Katerina Nikolaevna was a rare type who does not usually crop up in society. She was, in the highest degree, a simple and straightforward type of woman. I have heard—that is, I know for sure—that for this reason she was irresistible in society whenever she put in an appearance (and there were times when she used to absent herself from it completely). Naturally Versilov did not believe she was like this when he first met her but thought her, on the contrary, an impostor and a hypocrite.

Here—though I am running on a bit—I will quote her judgement on him. She asserted that he could hardly have had any other idea about her because 'an idealist who has come head first up against reality is always more likely than others to anticipate the worst in people'. I do not know whether this is generally true of idealists, but it was entirely true of him. I will append here, so to speak, my own judgement on him. It flashed into my mind as I listened to him. I had the impression that he

503

loved mother with a kind of humane, universal love, as it were, rather than with the simple love a man usually feels for a woman, and once he had met a woman whom he could love in this way he simply did not want that love, most probably out of sheer unfamiliarity. However, it may be that I'm wrong. Of course, I said nothing to him about this. It would have been tactless of me. I swear he was in such a state he almost made me pity him, he was so worked up, and at points in what he had to say he sometimes broke off and fell silent for several minutes as he walked to and fro about the room with a look of such malice on his face.

She soon got to know his secret then. Oh, maybe she flirted with him deliberately because even the finest women can be underhand at times like that—it's their unassailable instinct. It ended in a bloodcurdling rift between them and I think he even wanted to kill her. He terrified her and would probably have killed her but, as he put it, 'everything suddenly turned into hatred'. A strange time ensued in which he suddenly took it into his head to discipline himself—'in the way monks discipline themselves. Gradually and methodically you overcome your own will, starting with the silliest and smallest things, and end by achieving complete mastery over yourself and becoming free.' He added that monks took this quite seriously because through a thousand years' experience it had been elevated into a science. But more remarkable still was the fact that he did not conceive this idea of disciplining himself in order to rid himself of Katerina Nikolaevna but in the full certainty that he not only did not love her, he positively hated her. He was so certain of his hatred for her that he even suddenly conceived the idea of falling in love with and marrying her stepdaughter, who had been deceived by the prince. He completely convinced himself of his new love and made the poor idiot girl fall irresistibly in love with him, bringing her with this love, in the last moments of her life, complete happiness. Why, instead of her, he did not think of mother who was all the while waiting for him in Königsberg remained unclear to me . . . On the contrary, he had suddenly forgotten all about mother, not even sending her any money, so that it was left to Tatyana Pavlovna to save her. And then all of a sudden he went to mother 'to ask permission' to marry the girl on the pretext that 'a woman like that could not be a bride'. Oh, maybe it all contributed to the portrait of 'a bookish man', as Katerina Nikolaevna later called him. But why then do these 'men of paper' (if it's true that they *are* made of paper), why do they subject themselves to such painful torments and take things to such tragic conclusions? Still, that evening, I thought of things a little differently and was struck by the thought:

'Your entire development, all your spiritual self, has been achieved by suffering and struggle throughout your life, but her entire perfection has been achieved at no cost—and that makes for inequality. In that way women are dreadful.' I did not say this to flatter him, but heatedly and even indignantly.

'Perfection? Her perfection? She has no perfection!' he exclaimed suddenly, almost in astonishment at my words. 'She is the most ordinary type of woman, just a slut, and yet she ought to have every kind of perfection!'

'Why ought she?'

'Because, having the power she has, she ought to!' he cried spitefully.

'The saddest thing of all is that you're worked up now!' I couldn't stop myself from saying.

'Now? Worked up?'

He repeated my words, stopping in front of me in some bewilderment. And then suddenly a calm, long-lipped, thoughtful smile lit up his face and he raised a finger as if a thought had occurred to him. Coming to his senses, he picked up a recently opened letter from the table and threw it down in front of me.

'Read that! You ought to know the whole thing—and why you've made me root about so much in all this old rubbish! All it's done is bring back the hatred and the bad feeling!'

I cannot say how astonished I was. The letter was from *her* to him, of today's date and received by him about five o'clock that afternoon. I read it almost quivering with excitement. It was not long, but written so straightforwardly and sincerely that in reading it I almost saw her there in front of me and heard her speaking. Extremely truthfully (and therefore almost touchingly) she confessed how frightened she was of him and simply begged him 'to leave her in peace'. In conclusion she informed him she was now definitely going to marry Björing. Up till now she had never written to him about anything.

What I now gathered from everything he had said was this:

505

He had no sooner read this letter than he suddenly sensed that the most unexpected thing had taken place inside him—for the first time in the last fateful two years he did not feel the least hatred towards her and had had no repetition of that shock which had recently 'driven him out of his mind' at the slightest mention of Björing. 'On the contrary, I sent her my blessing from the bottom of my heart,' he said with deep feeling. I heard this with delight. It meant that all the passion and the pain there had been in him had vanished all at once like a dream, like a two-year-old incubus. Still unsure of himself he had hurried off to see mother—and lo and behold, he had arrived at precisely the moment she had become *free* and the old man who had yesterday bequeathed her to him had died. It was these two coincidences which had shaken him to the core. A little later he had given up looking for me—and I will never forget that his first thought had been of me.

I will never forget how that evening ended. His whole being was suddenly once more transformed. We remained sitting there until late at night. I will tell later, in the right place, how I reacted to this 'news', but now I will only say a few concluding words about him. Looking back on it now, I realize that what most charmed me about him was the humility he showed me, the truthful sincerity he demonstrated to me, a mere boy! 'It was an obsession, but God bless it!' he cried. 'If I'd not been so blinded by it, I would never perhaps have discovered so utterly and completely the one and only mistress of my heart, the true martyr to my love—your mother.' I took special note of these exultant words of his in view of what happened later. But at that moment he won me over completely.

I remember we became terribly happy towards the end. He ordered up champagne and we drank to mother and the future. Oh, he was so full of life and so ready to go on living! But we weren't happy from the wine because we only drank a couple of bottles. I don't know why, but by the end we couldn't stop ourselves laughing. We started talking about other things. He told jokes, so did I, and our laughter and jokes were in no way caustic or really funny, but they made us happy. He kept on stopping me from leaving. 'Sit down, sit down!' he kept on saying and I stayed. He even saw me on my way eventually. It was a fine night, just slightly frosty.

506

'Tell me, have you sent her an answer?' I asked quite casually, pressing his hand at the street corner.

'No, I haven't yet, and it doesn't really matter. Come and see me tomorrow and make it a bit earlier ... Oh, and another thing—have nothing more to do with Lambert, and tear up that "document" right away! 'Bye!'

Saying that, he suddenly walked off. I stayed where I was, so confused I couldn't decide whether or not to call him back. His mention of the 'document' had particularly upset me because he could only have heard about it from Lambert. I returned home very worried. How was it, I suddenly wondered, that such a 'two-year incubus', as he called it, could vanish like a dream, like an obsession, like a ghost?

CHAPTER IX

I

BUT I woke up the next morning feeling fresher and more lively. I even reproached myself, whole-heartedly and despite everything, for the degree of facetiousness and condescension with which I had listened to parts of his 'confession' the previous day. If it had been scrappy in parts, if some of the revelations had been a bit obsessive and incoherent, then he had hardly prepared a set speech for me, had he, when he asked me back to his place? He had simply done me a great honour in turning to me as his only friend at such a moment, and I would never forget it. On the contrary, his confession had been 'touching', no matter how much I may be ridiculed for calling it that, and if there were sometimes flashes of something cynical and even comic in it, then I was too broadminded not to understand and make allowances for its realism, without, however, besmirching its idealism. The main thing was that I had finally achieved a full understanding of the man, and I even felt a bit sorry and slightly annoyed that it had all come about so simply, since in my heart I had always set this man on such an extraordinarily high pedestal, right up in the clouds, and had deliberately clothed his fate in some kind of mystery, so that up till then I had naturally wanted the box to his heart to be harder to open.

Still, in the encounter with *her* and in his two years of suffering there had been much that was complex, since, as I put it to myself: 'He had not wanted destiny to dominate his life; he had wanted freedom, not enslavement to destiny; through the enslavement he had been obliged to humiliate mother, who had waited for him in Königsberg . . .' What's more, I considered this man, in any case, something of a prophet, because he carried the vision of a Golden Age in his heart and knew the future of atheism. And lo and behold the meeting with her had undermined everything, had distorted it all! Oh, I wasn't doing the dirty on her by taking his side! The way I worked it out, mother, for instance, would not have affected his destiny at all, even if he married her. I realized that, and that wasn't at all the same as his meeting with *her*. True, mother still wouldn't have given him a quiet life, but that would have been all to the good because people like him have to be judged differently and that's how their lives will always be.

There is nothing shocking about this. On the contrary, it would be shocking if they acquiesced in a quiet life and became generally the same as all run-of-the-mill people. I wasn't at all worried about his praise of the nobility and his words '*Je mourrai gentilhomme*'—I will die a gentleman. I considered what kind of a *gentilhomme* he was. He was a type of gentleman who gave up everything and became a prophet of universal citizenship and the main Russian concept of 'the coming together of ideas'. And although it was all so much nonsense—this 'coming together of ideas', I mean (which, of course, made no sense at all)—the good thing was that he had spent all his life subservient to an idea and not to some stupid golden calf. My God, hadn't I, in conceiving my 'Idea', bowed down before a golden calf, had I really just needed money? No, I swear, all I'd needed was the idea! I swear that, if I'd had a hundred million roubles, I wouldn't have upholstered a single chair or a single divan in velvet and I'd have eaten just the same kind of beef soup I eat now!

I dressed and dashed straight off to see him. I will add that, so far as his previous day's remark about the 'document' was concerned, I was now five times calmer than I was then. In the

508

first place, I hoped to have it out with him and, secondly, what did it matter if Lambert had wormed his way into his good graces and said something to him? But my principal joy came from a special sensation, the idea that he 'did not love *her*'! I was terribly certain of this and felt that a fearful stone weight had been lifted from my heart. I remember even the likelihood that occurred to me then—precisely that the crudity and senseless-ness of his last final outburst on hearing about Björing and the sending of that hurtful letter, precisely such an extreme act could serve as prophetic of, as a warning of a radical change in his feelings and a swift return to health and good sense. It must be almost the same as in an illness, I thought, and he would be back where he started—just a medical episode and nothing else! That thought made me happy.

'And so let *her* arrange things as she wants, let her marry Björing as much as she wants, only make it so he, my father, my friend, doesn't love her any more!' is what I often exclaimed to myself. However, there was a secret feeling I harboured which I do not wish to broadcast here, in these notes of mine.

Enough of that. And now, without any further ado, I will narrate all the horror which was to follow, all the facts, all the intrigues.

II

At ten o'clock, when I was just preparing to go out and see him, Nastasya Yegorovna appeared. I joyfully asked her whether she had come from him and was annoyed to hear she had not come from him at all, but from Anna Andreevna and that she, Nastasya Yegorovna, 'had left the apartment as soon as it was light'.

'What apartment?'

'The one I was in yesterday. It's the apartment with the baby, it's rented in my name, but Tatyana Pavlovna is paying for it . . .'

'Hey, that doesn't matter!' I interrupted her angrily. 'At least tell me if he's at home. Will I find him there?'

And to my astonishment I then heard from her that he had left before her—if she had left 'at first light', he had gone out before that.

'Well, would he be back by now?'

'No, sir, certainly not, and maybe he won't be coming back at all,' she declared, studying me with that sharp and furtive look and not taking it off me a moment, just as she had done on the visit I described when I was lying ill. The main thing that struck me was that once again secrets and sillinesses were rearing their heads and that these people evidently could not live without secrets and intrigues.

'Why did you say certainly not? What do you mean? He's gone to see mother—that's all!'

'I d-don't know, sir.'

'Why are you here?'

She announced she had come from Anna Andreevna and that she wanted to see me and was at that moment expecting me, otherwise 'It'll be too late'. This mystifying remark drove me crazy.

'Why too late? I don't want to go and I won't! I won't let her get the better of me again! To hell with Lambert—you tell her that, and if she sends Lambert here, I'll give him what for! Tell her that!'

Nastasya Yegorovna was petrified.

'Oh, no, sir!' She stepped towards me, clasping her palms together as if she were beseeching me. 'You mustn't be in such a hurry! It's an important matter, very important for you and for them, too, for Andrey Petrovich and your mother and for everyone . . . You must go to Anna Andreevna at once, because she cannot wait any longer! I assure you on my word of honour! You can decide what to do afterwards . . .'

I gazed at her with astonishment and repugnance.

'Nonsense, nothing'll happen, I won't go!' I shouted stubbornly, enjoying seeing her upset. 'Everything's changed now! Can't you understand that? Goodbye, Nastasya Yegorovna, I don't want to go and I don't want to ask you anything. You're just driving me crazy. I don't want to go poking my nose into your silly business.'

But since she did not leave and remained standing there, I, grabbing my fur coat and hat, went out, leaving her in the middle of the room. There were no letters and papers in my room, and on other occasions I had hardly ever locked up my room when I went out. But I had only just had time to reach the outer door when my landlord, Pyoytr Ippolitovich, came rushing downstairs towards me without hat or coat.

510

'Arkady Makarovich! Arkady Makarovich!'

'What?'

'Aren't you going to tell me what to do before going out?'

'No.'

He gave me a searching glance and was evidently troubled:

'About your room, sir?'

'What about my room? I've paid the rent on time, haven't I?'

'No, sir, I wasn't meaning about the money.' He suddenly smiled his long-lipped smile and went on giving me a searching look.

'What's wrong with all of you?' I shouted, almost driven mad. 'What more do you want?'

He waited a few seconds, still expecting me to say something.

'Well, all right, you can tell me what to do later . . . if that's the way you feel now,' he muttered, grinning even more broadly. 'You be on your way, sir. I've got to go to work myself.'

He ran up the stairs to his own room. Naturally, it all gave food for thought. I am deliberately not omitting the smallest detail of all the silly nonsense that occurred then, because every little bit contributed to the final show-down and fitted into its place, as the reader will become aware. That they really did drive me crazy at the time is the absolute truth. If I appeared so excited and annoyed, then it was precisely at hearing again in their words the same old tone of intrigue and secretiveness that had bored me in the past and was such a reminder of it. But I must continue.

Versilov was not at home and had left before it was light. 'He's gone to see mother,' I thought, sticking stubbornly to my own idea. I didn't put any questions to the nurse, a rather silly woman, and apart from her there was no one there. I dashed off to mother's and in such a state of anxiety that I took a cab after I'd only gone half-way. It turned out . . . *he had not been at mother's since the previous evening*! Tatyana Pavlovna and Liza were the only people with mother. As soon as I entered, Liza got ready to leave.

They were all sitting upstairs in my 'coffin' of an attic room. Downstairs in our sitting-room Makar Ivanovich was lying on the table and an old man was intoning the words of the psalter over him. I will not now describe anything that is not directly relevant, but I will note at this point that the coffin which had already been made and was there in the room was not a simple one, although it was black, but was lined with velvet and the pall covering the deceased was an expensive one and of a sumptuousness inappropriate to the old man and his beliefs; but mother and Tatyana Pavlovna had jointly insisted on it.

Naturally I did not expect to find them in a happy frame of mind, but the particular oppressive sadness I saw in their eyes, mixed with such care and anxiety, struck me instantly and I concluded in a flash that the old man's death was not the sole cause. I repeat that I recall it all perfectly.

Despite everything, I gave mother a tender hug and immediately asked about *him*. A look of anxious enquiry flashed in mother's eyes. I hastily mentioned that he and I had spent the previous evening together until late at the night, but that he had left home today before daylight after having asked me the previous night, on saying goodbye, to come and see him today as soon as possible. Mother did not react, but Tatyana Pavlovna, choosing an appropriate moment, wagged a threatening finger at me.

'Goodbye, brother,' Liza suddenly shot at me, briskly leaving the room. Naturally I dashed after her, but she stopped just by the outside door.

'I thought you'd think of coming,' she said in a rapid whisper.

'Liza, what's going on?'

'I don't know myself, but an awful lot of something. Probably it's the unravelling of what's called "an old, old story". He hasn't been, but they know something about him. They won't tell you, don't worry, and if you're sensible you won't ask. But mother's utterly crushed. I didn't ask why. Goodbye!'

She opened the door.

'Liza, are you all right?' I stepped out into the porch behind her. Her terribly miserable, desperate look cut me to the quick. She glanced at me not so much angrily as even a bit sarcastically, gave a bitter laugh and waved her hand.

'He'd be better off dead, God willing!' she hurled at me from the steps and went on her way.

She was referring to Prince Sergey Petrovich who was at that moment lying unconscious in a fever. 'An old, old story! What old, old story?' I thought challengingly, and it suddenly occurred to me I should tell mother and Tatyana Pavlovna at least part of

512

what I remembered of the confession he had made last night and the confession itself. It flashed through my mind that they were thinking the worst about him at this moment and that they ought to know the whole story!

I remember I started off very successfully. They instantly both looked extremely interested. On this occasion Tatyana Pavlovna's eyes literally bored into me, but mother was more restrained. She looked very serious, but a slight, beautiful, although somehow quite hopeless smile hovered on her face and hardly ever left it while I was speaking. I spoke well, of course, although I knew what I said could make little sense to them. To my surprise Tatyana Pavlovna did not poke fun at me, did not insist on accuracy, did not make facetious remarks as she usually did whenever I started to say something. She merely pursed her lips from time to time and screwed up her eyes, as if making an effort to grasp what I was saying. There were even moments when I thought they understood everything, but that could hardly be likely. I talked, for instance, about his ideas, but most of all I talked about the enthusiasm he had displayed the day before, how enthusiastic he had been about mother, how he said he loved her and had kissed her portrait.

On hearing this, they exchanged quick, silent glances and mother blushed, although neither of them said a word. But then, with mother being there, I couldn't mention the main point, which was his meeting with *her*, and so on and so forth, and most of all *her* letter to him of yesterday's date and the moral 'resurrection' he had experienced after receiving it. And that was the main thing, so that all his feelings of yesterday with which I had so wanted to please mother remained, of course, incomprehensible, although that was no fault of mine because what I could tell I told extremely well. I ended up in a state of complete confusion. They did not say a word and I found it very heavy going.

'Probably he's back now and maybe he's in my room waiting for me,' I said and stood up to leave.

'Be off with you then!' Tatyana Pavlovna declared firmly.

'Have you been down below?' mother asked in a low voice as we said goodbye.

'I have. I've paid my respects and said a prayer. He looks so peaceful and beautiful, mother! Thank you, mother, for sparing

513

no expense on his coffin. At first I thought it was a strange thing to do, but now I think I'd have done the same.'

'Will you be coming to the church tomorrow?' she asked and her lips quivered.

'Mother, what do you mean?' I was astonished. 'I'll be coming to the service today and, besides, tomorrow's your birthday, of course I'll be coming, mother dear! To think, he missed it by just three days!'

I left in a state of hurt and amazement at being asked whether or not I would be at the funeral service. If that's what she thought about me, then what on earth could she be thinking about *him*?

I knew Tatyana Pavlovna would catch me up and deliberately stopped at the front door, but on reaching me she shoved me on to the steps, followed me out, and closed the door behind her.

'Tatyana Pavlovna, does this mean you've not been expecting Andrey Petrovich either today or yesterday? I'm worried . . .'

'Hold your tongue. So you're worried—big deal! Now tell me what you left out of your story about what happened last night!'

I saw no need to hide anything and, almost in exasperation at Versilov, told everything about Katerina Nikolaevna's letter to him of yesterday's date and its effect—about him being 'resurrected' to a new life. To my astonishment the fact of the letter did not surprise her at all and I guessed she already knew about it.

'You're making it up, aren't you?'

'No, I'm not!'

'"Resurrected"—I ask you!' She smiled bitterly as she contemplated it. 'Just like him to be that! You're telling the truth about him kissing her portrait, are you?'

'Yes, Tatyana Pavlovna, I am.'

'With real feeling? He wasn't pretending?'

'Pretending? When does he pretend? You ought to be ashamed, Tatyana Pavlovna! You've got a mean, female soul!'

I spoke fervently but she wasn't listening. She was again thinking things over, despite the intense cold out on the steps. I was wearing my fur coat while she was simply in a dress.

'I'd ask you to do something for me, only you're so stupid,' she said contemptuously, with annoyance. 'Listen, go to Anna Andreevna's and see what's going on there . . . No, don't! Once

514

a fool, always a fool! Go on, quick march! What are you hanging about for?'

'I will not go to Anna Andreevna's! Anyhow, Anna Andreevna sent for me herself.'

'She did? Through Nastasya Yegorovna?' She turned briskly round as she said this, having been on the point of opening the door and going back in the house, but she slammed it shut again.

'I will not go to Anna Andreevna's!' I repeated with malicious glee. 'I won't go because you've just called me a fool, while I've never in my life been more clear-sighted than I am today. All your doings are as plain as the palm of my hand! No, I will not go to Anna Andreevna's!'

'I knew it!' she exclaimed. Again, she did not react to my words at all but continued with her own thoughts. 'They've got *her* all tied up now and then they'll just pull the noose tight!'

'Anna Andreevna?'

'Fool!'

'So who are you talking about? You're not talking about Katerina Nikolaevna, are you? Pulling what noose tight?' I was terribly frightened. An obscure but terrible thought crossed my mind. Tatyana gave me a piercing glance.

'Have you got something to do with it?' she suddenly asked. 'You're mixed up in something there, aren't you? I've heard things about you! Oh, just you watch out!'

'Listen, Tatyana Pavlovna, I'll let you into an awful secret, but not now. There's no time now, but tomorrow when you're alone, only tell me the whole truth now—pulling what noose tight? Look, I'm really worried . . .'

'I can't be bothered with your worrying!' she exclaimed. 'What's this about a secret you want to tell me tomorrow? Do you mean you really don't know anything?' Her eyes bored into me with their questioning look. 'You yourself swore to her you'd burnt Kraft's letter, didn't you?'

'Tatyana Pavlovna, I'm telling you again, don't pester me!' I, in my turn, went on with what I had to say without answering her question, because I was beside myself. 'Look, Tatyana Pavlovna, because of what you're hiding from me, something much worse may happen . . . After all, yesterday he was in the fullest sense resurrected!'

'Oh, you silly thing, be off with you! You little cock sparrow, you're in love too—father and son in love with the same one! Phew, what silly buggers you are!'

She vanished, slamming the door angrily after her. In a fury at the gross and shameless cynicism of her last words—a cynicism of which only a woman would be capable—I dashed off profoundly humiliated and hurt. But I will not describe the turmoil of feelings within me because I have already promised not to; I will simply continue with the facts, which will now explain everything. Naturally I ran round to his place again and again learned from the nurse he had not been there.

'Won't he be coming home at all?'

'God knows.'

III

Facts, facts! . . . Still, there is something the reader may not be aware of. I remember how oppressive all these facts were at the time and how hard they were to make any sense of, so that by the end of that day my head was spinning. In two or three words I would like to anticipate what happened.

What most worried me was: if he had undergone a kind of resurrection yesterday and given *her* up for good, where ought he to be today? Answer: with me, with the person he had kissed yesterday, and after me with mother, whose portrait he had kissed yesterday. But instead of doing these two natural things he had suddenly gone out before daylight and disappeared, and Nastasya Yegorovna was babbling some nonsense about him never coming back. What's more, Liza had talked about the unravelling of some 'old, old story' and the fact that mother knew something else about him, the very latest information. Then again there was no doubt at all that they knew about Katerina Nikolaevna's letter (I had been aware of that) and did not believe he had been 'resurrected to a new life' although they had listened to me attentively. Mother was crushed, while Tatyana Pavlovna had been particularly sarcastic about the word 'resurrection'. But if this was as it seemed to be, it meant that overnight he had had a change of heart, there was again a crisis, and all this after yesterday's enthusiasm, sense of uplift, and strong feeling! It meant that the so-called 'resurrection' had burst like a soap bubble and he was again consumed by the same

516

frenzy as when he had heard the news about Björing! I couldn't help asking myself what would happen to mother, to me, to all of us . . . and to *her*? What 'tightening of the noose' was Tatyana Pavlovna chattering about when she ordered me off to see Anna Andreevna? It meant that the noose was there—at Anna Andreevna's, and I'd only said I wouldn't go simply to annoy her! I was virtually on my way. But why was Tatyana Pavlovna talking about some 'document'? Hadn't he said to me yesterday: 'Burn the document'?

These were my thoughts and they also had me in their noose, but the main thing was that I had to find *him*. Once I found him I would get everything cleared up. I felt sure of this. We would understand each other instantly! I would seize him by the hands and clasp them tightly and I would find my heart full of warmly appreciative words to utter—I could not get this vision out of my mind! Oh, I would conquer the madness in him! But where was he? Where was he? And who should turn up at that very moment when I was in such a state of excitement but Lambert! I was only a few steps away from my room when I suddenly met Lambert. He gave a yell of joy on seeing me and seized me by the hand:

'It's the third time I 'ave been here . . . *Enfin!* Let's have some lunch!'

'What? You've been here before? Isn't Andrey Petrovich here?'

'Nobody's here. Leave 'em all be! You cretin, you got in a temper yesterday! You were drunk, and I've got something important to tell you. I've heard delightful things concerning what we were talking about yesterday . . .'

'Lambert,' I interrupted him, catching my breath and talking rapidly and sounding as if I were making a speech, 'if I let you detain me it was solely in order to be done with you for good and all. I told you as much yesterday, but you still can't understand it. Lambert, you're a child and as silly as all the French are! You still think you're at Touchard's and I'm just as silly as I was at Touchard's . . . But I'm not! I was drunk yesterday, but not from the wine. It was because I was worked up anyhow. If I encouraged you to go on churning it all out, then I was just having you on so as to find out what you were thinking. I was kidding you, and you just loved it and believed me and went on churning away. You know, the idea of marrying her was such nonsense even the greenest of schoolboys wouldn't be taken

517

in! So do you think I was? But *you* were! You believed you'd be accepted in high society and yet you've no idea what it's like there. Things are not all that easy there and she wouldn't be able to go off and get married just like that . . . I'll tell you clearly now what you're after. You want to nobble me so as to get me drunk and make me hand over the document to you and join you in playing some dirty tricks on Katerina Nikolaevna! So you're all wrong! I'll never come with you! Know this, too, that tomorrow or for sure the next day that document will be in her hands, because it belongs to her, because she wrote it, and I'll hand it over myself in person and, if you want to know where, then know this, it'll be through Tatyana Pavlovna, who knows her, in Tatyana Pavlovna's apartment and in her presence I'll hand it over and I won't want anything from her in return . . . So from now on and forever, Lambert, you've got your marching orders! Go away! Next time I won't be so polite!'

Having finished my speech, I was quivering all over. The chief thing and the worst thing that can happen in life, because it spoils everything every time, is if you show off. I got so worked up, devil take it, standing there in front of him that, ending my speech delightedly letting the words ring out and raising my voice higher and higher, I blurted out that quite unnecessary detail about handing over the document in Tatyana Pavlovna's presence and in her apartment. But I was suddenly mad keen to get the better of him! When I blurted out about the document so clearly and suddenly saw his silly look of fear, I just wanted to put the boot in by being accurate over details. And this boastful chattering on my part, just as if I were some babbling old woman, was later to be the cause of terrible trouble, because the detail about Tatyana Pavlovna's apartment was instantly registered by him, being the scoundrel and small-time wheeler-dealer he was. When it came to serious business he was a nonentity and understood nothing, but he had a nose for small-time stuff. If I'd said nothing about Tatyana Pavlovna, nothing serious might have happened. However, on hearing what I said he was terribly upset to start with.

'Listen,' he muttered, 'Alphonsine . . . Alphonsine'll sing something for us . . . Alphonsine was at *her* place. And here's something else—I've got a letter, a sort of letter, in which Mrs

Akhmakov mentions you. The pock-marked chap procured it for me. Remember him? You'll see, you'll see, come along!'

'You're lying! Show me the letter!'

'It's at home, with Alphonsine. Come on!'

Naturally he was lying and gibbering all this nonsense because he was frightened I might dash away. But I abandoned him there and then in mid-street, and when he tried to follow I stopped and shook my fist at him.

He remained standing there and watched me go, because he was probably already hatching a new plan. But for me surprises and chance meetings were not yet over . . . When I look back on that unfortunate day I have the impression that all the surprises and shocks literally conspired together and dropped on my head all at once out of some accursed cornucopia.

I had only just opened the door to my house when, in the entrance way, I bumped into a tall young man, with a long, pale face, of imposing and elegantly fashionable appearance, dressed in a magnificent fur coat. He was wearing pince-nez, but the instant he saw me he took them off (evidently out of politeness) and, politely raising his top hat but without stopping, announced to me, smiling courteously:

'*Ah, bonsoir!*' and went past down the steps. We recognized each other instantly, although I had only seen him once before in my life and then for an instant in Moscow. It was Anna Andreevna's brother, the young nobleman, Versilov's son and therefore almost the same as my own brother. He was accompanied by the landlord's wife, the landlord himself having not yet returned from work. The moment he had gone out I tackled her.

'What was he doing here? Was he in my room?'

'Not in your room at all. He came in to see me.' She spoke snappily and drily and turned back into her own room.

'No, that's impossible!' I cried. 'Please tell me why he came to see you.'

'Oh, God forbid I should have to tell you all the reasons why people come here! I think we can also look after our own business. Maybe it was a case of the young man wanting to borrow some money and wanting to get an address from me. Maybe I'd promised him last year . . .'

'When last year?'

'Oh, my God, it's not as if it's the first time he's been here!'

She walked away. The chief thing I realized was that there had been a change of tone. They were beginning to treat me rudely. It was clear this was again to do with a secret, because secrets were cropping up at every turn hour by hour. The first time the young Versilov had been here he had come with his sister, Anna Andreevna, when I had been ill. I remembered that only too well, just as I remembered that Anna Andreevna had astonished me yesterday by mentioning that the old prince might be staying in my room. But it was all so vulgar and horrid I could hardly make head or tail of it.

Slapping myself on the forehead and without giving myself a chance to have a rest, I dashed off to Anna Andreevna's, but she was not at home and I was told by the hall porter she'd 'gone off to Tsarskoe and probably won't be back until this time tomorrow'.

So she's gone to Tsarskoe, I thought, grinding my teeth, which means she's gone to see the old prince and her brother's been taking a look at my room! No, it won't happen! But if there really is some noose-tightening going on, then I'll have to defend 'the poor woman'!

I did not go home after leaving Anna Andreevna's because, in my feverish state of mind, I suddenly recalled the 'dive' on the canal which Andrey Petrovich was accustomed to visit whenever he was in a black mood. Overjoyed at the thought, I dashed there. It was four o'clock and already growing dark. In the 'dive' they told me he'd been there—''E came for a while and left, maybe 'e'll be back.' I suddenly made up my mind to wait for him there and ordered something to eat. At least there was a gleam of hope.

I had dinner there, even put in more orders so as to be able to stay there longer and spent, I think, about four hours there. I will not describe my sadness, my feverish impatience. It was just as if everything inside me was shaking and quivering. The noise of the organ, the patrons of the place—oh, the entire misery of it imprinted itself on my soul perhaps for the rest of my life! I cannot describe the thoughts that filled my head like a crowd of dry autumn leaves blown in a gust of wind. True, they were a bit like that and I confess at times I felt I was beginning to lose my reason.

But what caused me real pain—on the side, as it were, apart from the chief torture of my situation—was a persistently recurring and particularly venomous collection, as persistent and venomous as a late-summer fly to which you pay no attention but which buzzes round you, pesters you, and suddenly gives you a painful sting. It was no more than a recollection, something that happened which I had never spoken about to anyone. This is it, since I'll have to tell it some time.

IV

When it had been decided in Moscow that I would be going to St Petersburg, I was told by Nikolay Semyonovich Andronnikov that I would have to wait until the money for the journey arrived. I was not informed who the money would be coming from. I knew it would be coming from Versilov, but because I was consumed day and night at that time by dreaming about meeting him, so full of high-flown plans my heart almost stopped beating, I gave up saying anything at all about him, even to Marya Ivanovna. Besides, I had enough money of my own for the journey. But I accepted I ought to wait and meanwhile assumed the money would come by post.

Suddenly one day Nikolay Semyonovich on returning home informed me—as was his habit, curtly and abruptly—that the next day, at eleven o'clock in the morning, I had to go to Myasnitsky Street, to the house and apartment of a certain Prince V. and that there the young nobleman Versilov, son of Andrey Petrovich, who had arrived from St Petersburg and who was staying there with his schoolfriend, Prince V., would hand me the money needed for the journey. It seemed the simplest thing. Andrey Petrovich would quite likely have entrusted his son with this commission rather than send the money by post. But for some reason this news seemed unnaturally belittling and frightening. There could be no doubt that Versilov would like me to get to know his son, my half-brother, and that was how I portrayed to myself the intentions and feelings of the man about whom I dreamed. But it left me with an enormous question: how

521

would I, indeed how *should* I behave during this entirely unexpected meeting, and didn't it somehow pose a threat to my own personal dignity?

The next day, precisely at eleven o'clock, I presented myself at Prince V.'s apartment, a bachelor establishment but, as I had guessed, sumptuously appointed, with footmen in livery. I stood about in the hall. The sound of loud talk and laughter came from inner rooms. The prince apparently had other visitors apart from the young nobleman. I ordered a footman to announce me and I think I used a rather arrogant tone. At least, on leaving me to make the appointment he gave me what I thought was a strange look, one that was not even as respectful as it should have been. To my astonishment, he took a very long time to announce me, as much as five minutes, and meanwhile the same sounds of conversation and laughter continued.

Naturally I stood there and waited, knowing it would be improper and out of the question for me, 'such a little gentleman', to sit down in an entrance-hall where there were footmen. I, for my part, had no wish to take so much as a step into the main room without being specially invited—out of arrogance, perhaps, a keenly developed sense of my own dignity, but that was as it should be. To my astonishment, the remaining footmen—a pair of them—dared to sit down in my presence. I turned away, pretending not to notice, and yet began quivering all over and suddenly, turning round and stepping towards one of them, literally ordered them to go and announce me again *at once*. Despite my stern looks and highly excited state, the footman glanced at me lazily without getting to his feet and the other one answered on his behalf:

'You've been announced, don't worry!'

I made up my mind to wait no more than a minute or, if possible, less than that and then *leave for good*. The chief thing in my favour was that I was very respectably dressed. My clothes and topcoat were new and I had on a clean shirt, something Marya Ivanovna had made sure about for this very occasion. But I discovered later on, when I was already in St Petersburg, that these footmen had learned through the manservant who had come with Versilov that they'd been told 'an illegitimate brother, a student, will be coming tomorrow'. I am now quite sure about that.

A minute passed. It's a strange feeling when you make up your mind to do something and can't do it. 'Should I go or not? Should I?' I kept asking myself almost in a sort of fever. Suddenly the footman who had gone off to announce me reappeared. In his hands, clasped fluttering between his fingers, were four red banknotes totalling forty roubles.

'Here are forty roubles, sir!'

I blew my top. This was such an incredible insult! The whole of the previous night I had dreamed about the meeting between the two brothers which Versilov had arranged. All night I had feverishly wondered how I ought to behave without letting down and dishonouring the entire round of ideas which I had nurtured in my isolation and which I could take pride in no matter where I was. I had dreamed how I would be grateful, how I would be proud but of melancholy bearing even in the company of Prince V. and how in that way I would be admitted straightaway into his society—oh, I'm not sparing myself, so be it, so be it, I've got to tell this as well in every silly detail! And suddenly it all boiled down to forty roubles handed to me by a footman in the entrance-hall, after having waited around for ten minutes, and straight from his hands, from a footman's fingers, not even on a salver or in an envelope!

I shouted so loudly at the man he shuddered and stepped back. I instantly ordered him to take the money back and say that 'the gentleman should bring it himself'—in short, my demand was not, of course, coherent and made no sense to the footman. Still, I shouted so loudly that he went back. What is more, my shout had been heard in the main room and the talk and laughter suddenly stopped.

Almost at once I heard footsteps approaching—solemn, unhurried and soft—and the tall figure of a handsome and haughty young man (I remember him then as paler and thinner than he was today) appeared in the doorway, though remaining a step or so on the other side. He was wearing a magnificent red silk dressing-gown and slippers and he had a pince-nez on his nose. Without uttering a word, he directed the pince-nez at me and started scrutinizing me. Like some wild animal I took a step towards him and stood there challenging him, fixing my eyes on him intently. But he kept up his scrutiny only a moment or so, no more than ten seconds, and suddenly a hardly noticeable grin appeared on his lips, yet it was quite venomous, venomous for the very reason that it was hardly noticeable. He silently turned about and went back into the interior of the apartment as smoothly and quietly as he had come.

Oh, people like him are taught from childhood onwards, taught in their own families by their own mothers how to insult people and make them feel small! Naturally I felt small! God, how small and lost I felt at that moment!

At almost the same moment the footman with the banknotes reappeared, saying:

'Be so good as to take these, they're for you from St Petersburg. But you cannot be received now—"perhaps some other time when we're free".'

I felt he had added these last words off his own bat. But my sense of being lost and small still remained. I took the money and went towards the front door. I did it precisely because I felt so small and lost, since I had to take it regardless. But the footman, naturally wanting to run my nose in it, permitted himself the ultimate retainer's snub. He suddenly flung the front door open in front of me and, holding it wide open, announced self-importantly and pointedly as I went through:

'Permit me, sah!'

'You're a shit!' I roared and raised my hand at him but did not let it fall. 'And your master's a shit! You can tell him so right now!' I added this last and went quickly down the stairs.

'Don't you dare speak like that! If I informed my master he'd have you taken off to the police right away. And don't you dare raise your hand to me . . .'

I went down the stairs. It was a wide staircase entirely open to view and I could be watched quite clearly from above as I descended the red carpet. All three footmen came out and watched me over the banisters. I was determined not to say a word. One simply does not exchange abuse with lackeys. I went down the staircase without quickening my pace and even, I think, with deliberate slowness.

Oh, there are philosophers (shame to them!) who will say that all this was nonsense, a show of tantrums by a spoiled brat! Let them call it that, but for me it was something deeply wounding, a hurt that has not healed right up to the present moment of writing when everything is over and done with and all wrongs have been righted. Oh, I swear I don't bear grudges and I am not vindictive! There can be no doubt that I am always pathologically ready to get my own back whenever I feel I have been insulted, but only by complete magnanimity, I swear! Say I do get my own back by being magnanimous, so long as whoever has insulted me is aware of this and understands it, that's when I feel vindicated! Besides, I will add that, if I am not vindictive, then I do harbour rancour and yet at the same time I can be magnanimous. I wonder whether other people are like this.

Oh, then, on that occasion, I arrived feeling magnanimous, which was maybe a bit foolish, but so be it! Better to be foolish and magnanimous than dead serious and mean, commonplace, mediocre!

I have never told a soul about that meeting with my 'brother'—not even Marya Ivanovna, not even Liza when I got to St Petersburg. This meeting was just like receiving a shameful slap in the face. And here I was meeting this gentleman all over again when I least expected to, and here he was giving me a smile and taking off his hat and in the most friendly way saying: '*Bonsoir!*' Of course, it was food for thought ... But the old wound had been reopened!

v

Having spent four hours and more sitting in the 'dive' I suddenly rushed off in a frenzy—naturally once more to Versilov's and, naturally, once again I did not find him at home. There had been no sign of him. The nurse was bored and asked me to send Nastasya Yegorovna to her, as if that was all I had to worry about! I dashed to mother's house but without going in summoned Lukerya into the entrance way and learned from her he hadn't been there, nor had Liza. I saw that Lukerya also wanted to ask me something and maybe also wanted me to do something for her, but I had worries of my own! There remained the final hope that he had gone to my room, but I could not believe he had.

I have already said that I felt I was almost going crazy. And who do I suddenly find in my room but Alphonsine and my landlord! True, they had just come out and Pyotr Ippolitovich was carrying a candle.

'What the hell's going on?' I screamed at my landlord almost senseless with rage. 'How dare you let this bitch into my room?'

'*Tiens!*' shouted Alphonsine. '*Et les amis?*'

'Get out!' I roared.

'*Mais c'est un ours!* What a bear he is!' She skipped down the corridor, pretending to be frightened, and disappeared in a flash into the landlady's room. Pyotr Ippolitovich, still holding the candle, came up to me looking stern.

'Allow me to say, Arkady Makarovich, you should curb your tongue! With all due respect, Mademoiselle Alphonsine is not a bitch and, quite to the contrary, she is our guest, not yours, a guest of my wife with whom she has been on friendly terms for quite some while.'

'How dare you let her into my room?' I repeated, suddenly seizing hold of my head which had begun throbbing terribly painfully.

'It happened by chance, sir. I had gone in to shut your *fortochka** which I had opened to let in some fresh air. Since Alphonsina Karlovna and I were going on with what we had been saying, in mid-conversation she came into your room solely because she was with me.'

'Wrong! Alphonsine's a spy, Lambert's spy, maybe you are, too! And Alphonsine came here to steal something!'

'Have it your own way! Today you'll say one thing, tomorrow another. I have rented out my own apartment for a while, and my wife and I will be moving into a small box-room. That now makes Alphonsina Karlovna almost the same as a tenant here, like you are, sir.'

'You've rented your apartment to Lambert?' I cried in alarm.

'No, sir, not to Lambert.' He smiled his former long-lipped smile which now betrayed firmness rather than this morning's bewilderment. 'I assume you know who I've let it to and you're just pretending you don't know, solely to show off, which is why you're so bad-tempered. Goodnight, sir!'

'Yes, yes, all right, leave me alone!'

I waved my arms at him, almost in tears, so that he suddenly glanced at me in astonishment. Then he walked off. I latched my door and flung myself on my bed face downwards on the pillow.

And that was how the first terrible day ended, the first of the three final fateful days which bring my notes to a close.

CHAPTER X

I

BUT once again, in anticipating what happened, I find it necessary to clarify for the reader something beforehand because so many accidental things became mixed up with the logical flow of events that without such clarification it would be impossible to make sense of it. What is concerned here is 'the tightening of the noose' referred to by Tatyana Pavlovna. It involved the fact that Anna Andreevna had finally risked taking the boldest step she could take in her position. What a character—honestly and truly! Although the old prince, on the pretext of his health, had been conveniently wafted off to Tsarskoe Selo, so that news of his marriage to Anna Andreevna could not be broadcast in society and was strangled for a time at birth, as it were, the frail old man, who could have been made to do anything, still steadfastly refused to give up his intention and jilt Anna Andreevna who had proposed to him. For his part he was a real knight in shining armour, so that sooner or later he might suddenly up and put his intention into effect with irresistible force, something which is all the more likely to happen with weak characters, since they have a limit beyond which they cannot go. What is more, he was fully aware of the touchiness of Anna Andreevna's position. He had the utmost respect for her and recognized the likelihood of society tittle-tattle, jibes, and hostile rumours about her. All that stopped him from acting and had a calming effect was the fact that Katerina Nikolaevna had not once, by so much as a word or a hint, allowed herself to say anything bad about Anna Andreevna in his presence or give any sign that she might be against the marriage. On the contrary, she had shown the greatest cordiality and attentiveness to her father's bride-to-be. Thus, Anna Andreevna was placed in an extraordinarily delicate position, aware through her feminine intuition

527

that the slightest show of dissent towards Katerina Nikolaevna, whom the old prince also worshipped now more than ever precisely because she had been so magnanimous and dutiful about allowing him to marry—by the slightest show of dissent against her she would cause offence to all his tenderest feelings and arouse mistrust towards her on his part and even indignation. So this was how the battle lines had been drawn. Both contestants were competing against each other, as it were, in trying to be delicate and patient, and the prince in the last resort did not know which of them to be more surprised at and, as happens with weak but tender-hearted people, ended by beginning to agonize and blame himself for everything. His depressed state, so it was said, made him ill. His nerves were shattered and instead of his health improving in Tsarskoe Selo, as he had been assured it would, he was preparing to take to his bed.

Here I will mention in parenthesis something I discovered very much later. It seems that Björing had proposed that Katerina Nikolaevna should take the old man abroad, persuading him to go on some pretext or other and meanwhile letting it be known confidentially in society at large that he had completely lost his reason and obtaining evidence for this from doctors abroad. But Katerina Nikolaevna would have nothing to do with the proposal, or so at least it was asserted later. She had indignantly rejected the plan. This is all rumour from afar but I believe it to be true.

And then, when the matter had so to speak reached a final impasse, Anna Andreevna suddenly learned through Lambert that a letter existed in which the prince's daughter had taken legal advice about ways of declaring her father insane. Her proud and vindictive mind was alerted in the highest degree. Bearing in mind her previous talks with me and taking into account a mass of very minor incidents, she could have no doubt about the accuracy of this information. Then her firm, unbending, female heart hatched an irresistible plan of attack. The plan was suddenly, without any preliminaries, without any prior warning, to let the prince know everything, frighten him, shake him to the core and point out that what inevitably awaited him was the lunatic asylum, and if he were to stick his toes in, become indignant and refuse to believe it, then he would be shown his daughter's letter with accompanying words to the effect that 'there had once been the intention of declaring you insane, so now, in order to stop the marriage, it might happen again'. At that the terrified and crushed old man would be brought back to St Petersburg—*directly to my room*!

It was terribly risky, but she firmly believed in her own capacity to do it. Here, disgressing for a moment from my story, I will say, again anticipating what happened, that she was not wrong about the effect of her plan of attack—in fact, the effect exceeded all her expectations. The news of the existence of the letter acted upon the old prince a great deal more powerfully than she and all the rest of us had supposed. Until that time I had no idea the prince had got wind of the letter before then, but, like all weak and timid people, he had not believed the rumour and had dismissed it as firmly as he could in the hope of remaining untroubled by it. What is more, he blamed himself for being so ignoble as to entertain the suspicion. I will also add that the fact of the letter's existence also acted on Katerina Niko-laevna far more strongly than I had myself expected . . . In short, that piece of paper turned out to be far more significant than I had supposed and I was the one who had been carrying it around in my pocket all the time! But I have already jumped too far ahead.

Why though, you may ask, should the prince be brought to my room? Why should he be brought to live in the miserable cubby-holes people like me inhabit and be frightened out of his wits by our miserable circumstances? If he could not be taken to his own house (because everything could be messed up instantly if he were there), then why wasn't he being taken to a special 'sumptuous' apartment as Lambert had suggested? But this was precisely what was risky about the extraordinary step Anna Andreevna had taken.

The main thing was that the prince should be confronted by the document immediately after his arrival. But no way was I going to give up the document. Because there was no time to lose, Anna Andreevna, trusting to her own will-power, decided to set everything going without the document but simply by bringing the prince straight to my room. Why? Because by doing so she would involve me as well and by that means kill two birds with one stone, as the saying goes. She reckoned on acting on me by giving me a shove, a shock, a total surprise. She reasoned that once I found the old man at my place, saw his terror and helplessness, and heard their pleadings I would give in and hand over the document! I admit it was a cunning and clever plan and psychologically right too—and it almost met with success. So far as the old man was concerned, Anna Andreevna managed to spirit him away and make him believe her—in word, if not in deed—by telling him straight out that she was bringing him *to* *me*. I discovered all this much later. Even the solitary fact that the document was in my possession banished from his timid heart all doubts about its authenticity. He was that fond of me, that devoted!

I will also mention that Anna Andreevna never doubted for a moment that I still had the document and had never let it out of my hands. Most of all, she took a perverse view of my character and cynically relied on my innocence, my openness, and even on my sentimentality, while supposing, on the other hand, that if I had indeed decided to hand the letter to Katerina Nikolaevna, for instance, I would do so under certain special conditions and it was precisely these conditions she was rushing to anticipate by springing her surprise, by making such a leap in the dark and employing such a plan of attack.

Finally, Lambert backed her up in everything. I have already said that Lambert's position at that time was extremely critical. Weasel that he was, he was trying with all his might to lure me away from Anna Andreevna in order that we should jointly sell the document to Katerina Nikolaevna, something which he for some reason found more profitable. But since I had no intention whatever of surrendering the document until the very last moment, he had come to an extreme decision to try acting even on Anna Andreevna so as not to lose any chance of profit and so he wormed his way into her good graces right up to the last moment by offering his services and I knew he even proposed obtaining the services of a priest, should they be needed . . . But Anna Andreevna begged him with a contemptuous smile to do no such thing. Lambert seemed to her terribly crude and aroused in her a feeling of utter disgust, but caution dictated she should still use his services, including being her spy. However, I am not sure, even to this day, whether or not they had bribed my landlord, Pyotr Ippolitovich, and whether or not he received anything from them for what he did or simply joined with them in the conspiracy for the joy of it. But that he spied on me, as did his wife, I know for certain.

The reader may now understand that, though I was in part forewarned, I could in no way have guessed that tomorrow or the next day I would find the old prince parked on me and in such circumstances. What is more, I could never have imagined Anna Andreevna capable of something so audacious! To talk about things of that kind and drop hints is all very well, but to take a decision, embark on such a step, and actually accomplish it—that, I can tell you, demands real character!

II

To continue.

I awoke late the next morning, but I had slept unusually soundly and without dreams, something I recall with surprise, so that, on waking up, I felt so bright-eyed and bushy-tailed morally it was as though the previous day had not happened at all. I planned not to go to mother's house but straight to the church so that, after the ceremony, on returning to her house I could spend the whole day with her. I was quite certain I would meet *him* at mother's that day sooner or later—quite sure.

Neither Alphonsine nor my landlord were home. I had no wish to ask his wife anything and, generally speaking, I planned to end all relations with them and even leave my lodgings as soon as possible. So as soon as my coffee had been brought I again latched the door. But suddenly there came a knocking. To my astonishment it was Trishatov.

I at once opened the door and, delighted to see him, asked him to come in, but he declined.

'Just a couple of words while I'm here . . . or maybe I will come in because I think one's got to talk in whispers here. Only I won't sit down. You see the filthy coat I'm wearing. Lambert took away my fur coat.'

In fact he was in a threadbare old coat that was too long for him. He stood there in front of me without taking off his hat, looking solemn and morose, his hands in his pockets.

'I won't sit down, I won't sit down. Listen, Dolgoruky, I don't know the details, but I know Lambert's planning to do the dirt on you any time now, and that's for sure. So watch out! The pock-marked chap told me—remember him? But he didn't say what it was about, so I can't tell you anything more. I just came here to warn you. 'Bye!'

'Stay, Trishatov, please! Though I'm in a hurry, I'm so glad to see you . . .'

I had scarcely blurted this out when he said:

'No, I won't stay, I won't sit down. But I won't forget you were glad to see me. Oh, Dolgoruky, what's the point of fooling people? I agreed—of my own free will, quite consciously—to do all kinds of dirt on people and have sunk so low I'm ashamed to talk about it in front of you. I'm at the pock-marked chap's . . . Goodbye! I'm not good enough to sit down here.'

'Trishatov, my dear chap, that's enough . . .'

'No, look, Dolgoruky, I'm putting a bold face on it but I'm going on the game now. I'll soon have a much better fur coat made for me and I'll be racing about the place in style. But in myself I'll know I didn't sit down in your room because . . . because I'd passed sentence on myself, because I was a low-down bastard. It'll be a pleasant thing for me to remember when I'm disgracing myself and in a drunken stupor. Well, so long, so long! I won't give you my hand. After all, Alphonsine won't take my hand. And please don't come rushing after me and don't come and see me. We have a contract.'

The strange boy turned round and went out. I didn't know what to do, but I made up my mind to go and see him just as soon as I had our own affairs in order.

I will refrain from describing everything that happened that morning, although much could be recalled. Versilov was not in the church for the funeral and I think, judging by the looks on the faces of those present, no one expected him to appear before the coffin was borne out. Mother prayed devoutly and was evidently lost in prayer. Only Tatyana Pavlovna and Liza stood by the coffin. But I am not going to describe any of it. When the burial was over, everyone returned home and sat down round the table and I could still tell from their faces they did not expect him. When we got up from the table I went up to mother, hugged her warmly, and wished her many happy returns of her birthday. Liza did the same after me.

'Listen, brother,' she whispered to me, 'they *are* expecting him.'

'I can see that, Liza. I guessed as much.'

'He's bound to come.'

That meant, I thought, they have definite news, but I did not question them. Although I am not going to describe my feelings, all the puzzlement surrounding everything, no matter how bright-eyed and bushy-tailed I felt, suddenly weighed like a heavy stone on my heart. We took our seats at the round table in the sitting-room on either side of mother. Oh, how I loved being with her then and looking at her! She suddenly asked me to read something from the Bible. I read a chapter from Luke. She did not weep and did not even look very sad, but I had never before seen her face so filled with spiritual uplift. Deep thoughtfulness shone in her calm eyes, yet I had no way of telling whether she was anxiously anticipating something or not. We talked on and on. We began remembering all sorts of things about the deceased and Tatyana Pavlovna told a great many things about him I had never heard before. In general, if it had been recorded, it would have proved very interesting. Tatyana Pavlovna even altered her usual expression. She was very calm, very considerate, and most of all she was also very peaceful, although she talked a lot simply in order to distract mother. But there is one detail I remember especially. Mother was sitting on the divan, and to the left of the divan was a little round table with an icon on it laid ready for some purpose—an ancient icon, without a frame but with representations of haloes above the heads of saints, of which there were two. The icon had belonged to Makar Ivanovich, something which I knew full well and I also knew that the deceased would never be parted from it and considered it miraculous. Tatyana Pavlovna had glanced at it more than once.

'Listen, Sofya,' she said suddenly, changing the subject, 'why leave the icon lying there? Why not stand it up on the table with its back to the wall and light a lamp in front of it?'

'No, it's better as it is now,' said mother.

'All right. Yes, it would probably be rather showy like that . . .'

I had no idea what this was all about at the time, but the fact was that long ago Makar Ivanovich had willed this icon to Andrey Petrovich by word of mouth and mother was now getting ready to hand it over.

It was already five o'clock in the afternoon. Our conversation was still continuing when I suddenly noticed a shudder pass

533

across mother's face. She quickly drew herself up straight and was all ears while Tatyana Pavlovna, who was speaking at the time, went on talking without taking any notice. I instantly turned towards the door and a moment later saw Andrey Petrovich in the doorway. He had not entered through the front door but by the back way, through the kitchen and the corridor, and only mother had heard his footsteps.

I will describe the ensuing stupid scene moment by moment, word for word. It did not last long.

Firstly, at least at first glance, I noticed no change at all in his face. He was dressed as he always was, almost dandyishly. He held in his hands a small but expensive bouquet of fresh flowers. He came in and offered them to mother with a smile. She gave him a glance of timid bewilderment but took the bouquet, and suddenly a flush suffused her pale cheeks and happiness shone in her eyes.

'I just knew you'd take them like that, Sonya,' he said.

Because we had all stood up when he came in, on entering he took Liza's armchair just to mother's left and sat down in it without noticing he was taking someone else's seat. By doing so, he placed himself next to the little table on which the icon was lying.

'Hello, everyone. Sonya, I longed to bring you a bouquet today, on your birthday, and I did not come to the funeral so as not to bring a bouquet to the deceased. Anyhow I know you weren't expecting me. I'm sure the old man wouldn't disapprove of these flowers, because he willed us to enjoy ourselves, didn't he? I think he is somewhere here in the room.'

Mother gave him a strange look. Tatyana Pavlovna seemed to flinch.

'Who's here in the room?' she asked.

'The deceased. Let's forget it. You must know that the man who doesn't have complete faith in miracles is always the one most likely to be superstitious . . . But it'd be better if I explained about the bouquet. I don't really know why I brought it. More than once on the way here I wanted to fling it into the snow and stamp my foot on it.'

Mother shuddered.

'Yes, I awfully wanted to. Take pity on me, Sonya, and my

534

poor head. I wanted to because it was too beautiful. Is there anything more beautiful in the world than a flower? I was carrying it and all around were frost and snow. What a contrast—frost and flowers! But that's not what I mean. I simply wanted to crush it because it was pretty. Sonya, though I'll have to be off now, I'll be back very soon because I think I'm beginning to be frightened. I'm beginning to be frightened that no one'll be able to cure me of my fright except an angel like Sonya ... What's this icon doing here? Ah, I remember, it belonged to the deceased. It was an heirloom, his grandfather's. He had it by him all his life. I know, I remember now, he willed it to me. It's all come back to me ... I think it's a schismatic one ... Let me have a look.'

He picked up the icon, lifted it close to the candle, and studied it intently, but after holding it only a few seconds laid it down on the table in front of him. I was startled since all his strange remarks had been made so quickly I had no time to digest them. All I can remember is that a panic fear seized my heart. Mother's fright had turned into bewilderment and compassion because what she mostly saw in him was unhappiness. There were earlier occasions when he had talked just as strangely as now. Liza suddenly went very pale for some reason and, with a glance at me, nodded strangely in his direction. But Tatyana Pavlovna was the most frightened of all.

'What's wrong with you, Andrey Petrovich dear?' she asked anxiously.

'My dear Tatyana Pavlovna, I really don't know what's wrong with me. Don't worry, I am still aware that you are Tatyana Pavlovna and you're a dear person. I just dropped in for a moment because I wanted to say something nice to Sonya and I'm trying to find the right words, though my heart's full of words and I can't say out loud they're all so strange, really strange words. You know, I think I'm literally splitting in half.' He surveyed us all with an awfully serious look and one that expressed an extremely sincere wish to speak candidly. 'It's true, I am mentally splitting in two and I am terribly afraid. It's as if you have your own double beside you. You are yourself intelligent and in your right mind, but there's this other person just next to you intent on doing something completely silly, something that is sometimes quite outrageous, and suddenly you notice you yourself want to do this outrageous thing, God knows why, unwillingly, as it were, flying in the face of all you want.

'I once knew a doctor who was in church attending his father's funeral and suddenly started whistling. Really, you know, I was frightened to come to the funeral today because for some reason I was certain in my own mind I would start whistling and laughing like that unfortunate doctor, who ended up rather badly . . . And, you know, I really don't know why I've got that doctor on my mind today. He's sort of stuck there and I can't get rid of him. You know, Sonya, I've just now picked up that icon . . .' He picked it up and turned it about in his hands '. . . and you know I've got this terrible desire right now, this very second, to bash it against the corner of the stove, right there! I'm sure it'll instantly break into two halves—no more, no less.'

The main thing was that he said all this without any kind of pretence, not even jokingly. He spoke utterly simply and straight-forwardly and it was all the more terrible for that reason. And I think he really was terribly frightened of something happening. I suddenly noticed that his hands were shaking slightly.

'Andrey Petrovich!' screamed mother, clasping her hands together.

'Leave go of it, leave go of the icon, Andrey Petrovich! Leave go of it and put it down!' cried Tatyana Pavlovna, jumping up. 'You should get undressed and lie down! Arkady, get the doctor!'

'Hey . . . Hey, what're you getting so worked up about?' he said calmly, surveying us all with an intent gaze. Then he suddenly placed both elbows on the table and rested his face in his hands.

'I'm frightening you, but, dear friends, indulge me just this much, please sit down and keep calm—just for a moment! Sonya, it's not this I've come to you to talk about. I came to tell you something, but something quite different. Sonya, I'm saying goodbye, I'm going off again as I've been off several times before . . . Well, I'll be back again of course to see you—in this sense, you're irreplaceable. Who else would I come back to when everything's over? You must believe me, Sonya, that I've come to you now as to an angel, not to an enemy in any sense. What sort of an enemy can you be to me, eh? Eh? Don't get the idea I came here to smash this icon, since, if you must know, Sonya, it's just what I want to do . . . smash it!'

When, prior to this, Tatyana Pavlovna had cried: 'Leave go of the icon!' she had seized it from his hands and held it in her own. Suddenly, on saying these last words, he sprang to his feet, grabbed the icon from her and, waving it wildly in the air, smashed it with all his strength against the corner of the tiled stove. It flew into two equal parts.

He turned round towards us instantly, his pale face suddenly dark red, almost purple, and every feature quivering and working:

'Don't take this as being allegorical, Sonya! I haven't smashed Makar's inheritance, I've just done this to break something! Oh, I'll come back to you, I'll come back to the last angel on earth! All right, so take it as an allegory, that's how it was meant!'

And he suddenly dashed from the room, going back through the kitchen (where he had left his fur coat and hat.) I will not describe in detail what happened to mother. Frightened to death, she stood there, her clasped hands raised in front of her, and suddenly cried out after him:

'Andrey Petrovich, darling, come back! Come back to say goodbye!'

'He'll be back, Sofya, he'll be back! Don't worry!' cried Tatyana Pavlovna, quivering in a terrible access of rage, sheer brute rage. 'You heard, didn't you? He promised he'd be back! Let him go, the booby, let him have his last fling! When he's old and can't use his legs, who'll look after him then if not you, his old nanny? He'll tell you as much straight out, he won't be shy about it . . .'

So far as we were concerned, Liza had collapsed in a faint. I had been about to run after him, but instead I turned to mother. I put my arms round her and held her. Lukerya ran in with a glass of water for Liza. Mother quickly recovered. She sank on to the divan, put her hands to her face, and burst into tears.

'All right . . . all right, run after him!' shrieked Tatyana Pavlovna at the top of her voice, coming to her senses. 'Go on! Go on! Catch him up, don't let him get away! Go on! Go on!' And she tugged me away from mother as hard as she could. 'Oh, I'd run after him myself if I could!'

537

'Arkady, darling, do run and get him!' cried mother as well.

I dashed headlong out through the kitchen and the courtyard, but he was nowhere to be seen. Through the dusk dark figures of passers-by were visible in the distance. I rushed to catch them up and, having done so, looked each one in the face as I ran by. I ran as far as the crossroads.

There's no point in losing your temper with crazy people, I suddenly thought. Tatyana Pavlovna got mad with him out of sheer rage, which means he's not really crazy at all! Oh, I kept on thinking it was all *allegorical* and he was definitely intending to put an end to something, just as he had smashed the icon, and wanted to demonstrate the fact to us, to mother, to everyone. But there was also no doubt he had a 'double' at his side, no doubt about that at all . . .

III

However, he wasn't to be found anywhere and there was no point in running to his place, because it was hard to imagine he had simply gone home. Suddenly I had an idea and I raced off to Anna Andreevna's.

Anna Andreevna had already returned and I was admitted at once. I entered as restrained as possible. Without taking a seat, I told her what had just happened, mentioning particularly about the 'double'. I will never forget, and can never forgive, the avid, but pitilessly calm and self-assured curiosity with which she heard me out, also without sitting down.

'Where is he? Perhaps you know?' I insisted. 'Tatyana Pavlovna sent me to see you yesterday . . .'

'It was I who summoned you yesterday. Yesterday he was in Tsarskoe, he was with me. And now . . .' She glanced at a clock '. . . Now it's seven o'clock. That means he's bound to be at home.'

'I see you know everything—so tell me, tell me what it's all about!' I shouted.

'I know a good deal, but I don't know everything. Of course, there's no point in hiding anything from you . . .' She measured me with a strange look, smiling and speculative. 'Yesterday morning, in answer to her letter, he made Katerina Nikolaevna a formal proposal of marriage.'

538

'That's not true!' My eyes almost jumped out of their sockets.

'The letter passed through my hands. I conveyed it to her unopened. On this occasion he behaved in a most gentlemanly fashion and concealed nothing from me.'

'Anna Andreevna, I don't understand any of it!'

'Of course, it's hard to understand, but it's like a gambler who stakes his all while still having a loaded revolver in his pocket— that's what his proposal was all about. There were nine out of ten chances she wouldn't accept his offer, but he still counted on that one chance in ten and I admit I find it odd. Still . . . still, he may just have gone over the top, it may be that "double" at work, as you put it so well just now.'

'Are you joking? Am I really to believe you were the go-between? You're her father's bride-to-be, aren't you? Don't pull my leg, Anna Andreevna!'

'He asked me to sacrifice my destiny for his happiness, yet he didn't do so properly, it was all a matter of dropping hints and I simply read it in his eyes. Oh, my God, what more do you want? Didn't he go to Königsberg, to your own mother, to seek her permission to marry Madame Akhmakov's stepdaughter? That's quite consistent with his choosing me yesterday to be his go-between and confidante.'

She looked a trifle pale. But her calmness merely reinforced her sarcasm. Oh, I forgave her a great deal at that moment as I gradually began to make sense of the whole business! I considered it for a moment as she waited and said nothing.

'You know what I think?' I laughed suddenly. 'You were the go-between for the letter because it involved no risk for you, because there's not going to be a marriage, is there? But what about him? What about her? Naturally, she'll reject his proposal and then . . . well, what then? Where is he now, Anna Andreevna?' I cried. 'Every moment's precious now, every moment something bad may happen!'

'I told you, he's at home. In yesterday's letter to Katerina Nikolaevna, the one I took to her, he asked to see her *no matter what* in his apartment today, at seven o'clock prompt, this evening. She promised to be there.'

'She's going to *his* place? Why?'

'Why? It belongs to Nastasya Yegorovna. They could quite easily meet there as her guests . . .'

'But she's frightened of him! I mean, he might kill her!'

Anna Andreevna merely smiled.

'Katerina Nikolaevna, despite all her fear, which is something I've also noticed in her, has always felt, right from the beginning, a certain deep respect and wonder at the nobility of Andrey Petrovich's rules of conduct and the loftiness of his mind. This time she has entrusted herself to him in order to be done with him for good and all. In his letter to her he gave her his most solemn word as a gentleman that she had nothing to fear from him ... In a word, I don't remember exactly what expressions were used in the letter, but she had entrusted herself to him, so to speak, for one last time and, so to speak, by responding with the most heroic feelings on her part. It could be a case of both parties trying to outdo each other in the nobility of their conduct.'

'But there's the "double", the "double"!' I exclaimed. 'After all, he's gone out of his mind!'

'In giving her word yesterday to attend the meeting, Katerina Nikolaevna probably did not anticipate something like that.'

I suddenly turned round and started to run off—to him, to them, of course! But I came back from the main room for a moment.

'Maybe that's what you want! You want him to kill her!' I shouted and rushed out of the house.

Despite the fact I was having a fit of the shivers, I crept quietly into his apartment via the kitchen and asked in a whisper for Nastasya Yegorovna, but she herself immediately appeared and silently transfixed me with a terribly querying look.

'They're not here, sir. They're not home, sir.'

In a rapid whisper I told her, precisely and directly, that I knew about it all from Anna Andreevna and that I had just come from seeing her.

'Nastasya Yegorovna, where are they?'

'In the sitting-room, sir. Where you sat at the table, the day before yesterday.'

'Nastyasya Yegorovna, let me go there!'

'How can I, sir?'

'Not into that room, but the one next door. Nastasya Yegorovna, Anna Andreevna herself maybe would like it. If she didn't, she wouldn't have told me they were here. They won't hear me ... She'd want me to ...'

'And if she didn't?' Nastasya Yegorovna still transfixed me with her eyes.

'Nastasya Yegorovna, I can't forget your Olya . . . Let me through.'

Suddenly her lips and chin started working.

'My dear, for Olya's sake . . .'cos you've shown such feelings . . . Don't abandon Anna Andreevna, my dear! You won't desert her, will you?'

'No, I won't!'

'Give me your word you won't rush into their room and you won't make a noise if I let you in there?'

'I swear on my honour, Nastasya Yegorovna!'

She seized hold of my jacket and led me into a dark room adjoining the one where they were. She led me almost silently over soft carpet towards some doors and made me stop by the heavy curtains hanging across the doorway, raising one tiny corner to show me where they were.

I stayed there and she went away. Naturally I stayed there. I knew I would be eavesdropping on someone else's secrets, but I stayed. What else could I do? Wasn't it his 'double' there? Hadn't he smashed an icon before my very eyes?

IV

They were sitting facing each other at the very table where he and I had drunk to his 'resurrection' the day before yesterday. I had a full view of both their faces. She was dressed simply in black, as beautiful and evidently as calm as ever. He was speaking and she was listening to him very attentively and courteously. Perhaps she even displayed a certain shyness. He, for his part, was terribly worked up. I had arrived some way through their conversation and for a while could not understand a great deal. I remember she suddenly asked:

'And I was the reason?'

'No, I was,' he answered. 'You were just one of the innocent, proved guilty. You know there are people like that, don't you? It's the most unforgivable kinds of guilt that almost always incur the heaviest punishment,' he added and gave an odd sort of chuckle. 'For a time I had imagined I had completely forgotten you and I could laugh at my stupid passion . . . but you know all

541

about that. And yet what do I feel about the man you're going to marry? I proposed to you yesterday—forgive me for that, it was a silly thing to do, but I had no other choice. What could I do apart from something silly like that? I don't know . . .'

On saying this he burst into despairing laughter, suddenly raising his eyes to her. Till then he had kept his eyes averted. Had I been her at that moment, I felt I would have been frightened of that laugh. He suddenly stood up.

'Tell me how you could possibly have agreed to come here?' he suddenly asked, as if remembering the main point of it all. 'My invitation and my whole letter were silly . . . One moment, though. I can still make a guess at the reason you agreed to come, but why did you actually come, that's the question. Was it just out of fear?'

'I just came to see you,' she announced, eyeing him cautiously and shyly. Neither spoke for half a minute. Versilov again sat down and began saying in a tender, but emotionally charged and almost shaking voice:

'I haven't seen you for an awfully long time, Katerina Niko-laevna, so long I hardly thought it possible I could sit here as I am now, looking into your face and hearing your voice . . . We haven't seen each other for two years. We haven't spoken for two years. I had never imagined I would talk to you again. Well, let bygones by bygones, let what happens today vanish away tomorrow like so much smoke! I say bully for that, because again there's nothing to put in its place, but,' he suddenly added, almost pleading, 'don't just go away now! Since you've done your good deed, come on, don't just walk away, but answer me one thing . . .'

'What?'

'We'll never see each other again, so what's it matter to you, eh? Tell me the truth. Answer the one question sensible people never ask. Did you ever love me or had I got it all wrong?'

She blushed scarlet. 'I loved you,' she said.

I would have expected her to say that—oh, she was so truthful, so sincere, so honest!

'And now?' he went on.

'Now I don't.'

'And you're laughing at me?'

'No, I laughed just now because I knew you'd be bound to

542

ask: "And now?" That was why I smiled. When you guess right you always smile.'

I had a kind of strange feeling, because I had never seen her so cautious, so confused and even shy. He was devouring her with his eyes.

'I know you don't like me . . . and you don't love me at all, do you?'

'Maybe I don't. No, I don't love you,' she added firmly, neither smiling, nor blushing. 'Yes, I loved you once, but not for long. I stopped loving you very quickly . . .'

'I know, yes, I know you saw I wasn't what you wanted, but . . . but what did you want? Tell me again . . .'

'Did I ever tell you what I wanted? I'm the most ordinary kind of woman. I'm the calm sort. I like . . . I like happy people.'

'Happy?'

'You see I don't even know how to tell you things. I think if you'd been able to love me less, then I'd really have fallen in love with you.'

Again she gave a shy smile. The most complete sincerity flashed through her words. She could hardly fail to be aware that her answer was a final verdict on their relationship, explaining and solving everything. Oh, he himself should have realized that! But he looked at her and smiled strangely.

'Björing—is he a happy person?' He went on with his questioning.

'He needn't trouble you at all,' she answered rather hastily. 'I am marrying him simply because with him I know I'll be able to be my own calm self. My soul will be my own.'

'I've heard you've again grown fond of going out, of being in society?'

'Not in society. I know there's as much out of order in our society as everywhere else. But from the outside it still looks good, so if you live just to look in on things from the outside, then you might as well look in on society as anywhere.'

'I've been hearing the term "out of order" often. Were you frightened of me being "out of order" in those days—my chains, my ideas, my stupidities?'

'No, it wasn't that at all . . .'

'What was it, then? For God's sake, come clean!'

'All right, I will come clean, because I consider you a man of very great intellect ... It's this: I've always thought there was something ridiculous about you.'

Having spoken, she suddenly blushed as if recognizing she had done something extraordinarily indiscreet.

'For having said that, I can forgive you a great deal,' he said strangely.

'I didn't mean that,' she said hurriedly, going red in the face. 'I meant I was ridiculous ... for talking to you like a fool.'

'No, you're not ridiculous, you're just a depraved socialite!' He had gone terribly pale. 'I also didn't say what I meant when I asked you why you'd come here? Shall I tell you what I meant? There's a letter in existence, a document, and you're terribly frightened of it because your father, if it fell into his hands, could curse you in life and in death cut you out of his will. You're frightened of that letter—and you came here for that letter!'

He spoke almost shaking with rage and even with his teeth beginning to chatter. She listened to him looking depressed and hurt.

'I know you can do all sorts of nasty things to me,' she said, as if dismissing his words. 'But I came here not so much to persuade you not to persecute me as just to see you. I've been wanting to see you for a long time, I really have ... But I find you're just as you used to be,' she added suddenly, as if carried away by a special, crucial thought and even an odd and unexpected emotion.

'And you'd hoped to find someone different? After my letter about your depravity, that is? Tell me, you came here without any fear at all, did you?'

'I came here because I once loved you. But please, I beg you, you know—please don't make threats to me while we're here now, don't remind me of all my worst feelings and thoughts. If you could talk about something else, I would be very glad. Leave the threats till later, but let it be different now ... I honestly came here to see you and hear what you had to say. But if you can't, then kill me and be done with it, only don't use threats and don't tear yourself to pieces in front of me!'

She ended up with these words, expectantly studying him in an odd way as if literally supposing he could kill her there and then. He once more rose out of his chair and, looking at her fiercely, said firmly:

'You will leave here quite unharmed.'

'Oh, yes, you've given your word!' She smiled.

'No, it isn't only that I gave my word in my letter, but because I want to, and because I will, go on thinking about you all night long . . .'

'Torturing yourself?'

'I always imagine you're with me when I'm alone. I spend all the time talking to you. I wander through slums and visit dives and you're always there in front of me like a kind of exact opposite. But you're always laughing at me, just as you are now . . .' He spoke as if he were not his usual self.

'I've never, never laughed at you!' she cried in an emotionally charged voice and with the greatest sympathy written all over her face. 'If I've come here, then I've made every effort to ensure you shouldn't be embarrassed,' she added suddenly. 'I've come here to tell you I almost love you . . . Forgive me, I shouldn't have put it like that!' she concluded hastily.

He gave a laugh.

'Why don't you know how to pretend? Why are you always such a simple soul, why aren't you like everyone else? I mean— to say to a man you're about to ditch "I almost love you"!'

'I didn't know how to put it!' she cried all in a rush. 'It wasn't what I meant to say! It's because I've always been shy and tongue-tied since our very first meeting. If I didn't put it properly when I said "I almost love you", then it's what I thought—or almost, so it's why I said it, although I really love you with the sort of *general* love with which you can love everyone and you're never ashamed to admit to . . .'

He listened to what she said in silence, never once taking his fierce eyes off her.

'Of course, I'm insulting you,' he went on, still not his usual self. 'In fact it's what's called passion . . . All I know is that when I'm with you I'm done for; and without you, too. It's all the same with or without you. Wherever you might be, you're always with me. I also know I'm capable of hating you a great deal more than I love you . . . Still, I've long stopped thinking about anything like that, I'm past caring. I'm just sorry I fell in love with someone like you . . .'

His voice broke. He went on, as if he were trying to catch his breath.

545

'To you, it's crazy, is it, the way I'm talking?' He smiled palely. 'I think I'd spend thirty years standing on one leg if it would please you . . . so I see you pity me. Your face says "I'd fall in love with you, if I could, but I can't . . ." Am I right? All right, I've got no pride. Like a beggar, I'll accept any charity from you—any, do you hear? What's the point of a beggar having pride, eh?'

She stood up and went over to him.

'My friend,' she said, placing a hand on his shoulder and with inexpressible feeling in her face, 'I can't bear to hear you say a thing like that! All my life I'll think of you as a most precious person, as the greatest of hearts, as the most sacred thing I could ever revere and love! Andrey Petrovich, believe me really and truly, I have come here today for some good reason, you dear man, dear then and dear now! I will never forget the intellectual shaking you gave me when we first met. Let's say goodbye as friends, and you will always be the single most serious and delightful thing I ever had in my mind in my entire life!'

'"Let's say goodbye and then I'll love you" is what you're saying. I *will* love you, only let's say goodbye. Listen,' he declared, white as a sheet, 'do this last act of charity—don't love me, don't live with me! Let's never see each other again. I will be your slave, if you summon me, and I will disappear instantly if you don't want to see me or hear from me again, only . . . *Don't marry anyone else!*'

My heart was crushed when I heard that. The naïvely demeaning request was all the more pitiful and heart-rending for being so naked and impossible. Oh, of course, he was asking for charity! How could he possibly imagine she would agree? Yet he had sunk so low as to beg! To see him fallen so low in spirit was unbearable. Her face was suddenly contorted in pain, but before she could say a word, he had come to his senses.

'I will *ex-ter-min-ate* you!' he suddenly cried in a strange distorted voice which was not like his at all.

But she answered him equally strangely, also in an unexpected voice quite unlike her own:

'If I did do an act of charity for you,' she said suddenly, with firmness, 'then you'd avenge yourself on me later far more terribly than you threatened to do now because you'd never be

able to forget the way you've just stood in front of me and begged
... No, I won't listen to any threats from you!'

She ended almost indignantly, gazing at him with what
amounted to a challenge.

'"Any threat from you!" you say. Threats, you mean, from a
beggar! I was just joking,' he said quietly, with a smile. 'I won't
do you any harm, don't worry. Please go. I'll try as hard as I can
to send you that document. Only just go! Go! I wrote you a
stupid letter, but you answered it and you came here and now
we're all square. That way, please.'

He pointed to the door. She had been on the point of going
through the room where I was hiding.

'Forgive me if you can,' she said, stopping in the doorway.

'What if we meet one day as complete friends, reminisce over
what's just happened and laugh about it?' he suddenly asked. Yet
every inch of his face worked as if he were in the grip of a
convulsion.

'Oh, God grant we do!' she cried out, clasping her hands in
front of her, but studying his face fearfully and trying to guess
what he meant.

'Please go. We're both so intelligent, you and I, but you're ...
you're someone after my own heart! I wrote you a crazy letter,
but you were ready to come here to tell me you *almost* love me!
Oh, we're as crazy as each other! Go on being as crazy as that,
don't change, and then we'll meet again as friends—I swear we
will, I promise you!'

'And when that time comes I'll be certain to fall in love with
you, because I can feel it now!'

The woman in her could not restrain herself from flinging
these final words at him from the doorway. She went out.

Hurriedly and soundlessly I made my way through the kitchen,
hardly glancing at Nastasya Yegorovna, who had been waiting
for me, and went down the back stairs and through the courtyard
into the street. I just managed to catch sight of her as she sat
down in a hired carriage which had been waiting for her by the
front steps. I ran along the street.

547

CHAPTER XI

I

I DASHED to see Lambert. Oh, no matter how much I might want to make things seem logical and find the slightest sign of common sense in my actions that evening and throughout the night, even now, when I can look back over it all, I cannot envisage it in an appropriately clear light. It was all a matter of feeling or—better—a chaotic tangle of feelings among which I was naturally bound to get lost. True, there was one most important feeling which overwhelmed me and took precedence over all others but . . . but dare I say what it was? Especially as I wasn't sure . . .

It goes without saying I was beside myself when I burst in on Lambert. I even gave Alphonsine and him a real shock. I have always noticed that even the most feckless and dissolute Frenchmen are excessively devoted in their domestic habits to a certain kind of bourgeois orderliness, to the most prosaic kind of eternally ordinary and ritualized form of living. Still, Lambert quickly realized that something had happened and was overjoyed to see me there at long last, able finally to have me *in his grasp*. That's all he'd been thinking about day after day! Oh, how he needed me! And now, when he'd lost all hope of it, here I was suddenly right in front of him and in a crazy state, in just the state he wanted me to be!

'Wine, Lambert! Wine!' I shouted. 'Let's drink, let's have a party! Alphonsine, where's your guitar?'

I won't set the scene—that's irrelevant! We had a drink and I told him everything, everything. He listened avidly. I was the first to suggest we plan to send the whole thing up in flames. First of all, we had to contact Katerina Nikolaevna by letter . . .

'Maybe,' Lambert agreed, hanging on my every word.

Secondly, to make it convincing, we ought to send a copy of her 'document' with the letter so she could see we were serious.

'Sure we ought! We must!' agreed Lambert, constantly exchanging glances with Alphonsine.

Thirdly, Lambert should contact her himself, off his own bat,

548

in the guise of someone unknown who had just arrived from Moscow and I would bring Versilov . . .

'And maybe Versilov,' agreed Lambert.

'Not maybe, must be!' I shouted. 'That's essential! It's all being done for him!' I had to make this clear, drinking glassful after glassful. (We were all three drinking, but I think I alone must have polished off a whole bottle of champagne while they were just pretending.) 'Versilov and I will be in the next room—you've got to find a place with two rooms, Lambert!—and when she suddenly agrees to everything—the pay-off in money and the *other* kind, because they're all selling their bodies, these women—then Versilov and I'll appear and catch her in the act and Versilov'll see what a filthy bitch she is and be cured of her once and for all and kick her out. But Björing's got to be there as well to see what she's like!' I added in a frenzy.

'No, there's no need for Björing!' remarked Lambert.

'Oh, yes there is!' I yelled. 'You don't understand anything, Lambert, because you're stupid! On the contrary, there's got to be a scandal in high society, because in that way we'll get our own back on it and on her and she'll get what she deserves! Lambert, she'll give you an IOU . . . I don't need the money, I'll spit on it, but you can grab it and stuff it in your pocket with my spittle on it, just so long as I can crush her!'

'Yes, yes,' Lambert agreed, 'you do that, you . . .' He kept on exchanging glances with Alphonsine.

'Lambert, she worships, really worships Versilov!' I babbled at him. 'I was convinced of that just now!'

'It's good you eavesdropped like that. I'd never have thought you'd have spied on them! I didn't think you were clever enough!'

He said this simply to flatter me.

'You're talking nonsense, you Frenchie! I'm not a spy and I've got plenty of brains! You know, Lambert, she loves him!' I went on, trying hard to express myself clearly. 'But she won't marry him, she'll marry Björing, because he's a guards' officer and Versilov's just a man of great magnanimity and a friend of humanity, which means, in her way of thinking, he's comic, that's all! Oh, she knows how passionate he is and enjoys it, plays with him and teases him, but she won't marry him! She's a woman! She's a snake! Every woman's a snake, and every snake's a woman! He's got to be cured of her! He's got to have his eyes opened! Let him see who she really is and get her out of his system! I'll bring him to you, Lambert.'

'Right, right!' Lambert asserted again and again, pouring me more wine.

The main thing was he did his utmost not to annoy me or contradict me while getting me to drink more and more. It was all so crude and obvious even I couldn't fail to notice. But I just couldn't make myself leave. I went on drinking and talking and felt terribly keen to unburden myself completely. When Lambert went off to get another bottle, Alphonsine played somethng Spanish on her guitar and I almost broke down in tears.

'Lambert, you know the whole thing is,' I exclaimed with deep feeling, 'the man's got to be saved because . . . because he's under a spell! If she did marry him, he'd throw her out the very next morning after the wedding night because . . . because that's the way things are! Because a brutal, wild love like that is like having a fit, like putting one's head in a noose, like falling sick— and you've no sooner had full sexual satisfaction than the scales fall from your eyes and you have an exact opposite feeling— revulsion and hatred, a desire to exterminate and crush what you loved! You know the story of Abishag from the Book of Kings, don't you, Lambert? You've read it?'

'No, I don't remember. Is it a novel?' Lambert muttered.

'Oh, you don't know anything, Lambert! You're terribly, terribly ignorant . . . But, shit, I don't care! Oh, he loves mother—he kissed her portrait! He'll throw that other one out the next morning and go back to mother! But then it'll be too late, so he's got to be saved now . . .'

Eventually I started crying bitterly, though I still went on talking and drinking quantities. The oddest thing was that never once throughout the entire evening did Lambert ask anything about the 'document' or where it was. That is, he didn't ask me to show it to him or put it on the table. I think nothing would have been more natural, since we were planning to act on it. And something else: we merely talked about having to do it, about it being essential, but as to where it would all take place, how and when—not a word was said about that! He simply kept egging me on and exchanging looks with Alphonsine—and that was all!

550

Of course, at the time I was incapable of making any sense of it, but I can still remember that much.

It ended with my falling asleep on the divan fully clothed. I had a very long sleep and woke up very late. I remember that, on waking, I lay some time on the divan in a stupor, trying to sort out my thoughts and remember things and pretending still to be asleep. But it turned out Lambert wasn't there. He had gone out. It was ten o'clock. The fire was crackling in the stove just as it had been when I'd been at Lambert's the first time, after spending the night outside. But Alphonsine was keeping an eye on me from behind the screens. I had been aware of this because she had glanced round once or twice and looked at me and each time I had closed my eyes and pretended to be asleep. I did so because I felt utterly crushed and had to assess my situation. I was aware with horror of all the silliness and nastiness of the confession I had made to Lambert the previous night, the way I had plotted with him and my mistake in rushing to see him. Thank God, I still had the document! It was still sewn into my side pocket! I felt it and it was there! So all I had to do now was jump up and run away! It didn't matter a damn what Lambert might think afterwards! He wasn't worth thinking about!

But the person I was really ashamed of was myself! I was my own judge and jury and—oh, God, the things I felt then! Yet I am not going to describe that hellish, unbearable feeling and the consciousness of wallowing in such dirt and filth. Still, I must admit to it, because I think the time has come for it. It has to be mentioned in these notes of mine. So let's make it clear I didn't want to put *her* to shame and arrange for people to witness the pay-offs she would have to make to Lambert (oh, what filth that was!) just so as to save that crazy fool Versilov and get him to go back to mother, but perhaps because . . . because I was myself in love with her, because I loved her and was jealous! Jealous of whom—Björing, Versilov? Jealous of anyone she might look at, perhaps, at a ball or might speak to while I stood there in a corner ashamed of myself? . . . Oh, hell!

In a word, I don't know who I was jealous of over her. But I just had the feeling the previous evening, and was convinced, as sure as twice two is four, that she was lost to me, that this woman would reject me and mock me for being false and silly! She was completely truthful and honest, while I . . . I was just a spy who had certain 'materials'.

I had secreted all this in my heart ever since the start and now the time had come to draw up a balance sheet. But I will insist again and for the last time—maybe as much as 50 or 75 per cent of what I've written here is a lie so far as I am concerned! The previous night I had loathed her like crazy and later on like a roaring drunk. I've already said it was a chaos of feelings and sensations which I couldn't make head or tail of, but I've still got to admit that's how I felt because at least part of what I felt was real.

With irrepressible disgust and determined to wipe the slate clean I suddenly jumped up from the divan. The moment I did so Alphonsine popped out. I seized my fur coat and hat and told her to tell Lambert I'd been delirious the night before and slandered a lady, I'd done it for fun and Lambert mustn't dare come and see me again . . . I blurted it all out in stumbling, hurried French and, naturally, terribly badly, but, to my surprise, Alphonsine grasped it all and—what was more surprising still—even seemed delighted.

'*Oui, oui,*' she flattered me, '*c'est une honte!* It's a shame! *Une dame* . . . A real lady . . . *Oh, vous êtes généreux, vous!* You are a real gentleman, you are! *Soyez tranquille, je ferai voir raison à Lambert* . . . do not worry, I'll make Lambert see sense . . .'

At that moment I had to stare in bewilderment at her, seeing such an unexpected reversal of her feelings and probably Lambert's as well. However, I left without a word, my heart full of doubts and the whole thing making no sense. Oh, later on I got it all, but by then it was too late! Oh, what a hell of a scheme it was! I will stop here and explain everything later, otherwise the reader won't be able to understand it.

The point was that during my first meeting with Lambert, when I was thawing out in his apartment, I mumbled to him like a fool something about the document sewn into my pocket. At that time I must have suddenly dropped off to sleep on his divan and Lambert had then immediately felt my pocket and convinced himself there was some document sewn into it. Later he had more than once verified it was still there. For instance, during the dinner in the Tartar restaurant I remember he had several times put his arm round my waist. Having eventually discovered the importance of the document, he had concocted a plan of his own which I had never supposed he could. Like an idiot, I kept on imagining he was so keen on inviting me to see him solely because he wanted me to join him and act in concert with him. But no, he didn't invite me for that reason at all! He wanted me there to get me dead drunk, so that when I was fast asleep and dead to the world he could cut open my pocket and get hold of the document! And that's just what he and Alphonsine had done that night. It was Alphonsine who had cut open the pocket. Having got hold of the letter, *her letter*, the document I had brought from Moscow, they had taken a piece of notepaper the same size and sewn it back into my pocket so I wouldn't notice. Alphonsine herself had done it. And I, I had gone on thinking, almost to the very end, for a whole day and a half, that I was in possession of a secret and the fate of Katerina Nikolaevna was still in my hands!

A final word: the theft of that document was the cause of everything, of all the misfortunes that ensued!

II

I have reached the final twenty-four hours of my notes and I am at the very end!

I think it was about half-past ten when, in an excited condition but, so far as I can recall, oddly distracted, having finally come to terms with things in my heart, that I went back to my room. I did not hurry because I knew how I would behave. And suddenly, no sooner had I set foot in my corridor, than I realized a new calamity had struck, there had been another extraordinary complication: the old prince, who had just been brought from Tsarskoe Selo, was there, and with him was Anna Andreevna!

He had not actually been put in my room but in the landlord's old rooms adjoining mine. It turned out that the previous day certain alterations and redecoration—of the most superficial kind—had taken place in these rooms. The landlord and his wife had transferred themselves into the cubby-hole previously occupied by the capricious pock-marked lodger I have already mentioned, and he had been consigned God knows where.

I was met by the landlord who came flitting instantly into my room. He did not look at me as confidently as he had done the previous day but he was in an excited state—right on top of things, so to speak. I said nothing to him but, retreating into a corner and taking my head in my hands, stood there about a minute. He must have thought to start with I was merely pretending, but eventually he gave up and became apprehensive.

'Is something wrong?' he muttered. 'I've been waiting for you to ask you,' he added, seeing I made no attempt to answer, 'if you'd like this door opened so you can gain direct access to the prince's accommodation . . . rather than go round by the passage?' He pointed to a side door that had always been locked which gave access to the landlord's rooms and now to where the prince was.

'Look, Pyotr Ippolitovich,' I said to him, looking stern, 'please go and ask Anna Andreevna to come here at once for a discussion. Have they been here long?'

'It'll be almost an hour!'

'Off you go, then!'

He went off and returned with the strange answer that Anna Andreevna and Prince Nikolay Ivanovich were waiting impatiently to see me in their rooms. This meant that Anna Andreevna had no wish to visit me. I straightened out and cleaned up my jacket, which had grown crumpled during the night, washed, combed my hair—all without any hurry—and set off to see the old man, fully aware of the need for caution.

The prince was sitting on a divan at a round table, and Anna Andreevna, in another corner, sat at another table covered with a cloth, on which bubbled my landlord's samovar (more shiny than ever), and was pouring out tea for him. I entered with the same stern look on my face and the old man, noticing it instantly, literally shook and the smile on his face quickly gave way to an expression of fright. But I couldn't keep it up, laughed and held out my hands. The poor chap just flung himself into my open arms.

Without any doubt I realized at once who I was dealing with. In the first place, it was as clear as twice two is four that since I had last seen him the old man, who had been cheerful, more or less, and to an extent in his right mind and possessed of some character, had been turned into a kind of mummy, into a complete child, frightened and mistrustful. I will add that he knew perfectly well why he had been brought here. Everything had happened as I explained earlier, when I had anticipated what I had to tell. He had received a sudden and utter shock, and had been broken and crushed by the news of his daughter's treachery and the likelihood of being consigned to a lunatic asylum. He had allowed himself to be conveyed from where he was, scarcely aware, in his panic, of what he was doing. They had told him I had in my possession a secret and a key to a final solution.

I will say right away that the one thing he feared most of all was this final solution and the key to it. He was expecting I would come in with a judgemental frown on my face and a paper clutched in my hands—and so was absolutely delighted that I was ready to laugh and talk about something completely different. When we embraced, he shed tears. I admit I also shed a tear or two, but at once I suddenly felt terribly sorry for him because Alphonsine's little lap-dog started a tiny bell-like yapping and sprang up at me from the divan. He had never once been parted from this little dog ever since receiving it and even slept with it beside him.

'*Oh, je disais qu'il a du cœur!* I told you he had a heart of gold!' he exclaimed, pointing me out to Anna Andreevna.

'But how well you look, prince, what a fine, fresh, healthy look you have!' I remarked. Alas, it was the exact opposite—he looked mummified and I only said it to cheer him up!

'*N'est-ce pas, n'est-ce pas?* You mean it?' He was delighted. 'Oh, my health is surprisingly good!'

'Please have your tea, and if you'll let me have a cup I'll join you.'

'Wonderful! "Let's drink and be merry . . ." or whatever the song says! Anna Andreevna, give him some tea, *il prend toujours par les sentiments* . . . Feelings always get the better of him. Let's all have tea, my dear.'

Anna Andreevna poured out the tea, but turned to me suddenly and began saying with the utmost solemnity:

'Arkady Makarovich, we have both, I and my benefactor, Prince Nikolay Ivanovich, found a haven here with you. I consider we have come to you and to you alone, and we are both asking you for sanctuary. Please bear in mind that almost the entire fate of this saintly, most noble and aggrieved of men lies in your hands . . . We await the decision of your honest and truthful heart!'

But she was unable to say more because the prince was so horrified he almost shook with fright:

'*Après, après, n'est-ce pas? Chère amie!* My dear, please leave it, won't you!' he repeated over and over, raising his hands towards her.

I cannot express the unpleasant effect her words had on me. I did not reply and contented myself with a cold and solemn bow. Then I took a seat at the table and deliberately started talking about something else, various silly things, and began laughing and joking. The old man was visibly grateful to me and joined in enthusiastically. But his jollity, although enthusiastic, was obviously a little unsure of itself and could any moment have yielded to complete despair—that was clear at a glance.

'*Cher enfant*, I heard you'd been ill ... *Ah, pardon!* Didn't I hear you've been occupied with spiritualism?'

'It never crossed my mind!' I smiled broadly.

'Really? Then who was it told me about spiritualism?'

'It was that government official you've got here, that Pyotr Ippolitovich, he told you just now,' Anna Andreevna explained. 'He's a very amusing man and very entertaining. If you like, I'll ask him to come in.'

'*Oui, oui, il est charmant* ... Charming fellow, knows all sorts of jokes, but let's leave him till later. If we have him in, he'll do nothing but chatter—*mais après*. Just imagine, he was laying the table just now and said to us, "Don't worry, it won't fly away, we're not spiritualists!" Is it really true that spiritualists can make tables fly about?'

'I've no idea. I've heard it said all four legs rise up.'

'*Mais c'est terrible ce que tu dis!* But that's awful' He gave me a frightened glance.

'Oh, don't worry, it's all nonsense.'

'That's what I say myself. Nastasya Stepanovna Salomeeva—you know her, don't you? ... Oh, no, you don't ...—well, she believes in spiritualism and, just imagine, *cher enfant*,' he turned to Anna Andreevna, 'I told her they also have tables in government ministries and as many as eight pairs of official hands on each one all busy writing, so why on earth don't the tables dance about? Just imagine it if they all started dancing about! A rebellion by tables in the finance ministry or the ministry of education ... Whatever next!'

556

'You still say such funny things, prince!' I exclaimed, sincerely trying to laugh.

'*N'est-ce pas? Je ne parle pas trop, mais je dis bien.* Really? I don't say too much, but I say it well.'

'I'll get Pyotr Ippolitovich,' said Anna Andreevna, standing up. Happiness shone in her face since she was overjoyed at seeing how kind I was to the prince. But the instant she had left the old man's whole expression changed. He glanced hastily at the door, looked round him and, bending towards me from the divan, whispered in a frightened voice:

'*Cher ami!* Oh, if only I could see the two of them here together! *O cher enfant!*'

'Prince, don't worry . . .'

'Yes, yes, but we'll . . . we'll reconcile them, *n'est-ce pas?* It's a silly, superficial tiff between two of the finest women, *n'est-ce pas?* I place all my hopes in you . . . We'll sort it all out here. What a strange-looking place this is!' He gazed round him almost fearfully. 'You know something, that landlord—he's got such a face—tell me, he's not dangerous, is he?'

'My landlord? No! Why should he be dangerous?'

'*C'est ça.* Right. So much the better. *Il semble qu'il est bête, ce gentilhomme.* The man seemed stupid, that's all. *Cher enfant*, for Christ's sake don't tell Anna Andreevna I'm terrified of everything here. I said nice things about everything here when I arrived, including the landlord. Listen, you've heard about von Sohn . . . Do you remember?'*

'So?'

'*Rien, rien du tout . . . Mais je suis libre ici, n'est-ce pas?* Do you think anything like that'll happen to me here?'

'I assure you, dear friend . . . Don't worry!'

'*Mon ami! Mon enfant!*' he cried suddenly, clasping his hands together in front of him and no longer trying to hide his fear, 'if you really have something—a document, in short . . . If you've got something to tell me, then don't! For God's sake don't say anything! It'd be better not to say a thing . . . for as long as you possibly can . . .'

He wanted to fling his arms round me. Tears streamed down his face. I cannot express how my heart ached at the sight of the poor old man, who was like a pitiful, feeble, frightened child stolen from his hearth and home by gypsies and taken away to

557

live among strangers. But we had no time to embrace. The door opened and in came Anna Andreevna, but not with my landlord. She came in with my half-brother, Versilov's son. This new turn of events shocked me. I stood up and went towards the door.

'Arkady Makarovich, let me introduce you,' Anna Andreevna said loudly, so I was bound to stop in my tracks.

'I am only *too* familiar with your brother!' I cried in ringing tones, particularly accentuating the '*too*'.

'Oh, there's been a horrible mistake! I am so . . . so much to blame, dear And . . . Andrey Makarovich,' the young man started mumbling, approaching me with an unusually harassed expression and seizing hold of my hand which I was in no position to withhold. 'My Stepan got it wrong. He announced you so stupidly I took you for someone else . . . It was in Moscow,' he explained to his sister. 'Afterwards I made strenuous efforts to find you and clear things up, but I fell ill. You can ask her . . . *Cher prince, nous devons être amis même par droit de naissance.* Our birthright should make us friends, dear prince, shouldn't it?'

And the brash young man even dared place an arm round my shoulder, which was the height of familiarity. I dodged away but preferred in my confusion to leave without another word. Having returned to my own room, I sat down on my bed, distracted and excited. The whole thing was depressing, but I couldn't just abandon Anna Andreevna and leave her to her own devices. I was suddenly aware she, also, was dear to me and her position was terrible.

III

As I anticipated, she herself came into my room, leaving the prince with her brother who began telling him the very latest, freshly baked items of society gossip, which instantly delighted the impressionable old man. With a questioning look I rose silently from my bed.

'I have told you everything, Arkady Makarovich,' she began saying directly. 'You have our fate in your hands.'

'But I warned you I couldn't . . . The most sacred obligations prevent me from doing what you're counting on.'

'Really? That's your answer, is it? Well, it may be the end of me, but what about the old man? You'd better realize he may be out of his mind by this evening!'

'No, he'll only go out of his mind if I show him the letter in which his daughter seeks legal advice on how to have him declared insane!' I exclaimed fiercely. 'That'll be too much for him. He doesn't believe the letter exists, you know. He told me so.'

It was untrue he had told me, but it made my point.

'He told you that! I thought as much! In that case I'm done for! He's already been crying and pleading to be allowed home.'

'Tell me exactly what your plan was,' I asked deliberately.

She went red, out of hurt pride, so to speak, but she pulled herself together, saying:

'If we had his daughter's letter in our hands, we'd be justified in the eyes of society. I'd at once send for Prince V. .... and Boris Mikhailovich Pelishchev, friends of his since childhood. They are both respected, influential members of high society and I know that as long as two years ago they disapproved of certain things done by his callous and greedy daughter. They would of course reconcile him with his daughter at my request— I'd insist on that—but then the whole situation would be completely changed. Apart from that, I would then be counting on my own relatives, the Fanariotovs, to decide to support my rights. But the main thing for me would be his happiness. He would then finally understand and appreciate who was really devoted to him. There's no doubt I am counting more than ever on your influence, Arkady Makarovich, because you are so fond of him ... And who is fond of him apart from you and me? He has done nothing but talk about you in these last few days. He's been longing to see you, he calls you " my young friend". It goes without saying that from now on all my life my gratitude will know no limits . . .'

It sounded as if she were promising me some reward, perhaps in terms of money.

I interrupted her sharply:

'Say what you like, I can't!' I made this statement with a look of unshakeable determination. 'I can only pay you back with the same sincerity and explain to you my latest plan. I will hand back that fateful letter to Katerina Nikolaevna just as soon as I can, but on the express understanding she creates no scandal out of all that has just happened and gives her word beforehand that she won't spoil your happiness. That is all I can do.'

'It's quite impossible!' she announced, red in the face. The very idea that Katerina Nikolaevna might *have pity on her* was utterly abhorrent.

'I will not change my mind, Anna Andreevna.'

'Perhaps you will.'

'Ask Lambert!'

'Arkady Makarovich, you have no idea what problems may arise through your stubbornness,' she said severely and fiercely.

'So there'll be no problems—all right! My head's spinning. I've had enough of you. I've come to a decision, and that's that! Only, for God's sake, I beg you, please don't involve your brother!'

'But he's so keen to smoothe things out . . .'

'There's nothing to be smoothed out! I don't care, and I don't want to, I just don't want to!' I made these exclamations, holding myself by the head. (Oh, maybe I was being too high-handed with her!) 'Tell me, though, where's the prince going to spend the night? Not here, surely?'

'He will spend the night here, in your room, with you.'

'Then by this evening I'll find somewhere else!'

And immediately after saying these cruel words I seized my hat and started putting on my fur coat. Anna Andreevna observed me in puritanical silence. Oh, I was sorry for her, I was really sorry for this proud girl! But I dashed out of the room without leaving her anything more to hope for.

IV

I will try to be brief. I had taken my decision and I went straight off to find Tatyana Pavlovna. Alas, a great misfortune could have been avoided if I had found her at home. But inevitably failure dogged me the whole of that day. Of course, I went first of all to mother's in the hope of seeing her and, secondly, being more or less sure of meeting Tatyana Pavlovna there. But she wasn't. She had just left and mother was lying ill, with only Liza there to look after her. Liza begged me not to go in and wake up mother because, as she said, 'she hadn't slept a wink all night and now, thank God, she'd at last dropped off.' I kissed Liza and told her in a couple of words I had taken an important and fateful decision and was just about to act on it.

She listened without appearing particularly surprised, as if what I said was quite ordinary. Oh, they had all grown accustomed at that time to the way I was continually making 'final plans' and then going back on them! But now—now it was different! I went to the dive on the canal and waited there a bit in order to be sure of finding Tatyana Pavlovna at home. I will explain, by the way, why this lady was suddenly so essential to me. What I wanted was to send her at once to fetch Katerina Nikolaevna to her apartment so that I could hand over the letter to her in Tatyana Pavlovna's presence after having explained everything once and for all . . .

In a word, I only wanted what was owing to me, which was to justify myself and be done with it. Once that was over, I intended quite definitely to say a few words in Anna Andreevna's favour and, if possible, persuade Katerina Nikolaevna and Tatyana Pavlovna (as a witness) to come to my room and see the prince and there reconcile the two warring women, revive the prince's spirits, and . . . and . . . at least, there and then, this very day, make the whole lot of them happy, so that all that would be left would be Versilov alone with mother. I didn't doubt I'd succeed. Katerina Nikolaevna, out of gratitude for the return of the letter, for which I would seek nothing back from her, could hardly refuse such a request. Alas, I still imagined I had the document. Oh, what a silly and undignified position I was in without knowing it!

It was already growing quite dark and was four o'clock in the afternoon when I again called on Tatyana Pavlovna. Marya answered rudely that 'she was not back'. I remember very clearly the strange way Marya looked at me from under her brows, but naturally, at that time, I had no idea what it meant. On the contrary, I was overtaken by another thought. Vexed and a little depressed, on going down the stairs from Tatyana Pavlovna's apartment I thought of the poor prince who had so recently held his arms out to me—and I suddenly reproached myself for having spurned him simply because I was personally in a bad mood. I began anxiously imagining that something very unpleasant might have happened there in my absence and hurriedly set off for home. However, all that had happened there was the following:

Anna Andreevna, leaving my room in a fury, had still not given up hope. It must be made clear that she had sent someone round to Lambert's that morning, and then once more, but because Lambert had turned out to be absent on each occasion she had finally sent her own brother to find him. The poor girl, seeing how opposed I was, placed her last hope on Lambert and his influence on me. She had waited for Lambert impatiently and was astonished that he had suddenly abandoned her and vanished when until then he had hardly left her alone at all and been dancing attendance on her. Alas, she could have had no idea that Lambert, now that he possessed the document, had taken quite different decisions and was now deliberately making himself scarce!

Consequently, in her anxiety and with increasing alarm in her heart, Anna Andreevna was hardly able to muster the strength to keep the old man preoccupied, and his own anxiety meanwhile rose to threatening proportions. He began asking strange and frightened questions, even began glancing at her suspiciously and several times started crying. The young Versilov did not stay there long. When he left, Anna Andreevna brought in Pyotr Ippolitovich, on whom she had placed such reliance, but he proved not to be liked at all and even produced revulsion. Generally speaking, the prince regarded Pyotr Ippolitovich for some reason with ever-increasing mistrust and suspicion. And my landlord, as if quite deliberately, launched into talking about spiritualism and various tricks which he claimed to have seen on stage, such as one travelling showman who had cut off people's heads in public with blood flowing and everybody watching, and then he had stuck them back on the necks again and everybody had seen the heads and the necks grown together again, all of which had happened, he claimed, in 1859. The prince was so terrified and simultaneously so disgusted that Anna Andreevna was at once obliged to get rid of the teller of such tales. Happily dinner then arrived, having been ordered the previous day from somewhere close by (by Lambert and Alphonsine) from a remarkable homeless French cook who was seeking employment in an aristocratic house or a club. The dinner with champagne delighted the old man and he ate a great deal and prattled away happily. After dinner, of course, he felt tired and wanted to go to sleep and because he always slept after dinner Anna Andreevna had prepared a bed for him. As he fell asleep, he kept on kissing her hand, saying she was his idea of paradise, his sole hope, his houri, and his 'golden flower'—in other words, he embarked on a recital of eastern endearments. At last he fell asleep and it was at that moment I returned.

Anna Andreevna came bustling in to see me, folded her arms, and said she 'begged me, if not for her, then for the prince's sake, not to go out, but to go and see him as soon as he is awake. Without you he's done for, he'll have an attack of nerves. I'm frightened he won't last the night . . .' She went on to say she herself would have to be away for a couple of hours and so she was leaving the prince entirely in my care. I assured her I would stay there until evening and that when he woke up I would do everything I could to keep him happy.

'And I will be doing my duty!' she declared energetically.

She went out. I will add, anticipating what happened, that she drove off in search of Lambert, who was her last hope. Apart from that, she called on her brother and her relatives, the Fanariotovs. It is understandable what state of mind she would be in on her return.

The prince woke up about an hour after she left. I heard his groan through the wall and at once rushed in to see him. I found him sitting up on his bed in his dressing-gown but so frightened at being alone in a strange room with only one solitary lamp left burning that, when I entered, he shuddered, jumped to his feet, and cried out. I dashed up to him and when he saw it was me he began embracing me with tears of joy.

'They told me you'd gone to other lodgings. You took fright and ran away.'

'Who told you?'

'Who? Maybe I made it up myself, or maybe someone told me. Just imagine, I was having a dream and this old man with a beard walks in carrying an icon which had been broken in half and he suddenly says: "That's how your life will be broken in two!"'

'Oh, my God, you must have heard that Versilov broke an icon in two yesterday!'

'*N'est-ce pas?* Oh, yes, I did hear something! Nastasya Yegorovna told me yesterday morning. She was bringing my trunk here and the little lap-dog.'

'Well, that's why you had the dream.'

'Oh, it doesn't matter. Just imagine, that old man was shaking his finger at me! Where's Anna Andreevna?'

'She'll be back in a moment.'

'Where's she gone? She hasn't run away as well, has she?' he cried out as if he were in pain.

'No, no, she'll be back in a moment and she asked me to sit with you.'

'*Oui*, to come in here. So our Andrey Petrovich has gone clean out of his mind—"so swiftly and quite by chance"!* I always said he'd end up that way. My friend, stop a moment . . .'

He suddenly seized hold of my jacket and drew me towards him.

'Your landlord,' he started whispering, 'not so long ago suddenly brings me these photographs, all of naked women in various eastern poses, and begins showing them to me through a magnifying glass . . . I said I liked them, though I didn't mean it, you know what I mean, but surely it was just sluts like that they brought to that poor unfortunate man in order to get him drunk . . .'

'Oh, you're still on about von Sohn! Prince, forget it! The landlord's a fool, that's all!'

'A fool, that's all! *C'est mon opinion!* Be a good chap, if you can, get me out of here!' He suddenly clasped his hands pleadingly.

'Prince, I'll do everything I can! I'm all yours . . . Just give me a little time, dear prince, and maybe I'll be able to fix it!'

'*N'est-ce pas?* We'll up and go, but we'll leave the trunk so he'll think we're coming back.'

'But where'll we go? And what about Anna Andreevna?'

'No, no, I mean with Anna Andreevna . . . Oh, *mon cher*, my head's full of all sorts of rubbish . . . Just a moment! On the right-hand side in my case is a portrait of Katya. I stuffed it in there so that Anna Andreevna, and especially that Nastasya Yegorovna, shouldn't see it. Get it out, for God's sake, as quick as you can. Be careful, I don't want them to find us with it . . . Isn't there some way of latching the door?'

In fact I found a photographic portrait of Katerina Nikolaevna in an oval frame. He seized hold of it, raised it to the light and tears suddenly began pouring down his thin, yellow cheeks.

'*C'est une ange, c'est un ange du ciel!*' he cried out. 'Oh, she's an angel, she really is! All my life I've been in the wrong in regard to her, and now it's come to this! *Chère enfant*, I don't believe any of it, I believe none of it! Tell me, my friend, can you really imagine she wants to put me in a lunatic asylum? *Je dis des choses charmates et tout le monde rit . . .*' I say a few charming things, everyone laughs—and suddenly they want to put someone like that in a lunatic asylum!'

'It wasn't like that!' I cried. 'That's wrong. I know how she feels!'

'So you also know how she feels? Well, that's splendid! My friend, you've transformed me! So what's all this I've been hearing about you? My friend, get Katya to come here and they can both kiss and make up in front of me and I'll take them home and we can dispense with your landlord!'

He stood up, clasped his hands in front of me, and suddenly kneeled down at my feet.

'*Cher*,' he began in a mad, fearful whisper, shaking all over like a leaf, 'my dear friend, tell me the whole truth—where are they going to take me now?'

'My God,' I cried, lifting him up and sitting him on the bed, 'you don't believe me, do you? You think I'm also part of the plot? No, I won't let anyone lay a finger on you here.'

'*C'est ça*, you won't let anyone!' he babbled, holding me firmly by the elbows with both hands and continuing to shake. 'Don't let anyone get me! And don't you yourself lie to me because they *are* going to take me away from here, aren't they? Listen, that landlord, that Ippolit, or whatever he's called—he's not a doctor, is he?'

'A doctor? Him?'

'It's not a . . . a . . . lunatic asylum, this room, is it?'

But at that instant the door suddenly opened and in came Anna Andreevna. She must have been listening at the door. Unable to restrain herself, she opened it too quickly and the prince, who had flinched at the slightest sound, screamed and flung himself face downwards on to the pillow. There followed some kind of attack which ended in floods of tears.

'See what you've done!' I said to her, pointing at the old man.

'No, that's *your* doing!' She raised her voice sharply. 'For the last time, Arkady Makarovich, I'm appealing to you—are you willing to expose the devilish plot that's been hatched against a defenceless old man? Are you willing to sacrifice what you've called "your stupid and childish dreams of love" in order to save *your very own* sister?'

'I will save you all, but only in the way I described earlier! I'll be on my way again. Maybe in an hour or so Katerina Nikolaevna herself'll be here! I'll bring everyone together and then everyone'll be happy!' I cried out almost in a kind of ecstasy.

'Bring her, bring her here!' cried the prince frantically. 'Take me to her! I want Katya! I want to see Katya and give her my blessing!' he bawled out, raising his arms and trying to rise from the bed.

'See!' I pointed him out to Anna Andreevna. 'Listen to him! No "document" is going to help you now!'

'All I can see is that he could still help to justify what I have done in the opinion of society, but right now I am in disgrace! Enough of that, though. My conscience is clear. I am abandoned by everyone, even by my very own brother, who's frightened I might fail . . . But I'll do what I have to do and I'll stick by this poor old man, I'll be his nurse, I'll stay with him!'

There was no more time to lose and I dashed from the room.

'I'll be back in an hour and I won't be alone!' I shouted from the doorway.

CHAPTER XII

I

At long last I found Tatyana Pavlovna! In a flash I told her everything—everything about the document and everything about what was happening now at my lodgings down to the last detail. Although she herself understood only too well what had happened and could have grasped it all in a couple of words, my description took, I suppose, about ten minutes. I did all the talking and told the whole truth and held nothing back. She sat bolt upright in her chair, not moving and not saying a word, her lips pressed tight together, never once taking her eyes off me and listening to every word. But once I had finished she suddenly jumped up with such determination that I jumped up too.

'Oh, you little puppy-dog, you! So that letter was actually sewn into your pocket, and it was that idiot Marya Ivanovna Andronnikov who'd sewn it there! Oh, you beastly, blackmailing creatures! So you came all the way up from Moscow with the aim of conquering hearts and taking high society by storm and getting your own back on every Tom, Dick, and Harry because you were illegitimate, eh?'

'Tatyana Pavlovna,' I cried, 'don't you dare swear at me! Perhaps it was you yourself, with all your swearing at me, perhaps you were the reason right from the start why I've been such a bastard since being here! Yes, I'm illegitimate, I'm a bastard, and maybe I really did want to get my own back for being a bastard by really being a bastard to every Tom, Dick, and Harry and I'm not going to be blamed for that! But just you remember that now I've broken with the beastly blackmailers and got the better of my bad feelings! I will lay the document in front of her and just go away without even waiting for her to say anything. You will be my witness to it!'

'Give it me! Give me the letter at once, put it on the table! Or maybe you're lying, eh?'

'It's sewn into my pocket. Marya Ivanovna herself sewed it there. But here, when I had a new jacket made for me, I took it out of my old one and sewed it into this new one. Feel it! There it is! I'm not lying!'

'Give it me here! Get it out!' Tatyana Pavlovna raged on.

'No, I will not! I have told you over and over, I will put it down in front of her in your presence and leave without waiting for her to say a word. But she's got to see and know with her own eyes that it is I, I myself, who is handing it to her of my own free will, without any coercion and without any thought of reward.'

'Trying to show off again, are you? The puppy-dog's in love, eh?'

'You can be as nasty as you like. Maybe I've deserved it, but I'm not going to take offence. Oh, maybe I'll seem to her the shallowest kind of little boy who's been spying and plotting against her! But maybe she'll realize I've got the better of myself and I've set *her* happiness above everything else in the world! It doesn't matter, Tatyana Pavlovna, it doesn't matter! I tell myself loudly—Have courage and hope! Maybe this is only the first step I've taken in life, but let it be done properly, let it be done with dignity! And what if I do love her?' I was inspired to go on saying, my eyes flashing. 'I'm not ashamed of that! Mother may be an angel from on high, but *she*'s ... *she*'s a queen, a real earthly queen! Versilov will go back to mother, but I've got nothing to be ashamed of so far as she is concerned. After all, I heard her talking to Versilov when I was eavesdropping ... Oh, we're all three, you know, people *as crazy as each other*! You know something—*crazy as each other*—that's what he said, what Andrey Petrovich said! And maybe there are more'n just the three of us who are crazy as each other, aren't there? I bet you're a fourth— someone who's just as crazy! I tell you what—I bet you all your life you've been in love with Andrey Petrovich and maybe you still are! ...'

I will repeat that I felt inspired and madly happy but I didn't manage to finish. Suddenly, and unnaturally quickly, she seized me by the hair and jerked my head down once or twice with all her strength and then suddenly gave up and strode off into a corner of the room, stood there and brought a handkerchief up to her face.

'You puppy-dog, you! Don't you ever dare to say that to me again!'

She was weeping as she spoke. It was all so unexpected that, naturally, I was struck dumb. I stood there and looked at her, not knowing what to do.

'Oh, you're such a fool! Come here and give me a kiss, give this idiot a kiss!' she blurted out, weeping and laughing. 'And don't you dare, don't you dare say anything like that to me again! It's you I love ... and I have done all my life, you fool!'

I gave her a kiss. I will add, in parenthesis, that from that moment Tatyana Pavlovna and I became friends.

'Oh, yes! Oh, I know what it was!' she suddenly cried out, striking herself on the temples. 'What were you saying? That the old man was at your lodgings? Is that true?'

'I assure you it is.'

'Oh, my God! Oh, how sickening!' She started dashing in

frantic circles round the room. 'And they're just bossing him about there! Fools'll never learn, say what you like! From this morning, you say? Oh, that Anna Andreevna! She ought to be put in a convent! And that Militrisa, whoever she is, she knows nothing at all about it!'

'What Militrisa?'

'Your ideal woman, your earthly queen! So what's to be done now?'

'Tatyana Pavlovna!' I cried, coming to my senses. 'We've been talking all this nonsense and forgetting the main thing. It was Katerina Nikolaevna I was running to get, and they're waiting there for me to bring her back.'

And I explained that I would hand over the document only on condition that she immediately smoothed things out with Anna Andreevna and even consented to her marriage . . .

'Splendid!' Tatyana Pavlovna broke in. 'I've told her the same thing a hundred times over! Anyhow, he'll die before there can be any marriage. He'll not get married, and even if he does leave her—Anna—any money in his will it's all been allocated and left there already . . .'

'You don't mean all Katerina Nikolaevna cares about is the money?'

'No. She was frightened Anna had that document, and so was I. We were keeping an eye on her. His daughter didn't want to upset the old man at all, it was that Kraut, that Björing, who was worried about the money!'

'And after all this she can still want to get married to Björing?'

'Yes, what's to be done with someone as silly as that? Once an idiot, always an idiot, so they say. You see, he'll bring her some peace of mind, and what she says is she's got to marry someone and he seems the most capable of the bunch. And we'll just wait and see how much better off she'll be. Afterwards maybe she'll just drop her hands to her sides in despair, but by that time it'll be too late.'

'So why are you letting her do it? You're fond of her, aren't you? Haven't you told her to her face you love her?'

'Oh, I do love her—more than the whole lot of you put together—but she's still a mindless idiot!'

'Go and fetch her now, and we'll settle everything and take her to her father.'

'No, we can't! It's impossible, you little fool! That's what's the problem! Oh, what'll we do? Oh, it's sickening!' Again she started dashing to and fro, this time having snatched up her shawl. 'If only you'd got here four hours before, now it's eight and she'll have gone to have dinner with the Pelishchevs. After that she's going with them to the opera.'

'Oh, my God, we can't rush off to the opera! No, that's impossible! So what's going to happen to the old man? He may die during the night!'

'Listen, don't go back there. Go to your mother's, stay the night there and tomorrow early . . .'

'No, I'm not going to leave the old man, no matter what happens.'

'So don't! Yes, you're doing the right thing. You know what . . . I'll dash over to her apartment and leave her a note . . . I'll write it, you know, using our words (she'll know what I mean!), telling her the document's here and she must come here sharp at ten tomorrow—right on ten o'clock! Don't worry, she'll come! She'll listen to me and we'll settle the whole thing once and for all. You go back to your place and do your best to calm down the old man. Get him to bed and we can hope he'll last till morning! And another thing—don't upset Anna. I'm very fond of her, too. You're unfair to her because you can't understand what's happened to her. She's been deeply hurting, ever since girlhood she's been hurt. Oh, the way all your troubles have been heaped on my shoulders! Oh and don't forget to tell her I've taken it on now, and I'm putting all my heart into it, and she needn't worry, her name won't get dragged through the mud . . . In the last few days, after all, we've been at each other's throats, spitting and hissing and swearing like nobody's business! Well, off you go now! Oh, just a moment—show me that pocket again! Is that it . . . really? Really? Are you sure? Let me have the letter at least for tonight, eh? We won't eat it! You might let it slip through your fingers during the night, mightn't you? You might change your mind, mightn't you?'

'No, I won't!' I shouted. 'Look, you can feel it, but no way am I going to leave it here!'

'I can feel it's a piece of paper.' She fingered my pocket. 'All right, off you go! I'll go to her place and then maybe I'll slip into the opera—that was a good idea of yours! Go on, off you go!'

570

'Tatyana Pavlovna, just one thing! How's mother?'

'Still alive.'

'And Andrey Petrovich?'

She waved her hand dismissively.

'He'll get by.'

I ran off encouraged and full of hope, though things did not work out the way I reckoned they would. Fate dictated otherwise, and something different cropped up. Which only goes to show that fate really does exist!

II

I was still on the stairs when I heard a noise coming from my room and the door turned out to be open. An unfamiliar liveried manservant was standing out in the corridor. Pyotr Ippolitovich and his wife, both in a state of high anxiety for some reason, were also in the corridor and awaiting something. The door into the prince's room was wide open and a thunderously loud voice could be heard, which I recognized at once as the voice of Björing. Before I had had time to take a couple more steps I suddenly saw that the prince, trembling and in tears, was being led out into the corridor by Björing and a companion, Baron R., the very same man who had visited Versilov for talks. The prince was sobbing at the top of his voice, clinging to Björing and showering him with kisses; while Björing himself was shouting at Anna Andreevna, who was following the prince out into the corridor. He was threatening her and stamping his foot—in short, he was behaving just like a crude Prussian officer despite all his upper-class breeding.

It transpired later that he had somehow got it into his head that Anna Andreevna was guilty of something criminal and now undoubtedly had to answer for her actions before a court of law. Through ignorance of what had happened, he exaggerated it, as happens with many people, and consequently thought he had the right to act in a very authoritarian way. Chiefly he had not taken proper stock: he had been informed anonymously, as it turned out afterwards (I will mention this later on), and he had plunged into the whole affair in the sort of enraged state which even the cleverest people of his nationality get themselves into, ready at a moment's notice to brawl like so many drunken cobblers. Anna

Andreevna had reacted to this whole insulting affront with the utmost dignity, but I had not been there to witness it. I only saw that Björing, having led the old man into the corridor, had left him in the Baron's hands and, turning to face Anna Andreevna, had shouted at her, no doubt answering some remark of hers:

'You're a schemer! You're after his money! From this moment on you've disgraced yourself in the eyes of society and will answer for it before a court of law!'

'And you are mistreating a poor sick man and have driven him out of his mind! And you're shouting at me because I'm a woman and have no one to defend me!'

'Oh, of course, you're his fiancée, you're engaged to him!' roared Björing, breaking into malicious laughter.

'Baron, Baron . . . *Chère enfant, je vous aime!* I love you, dear child!' cried the prince tearfully, stretching his hands out to Anna Andreevna.

'Please go, prince, go! They're plotting against you, perhaps even against your life!' shouted Björing.

'*Oui, oui, je comprends, j'ai compris au commencement* . . . I knew it from the start . . .'

'Prince . . .' Anna Andreevna raised her voice '. . . you're insulting me and letting me be insulted!'

'Shut up!' Björing suddenly screamed at her.

That was too much for me.

'You bastard!' I yelled at him. 'Anna Andreevna, I'm coming to defend you.'

Here I cannot, nor am I about to start, describing things in detail. It turned out to be a horrible and squalid episode, and I suddenly abandoned all reason. I think I rushed at him and struck him, or at least I gave him a strong shove. He also struck me with full force on the head and knocked me to the floor. Recovering, I scrambled after them down the stairs. I remember that my nose was bleeding. A carriage was waiting for them at the front entrance and while they were getting the prince into it I once more flung myself at Björing despite being pushed aside by a footman. I cannot remember how the police became involved. Björing seized me by the collar and ordered a policeman to take me off to the police station. I shouted that he should come as well, in order to make a joint statement, and anyhow they shouldn't take me because these were my lodgings. But

572

because it was happening on the street and not in my lodgings, and because I was shouting and swearing and fighting like a drunk and Björing was in uniform, the policeman took me off. At this I went crazy and, resisting as hard as I could, I think I hit the policeman as well. Anyhow, I remember two of them suddenly appeared and led me away. I scarcely recall how I ended up in a smoky, tobacco-filled room along with a mass of different people, all sitting, standing, some waiting around, and some writing, while I still went on shouting and demanding to make a statement. But it was not just a matter of making a statement; it was complicated by my disorderly conduct and resistance to police arrest. What's more, I was looking far from my best. Someone suddenly shouted at me threateningly. The policeman meanwhile charged me with being in a fight and mentioned something to do with a colonel . . .

'What's your name?' someone shouted at me.

'Dolgoruky!' I roared.

'Prince Dolguruky?'

Beside myself, I answered with some extremely rude swearing and then . . . and then I remember being flung into some dark cell 'to sober up'. Oh, I am not protesting. Everyone has read the recent complaint in the papers from a certain gentleman who was arrested and forced to spend the night handcuffed, also in a detoxification cell, but he, it seems, was not guilty of any crime; whereas I was. I collapsed on to a bunk along with a couple of other men who were dead to the world. My head ached, my temples throbbed, and my heart beat like the clappers. I must have lost consciousness and I think I became delirious. I can only remember that I awoke at dead of night and sat up on the bunk. Instantly I remembered everything that had happened and realized what it meant. Placing my elbows on my knees and resting my head on my hands, I became plunged in deep thought.

Oh, I am not about to describe my feelings—they didn't matter at all—but I will say one thing: perhaps I have never in my life experienced instants of greater joy than during those minutes of reflection at dead of night, sitting on a bunk under arrest. A reader may find this strange—a kind of exhibitionism on my part, a desire to demonstrate my originality—yet it was exactly as I say. It was one of those moments that can probably happen to anyone, but occur only once in a lifetime. At such

573

moments people decide their fates, define their view of things, and tell themselves once and for all: 'That's what the truth is and that's where I have to go to find it!' Yes, those instants shed a light into my soul. Insulted, as I had been, by the haughty Björing and tomorrow looking forward to being insulted by that high-society lady, I knew only too well that I could take a horrible revenge, but I decided I wouldn't. I decided, no matter how much I might be tempted, that I would not divulge the document, that I would not make it known to the whole world (which was something I had toyed with). I repeated over and over to myself that, the following day, I would place the letter before her and, if necessary, I would endure instead of thanks her mocking smile, but I would still not say a word and I would then disappear from her life forever . . . However, there's no point in going on about it. As for everything that might occur to me here, how I might be arraigned and what might be done to me, I almost forgot to spare a thought for that. I lovingly crossed myself, lay down on the bunk, and fell into an untroubled, childish sleep.

I woke up late, when it was already daylight. I was alone in the room. I sat up and waited a long time for something to happen, about an hour in all. It must have been about nine o'clock when I was suddenly ordered out. I could go into it all in greater detail, but it would not be worth it because it is now all irrelevant. I simply want to stick to the main items. I will merely remark that, to my very great astonishment, I was treated unexpectedly politely. I was asked a question, I answered it, and at once I was permitted to leave. I left without another word and was pleased to read in their looks a certain surprise at someone who knew how to retain his dignity even in a situation like that. If I had not noticed that, I would not have written it down. Tatyana Pavlovna met me outside the police station.

I will explain briefly why it was so easy for me to be released. Early that morning, perhaps about eight o'clock, Tatyana Pavlovna had dashed to my lodgings—to Pyotr Ippolitovich, that is—hoping to find the prince still there and had then learned of the previous night's horrors and, chiefly, that I had been arrested. At once she had rushed to Katerina Nikolaevna (she, on returning from the theatre the previous evening, had had a meeting with her father, who had been brought to see her), had then woken her up, frightened her out of her wits, and demanded

I should be freed without delay. With a note from her she had instantly dashed to Björing and demanded from him another note 'To Whomsoever It May Concern' with a request from Björing himself stating categorically I should be released at once, 'having been arrested through a misunderstanding'. Armed with this, she had gone to the police station and the request had been met.

III

To continue with the main part of my story.

Tatyana Pavlovna, having picked me up, took a cab and brought me to her apartment, immediately ordered the samovar made ready, and washed and cleaned me up herself in her kitchen. Speaking in a loud voice she told me that at half-past eleven Katerina Nikolaevna would be there—as they had recently arranged—to see me. Marya, her cook, must have heard her saying this. In a few minutes she brought in the samovar but a couple of minutes later, when Tatyana Pavlovna suddenly called to her, she did not reply. It turned out she had gone out somewhere. I ask the reader to take special note of this. It was then, I suppose, about a quarter to ten. Although Tatyana Pavlovna was annoyed at her leaving without asking permission, she simply imagined she had gone out to shop and thought no more about it. Anyhow, it was of no concern to us. We were busy talking the whole time, because we had much to discuss, so that I hardly paid any attention at all to Marya's disappearance. I ask the reader to bear this in mind.

It goes without saying I was on cloud nine. I did not conceal my feelings, the main thing being that we were expecting Katerina Nikolaevna, and the thought that in an hour I would at last be seeing her—and at such a decisive moment in my life—made me tremble and shake all over. Eventually, when I had had two cups of tea, Tatyana Pavlovna suddenly stood up, seized a pair of scissors from the table, and said:

'Come on, let me have the pocket! We must get the letter out. We can't cut it out while she's here.'

'Right!' I cried and unbuttoned my jacket.

'Who made such a mess? Who sewed this?'

'I did, Tatyana Pavlovna.'

'I can see you did! Well, here it is . . .'

The letter was taken out. The envelope was the original one, but inside there was only a plain sheet of paper.

'What's this?' exclaimed Tatyana Pavlovna, turning it over and over. 'What's been going on?'

I stood there speechless and pale. Suddenly, in an access of weakness, I sank into my chair. I almost fainted at that point.

'What is this all about?' howled Tatyana Pavlovna. 'Where's the letter?'

'Lambert!' I jumped up, realizing what had happened and striking my forehead.

All in a rush, hardly catching my breath, I explained everything—the night spent at Lambert's and the plans we'd made, though I had already admitted to her the previous day I'd been in league with him.

'They stole it! They stole it!' I shouted, stamping about the room and clutching my hair.

'Oh, my God!' declared Tatyana Pavlovna, acknowledging the gravity of the situation. 'What time is it?'

It was about eleven o'clock.

'Oh, dear, Marya's not here! Marya! Marya!'

'What is it, mistress?' Marya suddenly called from the kitchen.

'You're back, are you? So what'll we do now? I'll fly and see her right away . . . Oh, you nincompoop! You nincompoop!'

'Right, then I'll go to Lambert!' I yelled. 'And I'll strangle him if I have to!'

'Mistress!' squealed Marya from the kitchen. 'There's a lady here asking for you . . .'

But before she could say who it was the lady in question came rushing headlong out of the kitchen, howling and wailing. It was Alphonsine. I will not describe what happened in any detail. The show she put on was a piece of play-acting, but I have to admit Alphonsine acted her role superbly. With tears of repentance and melodramatic gestures she rattled off an account (in French, of course) of how she had herself cut out the letter, that Lambert now had it, and that Lambert, together with 'that black villain', *cet homme noir*, were about to summon *Madame la générale* and shoot her right away, within the hour. She said she had learned all this from them and had suddenly become terribly alarmed because she had seen them with a pistol, *le pistolet*, and now

576

came rushing to us to tell us to go and save her and warn her against . . . *cet homme noir* . . .

'What *homme noir*?' cried Tatyana Pavlovna.

'*Tiens, j'ai oublié son nom*—I 'ave forgot 'is name . . . *un homme affreux* . . . *Tiens*, Versiloff!'

'Versilov! It can't be!' I yelled.

'Oh, yes, it can!' wailed Tatyana Pavlovna. 'Tell me, my good woman, without jumping about and waving your arms, what do they really want? Tell us, my good woman, sensibly and straightforwardly. I don't believe they want to shoot her, do they?'

The 'good woman' explained it all as follows (NB: nonsense, of course, I warn you): Versilov would be stationed behind the door and Lambert would show her *cette lettre* as soon as she entered the room, whereupon Versiloff would jump out and then they would have their way with her . . . *Oh, ils feront leur vengeance!* What's more, she, poor little Alphonsine, she feared the worst, because she was herself implicated, and *cette dame, la générale*, would be certain to be going there 'any moment now' because they had sent her a copy of the letter and she would see at once that they in fact had the letter and would be going to them, but it was only Lambert who had sent her the copy and she would know nothing about Versilov being there, since Lambert had introduced himself as coming from Moscow on a mission from *une dame de Moscou* (i.e. Marya Ivanovna Andronnikov).

'That's absolutely sickening! Sickening!' exclaimed Tatyana Pavlovna.

'*Sauvez-la, sauvez-la!* You must save her!' cried Alphonsine.

Of course, even at a superficial glance there was something implausible in this crazy account, but there was no time to think it over because in essence it all seemed terribly close to the truth. One could have supposed it very probable indeed that Katerina Nikolaevna, on receiving Lambert's invitation to go and see him, would first have come to us, to Tatyana Pavlovna, to find out what was going on; but that might equally well not have happened and she could have gone straight to them—and then she'd have been done for! It was also hard to believe she would dash and see Lambert, who was unknown to her, immediately on hearing from him; but it could have worked out that way, for example, because, on seeing the copy and being convinced they really had the letter, she could have gone—and met the same fate! The main thing was that we had no time at all to consider anything properly.

'Versilov'll do her in! If he's lowered himself to Lambert's level, he'll do her in! It's his double at work!'

'Oh, a "double" indeed!' Tatyana Pavlovna wrung her hands. 'Well, there's nothing for it!' she decided suddenly. 'Get your hat and coat and quick march! You, my good woman, show us the way! Oh dear, it's some way off! Marya, Marya, if Katerina Nikolaevna comes, tell her I'll be back in a moment and she should sit here and wait for me, and if she doesn't want to wait, then lock the door and don't let her out! Say it's on my orders! There'll be a hundred roubles for you, Marya, if you do that for me!'

We ran down the stairs. Without doubt we could not have thought of a better plan of action because, whatever happened, the main danger lay in Lambert's apartment, and if Katerina Nikolaevna did in fact come and see Tatyana Pavlovna beforehand, Marya could always detain her. Yet Tatyana Pavlovna, having already summoned a cab, suddenly changed her mind.

'You go there!' she commanded me, leaving me with Alphonsine. 'And die there if need be, understand! I'll be there in a moment, but first of all I'll call by and see if she's still at home because I'm a bit suspicious, you know what I mean!'

And she flew off to see Katerina Nikolaevna. Alphonsine and I set off for Lambert's. I urged on the driver the whole time and continually tried asking Alphonsine more questions on the way, but she took refuge more and more in exclamations and finally ended up in tears.

At the moment when everything hung by a thread, God preserved and saved us. We had hardly gone a quarter of the way when I suddenly heard a shout from behind. It was someone calling my name. I looked round—and there was Trishatov rushing after us in another cab!

'Where are you off to?' he cried in alarm. 'Why are you with her, with Alphonsine?'

'Trishatov!' I shouted. 'You told me the truth, this *is* a disaster! We're on our way to that bastard Lambert! Come with us—the more the better!'

'Turn back, turn back at once!' Trishatov shouted. 'Lambert's fooling you and so's Alphonsine! The pock-marked chap sent me. They're not at Lambert's. I've just seen him and Versilov on their way to Tatyana Pavlovna's! They're there now!'

I told my cab to stop, jumped out and joined Trishatov in his. Right up to this very moment I have no idea how I could have made such a quick decision, but I was at once convinced by what he said and decided to act. Although Alphonsine set up a frightful wail, we left her behind and I have no idea whether she turned round and came after us or went back to Lambert's. I never saw her again.

In the cab Trishatov managed to tell me breathlessly that something squalid was afoot, that Lambert had been in league with the pock-marked chap but the latter had betrayed him at the last moment and had himself sent Trishatov to Tatyana Pavlovna to tell her not to believe Lambert and Alphonsine. Trishatov added he knew nothing more, because the pock-marked chap had not told him any more about it due to lack of time, that he had himself dashed off somewhere and that everything was happening in a rush.

'I caught sight of you,' Trishatov went on, 'when you were on your way and dashed after you.'

Of course it meant the pock-marked chap knew everything about everything, because he had sent Trishatov directly to Tatyana Pavlovna. But it still posed a new puzzle.

To avoid further confusion I will explain what really happened and anticipate my story for the last time. Before, that is, I describe the final denouement.

IV

Having stolen the letter, Lambert at once contacted Versilov. How Versilov could have collaborated with Lambert I cannot say for the moment. That will come later. His 'double' was at work! But, being in cahoots with Versilov, Lambert had to be as cunning as possible if he were to lure Katerina Nikolaevna into his net. Versilov had told him to his face she wouldn't come. But ever since I had met Lambert a couple of nights before on the streets and boasted I would be handing the letter back in Tatyana Pavlovna's apartment in Tatyana Pavlovna's presence, he had arranged for a watch to be kept on her apartment in the sense that he had bought the services of Marya. He had given her a present of twenty roubles and then a day later, after the theft of the document, he had visited her again and in return for her complete co-operation he had promised her two hundred roubles.

That was why Marya, having overheard that Katerina Niko-laevna would be at Tatyana Pavlovna's at half-past eleven and that I'd be there as well, had instantly rushed from the house and taken a cab to Lambert's to let him know. This was precisely what Lambert wanted to hear, and what she had been paid for. At that very moment Versilov was also at Lambert's. In that instant Versilov hatched an infernal scheme of his own. They say there are certain times when madmen can be devilishly cunning.

The plan was to lure the two of us, Tatyana and myself, out of the apartment at all costs, if only for a quarter of an hour, but before the arrival of Katerina Nikolaevna. They would wait outside on the street and soon as Tatyana Pavlovna and I came out they would dash into the apartment, which would be opened to them by Marya, and there they would wait for Katerina Nikolaevna. Alphonsine in the mean time had to do as much as she could to detain us where and how she liked. Katerina Nikolaevna was due to arrive, as promised, at half-past eleven— certainly twice as early as we would be able to make it back. It goes without saying, by the way, that Katerina Nikolaevna had never received any invitation from Lambert and that Alphonsine was lying. Every detail of the scheme had been thought up by Versilov and Alphonsine had merely played the role of terrified traitress.

Of course, they were taking a risk, but they reasoned correctly that if it worked out, so much the better; but if it didn't, nothing would be lost because they would still have the document. But the scheme worked perfectly and could hardly have failed, because we could hardly have failed to dash after Alphonsine on the off chance that 'what she said might be true'! I repeat: there was no time to consider anything properly.

v

Trishatov and I rushed into the kitchen and discovered Marya in a state of great alarm. She had been shocked by the fact that when she had let Lambert and Versilov in she had caught sight of a revolver in Lambert's hand. Though she was accepting money for her services, a revolver had not been part of her calculations. She was quite bewildered and the moment she caught sight of me flung herself at me saying:

'The general's widow's here and they've got a pistol!'

'Trishatov, you stay here in the kitchen!' I ordered. 'The moment you hear a shout from me, come to my aid at once!'

Marya opened the door into the little corridor and I slipped into Tatyana Pavlovna's bedroom—into the little cubby-hole, that is, which had room enough only for her bed and where I had eavesdropped on a previous occasion. I sat down on the bed and at once sought a peephole in the *portière* or door-curtain.

But the room was already full of noise and they were talking loudly. I must add that Katerina Nikolaevna had reached the apartment just a minute after us and I had heard the noise of loud talk while still in the kitchen. It was Lambert who was doing the shouting. She was seated on the divan and he stood in front of her shouting like crazy. Now I know why he was so mad. He was in a mad rush, frightened there'd be no deal. I'll explain later what exactly he was frightened of. He had the letter in his hands. But there was no sign of Versilov. I held myself ready to rush in at the first sign of danger. I can only convey the gist of what was said, maybe because I cannot remember a lot of it, but at that moment I was too worked up to recall every last detail.

'This letter'll cost you thirty thousand roubles and you're surprised! It's worth a hundred thousand, but I'm only asking thirty!' Lambert was shouting loudly, in a terrible frenzy.

Although Katerina Nikolaevna was evidently frightened, she looked at him with a sort of contemptuous surprise.

'I see you've set some kind of trap here and I don't understand what it is,' she said, 'but if you've really got the letter . . .'

'Here it is! See for yourself! Isn't that it? I want an IOU for thirty thousand and not a copeck less!' Lambert broke in.

'I haven't any money.'

'Write out an IOU—here's some paper. Then you can go and get the money and I'll wait for it, but only a week—no more. When you bring me the money, I'll hand back the IOU and give you the letter.'

'You're using such an odd tone in talking to me. You're making a mistake. They'll seize that document from you this very day the moment I go and make an official complaint.'

'Who're you going to complain to? Oh-ho, what a scandal there'll be when the letter's shown to the prince! And where'll they get it from? I don't keep any documents in my apartment. I'll show it to the prince through a third person. Don't be stubborn, dear lady, just be thankful I'm not asking a great deal more. Someone else, apart from asking for this, might demand other favours . . . you know what kind . . . which no pretty woman could refuse under certain enforced circumstances, such as . . . Ha-ha-ha! You're a beautiful woman, you know that! *Vous êtes belle, vous!*'

Katerina Nikolaevna sprang to her feet, blushed crimson, and spat in his face. Then she set off briskly for the door. At this point Lambert, the crazy fool, brought out the revolver. Blindly, like the limited fool he was, he had believed in the effect the document would have. He had overlooked—which was the main thing—the kind of person he was dealing with, since, as I have already remarked, he considered everyone else's feelings were as base as his. From his very first word he had incensed her with his crudeness, while she, very likely, might not have been averse to some kind of financial deal.

'Hold it right there!' he yelled, infuriated by being spat at.

He seized her by the shoulder and showed her the revolver— for effect only, of course. She gave a scream and collapsed on to the divan. I flung myself into the room at the same moment as Versilov dashed in through the door into the corridor (he had been waiting there). Before I had had time to blink, he grabbed the revolver from Lambert and struck him as hard as he could on the head. Lambert buckled and fell down senseless. Blood gushed from his head on to the carpet.

On seeing Versilov she went white as a sheet. She gazed at him for several moments without moving, in inexpressible horror, and suddenly collapsed in a dead faint. He rushed to her. It all flashes before my eyes as I write. I remember the fright with which I saw his red, almost crimson, face and bloodshot eyes. I think he noticed I was there in the room but did not recognize me. He seized hold of her, senseless as she was, and with incredible strength lifted her up in his arms light as a feather and started pointlessly carrying her about the room as if she were a child. The room was tiny but he staggered from corner to corner, evidently having no idea why he was doing so. It was then that he went right out of his mind. He kept on staring at her face. I kept on running behind him, worried most of all about the revolver which he had forgotten was still in his hand and held right against her head. But he pushed me aside, once with his elbow, another time with his foot. I wanted to summon Trishatov but I was frightened of annoying him in his madness.

Finally I suddenly flung open the door-curtain and started begging him to put her down on the bed. He approached and laid her down and himself stood over her, gazed intently at her face and suddenly, bending down, kissed her twice on her pale lips. Oh, it was then I finally realized he was completely out of his mind! Suddenly he brandished the revolver threateningly over her but, as if struck by an idea, turned the revolver round and pointed it at her face. Instantly, with all my strength, I seized him by the arm and hollered for Trishatov. What I remember was we both struggled with him but he managed to free his arm and shoot himself.

He had intended to shoot her and then himself. When we stopped him aiming at her, he pointed the revolver straight at his own heart. I managed to jog his arm upwards and the bullet went into his shoulder. At that moment Tatyana Pavlovna burst screaming into the room but he was already lying unconscious on the carpet next to Lambert.

CHAPTER XIII

EPILOGUE

I

Now almost half a year has passed since that scene occurred and much water has flowed under the bridge, much has changed completely, and I for my part have long since begun a new life . . . But I will fill in the picture for the reader.

For me at least the first question was and remained for a long time: how could Versilov have collaborated with someone like Lambert and what aim did he have in mind? Gradually I came to an answer. In my opinion, at that moment—throughout that final day, that is, and the day preceding—Versilov had had literally no firm aim in mind and had even, I think, not considered it at all but had been caught up in a whole whirlwind of emotions. Besides, I entirely deny there was any real madness, more especially since he is not now mad in the least. But I undoubtedly make allowances for him having had a 'double'.

In fact, what is a double? A double—at least according to one medical book by an expert I have since read—a double is simply a manifestation of the first stage of a serious disorientation of the spirit which can have pretty bad consequences. Versilov himself explained to us with awful sincerity when he was at mother's the way in which his feelings and will-power were splitting in half. But I will repeat: what happened at mother's, when he split the icon in two, undoubtedly occurred under the influence of someone who was his double; yet since then it has always seemed to me he was partly acting out a kind of malicious allegory, partly showing how much he hated the women's expectations of him and resented their right to pass judgement on him—and so, in collusion with his double, he smashed the icon, as much as to say: 'There, your hopes of me are smashed in two, see!' In short, if there had been a double, it was all so much blarney . . . Yet that's only my guess. It is hard to be sure.

True, despite his worship of Katerina Nikolaevna, he always harboured the deepest and most sincere mistrust of her moral qualities. I certainly think that when he was standing outside the door at that moment he was looking forward to her humiliation by Lambert. But did he really want it even if he looked forward to it? I must repeat: I firmly believe he did not want anything of the sort and had not even considered it. He simply wanted to be there, then spring out, say something and perhaps . . . perhaps insult her, perhaps kill her . . . Anything might have happened at that moment. Going there with Lambert, he had no idea what might happen. The revolver was Lambert's idea, I must add. He went there unarmed. Having seen how proudly she behaved and, most of all, unable to endure the way that weasel Lambert threatened her, he sprang out—and there and then went out of his mind! Did he really want to shoot her at that moment? I

584

don't think he really knew himself, but he would certainly have shot himself if I hadn't jogged his arm.

His wound was not life-threatening and healed up, but he spent a fairly long time convalescing—at mother's, of course. Now as I write it is springtime, half-way through May, the day is beautiful and we have the windows open. Mother is sitting beside him. He strokes her cheeks and hair and continually glances lovingly into her eyes. Oh, of course, he is only half the Versilov he was! He cannot give up mother and never will. He has even acquired the 'gift of tears', as the unforgettable Makar Ivanovich put it in his story of the merchant. Besides, I think Versilov will live many years yet. Nowadays he treats all of us very simply and sincerely like a child, yet without losing his sense of proportion and tact and without saying anything unnecessary. His mind and his entire moral armoury have remained intact, although all his idealism has come to the fore. I will admit quite candidly that I have never loved him more than I do now and I regret this is neither the time nor the place to say more about him.

But I will mention one recent incident (and there have been many like it). By Lent he was better and he announced in the sixth week that he wanted to fast. I do not think he had fasted in thirty years or more. Mother was delighted. She began preparing special food for Lent, rather expensive, though, and exotic. On Monday and Tuesday I heard his voice in the next room chanting the words 'See, the groom is coming' and was overjoyed at the way he sang the verses. During those two days he said several fine things about religion, but on the Wednesday he suddenly put an end to his fasting. Something had suddenly annoyed him, some 'funny incongruity' as he laughingly put it. He had taken a dislike to something in the priest's appearance or the way things were in the church, but on returning home he had suddenly said with a calm smile: 'My friends, I love God very much, but I am no good at this!' The very same day we had roast beef for dinner.

But I know that nowadays mother often sits down beside him and starts talking quietly to him, smiling gently, about the most abstract matters. She has suddenly *grown bold* in his presence, though I have no idea why this should be. She usually sits next to him and talks to him more often than not in a whisper. He listens with a smile and strokes her hair and kisses her hand and the greatest happiness shines in her face. Sometimes he has attacks that are almost hysterical. At those times he picks up her photograph, the very one which he had kissed on that memorable evening, gazes at it with tears in his eyes, kisses it, reminisces about it, summons all of us to listen to him but has very little to say at such moments . . .

He has entirely forgotten about Katerina Nikolaevna, it seems, and never mentions her name. He has also said nothing about marrying mother. They had planned to take him abroad for the summer, but Tatyana Pavlovna insisted that they shouldn't and he himself didn't want to go abroad. They will be taking a holiday house in the country, somewhere in St Petersburg county. Besides, we are all still living at Tatyana Pavlovna's expense.

I must add one thing: I am terribly sorry that in the course of these notes of mine I have often allowed myself to refer to her disrespectfully and sarcastically. But I have written them always with the aim of imagining myself only too clearly as I was at each instant I was describing. Having reached the end of them and having almost written the last line, I have suddenly become aware that I have re-educated myself through the process of recalling events and writing them down. I repudiate much that I have written, particularly the tone of certain phrases and passages, but I will not cross out or correct a single word.

I have mentioned that he never says a single word about Katerina Nikolaevna and I even dare to think he has perhaps been entirely cured of her. It is Tatyana Pavlovna and I who sometimes talk about Katerina Nikolaevna and then only in secret. She is abroad now. I saw her before she left and visited her at home several times. I have already received a couple of letters from her from abroad and have written a couple in reply. But I have no intention of saying anything about the contents of these letters or what we talked about before she left. That is another story, a completely *new* story, and maybe it all belongs to the future. I do not even mention certain things to Tatyana Pavlovna. I will only add that Katerina Nikolaevna has not married yet and is travelling in the company of Mr Pelishchev. Her father has died and she has been left a very rich widow. At this moment she is in Paris. The rift with Björing occurred quickly and of its own acord—quite naturally, that is to say. I will describe how it happened.

586

On the morning of that final terrible scene the pock-marked chap, the very same man to whom Trishatov and his friend had gone, managed to inform Björing of the mischief that was being planned. This was how it came about: Lambert had still been hoping to persuade him to join him in his plan and, being in possession of the document, he told him all the details, the why and wherefore of what was being planned, even down to the final denouement when Versilov had thought up a way of deceiving Tatyana Pavlovna. But at the last moment the pock-marked chap had preferred to ditch Lambert, since he was the most sensible of them all and had the foresight to see the possible criminality of their enterprise. The main thing was that he considered Björing's gratitude a lot sounder than the fantastic plan devised by the inept and hot-headed Lambert, not to mention Versilov who had been driven nearly crazy with passion.

I learned all this later from Trishatov. However, I do not understand Lambert's relations with the pock-marked chap and have no idea what they were, or why Lambert could not dispense with him. But far more intriguing is the question as to why Lambert needed Versilov when he already had his hands on the document and could have done perfectly well without him. I now know the answer. He needed Versilov, firstly, because he knew all about the people and places involved and, secondly, Versilov was needed because, in the event of a muddle or everything going wrong, the responsibility would be his. Since Versilov did not need the money, Lambert was all the more ready to have him on his side.

But Björing did not arrive in time. He arrived about fifteen minutes after Versilov had shot himself, when Tatyana Pavlovna's apartment had a quite different look. Five minutes after Versilov had collapsed bleeding on the carpet, Lambert, who we all thought was dead, had climbed to his feet. He had looked around him in astonishment, suddenly realized where he was, and then gone off to the kitchen without saying a word, put on his fur coat, and left for good. The precious document was left behind on the table. I have since heard that he was not even all that unwell, but merely poorly for a while. The blow from the revolver had stunned him and caused him to gush blood, yet without causing any more serious injury. In the mean time Trishatov had dashed for a doctor, but before he arrived Versilov had already come to and even before that Tatyana Pavlovna, after reviving Katerina Nikolaevna, had taken her home. So that by the time Björing rushed in, Tatyana Pavlovna's apartment contained only myself, the doctor, the injured Versilov and mother, who, though herself sick, had dashed to be at his side after Trishatov had fetched her. Björing gave us a bewildered look and the instant he learned that Katerina Nikolaevna had already left he immediately went off after her without another word.

He was embarrassed. He saw only too clearly that scandal and talk were now unavoidable. However, no great scandal ensued, only all sorts of rumours. The fact of the gunshot could not be concealed, true. But all the main features of what had happened, all the essential things, remained almost unknown. Rumour had it simply that a certain V——, being in love, a family man, moreover, and almost 50, in a frenzy of passion, after declaring his love to a lady worthy of the utmost respect who did not reciprocate his feelings in the least, had shot himself when the balance of his mind was disturbed. Nothing else came out, and it was in this form that rumours made their way into the newspapers, with no names being divulged, only initials. At least I do know that Lambert, for example, was not asked anything about it at all.

Nevertheless, Björing, on discovering the truth, took fright. He managed, as things turned out, to learn about the eye-to-eye meeting between Katerina Nikolaevna and the completely infatuated Versilov a couple of days before the catastrophic denouement. This absolutely outraged him and, rather incautiously, he allowed himself to remark to Katerina Nikolaevna that it hardly surprised him there should be such fantastic stories flying about regarding her. At which Katerina Nikolaevna there and then broke off her engagement, without anger but without any hesitation. All her superstitious feeling about the wisdom of marrying such a man went up in smoke. Perhaps she had already seen through him long before, or maybe, after such a traumatic experience, some of her ideas and feelings had suddenly changed. Here my lips are again sealed. I must simply add that Lambert vanished away to Moscow and I have heard that he's really dropped into it there. And Trishatov has long since vanished, no matter how hard I have been trying to trace his whereabouts right up to the present time. He disappeared after the death of his friend '*le grand dadais*' who shot himself.

I have mentioned the death of the old Prince Nikolay Ivanovich Sokolsky. The dear, kind-hearted old man died not long after the events described—about a month later at night, in bed, from a stroke. I never saw him again after the day he spent in my room. They say he became much more rational in the course of that month, much calmer, and no longer appeared frightened, shed no tears, and never once in the whole time said a single word about Anna Andreevna. All his love became directed to his daughter. Katerina Nikolaevna on one occasion, a week before his death, suggested he might like me to visit him to cheer him up, but he even made a face at the idea. I mention this fact without offering any explanation. His estate turned out to be in order and, apart from that, he left a very considerable capital sum. Up to a third of it, according to the old man's will, was to be divided among his innumerable goddaughters. Everyone thought it extremely odd that there was no mention of Anna Andreevna in his will. Her name had been omitted. However, I know for an absolute certainty that a few days before his death the old man summoned his daughter and his friends, Mr Pelishchev and Prince V., and ordered Katerina Nikolaevna, in the likely eventuality of his early death, to assign sixty thousand roubles of his capital to Anna Andreevna. He expressed his wish precisely, clearly, and succinctly without permitting himself a single expostulation or a single explanatory word.

On his death and when his affairs were being settled, Katerina Nikolaevna informed Anna Andreevna through her lawyer that she could receive the sixty thousand whenever she wished, but Anna Andreevna turned down the offer, caustically and tersely. She refused the money despite every assurance that it had been the prince's wish. The money is still there waiting for her and Katerina Nikolaevna is now hopeful she will change her mind. But I know she won't. I know this for sure because I am now one of Anna Andreevna's closest friends and confidants. Her refusal has caused quite a stir and a lot of talk. Her aunt Fanariotov, who was extremely indignant to start with at her scandalous liaison with the old prince, has suddenly changed her mind and since the refusal of the money has solemnly made public her respect for her. On the other hand, her brother has finally quarrelled with her for good and all. Though I visit her frequently, I cannot say we discuss intimate matters very closely. We never mention the past. She is glad for me to visit her, but she always talks to me in a rather vague way. Among other things she has firmly assured me she wants to become a nun. That's a recent topic of hers. But I don't believe it. I think it's sour grapes.

Something really sour, something really bitter is what I have to say about my sister Liza. This is a case of real unhappiness. What are all my petty failures by comparison with her bitter fate? It began with Prince Sergey Petrovich failing to recover and then dying in hospital before his trial. He died even before Prince Nikolay Ivanovich. Liza was left abandoned with her child as yet unborn. She shed no tears and even appeared outwardly calm. She grew resigned and composed, but all her former warm-heartedness became buried somewhere deep inside her. She accustomed herself to helping mother and looking after Andrey Petrovich in his convalescence, but she became terribly withdrawn and taciturn and would never look at anyone or anything directly, as if nothing mattered to her and she were just passing by. When Versilov was better, she took to sleeping a great deal. I brought her books, but she never read them. She grew frightfully thin. I could never bring myself to comfort her, although I often had that in mind. In her presence I could never make myself go up to her and I could never find the right words to say in trying to talk about it. That was how it went on until something terrible happened. She fell down our steps—not far, only three steps in all—but she lost her baby and the miscarriage laid her low almost the entire winter. She is now no longer in bed, but she will take a long time to recover fully. She is as taciturn and withdrawn as ever with us men, but she has begun talking a little to mother. Of recent days there has been a bright, springlike sun high in the sky and I have constantly been reminded of that sunny morning last autumn when we walked so joyfully along the street, with such hope in our hearts and such fondness for each other. Alas, what has happened since then? I am not

590

complaining. I have embarked on a new life—but she? Her future is anybody's guess. Now it even hurts me to look at her.

Three weeks ago, however, I managed to tell her some interesting news about Vasin. He had been set free at last. I had been told that the sensible man had given the most accurate account of himself and furnished very interesting information which entirely justified him in the opinion of those upon whom his fate depended. What is more, his notorious manuscript turned out to be no more than a translation from the French—material, that is to say, which he had gathered purely for his own use with the aim of turning it into a worthwhile magazine article. He is now living in the provinces. His stepfather, Stebelkov, still languishes in prison in connection with a case that is, I hear, becoming more ramified and complex the longer it goes on. Liza smiled oddly when she heard about Vasin and even remarked she knew it would have worked out that way with him. But she was evidently pleased—pleased, of course, that the late Prince Sergey Petrovich's meddling had done no harm to Vasin. I have nothing further to say here about Dergachev and the others.

I have reached the end. The reader may like to know what happened to my 'Idea' and what my new life is, the one beginning for me now which I have talked about so tantalizingly. But this new life, this path which has opened up before me, *is* my 'Idea', the very same one as before though in a completely different form and therefore unrecognizable. Yet none of this is to go into these 'Notes' of mine, because it is an entirely different matter. My old life has gone for good and my new life has scarcely begun. Still, I must add one essential thing: Tatyana Pavlovna, my sincere and beloved friend, has been pestering me almost every day about applying for a university place as soon as possible, because, as she puts it: 'You can start having ideas later on, when you've done your studying, but now's the time to start studying.' I admit I have been thinking about her suggestion but I have no idea what I will decide. Besides, I reacted to her by saying I had no right to start studying now because I will have to work to support mother and Liza. But she has offered her own money for that purpose and has assured me there will be enough to pay for everything during my time at university.

I decided to ask someone for advice. Surveying those round

591

me, I chose someone after meticulous and critical consideration. He was Nikolay Semyonovich, my former mentor in Moscow, Marya Ivanova's husband. It is not a question of my needing advice, but I simply wanted to hear the opinion of this completely objective and even rather coldly egotistical man, yet one of undoubted intelligence. I sent him my manuscript, asking him to keep it a secret, since I had not shown it to anyone, least of all to Tatyana Pavlovna. The manuscript was returned to me after a couple of weeks accompanied by a fairly long letter. I will now offer a few extracts from this letter, finding they contain an overall view and one that is rather enlightening. Here they are:

III

'. . . And you have never, Arkady Makarovich of blessed memory, used your leisure more usefully than at the present time in writing these, your "Notes". You have provided, so to speak, an intelligent account of your first stormy and risky steps in life. I am firmly of the belief that in doing so you really can, as you put it, "re-educate yourself" in a great many ways. I will not permit myself, naturally, to make the slightest criticism, although every page offers food for thought . . . for example, the fact that you were so stubborn in keeping the so-called "document" to yourself for so long is entirely characteristic of you . . . But that is simply one of a hundred such observations I could make.

'I also value very highly the fact that you resolved to tell me, and me only, it appears, the secret of your "Idea". But as regards your request for my opinion of it I must refuse categorically, firstly, because there would not be room enough in this letter and, secondly, because I am not yet ready to answer, I need time to mull it over. I will simply remark that your "Idea" is notable for its originality, while young people of today tend mostly to pounce on ideas not of their own devising but ready-made ones, and there are not many of these and they can often be dangerous. Your own "Idea", for example, saved you, at least for a time, from the ideas of Dergachev and company which were without doubt not as original as yours. And, finally, I am entirely in agreement with that estimable lady, Tatyana Pavlovna, whom, though I have known her personally, I was not in a position to appreciate to the extent that she deserves. Her idea that you

592

should enter university would be highly beneficial for you. Knowledge combined with life will undoubtedly open up to you, in three or four years, much wider horizons of ideas and aspirations, and if after leaving university you again want to turn to your Idea there will be nothing to stop you.

'Now permit me, without any specific request on your part, to express quite openly certain ideas and impressions which have occurred to me, both in an intellectual and a spiritual sense, while reading these extremely frank "Notes" of yours. Oh, yes, I am at one with Andrey Petrovich in thinking that there were real grounds for anxiety over you and your *isolated* boyhood! There are a great many boys like you, whose gifts really do always threaten to develop for the worse either into a Molchalin-like* subservience or into a covert desire to overthrow the status quo. But this desire to overthrow the status quo springs more often than not from a likely covert yearning for order and "nobility" (I use your own term). Youth is pure because it is youth. Perhaps it is precisely in such early, youthful outbursts of madness that the yearning for order and the seeking after truth really originate, and who is to be blamed if certain young people today see this order and this truth in such silly, such comic things that you haven't the faintest idea how they could ever have any faith in them at all! I will remark in this connection that previously, in the fairly recent past, only a generation ago, there was no need to feel such pity for these curious young people because in those days they almost all ended up becoming part and parcel of the higher cultural layer in our society and blending with it into an integral whole. And if they were conscious, at the outset, of all the disorder and haphazardness in their own lives, of all the absence of true nobility in their family circumstances, the absence of a native tradition and of beauty in finished artistic form, then so much the better for them, since they could then consciously set out to achieve such things in later life and by that means learn to appreciate them. Now the situation is different because there is now almost nothing to which they can feel an attachment.

'I will explain what I mean by analogy or by example, so to speak. If I were a Russian novelist and had enough talent, I would always make sure of choosing my heroes from the Russian hereditary nobility, because it is only among that type of cultured

Russian that an appearance of beauty and refinement in living is possible, something so essential in a novel if it is to leave an elegant impression on the reader. In saying this I am being quite serious although I am myself, as you well know, in no sense a member of the Russian nobility. Pushkin long ago made mention of the subjects suitable for future Russian novels when he referred in *Eugene Onegin* to "the traditions of a Russian family"* and, believe me, that really sums up everything we have so far had that is truly beautiful. At least that sums up everything we have so far had that is in any way a finished product, as it were. I do not say this because I approve unconditionally of the rightness and truthfulness of this beauty. But there were finished forms of honesty and duty in such a milieu, whereas nowhere else in Russia, apart from the nobility, were there any finished forms at all. In fact, elsewhere nothing had even been begun. I say this as one who has no axe to grind and is seeking a quiet life.

'Whether the honesty to be found there was admirable and the sense of duty right and proper is another matter. More important, so far as I am concerned, is that the forms show signs of finish and the orderly pattern of life is not prescribed from outside but evolves from our own experience. My God, the most important thing we can have is some orderly pattern of life we can call our own! It is what we have hoped for, so to speak, our chance to have a rest—something really finished, really constructed, and not the everlasting piles of rubbish, not the woodchips flying everywhere, not the trash and garbage from which absolutely nothing has come in the last two hundred years!

'Don't accuse me of Slavophilism!* I say this out of pure misanthropy because I am heavy at heart! Nowadays, in the fairly recent past, something exactly opposite to what I have described has been happening among us. It is no longer a case of scum attaching itself to higher echelons of society, but now it is a case of bits and pieces tearing themselves free of that beautiful type in gay abandon and combining with all who are envious and disruptive. And it is a far from unique thing that the very fathers, the very founders of those former cultured families should now make fun of what their children might want to believe in. Moreover, they take pleasure in not hiding from their very own children the way they lust after their sudden right to dishonour which has sprung up among them in whole droves. It is not about the real progressives that I am speaking, dearest Arkady Makarovich, but about that ragtag and bobtail, countless in number, of whom it is said: "*Grattez le russe et vous verrez le tartare*", or "Scratch a Russian and you will find a Tartar". Believe you me, there are not as many genuine liberals, genuine and whole-hearted friends of humanity, among us as it may once have seemed.

'But this is all philosophizing by the way. Let's return to our imaginary novelist. The position of our novelist in such a circumstance would be quite clearly defined: he could only write historical novels, since there are no longer beautiful types in our time and if there are any remnants remaining then, judging by the opinion prevalent nowadays, they have not retained their beauty. Oh, in a historical novel you can describe whole masses of extraordinarily pleasant and delightful details! You can even so enthral the reader he may mistake the historical scene for one that is possible nowadays. Such a novel, written by a great talent, would belong not so much to Russian literature as to Russian history.* It would provide an artistically finished picture of a Russian mirage, but one that really existed so long as no one guessed it was a mirage. The grandson of the characters depicted in a picture showing a cultured upper-class Russian family over three generations in a Russian historical setting—such a descendant could not be portrayed otherwise than as rather misanthropic, isolated, and undoubtedly miserable-looking. He would even look somewhat out of place, someone the reader would be convinced at first glance was on his way out and to whom the place could not belong. Another moment and even this misanthropic grandson would himself be gone, to be replaced by new, so far unknown characters and a new mirage. But who would these characters be? If none of them was beautiful, no further Russian novel would be possible. But is it only the Russian novel that would then be impossible?

'Rather than go on about this, I'll turn to your manuscript. Look, for example, at Mr Versilov's two families. Let me be utterly frank now. Firstly, I will say little about Andrey Petrovich himself, save that he is, however, from the original aristocracy. He belongs to one of the oldest families of the nobility while at the same time belonging to the Paris commune. He is a genuine poet, loves Russia, and yet completely denies its value. He has no religion, but he is prepared to die for almost anything vague, which he cannot name but in which he can passionately believe, on the example of many, many enlightened Russian Europeanizers of the St Petersburg period of Russian history.

'That is enough about him. Now about his legitimate family. I will say nothing about his son. He doesn't deserve it. Anyone with eyes in his head can see what will happen to scum like him and what they can do to others. But then there's his daughter, Anna Andreevna—she's a girl of character if anyone is! She is someone a bit like the Abbess Mitrofania*—naturally without suggesting she is criminally inclined, which would be unjust of me. Tell me now, Arkady Makarovich, that this family is something accidental and I would be delighted. But it would surely be more just, on the other hand, to conclude that many, many such undoubtedly legitimate Russian families are transforming themselves irresistibly, *en masse*, into *accidental* families and blending with them in a common discord and chaos. It is a type of accidental family you are partly describing in your manuscript. Yes, Arkady Makarovich, you are *a member of an accidental family* in complete contrast to all our recent types of legitimate hero who had boyhoods and youths quite unlike yours.

'I confess I would not want to be a novelist trying to describe a hero from an accidental family!

'It would be thankless work and one lacking formal beauty. In any case, such a type is a matter only of current importance and cannot, for that reason, have any artistic finish. Serious mistakes would be possible, and exaggerations, and oversights. In any case, far too much would have to be guesswork. But what choice does a writer have who has no wish to write historical novels but longs to write about matters of current importance? He has to guess . . . and get it wrong!

'But such "Notes" as yours could, I think, serve as the basic material for a future artistic work, for a future picture of a disorderly but already vanished epoch. Oh, when what is topical has ceased to be and the future has arrived, then a future painter will seek beautiful forms even for depicting all the past discord and chaos! That is when "Notes" like yours will provide the basic material and could prove sincerely useful despite all their chaotic and accidental character . . . At least certain truthful

596

features would survive through which it may be possible to guess at the innermost spiritual world of someone on the eve of manhood at that tumultuous time—an insight of no mean value, since it is from those on the eve of manhood that the generations are made . . .'

EXPLANATORY NOTES

(These Notes are drawn principally from the first definitive edition of the works of Dostoevsky, F. M. Dostoevsky, *Polnoe sobranie sochinenii v tridtsati tomakh*, vol. xvii (Nauka, Leningrad, 1979), 360–426.)

11 *'Anton the Unlucky' and 'Polinka Saks'*: *Anton the Unlucky* (*Anton Goremyka*, 1847) by D. V. Grigorovich (1822–99) and *Polinka Saks* (1847) by A. V. Druzhinin (1824–64) were characteristic short novels of the 1840s which epitomized the liberal mood of the decade in their pleas, respectively, for the oppressed peasantry under serfdom and for female emancipation.

24 *Kuznetsky*: a fashionable shopping street in Moscow, also known as *Kuznetsky Most*.

49 *Duc de Berry*: it was not the murder of Duc de Berry in 1820 that gave rise to the wealth of James Rothschild (1792–1868) but his timely receipt of the news of Napoleon's defeat at Waterloo in 1815.

50 *Petersburg side*: or Petersburg Island, an island on the northern bank of the main channel of the Neva linked by bridges to Vasilevsky Island and the central, administrative areas of the capital on the southern bank.

51 *'Quae medicamenta . . . ignis sanat!'*: 'What medicine will not cure, iron will; what iron will not cure, fire will.'

60 *all these rational ideas . . . phalansteries and so on*: Arkady here demonstrates his hostility to the ideas of Fourier (1772–1837) which so enthralled members of Dostoevsky's generation and which he first encountered at meetings of the Petrashevsky group in the 1840s.

84 *Harpagons or Plyushkins*: Harpagon is the hero who epitomizes miserliness in the famous comedy *L'Avare* (1668) by Molière (1622–73), as does Plyushkin among the portrayals of landowners in *Dead Souls* (1842) by N. V. Gogol (1809–52).

89 *Russian railway magnates*: those named in the Russian text are V. A. Kokorev (1817–89), S. S. Polyakov (1837–88), and P. I. Gubonin (1825–94).

Low: John Low (1671–1729), an Englishman, opened a bank in

599

Paris with government backing in 1716. The bank collapsed in 1720 causing government bankruptcy and widespread hardship.

93 *Talleyrand or Piron*: Talleyrand (1754–1838), French diplomat and master of diplomatic intrigue, notorious for his ability to stay in power under many different administrations; Piron (1689–1773), famous French comic poet, author of comedies and operettas, well known for his epigrammatical wit.

95 *for me . . . aware of this*: from the Little Tragedy *The Miserly Knight* (1830) by A. S. Pushkin (1799–1837). Arkady's 'Idea' owes something to this source, as becomes clear later in the novel.

98 *Bismarck's idea*: this presumably involves his axiom that great questions are not solved by speeches or majority votes but by 'blood and iron'.

111 *'Genevan ideas'*: the reference is presumably to the ideas of J.–J. Rousseau (1712–78) who was Genevan by origin.

112 *Eliseev's and Balle's*: well-known produce stores in Moscow and St Petersburg.

114 *Into desert regions I depart*: the first line of a popular song first published in 1790.

118 *Krylov*: I. A. Krylov (1769–1844), famous Russian fabulist.

Woe from Wit: usually dated 1824 and composed before the Decembrist Revolt of 1825 but banned and not fully published until 1861, famous satirical comedy by A. S. Griboedov (1795–1829). Versilov was playing the role of the hero, Chatsky, whose wit leads him to be considered mad.

137 *this provincial Uriah*: in the Old Testament (2 Samuel, 11–12) King David fell in love with Bathsheba, wife of Uriah the Hittite, and arranged for Uriah to be killed in battle so that he could make her his own wife; for which the prophet Nathan condemned him as having committed a sin against the Lord.

139 *Swarthy, tall and straight*: a quotation from the poem 'Vlas' (1854) by N. A. Nekrasov (1821–77) describing a peasant figure very similar to Makar Dolgoruky.

154 *Brest–Graev*: a reference to shares in the newly floated company of the Brest–Graevo Railroad which were advertised in a number of newspapers in 1873–4.

155 *'The charming girl . . .'*: a line from Pushkin's poem 'The Black Shawl' (1820).

'petticoat prophet': an oblique reference to the likely resemblance between Versilov and P. Ya. Chaadaev (1794–1856) whose first

600

Philosophical Letter, published by error in 1836, was an elegant and prophetic criticism of the intellectual and cultural backwardness of Russia.

196 *'The lie . . . lowly truths'*: from Pushkin's poem 'The Hero' (1830).

216 *the late tsar*: presumably Emperor Nicholas I, who reigned from 1825 to 1855; the site of the (supposed) stone near the Pavlovsky Barracks was on the corner of Millionaire Street (or Khalturin Street) and the former Field of Mars.

Tsarskoe Selo: 'Tsar's Village', some distance from St Petersburg, where the tsars used to reside prior to 1917. Renamed Pushkin in 1937.

Montferrant: A.–R. de Montferrant (1786–1858), of French extraction, was the architect of St Isaac's Cathedral, the Alexander Column, and several houses in St Petersburg.

219 *Pyotr Ippolitovich*: his story derives from a collection published by V. I. Dal´ (1801–72) in 1862 and later used by L. N. Tolstoy in his *Reader* (*Azbuka*) in 1872 to illustrate Russian peasant quick-wittedness.

in front of all the senators: popular legend held that a ghost had appeared to King Charles XI of Sweden (1655–97) warning of a threat posed to the future King Gustav III (1746–92). Legend also held that Emperor Nicholas I had been summoned to the Senate and forced to kneel before it. He had been rescued by his brother Constantine.

Chernyshev: Prince A. I. Chernyshev (1785–1857), Minister of War 1832–52.

227 *the 'Geneva ideas'*: the reference is supposedly to such ideas as socio-economic equality, the denial of religion and Christian ethics, the quest for universal human welfare and contentment, all of which tended, in Dostoevsky's view, to characterize socialist thought in Europe post-1871.

228 *Horatius*: according to legend, Horatius sent his three sons to defend Rome in a duel, from which only one returned undefeated.

Somewhere in the Koran: there is possibly a confusion of references here. Pushkin, in his cycle of short poems, 'Imitation of the Koran' (1824), refers to the prophet's word as not being offered to 'the disobedient', while in his 'Verses composed at night during insomnia' (1830) he used the image of 'life like the racing of mice'; but nowhere in the Koran is there such a clear identification of 'the disobedient' with 'mice' as is suggested here.

601

243 *mont de piété*: established as a savings bank in Paris in 1777. Stebelkov was based on a certain Kolosov who set up a savings bank in Russia in 1869. Like Stebelkov, he had some training as a doctor and in midwifery, but his criminal activities came to a head in 1874 with a notorious attempt to sell forged shares in the Tambov Railroad. The court case attracted Dostoevsky's attention.

297 *Zershchikov's*: A. S. Dolinin, the noted Dostoevsky scholar, has suggested (*The Last Novels of Dostoevsky* (Moscow-Leningrad, 1963), 150–2) that Zershchikov was probably based on a certain retired army captain Kolemin who was brought to trial in 1874 for conducting an illicit gambling establishment.

322 *Rohans*: an ancient princely line related to many of the royal families of Europe with a family motto: 'Roy ne puys, Duc ne deygne, Rohan suys' ('I do not aspire to Kingship, I do not deign to be a Duke, I am a Rohan').

323 *the forgery of railway shares*: A. S. Dolinin (*The Last Novels of Dostoevsky*, 142–9) has pointed to Dostoevsky's use of the trial of Kolosov in 1874 (see above) as the basis for his sub-plot involving Prince Seryozha's forgery of shares.

333 *'Quelle charmante personne . . .'* : 'What a charming person, eh? The Song of Solomon—no, it's not Solomon, it's David, who took unto himself a beautiful young girl to bring him warmth in his old age. Besides, David, Solomon . . .'

Paul de Kock: (1794–1871), very popular French romantic novelist.

351 *an ancient Moscow church*: a seventeenth-century church stood next to the Souchard school in Moscow which Dostoevsky attended as a boy, but the church described here bears a close resemblance to one in a street where Dostoevsky's wealthy relatives, the Kumanins, lived.

356 *Le Page pistols*: possibly a reference to wheel-lock pistols for which the Parisian gunmakers, Le Page, were famous.

360 *'Mais vous n'avez pas dormi . . .'* : 'But you haven't slept at all, Maurice!'

'Taisez-vous . . .' : 'Shut up! I'll sleep later.'

'Sauvée . . .' : 'Saved!' . . . 'Sir, sir, never was there a man so cruel, such a Bismarck, as this one, who regards all women as filthy and worthless. What is a woman in our time? Fit only to be killed! That's what the Académie française thinks . . .' The phrase 'Fit only to be killed!' derives from a notorious pamphlet *L'Homme-femme* (Paris, 1872) by A. Dumas-fils (1824–95) which advocated

602

the killing of unfaithful wives. A. Dumas-fils was received into the French Academy with due ceremony in February 1875.

361 '*Hélas! de quoi m'aurait servi* . . .': 'Alas! What good would this discovery have been if I had made it earlier, and would it have been better if I'd concealed my shame all my life? Perhaps it's not right for a girl to speak so openly to a man but I confess to you that if I had a wish to be granted I would want only one thing: to plunge a knife into his heart, but with my eyes averted so his frightful look wouldn't make my hand shake and take away my courage! He killed that Russian priest, sir, and tore out his red beard and sold it to a barber on the Kuznetsky, just next to the house of Andrieux—you know, the one selling the latest Paris fashions, linens, and shirts . . . Oh, sir, when friendship gathers together round a table one's spouse and children and sisters and friends, when the joy of life burns in one's heart—tell me, sir, is there a greater happiness than this, which all people enjoy? But he mocks it, this execrable and incredible monster mocks it, and if it hadn't all been arranged through Monsieur Andrieux, I'd never, never . . . But what's wrong, sir, what's wrong?'

362 '*Mais ce n'est pas loin* . . .' 'But it's no distance away, sir, no distance from here, there's no need for your fur coat, it's just next door!'

'*Il s'en va* . . .': 'He's leaving, he's leaving! . . . But he'll kill me, sir, he'll kill me!'

377 *Gennadian monastery*: this perhaps refers to the monastery founded by Gennadii of Kostroma in 1565.

405 *. . . on the fifth day he hanged himself*: Dostoevsky drew such instances from cases reported in the press in 1873 and 1874, particularly during his editorship of the journal, *The Citizen* (*Grazhdanin*).

415 '*my own clothes do abhor me*': the quotation is from the Book of Job 9: 30–1.

439 *in Archangel, in Kholmogory*: it is possible that the prince's references to Archangel and Kholmogory were due to the fact that the famous scholar, scientist, and man of letters, founder of Moscow University, M. V. Lomonosov (1711–65) was born near Kholmogory.

443 *Kammerjunker*: 'Gentleman of the bedchamber' or 'junior chamberlain', an honorary title bestowed by the Russian Emperor for distinguished service. It was the lowest rank of courtier in the Table of Ranks created by Peter I in 1722.

452 *'Monsieur le prince . . .'* : 'Prince, could you spare us a rouble, not two roubles, just one?' . . . 'We'll return it.'

453 *'Dites donc . . .'* : 'Tell me, do you want me to bash you on the head, my friend?' . . . 'My friend, here's Dolgoruky, my other friend.'

'Mademoiselle Alphonsine . . .' : 'Mademoiselle Alphonsine, will you kiss me?'

'Ah, le petit vilain . . .' : 'Ah, the horrid boy! . . . Don't come near me, you'll make me dirty, you big booby! You know what I'll do, I'll throw you all out!'

454 *'Mademoiselle Alphonsine . . .'* : 'Mademoiselle Alphonsine, have you sold your lap-dog?'

'Je parle comme une dame russe . . .' : 'I'm talking Russian like a Russian woman at a spa . . .' 'What is a Russian lady like at a spa and . . . where's the pretty watch Lambert gave you?'

455 *'Nous avons . . .'* : 'We've got a rouble we've borrowed from our new friend.'

460 *Madier de Mangeot*: (1814–92), French left-wing politician, forced into emigration under Napoleon III, but prominent in the French national assembly after 1871.

461 *'And the years go by . . .'*: the words, slightly misquoted, are from the poem 'It is boring and sad' (*I skuchno i grustno*, 1840) by M. Yu. Lermontov (1814–41).

462 *Stradelli*: A. Stradelli, seventeenth-century Italian composer.

463 *Because it's innocent*: Trishatov greatly exaggerates what is a minor, sentimental episode in *The Old Curiosity Shop*, endowing it with tragically universal, pan-European significance.

465 *Milyutin shop*: a group of shops on the Nevsky Prospect built in 1735 by Count A. Ya. Milyutin. They no longer exist.

490 *Herzen*: A. I. Herzen (1812–70), the most outstanding Russian advocate of liberalism in the nineteenth century and a political philosopher and memoirist of the first rank, left Russia for voluntary exile in the West at the end of the 1840s and became, through his London-based journal *The Bell*, a very influential critic of the tsarist government and a scourge of its injustice and corruption in the post-Crimean War period, especially between 1855 and 1863.

491 *Claude Lorraine*: (1600–82) Dostoevsky's favourite painter. While in exile in Dresden he saw the painting many times and used it as an image of an ideal 'Golden Age' in Stavrogin's 'Confession' in

the banned chapter of *Devils* (or *The Possessed*) and in his study of suicide 'The Dream of a Foolish Young Man'.

492 *the Tuileries*: a former royal palace, it was destroyed during the struggle between the Paris communes and government forces in May 1871 after the defeat of France in the Franco-Prussian War.

498 *Heine in his 'Christ on the Baltic'*: the poem by H. Heine (1797–1856) from the cycle *The North Sea*, first fully translated into Russian in 1872.

502 *Othello's last speech . . . Victor Hugo's 'Les Misèrables'*: presumably this refers to the penultimate, rather than the last, speech by Othello; to the final scene between Onegin and Tatyana in ch. 8 of Pushkin's *Eugene Onegin*; and to pt. II, bk. 3, ch. 5 of *Les Misèrables* (1862) by V. Hugo (1802–85).

526 *fortochka*: small hinged pane used for ventilation when the windows are sealed for the winter.

557 *von Sohn*: a government official of that name was murdered in a Moscow brothel in late 1869 and the case became the talk of St Petersburg in 1870. Dostoevsky made use of it in connection with the plotting of *Devils* (or *The Possessed*) and referred to it specifically in *The Brothers Karamazov*.

564 *'so swiftly . . .'*: a slightly inaccurate quotation from *Woe from Wit* (1824), the satirical comedy by A. S. Griboedov (1795–1829), which sardonically emphasizes the unlikely rapidity of Chatsky's madness.

593 *Molchalin*: a character in Griboedov's satirical comedy *Woe from Wit*, who finds favour with the heroine and his prospective father-in-law through his fawning sycophancy.

594 *'the traditions of a Russian family'*: the reference is to a line from ch. 3 of Pushkin's *Eugene Onegin* (stanza XIII).

Slavophilism: a conservative socio-political and religious doctrine which arose in Russia in the 1840s and advocated an indigenous, rather than a Western, approach to Russian problems. It repudiated the Western orientation of Peter the Great's reforms at the beginning of the eighteenth century and believed that Russia should seek its true identity in a conservative utopianism based on the Orthodox Church, the autocracy, and the peasant commune.

595 *Such a novel . . .* : the reference is to L. N. Tolstoy (1828–1910) and his great historical novel *War and Peace* (1869).

596 *Abbess Mitrofania*: *née* Baroness Rozen, a former lady-in-waiting at the imperial court, who was brought to trial in 1874 accused of forging financial documents for the benefit of her monastery in Serpukhov.